## PRAISE FOR JONATHAN GASH AND THE CLARE BURTONALL SERIES

'Brilliantly successful: the previous novel that *Different Women Dancing* reminds you of is *Brighton Rock*.'
*Sunday Times*

'A smashing new crime novel.'
*New York Times Book Review*

'Light years away from the jovial roguery which Gash has made his own, but just as distinctive.'
*Literary Review*

'Gash is on top form as he introduces Dr Clare Burtonall . . . Promises further entertainments to come.'
*Publishers Weekly*

'A woman doctor and a streetwise gigolo make an offbeat pairing in a brilliant thriller.'
*Peterborough Evening Telegraph*

'An absorbing new character makes a terrific debut in *Different Women Dancing*.'
*Highbury and Islington Express*

'An exciting and readable novel from the creator of TV's *Lovejoy*.'
*Books Magazine*

'A smooth, sexy suspenser . . . The promised series is cause for rejoicing.'
*Kirkus Reviews*

'Well-crafted, involving stuff, as ever with Gash.'
*Crime Time*

'A classy tale of stark urban underworld life.'
*Newcastle Upon Tyne Chronicle*

'This fast-paced thriller will delight Gash's deserved legions of fans.' *East Anglian Daily Times*

# prey *dancing*

Jonathan Gash is the author of the hugely successful Lovejoy novels, which were adapted into the long-running BBC TV series *Lovejoy*, starring Ian McShane. His latest Lovejoy mystery – the twenty-first in the series – which is entitled *A Rag, a Bone and a Hank of Hair*, is available in Macmillan hardback.

Jonathan Gash is also a doctor specializing in tropical medicine and lectures worldwide on the subject. He is married with three daughters and four grandchildren and lists his hobbies as antiques and his family.

*Prey Dancing* is the second novel in his series of medical thrillers featuring Dr Clare Burtonall and Bonn, following *Different Women Dancing* which is also available in Pan Books.

*By the same author*

Firefly Gadroon
Gold from Gemini
The Gondola Scam
The Great California Game
Jade Woman
The Judas Pair
Moonspender
Pearlhanger
The Sleepers of Erin
The Tartan Ringers
The Vatican Rip
The Very Last Gambado
The Lies of Fair Ladies
The Grail Tree
Spend Game
Paid and Loving Eyes
The Sin Within Her Smile
The Grace in Older Women
The Possessions of a Lady
Different Women Dancing
The Rich and the Profane
A Rag, a Bone and a Hank of Hair

*Omnibus editions*
Lovejoy
Lovejoy at Large
Lovejoy at Large Again

*As Jonathan Grant*
Mehala, Lady of Sealandings
Storms at Sealandings
The Shores of Sealandings

JONATHAN
GASH

# prey
# *dancing*

PAN BOOKS

*For Lal and Richard,*
*Jackie and Bill,*
*Yvonne and Rich*

First published 1998 by Macmillan

This edition published 1999 by Pan Books
an imprint of Macmillan Publishers Ltd
25 Eccleston Place, London SW1W 9NF
Basingstoke and Oxford
Associated companies throughout the world
www.macmillan.co.uk

ISBN 0 330 36905 9



9 8 7 6 5 4 3 2 1

A CIP catalogue record for this book is available from the British Library.

Phototypeset by Intype London Ltd
Printed and bound in Great Britain by
Mackays of Chatham plc, Chatham, Kent

'There are three kinds of human beings: men, women and women physicians.'

Sir William Osler

# 1

**Upper** – a female who hires a male for an episode of sex

'The patient died about twenty past midnight,' the night nurse said.

'No, nurse,' Dr Clare Burtonall whispered. She was worn out by reporting sloppiness. 'Not *about*, please.'

The night nurse said quickly, 'That's what it says in the Cardex, doctor.'

'Did you enter it?'

'Yes, doctor, but—'

'Then that too is imprecise. Help me, please.'

It was four in the morning. Clare had been summoned at ten minutes past three, and driven along the silent roads to the District General. She always made a click entry in her auto-record to register phone messages. Heaven knows why, she thought dispiritedly. She hardly ever checked the wretched thing.

The nurse stood. 'Help with what, doctor?'

Clare surveyed the ward beyond the glass partition of the secure Infectious Disease unit. Patients were sleeping, except for one woman moaning softly, being specialed for drug overdosage. Night nurses sat, heads together, writing their reports, doubtless with accuracy.

'Help as in assist, please.' Clare thought maybe she had

been too harsh. The nurse wore the hatched blue of the second-year trainee. No hat, of course, nowadays, no starched apron. 'To lay the patient out.'

'I'm sorry, doctor?'

The night nurse's refusal trailed off. The seated nurses became aware, and peered down the length of the ward. Clare drew the curtains across the partition as if to cosset the dead girl.

'What is the problem, nurse?'

'Nursing staff don't lay out any more.'

'Don't *what*?' Clare stared. Two patients on drips, green-hooded lights showing the transfusion chambers in relief against magnolia-coloured walls. 'It's routine nursing duty!'

'Don't lay out dead on this ward, doctor.'

Clare drew breath. More new Admin. manoeuvres?

'Since when, nurse?'

'The SNO published new instructions, doctor. AIDS patients—'

'Then what *do* you do? Dispose of patients down some chute like so much rubbish?' Clare felt a headache begin. She hadn't had a significant migraine since she'd taken up using – no, a hateful word – taken up *with* Bonn. She let the nurse see her contempt.

'We body-bag them, then porters move it to the mortuary.'

'And the drips? Transfusion lines?'

The senior night nurse, sensing a dispute, started down the ward towards the small island of light cast from the infection-containment facility. Nurse McHenry stood taller than Clare. That and her air of aloof unconcern did nothing to lessen Clare's anger.

'Then I refuse to certify the patient as dead,' Clare

whispered, furious. 'And I prescribe a hygienic blanket bath *in situ* for her.'

'That isn't allowed, Dr Burtonall,' Nurse McHenry said coolly. 'I can see no signs of life in this patient. Nurse Widdowson, please draft your patient report.'

'Yes, Nurse McHenry.' The junior nurse thankfully withdrew.

Clare faced the senior nurse. Her face felt hard as cardboard, her cheeks prickling with rage. 'May I know what nursing you *do* offer?'

'None, doctor.' Nurse McHenry looked at the corpse. 'I switched off the emergency night buzzer on the patient's pillow, removed the headphones.' She was sure she would win. 'It's an AIDS case. We restrict nursing to life-support.'

'You bag her mortal remains and bin her?'

'As Admin. lays down, doctor.'

'No, nurse. What you are saying is that your humanity is terminal.'

'When the case dies,' Nurse McHenry intoned, staring with frank disgust at the dead girl, 'we concentrate on disposal. That is the SNO's one instruction.'

'If that's your one conviction, nurse, then cherish it, cherish it.'

The charge nurse, sensing that she had been on the receiving end of some barbed quotation, angrily marched off down the corridor. Clare quietly went down to the sluice room, and started preparations to do the job herself.

Jesus, she thought in despair. The SNO, Senior Nursing Officer, was all too often a fat coffee boffer whose only nursing experience was bandaging one swollen ankle forty years before and who had found it too much like hard work. Now in a splendid office, the SNO laid down rules for some distant incomprehensible war game, an idiot general who never saw a battlefield.

Well, Clare thought, gritting her teeth, there'd be a mighty battle in the morning when the SNO deigned to drift in to work ready for her Danish pastries and hot sweet tea. She'd find a welcome. Dr Clare Burtonall would make sure of that.

First, poor Marie Cullokin's body awaited the last offices.

Clare gowned up, still fuming. Whole sentences – outrage, indignation – formed, ready to be spat out at Admin., but even as she fastened the gown, selected the gloves, located the visor that would protect her against splashes, she warned herself against temper. She was a bad arguer, unable to damp down the fires that flared when she saw patients abused. Alive or dead, there could be no compromise. Steady, Clare, she thought, keep control. It was still night, and Marie Cullokin had to be laid out since, Clare could not resist adding, the entire Farnworth District General Hospital had decided to doze instead.

Alone in the microbiological-containment side unit with the body, Clare mentally listed the precautions.

She donned a long protective apron. Over that, an absorbent disposable gown. Her head was doubly covered, within moments becoming insufferably hot and humid. On her face was the swivel visor. She wore heavy rubberized boots, wellington type, which she hated. Her hands she covered with two layers of gloves, nitrile and latex. She wheeled a double-bowled trolley in clear sight of the silent nurses – they were so preoccupied with their notes – and into one dispensed a phenolic disinfectant. Warm water, to avoid excessive heat dangerously precipitating virus-shielding protein on to instruments.

Hypochlorite, being corrosive, was strictly out. Lingering in or on the body, it could release chlorine. Even traces of the gas, once freed, could react with the formaldehyde so commonly used in pathologists' morbid-anatomy rooms, and create the highly dangerous bis-chloromethyl ether, a powerful cancer producer. Okay, Clare told herself, excessive caution perhaps. A small chance, but why take it?

Quietly she began work.

Marie Cullokin had arrived in hospital in a debilitated state, already dying from the complications of her immunodeficiency virus. Her intercurrent infections were complex and serious. After only two weeks, she had become almost moribund.

In her last lucid moments, Marie was brave. 'Tell Jase one word, Dr Burtonall, please.'

'Yes, Marie. What?'

It would be love, hope, remember, take care. Clare had heard it all. She was unprepared for what Marie eventually came out with.

'Forgive. Tell him forgive.'

'Does he visit you, Marie?' Clare recalled asking. Forgive whom? Marie herself, for some denial or transgression? Clare knew better than ask.

'No.' Marie had tried to smile. 'He can't always get away.'

'Does he work nearby? I could deliver a letter.'

'No!' The refusal came out with force. 'No. They don't let just anybody on to the wharf, see, doctor.' Marie's voice spent itself. 'Pollen, see?'

The conversation was strange. Clare quickly excused

the dying girl, facing her plight with almost unbelievable fortitude.

'Jase'll come when he can, doctor.'

'Is he your boyfriend, Marie?'

The admission notes – Clare's own, for it was she who had made the transfer to the hospital's Infectious Disease unit – revealed little.

She checked everything. Phenolics to disinfect. The sealable containers, metal containers for 'sharps', anything with needles or that could cut. The infusion and tubing. Some unthinking soul had yet again provided polyvinyl chloride body bags in the hospital's CDK, Complete Disposal Kit. Clare's anger flickered, but she was too tired to rage any more against the system. Polyvinyl chloride bags were shunned when it came to cremation on account of the emission of highly toxic dioxins, as products of burning. Atmospheric pollution was now a highly sensitive political issue, and not before time.

Clare cut free the dead girl's ward nightgown, bagging it carefully. Slow movements, she'd been taught in her pathology practicals as a student. No splashes, lessen aerosols, keep turbulence to a minimum. The sheets would have to go, and all the bed linen.

The two-layered protectives under the body were in place. She washed the cooling form – slowly, slow – blotting rather than wiping, meticulously bagging the towels and absorbent papers. It was all a matter of consistency, gentle handling bagging up immediately with deliberate care. And making sure every container was sealed before the next stage, disposal of all garments and the final phase of self-decontamination.

The dead girl's orifices she carefully packed, firming up the absorbent materials by steady pressure. The jaw she supported with a bandage tied round Marie's head, concealing it under the girl's sparse hair. Nostrils, ears, anus, vagina. She flexed the dead Marie's knees, leaning her shoulder in to support the lower limbs in the lithotomy position. The use of endotoxin-free saline, and of slender packing-gauze strips made of fibres artificially cleared of cottonwool's natural oils, was essential, for otherwise medical microbiology's cultures of pathogenic organisms would all be invariably reported as negative, and Clare would have to take the clinical pathologist's endless ribbing. With non-toothed surgical forceps she located the urethra by parting the girl's labia, and gently packed the minute orifice. She left the ribbon gauze protruding, to help Dr Wallace at post-mortem, and with a grunt of effort lowered the corpse's legs.

She rested a moment, then used Marie's own comb from the bedside table, making a rather unsuccessful show of tidying the hair. She tied the big toes together with bandage, foolishly slipping cottonwool between to prevent chaffing. As if that mattered now.

The last thing was to see the eyes closed. No large pennies nowadays. She held the eyelids down a moment or two. Not bad. Clare felt a twinge of sorrow. A cornea from a dead patient was valuable, if slickly containered and shipped to the ophthalmic surgeons, but they would bluntly refuse corneas from an AIDS patient. Pity. Such a waste.

Forty minutes later, Clare stood looking. The dead girl's arms and thighs showed the needle marks, the infected pustules from self-administered drugs – Clare never did get to the bottom of the story, the police shrugging at yet one more addict leaving the city's drug areas for her final sojourn in hospital. Treating terminal infections was a losing fight. Clare put sealing dressings on each injection site.

Goodnight, Marie, she thought. Brave girl, taking her last leave of – who? Jase, was it, who worked at the wharf with 'pollen', in a restricted area? She determined to pass the message on: *forgive*.

Marie had deserved better last offices than Clare's shaky efforts. The old women on Farne Island, where Clare once worked as a GP, would have done a better job. She sighed. She would ask the porters to be especially careful when moving the girl to the mortuary. Much difference that would make.

A score of reports and warnings had to be written about the deceased. That was Clare's task, would take her well over an hour.

*That* was the true rubbish, not poor Marie Cullokin, rest her.

# 2

**Goer** – a male hired by a female for sexual purposes

CLARE HAD A bath, changed into the spare clothes that she always carried. Books should be written about doctors' internal clocks, she thought. The problem wasn't getting along with patients, staff, finding instruments for surgical ward procedures, knowing where the pharmacy was. The age-old problem was one's internal biorhythms. Like, what to do at five-thirty in the morning in a ghostly hospital?

There were other difficulties. She lived too far out to justify driving home at this hour. Also, she was determined to wage her own special war against Admin. She owed it to the dead girl.

She glanced at her watch – the hospital clock on the blink, of course. She decided to go down to the communal waiting area, a sordid place where chairs and low tables were being shifted by cleaners trundling vacuum machines. Unbelievably there was a lingering stale smell of cigarettes. Clare put coins into the coffee maker for some unspeakable liquid. There had been a move to prevent smoking, but freedom had raised its troublesome head. The anti-smoking lobby had been defeated on moral principles – *that* old one.

The cleaners drifted off down the corridor. Clare sat, making sure her handbag was safe. By chance, she had placed herself directly opposite the public telephones. Expression of a subconscious wish?

Certainly not, she answered herself testily. She hadn't even given phones a single thought.

Tired, she sipped the hot coffee. A surgical houseman she did not recognize strode through, stopped, patted the pockets of his white coat, struggling to think of things forgotten. How well she remembered that feeling of stupefying tiredness, when you could no longer remember if you'd paused for a drink of water or been to the loo. Legislation was afoot to limit working hours – for everybody except doctors. Happily, her houseman days were gone for ever.

Reluctantly she decided to phone Clifford. Her husband would just be getting up. Their housekeeper Mrs Kinsale wouldn't arrive until half past eight.

'Hello?' Mercifully answering on the first ring.

'Clifford? It's me. I've finished in the ward, but I'm waiting to see Admin. Something's come up.'

'You won't be home before I go? I meet city planners at ten.'

Careful, she warned herself. She herself might have an appointment. They kept a communal calendar, tried to keep it up-to-date. 'You're down for the cardiac surveillance unit, ten to six?'

'That's tomorrow,' Clare said. 'And thank God. I'm doing in-patient documentation once I'm finished here.'

'Can you meet for supper, say, six-thirty? I'll be done by then, and it's quite a time since . . .'

She let it hang for a moment. He was at least trying. She ought to respond, keep up appearances despite the absurdity of the whole thing.

'That would be nice.' Time to introduce a note of levity,

so the call would not end with another of their dreadful silences. 'I warn you, Clifford, this week will be hell. Today, I shall have an unholy scrap with the desk dozers, so be warned!'

He gave a convincing chuckle. 'I'll tread carefully, darling! See you at teatime.'

Ridiculous, she thought, returning to her cold coffee. Twenty-eight years old, a professional woman eminent in her career, and she was still hesitant about so many things.

Inherited anxieties were as foolish as a married professional couple – guess who – making polite conversation, when they cohabited in a state of guerrilla warfare. Clifford had been trying to make peace ever since . . . Clare closed that particular mental avenue.

Two nurses came through the silent lounge. One used a phone while the other listened closely. They left talking discreetly, probably some boyfriend issue.

More cleaners passed, then an anxious medical registrar, bundles of notes already in his arms, his spectacles gleaming as he gave her a grin. Dr Phil Morreston, tipped for high consultancy appointments, currently writing a paper on respiratory susceptibilities in intractable neurological disease. He'd been refused funds to extend his research into the elderly. Clare had expressed sympathy when they had talked in the hospital canteen, Phil wrily joking, 'An interesting exercise in priorities, Dr Burtonall!' making her laugh.

The phones were still free.

Dr Morreston was coming back. He'd remembered something.

'Got a second, later today, Dr Burtonall?'

'For you, Dr Morreston, anything.' She rolled her eyes to make it an exasperated lie. This was the last thing she wanted.

'I heard about your cracking row in Inf. Div.' His expression grew grave. 'How do you stand on PVS?'

PVS was bitterly controversial among doctors. Everyone differed about the persistent vegetative state. Should life-maintenance services for a patient in seemingly terminal coma be turned off so the patient died? Or should the moralists be listened to, and the combative religious orthodoxies be allowed to force doctors into actions they opposed? Should relatives decide? It was dangerous ground.

'Dr Boucher knows where *he* stands, Phil, so the question of my morals doesn't arise.' Clare had already had a run-in with Phil Morreston's senior, Dr Paddy Boucher.

'He's giving me *carte blanche*.' Phil stammered slightly when agitated. 'I wouldn't ask you, only the patient's going to be the subject of a CPC. I wondered if you'd moderate for me.'

The clinico-pathological conferences, CPCs, were arenas arranged in the Baron lecture theatre. Anyone from the medical school was allowed to attend and chip in. Each weekly CPC was seen differently. To junior doctors it was a war game, where they could shine by displaying medical knowledge. To older consultants it was a trial, the wilder impulses of their registrars against common sense. To medical students it was a source of amused folklore about this consultant's erudite backhanded swipes at clinical rivals, or about that surgeon's wry digs. Moderating Phil's CPC was something she could do without today.

'I wouldn't ask, Clare, but I'm afraid I'll have Dr Carrillon in.'

Clare drew breath. Dr Anita Carrillon, an ambitious doctor who had worked extensively in Mediterranean countries, saw religion everywhere. She was regarded as a pain, but had a few foci of support. She was Clare's age, greedy for influence, Clare thought waspishly, way beyond her wisdom.

'I'm so sorry, Phil. I'm not establishment staff. Plenty of staff doctors want a go. I'll try to come, though. Two o'clock?'

'Yes, usual time.' In spite of her refusal he looked relieved. 'The case is that patient with the head injury, six months back. The relatives want out. We're being lobbied by AML.'

The anti-murder lobby, as a number of lay people called themselves, saw the removal of life support from patients who'd shown no sign of consciousness for several months as plain murder, and constantly threatened legal action even against open discussion. The hospital had already been picketed, and nobody on the staff – Dr Carrillon excepted – wanted to repeat the process.

Dr Morreston left with a nod of thanks.

Clare looked. Those phones, still free.

Soon patients' relatives would start arriving, thinly at first among the hospital staff, then in hordes. Once Admin. started drifting in – Clare pointedly refused to think of their arrival in any other way – then the phones would be continuously occupied. The chances of using a phone to arrange a possibly clandestine meeting with some male would be nil. She would have to use her car phone, or wangle a call from the ward handset. That would be far too compromising in these days of recorded calls. A woman had to be doubly cautious, a woman doctor trebly so.

The thought of making such an arrangement hadn't entered her mind.

A chattering group of nurses coming on day duty passed through the lounge, one laughingly shushing the rest as they crossed to Out-Patients. Clare analysed her feeling.

Relief, that they hadn't stopped to use the public telephones? Could be. Clifford was now out of the equation. This evening's supper would have to take care of itself. And the same for this afternoon's CPC, featuring Dr Phil Morreston against the redoubtable Dr Anita Carrillon's entrenched opinions.

Clare should be free after the Admin. battle over the dead AIDS girl, if she played her cards right. There would still be her cardiac surveillance notes to do.

Poor Marie Cullokin, though. Pass on her last vital message to Jase. Who worked at some wharf, with pollen. She would have him come to the hospital. Probably the youth would call soon anyway. He would be notified of Marie's death, Admin. indolence permitting.

The phones were still free. A chance?

Doors were starting to go, telltale wafts of air cooling Clare's cheek. These were the tricks doctors learned in houseman years – 'intern', as the Americans said, such a graphic hint of confinement! She waited as some clinical pathology technicians passed, always carrying files and textbooks. Just for one minute no doors blew air along corridors, no feet clattered on the tiles.

As if on signal, three adults came and sat at a nearby table, huddled in conference. Clare couldn't help overhearing.

'We ought to talk to the doctor,' one woman said to the man. The argument was obviously not new.

'We ought to let Uncle Jerry know we're here,' the man said.

'See the ward sister,' the second woman said. 'Doctors'd tell us nothing.'

'Why not? We're next of kin.'

The second woman said in anger, 'Some lawyer's been sniffing round. You know what they're like.'

'Sheila's right. There's his house. There's a limit to how long they hang on, isn't there?'

Clare heard them settle their tactical plan, first the ward sister, then Uncle Jerry's doctor, see if their sick relative was still able to sign things or was he too far gone. She watched them leave, couldn't help scoring the women's clothes down on points, a thoroughly useless blow on poor helpless old Uncle Jerry's behalf.

The lounge area fell silent. It was one hint too many. She went to the phone, dialled. Clare kept looking about in case someone might overhear. She always felt a nervous quivering in the pit of her stomach, so silly after all this time.

The saccharine sweet voice she knew so well by now came on. 'Pleases Agency, Inc. How may I help you?'

'This is Clare Three-Nine-Five. An appointment for late this morning, please.'

'Very well. Eleven o'clock?'

'If you can.'

'That's fine, Clare Three-Nine-Five. Might I ask for your preference?'

'Bonn.' Clare almost spat the name, angry that the stupid woman would assume she'd want to change, for heaven's sake. 'Please,' she added by way of apology.

'Do you prefer any particular venue, Three-Nine-Five?'

'Somewhere different this time, please.'

'Certainly.' A pulse, then, 'The Time and Scythe Hotel?'

'At the north end of Bolgate, that one?'

'Yes. Your suite number will be 482. Repeat, please.'

'Room 482, eleven o'clock. Bonn.'

'Thank you, Clare Three-Nine-Five. Please be assured that the Pleases Agency is always attentive to clients—'

'Thank you.' Clare cut the woman's practised prattle short, replaced the receiver just as her coins ran out.

She was too tired to read, and too pleased by the success of the booking to rest. Instead, she went and had breakfast at the hospital canteen as soon as it opened at seven. Normally she would have brought clinical notes to read through, but this morning felt too edgy on several counts. There was Clifford. Then cudgels for poor dead Marie. Then the pleasure of slipping between the starched white sheets in that hotel in Bolgate. She found herself smiling in anticipation, making some physiotherapist smile back in mistaken greeting. Clare quickly composed her features, and tried to look preoccupied with higher thoughts.

# 3

**Crossing** – forbidden sexual congress between a goer and a female prostitute in the same employ

RACK FELL IN with Bonn as he emerged from the Butty Bar.

'Whyn't you have your brekkie, Bonn?'

'I had breakfast two hours gone, Rack, thank you.'

Rack sighed. Every answer Bonn ever gave made him want to shake his head. Thank you, beg pardon, not at all, wasn't frigging *natural*. They crossed by the Bolgate Street traffic lights, Rack taking a newspaper from Fat George.

Bonn slowed. 'Rack. Pay him, please.'

'Christ's sake, Bonn,' Rack cried, exasperated. 'Martina fucking *owns* George and the frigging city centre and Grellie's girl stringers and Waterloo Street *and* the Shot Pot and—'

'Language, Rack,' Bonn said patiently. 'It is wrong to steal.'

Rack thought, I don't believe this. Except he did. But you couldn't disappoint Bonn because if you did Martina would go galactic, Grellie wouldn't speak for a week – okay, maybe an hour but you'd pay somehow, Christ how Grellie'd make you pay. Bonn himself would never mention this terrible episode when he, Rack, his trusty loyal stander and mate, took a paper without paying and so threatened civilization as we fucking knew it. And did Fat George even notice? Enough to make a saint swear.

'I'll pay him when I pass next, Bonn,' Rack said. 'It's not honesty makes you tell me off, Bonn.' There wasn't time to develop the theory, because he'd a message to give. 'Eleven o'clock, your next go. Clare Three-Nine-Five in the Time and Scythe, Bolgate Street.'

Which made Bonn stand still. Rack thought, aha!

'Far end of Bolgate Street,' Bonn said, not being addicted to questions.

'It's early, innit?' Rack, asking the questions Bonn ought to.

'Somewhat.' A crowd dashed across the zebra crossing, heading for the trains. They stood to let the rush dwindle.

'Women never come early.' Rack perused the paper, gave up in exasperation when Bonn said nothing. 'That mayoress who booked you a month back. She comes council days.'

Listen to me, Rack thought. I'm fucking bewildered, talking my own conversations when Bonn ought to be saying his bits. Minding a goer like Bonn was weird.

'I have forgotten, Rack.'

Bonn never forgot. The mayoress was from beyond Bury, and wanted her shag before her council meetings began. She was in political trouble now. Rack reckoned she'd be out of it until things cooled and the newshawks stopped following her from the Party Central Office.

'I would appreciate it if you could find Grellie, please, first.'

Rack widened his elbows to stop Bonn getting jostled by pedestrians. The morning pavements were crowded, schools breaking up. When was Easter?

'Grellie's having breakfast in the Volunteer.'

'Thank you.' Bonn knew better than argue. He never

knew if Rack had some system of signals indicating where everybody in Martina's syndicate actually was.

'Hey, Bonn,' Rack said. 'They're going to blam somebody at the canal gates. Maybe some shooters, I dunno. Can I say you're booked up for the rest of the day?'

'As you suggest, Rack. Thank you.' There would be nothing in the *Standard*, early or late edition, about the coming crime. Rack had the attention span of a gnat, but his street susswork was accurate.

Grellie, head of the working girls on Martina's strings who trawled the main square as far as Waterloo Street, saw them and turned to intercept. She was coming from the direction of the Volunteer Arms by Deansgate. Intuition? It was as if Rack actually bleeped people, but so far Bonn hadn't spotted how.

Rack said, 'Good that you want to see her, Bonn. She wants a word.'

'Into the gardens, I think.'

Rack said no, go into the shopping mall.

'Because you've not much time. It'll be about that lass who's a dope-nutter. Ankles, redhead with a step-brother jugged up three months, remember her? Four years, with GBR.'

Bonn watched Grellie approach. She was attractive, casual, and her cool vigilance shone with a kind of luminescence. Rack's precise foreknowledge couldn't be simply all guesswork. This was an instance. GBR, good behaviour remission, was discretionary, but Rack knew how far it would operate in Ankles's step-brother's favour in some future parole panel in some distant gaol.

'I'd need the full story, Rack, please,' Bonn said, voice low.

Rack was disgusted. Like, they weren't in Victoria

Square, teeming traffic circling in a rubbish one-way system round the central gardens, the immense bus station with its shoddy nosh caff and kiddies' playground, people from the shopping mall in hundreds, hordes more to London Road railway station. And Bonn here talking like in some library, hush Rack everybody's reading.

'Ask me,' Rack said, challenging Bonn to pop some question about any of the girls, maybe sixty not counting the wheel-peelers who paid Martina direct to be franchied – franchised to operate in the area – and who went separate, though Rack even knew all about those. A direct question from Bonn would be a victory.

'Thank you, Rack. I probably won't have time to see Martina before the next woman.'

Rack waved to Grellie. They drifted into the Azda shopping mall, warmth engulfing them. 'I'll be outside.'

The mall could have been anywhere. The same birdcage with budgerigars, the same ceaseless water clock, escalators to echoing floors, multinationals selling electric goods, clothes, toys so brightly coloured they made choice impossible. Bonn preferred the barrows in Market Street, where the Worcester Tea Rooms laid a genteel cloak over its true functions and where the Café Phryne provided comfort for ladies who required rather personal encounters.

Bonn found a seat by the enormous herbarium. Grellie sat by.

'Morning, Grellie. I'm glad you came.'

'Morning, Bonn. Today's going to be hectic.'

Grellie was pretty. No other word would do. It was unusual, in one who operated whole lines of girl stringers. Any lass with that harsh responsibility soon became emotionally dowsed, suffused by strain and responsibility. What was once an untouched, even aloof, beauty became a sour creature of callous ferocity. Oddly, Grellie somehow remained intact, but at what cost? Bonn liked Grellie, not only for her kindness to him when he'd arrived from nowhere.

'I was hoping for a quiet start.' Bonn made the wry comment a joke.

She laughed. He noticed her hair was different.

'That'll be the day. Ankles has already had a scrap, that drummer at the Palais paying her in scag.'

'Poor lass.' Ankles was a girl suddenly paying too much for her drugs at the Ball Boys disco near Manchester Road, north side of the square, everybody in the syndicate on about it. Rack had told Bonn the lads were taking bets on Ankles lasting less than a week, eleven to five.

'I'm sick of her, Bonn. It's time she went.' This was the wrong beginning. Grellie wanted clean pleasantry, not social pathology. She quickly cut across Bonn's compassion. 'I'll think it out.' She angled towards him. 'Look, Bonn. Don't let me speak out of turn.'

'You never could, Grellie.'

Her eyes shone. She patted her hair, pleased.

'You know I said once you'd got settled in at Martina's?' It was common knowledge, after all.

'It's a nice room, very comfortable, thank you.'

Grellie breathed relief, the hurdle passed.

'I was wondering if you'd given any thought to, well, you and me.'

She looked about the mall concourse, children in push-chairs, old men yakking, women heading for the coffee balcony, teenagers laughing with extravagant body language. Grellie's offer was made from a generous soul.

'I would like to.'

'You would?' She stared. 'Me?'

'The difficulties are serious,' he said. A dog came, sat before him. Bonn absently reached and stroked it under the chin. She watched his gentle hand move. 'People know too much about you, Grellie. And me. It's like trying to keep secrets in a huge family.'

'Rack.' Grellie named the main problem. Nobody knew how deeply Rack was in with Martina. Were they cousins, as rumour said? 'He still wants to pair us off. He ran a book on us until Martina put a stop.'

'I heard,' Bonn said. 'It was improper.'

An old man rocked past, the rubber ferrule of his walking stick squeaking. It must have started raining. People were coming in shaking umbrellas, undoing plastic hoods from pushchairs.

'I played hell,' Grellie said with a relaxed smile.

Bonn was amused by the incongruity of her expression. She watched his smile begin, slowly take over his face, spreading until it occupied his features in a great grin. She wanted to touch, but word would have got back to Martina within the hour, and then what?

'There's one possibility, Bonn.' She saw the dog go after its master, glancing back at Bonn. Even fucking animals, she thought in wonderment.

His smile died. 'It would have to be sound, Grellie.' He too looked after the dog. 'Crossing over between goers and working girls is not allowed.'

'It would be absolutely safe, Bonn. I have a relative, works near Altrincham. She has a maisonette near Colne. I sometimes go there.'

'That would hardly be the place, Grellie.'

She thought, at last I'm discussing it. Me and Bonn. Sodding Martina could go and jump off the viaduct, take her lame leg with her.

'My cousin'd sell it, then buy another place in her own name. Her bloke's a canal worker, St Helens. They'd live in his flat. Martina's syndicate doesn't run as far as Liverpool. It's like on Mars, from here.'

'You would buy the cousin's new flat, then.'

'No. She would swap ownerships. You and me'd just meet there. It'd only need a decent cover tale.'

'Decent is right, Grellie.'

'Bonn.' She drew breath, risking offence. 'You're not just saying this?' She felt stiff inside and had to look away. 'I don't need pacifying, is all I'm trying to say.'

'I like you, Grellie. The question is your cousin's new place.'

'As long as she didn't have to fork out, she would buy wherever.'

Bonn saw Rack appear at the mall's main entrance. He carried an umbrella. One problem with Rack was, Bonn never knew where Rack lurked between one reappearance and the next. Perhaps several minions earwigged wherever Rack was not? He rose.

'Grellie. About Ankles.'

'I'm binning her, Bonn. I can't have this drugs business. It's getting out of hand. I've hung my washing. The girls know the rules.'

'A drummer is supposed to be causing it all, they say.'

'Him too. He has to go. I'll tell Rack.'

'I wonder if you are being a little hard, Grellie. Perhaps a talking-to . . .'

'Perhaps, Bonn.' Now she would never know if this was Bonn's suggestion of a topic fabricated to allay Rack's suspicions, or whether Bonn was making a plea for clemency. She hoped it was the former. The girl had already caused enough trouble.

She rose, making sure she smiled for watching eyes. 'It would have no effect. *Listen* to me! I'm starting to talk like you! Better not let any of the girls hear me, or they'll think the worst. The best!'

'I also hope, Grellie,' Bonn said. 'Thank you for your time.'

She turned quickly away and headed for the nearest boutique, not wanting to be caught looking.

'Twenty minutes.' Rack came up. 'Stop here. It's teeming down. I'll get a taxi. Okay?'

'Yes, thank you.' Bonn halted Rack's dash by a gesture. 'I think Grellie may be a little harsh over Ankles, Rack. You might suggest a period of probation.'

It was in the taxi that Rack told Bonn about Ankles. Grellie had already sacked the girl, no question of having her back. The drummer at the Rowlocks Casino had been bagged early this morning.

Bonn wondered why he'd been put through the hoop so long after the events. He wanted to ask Grellie, but would not dare. Had he been too frank? There was just a chance that, if anyone had taped the conversation, he just might – only just – be able to imply that he was only being kind.

The problem was Martina, who was virtually all powerful. Posser, her sick dad, was as much a friend as any old man could be, but risks were everywhere. Bonn wanted routine.

They alighted a hundred yards beyond the end of Bolgate Street and the Time and Scythe Hotel. Rack gave Bonn the opened umbrella.

'Ten minutes,' Rack said. 'Room 482. Her motor's in the pub car park, but she won't have gone in yet.'

Hasn't? thought Bonn, or did Rack really know for

certain where Clare Three-Nine-Five was at this very minute?

'Thank you.' Bonn paused. 'Rack, Grellie spoke as if she was still thinking what sanctions to impose.'

Rack grinned. 'That's Grellie's way, Bonn. Gotter be careful with birds. Say one thing, mean anything. Know why? It's different grub, see? Birds eat different things. Tell you about it after you've done.'

'I look forward to it, Rack. Thank you.'

Bonn entered the hotel, and made his way to 482.

# 4

**Stringer** – a female street prostitute of a group allocated a particular beat

'It's strange, Bonn,' Clare said after he woke.

Room 482 was sparser than the suites she'd become used to in the Hotel Vivante. Lovely freesias, however, the curtains a bright admix of floral patterns. The place was spotlessly clean, and she really envied the Time and Scythe for the bedside lamp, an amber parchment design she had been hunting for months.

This was their established pattern now. At first her uncertainty, and Clifford's criminal involvements, had brought this about. Had anyone suggested that she, a practising doctor, would hire a male for the most intimate purpose, she would have been outraged. Now? Now Bonn was part of her life. What Clifford did she no longer cared. She was trapped, yes, but shared her prison with the one she wanted most.

Not true, though, that she didn't care about Clifford.

The truth was that she'd never really known what he was doing. The facade had been shored up by glib lies. Ostensibly Clifford was an investment counsellor for major city companies. Only a chance encounter had brought her to her senses, and caused her to meet Bonn.

Admittedly Bonn was her hireling for sexual gratification.

Clifford knew, or suspected. She however *knew* that her husband was involved in city crime, and that he used marriage as a cloak of respectability. They lived in deceit, but the chains were of Clifford's making. She could manage, as long as she had Bonn.

She looked along the pillow at him, and found his eyes still closed. But his breathing had changed, so he was awake and giving her a minute to adjust. He knew how awkward it had been for her. She wondered, was it simply that Bonn was more careful than most?

He was eight years or so younger. Background, a void. Origin, somewhere in the north but no exact spot. She never asked for details of his parents, siblings. He never volunteered.

'Strange,' he repeated, eyes shut. Nor did he ask questions.

'Circadian rhythms,' she said.

When booking him that first anxious time, almost driven out of her mind to find someone to help her find if her husband was implicated in murder, she had automatically given her first name when asked by the Pleases Agency's telephone lady. She had cursed herself back then, but now no longer cared.

'Circadian rhythm. The automatic timing mechanism that keeps *Homo sapiens* in step with the rising and the setting of the sun. We're all in synchrony.'

'I sometimes wonder.'

She smiled. 'Don't go philosophical, darling. Not after what we have done to each other. I couldn't stand it.'

'With,' he said. His eyes still hadn't opened, yet she felt he was observing. 'Done with. Not done to.'

'Is that too crude, Bonn? Maybe one of us did it *with*, the other *to*?'

'Circadian rhythm,' he reminded.

She laid her leg over him, heeling against him the firmer.

'There's the day–night clock in each of us. We doctors think there's another one. It serves as a kind of an episodic timer, as if we had an hourglass within. It works by trickling dopamine molecules from one chemical state to another, drip-feed. Our bodies can thus time shorter intervals.'

'How marvellous.'

Laughing, she pulled him over her, gasping at his weight.

'These theories, Clare. Doctors ought to be free of speculation. You're as bad as my stander.'

That interrupted her humour. She knew that each goer for hire in Bonn's syndicate had a guardian, who stood guard while the goer met the lady client. It was a sorry reminder at a moment when she didn't want reminding.

'Why? What theories does he have?'

'Every yard he'll explain why traffic is noisy, that steam would be quieter but the Government won't buy the coal. That church spires stay up because of the prevailing wind. That grass can be made to grow inverted, but farmers block the patents. That nurses are all heavy smokers, politicians trained in a secret school on the Isle of Man by Americans.'

'And I'm as crazy as that?'

'Your ideas sometimes sound so.'

She knew it was a joke, Bonn making comparisons with the way she first felt when coming to him as a client.

'You mean when I spoke of love as a chemical phenomenon?'

'That's the one.'

'It isn't as silly as it sounds, Bonn.'

His eyes were open now, and she'd missed the event. She always liked to see his eyes dart into wakefulness, their instantaneous wariness swiftly changing into quiet appraisal.

After that alertness, he was Bonn as she knew him, half smiling, apologetic, accepting. And, most importantly, hers for the hire.

'Not silly. Sad.'

His other characteristic, sadness and sorrow in various degrees.

'It doesn't supplant fondness.' She evaded the most emotive word of all. 'Desire, compassion, respect, admiration, the comfort of another.'

'People think it does.'

It was when they'd first made love. She had deliberately hired him in revenge, after learning that Clifford had caused a death simply to protect his own position. She had been like a spoiled brat, desperately angry, wanting to get back at her husband. Bonn had carried out investigations on her say-so. Once she was sure of Clifford's guilt, and that she was powerless to expose him because of her gullible complicity, she had cold-bloodedly phoned the Pleases Agency and hired Bonn. Of course she had deceived herself with all kinds of emotional manoeuvres. Then she found herself a regular client, blandly paying the Agency's fees, always seeking Bonn when days filled with problems. A placebo? No, he was more than that.

Having come this far, she now had a hundred explanations to assuage her guilt. Bonn, she told herself, was auto-psychotherapy, badly needed after times in clinics, at the hospital, when her emotions were damaged by patients' suffering. Or – another explanation, almost as good – she was deprived of sex now that Clifford had put himself beyond the pale. How could she make love with a husband who had manipulated her into giving him an alibi? Impossible. So what was she to do, live like a nun because her husband was virtually a killer and a crook? She had taken the only way, for a professional woman determined to control her own life. She simply hired necessary support services – think of Bonn as no more than that.

It was totally justifiable. If a person – man or woman, married or single – grew hungry, why, what was more natural than going out for food? Yet nobody claimed that was a betrayal of family life, did they?

Bonn was hinting at something they had talked of when first they had made love. It had been in the Vivante, the hotel Bonn's agency seemed to use most. She even remembered the room.

She had spoken of the chemical theory of love. He had not laughed or made fun, just listened. The first stage, of sight and scent of another person, pheromones worked to attract the opposite gender, Then the phenylethylamine, the famous 'rush' molecules which, with neurochemicals like norepinephrine and dopamine, zoomed a person to elation and a state of excitement at the prospect of forthcoming sex. Endorphins, so like morphines, bring tranquillity to the process, a sense of ease and comfort. Oxytocin was supposed to be the famous 'cuddling chemical', when orgasm reigned and life chugged into some bliss-filled superstratum.

'I have reached stage five,' Bonn said.

She was startled at his perception, but quickly came to. 'So have I.'

'It seems too slick to be true.' A pause. 'For me, I mean.'

Clare reached down and stroked his flank, drawing his hand onto her breast.

'I don't like it being chemistry. The last stage is when duty and the temptation compete – the beautiful secretary enticing him, the handsome male attendant attracting her.

It's too laid-down.' She felt sudden distress. Her eyes filled. 'Bonn, look at me.'

He obeyed. 'You are beautiful, Clare.'

'I wish I knew if you were you.' She gazed at him, her vision blurred. 'I lose sleep thinking about what you say. I kept asking myself: Does he say the same things to all his women? Does he practise answers? Does he feel?'

'They are not "my" women, Clare.'

'Us, then, whoever we are.'

'You know the answer, or you would never have asked.'

'I tell myself it shouldn't matter.'

'You see, Clare, you knew all the time. When you first hired me, I was what you wanted me to be. I made myself so.'

'And now it's different?'

'No. It's the same. I am to be what you want. Except that now I want you to continue hiring me.' His hand kneaded her breast. 'I have purpose, where you are concerned.' It took time for him to add, 'With you, I would even settle for less.' He smiled, with apology. 'It's a shameful admission, for one of my persuasion.'

She had almost begun to speak before she caught herself and managed to stay silent. No more, she warned inwardly, not another word. His mouth sucked on her breast. She groaned once at the stimulus, and then tugged him so he splayed over her.

They made love. She glanced at the bedside clock just before he entered her. She gave a gasp at the quite audible dry susurrus, glad that he seemed oblivious. It was important to her that he behaved as a preoccupied lover. Her thoughts ended in oblivion, the destiny of all theories.

*

'We have ten minutes, Clare.'

She lay drenched in his sweat, relishing the way the damp sheets clung after love. Not, she corrected herself quickly, 'making love'. After sexual congress.

'Did you know the Victorians called sexual intercourse "conversation"?'

'Yes,' Bonn said.

His reply was muffled, yet he had wakened first this time. Conscience, she knew, or consciousness of time's passing, ruled his days. She could not stay beyond one hour, unless she booked beforehand and of course paid accordingly. The memory returned of her dithering when she'd hired him for that first calamitous encounter, when she'd suggested that he act as her private investigator to see what Clifford was up to. The television, she remembered, smiling. She had put the money on the TV set, her face scarlet.

'They had conversation bonnets, with the neb aslant,' Bonn murmured, 'so they could kiss without turning. And conversation chairs, double ones facing opposite ways.'

'Clever old them.' She raised herself, tutting. He made to rouse but she shook her head. 'No. Don't see me out, Bonn. Let *me* leave *you*.'

It was as she was dressing that she brought out the question.

'Can I ask, Bonn?' When he made no reply, she told him about a patient who had died of AIDS. 'I'm going to have a row with a senior nursing officer. They "weren't in" this morning.' Clare made a falsetto out of the postponement. 'I'll snare them this afternoon, though, God help them.'

'Amen,' Bonn said.

Clare paused, drawing on her stockings. Now, there's a thing, she thought in surprise; stockings! Had I known, when I dressed during the night to respond to Nurse McHenry's call, that I would hire Bonn this morning? Normally she wore tights, for simplicity. So much for the all-conquering biochemical and neurophysiological mechanisms.

'Her boyfriend works on some wharf or other. I've no address. Jase loads pollen. I'm sure that's what she said. She's died. I need to pass him her message.'

Bonn had gone very still. 'Pollen, at a wharf. I suppose it is this city, Clare, and not somewhere like Liverpool.'

'She implied it was here. He doesn't get much time off.'

I'll bet, Bonn thought. Haleys Wharf, the canal where 'pollen', street drugs, were sold of a night.

'If I hear anything,' he said, wondering how to explain.

'Sorry there's not much to go on, darling.'

Darling, she admonished herself, plus stockings! She'd be wearing transparent underclothes next, with spike heels. Give the clinic nurses something to talk about, that would.

Bonn could have taken Clare to the very spot. 'One thing, Clare. I don't think you ought to ask around, not generally.'

'No?' She felt something amiss and studied him. 'Is everything all right?'

'Yes, thank you,' he said politely. He was still naked.

She bent, put her mouth on his. This act wasn't something she could think of as kissing. When first she'd . . . not kissed, but osculated . . . he'd said, reading her mind, 'Prostitutes never kiss, Clare.' He had uttered the words softly, but into her with such a terrible directness that she'd recoiled, alarmed at the intensity. And now look at her, osculating away. Hussy. She left money on the television, smiling to herself as she did so, and left with a backward glance at him there on the pillows, looking. She didn't understand his look, but that was nothing new.

# 5

**Key** – a goer who controls a group of goers, usually three or four in number

RACK WALKED PAST Frondy, the dishevelled artist whose pitch was at the Bradshawgate corner of Victoria Square.

'Stopped using that black grot, Frondy?' Rack asked, not pausing.

On his second stroll by, the artist answered. 'Charcoal costs a frigging fortune. I uses pencil, ten pence.'

Rack judged Frondy's sketch, which looked crap. 'It's crap. What is it?'

'God knows. Sold two yesterday, though.'

Rack was here to collect whatever news his grass had. Frondy was once a legit student at the City Art College, until he got slung for selling herbal ecstasy. After that he drifted, until he hit on begging. He set up his easel, canvas, with brushes and whatnot, and wrote a notice, the final version of which now read POOR ARTIST PLEASE HELP. At first he made highly accurate observations about the northern public. An adverb was counter-productive, so GENEROUSLY caused donations to dry instantly. Exclamation marks had the same effect.

Another thing. When yobbos came ripping through the square and up-ended his easel and stood jeering and squirting his paints over him, hobbling crones and wheezing gents immediately rallied to his rescue, beating the tearaways with brollies. And these were ancient frails who'd battled through real tank-and-bomb wars. They said things like, 'Poor man, because fair's fair,' and that. Invariably Frondy's take after such episodes rose sharply, so he hit on the idea of hiring a load of doozes to roar in and rough him up. Rack put a stop to it because it gave the square a bad name.

Frondy obediently streamlined his whole operation, discarded his easel and simply stood there and sketched. The plod, he'd explained when asking Rack could he do it, can't move you on for sketching, could they? Rack told him fair enough, but to give a third of his daily take into the Waterloo Street girls' pot, which Frondy knew was only fair. In payment, Frondy told Rack what mother he could gather, mother being trustworthy news.

'Some teacher's around, Rack, asking about goers.' Frondy swore as a passing motor splashed him.

'By name?'

'Nar, just general digging.' Frondy glanced, warily judging how his next words might go down. 'I told her I'd maybe have some news later. That all right, Rack?'

'What news?' Rack didn't like people making decisions.

'Dunno. Whatever you tell me to say.'

That was more like it. 'What's she a teacher of?'

'Shot me some line about sociology, researching street behaviour.' Frondy saw Rack's unease, so offered more. 'Middle height, brown jacket, white collar, slacks, shoulder bag, no hat. Thirty-one? Birds' ages, all look the frigging same nowadays.'

'Good lad, Frondy. Don't name the Pleases Agency.'

'Right, Rack. One thing. That pimp, you broke his leg—'

'I what?' Rack was on instant heat. 'How'd I know the fucking tram'd creep up?'

'That's what I meant,' Frondy agreed quickly. 'Ought to have loud hooters like in Bispham. Well, he's gone to London.'

'Hopped it did he? Wise lad. Taddah.'

Rack shelved the sociology woman for the minute, and moved on to the Butty Bar at the junction with Mealhouse Lane. It was Rack's own patch. He entered shouting cheery insults to the counter girls and demanding food, tea, news of the Wanderers' latest fiasco, football nonsense. A dozen people were in watching the steamed windows.

'Rack.'

The girl who joined him was a stout, thickset lass whose face looked assembled from left-overs. That didn't mean Jessie was ugly, merely disordered with her white-streaked hair and odd earrings. She thought it trendy to have eyeliner only on her left eye, one cheek rouged and the other a ghostly white, lipstick one side of her mouth when just one lip would have been better. Rack never knew what to make of Jessie. Even her shoes didn't match. Today she'd gone still further, stitched on a different-coloured sleeve to her coat, but who the fuck, Rack thought in wonder, needed three sleeves when you'd only got two arms? She looked ridiculous. Find the other two halves of Jessie you'd have a smashing pair of bints you could do something with. But this? He put it all down to fashion. He'd ask Bonn about Jessie, was she off her trolley or just artistic. Grellie let Jessie charge punters over the odds for gob jobs but not on Grand National race days. Rack didn't know why. It was women.

'Jessie,' he greeted, then bawled for beans, seeing an inadequate meal on the way. The counter girls scurried in retreat, shouting laughing abuse back because they'd made the mistake deliberately simply to provoke. 'Your gear's all odd, Jessie.' He wondered about tact. 'You look crap.'

'That new manageress, Worcester Club and Tea Rooms? She's agate, asking all sorts.'

'Oh, aye.' Rack repeated the phrase, narked at how it didn't come out right like these northerners could say it, him being a Londoner. Their word 'agate' seemed to mean anything you liked. 'Who about?'

'I think she meant Bonn. It were yesterday.'

Rack's grin suddenly failed to match his eyes, though nothing changed that you could see. Photograph him a second earlier, then now, the snaps would seem identical, but she felt something go, and went cold.

'It wasn't me heard it, Rack, honest to God,' she almost yelped. 'Connie's over there now to suss her out.'

His extrovert joviality came back like a swift invisible thaw. He guffawed as the counter lass tried again, laying knife, fork, condiments as her ally brought the steaming plate.

'About time, Tansy. I bin here an hour.'

'One of these days you'll get struck by lightning. And no grumbling about the bacon, either!' she scolded. 'We've had enough from you this week!'

It was all so innocent, but Jessie knew better.

'What've I to do, Rack? I don't want to get it wrong. Mrs Judith Alexander, the manageress, forty-three, is all I know so far.'

'You done right, gal. Do as Connie says, and tell her you tellt me, roight?' Rack's returning Cockney was a clue: all wasn't well, the news troubling him.

'Yes, Rack. Thanks.'

Jessie went then as he started his grub, heard him shout calamity because the toast was slow coming, still cracking jokes, everybody in the place falling about as football cat-calling started up. She breathed relief as she went out into the rain and traffic where it was safe.

They were assembling in the Pilot Ship Casino's upper rooms, where the agency's phones operated. Martina called it 'the control office', to Bonn too pompous for two rooms and a small kitchen thing with a bathroom down a creaking corridor. Two ladies of a certain age booked incoming requests, knitted, and made themselves tea.

Martina was already waiting. Her limp would remain unseen, seated as she was by the obsolete ironwork grate, hob and all, when the goers started arriving. Miss Rose and Miss Hope were all a-simper in the adjacent room on floorboards from hell, but hoping to hear everything because they only rarely got to see goers. Excitement had taken hold. Martina had to reprimand Miss Rose for failing to pick up the receiver within the prescribed three rings. They were thrilled when Fret Dougal, lanky and smiling, put his head round the door to ask if he was in the right place.

'He's the Accrington one,' Miss Rose whispered. She had been a school headmistress, and was supposedly the harder case.

Miss Hope was astonished, whispered back, 'He doesn't look like I'd imagined! I was sure he'd have brown eyes. They're blue!'

Grellie came clipping upstairs, calling a casual 'Ciao, girls!' Disappointed, the two wanted heavier footfalls.

Resentment emboldened Miss Rose. 'I think,' she told her oppo, bridling, 'that we should be allowed in, don't you? I mean, who does the bookings? We do! We can't even *recognize* the goers, let alone the keys.'

Miss Hope said nothing. She hoped she might be allowed to make coffee and take it in. She daren't criticize. Luck was a volatile friend. She lived rent-free, was paid an executive salary with free expensive holidays. Her only talent was astute caution. This meeting, like dubious calls, was a test of that quality. She was determined never to jeopardize her position. Her first glimpse of Martina's beautiful doll-like countenance had been sufficient warning – such beauty was the serenity of a quiescent volcano capped by glittering snows.

'Don't say anything.' Miss Hope couldn't even think of a challenge. 'Martina's still in a fury over That Woman Yesterday.'

But Miss Rose was all excited by TWY who had rung in wanting Bonn to father a child. Miss Rose was ecstatic because she, nobody else, had taken the call. Having to refer it to Martina still rankled. Miss Rose saw herself – she went giddy – entering a roomful of keys, head goers all, and reporting directly to them. Miss Hope had no luck, except for one exploratory call, as yet unconfirmed, that she suspected might even be from some convent. Miss Rose thought her fanciful. They listened in silence as the keys went in one by one.

In the next room, Martina welcomed each arrival with a smile.

'Are we all needed?' Fret asked, folding his length on to a chair. 'The film school's got the city clagmired up again.'

'This is the quorum, Fret.'

Canter was astonished. He alone among the keys had a phone service that operated in tandem with the control office. It was needed because his firm of five goers, largest in the Pleases Agency, served towns in a radius of a dozen miles. He was twenty-three, had a penchant for fast cars that Martina secretly deplored. Her father Posser condoned Canter's hobby, letting Canter shut down whenever there was motor racing at Brands Hatch. Martina simply couldn't see the point of driving round a circuit.

'The cinematic college is harmless,' Bonn observed.

'That's true, Fret,' Grellie said, obliquely sticking up for Bonn. 'People like to see them about.'

'It's their bloody cables I hate. Traffic's bad enough.'

'Thank you,' Martina said. The issue closed.

She gave them a moment. No sounds got through from the Pilot Ship Casino below. It was jointly owned by the Pleases Agency with some holding company Posser had used in the early days. She began by mentioning this.

'Our problem is mostly for Grellie, secondarily for you keys.'

Martina took them in with a glance. Faulk Faulkner from Horwich, dark haired and silent, edgy in company of more than two or three, sat frowning, head down. Bonn, next to him on a straight upright, then Grellie, chewing gum to point yet another distinction. In the armchair Canter, and opposite on the low boudoir chair Suntan, who alone had two standers to watch out for him. Suntan had done time in prison for knifing a Leeds drunk. Martina had never excavated the details, though she knew that her dad liked Suntan, seeing his own youth in him.

'We taking the Pilot Ship over?'

Martina did not smile at Grellie's accurate guess. 'We might.'

'Staffing's the difficulty. Pit bosses are easy come by, but croupiers are a pig to hire, Martina. Security's somewhere in between—'

'Thank you.' Martina cut her lecture short. 'Honchos are down to Rack, not you.' Grellie quietened at the rebuke. 'I can do a deal with east-coast casinos, bring in four pit bosses to the Rum Romeo, shell off our own people to run the Pilot Ship.'

'Is anything wrong, Martina?' Fret asked.

'I hate that Blackpool Kiss system.' Martina gazed candidly at Grellie. 'It's too well known. It takes too long. It doesn't summon a sub, if the pit boss is elsewhere.'

Croupiers used the Blackpool Kiss system to summon their pit bosses when problems arose. It was done by simply kissing the air loudly while keeping on dealing. The pit boss then came hot-foot to sort problems. Substitute pit bosses were notorious fly-by-nights.

'Then we have a floater, Martina.' Grellie had to fight her corner, since she provided the Rum Romeo's girl croupiers. Any new girls taken on at the Pilot Ship would be down to her.

'It's costly. Rotation always causes argument.'

'It's either one or the other, Martina.'

This wasn't exactly truculence, but was out of character. The mood until then had been one of ease.

Bonn remarked, 'I assumed the Pilot Ship had no difficulties, Martina.'

'It hasn't, Bonn. Opportunity presents itself for a buyout.'

Listen to them, Grellie thought, talking as if halfway through some suspended combat. She worried for Bonn.

'Is this anything to do with city redevelopment?' Suntan wanted to know. 'We might get sidelined, find ourselves out of Victoria Square.'

'That's part of it.'

'Then buy them out, Martina, and have done.' Suntan grinned. 'Next!'

Grellie stayed in. 'I'd be careful, Martina. We've the Café Phryne – not my responsibility, sure. The Bouncing Block health centre in Moor Lane. The Barn Owl mill conversion, the Shot Pot on Settle and Bridge Street, the Rum Romeo in Mealhouse Lane, a score of girls to each of four strings. It's hell of a lot. We're stretched thin.'

'Your helpers will be increased soon, Grellie. Right.' Martina fixed Faulkner. 'Faulk, those presents. What are you playing at?'

The dark-haired key cleared his throat nervously. 'A Rolex, a camcorder, a designer jacket, cuff links. All from one client. I reported.'

'Thank you, Faulk. Opinions without jokes, please?'

Canter stirred. 'We all have the same difficulty, Martina. Clients state possession. It leads to trouble.'

'Tell them at the outset,' Fret Dougal said. 'I do. An upper buys you a pullover, seems harmless. But wear it? It's like a signal. Don't wear it, it's a disappointment, see?'

'This is the reason I like Grellie's girls to go on as they are,' Martina said. Bonn realized she was more worried than she seemed.

'If we ran a pimp system,' Grellie took up, sensing the same, 'we'd have working girls scrapping over the presents they gave their pimps. It's inevitable. Pimps lead to fights, even killings. That girl in London only last week, wasn't it drug poisoning over a *scarf*? Our way, they can keep a bloke of their own. How they play it is up to them.'

Martina pressed, 'And the goers, Grellie?'

The girl hesitated. She knew her worth, but was unhappy talking in an area that wasn't properly hers.

'I don't know, Martina. Couldn't you simply ban presents?'

'How, though?' Suntan asked outright. 'Give the ladies a written rule card?' He shook his head. 'I've one upper, regular as a town-hall clock, would see that as a challenge.'

Faulk agreed. 'Ladies feel they've a right. That's the trouble. But punters give Grellie's Waterloo Street lasses presents as a duty.'

'Leave comparisons out, please,' Martina ruled. 'Bonn?'

'I have the least experience of any key here – any key,' he quickly amended when Suntan grinned and raised his eyebrows. Bonn was the newcomer. 'Forgive my presumption. Maybe each event has to be treated individually. One lady would be mortally offended if her gift is refused. Another might understand.'

'No, Bonn.' Faulk took courage, seeing the lanky Fret nod. 'They're always furious.'

'It's only part of a wider question.' Martina didn't need to consult notes. 'Look at examples. Two flight tickets to Singapore. Time-share villa in Torremolinos. Summer in Monte Carlo. A yacht in Guernsey. So it goes on. There are,' she said without looking at Bonn, 'currently skirmishes with lady clients insisting on cruise holidays with particular keys. These are Greek gifts.'

'Charter tour, then?' A little of Grellie's bitterness showed through the remark. None of this was likely to come her way. If a punter wanted one of her girls that bad, a girl who wanted out would just up and off like as not. All girls were instantly replaceable, gender being what it was. But goers who were promoted to key were rare and astronomically costly.

'Out of the question, Grellie,' Martina said evenly.

'Then we play each off the cuff,' Fret Dougal said. 'Isn't that it?'

Canter was even firmer. 'I'd make them take it back, thanks, missus, but no thanks.'

'This doesn't help, though,' Bonn said. 'I suggest we allocate blame to someone. Unnamed, of course. We reject each gift with every appearance of sorrow. We say, truthfully, that we would get into serious trouble were we to accept any present, blaming some controller we daren't question.'

'Meaning me?' Martina asked.

'I'm sorry, Martina. It's my experience, paltry as it is, that ladies seethe more vehemently at another lady.'

'They seethe for nothing,' Grellie added, still bitter. 'One of my Station Brough girls did a punter last week whose missus came with him—'

'Thank you, Grellie,' Martina interrupted. 'All of you may leave. Motors are available.'

All was decided, Martina style. Well, Suntan told Bonn on the stairs as they left, with Posser you just got do this, do that, no opinions asked.

'Democracy, Bonn, lad,' Suntan said, laughing, 'has reached the bastion of autocracy!'

Bonn smiled, and went out into the rain.

# 6

**Tuber** – a criminal who uses a gun

NOON WAS A pig, to clubbos. 'Get midday, the day bee*geen*,' Noddo told everybody who got to the Rowlocks Casino on the Liverpool Road, which older loles still called Deansgate. The road was supposed to run straight to Liverpool but, typical of the decaying city, didn't.

'This too early, ma man,' Beaky Divine said.

'That's the point,' Noddo said.

Noddo believed that, say something opposite straight out, as if you alone could see they were wrong, every single one would back down. Like now, Beaky Divine looking shivery, shoving his hands up his armpits for warmth and making comic chattering noises. Wolves back down, top dog bark loud enough.

'How many we got?' Jase asked.

Noddo looked at Jase. Loles was trouble. Never take no, didn't chuck the sponge in when the boss showed a fang, not they. Jase was white, riddled with coch – the in-word for mainliner powder, once a day minimum. Typical lole, Jase was. He'd retreat, say fine, sure. Then, lole-like, come roundabout, like that kiddies' nursery rhyme Noddo'd learned in school, Kingston, Jamaica, *Here we go round the mulb'rry bush, the mulb'rry bush*, except loles didn't need no cold and frosty morning. Not they. Different from Kingston yardies, except Barbados folk were more similar to loles than anybody in Jamaica, for which there was no accounting, cricket or anything else.

'Who's coming?' from Jase. 'That's what I mean, Noddo.'

See? Roundabout, never mind he'd already been dissed. Same dig, different shovel. Once a lole, always a lole, which pissed Noddo off.

'Let's wait and see, shall we?' Sanj said.

Sanj, more problems, was from some unknowable eastern country. So he said, but he meant Trafford Park and could only talk English, which he did like some politician wangling votes. His breed was secret lole, talked better than most homegrowns.

Noddo didn't trust words. Look at today. He'd come in to the Rowlocks Casino, sniffing the stale fag smoke like it was pure scent, chattering women cleaning tables and shaking dust so nobody could breathe the fucking air. He'd gone to the office where Rowney the owner sat yakking on some blower with his tart scratching herself gazing glass-eyed into space, and chucked a wad of notes in, never mind where it went, closed the door, not a word.

Which sealed the deal. Notes is votes. Noddo wouldn't be disturbed at the tunes end of the casino. Nobody would come hoovering saying move your feet like they was your mam, saying no when you wanted a drink if the bar wasn't open. Rowney was too scared to do anything but fold.

'As long as we keep distance,' Coffee chipped in.

Coffee was Noddo's favourite, a quiet halfie – fifty per cent Kingston wasn't bad as colour goes, but some bad-mouthers were saying he was half spic, namely and to wit Puerto Rican, which could be calamity if true yardies started believing. The reason Noddo liked him was he was oddness. Like, Coffee played the English straightie tin whistle, half-finger stopping so slick the sound came out like treacle but so fast you thought the fuck *was* that? Better, he was a slow leg-spin bowler, Finsbury cricket nets, un-fucking-believable, get knocked all over the park first innings then go through them like a dose of salts second innings, eight for thirty-nine. And Coffee crossed himself in church with his whole hand so women thought he had the magic voodooing like fucking Haiti.

'That's right. Keep distance,' Noddo agreed, except distance from what? No accounting for Coffee, things he said.

From Jase, 'One motor's plenty.'

'One motor can get fucked up's no good, man.'

'Then we choose good wheels.' Jase showed his palms like what's the problem? See, a lole.

'Two sets is good. One is neff.'

'One,' said Coffee slowly, thinking how to clear things so everybody would leave Noddo to decide, 'is known ridic'lous. Two is essential, Jase.'

'First car does the pop.' Jase, lole, wouldn't be shaken. 'What's the second for?'

'The second car's for back-up.'

Jase sighed. This too got up Noddo's nose, the lole head jerk that signified exasperation, in particular with who was getting the benefit of the head jerk. It was always accompanied by a half-deep breath, then a long slow breathe out so by now the whole frigging audience was dissing the mark, like he's an idiot not understanding what's being said here. Noddo'd tried to do it in front of the mirror until Fluella said he looked stupid and anyway it was a lole thing.

'What for back-up?' Maybe Jase's coch was making him

insolent. Matters didn't usually get this far. 'Back-up's just telly talk, them poncey Friday serials when there's fuck all else on.'

'I think we should wait and see,' from Sanj. He looked round, the diplomat.

Beaky Divine hissed almost inaudibly, while Coffee said nothing.

Noddo thought it was high time Jase got lost. Except for one thing. Jase was the tube man. Give Jase couple hours, he'd make a howitzer from anything with a hole in it. And Jase was good at grenades, that time down the Mersey when somebody did Raser's boat. Okay, so Raser's boat was only decoration. That wasn't the point, when people were getting disrespect from other hobbles. Everybody carrion, picking over remains, whether the dissed hero's alive or dead nobody cares.

Jase was essential.

But one day, and Noddo was thinking tonight was it, Jase would go too fucking far. Thinks he can say anything because he knows tubes, rule the roost maybe? Wasn't because he was lole, no. It was because he was a track hacker, a mainliner, needed white pollens soon twice, three times a day, it was good fucking night Vienna.

Then where would Noddo's yard be, no tuber? On a slag heap down Stretford, that's where, every single one of these faces thinking Noddo was a prat. Coffee had a cousin who was a tube man who Coffee said was good as Jase. Swap time?

'Point is,' Jase was telling the whole wide world, vacuum cleaners doing their howl that got right up Noddo's nose, 'we should be in and out fast.'

'We will be, Jase,' from Sanj, Sanj the driver.

'Two cars is making sure,' Noddo said. 'Like that time at Massey's Kestrel Mill, ten seconds, we gone.'

'It was half a minute, Noddo.'

Jesus Christ, Noddo marvelled. Un-sodding-believable. Couldn't he see he'd been given his orders, shut the mouth when Noddo said enough?

'Who was timing?'

'Me. I set my watch before we went in.'

Sanj did that sniff eastern folk were good at, two long rubbery throaty croaks then a rough rasp that made even Jase lean away.

'Timing leave to Noddo,' Coffee said. 'Several generals can't conduct one battle.'

Noddo was proud. Coffee, halfie or no halfie, was real educated. People didn't know that the University of the West Indies gave the same degrees as London University, no crap, same-same. Coffee had done a whole term there. Brilliant. It showed, when some burke like Jase queered the game.

In came Bunce, tall and gangly, gold teeth a-gleam, head shining from special oils that cost a mint, glitzy gear like from some fairground. He too was a coch user, but nothing like Jase. Also, Bunce was a slow learner but not slow like Coffee. With Coffee, slow meant clever. With Bunce, slow meant wall thick. He was loyal, cheerful, kept Noddo's laws. It was Bunce who'd done Last Ben on the railway, making it hardly worth the police looking. Bunce was vital. Like Jase was vital. Like Coffee was vital. Like Beaky Divine was almost vital. Like Sanj was nearly almost not vital.

'Is that it, Noddo?' from Coffee.

'That's enough. Two cars is plenty.'

Noddo said that for Jase's benefit, but Jase was already

starting to rub his wrists against his belly like junkies did when hotted out from too much time betweens. Soon Jase wouldn't remember a frigging thing. Must be something real good in drugs.

'Hey,' Noddo shouted to nobody in particular. 'Get that door shut.'

A man rose from behind the bar where he'd been slumbering, shuffled to the entrance.

'We do the Falkland Street shed,' Noddo announced to his yard.

'The Oldham lot did it last week.' Inevitably Jase, nobody like loles for Memory Lane.

'They got shelts on it now. That's *why* we do it.'

Shelts were ordinary people set to do mundane jobs around a street drop, an illicit drinking 'still', anywhere a yard called its own.

'We do a drive-by. One pass, KB and that's it.' KB for kaboom, one sweet shot from a car window.

The shed belonged to a different yard. The reasons were obscure, known only to Noddo, but concerned Fluella his half-sister, or who said she was which amounted to the same thing. Okay, she got herself sawed now and then by neighbours, no harm done.

But when Fluella got talked down by any young jock, that's being seriously dissed and couldn't be tolerated or where would the human race be? The two shelts responsible would be on the flagstones tonight, the Janesons, Irvine and Hebrew respectively.

'Hebe and Irv Janeson will be outside the shed. You all know it. Falkland Street corner.'

'How'll we know them, Noddo?' Jase, thank Christ focusing at last.

'One car,' Noddo explained pointedly, 'drives past slowly, checks. Then the other, see?'

'Me in the second,' Jase said, satisfied at last.

'For fuck's *sake*. I go past, check it's the Janesons, nobody else. Then I start back. They'll see, think what the sodding hell's coming, see?'

'Then we do the drive-by?'

'No drive-by, Jase. You're on the flags beside them, see? You pop them, stroll off. We drive home, whatever. I plant witnesses, see these wicked motors filled with tubers, guns going off, give car numbers fine anybody asks.'

'It's very good,' said Sanj.

Coffee added slowly. 'It can't be faulted.'

Noddo gazed fondly at Coffee. That was real education, 'it can't be faulted'.

'Which only leaves one great hole,' Jase said.

'What?' Noddo felt betrayed by the junkie lole, pecking, wearing away till the threads showed. Disbelief's the road to ruin.

'Me.' Jase gazed round, still scratching. 'I tube the Janeson shelts, I'm left there like a spare prick at a wedding. I wait, tell the plod I'm just out for a stroll? What?'

'You walk off round the corner.'

Jase didn't believe his ears. 'Walk, with more fucking weapons than that?'

Noddo grinned, having them on, their faces gone serious.

'A car'll be *waiting*. Bunce's. Got that, Bunce? Hire it fair and square, like some girl'll do the paperwork.'

They all smiled, Noddo laughing outright now they saw how clever he was. Even Jase smiled, sheepish.

They went to the bar for a celebration drink. Noddo sent Coffee to tell Rowney he could open up. Jase alone didn't stay, said he had somebody to see at the hospital, his bird poorly.

'Do please wish her well from us all,' Coffee said.

'That's it,' Noddo said, proud. 'Say it just like that.'

# 7

**Diss** – disrespect, mortal offence

THE HOSPITAL SEEMED dowdier than usual, Clare thought as she parked her huge old maroon Humber SuperSnipe. Deliberately she left it where it would be best noticed. Colour is as colour does, one of Sister Assumpta's maxims at the convent during art class. What had any of that teaching meant? she wondered in exasperation. She warned herself to stay calm. Bonn had satisfied her physical need, but she still felt combative.

The Admin. offices were on the third floor. The corridor had a peculiar aroma. Polish on the ornamental floral stands? Chrysanthemums were available all the year round, a cheat, the lazy lady's cop-out. Thick Wilton carpets, air conditioning, heating above comfort zone, the hallmarks of administrators in their maven havens. Careful, Clare, she lectured herself sternly, none of that. She tried to adopt Sister Assumpta's bland smile – worn to gloss over the shocking Expressionists, catastrophically a compulsory element in Modern Art.

Clare was told to wait by a typical Admin. secretary. Varnished, Clare labelled the woman, and overweight, a stone and a half, twenty-one pounds of surplus blubber.

Mentally she apologized to her, remembering her earlier resolution. Peace. No rows, not today.

She was finally called in. Mrs Mandel rose with a smile of welcome much blander than Clare's own, to her annoyance. Same convent, perhaps?

'Good afternoon, Mrs Burtonall,' the SNO said. 'I'm sorry I couldn't see you earlier.'

The deflection was there, Clare noted, taking a chair. The deflection was her own word for the concealed mental sneer with which bureaucrats turned enquiries away in the hope they would vanish. Their true function. Clare caught herself thinking this with dismay, for she was pretending friendliness, to ask about how deceased patients were treated. Mrs Mandel had scored first.

The SNO was a thin, almost cachectic, woman, her face masked with cosmetics. Her plain blue suit was adorned with a crocodile brooch, genuine diamonds if Clare was any judge. The traditional hospital badge, awarded to nurses on State Registration, was absent. Junior nurses wickedly joked that the qualification for SNO was the ability to pretend that they had gained their SRN *before* university degrees in nursing came in. Clare warned herself to concentrate, fight for Marie.

No 'doctor', for that would belittle office staff. Clare smiled pleasantly. Anything for the dead girl. The thought of the lonely corpse in the Infectious Disease cubicle strengthened her. Once promoted, desk baskers dropped the plain, 'Can I help you?' of the sales assistant. Power lived with them. Anybody entering their portals was a supplicant for favours, not someone entitled to service.

'Thank you,' Clare began brightly. 'It's about deceased patients. I was present after a patient died early this morning, and wondered about nursing practices.'

Mrs Mandel smiled. Clare kept her cool, but vowed one day to analyse SNO smiles. It was a smile that announced, tiredly, how forbearing bureaucrats were with misunderstanding minions.

'Nursing practices are laid down.'

'I do appreciate that,' Clare said.

She kept her smile open and frank. The other's expression relaxed, in the certainty that no copy of nursing procedures had strayed to the undeserving.

'My query relates to the last offices, Mrs Mandel. Will nurses no longer receive any supervised instruction about preparation of the deceased?'

'That is correct.'

'So the patient who dies of, say, AIDS, is . . . ?' Clare pretended hesitancy.

'Disposal begins as soon as the case is declared dead by the attending medical officer,' Mrs Mandel said smoothly.

Case? Disposal? Clare's mind shrieked the words, but she kept her poise. 'Which takes the form of, ahm . . . ?' she prompted.

The SNO's assurance rose even higher. Soon she would reach pomp.

'Total bagging of the case, with Danger of Infection labelling as recommended by the ACDP in accordance with the HSWA as amended.'

Here come the initials, Clare noted. Eponyms aren't too bad, because at least they suggest that some doctor of old had studied some disease and identified the damned thing, or tried to. But Admin. paper prattle shrivelled everything into an assemblage of initials. Use enough acronyms, you could baffle everybody and get away with murder, actual and symbolic. Clare wondered if there was a term for it, acronymania, perhaps? Acronyms had really boomed with the Advisory Committee on Dangerous Pathogens, and the Health and Safety at Work etc. Act, had fired them into orbit.

The woman's smile grew. 'As the authorities advise, disposal of the remains must be careful, you see.'

Thank you for that, Clare thought. She rose, smiling. 'Yes, I do see,' she said affably. 'I appreciate your time, Mrs Mandel.'

With surprise, the SNO watched her visitor take up her handbag. It swiftly turned to consternation as Clare made for the door. She followed.

'Wasn't there something else?' she asked.

Clare paused, putting on a little surprise. 'No. Should there have been?'

She was under no misapprehension. Mrs Mandel knew every word of Clare's brush with the nurses in the early hours and had been prepared for a fight. Clare felt that she herself had boxed clever, disarmed the woman by not contesting an inch of ground. Let the woman stew.

'I just wondered,' said the SNO with a half laugh, 'if something was perhaps causing concern.'

'Why on earth should you think that, Mrs Mandel?' Clare said, hand on the door. 'Unless you know a great deal more than I!'

She left then, cutting off the woman's next comment. Clare said a bright good afternoon to the desk pest, and swung out.

In the lift she glared at herself in the wall mirror, almost incoherent with fury. Disposal? *Disposal?* As if poor Marie Cullokin were nothing more than debris to be thrown out in a body bag. The term 'case' too was an affront. The medical world had gone mad. Jesus, weren't people simply people any more, human beings to be accorded a little dignity?

She went to Hospital Records, and quizzed a young clerk. The girl was eager and pleasant, and provided Clare with every help tracing the sparse details of Marie Cullokin, deceased.

'The address is a care-of, doctor. Next of kin's left blank.'

'Is nothing more known? Past out-patient records, anything?'

'Not here, I'm afraid, Dr Burtonall. Look. Let me have a go later this afternoon. I might turn something up.'

Clare didn't want clerical staff to be so willing. Today, she wanted to condemn the entire hospital bureaucracy, damn the lot of them. Now this kindly cherub was treacherously defusing her anger.

'I'll see what I can find, put it in your pigeonhole.' The girl hesitated, and went for it. 'It's that girl who died of AIDS, isn't it? Poor thing. I'll do what I can.'

Clare went, deprived even of exasperation. The CPC must have been going at least half an hour by now. She thought about it, decided to go and sit at the back. She could listen, at least take in the arguments for an hour, then she would drive home, change, and eat with Clifford.

Martina had Miss Rose in after she handed over to Miss Hope.

'The woman,' Martina said. Miss Rose had to cup her ear, so quietly did Martina speak. 'Patsy Two-One-Three.'

'Who . . . about a baby?'

'Scrub her.'

Miss Rose stared. 'Cancel a client? But she wants a meeting. She has lawyers, doctors, and everything.'

Martina said nothing. The silence hung. Martina looked so intimidating Miss Rose was frightened to move.

'Miss Rose,' Martina said after a protracted time. 'Are you happy?'

The telephonist went pale. The sack would mean losing every perk and penny.

'Yes, Miss Martina! I've never been so—'

'What did I just say?'

Miss Rose swallowed. 'Delete Patsy Two-One-Three, Miss Martina.'

'What *will* you do?' Martina's gaze seemed one of mere curiosity.

'Exactly as you say, Miss Martina.'

For a moment Martina wondered whether to take the matter further, perhaps have Rack send a honch to straighten the importunate woman, but finally decided to let sleeping bitches lie. Have a child by Bonn, indeed.

To his surprise, Bonn found Rack gambling. This was new. He'd never had to seek Rack out before. He'd never found him doing the green-eyeshade bit hoping for a running flush in the Lagoon on Waterloo Street. Bonn had had to get Askey – calf-lick, bulbous head, so like the long-dead comedian that folk called him Arthur, complete with the khaw-khaw laugh straight from the old films. Bonn said, 'I need Rack, please,' and the old messenger had scooted while Bonn talked to Reenie, bonny girl stringer whom Grellie, some hinted, was going to promote to head a whole string of street girls. Four minutes later, Grellie in the municipal gardens glowering at Reenie to cut away from Bonn this instant and get back whoring the Station Brough where she belonged, Askey came panting up to say Rack was gambling in the Lagoon.

'Thank you, Reenie, for your time.'

'Whenever, luv,' and there went Reenie, waggling cockily to show Grellie she couldn't touch her because Bonn wanted to talk so what was she supposed to do, walk away like Grellie's stringers were slags with no manners?

Women's wars gave Bonn a headache.

He entered the Lagoon, passing the honchos who stood straining stitches of their smart frockcoats, and ran the gauntlet of the Lagoon's smiling fishnet girls – three of them hoping to be stringers soon, which Grellie was flatly against, some contest with Martina. Bonn hoped the bonny trio would make it, because every man, saint or sinner, wanted to see pretty street lasses. The pickings were due soon, when possible prostitutes (nobody ever used that word in their right mind, Grellie and Martina in unique agreement on this), when possible working girls got chosen. The alternatives waiting to engulf rejects were stark: whoring, or routine eight-to-five slogs for ever and ever.

Rack was there. His flush went pop. Bonn waited, seeing the slick dealer Bellidge do the one-handed table cut shift, then the two-handed, then the one-hand hop, pages 650 to 652 in Scarne revised cubed, showing off, laughing. Bellidge campaigned – his word – Parliament to enforce the term 'queer' to specify homosexuality, eliciting tired responses from Home Secretaries to the effect that the English language was the free property of all and please could he stop fucking up their days with such gunge. Bellidge said the refusal was a plot.

Rack lost a second game. Then a third. Then fifteen minutes of successive plunges, and over a thousand quid down the chute. Bonn wondered was Bellidge doing more than just play.

Time passed. Bonn grew concerned for himself, then Rack. The order in which his anxiety focused was immoral. He felt ashamed but said, 'Rack, please,' and walked to a table near where several gamblers, wreathed in smoke, clinked glasses against their diamond cufflinks and glowered balefully at a roulette wheel that wouldn't do the right thing.

'Wotcher, Bonn.' Rack was spritely with uncontrolled joy. 'See that shuffle? Bellidge is working a whole section of Scarne.'

Bonn spoke softly. Evita, named for some musical, or not, was the croupier, and deliberately hung out her calls to cover Bonn's quiet words, good girl.

'I need another goer, Rack. Please hint it to Martina.'

'Yeah?' Rack looked thunderstruck. He glanced back at the table's uproar over something Bellidge was doing. 'How soon?'

You had to hint like a salvo. Rack had limits.

'Forthwith,' Bonn said. 'I am sorry to interrupt your game, Rack.'

Rack was still digesting this as Bonn smiled his miniature smile at Evita. She watched him leave. Bonn's glance said sorry, he would have stayed but he couldn't take the emotions, the smoke, the raucous din. It also said thanks for helping him to find a quiet corner to tell Rack whatever it was. It also said he was saddened by Rack's presence in the Lagoon. It also said Bonn would have rather been sitting beside Evita in seclusion where they might have spoken a word or two, but maybe another time. She watched, but he didn't glance back.

Bonn walked to the little caff in Argyle Street by the

Weavers Hall and got a black coffee. He needed more assistance.

Usually, a goer who was promoted to be a key – head of a few goers – managed his own way. There were exceptions. Canter served a stretch of South Lancashire, had five goers, the ancillary fifth operating in a circuit Bonn had no reason to explore. So what if Canter did mainly housewives who saved up for one-offs? Faulkner from Horwich coped by asking to have his clients reduced. Martina had gone ballistic, Rack's words, but gave in. Zen, a nice bloke who had given Bonn kindly advice the day Bonn was raised to key, simply farmed clients to other keys, no bones about it.

So on down the list. Commer the Liverpudlian, Suntan the ex-knifer from Leeds, TonTon Atherton, Angler, all were hardly enough for the rising demand. The increase in Bonn's bookings was now out of hand. Rack ought to have said something off his own bat without being winkled out.

'Bonn?' Rack entered, breathing heavily, having run through new rain. 'Done it. Martina's not a load of laughs about it.'

'Please sit down. Coffee, I think.'

'Ta.' Rack leant close. 'I hate here, Bonn. It's not Martina's. We've to frigging well *pay*.'

'Of course.' Bonn waited, but Rack said nothing to explain his gambling. 'I was surprised to find you playing cards, Rack.' And not doing your job of looking out for your goer, but Bonn did not say.

Rack grinned, wagged a hand, and a shabby man Bonn had noticed cadging on the pavement near Reenie straightened up and left.

'That's Devlin,' Rack said, hugely pleased because he'd tricked Bonn. 'An old music-hall bloke. I had him watch you while I sussed Bellidge.'

'Oh, dear.' Bonn felt sickened and relieved. 'I'm so sorry, Rack.'

'Bellidge is milking the wheels. Fucking loon, cameras everywhere.'

So Bonn's suspicions were correct. The dealer was cheating on the Lagoon's customers, roulette and cards, a whole system.

'I do hope Evita is not involved, Rack.' Please God.

'Not her. She's too much nous.'

'And I do hope no harm will come to Bellidge.' *Deo volente*.

'Bonn,' Rack said, 'hope's your fucking trouble.'

By then Rack was rolling in the aisles, everybody at the counters and tables turning grinning to see who was being an idiot. Indeed, Bonn thought, waiting out Rack's gusts of hilarity at Bellidge's coming doom, hope was a terrible liability.

Maybe he was simply tired. He needed a fourth goer.

# 8

**Poll(en)** – any illicit drug, esp. in powder form

'MARTINA'S SCREAMING TO see you, Bonn. Well? What?'

Rack decided he'd been too lenient. Keys like Bonn got carried by the standers, fortsies, honchos, leggers, bens, the helpers who made the syndicate work. Or, at any rate, who did as Martina said.

They were on the corner of Waterloo Street, the girl stringers busy trolling office workers coming in from the city outskirts to the bus station. Rack was already exchanging shouts and mock derision with them.

'I mean yes or no about using Grellie? Time you did, Bonn.'

'Thank you for asking, Rack.'

Bonn resumed walking, heading towards Greygate, the square's south-east corner that syphoned traffic off to London and the south. Rack walked backwards, elbows flying, clearing a path for Bonn through the pedestrians.

'A bloke must have his own woman, Bonn. It's like feeding falcons.'

Bonn slowed. Even for Rack this theory was wild. 'Falcons.'

'Get scurvy, if they don't get fish. They can't sing straight.'

Falcons sing, straight or otherwise?

It was generally famous that Rack had tried to pull Grellie, when first she'd become a power in Martina's empire, namely Victoria Square and near. He'd failed. Therefore it was his duty to team her with Bonn. He urged this every day, but not in Martina's hearing because she went galactic when anybody mentioned Bonn, even though Bonn now lodged in her ailing dad Posser's Bradshawgate house. Rack knew he could arrange folks' lives hell of a sight better than they could. It galled him.

'Rack. Pollen here in the city.'

Rack swivelled, bawled across to three girls standing under the jeweller's awning, end of Quaker Street that led off, 'Tell Vee her team's had it tonight, three nil or I'm a Dutchman.' Bonn listened for hidden messages. Rack resumed in his ordinary voice as the girls' catcalls came wafting back, 'I know you get plenty of grumble, Bonn. But it's sense. Scientists proved it with that steam train.'

Too many theories today, Bonn told himself. 'I'll find Martina in the snooker hall.'

Rack did a pavement dance. 'Here, Bonn. Martina'll be hopping mad about them Rotterdam coaches. Put a good word in for them, okay?'

It was hard to keep up. Bonn thought, Holland? Coaches, Martina furious?

'My next go should be fairly soon, Rack.'

Rack sighed. 'Bonn, you're a bleedin' pest. Why don't you ask straight out, when's my next shag? Instead, it's all round the frigging houses.'

Bonn wondered, yes, why don't I? Then it came, surprising himself.

'Assuming that a lady will hire me might sound rude.'

Rack gaped. 'Every upper wants to book you, Bonn.'

Anybody else, he'd have said straight out, You're off your fucking head, wack, but this was Bonn and he'd rather risk a ballocking from Martina than one of Bonn's forgiving quiets. 'You're a queer fucker, straight up you are.'

Bonn saw his stander's exasperation. 'It might appear vain, Rack.'

Sure, Rack thought, let's all worry our balls off in case anybody thought we was snotty.

'Frigging nutter, you,' he told Bonn, fondly because Bonn was a matter for pride. Nobody else had a key remotely like Bonn, come from nowhere only months ago, and now everybody looked up to him.

'Pollen's not pollen,' he said by way of reward. 'Not them butterflies that eats flowers. Pollen's drugs, doves, lifters, crack.'

Drugs? 'Thank you, Rack.'

'The pollen's down the wharf. I told you, the shooting, dinna?'

Bonn wanted Rack to reveal how he knew, how came the pollen word into the language, but couldn't bring himself to ask. The relationship with Rack, Martina's chief stander, could not be jeopardized.

'Rack. This shooting . . .' Bonn trailed off, not knowing how to go on. He righted a wheelie that some old dear was struggling with at the traffic lights. It looked stolen from the Tesco supermarket, but so?

'Nothing nobody can do, Bonn.'

Bonn replied unhappily, 'As long as somebody thinks of saving life.'

'Oh, they do, Bonn,' Rack said with a wide grin. 'They think of people getting out from under.'

'Let them show mercy,' Bonn said almost to himself.

'Martina's just sent Osmund to find you, Bonn,' Rack warned. 'Best get on or she'll marmalize yer. And me.'

Bonn had actually crossed over at Greygate, and was cutting behind the Granadee Studios where they made the soap opera about northern people and that pub, before the ambiguity of Rack's grinning reply struck. Could Rack have meant that intending gunmen blocked avenues of escape?

He entered the Shot Pot Snooker Emporium, a place of miracle gloaming and cones of amber light cast on to green tables, and strolled slowly down. The teams were already practising. There always seemed to be championship matches on the go, lads training and complaining, setting up rehearsed shots and arguing chances.

Several of the players greeted him. He knew to stop, motionless, if somebody was taking a shot, wait before moving on past, watching for a raised elbow, a lifted cue. Wars had been fought for nudging a player in mid-stroke.

'Toothie stayin' home tonight, Bonn!' from Toothie, one of the lads from Moss Side. He did occasional jobs for Rack on retainer payment. The jobs Toothie and his oppo Fren – equally slim, equally given to West Indies slang shelled from gold teeth – did for Rack Bonn hated to think about.

'I'm not sure what you mean, Toothie.'

'T'ank Gawd fer dat!' Toothie rolled his eyes in a slangy take-off.

People roared with laughter, some unexpectedly teeheeing like in ancient comic books. Bonn smiled and went to Osmund's cubicle. The old man was playing patience, red four on a black five, immaculate as ever, near the rails of dusty coats, the umbrellas that never saw wet, trilby hats long since showing the protruberance of the hat pegs on which they hung.

'Osmund. Good afternoon.'

'Think any of them stands a chance, Bonn?'

'The championship,' Bonn guessed. He thought the snooker hall, with all its grime and smoke, quite beautiful. He'd thought so when he'd first come in blinking, wondering what place this was.

'No. At surviving to forty, son. Smell.' Bonn inhaled experimentally. 'Ganja, son, that's what. Come nine tonight they'll be falling over each other like a sack of puppies. Just look at them. Can't stand straight now, and it's barely teatime.'

'Good footballers, though.' Bonn pointed, red queen on the King of Spades, but the old man was there before him.

'Footballers? I've shot 'em! Think of Wilf Mannion. Know what, opponents clapped Mannion off the pitch at an international! They're no good now.'

'Martina, Osmund, please.'

Bonn wanted to ask, but the old man, neat in his waistcoat with his football medals, white starched collar and dark strip tie, would never say how it worked. The clothes racks slid aside, and Bonn went through into the small cupboard. Lucky not to be claustrophobic. He stared at the safety notice he knew by heart, and the side wall moved. He walked down a corridor so short it was almost part of Martina's room.

And there she was, beautiful, blonde. The furnishings were spare, rejects from government surplus. Her desk looked unused, a blank sheet of paper before her, one pencil. Nowhere to sit.

'Good afternoon. Martina, this is a non-office. Your cloak-and-dagger entrance. My latest notion is that you keep it like this because it pleases Osmund.'

Osmund had been Posser's friend in the old days. They'd

soldiered together, when war was war and not scrapping drug gangs.

'I have little time.'

Martina's voice was mellifluous. She should have been a radio announcer, lifting the ratings on to a decent footing. Or on television, with that stunning loveliness. Instead? She headed her father's empire. He waited for those mysterious Rotterdam coaches Rack mentioned.

'Ticket touts have asked for franchies in the square.'

Bonn remained standing, no choice. Franchises were given only when the grantor had muscle, honchos, power to protect the franchisees from rivals. Ticket brawls came a-plenty when United played at home.

That Martina asked his advice was unusual. Posser, who had built the syndicate from nothing, was the one to tackle about this. Posser knew the Trafford touts, once ran with them back when.

'I would be inclined to ask Posser,' Bonn said.

'Posser's too poorly.' She waited a pulse. 'That's another thing.'

'I do hope your father hasn't had a setback,' he said politely.

Posser was always Posser to Martina when she was at work. Only at home did he become Dad.

'I'm worried, and want your advice.' She looked aside, casting her hair on to a shoulder.

'I didn't see him this morning.'

Bonn was always down first, to make his own breakfast – porridge made Lancashire style, plain oats and water alone. Then grapefruit, tea with skimmed milk. Posser roused in mid-morning for breakfast before taking a slow perambulation round the triangular greensward of Bradshawgate where he'd been born.

'He is ailing badly today.'

'Perhaps this evening we might have supper out.'

'Very well.' She spoke stiffly. Bonn wondered if she were embarrassed, but that was his peculiar torture, never hers. 'I'll make the pretext, you fall in.'

'Thank you.' Still no coaches to Holland.

'The touts are pressing. I have to answer soon.'

'Have we the clout, is the question,' Bonn said. 'Rack would say yes. I worry we are over-extended.'

'There's the police, and the media. I don't want my standers and honchos battling Station Brough every time there's a game.'

'Paying them would be a fortune.'

'I balance the books, Bonn,' she said sharply, 'no one else.' He nodded. She gathered herself. 'There's other trouble coming, Rack said. I want everything shelved. You've done the go with Clare Three-Nine-Five? I'm standing all the goers down.'

'This is unprecedented, Martina.'

She smiled at his reticence. 'Some shooting is predicted. All goers must have legitimate alibis tonight.'

'As you wish.'

'You have two regular lady clients pencilled for today in the Hotel Vivante. I've told Miss Charity to defer them if they call. Rack will spread a story of some stripe being searched for, protection of the ladies our paramount concern.'

'I'll remember.' Stripe meant stolen items.

'The last thing is, some coach smokers want us to do their bookings.'

'Smoke coaches are a nuisance, Martina.' He added hastily as her expression hardened, 'Little profit for a lot of aggro.'

'Public attitude to drugs is weakening.'

'Public attitude is manipulated and uninformed.'

'I mean the ones who matter, Bonn.'

'Among the people we tend to see, Martina, attitudes are drifting, but not among the rest.'

'Where's the harm?' she asked, straightening her leg with a small grimace. Bonn thought, surely a softer chair would be more comfortable? 'A group of ganja smokers puff their way through the Channel Tunnel. Their charabanc reaches Amsterdam, junky shops open for their arrival. They smoke their heads off, come back singing what great people they are, all Dick Turpins and Diamond Lils. It's only playtime, cocking a snook at teacher.'

Bonn hesitated. 'They go in convoy from London, I believe.'

'So we allocate places here, give a creative price.'

'I can't see the benefit for us. Unless . . .'

'Unless it lets us into other syndicates? That what you mean?'

She controlled her exasperation. Living under the same roof, not exactly together, yet they spoke as distant strangers. Things would be a deal better if he opened his mouth now and again and actually spoke out. She didn't say it. She and Bonn had been lodger and landlord's daughter for two months, behaving with courteous civility, straight Jane Austen but in the wrong millennium.

In a way, her non-relationship with Bonn was emblematic of the city, stuck between coastal Liverpool and the big inland conurbations. Drugs, not county lines, zoned the new boundaries, defining the manors of different mobs. So far Martina's syndicate, with the Pleases Agency, Inc. its flagship, had managed by keeping out of drug rumbles.

'You could ask, Bonn,' she said quietly. 'I trust that you have the syndicate's best interests at heart, unlike many.'

He watched her think, far too deeply to entrust any doodle to that blank sheet of paper or to wear the valuable point of that unused HB pencil. It would have been amusing in some corporate business. Here? Here, nothing amused anyone. She still had given no clue as to what exactly he was to ask.

'Please say how it will affect us, Martina. My goers need my guidance. I'm thinking of reinstating Galahad, after that misdemeanour which made me suspend him.' Galahad, a majestic if simple body-builder, was on Bonn's firm. He had been sanctioned for defaulting on lady clients.

'Don't let his punishment be too light. I'll let you know about the coaches.'

'I shall fall in with whatever you decide.' He coolly gave her time. 'The ticket hicks, I believe, should be left well alone.'

'I heard you before, Bonn. That's all.' She opened an empty drawer in the desk. She closed it, so much work to be getting on with.

Bonn said his thanks, and left, waving to Osmund.

'Rack's outside with orders, Bonn,' Osmund called after. He had one of those directional voices, somehow able to project words as if along an invisible speaking tube to one listener even in a crowd.

'Thank you, Osmund.'

'Hey, Bonn! Watch this, trickle red-black-red, in off that blue, okay?'

'Well done, Toothie.' Bonn went out into the daylight thinking of pollen.

# 9

**Suss** – to examine, investigate, to subject transgressors to a trial

SHE DROVE ALONG Deansgate. Traffic on Derwell Bridge held her up, of course, in the way of bridges. Resignation was on her. Perversely she turned the opposite way, and found herself on one of the quieter streets heading northwest. Before she had gone a hundred yards she saw Bonn. She almost stalled, pulled to the kerb. No traffic wardens, but inevitably a no-parking zone.

He had not seen her. She switched off, alighted, locked the door, searching for him among the pedestrians. He could have gone into a shop – Bonn, shopping? Retailers, a bank, a motorcycle place with thick ugly machines fungating on to the pavement amid garish notices. Still looking, she crossed in haste among mothers, grandfathers with pushchairs, teenagers shouting jokey slang. Where had he gone? To find him accidentally would be an opportunity, the priceless kind she'd been denied. Deliberately she avoided glancing at her reflection in a bakery window, scared she might see a predator's face.

Quickly glancing into shops, she hurried on. She pretended to enter the bank, no luck. Then half-opened the insurance company's door, made a gesture of apology at the girls' expectant faces. Bonn had vanished. Heart sinking she scanned the pavements both sides of the street, more of the same resignation she'd been feeling all day.

Then she noticed. Could he have entered the church while she was cutting to the kerb? It was large, clumsily misplaced, its architecture mistimed in this busy street.

She went into the gloaming, and almost immediately saw him.

A service was going on, priest at the altar, a scattering of congregation, some elderly acolyte with bad feet. A faint bell clonked. The people muttered. No incense, she noticed. Should there have been? Bonn was leaning against a pillar. He appeared watchful, yet didn't seem to be watching, definitely not taking part. As wrong here as elsewhere? She sat in the rearmost pew, working out what to do.

Sooner or later he must leave. Wasn't it simple? When he made to go, she could easily be in the porch and, with surprise, say, 'Hello! Fancy meeting you . . .' Or some inept such. A predator indeed.

Bonn glanced at the altar, then returned to his reverie. The congregation then stood. Clare was impressed. He must have known they were due to rise, a move delayed by the old acolyte's tardiness. She marvelled. Was the ritual as familiar to Bonn as some well-known tune inexplicably given a crotchet's extra dot, making a hiatus where none should be?

What had impelled him here? Perhaps it was sanctuary, from intrusive clients such as I am going to be any minute now? Nostalgia?

A girl approached him, whispered, Bonn tilting his head. Clare felt condemnatory: very young, say Bonn's age, tartily hard, lipstick a scarlet glare, hair a mannish helmet cut, dress brilliant slabs of colour of differing materials, tall boots for God's sake.

Bonn didn't even nod. The girl hesitated, didn't say more. Then went, trying not to make her steps echo from the marble floor.

Clare quietly moved into the church porch where she read the notices over and over. Quarter of an hour later Bonn came. She had almost given up hope, was wondering whether to go back in and say her phoney hello in the aisle. What she did was almost unbelievably clumsy. She turned to greet him, but then saw a smallish dark-haired youth by his side. Bonn merely nodded to her. She could do no more than smile distantly, and pass him quite as if she was going in.

Minutes later, in her Humber, she fumed at her ineptitude: 'What are you playing at?' she asked out loud. 'You didn't even open your mouth.'

Worse, some trollop could swagger up and speak openly – all right, fine, only a message – but still the harlot had greater freedom. It was an affront so outrageous Clare was almost apoplectic. Bonn would have acknowledged anyone in a church porch, as he had her. The tart received *attention*, though, spoke and was listened to. Clare felt like poisoning the bitch.

Using her mobile phone, she dialled the Pleases Agency. Her voice was harsh. She cut off the lady clerk's closing pleasantries. It was time to be blunt. She'd let things go too far before speaking her mind.

Clare drove home, deliberating. The old maroon Humber was back in her affections. Once, the vast trundling saloon had been a friend; then anthropomorphism could take a running jump. She had met Bonn and forgot that silly affectation. Today, the old vehicle was a pal. Clare had always detested whimsy, giving nicknames to cars or bicycles, but here she was, being silly again.

The journey seemed too short. Where she usually had to fight to the middle lane for the A666 switch, motorists today deferred. Huge pantechnicons that usually frightened her, swaying on high wheels that blinded in the wet, this particular late afternoon let her go, helpful headlights flashing.

Clifford was in. Mrs Kinsale had left notes about the dinner in the oven – a woman of many instructions, scribbles commanding countdown attention.

He was affable, with the tea ready and keen to talk, this time not about computers. Clifford was a computer wizard, but said there were youngsters in his office who left him standing.

'Had a good day, darling?'

'Darling' was surely redundant, in their state of emotional separation? 'Not really.'

'Sorry you got a night call.'

He poured the tea with a man's careful solemnity. She wondered what was coming, seeing signs.

'That was the issue. Well, its consequences.'

She sighed, shook out her hair, trying for normality. They lived as if in a state of truce, threatening forces on the horizon, invasion likely.

'Who was it this time?'

That 'this time' rankled, but she didn't pick him up.

'Admin.'

Clifford laughed. 'I might have known. What now?'

*This* time, she translated. Was she such an endless complainer? And if so, was this something new, since she'd met Bonn? She had enough excuse, she frankly admitted to herself, since Clifford was to blame. His criminality had driven her to Bonn.

'Once, nurses did the last offices for a patient who died.

That's what they were called, the last offices. Washing, removing transfusions, whatever.'

Clifford's hand poised with his cup. He was always a good listener.

'And didn't they do it?'

'They don't, any more. They just "bag up" – their phrase – the poor patient for disposal, as if she were garbage.'

'Did you win, darling?'

He was serious. Clare suspected he was brewing a question. Not a personal problem. It would be some way of using her. He had already compromised her this way.

'No. I did it myself.' He almost asked, but baulked, queasy. 'Then I had a row with the senior nursing officer.'

'Who is she?'

Clare was surprised. Clifford tended to shun the personalities of her world.

'She's a political animal. Mrs Mandel, Lucile of that ilk. I lost that fight as well.'

'Tough luck. Maybe your stand will make them think, eh?'

'Or not.' Clare sipped the hot tea thankfully. Another friend.

'Is she in charge of the pharmacy too?'

Pharmacy? 'No. There's a separate pharmaceutical unit.'

'Do they do tests on people?'

Tests now? Closer and closer.

'No. The laboratory's biochemistry section does that. They test out-patient samples and in-patient specimens all as a group, run the tests through together. There's no point in separating them.' She eyed him. 'Why?'

'Oh, something somebody was saying. I visited the new stands.'

Recently there had been a massive input of government

money to redevelop the city centre. Clifford had mobilized an investment group, buying into the marinas, sports stadiums, condominiums, new hotels, a huge array of roadworks for illegal motorway fee-ons, not to mention the inevitable shopping malls and leisure parks. The projected completion date was several years ahead, but city areas were already heavily excavated.

'Teams are already training there.' Clifford grimaced. 'Parks are easy. Break an area, cover with topsoil, grass or artificial turf, it's usable. Sell fast-food franchises, and money comes in.'

'Why the pharmacy interest?'

'Trainers are anxious to have a drugs avenue.'

Avenue was a strange term. She knew Clifford. 'Do you mean a laboratory for testing athletes? Anabolic steroids? Performance enhancers like EPO?'

'Yes. I'm only supposing.'

As we both are, Clare thought wrily, each supposing away. No hormonal enhancers for *this* conversational performance. Yet Clifford's sudden interest felt odd.

'How come they ask you about pharmaceuticals?'

He shrugged, offhand. 'Investors are interested.'

'And they want athletes tested?' She had too much on her mind for this. 'Use a private lab. It needn't be a hospital thing.'

'Prescribing seems the bugbear.'

She felt cold. This was it. 'Prescribing?'

He caught himself, smiled easily. 'Not as such, darling. I mean, are tests simple things anyone could do, or specialized lab work? Athletics meetings have all these rules.'

Mrs Kinsale had rationed the bloody biscuits again, two Peak Freans. It was piteous, a professional couple letting themselves be tyrannized by some silly old bat.

'It's very technical, or the results would be meaningless.'

Clare wanted a bath. Usually, she let Bonn's sweat linger, relishing the sinny tingle of it on her skin. This conversation was going bad. It was the same feeling from when she'd learned of his double life.

'What do they do, exactly?'

She went warily into a possible ambush.

'There are several ways. Gas chromatography's the most famous, I suppose. Then high-pressure liquid chromatography. CE, capillary electrophoresis is the best, being a sight cheaper. It's the method of choice for those illicit drugs that are always being seized on transporter lorries among daffodil bulb shipments. But some – erythropoietins, human growth hormones – are beyond even Olympic labs.'

Clifford pulled a face. 'I've always regretted my lack of technology.'

'You've never said that before.'

'We're still learning about each other, darling!' he said, laughing.

For an instant Clare saw him as he had been when first they'd met, his charm warming the heart. Now, she saw it simply as a mask behind which he sniped at others. She would never be deceived again.

'Could you have a sample analysed, for Mr Farnham?'

Tom Farnham she'd once or twice met at Clifford's charity functions, an edgy coarse millionnaire. Three times divorced, he was a tough development agent.

'One?' She thought a moment. Maybe Dr Kensington the clinical pathologist, a friendly South African with leanings toward rapid-diagnostic techniques, would run one. 'I suppose. Why, though?'

'Just to see what and how.'

She ought to have been more cautious, but tiredness disarmed her. 'I'll ask, if you like.'

'Did you say Mrs Mandel?'

'Yes,' Clare said, sharply coming to. 'Do you know her?'

'I think I just saw her on the news.'

'On the *what*?'

'I had the telly on, racing at Uttoxeter. Oh, I laid the table for later.' He collected the tea things. 'Something about AIDS and hospital policy.' He added hurriedly, 'Don't blame me if I got it all wrong.'

She clicked the remote. 'Are you sure?'

'She mentioned some girl who'd died.'

'When's the local news? They re-run, don't they?'

Clifford saw Clare leaning intently towards the TV set. He smiled to himself. Easier than he'd thought. Get her to authenticate one test, the rest would follow like night after day. She'd be in, with no way out. Clifford went to check on the supper, blessing Mrs Kinsale's obsessional written instructions. She'd been good to him ever since he was little, the perfect housekeeper. Marvellous that she had stayed on after he'd married. Mrs Kinsale was a godsend, and that was the truth.

The new halfie who called herself May tried to speak to Bonn near the Conquistador Bed and Grill, Quaker Street, but got budged by Connie, Grellie's sort of lieutenant.

'I do suppose May is all right,' Bonn said as he passed Connie at the shoe emporium that was failing to become a minimarket.

Connie snorted, clicking along on steel heels, a tiny Sunderland girl with a reputation for bottle cutting.

'That one? It's all I can do to stop the little cow swarming all over the football coaches.'

'She looked anxious.' Bonn was pleased that Connie walked with him. That 'little cow' was a laugh, because May was a head above Connie the dynamo.

'Well she might.' Connie smiled at Bonn. Like a child, taken in by any scheming stringer, even that Danielle on the yellow string, who was sinning, 'crossing' by shagging Galahad, one of Bonn's own goers. All this so far unknown to any except Connie who'd got it from Manko, a druggo who owed Connie for keeping her mouth shut. 'It'll end in tears, Bonn.'

'Oh, dear.' Bonn's pace faltered.

Connie almost laughed. Shocked, that an attractive tart could be scheming enough to try to wheedle his support. Like a little lad, him.

'She's dick-struck, Bonn. I'm wondering what to do. I hate sly.'

'Indeed,' Bonn gave her gravely, sounding eighty instead of barely twenty, his charisma and innocence making him talk like a minister.

'You never know what's going on, do you,' she said.

'True, Connie.'

'Any time, sweetheart,' she said, mischievously adding, 'Don't tell Grellie I said that.'

Bonn smiled, part held back, because talk like this embarrassed. The girls had a knack of slipping in and out of flippancy with a kind of loopy grace. Men couldn't do it without sounding either lascivious or wholly inept.

He walked into the Shot Pot thinking. Rack easily coped with a girl's repartee, even if she was trolling the square in the dark hours. Rack'd catcall, checking up, laughably abusive yet reassuring. Bonn would have liked to be so, but a separateness lay in him.

'She's in, Bonn lad,' Osmund told him.

Osmund was worried. Martina wanted the old man to become her driver. Osmund thought it too much responsibility. A young honcho, tough and fast, aye. An old cock who was scared of the city traffic? No. It was unresolved, two days now. Bonn went through.

'You wanted me, Martina.'

'Yes. Thank you for coming so promptly.' Bonn's mind rattled through recent events, seeking sarcasm. None. A manoeuvre, then? 'A sister syndicate wants us to judge a problem.'

She looked so elegant, more beautiful than all Grellie's girls. Her lameness, she erroneously believed, ruined her. Bonn was mystified by the astonishing faith women had in appearances, when every woman has her own beauty. Like saying a star's no good because it looks thus or thus. A star is a star, when all's said and done. He couldn't understand it. Cleopatra was stunningly beautiful, though tiny, less than shoulder height on any modern lass. So?

To *judge* a problem? What sister syndicate?

'It's serious. Some working girls are synding up to collar territory, start paying off police, franchise half a town.'

'It sounds enormous.'

'It is. Three syndicates are needed to do the suss, decide what.'

'Like a trial jury,' he observed.

'It is exactly that. I want you to come with me.'

Bonn thought her words through. His seminary had been no place to learn street slang. He usually did best by listening or asking Rack to translate. Martina was telling him that another syndicate's working girls were trying to go independent by pinching punters and holding back money. They had to be punished. Martina had been asked to hear the transgressing girls' defence at a suss, a drumhead trial.

'I hope not to adjudicate on anyone.'

'You hope wrong.' Her lovely eyes met his, blue wine.

His reply took a time. 'I'm afraid I must decline, Martina. I would be frightened. The predicament, discarding individuals for the greater good, always causes me difficulty.'

'You mean you'd be useless? Why?'

'I could suggest a substitute key with no such inhibitions.'

She matched him in tone. 'That's all. On your way out, tell Osmund I want Zen to accompany me.'

Zen was once a used-car salesman. He had risen fast, been promoted to key a year after Posser took him on. He was the image of an ideal goer, remarkable for his gleaming teeth and perfect physique, and worked hard to stay perfect.

'Very well, Martina. Thank you.'

She had not even hesitated.

# 10

**Leech** – to dilute any injectable illicit drug

THE DARK CAME too slow, Jase told the others.

'Lole talk,' Noddo said. 'Me? I *want* slow. Home, night take decent time.'

They were in the hire-car depot; the Kingston lads said dee-poh, like Yanks. Jase ignored them, watched the TV news, the set high on the wall. Gordge owned the place, wouldn't have the BBC on at any price, when the world was screaming to watch United's two goals. Unbelievable.

Jase was the tube man, didn't want chat. He'd toked a little, swum in the famous River Ganja sprawled on Marie's settle. He'd go and see her after this, Bunce drive him to the hospital, build alibi.

He felt sensitive. His own origin was Sally Gap, County Wicklow, where they made that soapo of the Lancashire priest and the barmaid who liked him only he was too fucking thick to notice, that one. Back home, you could *feel* background. It, he was proud of the word, *pervaded*. He'd been good at composition at school, Father Charnley never raised a hand, unlike the other bastards. Christian Brothers? Jesus ought to keep a book, only Jesus was too fucking good to be true.

Maybe they'd spring Marie for the weekend? He missed Marie.

Sanj came in. Always looked as though he'd been running, Sanj. A good driver, but too careful. Stopped at the frigging traffic lights once, after Beaky Divine and Bunce done the jewellery shop in Preston Road, the plod wahwahing about the whole frigging county. Could you believe some people? They'd only got away because the car broke down and they'd pulled in to Morston's Garage in Cromwell Street. Rely on accidents, accidents was like luck, never there when you needed.

Jase's tube was a dee-bee shotgun, no Purdey but serviceable, seven cartridges. Shotgun licence in his inside pocket. His mate Pol was teed up to say sure, he expected Jase any second, in the morning they would shoot crows in some farm – trust Pol for details, clean as a whistle. If after the shooting Bunce maybe pulled some loony trick like, 'Hey, let's stop at this pub,' crazy like these nerks tended to, Jase could eel off, head for Pol's semi-detached bungalow, Pendleton.

Don't anybody worry, either. Jase had ways of cleaning a shotgun on the hoof. Best way, piss down the barrel. He'd already checked the all-nighter gents loos, Liverpool Road near the old terminus, so he could slip in and clean the shotgun. The plod could link a cartridge case with a particular shotgun, but not if you filed the prodder down. Jase had his file ready, safe was best every time. Now, though, some tube blokes wouldn't even have a beer without a PM-5 nicked from the SAS, their very favourite weapon, spray like a hose. But that was the thicko's way. Jase's way: think first *then* use his tube.

Beaky Divine came in, grinning, easy. There's another thing, Jase thought. Noddo was always Noddo. Sanj was never anything else but Sanj. Coffee was just Coffee, careful peacemaker. But Beaky Divine was always Beaky Divine in full. Nobody'd ever call Beaky Divine anything else.

In came Coffee. The full set.

Noddo said fine, that was the team. He spoke like he wasn't trying to peer, wondering where the fuck the tubes were. Jase lolled in the bursting armchair, a derelict from the Flash Street tip.

The news woman came on, brief, only Independent TV, not BBC, like adverts and quick go together.

'Time for a fag,' Noddo said. Two lit up, Bunce and Beaky Divine.

'They call these talking heads,' Noddo said. 'TV producer juss push buttons, she talks, see?'

The woman was speaking, plum in her mouth, somebody died of AIDS.

' . . . hospital in the forefront of infectious diseases.' She really couldn't be bothered, all best forgot.

'Hear about that bamba claat down Salford?' Bunce started saying.

'Shush, please, Bunce,' Jase said. Bunce talked all the louder, laughing and slapping his knee.

'Took a bet his fren' wouldn't pick three winners a whole *week*.'

'Shut it, Bunce,' from Jase, eyes on the screen.

'He get none! Losses his fucking flat, you believe it?'

Sanj said, 'I've never been placed in any classic in seven years. I do two horses.'

Another woman now, to camera, '. . . die of AIDS wasn't Marie's fault. Hospitals never apportion blame. We deliver the care patients need . . .'

'Who has?' Noddo said. 'Gran' National, I lost seven hundred. When a fucking favourite ever win *that*?'

'Is this today's news?' Jase asked everybody.

'Rough Something, seven to one favourite, remember? Stewards Enquiry, blocked that Encore Something at fourteen to one.' You couldn't argue. Sanj had a fantastic memory.

'Shut up, please,' from Jase, staring up at the screen.

'Seven hun'red's no pissing joke. That *loss*, man.'

'So,' the interviewer ended, turning towards the camera, rain shining on her hair, 'our hospital can be proud of maintaining its tradition.'

Noddo said, 'Less go.' He flicked his fag end. It hit the wall in a shower of sparks.

The TV showed young ballet dancers in a hall of mirrors.

'Jase go first. Bunce drop you Farnworth Road.'

'Right,' Jase said dully.

'Four minutes, Jase,' Coffee said, ever meticulous. 'Fluella's in the blue Ford you used for that darts champion, okay?'

'Ever'body got it?' Noddo said, narked because a customer outside was knocking on the glass door. 'Fluella drive by, no signal, then Jase do it?'

'Bunce,' Coffee said. 'Forty yard down the side street.'

'Never get outa them cracks,' Bunce said, laughing, setting Sanj grinning and Beaky Divine making twat gestures, index fingers touching and thumbs the same. 'No God's diamond, they.'

Jase watched them. The TV talked about his Marie, AIDS you don't get better from, and these erks were laughing.

'Jase, no runnin', Jase. Bunce start off slow, take time, okay?'

Jase said, 'Bunce will be waiting in the back street?'

'Got it.' Bunce did a shuffle step, Beaky Divine would clap at anything.

'The quietest drive-by in the whole wide worl', got that?'

Noddo gave Bunce his special look as they left, Jase following head down. Beaky Divine thrust his face at the startled would-be customer and yelled, 'You fucking deaf? I shoutin' we're closed, you don't wanna hear, prat?'

'Sorry, sorry,' the man stammered, and hurried off along the pavement.

Beaky Divine turned. 'You believe these people?'

Coffee smiled shyly. 'Good luck, ever'body.'

Sanj said, 'I'm sick of Hondas. Whyn't we get new wheels?'

'Hondas what we got,' Noddo told him. 'Two motors.'

Jase was dropped near the corner. Never at, always near. You had to first test the water. These halfies, even the cheery Guadeloupes, wanted like some crazy western, shooting out of stagecoach windows. There was proper, and there was crazy.

He felt the double-barrelled sawnie in his left trouser leg. Like, who'd think a bloke would bring out a dee-bee tube with his *left* hand? Nobody.

That horse of a bitch, talking on telly about Marie. Marie died, the horse bitch tellt the camera, smiling like a fucking plate smiles back, you eaten everything off it, done its job.

Marie, gone.

AIDS he knew about. He'd shagged Marie every way you could dick. He'd shared like Marie'd shared. Needles they gave out at the downie behind the Camberwell church, needles on the pavement causing havoc, parents riled, police charging in removing coch got from panel doctors' legit scrip.

Needles got legit were clean, right? That didn't mean he had it too, did it? She'd not been well, okay, when he'd put her in Casualty. Nurse he'd collared'd been snooty, I'm on paediatrics, what was that, feet or something, unwilling to take Marie until he'd seized a fucking wheelchair. If it hadn't been for that woman doctor who'd come by and said, 'I'll see to her,' and he'd scarpered, off like a ferret.

Marie gone, leaving him with what? No fuck, AIDS a possible, no methadone to share by leeching Marie's scrip and using the other. They could buy legit from a methadone swap, two bulges for one, four from two scrips. Now, he was down to just himself for pollen.

There were ways. Noddo couldn't be trusted. Once a yardie always a yardie. What if some new tuber came, say fresh out of the army, bringing grapes and clay, grenades and Semtex lookalike? Noddo would marry the fucker for that.

Then Jase would go to the wall, Noddo doing one of his sly winks he thought nobody saw, except Jase who watched reflections in glass doors while Bunce grinned his golden grin and danced for Beaky Divine to clap.

Jase wasn't born yesterday.

He saw the Janeson brothers on the pavement outside the off-licence, light streaming from the window. Why did off-licence shops have such wide windows? A mystery question. Marie's crack answer always was, they'd ask God like, Hey, God, how come off-licence shops have big windows? Jase imitating God on some fucking great lavvy, Marie falling about.

Except Marie was already at God's right hand. He'd forgot whatever the prayer was. Was that how it began, this AIDS thing, forgetting things? He been good learning poetry at school.

Some old dear trogged along the pavement. No cars, thank Christ. He saw a blue Ford go past, Fluella, calm as you please, no signal being the signal to tube the Janesons.

Jase started walking, now not really caring Marie was asking God them playtime questions, pissed out of their minds or stoned into them.

The Janeson brothers were peering after Fluella's motor, talking probably how they could shag her till she screamed for mercy like Noddo talked, like nobody else ever thought of cunt. Strange the way things happed out. Jase's heart was broke, Marie leaving and no scrip. Marie was good at leeching, mixing baking powder or chalk she dissolved in water, making the white chalk come back by heating so you got left powdery chalk that would – presto! – mix with anything and look real.

Marie, his shag, with God. Heavy.

Ten yards and walking at them into the slices of amber light, Jase was astonished to find he was actually bored fucking stiff.

The Janeson lads laughed, watching him come, him the slow-striding innocent lole. They'd start fucking dancing any minute, 'Hey, lole, do this?' with a tapdance or lurp, rattling out paradiddles on the flagstones. He'd just go, 'Hey, no, who teaches you that?' Keep them happy until he pulled their plugs.

Which was Hebrew and who Irvine, Hebe older, was that right? He came into their light.

'Hey, ma man. Watch!'

Hebe doing a tap, a sping, winging, arms out loud.

Jase started his grin. He could see nobody in the off-licence. A car went past, too slow, that silly fucker Beaky

Divine enjoying the tap show, thick as a brick. Had Noddo the sense, put himself in the first car?

'Do it, lole, or we takes your folding!'

The two brothers laughed, whooping. 'Ken y'do this?'

Jase thought, for you, Marie, tell them welcome, okay? He pulled out his tube, thumb over the cocks because he'd heard of some Wigan tuber who'd got it caught on his pocket and binned himself.

Jase said while they froze, one almost in mid-air, 'Can you do this?'

He pulled on one, Irvine it must be, then as Hebe made to run he pulled on him across his knees.

Cool, he loaded two more cartridges, taking time, and pulled into their faces one after the other. The first was already done for, but Hebe was howling please mercy and you fucker stuff. Jase was disgusted, him and his fucking dancing. Waste time, look what happens. Plans go out of the window. His teacher used to say that, plans go out of the window.

He walked quickly away, ignoring a car slowing on Liverpool Road, inquisitive fucker should mind his own business. Ten to one he'd have a car phone, dial the plod. It's the way folk got theirselves in trouble.

In the side street, no Bunce. No wheels, no escape.

Not making a meal out of running like some criminal, he made the back alley. Still no car.

It was as he'd guessed, the Noddo wink. He walked down the back entry, testing yard gates. He wanted ten minutes, some old dear so far fucking gone she'd think he was her nephew visiting from Nott End, him going hello auntie to the barmy old sod.

It was a disgrace, the people you had to work for.

No gate open. He wasn't going to clobber his way into

some staring family's two-up two-down, no. And he was too shrewd to dump his tube in some dustbin. His cousin made that mistake, done fuck all except hold up some half-baked Bromsgrove post office.

In ten minutes he reached the bus station. He caught the Turton bus, sat listening to an old couple. They'd been to the pictures, hadn't liked the violence, nothing on these days except American gangsters. He joined in, said no, not pictures like he used to go to with his mam. They was real films.

They said the same thing over and over. At the terminus, he got off and dossed in a disused mill. He slept thinking of Marie, blaming Noddo, blaming that fucking lady doctor who'd let his Marie die. He felt rough.

# 11

**Tanker** – one who inflicts physical injury on the directions of another

HASSALL FELT IT, being on the Force. Ignore the ludicrous nicknames – filth, pigs, Old Bill, the plod, ploddites – it remained an ignominy. Walk round the square, like he was doing, and people avoided his eyes even if they didn't know. If they did, why, what was one more middle-aged portly bloke, hardly the sharpest dresser, looking lost?

And take parties, back when he'd gone to parties, keeping in with promotion rivals. Lay folk would say, 'Oh, police, are you?' with a kind of enthralled awe. Then they'd tell him tales of lunatic driving, domestic mayhem, or the daftness of uniformed squaddies.

He sat on a Bradshawgate bench facing the bus station. He liked to see folk behave. Schoolchildren coming from the buses to Greygate's massive Textile Museum, hesitant couples in from the moorland to shopping centres. Hassall liked scenes.

His great sin was chocolate. He was doing this low-fat diet. The only slimming effect was that you starved while reading the small print, checking foods had less than 5 per cent fat. By the time you'd got your specs out and read the damned label you were past caring. Today, he'd resisted.

Two benches away – there were five pavement benches, to sit and inhale pollutants – sat an elderly man, wheezing, pressing his hands down so his chest got a fair whack. When he had to relax, his breathing would worsen, then he'd lift himself once more. The cotton worker's chest, phlegm spat every ten yards, lips purple by seven of an evening. Hassall was local. He knew.

Posser was the old man's name. Father of Martina, of the Pleases Agency, Inc. which hired out males – jessamies, cicisbeos, goers, jessies. No real harm. Prostitution was not illegal, after all, and a good job too, or where would we all be? So what, if a woman paid a bloke? Hassall looked through the circling traffic into the central gardens. Already the stringers were out, poaching blokes from commuter trains. Was there a difference? In popular conscience, yes. The female prostitute was a whore, condemned by church and society. The male hireling? That was somehow different. Fascinating, not so vilified, God knew why. Was it, these feminist times, because a woman was justified spending her gelt as she wished, yet the male punter who hired a whore was a victim? Hassall chuckled at the paradox. A wanton woman was a harlot, the dissolute man a gay dog; the former shunned, the latter admired. A strange, ancient imbalance.

A student camera crew was filming outside the posh Weavers Hall. Hassall watched. The university had fallen on hard times, arts faculties now walking on their welts. The film school was its hope.

'Excuse me, sir,' somebody said.

He looked up at the girl. Duffle coat, thick sneakers, bleached jeans, she could have stepped from any of the past three decades. He worried they were unwashed, this concern his wife's doing.

'Are you a local, please?' She was embarrassed when he didn't reply. 'We're interviewing locals, if we can find enough.' She laughed self-consciously, flinging her hair like they did.

'How local?'

'City born,' she said hopefully. 'Working in city confines, and has raised a family here.' Like a catechism.

'I don't quite qualify, miss,' he lied. 'Wish I did. But I happen to know that old gentleman is born and bred. Ask him.'

Doubtfully she examined Posser. 'He doesn't seem very well.'

'He'll like talking to you, luv.'

Hassall watched her go to Posser, glance at her camera mob – all nine of them smoking, drinking from garish red tins, idling like some driverless motor. Theirs was a barbaric world, that found justification in the nostalgia industry. Reading history got him down. The Regency days got off on some imagined Arcadia of the Ancient World. The Victorians, living in stewpots from hell, reminisced about halcyon Georgian times. Edwardians lingered longingly on dream-a-day memories of their grandparents' age. Now? Now we sing World War II songs and dress up for Good Old Days jubilees – nothing now's worth anything, but it was luvverly Way Back When. Hassall thought it a way of telling youngsters they didn't matter a toss. Nostalgia or bust, today's dogma. No wonder youngsters only woke to get stoned. Maybe they saw through the sham?

Windsor's car zoomed up, screeched to a halt. So much for tact. Hassall strolled to board.

The film crew were setting up round Posser. Hassall said nothing to Windsor. He'd like to see the footage, if he got a minute.

*

'They're all failed motor mechanics,' Rack told Bonn in Waterloo Street. 'Know why?'

'No.' It was too early for Rack's theories.

'Bonn? You're wanted. I'm sorry.'

'Morning, Grellie.' She looked stunning today in the watery sunshine, slim, red jacket, silk cravat, harlequin ankle shoes, complex dark specs.

'It's the spanners,' Rack persisted, enjoying the tangle of students at the street corner. The City Art College film unit was out to prove itself. 'They can't hold them. Know why?'

Near the Lagoon, that card-sharp place of occasional violence, they paused because a trio of students in frayed leathers ordered them to during some filming. Bonn counted thirty-nine, including four students in canvas chairs, smoking, aloof.

'Four cameras,' Bonn said. 'Only one seems needed.'

'Measuring light,' Rack explained, 'while you're not looking.'

'Bonn.' The lovely girl was distressed. 'I'm so sorry. I wouldn't have it happen for the world. Martina's sent word.'

Rack could hardly speak for laughing. 'It's the picking. Martina says make up the four!'

'I'm really sorry,' Grellie said, near to tears. 'I asked her to let you off.'

A film student stalked over. 'Here, you! Shut it.' He pointed at Rack, glaring. Bonn wondered, if Rack already knew Martina's command, why hadn't he mentioned it in the Vallance Carvery an hour since?

'Please don't worry, Grellie,' Bonn said.

'But don't you have an upper at two o'clock today?'

Now how did Grellie know that, Bonn thought, if he

himself did not? She must have seen Martina. He supposed everything was all right.

'I'm uninformed,' he replied, careful not to offend.

A huge bearded student approached with three consorts, two of them girls. He shoved Bonn, bellowing, 'I said shut it, mush. We're filming here for Chri—' He screamed, fell back clutching his hand.

Bonn didn't see, it was so fast. Rack, shifting position on the railings, seemed to flick a hand and touch the big youth's arm.

'He broke my fucking hand!' the big student yelled.

The student's fingers projected at the oddest angle. It made Bonn feel ill.

'Grellie's got ten girls coming,' Rack said conversationally, still chuckling. 'The Barn Owl. I wus going to tell you.'

Grellie gave Rack a tight-lipped stare. 'There's no need for violence.' She drew Bonn away. 'Are you all right?'

'Yes, thank you.'

'It's their nature.' Rack shoved a way through the crowd. 'They eat wrong. Know why?'

'Rack,' Grellie gritted out. 'One more word from you.'

'What?' he demanded, all indignation. They came clear of the press. He paused dramatically, astonished at her anger. 'What'd I do? I'm to stand there like a fucking lemon, let my goer get clocked round Victoria Square and do sweet sod all?'

'Watch your tongue,' Grellie hissed.

'I'm to tell Martina, I stood there, Martina,' he said in mad falsetto, 'Bonn's coming to pick her new whores, this gorilla knocks my key about and I stand there like a prat?' He obstructed their progress. 'Will you tell Martina, Grell? Because I fucking won't, tell you for nothing.'

Bonn said, 'Rack, please give Martina apologies, say I am on my way. Give me a moment.'

'Right.' Rack went, thumbs in his belt, shouting to Grellie's stringers at Greygate.

'He might have told you, Bonn. Are you all right?'

There were benches by the square's southeast corner. It wasn't all that warm, but the wind had abated and there was a fitful sun. They sat as a crocodile of children moved towards the famed Textile Museum.

'There were only nine girls,' Grellie told Bonn, giving him time to recover from the gruesome sight of the student's hand. 'There's always extras.'

'I will feel superfluous, Grellie. Rack already knew.'

'He does that, God knows how.' Bonn wondered, God, Grellie and possibly Martina? There was pandemonium at the filming, students crowding round, a policeman approaching.

'It's usually you, Martina and Posser, who pick,' Bonn said. 'I won't know what to ask.'

'That doesn't matter.' She was worried about Rack's rash act, but Rack had been right. You couldn't have Bonn shoved about. The square was always watching, which was half Grellie's trouble.

'You will do right, even if it's nothing, Bonn.'

She smiled to make the double meaning clear. They took the George Street dogleg, passing the office block where Burtonall's firm occupied the fifth floor. At the Barn Owl, one of Grellie's girls joined them by the mill gates.

'There's sixteen, Grellie,' she said. 'Rack's just told me.'

'Ta, Valerie. Get back on hock.'

The girl begged, 'Grellie, can't I see you choose the new girls?'

Grellie smiled brightly at Bonn and let him walk on up

the worn steps. He had barely gone when Grellie lashed Valerie across the face.

'Listen.' She pulled the girl close, to speak the softer. 'I decide who's pushy. D'you hear?'

'Yes, Grellie.' Valerie wept, her face stinging.

'The square thinks the syndicate rule you girls, but they're wrong. It's me.'

'Yes, Grellie. I'm sorry.'

'Talk me down in front of Bonn, I'll pop you.'

Grellie thrust the weeping girl away, fuming. The bitch's ambition would ripple the pond for weeks, and still end in her being given the push. It was always the way. They either stayed in line from the start, or went wrong. And exactly who'd spread the herd word? Things were coming unstitched, somebody picking away, .busy, busy. Now she'd have to speak to Martina, which she hated. Not like when Posser was the word man. Jesus, she groaned inwardly, catching up with Bonn as he made Martina's floor, hark at me: Posser still alive across Bradshawgate, and I score him like a dead pharaoh.

There was a babble, girls talking. Always some loudly showing off, others scared, defiant, or brazening out, God knows what guilt trailing them. Others would never know what guilt was, or think it a joke. Women, Grellie thought, what a lot we are.

'Was that necessary, Grellie?' Bonn asked quietly as they entered the enormous room.

'I'm afraid so, Bonn. Poor girl.' Grellie plastered a benevolent smile on for Bonn's benefit, thinking Poor girl? She felt like strangling the pushy cow.

The huge mill had been converted into a miscellany of workshops. The Pleases Agency rented a vast derelict carding room. The rectangular windows were blacked by roller blinds, enormous inept abstract paintings hanging between. Chairs were arranged in a crescent about a coal stove.

Martina sat there, pale with rage. Miss Charity, an elderly chintzy woman looking fresh from Evensong, garbed in black, sat primly by. Her rimless spectacles were, Bonn believed, superfluous. She had worked on the Ainsworth estates with Posser when young, but now served the Agency.

'I see you made it,' Martina said, ice.

'I apologize.' Bonn gave Grellie a chair. 'My fault entirely.'

'Miss Charity? Please keep record. Grellie, get them in. I don't want to waste all day seeing dross.'

Grellie swallowed the insult. She did the preliminary selection.

'I don't know how there's so many, Martina,' she said equably. 'They just come. The herd word, see.'

'Get on with it.'

Grellie thought, unfairly, Martina never says my name. She went to the fire exit and brought in a girl. She was pudgy, her makeup overdone, hair trendily flounced. She wore jeans, one knee frayed to show attitude. She stood eyeing them.

'Who's the boss?' she quavered. Bonn tried to smile when her gaze touched him, but failed.

Grellie returned to her seat, frankly inspecting the girl. 'Just answer.'

'Name, age, what do you do?' Miss Charity intoned.

'Dawn, seventeen,' the girl said, riding her voice. She must have been shoved in first by the others. Or had fought? 'What do I *do*?'

'What work,' Miss Charity said. 'For the punters.'

The girl looked uncertain. Grellie explained.

'Dawn. Have you done street work? If you haven't, say so. If you have, say how – car pumps, gobs, knee-tremblers, what? And what for.'

'All them, a few times. For money, clothes. I tried pub jobs, but girls scrapped me over it. A friend told me about a string.'

'You know the difference, tell me,' Martina said.

'Stringers get took care of, money saved. You're looked after if you fall poorly. A string's like a good pimp.'

Grellie hastily took over at Martina's sudden glare. 'There's rules, Dawn.'

'What rules?' Curiosity lessened the girl's truculence.

'About having your own feller, drugs, booze, fighting, money. And what streets you work.'

'Who makes the rules?'

'I tell you.' Grellie made it sharp. 'If you're told not to work a street, you don't. If you're told don't work football crowds, you don't even if you could make a fortune. Row with some girl, you tell in. Like that.'

'Turn round,' Miss Charity said. Dawn obeyed. 'Again.'

Bonn felt ashamed. The women were aware of his discomfort.

'Have you any street relatives or friends?' Miss Charity asked.

Dawn shrugged. 'No.'

'Have you ever been pregnant? Married?'

The girl was incensed. 'What d'you take me for? I'm not stupid!'

'Have you a place to live?'

'I can find somewhere.'

They inspected her a moment longer, then sent her to wait.

'Yes or no?' Martina asked quietly.

'Far as I can tell, yes.' That from Grellie. Miss Charity sniffed, but did not demur. Martina looked at Bonn.

He said, 'I wonder about her home.'

'That's her business,' Martina snapped. 'We aren't nursemaids. Yes, then.'

'Dawn.' Grellie beckoned the girl. 'We'll take you on trial. Find the Butty Bar, north side of the square, Mealhouse Lane. Ask the counter girls if Molly has been in. Just say that. Then wait. Say it back?'

'Butty Bar, has Molly been in, wait.' Dawn hesitated.

'Molly will talk you through your street work and find you a place.' Grellie added bluntly, 'Do right, you go on a string. Cross me, you're binned.'

They watched her leave.

Martina's gesture kept Grellie silent. 'What, Bonn?'

'Perhaps we ought to ask more.'

'About what?'

He was not able to explain well, and said so. 'It's so different, Martina. The clients who hire me have something reasoned.'

'What's reasonable?' Martina asked, and when he couldn't reply insisted.

'I think women use me to explore their own lives.' It wasn't much, so he went on, 'They feel time passing, or that they're missing out. They become frantic telling me.'

'Age is everybody's problem,' Martina said, angered at this chat with only one girl yet seen and a crowd to do.

'Or they feel opportunity slipping away – marriage, children grown, friends perhaps starting new jobs, out of things.'

Martina's irritation was undiminished. 'Bonn, nobody can explain all the wrinkles in the goer game, but what's that got to do with picking tarts?'

He felt uncomfortable. She wasn't usually this intense.

'Perhaps I ought not to have spoken, Martina.'

'You don't get out of it like that.' He'd never seen this cold passion before. What had he done, but be late when Rack broke a student's fingers? 'Explain, please.'

The others were silent. Not even Miss Charity dared interrupt, and she'd bathed and dressed Martina as a little girl.

'I am not evading.' He gathered his thoughts, found a way. 'Traditionally, men "do that", implying that hiring another person for sex is a consequence of gender. When women prostitute themselves, apologists condemn.'

'So?'

She was trying to hurry him into losing his thread. He deliberately paused, only to rebuke himself instantly for the tactic.

'Men are condoned, women blamed.'

'Will this take long, Bonn, darling?' Martina cooed with such venom that Miss Charity gazed at her in astonishment. Grellie's heart soared. The endearment told her Martina and Bonn were still strangers.

'If anyone has a valid justification for using prostitutes – I mean that term – it is women. The lady clients I serve have reasons for hiring me beyond the physical act. Some want to test their physical responsiveness, fearing they've lost something – with me, they discover it's there still, and rejoice. Some want to act out a dominance they never could elsewhere. Some women want to experience shame, or some other emotion they've never felt before.'

There was silence. Somebody opened the door, looked in, quickly withdrew from the tense faces. The hubbub that washed in ended abruptly.

'Do they confess this?'

'Not "confess", Martina,' Bonn said politely. 'Get round to telling me, is a better way of saying it.'

'Every single one?'

Martina was now frankly curious. Grellie marvelled. Had these two never even fucking well met? They lived under the same roof, for Christ's sake. But it was all to the good.

'Many.'

'Is this leading somewhere?'

'Yes.' He was apprehensive now. Grellie glanced swiftly at Miss Charity. The old lady must often have seen Martina go into one, and wasn't going to exchange knowing glances. Grellie prayed, don't say it Bonn, darling, don't say it.

'An upper who hires me has a purpose other than mere *use*. It may include an element of abasement, whatever, but it never seems only that.'

'Whereas . . . ?'

'Whereas here, Martina, we're selecting cattle.'

'You don't like it, this hideous process?'

He waited until her breathing slowed, then said calmly, 'It's setting them lower than need be, service beasts of burden.'

'You want us to applaud them, for wanting to be whores?'

'No, Martina. We ought not to shame them.'

Martina looked at the other two.

'Does either of you two ladies know what Bonn is on about?' She continued, as Grellie stirred, 'Because I frankly do not.'

'Perhaps it's because I am here,' he said.

'Perhaps it's because you are concentrating on the tarts and not on what you've been called to do,' Martina said harshly.

'Martina,' Grellie tried.

'*Quiet!*'

Martina steadied herself. She could have paced in showy threat, or stalked out. Lame, she battled on.

'Listen, Bonn,' she said, her tone not unkindly. 'I, Miss Charity, Grellie, Posser, the rest all admit the difference. We send girls out, give a service. It pleases everybody but the City Watch Committee's loony vigilantes.'

'I regret—'

'Bonn.' Martina was imperious and unyielding. 'Make no mistake. Our girls would be on the streets *whatever*. Out trolling. We just make them less incompatible with society. We cut across all barriers of race, creeds, ethnicity. We stock Christians of every sect, two Buddhists for God's sake. We've Muslims, Jews, we've don't-know-whats. We keep them clean, a doctor four times a year, and I – I, me – bear the expense. Pleases Agency does more for equality than any legislation. Do you disagree?'

'No.'

'Furthermore,' she coursed on, winning, 'we keep drugs out. But cleanliness is bought, Bonn. It costs. Grellie? That girl, defaulted on her medicals . . .'

'Last month? Sheila, Scotch, from Leith, auburn, with—'

'That'll do,' Martina said rudely. 'Sheila defaulted, so we got rid. She's *one* reason we're recruiting today. Who gets attacked most in these charming little islands of ours? Prostitutes. Who suffer drugs most, carry most disease, get blamed, exploited, pay thousands *a week* for a rat-infested room with two planks and a soiled sheet?'

'I know this,' he said, distressed.

'You, Bonn, as a key are doomed to be a millionaire. You also have a highly paid stander, to beat the bushes as you pass. You can live anywhere within Posser's rules. Your investments are handled by a clever girl who sees the Inland

Revenue doesn't bother you. You have influence and autonomy. Is this true?'

'Yes.' He had never felt so unhappy.

'Yes,' she repeated. 'Problematic as it is, tarts selling themselves to men is a wider business. It's better known, and stems from men's hunger. Whoring is the standard music-hall joke. But some whores are a cut above. They are, in fact, ours.'

'I accept this, Martina.'

'Then relearn it! Before you came, less than half our tarts had savings. Now, there's . . .' – she leaned for Grellie's quick murmur – 'only eighteen who don't. We've chastised under a dozen in the past three months. Anywhere else, they'd have been maimed, maybe even topped. Talk morality if you like, but don't let your anguish warp our pickings. We look after them better than they can themselves. Dislike the process, but don't get in my way.'

She waited, finally sighed and made an erasing gesture.

'Do you understand?'

'Yes, Martina. I apologize.'

'It is accepted.' Tiredness calmed her. She forced herself. 'Next.'

They went through the lot. By the finish they were seeing one every fifteen minutes. Bonn sat, concealing his grief.

They picked twelve from the twenty-two who eventually came. The majority were young, or said they were below twenty-four, the acknowledged stalling age for stringers. They selected two over thirty. Martina declined an obvious thirteen-year-old, to Grellie's chagrin. The girl caused an argument. Grellie stressed the advantage a youngster would bring to her blue stringer team, if only for a joiner, a girl to take an incomplete part in a triple sex act. Martina vetoed her.

One woman caused Bonn particular thought. Trish was thirty-seven or so, he judged, children now off her hands, and whose husband had gone south beyond recall. She frankly asked how to join, having overheard two girls talking about the Barn Owl pickings and coming on the offchance. She lived in a bed-and-breakfast, worked as a school cleaner, and wanted a new life before it was too late.

The four flatly disagreed. Grellie said a blunt no. Miss Charity was equivocal. Bonn wanted her accepted. After all, he quietly persuaded while Trish waited anxiously, he made love to women a deal older. Trish was attractive and obviously commonsensical.

Martina rejected her. When Trish had gone, silent and pale, Bonn asked why. Martina looked and said to Grellie, 'You tell him. He'll never learn from anything I say.' That was it.

Rack met him on the way out. Bonn would barely have time for tea before he was due at the Hotel Vivante for his next lady.

'You'll like this one, Bonn,' Rack told him, jaunty as ever. 'She's come in a Ferrari. Her husband'll wait in the hotel lounge. She's that singer – you know, on the telly?'

'How pleasant, Rack.'

'Singers are kinkier. Know why? Their vocal cords.'

Bonn said, tired, 'Please find somebody who judges body-building competitions, weight lifting, that sort of thing.'

'Great!' Rack did a pavement dance, amusing shoppers. 'We going to rig a bet?'

'Not quite, Rack.'

Rack sobered. 'Watch it, Bonn. Here comes Gentry, wants to be a goer.'

Bonn sighed inwardly. The pickings had exhausted him. He set his features to a smile as the thief fell in and accompanied him to the café.

'Yes,' Posser was still giving it, ten minutes after they'd begun questioning him. 'Our school was in Fletcher Street. Not there now. C. of E. Infants.' He wheezed, raised a hand to stay interrogation. 'Miss Anderton's class.'

'Was it happy?'

Posser gave them a keen glance. The girl was pretty yet somehow dulled, as if she'd been left out in all weathers and her patina gone.

'We didn't ask that,' he puffed. 'Not even of ourselves. Everything seemed God-given.'

'How do you answer the youth of today?' she pressed.

'What's their question, luv?'

'Oh.' This made her uncertain. 'I suppose feeling that your generation didn't address the right concerns, pollution, racial issues, social justice, unemployed.'

Posser worked on his breath. 'What's the question exactly?'

'Well, those issues, really, is sort of what I'm saying.'

Posser glanced at the others. Had the language changed? 'Your question . . . ?'

The girl grew agitated, consulted her clipboard, black with notes.

'What are the differences between then and now?'

'Talk,' Posser replied instantly. 'People can't talk. Like they don't hear the sense of things.'

Relief, on sure ground. 'They don't communicate.'

'No, luv.' Posser inhaled, hard getting going. 'We didn't say very much, not most of the time.'

'He's hostile, Evadne,' some other youngster interrupted. 'I mean, keep it for reference, but, like, y'know? Ta, dad. We'll try the shopping mall. This fucking traffic's too much.'

'Another minute, Bruce,' the girl begged. 'I'm just going on to—'

'Not at all,' Posser said.

They paused. 'Eh?'

Bruce was commandant. Posser watched them talk. They didn't seem to do it with any purpose, presumably waiting a mood moment.

He shouldn't have been picky. He'd been wondering lately about age. Martina was coming up to foot-tapping time, those twenties years when a woman started looking beyond tomorrow, next week. Since the lad had moved into their house in Bradshawgate, sharing evening meals, Martina's behaviour was more directional. Like, she'd always planned her working day – her cramped office behind the snooker hall at a certain time, then the phone check on Miss Rose, all that.

But now? Now, Martina considered Bonn's presence. She would stay longer after breakfast, have coffee, and still be out before Mrs Houchin the housekeeper, whom she disliked, arrived. It wasn't just her dad getting old, his tablets checked, Dr Winnwick's vigilance to consider, no. It was a greater willingness to be about.

The fact was, Posser warned himself ruefully, he'd come to the end of the road. He ailed. He, Posser, boss founder of the Pleases Agency syndicate was soon for off, no two ways about it. Then what, for Martina?

He'd engineered Bonn's staying with them in Bradshawgate with, that legal phrase, malice aforethought. Frankly he wanted Bonn and Martina hitched. However the young went about it these days, he wanted them an 'item', didn't folk say? His daughter was rich, influential, and dazzlingly bonny. The lad of course, whom he'd met on the very day Bonn had deserted his crumbling seminary, was ideal. Surely Martina knew this deep down? She'd not said anything.

The trouble was, Bonn's occupation was hardly 'ideal', but so? God, he'd started the Agency with only himself, decades agone, and now look at it. Bonn was right for Martina.

The question was, how could he wangle, coerce, compel this pairing of two ideal individuals? Martina was headstrong. Well, Christ's sake, she had to run fourteen premises, over eighty employees, and let only four people be shown on the books. It called for sharp business acumen and brains, which Martina had aplenty.

Dr Winnwick's last visit had been grave. The prognosis was bad. He'd said it outright, when Martina was halfway down the stairs. Fair enough. Posser knew he meant make decisions soon, arrange things. There'd be no time later. Bonn and Martina must marry, finish.

The film students were on the move, gathering their gadgetry and drifting. Refugees, from a distance, bereft. They were probably muttering that Posser was a cantankerous old bastard, blaming him for not replying exactly as they dictated. They were right. Posser and his generation were to blame.

Then he asked himself why, though? And immediately answered: Because they are young. He burst into laughter, almost cackling himself into a coughing fit.

One of the students heard him, said, 'Silly old fart.' Which made Posser laugh worse, almost finished him off. He hoped Hassall enjoyed the movie.

# 12

**Yardie** – one of a criminal group affiliated by kin or origin (Jamaican slang)

Bonn and Martina took a taxi from Bradshawgate to a quiet Italianate restaurant beyond the cathedral. Only six other couples were dining. Bonn wondered if Martina had papered the place with people of her choice, but couldn't ask. Instead, he mentioned her dad.

'Posser knows, I think.'

She was beautiful, lustrous in the low lighting. It must be almost unbearably distressing for her to see girls like, for instance, Grellie, able to swing along carefree. The lameness was some old injury, he'd heard from Posser who, fatherlike, blamed himself. The mother was an indistinct blurry figure never referred to. Bonn had not yet learned why. No, he corrected himself sternly, delete *yet*, for that implied a spymaster's vigilance. He was resident in the same house, that was all. In Martina's words, when he'd arrived from Mrs Corrigan's dingy terraced in Waterloo Street, it was a matter of convenience.

'We must have communicated it to him, Martina.'

'Do you mean I've been thoughtless?'

'You, Martina, no. I'm afraid that I might have.'

'You?' Startled, she became lovelier still, her eyes shining in the candlelight. 'But you didn't know that I . . .'

'I might have let it cross my mind.' He stared at the roll he had broken. 'Posser is astute.'

'Yes.' She was mollified, glanced about for waiters. 'When I was little, we were left, me and Dad. He was marvellous. I can remember just flashes unbidden, isn't that what they say?'

'Sometimes.' She made a smile of deferral at his pedantry. 'I try to excavate memory. It is never pleasant. I feel a sense of trouble, like an engine that never works.'

'Dad took a job with the Ainsworths, their moorland estates. It was a proper job,' she interposed quickly, as if at criticism. 'Supervising the stables.' Her eyes fixed on distance. 'I started at a convent school, Mount St Joseph's, very prim. I was handicapped, of course.' She tried to laugh. 'No tennis or netball for the likes of me. Swimming was different. You could say I excelled – in the water.'

'Like Lord Byron.'

'That's it.' She smiled better. 'Without his success in other directions.'

'By choice, Martina.' They stayed silent a moment. Both were speaking of the same thing, her possible choices.

She raised a hand, small and painterly. A waiter came. Bonn wondered, did they normally fuss so, or was it response to this lovely woman's aura? There was always the possibility that Martina actually owned the restaurant.

'Mrs Mildred, I called her. She had an ancient title nobody uses, older than most monarchies. Her husband was in a nursing home, some war illness. Mrs Ainsworth took me to see him. She cried. He was bedridden, so thin. I remember her saying, "He loves wallflowers so!" We took bunches. They filled the room.'

'I wish we could choose our memories.'

'We might hate it.'

'I wish we might.' For him, this was insistence.

She seemed to shake herself, and spoke on wistfully.

'I liked Mrs Mildred. Servants, women from Rivington village, men about the grounds, and a housekeeper.' Martina shrugged prettily. 'You'll have guessed what Dad was to Mrs Mildred. The clever arrangement to serve her purpose. Respectability was the cloak.'

'The housekeeper and the others must have known.'

'I'm sure they did.' Martina sighed. 'I was oblivious, of course, being young. Then Mrs Mildred passed away. I couldn't understand the terrible rows, why we were hated. The Ainsworths fought tooth and nail. Dad finally settled for a percentage. We left them wrangling and scrapping. Hateful, hateful.'

'Home to Bradshawgate.'

'Yes.' She coloured. 'It must have been common knowledge that Dad was Mrs Ainsworth's kept man.' She had to pause. 'It's always difficult, parents having sex just like, well, you know.'

'You mean the school.'

'Word got out. The girls' attitude changed. Nuns spoke in corners, changed the subject when I came.' Now she frankly blushed. 'Their dreadful heartiness. "Oh, *there* you are, Martina! We were just wondering, weren't we, Sister Cecilia?" I wasn't of their persuasion, an extra opacity. Me and three other girls were separated during their religious services.'

'You felt excluded.'

'The nuns' motive was to protect our fragile alien theologies, but it *felt* like ostracism.' She suddenly laughed, at ease. 'One girl was called Lana. She used to sing phoney chants in hilarious nonsense words. We were supposed to be in Private Contemplation – our exclusion zone. We choked laughing. A nun punished us for it, God noting it all down, you see.'

'Then Posser started the Pleases Agency, and you never looked back.'

Never looked back, Martina thought. Forward?

She watched him eat. Fast, almost as if getting food out of the way so he could back away into that private dream time she was beginning to recognize. At first there had been curiosity, even worry – where he was going to sit, should she stock everything, let him find his own way among victuals.

It had become easier once the evening ritual was established. Mrs Houchin oversaw the two Bowton cleaners who came two days a week. But that was all underpinning. The substance was what to say, how to behave.

She and Dad had lived alone since his condition had worsened and he'd stayed home. Bonn had lived with them two months. The mistake, she acknowledged, had been to choose two of his goers for him, Galahad and Lancelot with their problems. She should have trusted Bonn's judgement.

'She must have been nice, your Mrs Mildred Ainsworth.'

Martina still felt ashamed. 'Much older than Dad. I suppose I was like her grandchild. I know she loved me. And she must have been head-over-heels for Dad. She always had us to evening meals.'

A police car went past, silencing restaurant conversation. A waiter went to the window. Bonn thought, are we near the canal?

'She must have truly loved him.'

Another car wahwahed past. Martina glanced at her watch. Bonn wondered why she had chosen the place.

'I keep thinking that,' she said, frowning. 'Adored? I find it difficult to match words to feelings. Dad loved her, in a way, as good as admitting it. Fondness? Companionship, friendship even? They might all be in there. Maybe he just *liked* her.'

'It shouldn't worry you, Martina.'

She watched as he separated part of his fish. He had chosen a gratin of skate and mushrooms. She would have cooked it a little different, with less sauce. Food textures were underestimated, a Lancashire sin. He always seemed to need bread. She passed him another roll.

She went on, 'It recurs. Once just vague suppositions, now it's a distinct worry. I need to *know*. Did they truly love, or was everything expediency? Love means it was all justifiable.' Her face was flaming. 'Expediency means it was ugly but whitewashed.'

'They were lovers, Martina. That is enough.' He touched her hand. 'Think in extremes. At the opposite pole is what the housemaids and estate workers were doubtless saying, that the mistress Mrs Ainsworth had bought herself a lover to supplant the infirm husband.'

'I *hate* that they were thinking it all the time I grew up, me not understanding. The remarks of the housekeeper to the baker weren't kindly quips. They were carping cruelties, spoken in code over my head.'

'Don't, Martina.'

'I'd like to,' she said bitterly. 'You don't know how often I've felt inclined to send Akker or Rack, seek them and punish the lot of them for their jibes at an uncomprehending child. The little girl is now grown.'

'You've thought of buying the estate.'

She was startled at his perception. 'Yes. There's a housing estate, quite a sprawl, but the lodge is still there. It's a restaurant.'

'Put it from your mind.'

Two more police cars went past, then an ambulance, waiters explaining the goings-on to couples at tables.

'Dad needs daily attention. Mrs Houchin's good, and the cleaners. Dr Winnwick calls, the district nurse.'

'Posser's said nothing directly.'

'Dr Winnwick did yesterday.' She laid her knife and fork down. 'He thinks it's advisable. Said there's a score of decent . . . "homes" seems wrong. Quite near.'

Bonn imagined old Mr Ainsworth surrounded with flowers in the nursing home, receiving visits from his elderly wife and her hired lover's pretty child. Mrs Ainsworth herself must have dressed Martina up in a colourful ribboned summery dress for the occasion. That too must now seem deception in Martina's memory, not an outing gay with innocence.

'You see, Bonn, I never thought it would come to this. Not to Dad. I'd always assumed we were permanent.' She looked away. 'Those police cars are having a time of it.'

'Some accident, perhaps.'

She let him pour wine. 'Mrs Judith Alexander, Bonn. New manageress, Worcester Tea Rooms. Wants you, overriding priority. What do you think? A pushy lady.'

'Whatever you decide, Martina,' Bonn said courteously. 'Myself, I'd invite her to take her turn.'

'That's settled, then.' Innocence puzzled her. Bonn's was so extreme as to be a true ailment. Other goers would see the status a new client might confer. But already Bonn the Innocent was back to Posser.

'Posser was blunt about his hopes, when I was invited.'

Her colour returned. It had been awkward, that first evening. Supper had been stilted. Posser had done his casual best.

'I know.' She made it an apology. 'You guessed?'

'It didn't alter my pleasure.'

'Thank you. What do you think, Bonn?'

'I think Posser absorbed the sense of things from Dr Winnwick, from you, me too. He's weaker, can hardly walk round the green.'

'Don't feel pushed into obligations.'

'I never feel pushed, except in business matters.'

Martina smiled with relief, his mild reproach an attempt at humour.

They spoke of other things, the redecoration of the house at Bradshawgate, and garden problems. Creepers were damaging the pergola, Bonn learned. Clearly it was time she got somebody in to take strict measures. The herbaceous border was simply driving her mad, she wouldn't put up with it. What did he think?

He floundered, hardly knowing one plant from another. He liked remembered bright colour – fuchsias? – at the seminary, and garish azaleas. Rhododendrons got everywhere. That was all he knew.

'Fuchsias, maybe,' he offered.

She didn't point out that they already had several varieties. She realized that she had never even seen him in the back garden. Did he think it restricted?

She said, 'Good idea. We'll make a plan.'

Clare knew she had a temper. 'Your temper,' Sister Conceptua had lectured her after a bad episode of clothes-flinging, 'will get you in serious trouble. Remember, once expressed it cannot be undone.' Was that the noble nun's one gem, remembered now Clare was lying beside her hired lover in a state of repletion? Clare had timed the move. First, let love happen. Now he was awake. Time for it.

'Bonn? That girl, in church.'

'It goes against the grain.' And explained to her surprised pause, 'Talking in church. I got punished when I was little.'

'She knew you when you were little?'

'I am puzzled by all ritual.'

Why was he so evasive? Would it matter if she knew how long he'd known some slut? She tried for control, almost immediately lost it by telling herself, all right, fine; if he can ignore my questions I'll ignore his. Ritual, indeed.

'She at least spoke to you.' There, Sister Conceptua, my temper coming out. 'I couldn't.'

'It protects you.' All this time he'd lain on his back, eyes closed.

'Cutting me dead protects me?' She felt like hitting him.

'Distance. People might be watching, ready to make five. You have reputation, marriage.'

Her anger grew. She saw he'd been somehow ready. His remark about ritual should have forewarned her. He'd been silently digging trenches.

'Marriage!' She spat the word. 'Will you answer if I ask?'

'Try.' He looked at her, then away. She ignored the sadness in him. If she had obligations, then so had he.

'I can't take this much longer, Bonn.' Furiously she plumped the pillows. 'How long have I known you?' When he remained silent she let go, shouting, 'We've never even had a meal together! All we have are these bloody awful hotel rooms!' She flung off the bedclothes and stalked into the bathroom.

He had not moved when she emerged, her rage undiminished.

'Tell me, Bonn, how these affairs evolve,' she got out, choking. 'Do they "settle down"?' She made her voice a mad coquettish soprano. 'Or do they "go to the bad" and cause loony divorces? Because I'm telling you I won't put up with it a moment longer.'

She hurled herself into bed and sat upright, seething. He turned to look.

'What do you want?'

She wondered if she'd finally got through.

'I want you. I feel you want me.' She fought down her anger. 'I can't see any end, as we are.'

'What, then?'

'For God's sake! I want us to be able to see each other! Go out, away from the city, anywhere! I'm stifled.' She felt helpless. 'It's unfair, you putting the onus on me to ask. And that bitch.' She jolted herself, remember to stay on the rails. 'Has she her own man?'

'Stringers are allowed.'

Talking like a Government White Paper, she thought in despair. 'Then why can't you have a woman of your own?'

'I could.' He spoke so quietly she didn't take it in.

He crossed his hands behind his head and gazed up. She knelt, staring. 'You could what?'

'A goer is permitted one lass.' He added, reflecting, 'I wonder if a goer could marry. I suppose one could.'

Could one, would one? She stifled an insane urge to giggle. She'd almost won. Cautiously she entered the arena.

'If your goers asked, would you let them?'

He took his time. 'I'd have to know who, the morality.'

'And you?'

'Me what?' But he knew, he knew.

'If you wanted, maybe marry someone later?'

He thought. And thought. He said, 'I should be scared.'

'Why scared? Did your parents fight like cat and dog? Unhappy home? No home at all?' She, trained expert interrogatrix, couldn't hold back because she'd come too far. 'You're not scared of me, Bonn.'

'Here, no. There, though . . .'

Wildly she thought, God Almighty, is it leap year? How close can words get, with him?

'Bonn. We'll make a home. You can keep on doing this, but we'll be a pair. Then when you're ready . . .' She didn't give an inch, kept going. 'If you'd allow your team, why not yourself? I'd not let you be scared.'

He raised himself, looked into her. 'Would you not, Clare.'

Her voice went shrill. 'Oh, fine! Now you don't trust me to do a single thing?' She leapt from the bed and started to hurl her clothes on, yelling.

'You know what your trouble is? It's bloody arrogance!' She had trouble with her skirt zip, tore it in temper. 'You're in hiding, like a kid who doesn't want to be found out!' She wrestled into her blouse, tucked it in anyhow, grabbed her shoes, shook one at him by its heel.

'Your reserve is emotional claptrap. It's blackmail! To stay aloof from the rest of us!' She was more or less dressed, awry, yet she managed to sneer. 'You know what, Bonn? I actually pity those poor bitches you service. They're thinking how you admire them. Poor bloody fools. We both know they're nothing in your eyes. Because you're blind as a bat.'

She was trembling, sickened by the whole dismaying shambles, but made herself go quite still at the door and say, quivering, 'I'll tell you something else. I'm no longer one of your money-spinning harem. You hear me?'

And left, slamming the door. Mercifully, no one else was in the corridor. She felt ill, malaise swamping her, almost vomited on the hotel carpet. In the Humber, driving anywhere, she remembered she hadn't paid Bonn and thought, damn the payment, damn the agency, damn Bonn. Let them sue. He was consigned to oblivion. From now on, he might never have been.

The morning was full of problems. Rack loved days that started so brilliant. He was jauntier than ever meeting Bonn.

'Grellie says she's running a frigging zoo,' he said, almost bouncing as they neared the Vallance Carvery. 'She's threatening to do Jemima herself.'

'How difficult. I hope neither is hurt.'

'Look,' Rack said, exasperated. 'I want response, not tut fucking tut. Tell news as it is, Bonn, you give me how frigging difficult?'

'Abate your language, please, Rack. We're in public.'

Rack stared at the teeming traffic of Victoria Square pouring down the station slope from the London express, motorists clagging up the Warrington exit, a heaving mess, and Bonn says hold the slang like the HGV wagon drivers would swoon for smelling salts if they heard? No wonder everybody treated Bonn like he was from Planet Mars.

'I'll abate, Bonn,' he said, and threw in his astonishing chunks of news. 'There's new franchies to settle. Women's boxing.'

They stood, wind gusting about the pavements by the Deansgate mall. Rack leant on the pedestrian railing.

'I cannot imagine women boxing,' Bonn said.

'It's big money, Bonn.' Rack wanted to persuade, no telling what Martina might ask Bonn of an evening beside her fireside, Bonn reading there. 'Martina's going to be asked, let the ZeeZees do it, them Dutch lot. They're keen. I reckon it's cheese and them iron ball games. Know why?'

Iron ball games? Bonn nodded, his way of saying please, no more theories.

'There was shooting, Rack.'

'Eh? Not Chelsea fans this time.' Rack cackled at his crude joke. Bonn didn't smile. 'Them Janesons got done. One's on life support. Must hurt, pipes in you, d'you reckon?'

'They were shot, then.' No escape, planned or otherwise.

'Wharfies are saying it's Noddo's pollen mob, as did the Moss Side drive-by.'

'I suppose they think there was just cause.'

Rack sighed, some blokes get tubed, and Bonn wanting it was nobody's fault.

'You shagged that woman – Servina Four-One-Nine, writes them history books? – she's booked for two this afternoon. She wanted the same room as last time, but she'll have to make do with Room 251.'

Rack had seen the client's photo in a bookshop window, a rare instance of a woman's true identity intruding.

'She will make a formal complaint, Rack.' Bonn never liked to disappoint.

This was what really pissed Rack off, things that weren't his fault but for which he'd get ballocked by Martina, stupid hotels not doing their job. Bonn wouldn't even get mentioned, when a word from him would straighten the hotel management, especially the new woman owner of the Conquistador Bed and Grill who was barbary as hell. Martina's law was that keys weren't to get involved. What she meant, Rack thought, aggrieved, was that Bonn didn't do scrubbers' jobs. Martina was a fucking nuisance. If only Posser would come back.

'We must endure, stay within.'

Bonn warning him to obey Martina's laws now? Rack said disgustedly, 'Anyhow, the bird wants to ask you abroad.'

'Overseas.'

Rack was pleased, tricked Bonn into raising an eyebrow. He laughed, feeling the brains of the outfit.

'She's got a history story, women in them frocks, blokes on horses.'

'To reside, I take it.'

'Don't be daft. On a frigging ship, sun and cold beer.'

As long as it wasn't Calabria, Rack could have said. His dour Mama came from there, as did his sainted Papa, fucking non-existent waster. Calabria should get fired into space and forgot.

'I daren't. Martina banned cruises.'

'What if she says you're to go?'

'That is highly improbable.'

'It won't stop Servina Four-One-Nine from creating. Watch out. She'll have it in for us.' But not for Bonn.

'Please stay close to hand.'

'I've marked Stan Cullenough's card. He'll be some fireman, in case.'

'Thank you.' Bonn disliked knowing the details of the standers' arrangements. Rack hadn't yet failed him, so the fewer technicalities the better. Stan he already knew, a dour older man who made a convincing fire officer, traffic warden, commissionaire; just give him ten minutes to garb up.

Askey, diminutive messenger the image of the dead comedian, came up with a message, muttered it to Rack, then returned to the bikers draped about the Triple Racer, south end of Bolgate Street.

'Second client,' Rack said. 'You did her friend two months gone.'

'She said so openly!' Bonn marvelled.

Women's things were too secret, Rack thought. If they were a bit more open the world wouldn't be in such a bloody mess, but no. They wanted nobody ever knowing what or why or who with. It wasn't natural.

'It's rather unusual, Rack.'

'I know. Martina's law, clients come first.'

When he first started, Bonn remembered, it had been Posser's law. This was a measure of the old man's atrophy.

'Rack, I hope the shooting was nothing to do with the syndicate.'

'Nowt, Bonn. Some footballer's getting blacked from the Rum Romeo. Martina'll want the word out about threeish, she's not decided yet. And a lady comed in the Phryne, asked Carol. Go on.' Rack fell about laughing at Bonn's embarrassment. 'Ask why.'

The Café Phryne was a discreet tea place off Market Street. It was owned by Martina's syndicate and in the hands of Carol, a petite clever girl with a talent for design. It was confidential, for ladies who were still dithering whether to take the plunge and become clients.

'She wants you to speak at some Ladies' Guild!' Rack roared, causing heads to turn. 'Tell how the city's wicked streets really is!'

He could hardly stand up for laughing at Bonn's discomfiture.

'That's out of the question, Rack.'

Rack regained control. He leant close, in all this public, and said, 'Martina says you're to do it!' Then he let go, laughed until tears streamed down his face.

'Oh, dear,' Bonn said, causing Rack even more hilarity. This lunacy would send anybody into orbit. From Bonn it scored oh, dear, frigging things Martina decided.

'Carol will point her out, I trust.'

'You trust right, wack,' Rack said graciously. 'Hey, tell that writer bird I've a smashing story. Geezer in Atlantis has two brains—'

'Rack,' Bonn interrupted. 'Several problems.'

'Serious.' Rack went sober. 'Galahad's a bad lad, Bonn. He's crossing. Girl calls herself Danielle. Know her? It's why Grellie's scratching everybody's eyes out this morning.' He could see that stunned Bonn, Bonn's own goer sinning.

'How disappointing of Galahad.'

'It's not a talk thing, Bonn,' Rack urged. 'It's *got* to be a tanking. Others get to know, all hell's let loose. Grellie'll agree.'

'I do hope Grellie isn't too punitive.' It was Grellie's place to punish.

'She'll want carnie, Bonn.' Rack decided to go for it. 'Time you shagged her, Bonn. Regular, not a knee-trembler up some alley.'

Bonn winced. 'Thank you, Rack. I shall speak with Grellie. Please find Galahad. I want Lancelot and Doob there too.' Lancelot, the mogga dancer becoming famous, and the ex-pickpocket Doob, comprised Bonn's firm.

'I told them.'

'I shall see Grellie before Servina Four-One-Nine, please.'

'I already told Grellie. She'll have her dinner at the Vallance.' Rack snorted disgust. 'Frigging salad. Make sure she gives you solid grub.'

Bonn was mystified. How on earth did Rack know?

'Get in her, Bonn.' Rack walked with him. 'Bloke doesn't have his own bird, his ears go first, can't hear. Know why?'

'Finish your problem list, please.'

'Jemima's rattling Grellie's cage. Had a scrap with that

blower in Vicko's Palais band.' Rack spoke with disgust. 'Honchos separated them. Jemima's laid up, her leg gone bad. Know why women barney different? It's their hands. Aren't proper formed when they're babs, see.'

'That shooting, Rack. The police might be around.'

'Already are. Fat George got interviewed first thing, then two of our girls sleep over Station Brough. Been in the Butty Bar trying to get free grub. That Hassall done his gym stint this morning. He's left the square.'

'The sergeant . . .'

'Windsor, sandy-haired git. Remember he wants to prove you aren't doing traffic surveys? Pillock. Oughter get a proper job.'

'Thank you, Rack. I appreciate the news.'

'Okay, Bonn.' Rack felt proud, praised like that. Bonn didn't say that kind of thing to just anybody.

Clare felt sombre. On the way in, she had phoned the Pleases Agency, to explain she had forgotten to leave payment. And was told no, payment had been made, thank you. She had made some commonplace, realizing Bonn must have made over her fee. It depressed her more than any anger he might have shown.

Sister Gascoine in Ward 3A told her that a policeman was waiting downstairs. Clare met him in the main cafeteria. He declined coffee. They sat apart on an uncomfortable window seat. The policeman didn't seem quite so rheumy since they'd met last.

'Are you exercising? Vitamins? The right food?'

'Doing all that, Dr Burtonall.' He pretended indignation. 'I've been at that Bouncing Block behind the Weavers Hall, off Market Street. It's killing me. Must be good for my health.'

'So you'll shun my cardiac survey?'

'I'm keen as mustard. It's just that there's been a serious event. Call to arms, sort of.'

'The men can't come?'

It had been difficult, the inclusion of a police contingent in her research. There was the Police Federation gauntlet, the natural aversion to a health scrutiny, all of that. She had spoken at Central, 'selling her product', as Dr Paul Porritt cracked. It was Paul's brain child, to amass cohorts and match social behaviour – drink, food, hobbies, psychiatric profiles, family – with occupations. Mr Hassall had been surprisingly willing. Acceptance was on a volunteer basis.

'The lads are eager. It's cut down on smoking, I can tell you.'

They both made false chuckles, then quietened. Hassall seemed uncomfortable in hospital surroundings.

'It's these uniforms, those blinking folders doctors carry all the time, keeping tabs on us.'

'Confidential, Mr Hassall.' She'd said it often enough.

'Confidential's an elastic term nowadays, doctor.'

'Not with me,' she replied, tart. 'I alone will keep the cardiac code. Dr Porritt supervises encoding. The statisticians do it in blank.'

'So I've only to stop the lads ogling the nurses?' Hassall harrumphed. He held his hat, his eyes following the staff coming in for their break. The self-service queue was noisy, crockery clattering.

'We could come to you,' Clare offered.

That surprised him. 'Can you? What about your equipment?'

'We're mobile. We've already been to a pottery, and a

garment place outside Halliwell.' She smiled, wanting him to agree. 'Medicine's in the jet age.'

'Have you dates? I'll check, and see what.'

She wrote three, tore him the slip. 'I'll need notice.'

'Here comes Sergeant Windsor.'

The sandy-haired officer nodded as Hassall waved acknowledgement, and retreated to the stairs.

'Best be off. He's been sniffing round the pathologists. I honestly wonder about these young blokes. He's bought a forensic pathology tome, can hardly lift it let alone read the damned thing. He looks through and says *snap!* like in the kiddies' card game, two pictures the same gets the prize. Beyond belief.'

'It shows he's willing. Is it that murder?'

'See,' he said heavily, 'this is what baffles us, doctor. Medicine's got a secret folklore, hasn't it? Lay folk must think the same of us police.'

'No, Mr Hassall.' Clare felt kindly. 'We see you as homogeneous.'

'Is that so.' He wasn't interested. 'What worries me is, do you talk among yourselves? For instance, was last night's drive-by shooting the main topic of conversation this morning?'

'Not unless we happen to be there when something comes in. Doctors talk of cases, have to. And we have the CPCs, clinico-pathological conferences.'

'Do they still do open ward rounds?' Hassall surprised her by asking. He smiled. 'My sister used to like those.'

'Is she a doctor?'

'In Leeds. Was always scared stiff of being asked questions.'

'Poor thing. I know the feeling.'

Hassall waved at Windsor's evident impatience. 'Two

were shot, deliberate. Drive-by, by some accounts, not so says a passing motorist. Don't know what to believe.'

'Was it drugs?'

'Why do you ask, Dr Burtonall?'

'It's always in the tabloids, isn't it?'

'Much they know. Make up half, invent the rest.' He rose, stiff. 'I must stop cavorting about in the gym. They always put me next to some thin young pillock – sorry, doctor – who can do the splits. Bloody mirrors show every inch of flab. They call it encouragement.'

'You'll get no such hassle – sorry back – from me. We'll simply test you, and jot it down. What does the police standard fitness include now? Is it still jogging a mile and a half in under 12 minutes?'

She walked with him to the exit. The intense, overactive Sergeant Windsor came forward.

'The pathologist's doing the PM now, Mr Hassall. He says we can go.'

'You.' Hassall nodded thanks to Clare. 'I'll visit the scene of the crime.' He spoke drily, as if mocking his own contribution. And added, as Windsor shot off taking stairs two at a time, 'Drugs is easy. We've already got suggested names. Oh, how's Mr Burtonall?'

'Clifford is well, thank you. I'll tell him you asked.'

'His name's up on the marina complex.' He started down, Clare with him. 'I suppose it'll be named after him, the Burtonall Leisure Park?'

'Don't overestimate Clifford's altruism. He's in it for money.'

'Pleased to hear it. I like pure motive. Even greed. It's when it's mixed with others the problem starts.'

They reached the ground floor.

'Why didn't you want to see the autopsy, Mr Hassall?'

'You've been seeing too many pictures, Dr Burtonall. All I want is the blunt report. And there's that smelly chemical.'

'Formaldehyde?'

'Clings so you stink of it. Also, it won't be so blinking noisy without Windsor. Never leaves me alone, him.'

He said his thanks and departed. Clare wanted to prolong the conversation, but thought better of it. Odd that he'd asked after Clifford.

And the day was unexpectedly clear, her surveillance clinic – examining twenty or so policemen – now void. She wondered what to do with so much time.

# 13

**Sawnie** – a cut-down smoothbore shotgun

Some goers – TonTon Atherton was one – were maniacal about hotel rooms.

'You can't be too careful,' Ton preached one time the keys were called to the Barn Owl mill. 'I take an hour going round the place. Bed linen, phones, TV, flowers. I do it myself.'

Bonn looked slowly round Room 251. The Vivante Hotel was not quite superb, but safe as houses, especially with Rack out there. Bonn trusted the Vivante. TonTon Atherton was from Liverpool, where edges frayed, so only trusted caution.

Servina would create, Rack warned, because she couldn't have the same room as before. Why, Bonn didn't enquire. Life was simply so.

The last go with Servina Four-One-Nine had been interesting. Bonn forgot every upper the instant she left, his selective forgetfulness a knack of mind. Mostly it worked, unless he received warnings like this room problem. Most goes caused no difficulty. One lady, an important councillor's wife from the Wirral, craved flagellation, which at the time had been beyond his experience, him a new goer full of trepidation. She had complained, but merely to provoke him. He'd taken Posser's advice, and done the required deed. The lady was now a regular upper, the act part and parcel in the sex. She paid. It was her wish. Life was simply so.

This Servina lady, he would go gingerly. Martina could not tolerate a complaint.

Bonn went into the service room and put water on to heat. Coffee, tea, the potpourris fragrant, all in hand. The suite's wide window had a view of the Royal and Grandee Hotel, then the ornate Vallance Carvery where racing punters congregated, before the squat mass of the Granadee TV Studios.

Time.

A knock came. Bonn opened to Servina Four-One-Nine.

She was dressed in a pale blue trouser suit with what looked like leather clogs – orange? Fashion was beyond him. Her hair was blondish, a profusion of ringlets. Blue eyes, cherubic, teeth dentists slaved to maintain. She stormed in, already worked up.

'What's the idea?' She slammed the door. 'I said *my* room!'

'I insisted on this, Servina.' Was a lie necessarily bad?

'*You* changed it?'

Bonn stood there. A lie was undoubtedly a lie, but theologians accepted a mental reservation. He would work it out in lantern hours.

'Servina. Somebody was working the travel agencies, asking who was famous. So far they have only reached the Royal.' Would that appease this harridan?

Servina lost impetus. 'Were they asking about . . . ?'

'Not you, darling, no.' Rack checked every day, the syndicate paying all round Victoria Square. Rack's standers knew the newshounds, the games they played.

No hair-flinging now. Servina's hand moved to her throat, genuine pearls in a double choker.

'Are you sure, Bonn?'

He made his voice catch slightly. 'I won't have intrusions, Servina. Not after meeting you.'

Slowly she moved into the room. 'You did right, Bonn.' She smiled, rueful, sat by the window. 'I came here in a hell of a temper!'

He smiled back. 'I'm going to keep out of your way!'

She said, mollified, 'Don't. That acid bitch on the phone did it, telling me what I could and could not have.'

Acid bitch? The phone ladies were the meekest creatures imaginable.

'They're automatons,' he said, placating, lies thick and fast. 'They have to stay within the rules. They know nothing.'

'I'm glad to hear it.' She laid her handbag aside.

'I'm on your side, darling.'

'Literally?' she asked mischievously. 'I've got a plan. You and I are going on holiday!'

Here it came. He pretended surprise. 'Are we?'

'To sun, sea, ancient colourful cities!' She gestured to the window in disgust. 'Away from this drabness.'

'I'd love to, darling.' He'd had enough. Martina could fight this one.

She stretched out her arms, wriggling her fingers.

'It's important, Bonn. I still feel I hardly know you. We need time to ourselves.'

She looked up at him, her hair falling back. She pulled him close. He almost stumbled.

'You're kind, Servina. Think of the expense!'

'Hush, darling.' She smiled, reaching round him. 'You don't know how *freeing* you are to me. Do you remember how timid I was, first time? I wouldn't have come if I hadn't been desperate.'

'You looked superb, so cool.'

'Having to hire. If it's not shameful it's at least decadent.'

'No, Servina.' He put his hands on her face. 'You brought the burden laid on you by people who'd cowed your mind. They made you please everybody else, instead of thinking of yourself.'

'That's true!'

'Your body rebelled as your mind preached *their* doctrines.'

She pressed hard to him. 'You're so comforting, Bonn. It's exactly how it was.' She tugged at his belt. 'Tell me more, darling.'

'If you insist, Servina.'

'Oh, I do, darling.' Her voice was husky. She drew the leather free, slowly slid the buckle down its length.

'Galahad's with Danielle now, Bonn.'

Which was the only news on earth that would make Bonn halt like that.

'Get Grellie, please, Rack.' It had come at last.

Rack grinned. 'She's waiting. She knows where. I tellt her.'

Grellie arrived with a much taller lass they called Lorna. As with other girls Grellie put on station trolling, Lorna's was a new name, adopted only two months before. Lorna was plain but meticulous, with a wariness about her. If Bonn remembered rightly, she'd stabbed a Soho punter. Lorna was honest, helped out at the Bouncing Block gym, doing massage and sauna punting there on Grellie's say-so.

It wasn't satisfactory, but Grellie needed a more physical girl to serve as her lieutenant.

'Lorna's here to help, Bonn,' she explained.

'Good afternoon, Grellie, Lorna.' He hesitated. 'I believe it would be wise to separate, approach from different directions.'

Rack rolled his eyes at Grellie, the bleedin' obvious.

'It's sorted. You go in one motor, Bonn, me and Grellie, Lorna in a third.'

'Oh.' Bonn coloured, looked at the pavement. 'I apologize.'

'Okay.' Grellie smiled at Bonn. Lorna was expressionless. Rack thought hard, having embarrassed his goer, and came out with a ponderous reparative stroke of genius. 'You telled me to do it, remember, Bonn?'

'No, Rack, but thank you.'

Nobody was deceived. Grellie took Bonn to one side while Rack chatted to Lorna, only numbers as usual.

'Galahad's using Danielle, Bonn,' she said quietly. 'Be prepared.'

She was under no illusion. Bonn was green as grass. It was his gravity, his air of apology, that captured the girls' attention. He was so distinct, even though his clothes looked true off-the-peg mundanity.

'I heard, Grellie. What a shame.'

Grellie quelled her exasperation. Action, not sympathy, was called for.

'The question is, Bonn, how far will you say we can go? I don't want this a vicarage tea party. Somebody's got to suffer.'

'Very well.'

Bonn seemed so sad. That was it, Grellie thought. His sorrow iced the gingerbread, on the side of the sinner.

'I want punish, hence Lorna.' Grellie hesitated, baulking at forcing Bonn. 'Maybe Rack wants to make an example of Galahad too?'

'And as for Martina,' Bonn prompted her drily.

'You know Martina,' Grellie gave him, too tartly. 'Sorry, Bonn.'

'I understand.'

But did he? Grellie went on, 'Well, God alone knows. Martina'd have Galahad done over and binned, like as not.'

She looked at him as she said it, but he gave no sign. Maybe Bonn truly didn't know what Martina was like? Strange things happened, and Bonn was the one for strangeness, God's truth.

Bonn looked where Rack and Lorna were laughing, Rack in mid-theory, clouds making cars go faster, something of that sort, the tall girl shoving him, no, you're making it all up. It was an outing for ice cream. Here, two yards off, he and Grellie were deciding lethality.

'I admit Galahad has to go, Grellie, if he is found transgressing.'

Grellie could have hugged him with relief.

'That's good, Bonn. It's only fair.'

Why must I reassure Bonn like this? she wondered. Listen to me, psychotherapy class, fool that I am. She got in the taxi. Rack embarked with her.

Bonn entered a taxi alone, smiling apologetically at Lorna, but a third was already waiting. She gave a shy return smile. The three motors left Victoria Square by different exits.

Bonn had never been to this part of the city. The cab dropped him between sombre warehouses and terraced houses, with seven-storey blocks of flats rising about a tired acre of worn green. Swings, a defaced pavilion, somehow proved the district's character. He thanked the driver, no payment.

Rack's taxi was already drawing away. Grellie gave no sign of recognition, merely waited until she was sure Bonn saw where. They entered the nearest block and met Lorna in the foyer.

The lifts were damaged, every wall a jumble of graffiti. Bonn wondered, who *does* these? He had never seen anyone hard at it, spray can in hand. Glass shards and plastic dross littered the floor. Rack raised a finger, leapt the stairs three at a time.

He paused on the third floor outside a chipped blue door. Bonn wasn't surprised when he produced a key, turned it silently pulling hard, a thief's trick to minimize noise. Rack went first, opposing his thumb and four arched fingers – possibility of a dog.

They followed, Grellie second, Lorna last, and stood in the passage as Rack closed the door. The place seemed vacant, but Rack jabbed a forefinger at the second door on the right, tilting his head: somebody sleeping.

The door was ajar. Galahad and Danielle were sprawled in bed. The body-builder was huge, lying on his back, mouth agape. Danielle was prone, uncovered.

It was proof enough. Bonn touched Grellie and nodded. He was convinced. Rack raised his eyebrows, offered him the next step by a raised palm. Bonn demurred. Rack slapped Danielle's rump.

'Let's have yer!' he barked. 'Up, the two of yer.'

His Cockney accent always returned with his bruiser's attitude. The lovers' startled grunts saddened Bonn.

Rack plumped himself on the bed.

'Just see the two of yer,' he said, disgusted. 'Going "What, what?" Stay there.'

Galahad had made to get out of bed. Rack shoved him down. Danielle, gaping, leant against the velour.

'The fing is,' Rack continued, 'you bofe knowed. Am I right?' His sudden howl, *Am I right?*, made them all jump.

'Yes,' Danielle said faintly. Galahad nodded, bleary.

Rack said, 'Nar, Grellie's come ter say what yer do. Bonn's here ter see trufe, so liss'n.'

Grellie held on to Bonn's arm in condolence.

'This is your flat, Danielle,' she said. 'Make it over, to sell. It'll be shared among the girls. I want your every last penny. Leave the city today. Do you understand?'

Danielle began to cry, her breasts wobbling.

'It's on a mortgage, though, Grellie,' she wept. 'I don't—'

'You know the Pilot Ship casino, Waterloo Street? There's a lawyer, side entrance, called Mr Verreker. Tell me it?'

Danielle blubbered the instructions, reaching out. 'Grellie. We did nothing wrong. This is the very first time—'

'Liar.'

Lorna stepped past Bonn at Grellie's gesture and lashed Danielle across the face. The girl's head flopped back, struck the wall a thump.

'Midnight, Danny.' Grellie wagged a finger. 'If you're here after midnight, it's sleepy wheels. Say it?'

'Sleepy wheels, midnight. Mr Verreker at the Pilot Ship.' She wept. 'What about my pollen?'

'Hand it in. Lorna'll be with you.'

Galahad looked about for his clothes.

'Bonn,' he pleaded. 'Look. I done everything you ever said. It's not just me. Everybody crosses over.'

They went silent. Only Danielle's weeping allowed time to creep by. Distantly, some child shouted a repetitive 'Ah-ah-ah,' in private song punctuated by a banging, maybe a spoon. Bonn didn't know what sleepy wheels meant.

He said, 'It's all very sad,' and left, stood in the vestibule until they came down. One taxi was waiting for the four of them. All the way to the city centre Bonn said nothing. They alighted between the Phoenix Theatre and the TV studios.

Bonn went to the Butty Bar. Doob the ex-pickpocket came in a few minutes after and sat opposite.

'Rack told me the Shot Pot caff, Bonn.' He knew something was wrong but not what. 'Can I agree a go soon after three this aft?'

'No, Doob,' Bonn said. 'Please decline.'

Doob drew breath to say Martina wouldn't like that, but didn't speak.

Ten minutes later Rack came, chatting merrily to the girls, pulling their legs and giving out some daft new theory. Bonn rose and left to sentence Galahad. It was all tragic.

# 14

**Working girl** – a prostitute

THE ONLY ADDRESS Clare had for Marie Cullokin was 'c/o Haleys Wharf', no phone number. She drove her old maroon car into the derelict canal area.

Buildings, Clare thought, leave them untenanted, become gaunt like folk unloved. Like patients unvisited. Like the elderly batting out time in non-home homes. She shivered, drove slowly along the cobbled street, looking at windows.

No Jase Cullokin fitted the electoral list for 17, Haleys Wharf.

Warehouses, small workshops, a couple of gutted places, a few terraced houses with curtained windows. Distantly, four half-tower blocks, balconies, a woman hanging clothes by metal-framed doors.

Clare halted at a thoroughfare with a corner shop barred and shuttered. Graffiti marked civilization, or its departure. Nobody was about. A commercial van was parked further along, but looked as if it had been there a generation. Nobody to ask. No shops, except a grubby café she didn't want to risk, steamy windows, smoke emerging from a vent. A canal bridge. She felt odd, prickly, as if Haleys Wharf was inspecting her, had watched for her coming.

Two children laughed on the end steps. One shouted down. There must be cellars, for old style hand-loom weavers. A deserted chapel showed ragged-tooth rafters against the grey sky. She shivered. Poor Marie Cullokin, poor Jase, poor children, come to that. The International Classification of Diseases gave the world's worst killer as Z59.5 – Extreme Poverty. Pampered WHO bureaucrats should leave their overpaid jobs in Switzerland and move here.

Clare reprimanded herself and drove to the end of Haleys Wharf, wondering if she should take a chance and ask for directions. There was a canted children's roundabout of the sort called the Wedding Cake, but no fond grandparents taking infants out to play here. What had happened? She thought of Clifford. If her criminal husband was hauling the district into the modern world – new housing, a marina, parks with bowling greens – then what was money crime against such utter calamities as this?

She saw a taxi. A young man emerged from the entrance of the flats. Three other figures joined him, two of them girls. They got into the cab, which drove off.

The figure looked familiar. Bonn? She was too far off to see. Was she imagining him, still distressed over things she'd said?

A shrill whine sounded, bandsaw perhaps, down the grim street. She turned the Humber, so gaudy and distinct. No way Bonn could have failed to see her, if it had been he.

There was a warehouse door, one leaf of two open, fraying at the bottom. Inside she could see men with welder's hoods in weird light. It looked hellish. With sudden determination she alighted and entered.

The workshop floor was coated with metal filings. The iron smell – blood and coffee, she thought – was overwhelming. Three men in overalls were at the work-benches, one hauling on gantry chains. Four cars lay in carcass state.

'I wonder if you know where number seventeen, Haleys Wharf is,' she called over the scream of machinery.

One man raised his visor on a surprisingly aged grinning face. 'This is Haleys, luv. There's no numbers now the houses're gone.' He glanced at the Humber. 'Sorry a nice lass like you's wanting places like this.'

'I'm a doctor, trying to trace next of kin at this address.'

He hesitated, gauging her. 'There's just that place by the canal's turning pool. I shouldn't go down there.'

He shouted to the others. One called to try the shacks on the canal, returned to his welding. She said her thanks, and went to sit in the car. Nothing for it. She would have to resort to extreme measures. That pompous Admin. bitch must sweat for a living.

She would ask Bonn. It had been him, she was certain. She fired the ignition, and fled the dying district.

Mackay caught Hassall on the way to interview Noddo.

'Not coming to the ARV meeting, Hassie?' Mackay was of a rank with Hassall, his elfin grin masking his total hatred of disorder.

'Nar, Mac. Armed Reconnaissance Vehicles are ridiculous. What, two lads vaporizing the taxpayer's money, pretending they're Yank TV cops? What city needs that?'

Hassall said it loudly. The station lads had a standing bet that nobody could wipe Mackay's merry grin off by Christmas. Hassall's crack nearly did it.

'Section Three of the Criminal Law Act—'

'Sorry, Mac, it's only hunting statistics.'

'Eight thousand four hundred handguns stolen—'

Hassall left him and entered the room where Windsor waited. He got down to it after the PACE nonsense, Noddo and his lawyer watching the Police and Criminal Evidence Act ritual with unconcealed hilarity. Section 25 was always a laugh.

Hassall asked Noddo, 'You talked with Jase last night?'

'Dunno.' Noddo placated his lawyer, hands raised, doing his noble citizen. 'I were in the Rowlocks Casino.'

'You don't remember, sir? Our informants place you there.'

'I can't ree-call everybody, I having a quiet drink.'

The lawyer interrupted, 'This line of questioning—'

'One more, sir, then I'm done.' Hassall felt Windsor stir, itching to kick the mouthpiece. He'd go far, a sergeant destined for promotion.

'What's he like, this Jase?' Noddo put in, casual.

'Exactly like the young man you were with in the Rowlocks.'

'Who else was with you?' Windsor interrupted harshly.

Hassall gave Windsor a long stare. With a firework you lit it and stood clear. It said so on the packet. Promotion, but no common sense. To Noddo he did his cardboard cut-out smile. 'I can't imagine you drinking alone.'

Noddo shrugged. He had been here many times. He would mimic this lole Hassall, make his yardies laugh, that waterpistol leaning by the door – seen too many Yankie fillums, he trying the nice-cop-bad-cop gunge. Noddo could eat him for breakfast, still have Kellogg room down there.

Hassall should have remembered to bring in a pretend report from some informant.

'You spoke with at least three others?'

'At least,' Noddo said, lazy. 'Barman, some women sweepin'.'

'An empty casino?' Hassall tried his bored smile, this time better. He'd definitely touched a nerve. It was a guess based on averages – five to a yardie hit-team, Noddo keeping well out left four, Jase on the run meant three. Who, then?

'I wus thirsty, man, like that.'

'You drinking alone doesn't fit, so stylish.'

Noddo was pleased but knew the game. He wanted to say the Ali zinger, 'Hey, you ain't dumb as you look!' but that would piss Mr Bernstein's ulcer off.

'So who were these other three?' from redoubtable Windsor.

Hassall wondered why it was always him got the short straw. There was that solemn young sergeant – Boatman? – taking law in night school, he'd heard was good. And, not to make too much of it, quiet.

'Weren't there four, sir?' Hassall said to Noddo.

He'd get a requisition in, put mirrors on that opposite bloody wall to glare at Windsor any time he wanted. They'd turn the requisition down, of course. What, Mr Hassall, glass for cut-throats in the interrogation room? Denied, etc.

'Four,' Hassall said. He tried to look like he was thinking over some report. 'A white male and three others. No females.'

'Hey.' Noddo leant forward. 'Talk to Rowney. He *own* the Rowlocks.'

'I already have.' Hassall waited, but nothing. 'Do you know anything about cars which passed the off-licence immediately before the shootings?'

'Identify the cars, Mr Hassall,' from Bernstein. 'Which is not to say that my client—'

'Ta, Mr Bernstein. Well, sir? Do any of those vehicles belong to you?'

'Dunno, Mr Hassall. My motor's laid up. Being welded.'

'An accident?' Windsor barked.

'Nope. Hate that shine, man!' Noddo rocked with laughter. 'I changed the colour twice, sick of blue.' He swung on Bernstein. 'Ain't you sick of blue?'

'You couldn't have done the driving,' Hassall said urbanely. 'It was good.'

'Hey!' Noddo too was playing. 'My driving best on the manor!'

'I'm sure, sir.' Hassall grinned, went for the joke. 'When my lads have their cameras out, eh?'

Noddo laughed, slapped his thigh. 'That's it, man!'

Hassall's grin hadn't faded. 'Somebody dissed Fluella, was it?'

'Fluella?' Noddo cooled, some trap here, him walking round the door. 'Not seen her mebbe a month.'

'Are you definite, sir?' Hassall overdid the surprise, making sure Noddo got the acting.

'My client does not have to answer that.'

Hassall nodded. But he really did wish there weren't so many American procedurals on TV. Even the frigging mouthpieces were talking Bronxspeak. Only last night, on some BBC cop-shopper, a telly chief constable had read a suspect his Miranda rights, the whole USA You-have-the-right verbals. Beyond belief.

'I shall be seeking Fluella's comments, sir. The identity of your other friends, though. Could you possibly help us?' Hassall acknowledged the lawyer's agitation by tapping his watch, he'd end soon.

'How'd I know people not there?' Noddo could also overact.

'If you do recall, we'd be obliged if you'd phone in.'

Hassall walked them down the corridor and on to the steps.

'Who does your resprays, Noddo?' he asked, casual. 'I get a motor again, I'd hate that red metallic like on yours.'

'Some wall-eye down the wharf.'

'Sanj doing it on the cheap?' Hassall spoke even more offhand. 'I reckon I'm the only bloke pays full whack.'

Noddo said nothing, wanting to answer flashy but not knowing where an answer might land.

Hassall continued, 'My motor lads say red for safety. I'd stick to it, if I were you.' He thought, deliberately frowning. 'Did you say blue, Noddo?'

'I juss talking colour.'

Hassall said so-long, and collared Windsor. It was no use ballocking him. He wouldn't understand.

'Look. Find Sanj. Talk. Hang on to the concept, no aggro, just chat. Ask what he was doing at the Rowlocks. Be quiet and smiley.'

'Have we an informant?' Windsor asked, a hound on scent.

'Wish we had,' Hassall said, weary. 'Pretend.'

The SNO was just about to leave when Clare dropped by. Mrs Mandel didn't rise to greet her, the Admin. boss ready to repel boarders. The plush office's flowers were gorgeous.

'I'm sorry to intrude, Mrs Mandel,' Clare said, acting breathless. 'Only, I've come to ask your help. I do hope—'

'Help on what?' Too sharply, which pleased Clare.

'I received rather an odd phone call last evening. You do remember Marie Cullokin?'

'I remember. Yes?'

'Somebody said he was Marie's next of kin. He threatened to sue the hospital. Of course, I was just simply flabbergasted.'

Mrs Mandel went pale. 'Sue? For what reasons?'

'That's the question,' Clare said, happy in the lies. 'I gave him your name. He intends going to the newspapers.'

'*You* attended her, Dr Burtonall!'

Ah, Clare thought, jumping out of the windows now, Mrs Mandel? Nothing restores status like a lawsuit.

'His complaint was your breach of confidentiality.'

'Confidentiality?'

'Marie's medical details were evidently disclosed to the public,' Clare coursed on, acting far too young for the scene. She felt she had the right. 'Of course I denied the whole thing. Nobody in her right mind would rush on to TV with such a gaffe.'

'I spoke,' the SNO said in a choked voice, 'to anticipate any criticisms about your handling of the case.'

'Oh, I'm sorry,' Clare said sweetly, thinking, you stepped into the firing line to defend *moi*? Such nobility! 'I hadn't heard.'

'What's his name and address?' The SNO's face was ugly with fear.

'I haven't it. I thought you would know, Mrs Mandel.' As you are required, in fact. Clare added, feckless now, 'He's writing to the Ombudsman.'

'The . . . ?'

'The Health Service Commissioner,' Clare explained, hoping her pedantry would madden. 'Church House, Great Smith Street, I think.'

Mrs Mandel buzzed the intercom. Clare rose.

'Please wait, Dr Burtonall. I'd like my secretary take down the gist—'

'So sorry, Mrs Mandel.' Clare moved quickly to the door. 'I'm so far behind in cardiac surveillance, what with one thing and another.'

She left, satisfied. Let the idle cow do some work for a change and find the elusive Jase. Save Clare a fortune on petrol.

While driving home she wondered if she shouldn't call Hassall. Or would Mrs Mandel think of that, now out of hibernation?

Bonn, down that seedy, unsavoury district of Haleys Wharf. He'd know how to find Marie's Jase. Her heart ached.

# 15

**Straw** – a false alibi

'I GOT NEWS,' RIO told his mate. He sang the word, 'Money!'

'Oh, aye.' Dum rolled his eyes. A Gooj, second generation, considered himself handsome and talented. It was nearly true. 'Not another football scam, please.'

They were in the War Torn, a place of ill-repute, Salford.

'Cast iron, Dum.' Rio knew Dum thought him a duckegg, but this time he had it. 'What we got?'

'Nowt.' The band started up, some tired stripper kidding herself it was Hollywood. The lads growled. She became enlivened.

'That's just it.' Rio knew he was handsomer than Dum. Some had it, some didn't. 'I had a mate, Zen. He did cars. Know what he does now? He shags. For hire.'

'Eh?' Dum gaped. 'They do that?'

'All the time. This tart tellt me there's goers. Get hired, make a mint.'

Dum was dazzled. 'All the cunt they want, and paid? Jesus.'

'We gotter get in there. Who's got a caravan trailer?'

'Not you, not me.' Dum's face broke into a grin. 'But we can get one.'

'I mean luxury, mind, Dum,' Rio warned. 'No tat.'

'Then what?'

'We put the word out, and start. Couldn't be easier.'

Posser's summons didn't worry him, but Rack's intent face worried everybody else as he strode, hunched, to the Volunteer.

There he found Posser at one of the iron tables looking out of the window into Deansgate traffic, breathing not bad today, cooler weather.

'Get your ale, son.'

'No, ta.' This was serious. Rack knew Posser. 'What?'

'Zen, Rack?'

The stander controlled his astonishment. 'Zen? Straight, knows when he's well off. I'd give him the benefit, Posser.'

'So would I. Tell me.' Posser listened amiably while Rack expounded Zen's character.

'Bonn likes him, which counts. Zen doesn't do cars since you barred it. I'd know if he did. Limits his work when he's worried about his frigging weight.' Rack snorted. 'Training circuits, Bouncing Block gym with Prand. What?'

'Calm down, lad. Only, Zen knowed a bloke called Rio?'

'Accrington, pals up with a Gooj called Dum from Leigh?' Rack was getting edgy. 'Rio's in motors, Posser. Nowt to do with us, less you say.'

'He's starting up a wank wagon, Farnworth side.'

Rack felt his gorge rise. First, he'd not been told, here he was learning it from Posser, no less. Second, what the fuck was a moron like Rio thinking of, an ape like him? 'The bastard.'

'They've got to learn, Rack. Reckons he can cock a

finger, tell all his mates how he's done us over, you, the rest.'

'How soon?' Rack asked, praying say now, say now.

'Any time from this aft.' Which meant now.

Ta, God. Rack's face felt tight. The syndicate was down to Martina, Posser, the goers, with Grellie and her stringers. But diss was down to Rack. His throat went thick as a tree trunk.

'Make sure you got the straw, Rack. Use Florence's lot through the Vallance Carvery, something this size.'

'I'll only need three, Posser,' Rack said, aggrieved, 'not a fucking army.'

'Use Florence,' Posser ruled. Straw was alibi hard enough to satisfy the most ardent plod. It was supplied by plants, women held on a promise of good money. They testified what they were told. Their perjury was laid out in detail they simply learnt off by heart. 'She's got plants who'll sing Handel's *Messiah*. Son, take care, eh?'

'Can I go?' Rack was murderous.

'Just take care.' Posser sighed, watched him shoot out of the doors. Young folk. Hurrying was all their trouble.

Hassall hated newshounds, broadcasters. He could hear them grumbling in the other room, no homes to go to.

'They're just newsagents,' he told Windsor, who was doing his exasperated eye-rolling. 'But they have their uses, like now.'

'Spread news?' Windsor gave back, a kid in a lesson.

'Wrong. Spread our balderdash.' Hassall took the list. 'Know what hurts me, these exercises I'm doing? My bum muscles scream blue murder. How many witnesses?'

'The motorist who passed. A woman who phoned in, anonymous. Four descriptions of cars. That's it.'

'The city's tubers are how many?'

'Seventeen, narrowed down to four.'

Half a chance, Windsor'd give him their dentition and school reports. But neuroses meant promotion these days. Slim Tim here'd go far.

'Four who?'

'Five are already under investigation, so unlikely. One's banged up—'

'Not the rejects,' Hassall said patiently. 'Who remain?'

'That weirdo keeps grenades in his attic, says he's a legit collector. He's under surveillance, Winstanley's there now. Jase, no other name, answers the description and pals with Noddo. Another, no name but in Leeds. And the new one, Devalier, contract tube bloke for yardies everywhere.'

'Jase, then?'

'Haleys Wharf, last heard of. His girl's a druggo.'

'How do I say that?' Hassall pointed, spelled slowly. 'Guayaguayare?'

'I think the report's wrong – if Noddo did it, that is. His yardies are Salt Ponders.'

Like drawing teeth. 'Let me in on it, Sergeant Windsor, please.'

'They're named for different accents, place names. Jamaica, Trinidad, Bradford even. All different.'

'Odd, this Jase, tubing for Noddo when his girl's a druggo for some anti-Noddo mob, eh?' Hassall felt charitable. This was good. It either eliminated Jase, or made him the shooter. 'He done time?'

'Can't be sure. We lack ID.'

'Trust motorists. Will the bugger let himself be quoted?'

'No. He's a shopkeeper from Truro. No,' Windsor put in quickly. 'He'd his wife with him.'

Hassall listened to the grumbling in the press room. 'Hark to that idle lot. Moan, moan. It isn't as though they actually slog for a living, is it? We do their work for them. Got my statement typed out, have you?'

'No.' Windsor was startled. 'You didn't say that.'

Hassall sighed. They'd have him carrying the pots and pans next. 'Okay. I'll blag it. You'd better come in, in case they ask summert barmy.'

'Right, Mr Hassall.' Like, forward the guns, Hassall thought, honest to God, and said out of the side of his mouth as they went in, 'Get the Truro couple for a chat somewhere else, when you've got rid.'

'Roger,' said tight-lipped Lieutenant Carruthers, ready for the assault on the Khyber. Hassall marvelled. The silly sod actually did say it, Roger, like in the comics. He'd go far, no shadow of doubt.

They gathered in the Shot Pot's back room, all alcoves. You could get a beer there without a struggle.

The lads were cheering trick shots. Tonto, Toothie's Guadeloupe cousin, would bet on any colour doing anything. Bonn wished they wouldn't scream, but Toothie said they were born like it. His great snooker enemy and friend was Pencey, a Ghana lad with a propensity for defeat.

Beth served, Grellie's section girl. She hid the kitchen behind partitions that she controlled with some electronic zapper. This innovation truly disgusted old Osmund, who thought the nation was becoming soft. He kept saying that one day soon he'd reinvent the door handle, make a mint.

She was a pretty nineteen, lived Moss Side with an

antique dealer, a dud. Grellie kept asking Beth to join her green string, make a fortune, her own property in eight Lady Days. No more knee-tremblers in alleys, enjoy free shopping. Beth hadn't the nerve, so meanwhile the Station Brough punters were in paradise, a lovely young shag like Beth doing it for a few quid. It didn't make sense. Rack said make Beth do as she was told, but Grellie said Rack should shut up, it was a free country.

Doob came in, sober and furtive. The pickpocket was neat now, no longer a wino. A suit, casual loafers, looked twenty-three when as a drunkie he'd looked fifty. He even had haircuts at Ellie Freedo's, which cost the earth, but he could afford the earth now he was one of Bonn's goers. Against Martina's wishes, which only went to show.

Galahad stood there, for once not looking in the mirrors. He sagged, had lost muscles but was still a monument to pumping iron and mad nourishment. Danielle was waiting outside with Grellie's Lorna. Bonn didn't know why. He'd not expected her.

'Bonn!' Lancelot exclaimed when Bonn entered, Rack following. 'How long will this take? I'm rehearsing mogga dancing.'

'Your new partner's crap, Lancelot,' Rack said.

'She isn't!' Lancelot stared at Rack in horror. 'Is she?'

'Dark hair, good figure, won Latin-American finals?'

'No. Blonde, second in the North of England.'

'I'll drop by,' Rack promised, magnanimous. 'Me and Bonn saw the one I mean. Bonn'll recognize her.'

'You will?' Lancelot almost broke down in relief. 'Thanks, Bonn.'

In these circumstances Bonn couldn't rebuke Rack, but he was saddened by his stander's lies. Fine, yes, lies got the meeting underway, but at what cost? He would have to make a remark. Rack would go into one, but had brought it upon himself. Lancelot could have been brought to heel more easily, and saved Bonn time, and the career of the girl who danced with Lancelot, whoever she was. Now, Lancelot was a nervous wreck.

'Meeting, please,' Bonn began, looking at his hands when Beth asked what. She quickly left. 'Rack.'

'Ta, Bonn. Galahad? Come 'ere.' Cockney, hard, quiet, not at all Rack's street voice.

The muscle man moved across and stood.

'Toothie?' Rack bawled suddenly. 'Shut that bloody door.'

The partition clunked into place, the snooker noise silenced.

'Galahad wuz shagging crorsst the line,' Rack said for everybody's benefit. 'Danielle, Haleys Wharf. No frigging excuse, Galahad.'

'It was just—' Galahad tried, but Rack glared.

'Galahad, mate. You wus already dunned fer shedding clients, saying you wus booked when you wasn't, right?'

No answer. Rack straightened an arm, brought it slowly round so his finger pointed at Galahad.

'Right?' Rack slammed his right hand down on the table, and yelled, 'Fucking right, clorf ears, yiss er no?'

'Yes, yes!'

Rack glared round, snorting with rage. Bonn wondered, real or simulated? It looked scarily genuine. 'Got aht to say? If yer have, say it.'

All were silent.

'Doob?' Rack said. 'Spit it aht.'

'No,' Doob said. 'I'm sorry, Galahad.'

'Shut that, Doob. We're the ones sobbin' in our slop. Lancelot?'

'Eh? No.' Lancelot was wondering miserably about his dancing partner.

'Then that's that. Bonn?' Rack ignored Bonn's look of supplication. He reckoned he did a fine gangster imitation. With green eyeshades, bishop sleeves, silver elastics on his arms, he'd look really great.

'Thank you, Rack. Galahad's assets, please.'

'He owns the Bouncing Block, half franchise.' Rack also wanted a mirror. 'That's fifty per cent, dude.'

'Rack,' Bonn said, tired of Rack's put-on voices.

'And two building society accounts in different names. Galahad Treviso Chestersohn is one. The other's a woman's name, Geralday Price Washto. Know what?' Rack waited, but nobody wanted to know. 'I reckon he made them up.'

'Thank you, Rack. Go on.'

'He has a mortgage on some flat, a frigging right dump. An' he bought a motor three days back, di'n't yer, Geralday?'

'Very well,' Bonn said, hating this. 'Galahad. Transfer all your assets to the company, via Martina's lawyer. Rack will take you. Sign your flat over. Close your accounts down and hand the wadge to Rack. Your motor, sign over to persons Rack will designate. Your gymnasium franchise assign to Prand.'

'Prand?' Galahad reeled. 'I beat him in the Body Masters.'

'I'm so sad, Galahad.' The big man recoiled as if whipped.

'Bonn means nah, Geralday, see?'

'Please give him a few moments to adjust, Rack.'

Rack thought, He's had a fucking few moments fer Christ's sake, but kept quiet.

'I've got nothing else, Bonn,' Galahad said.

'You sure?' Rack did his slam and glare.

'Galahad,' Bonn said. 'You disappointed me.'

Galahad wept openly. Rack groaned in disgust.

'Thank you for attending,' Bonn told everyone. 'Rack, see to it. Send Prand to me when you can. Doob, Lancelot, carry on as usual.'

Lancelot caught Bonn up so they went through the snooker hall together. The lads were quiet, glancing, lighting cigarettes, wondering what.

'Bonn?' Lancelot said, worried sick. 'Will you come to the Palais Rocco? My partner'll be there. I almost lost the semi last week with that nine-legged Wolverhampton mare. You know how many hours I practise for one single step change?'

'Sixteen,' Bonn said, worn out.

'Six*teen*!' Lancelot agreed dementedly. 'You just come along when I'm really on song.'

'I'll be there, Lancelot. Please say nothing to the girl.'

Reassurance was a therapy all goers seemed to need. He would ask Posser tonight was that always the case.

Grellie was sitting in the central gardens watching the old men play walk-about chess. He went to sit with her, ask what had she done with Danielle.

She budged up, giving him space. 'Don't cry, darling,' she said.

Bonn's eyes were dry. 'I just hope I've sanctioned him sufficiently, Grellie.' He meant for Martina.

# 16

**Cushy, cushti** – profitable, easy (romany)

'THE PATIENT WAS brought in after a drive-by shooting,' Dr Steve Burnden said when Clare asked. They were in the doctors' mess, a ramshackle three-storey house in the District General Hospital patch. The ground floor was their sitting room. 'Young bloke, what, twenty or so. Brother killed outright.'

'Shotgun?' Clare asked the neurosurgeon.

'I forgot you'd been a pathology registrar. Yes, a mess.'

They were alone, except for a paediatric houseman, Trudy Nelson, sleeping flat out with a pile of notes sliding off her lap.

Steve was a large and shaggy Sheffield man, not given to flights of fancy, but cunning. He'd made more court appearances than most, neurosurgery a hell of a trade, his saying.

'Wasn't it a bit precise, two at one go, I mean?'

'Look at Mr Kennedy.'

'Who's doing the post-mortem?'

'Dr Wallace, tomorrow. Coroner's list.' Steve scribbled himself a memo. 'Hebrew Janeson's going to be a PVS.'

Clare thought, oh no. 'How soon will you be able to say?'

'You know the Royal College of Physicians. They changed "persistent vegetative state" to *permanent*, nothing better to do with their time.'

'Come on, Steve,' Clare said with some asperity. 'A working group's only a working group. Your patient's entering the CVS, "continuing". Is the head wound extensive?'

Steve grimaced exaggerated agreement. 'Looks done close up. He's got abdominal wounds too.'

'Prognosis, doctor?'

'Mister, if you please.' He grinned. 'Those bloody Dr Kildare programmes ruined us surgeons. We work our youth away to become "doctor", then slog another decade to become a surgeon and "mister" again. It's ludicrous.'

'It's merely archaic. Think of us women.' Clare smiled, to lighten the moment.

'Anyway, the heat's off you locum doctors. You can always scarper.'

Clare winced. There was truth in what Steve said.

'You've scored the patient?'

'On the Glasgow Coma Scale? A bit early. He'll settle into brain-stem death any sec. A1, B1, sort of, to B2. It's a sod. I wonder do these gun idiots know which neural pathways to aim at.'

Assessment by means of the Glasgow Scale was virtually routine, for evaluation of 'vegetative' patients. It was based on three categories of response, in each of four numbered grades: eye responses A, motor functions B, and verbal reactivity under C. Despite the Coma Scale's brevity, there were still arguments about finer interpretations, especially in prolonged VS patients.

'C1, I suppose?' Meaning no response.

'They're doing the central metabolism now. It'll be nil, or near zero.'

'And EEG?'

'Virtual electrocerebral silence. 'Course, one house surgeon made a summer out of a theta nudge. You know what housemen are like, unwilling to face the obvious. A bit of reflex spinal movement, he said, but I don't know.'

'We were all like that. It sounds like death in a fortnight, wouldn't you say, Steve? PVS?'

'As ever. The police have been. God, I hate their excitability.'

'That reminds me,' Clare said, stirring. 'I've got a shoal of them signing for Dr Porritt's cardiac project. I've an athlete to test in an hour.'

'Clare,' Steve said before letting her get away. 'You know the RCP recommendations? Two doctors, separate examinations?'

'Yes,' Clare said, wary. 'Individual.'

'Would you be our second PVS assessor? Only, you'd be completely independent.'

'Of course,' she said, rising, thinking, what am I saying? 'Better get on.'

She left the neurosurgeon and the dozing paediatric house doctor, and made her way to the cardiac surveillance unit. On the way, she was handed a note from Reception. Some anonymous youth had phoned two hours before wanting to speak with 'the lady doctor who'd done Marie'. She thought, Jase?

The fiction she had devised for Clifford's friend's athlete was that he – she? – had volunteered for the cardiac surveillance project, and that it was reasonable to take samples of blood and urine for anabolic steroids, considering the publicity there had recently been about them.

She reached the unit, and found not one but thirty-six athletes waiting in a queue.

The elderly Truro couple were still there. The man rose.

'Excuse me.' Mr Widden was sweating. What else in such thick tweeds? Hassall wondered if they'd assumed they were coming to another country, so cold up north. 'How soon will you let us go?' The man's deep bass vibrated, probably a mainstay in the church choir.

'After another couple of details, Mr Widden.' Hassall smiled at the lady. He signalled Windsor to take over.

'Only, we've to be back first thing tomorrow,' Mrs Widden said. 'Our grandchildren go swimming. George sees to their schoolbags.'

Hassall wondered why Sergeant Windsor got on so well with the couple. His own smiles never worked.

Windsor had drawings out. Hassall watched, sulking. The sergeant was brisk, sure of himself, guessing when to josh their memories. A performance.

'Is there anybody here, any bobby in this room, who's the same size as the young man you saw?'

The Widdens scanned the place. Four or five uniformed police had gone through. Six clattered consol keys. The couple discussed shapes, heights, decided they were all too beefy or too tall.

'That young man who carried that box a few moments agone,' Mrs Widden said. 'Don't you think, George?'

They narrowed it down. PC Gaffney was fetched, narked at being interrupted sifting narcotics records.

'You don't mind, do you?' Mrs Widden asked. 'Was it your break?'

The constable stood obediently, was made to turn round,

the lads all grinning, two women constables hiding laughs. Hassall was ready to give them a mouthful. Police work was all watching telly screens. Now this, in a squad room. Like a fitting for a bloody frock.

'You're exactly his shape,' the lady said. 'My eyes are better than my husband's. It's farming, chemicals.'

'My uncle says that, Mrs Widden,' from Windsor. Hassall felt out of it. 'It's as bad on the fells.'

'Is it, dear?' she said with sympathy. 'Is your uncle retired? George retired three years ago, didn't you, dear? He's never looked back.'

'This, then?' Windsor shuffled transparencies like a card sharp.

'Sloppy jeans, frayed at the ankles. And great canvas boots with thick soles.' She clasped her hands on her lap, bridling. 'Our grandchildren have those laces. It's a wonder they don't trip themselves up. They won't be told.'

Hassall said he had to go. So it was Jase, but how come? On the pavement, on his tod, no wheels?

He looked back through the partition at Windsor, who was enjoying himself, manoeuvring the old couple into disclosures. Remembrances of things past. Was that a song title? He left, jokily told PC Ferdiham he was deputized and it was Jase they were looking for. Hassall hoped to Christ he never remembered the melody; he'd never get it out of his head. He told Ferdiham to tell Windsor to follow on to Haleys Wharf.

'Deputized?' PC Ferdiham said, mystified, but only when the door swung to behind Hassall. 'Yon's been reading too many westerns.'

Hassall heard the remark. Police work was far too serious to leave to adults.

At the door they caught him, Frank Wilmslow from,

chuckle, Wilmslow in Cheshire. A quiet bowls player, a mere twenty-odd, did weight-lifting, unmarried and, it was said, likely to remain so. His fiancée had wed a taxi driver.

'A lady at the hospital needs you to ring, Mr Hassall. Urgent.' Wilmslow passed him the note. 'Mrs Mandel. That's her extension.'

'Ta.' Hassall wondered, Now why did I think of Clare Burtonall?

The bus was on time, a miracle.

Jase felt uncomfortable, wondering how folk actually wore clothes like this. He'd got them from a cottage only yards from the bus stop. Nicking was the easiest thing on earth.

He'd slept well in the barn. That TV woman had said Marie died of AIDS. Which meant, didn't it, that he'd got it too, shagging Marie every how, and they'd pooled needles. He'd phoned the hospital, got nowhere.

The bus rumbled between cottages on the sloping moorland. He'd maybe done wrong to drop his gear, but he couldn't carry his jeans and bomber jacket over his arm, could he? Bad enough wearing the tube down his leg with this gear. Suit, Christ's sake. Who wore suits but undertakers? The best thing was the credit card, easy peasy, some old crone in a garden busy with plantpots. What a frigging life, highlight of her day somebody giving her a good morning. Nip round the rear, swarm over her wall while she trilled and trowelled. Beyond fucking belief, people's lives. Told a yarn, she'd have made him his tea.

He'd no scrip. Marie always kept it. Lately, she'd done nothing but sleep, too tired even to sol up the scrip. He'd ballocked her proper for that. His anger was what took her to the doctor's. She went for too many blood tests. Doctors experimented with you, the bastards, and what good did it do?

The shopping bag looked authentic. No rabbit pockets in these kecks, like he'd made for himself in his other clothes. Marie'd stitched real chandler's twine, wouldn't break so shoppers wondered, hey, that lad's dropping fucking guns.

Jase saw the brown moors above Dunscar. Couple of miles, he'd be back in civilization. He was beginning to shake, though he'd nicked the old biddy's sugar. Lumps, thank God, keep going somehow, reach the wharf.

Bunce who'd not been there. Jase knew anyway, deep down. What had Noddo told the others? That Bunce wouldn't be there when Jase came lamming round the corner, tee hee? Jase then get caught red-dicked, toodle-oo, lad, see you some other existence?

It left Noddo in the clear. The city would wonder why some loony tuber had gunned the Janesons down, think it a plain drugs pop. Noddo's stock would rise, nobody more impressed than people who whispered about possibles, the way folk with no lives of their own got their onions.

Tall and gangly, gold teeth on the gape, Bunce'd be killing hisself, hey, I ten mile off, Jase come runnin', tee hee.

'What's that, son?' Some lady turned on the seat in front of Jase.

'Sorry, missus,' he said. 'Laughing at something a friend said. Tee hee.'

'In her flat, then,' Bonn said to Rack, nearing the new woman's house.

'Yip. It's safe. It's a gater.'

Gaters were becoming popular, blocks of flats where a guard controlled ingress and intercoms ruled.

Rack drove barely above the speed limit, sarcastically making Fangio noises because Bonn kept saying slow down, please. Rack would get a reputation for driving like everybody's auntie. The other worst thing, he'd not squealed the tyres once since collecting Bonn from the Vallance Carvery. Driving Bonn was a pain.

'Her husband's straight, just interested. She's not new, been in once. She hates hotels.'

'I shall look for cameras.'

'Know what?' Rack said, slowing among neat suburban gardens and trellised garages. 'Homers're more interested in money than sex, see?'

No, Bonn did not see. He wondered where Rack would wait.

'Money can't be right, Rack.'

'It is, Bonn!' Rack cried, urging him to logic. 'Next road on the right. A woman wants to pretend *she's* on the game, see? You're the nearest she can get.'

Bonn still didn't follow. Because they were nearly there he said, 'The woman who hires me is playing at being a—'

'Whore! You got it!' Rack was only disappointed he wouldn't have time to really explain, because it was all due to having bad feet, and here was the gate.

The security man stepped out. 'Flat Fifteen?' he asked. 'One hour?'

'Thank you,' Bonn said, and they were through.

'See?' Rack was indignant. 'We could have been Jack the Ripper. What a burke. Don't knock for two minutes, okay?'

'Very well. Thank you for the lift.'

Rack parked, marvelling. Thanks for the lift, when

Martina paid a fortune for motors? Fall down on the job of getting your goer to the next lady, Martina'd crisp you. It was a real shame, Rack thought, going to tell the gate man his passenger had to fly to Venezuela and they'd hold the plane at Ringroad Airport. The shame was, Bonn would be cool if he shagged Grellie regular. A bloke without a bird got twisted. Women without a man had it easy, not really needing men.

Bonn knocked on the door after two minutes.

A woman opened, a little nervous, her husband standing behind. He had dressed for the occasion, shirt, tie, smart shoes as if ready for out.

'Hello. I'm Bonn.'

How the woman greeted you was always a clue. Hello, good morning, afternoon, all seemed difficult.

She was not quite blushing, a little breathless as she admitted him.

'Cherie,' Bonn said. 'Nice name.'

'I'm Ryde,' the man said. Bonn thought, Ryde? From some film? If he said so.

'Hello, Ryde. Thank you for booking me.'

'Would you like—?' the wife began. Her husband cut her short.

'I want to watch the start,' he said, as if expecting rebuke. 'It's that or—'

'As you wish, Ryde.'

It was at this point Bonn always wished he had something – folder, leather case, maybe – to lay down, show he'd fall in with the lady's wishes. But that would have made him a performer carrying props, the last impression he wanted to create. A lady deserved better.

Ryde concealed his surprise with a few throat clearances. 'You do her in there.'

Cherie hung back, smoothing her dress. Bonn smiled, took her hand, walked her in.

'I'm so pleased, Cherie. I expect it was a big decision.'

'Oh, well.' She looked uncertainly back at her husband. 'I . . .' She reddened, not sure whether to admit that she had used the Pleases Agency before. 'It's what seemed best, really.' She searched for her husband's coined name. '*Ryde* said we should send out for someone, instead of my going out alone.'

'Whatever pleases you, Cherie.'

The bedroom was in gloaming, no lights except for a fluorescent over a print of a Victorian cottage scene, a woman in an apron, two children gathering flowers, winding paths between trees. Cameras?

'Have I to . . . ?' Cherie stood uncertainly.

'Let me.'

The coverlet was turned down. He sat on the bed and drew her to stand before him. Ryde watched. Bonn held Cherie's hips.

'Ryde? You watch from outside, not here.'

'Look,' Ryde said hotly. 'If I'm—'

'No, Ryde. Close the door when I tell you.'

'I'm paying!' But Ryde stalked to the door.

Bonn smiled up into Cherie's face. She was breathless with anxiety. He started to undo her dress. 'Say when you want it to be just us.'

'I want to hear what you're saying!' Ryde shouted.

Bonn pressed his face against Cherie's body, inhaling.

'I want to go slowly, Cherie.'

She said, 'Yes.' Her head turned, checking her husband was still there. She whispered down, 'I don't want him there.'

'I'll see to it.'

'He'll get mad.' She mouthed the words.

Bonn slipped his hands inside her dress, and embraced her thighs, the skirt falling over his forearms. 'It's what *you* want.'

Gingerly she touched his hair. 'Can I decide?'

'Now, Cherie?' He was getting used to that name. 'Close the door, Ryde.'

'I said I wanted—'

'Ryde,' Bonn said, his eyes on Cherie. 'If you please.'

He parted her dress and slowly shelled it from her so it fell to the carpet. One by one he removed her underclothes until she was naked, held the bedclothes for her to slip in, and stood looking down.

The light faded as the door clicked shut. Bonn stripped, eeled in beside her, and brought her close.

He said along the pillow, 'You see how easy it is, when it's your day. Now remember, Cherie, you've all the time in the world.'

# 17

**Homer** – the hiring of a goer for sex, by a woman in her own dwelling

MARTINA GRASPED THE nettle immediately supper ended.

'Dad? Bonn and I will go for a run out. Is that all right?'

'Yes, love.' Posser was in his chair before the fire. 'Somewhere nice? Is Bonn driving?'

She coloured. Their recurrent joke was that she dared not ask Bonn if he could drive. Posser laughed about it. He'd said once to her when Bonn was out, 'No motors in a seminary!' She never enquired into Bonn's past, and now it was too late. Partly it was Posser's fault, who had met Bonn first and taken him on. But that seminary word. She'd looked it up in the dictionary, like a fool.

The Bentley came on time, seven-fifteen. Martina kissed Posser and Bonn said so-long. They set off, the driver Martina's constant anonymous man with the pitted-skin neck and cropped hair.

'It's a shame,' Bonn said as they went through Victoria Square. 'Gas fires. Imitation. Posser probably grew up with proper coal fires.'

'It's hardly as safe.'

They were both on edge, worried about visiting an old folks' home on the sly, Posser thinking they were going out to some cinema. Martina would have to concoct some tale. Soon she would have to admit her deception, that she was looking for somewhere to send him. Posser still had ways of knowing what happened in the city. The chances were he had already detected their duplicity, and that he was already on the phone, sussing. Martina pondered mortality.

Mrs Ainsworth had servants galore in her great house. The venerable old lady, Martina supposed, had been past making sexual demands on Posser towards the end. She'd seen her dad cry when Mrs Mildred passed away, the doctor coming downstairs with slow tread saying it was any moment, please go up.

Martina thought, this final journey comes to all, when we're unable to bath ourselves, eat even, needing fitter folk to clean and dress us, tell us what. Here she was with Bonn, a stranger, travelling out of the city to arrange her father's last real trip. Was there no alternative?

The Bentley took the Bolgate Street exit. Neither she nor Bonn looked at the Time and Scythe Hotel as they passed it.

The place was reassuring. Martina and Bonn alighted.

'We shall visit about an hour,' Martina told the driver.

Visit, Bonn noted. Not here for an appointment to see about moving Martina's father in. He settled the fiction in mind.

The matron was a rotund cheery woman with a fixed grin, every word spoken through a mirthless rictus. Yet Mrs Calderwood behaved pleasantly enough and offered tea before showing them round. Martina explained about an elderly relative.

'We've been recommended,' Martina said, 'my cousin and I.'

'Of course!' the grin said. 'You wanted to see for yourselves!'

'We have no experience, matron,' Bonn added, taking Martina's deceit on. Cousin was pleasant. 'Please explain as we go. Even,' he added apologetically, 'obvious things. You're the expert, after all.'

'Of *course* I shall, Mr Brooks!'

She ushered them. The home had been purpose built some ten years before. Mrs Calderwood bustled ahead, mentioning fire doors, dining arrangements. Each guest had an individual room. There was a communal dining room, three sitting rooms. Surveillance was as vigilant as privacy allowed.

'Could we see a typical room, please, matron?'

'Certainly! This one is vacant at the moment.'

The room was on the second floor. ('Not exactly a tower block, Miss Brooks!' from merry Mrs Calderwood. 'Safety, you see!') It was quite spacious, held a single bed, an armchair, and a small table with two upright chairs. Flowers, a window overlooking trees and a pond with ducks near a paved area set with garden furniture. A pergola on a raised pavement lent colour.

'There's hardly any traffic noise, even in summer!'

'Marvellous,' Bonn said. 'Your residents must be very happy.'

'We have few complaints!' Mrs Calderwood pointed out the safety circuit, auto-dimmers, remote control television and radio. 'Limited sound, of course, so as not to annoy!'

Martina nodded, smiling but silent while Bonn fielded Mrs Calderwood's determined soliloquy.

'We have entertainments, visitors who bring their little

shows!' The matron led the way to the communal lounges. 'They're quite a popular feature of the home!'

The door opened on a wide room. A dozen elderly folk were seated in comfortable chairs. One was being given a drink through a tube by a middle-aged helper. Another was shaking badly, the tremor causing her covering blanket to slip. A comedy film was on the screen. The folk were silent.

They were shown a reading room, where two ladies were knitting and three played cards. One old man read his book in a corner.

After an hour they were shown out. To Bonn it had been a time of endless pleasantries. Martina managed to prevent Mrs Calderwood from waving them off.

Their drive back to the city was in silence.

An hour after Posser had gone to bed, Bonn was reading when Martina at last came into the living room. He put his book down.

She took the opposite armchair, ready for terrible thoughts. 'I've just been up. Dad's asleep.'

Her lovely eyes filled. She tried to speak. Bonn switched off the main lights, leaving only his table lamp.

'Sorry, Martina. I forget. The lights are like a fairground.'

'You see, Bonn,' she said as if continuing a conversation, 'it isn't as if I had sisters I could call on, a brother to talk things over. It's so hard.'

'I believe that.'

'I used to pretend I had aunties, a kindly uncle to take me walks. It was always my fictional uncle who'd somehow straighten my lameness so I could run home and Dad's face would light up!'

She blotted her tears and went to sit on the ottoman, hugging her knees and staring into the fire.

'Did you see their faces? The old lady being fed.' She shivered. 'That man looked up as we entered. Did you see?'

The man had been about seventy, as far as Bonn could judge. He'd worn a woollen pullover that had seen better days. His appearance was that of an artisan, maybe a mill craftsman. Bonn mentally invented a history for the old gent, a wife who'd died, children convincing themselves that their duty was discharged by putting the father into 'care facility'.

The instant the matron had ushered them in, the lone reader had raised his eyes. Hatred, Bonn had realized with a shock, hatred for yet more young betrayers looking to salve their consciences, so they could depart saying the place was 'really nice'.

'He hated us, Bonn.' Martina wept again. Bonn didn't know what to do. 'What if Dad hated me like that? I couldn't bear it.'

'We'll have to think.'

'You see, we were left when I was little.' She sobered, tried hard. 'Dad looked after me, even when we moved to Mrs Ainsworth's. He was' – she glared defiantly at Bonn – 'a stablehand, as I told you. Just us, Dad and me.'

'He must have seen a lot of changes.'

She tried a smile of reminiscence. 'Dad says the city is a sinking convoy, debris and survivors.' She looked at Bonn in challenge. 'And it's come to this. Sometimes he needs lifting, and I can't do it.'

Bonn drew breath to make the offer, but Martina shook her head.

'No, Bonn. A fulltime nurse, here, with our syndicate? I

couldn't have that. Dad would go crazy. What else *is* there, but a home?'

'I'll think of something.'

'Will you, Bonn?' She gazed at him. 'Will you?'

'Promise,' he said. 'I'll find a solution, to please us all.'

They sat before the fire in silence, thinking of the hatred in that old man's eyes.

The Bone Diver in Salford was heaving, smoke, booze, noise. Rack laughed, ready, the bliss of coming rumble an ecstasy. Toothie and Henno were listening to the music beat, Toothie already spot jiving, loving it.

'Two more minutes, Toothie'll want to forget the job, Rack.'

'You see he doesn't, Henno.'

Toothie, dancing among the sweaty crowd of drinkers, heard but wasn't offended. He knew he was the one, not Rack or his pal Henno from Welsh Wales. Dancing was simply stirring coals. He tittered, wanting to be done, take up his golden cue that tonight would set the Shot Pot alight.

'No drinks,' Rack ruled.

'Just one pint, Rack bach.'

'No drinks. Wait till after.'

Henno sulked. Sulking was Henno's trouble. Good pal, but his sulks sometimes lasted days. Rack decided to move, no good drawing it out when there was carnie to be done. Carnie was too neglected, had to be seen. Herd word was important.

'Come on.' Rack signalled Mya, saw her press through the crowd to join Rio and Dum.

The girl was smart, drew both to the Bone Diver entrance, and vanished into the ladies' loos. Rack gave

Toothie and Henno the nod and went outside into the cool Salford night. The car park was virtually empty, a few snoggers clamming up.

They emerged in less than a minute. Rack was by Rio's motor. Rio and Dum came strolling up, looked at each other uncertainly, the club's on-off signs bathing their faces in green, red, yellow. Rack wished then that he'd brought a cheroot. He could spin a gold coin, American.

'Ta, Mya,' he said. 'Push off.'

'Here, what is this?' Rio started, but Toothie clouted him with an iron from behind, which ended chat.

Dum squealed as Henno jabbed a brick into his kidneys, and sank to the tarmac. Rack thought, Dum actually weeping? Christ's sake, it was a queer fucking world. Crying like a tart and going oooh, my back?

'Listen,' Rack said. 'Your trailer catches fire tonight. Do it.'

Rio asked, coming round, 'Who're you?'

'Shut it, Rio. That trailer you went halves on with Tommo? Well, set it afire one hour from now, okay?'

'What *is* this?'

'Say that one more time, swelp me I'll do you. Both of yer, smash that Daimler's windows and stab its tyres.'

Rio tried to run. Toothie clobbered his shin with the metal rod and he fell groaning. Rack heard a bone crack. He'd deliberately told Toothie no bones. He looked up into the drizzle. God, he prayed, give me fucking strength. Do people never listen?

'That Daimler's Tommo's,' Dum said, panting though he'd so far run nowhere. 'He'll kill us.'

'Dum, I want both of you smashing it when folk come running, okay?' Rio's rolling around and clutching was making him laugh, and Dum was pathetic. 'The alternative's really bad news.'

'Shall we do it?' Toothie asked, thinking snooker, 'hell of a sight quicker.'

'No. Tommo's goons must see.'

'Why is this?' Rio begged. 'We done nowt.'

'You tried to start up as goers, right? Start smashing, or the world ends here.'

They went then, Rio weeping and hopping. After a few moments Rack heard the crash of glass. He counted seven before he turned and waved at the Bone Diver. Instantly Mya, carefully watching, screamed. Dum and Rio legged it to their own motor, screeched off without lights.

Gone. Rack walked casually inside as people started running out. Mya was doing her oh-my-God act in the foyer. Rack walked past her. Rio and Dum's trailer would be already well ablaze by now. Rack'd had the foresight to sugar Rio's petrol tank and deflate his tyres, so Tommo's chasing goons would catch them halfway, with horrible results.

Some folk have brains, he told himself, pleased. It was having special lungs when you were five. He'd explain it to Bonn, see what he said.

# 18

**Knick-knock** – reprisal between criminal groups

'DO YOU KNOW what I've had to do?' Clare blazed, marching about her living room. Still sickened over Bonn, she was ready for battle.

Clifford was being amazed, with what sincerity she could only guess.

'Listen, darling—!'

'Listen?' Clare halted. 'You said *a* sample. You sent a horde!'

He looked aggrieved, as if she was creating problems.

'I honestly can't see why you're so steamed up.'

'You said one.' She showed him her index finger. 'Instead, I've to take blood and urine samples for anabolic steroids from thirty-*six*, you idiot.'

He caught her, begging, 'Please listen.'

She shook herself free. He hadn't a notion.

'You think it's so simple? A drop of blood, a specimen in some jar, and it's done? Can't you understand that it's only then that the work begins? The samples have to be analysed. It costs actual money – the stuff you're such an expert on!'

'Money?' Now, that he understood.

She calmed, but her teeth were clenched. 'Clifford. If I sign for six dozen samples, at God knows what cost for each one, the clinical pathologist demands which fund will pay. The surveillance subvention is allocated for research. It will look as if I'm running a clinic on the sly!'

'Why not send them to an outside laboratory then?'

'I'll have to. Or discard the samples.'

'No,' he said quickly, 'don't do that. Look. Where would private samples normally go for athletics?'

'There are commercial labs.'

'There, then!' Clifford urged.

'You're not listening! Analysis is expensive, not just drop-blot test. Adapted capillary electrophoresis alone—'

'I'll make a couple of calls, darling.' He bussed her cheek before she could turn aside. 'Give me ten minutes.'

She was still angered. 'I'll have to explain the mix-up to Dr Porritt.'

'I'll give Tom Farnham a ring, sort it out.'

She watched the news – mercifully free of Mrs Mandel – until Clifford returned. He was beaming.

'All done!' He drew her to the couch. 'There's a commercial laboratory in Droylsden. Materials, industrials, pharmaceuticals. The scientist's Dr Julia Pickard. Tom Farnham's guaranteed payment.'

Clare nodded with reluctance. She would have to go through with it. At least she could pass the whole thing off with near-truths. Maybe she could incorporate the athletics teams as some sort of quality-control cohort, and portray Clifford's colleague Farnham as a benevolent contributor? She would be as frank as she dared, say her husband jumped to conclusions.

Clifford watched her expression chart her thoughts. Clare had played her part just as he'd expected. Now she was in until, he thought with a concealed smile, death do us part.

*

At the Shot Pot the hullabaloo was beyond belief. The Bury lads were yelling predictions, they'd whitewash the Wiganners. Toothie and Pencey already laying heavy bets were next in the knockout.

It was getting personal. Opponents were trying to bribe the judges, two morose Trafford Park octogenarians who wouldn't take free snuff, let alone snooker money. Osmund kept trying to quieten them. 'Immigrants,' he censured, though most were Lancastrians with accents broader than his own.

Martina heard none of this, except the faint noise when Osmund operated the lock. She watched Akker enter.

Akker, a Burnley man, could pass for a teenager but was well over that. He looked bloodless, death's door features, thin and wan. Forever young, Martina thought.

'There's a problem, Akker. It's Galahad.'

Akker blinked, the last name he'd expected. He only knew Galahad as a giant body-builder, a goer on Bonn's firm, preselected by Martina's own decree. He said nothing. He wouldn't have been summoned unless there was serious work on.

'Have you seen Galahad lately, Akker?'

'Aye.' He thought, listing places, times. 'I saw him come second, northwest hefters or summert, two month since. He created, said he'd won. Rack had to tone him down.'

'What else?' Martina hadn't heard of the incident. Insignificant, or Rack would have come barging in wanting to hang everybody.

'Him at the snooker hall with Lancelot, a row, mutter mutter, come to nowt. Him in a taxi, his stander got peeved, ready for a barney but clemmed up. A fortnight back.'

She knew of those, only routines.

'It's a problem, Akker. I want some act. It can't be left.'

He cleared his throat. 'Right. In the city?'

'Better outside. I'd like a gap.'

'How long?' Akker was disappointed, but women didn't have to do the job. They – Martina too, even – thought it was like posting a fucking letter, ordering from Freeman's catalogue. Carnie wasn't anything of the sort.

'Give them maybe ten days. Can that be done?'

'Depends where he goes.' Akker noticed something. 'Them?'

'Galahad and Danielle.'

Rumours had been right. His pale brow cleared. This was easier.

'It's best done soon and quick, Martina.'

'I know that,' she said, patient. 'Do it alone. I don't want a squad of tankers like foxhounds.'

Foxhounds? Akker had never seen one. Tankers were folk like himself, bludging on demand.

'How, is your job, Akker.'

He stood there while she made her mind up. Her prettiness mesmerized. She was like some synthesized doll, every ingredient made to perfection's measure. Bonn now lodged with her and the old man. If Grellie was right – he'd overheard Cleo telling Bridget the Sunday previous – Bonn hadn't stuck Martina even once, which was highly weird, her the ultimate dazzler and Bonn's feet under her table. There was simply no telling. Look at Galahad, in paradise, money and grumble guaranteed, chucking it away for Danielle, a flag scrubber. Was anything straightforward any more?

'Perhaps it will have to be some motor, Akker.'

He groaned. There were so many tabs on wheels these days it was like leaving a trail for the plod. Registrations, serial numbers all over the fucking engines like confetti, not to mention cameras on every sodding motorway.

Conting out with some southern mob he really detested, and he wouldn't hire Yorkshire Ridings tankers for a gold clock.

'I take it you don't care for the idea?' the lovely Martina said, like she'd turned a wrong page. You had to give it to Martina. Calm, go and top Galahad and don't forget Danielle, and close the door there's a draught.

He caught himself being watched in mid-think, and thought, careful now. She must have talked it over with Posser, and Akker wasn't going to gainsay *him*, poorly or not.

'Contracting out's always on the kilt, Martina. I like things cushti.'

'Do motors always have to be contracted out?'

'No. But cars are traceable.'

'Brum, then?'

He thought that one out. 'Birmingham, aye, but we don't want to upset their local lads, bring a knick-knock.'

Martina also didn't want reprisals. 'London, then?'

'I wouldn't, Martina. Everybody's hoofing from the Smoke, cameras on every street lamp. Motorway, tank Galahad and the bird up aforehand, is what I'd do.'

'Then why contract out at all?'

He shifted uneasily. How to put this? He'd only once seen this beautiful girl in a temper, and didn't want to be here for another. Women were bad judges of venom. They had plenty, but didn't know when.

'Dogtrack talk is a working girl here's been serving from Haleys Wharf with some canal yardies.'

'Danielle?'

He nodded. 'Galahad too.' Then he almost shouted, seeing her expression cloud, 'Just what they're saying.'

Why hadn't Rack brought this tale in, Martina thought

in anger. Instead, she got to hear from passing villers like Akker.

'Which way would they go, if Galahad got a car, money, pollen?'

He tested directions inwardly. 'Leeds.'

'Then there. Cont out if you have to, but don't tell me.'

'Awreet. Who'll see to our end, though?'

'Rack,' she said, unhappy though, because why *hadn't* Rack come in to tell her?

'Then it doesn't matter when,' Akker said, relieved.

She took up her pencil. 'Do it any time you like.'

'Tadda, Martina.'

She would go home early and tell Dad. It was different from the way he'd advised. If he said no, she'd pull Akker off. If he said fine, she'd let it go ahead. This wasn't her fault. She must hold on to that, so Bonn wouldn't suspect.

One vital point. In view of what she'd just ordered, she couldn't let Galahad be sanctioned as Bonn had decided. Even the plod would smell something odd. She would have to rescind Bonn's sentence, let Galahad keep the gymnasium. It would only be for a little while, until his coming motorway accident.

She'd tell Bonn to give Galahad another chance, let Bonn talk her round maybe, show her charitable side. He would be pleased. She warmed at the thought of alleviating his perennial sadness.

The truly sad thing was that if people only did their job honestly things like this wouldn't have to happen. They brought it on themselves.

Rack caught Bonn as he met Grellie. She was in her best gear. Her hair, loose and uncontrolled, was the one thing she chose to worry about, shaping her lovely face's contour with the right cut. Needless worry, Bonn told her when she went on about some new shampoo, but reassurance only served doubt's purpose.

'Grellie'll have to wait, Bonn.' Rack was laughing. 'That Mrs Fennimore's in the Phryne, Ladies' Guild. Carol's screaming for you.'

Grellie made a what-now gesture of despair at another postponement, furious, to sulk where the old men were playing chess on the paving. Bonn felt things were awkward. The pace was somehow wrong.

He cut through Quaker Street, and then the street market to the Café Phryne.

Today it was in muted pastels rather than dense primary colours, national dress Carol's theme. The lovely dark-haired girl had used low lighting to show materials – smocking, tartan, Welsh umbers and Ulster tweeds in clever array – that drew the eye. Quiet was Carol's way. From the outside, it could have been any small tearoom. Inside, it was cosy, welcoming, not so frantic that it dissuaded a lady who wanted a few minutes. Perhaps a dozen ladies were in.

'You'll find your own place?' Carol asked pleasantly.

He took Carol's cue, her five words indicating the fifth alcoved table along the far wall.

A lady was seated at the nearby open table. Carol was also clever with flowers. It would have been tempting to select enormously daunting table centres, festoon the alcoves with arrangements. Instead, here a small Wedgwood vase held small marigolds, there a plain Chinese celadon vase carried three anemones. Serenity without ostentation. Rack said Carol went too expensive, displays changing every time you blinked. Bonn disagreed, said let Carol order what she wanted. Martina too agreed, because the Phryne brought a steady trickle of clients to the agency. Economy was sometimes absurd.

Bonn asked for tea. Carol came over.

'Bonn? Message for you.'

He opened the letter, scanned the blank sheet, folded it away. He caught the gaze of the lady at the adjacent table.

'I'm always scared it will be serious news,' he said, smiling.

The lady was matronly smart. No dietary problems, honed to slimness by diligent masseurs, here was a lady whose position was maintained by vigilance. Bonn felt a faint apprehension. He signalled as much to Carol, hands to his cheeks as if checking that he'd shaved.

'You are Bonn?' The lady met his look. 'I heard the girl.'

'Yes. May I know with whom I have the pleasure of speaking?'

'Mrs Fennimore.' She was used to authority. 'I made inquiries.'

Bonn smiled. 'Sorry. I should have been earlier, Mrs Fennimore. Duties.'

'I have heard about those.' She was forty-six or so, obedience in others her satisfying norm. She added with meaning, 'From Andrea Quartermaine.'

Bonn said evenly, 'I never recollect names.'

Mrs Fennimore drew herself up a moment, then relaxed. 'How would you feel about speaking to a Ladies' Guild?'

He had his orders. 'Will you be there?'

Her look was steady, amused. 'Would you like me to be?'

'Very much, Mrs Fennimore.'

'Then I shall be.' She drew a gold-clasped notebook. 'Shall we arrange a date?'

# 19

**Still** – a place where drug dealers prepare illicit drugs for sale

The vast city library was a waste of space. Jase thought it absurd. Who wanted libraries? He asked a specky lass at some counter about hospitals.

'I want the name of a woman doctor,' he told her. She asked him a load of crappy questions, finally gave him two massive red volumes filled with a million names. He left in disgust, thinking it fucking useless.

He rang the hospital, asked again for the name of the woman doctor who'd treated Marie Cullokin. A snotty bitch said ring Administration in the morning.

'I want to know now,' he said.

'Admin. have closed. They've all gone home.'

Typical, Jase thought. All gone home, leaving sick folk dying all over the fucking place. Like that woman doctor had, with his Marie. He'd ring her number all right, see if he wouldn't. He felt ill.

It was dusk when Hassall reached Haleys Wharf. He left his engine and car lights on. Never mind the planners' fine watercolours in the Central Library. This was the real city, necrosis writ large, a mess of refuse, broken glass, buildings gaunt and broken. It was a void, lonely workshops trying to keep its decaying old heart beating. The blinking planners should be dragged down here, actually take a gander.

Hassall remembered, his mind wild sometimes, that he'd been to school with a girl from Haleys Wharf. She'd had a little dog. He'd never seen it. Her dad was a millwright, a skilled engineer, made for life – as folk back then said, for the mills were omnipotent, and affluence was the reward of those who slogged. Die of industrial disease, but look what you created!

Aye, look. He stood, his motor going um-um-um.

Haleys Wharf ran by a canal, back yards abutting on the towpath. Empty warehouses and a mill opposite were the honeycomb playgrounds of tearaways now, places to avoid. Here was the culture medium for new generations, the spaced-out who lived to toke, smoke and poke, and who demanded nothing but a supply and a mattress to 'come down' on. Every disco had to have its crash pad along a gloomed-out wall, every child had to know the language of ganja and the next new scag.

Population? About three hundred, Hassall registered in silent answer, all of no fixed abode. Industries? Bodywork factories, run by workmen who shut their wheels in with them as they worked, who brought their baggins – lunch – so that, tough as they were, they needn't risk a stroll to the one remaining caff.

Future? Ask the graft-ridden city councillors. Prospects? Nil. Just don't ask the police, because we haven't a blinking clue when the place will finally dissolve into grot.

A couple of houses were still inhabited, incredible, lights on in dingy front rooms. Nobody about, this hour. The panel-beaters had gone. The pub beyond the green was struggling awake for its evening stint. He heard shouts from youths still kicking a ball.

A motor raced round the corner, slithered to a halt.

'Hello, Sergeant Windsor,' Hassall said aloud to Haleys Wharf.

The sergeant disembarked, locked his motor. He'd a flashlight and walked with an ostentatious stiffness, half a dozen truncheons probably stuffed down his trousers. Reproachfully, Windsor switched off Hassall's engine, locked the vehicle, handed him the keys.

'I came as fast as I could, Mr Hassall,' Windsor got the rebuke in, 'when I heard you'd come on your own. A Mrs Mandel from the hospital rang, just missed you.'

'I forgot her.'

'She wants assistance in locating Jase, this address.' Windsor ahemed. 'I checked. There's no number seventeen, Haleys Wharf.'

'Let's risk it, while there's a slice of light.'

It was almost dusk. Hassall turned across a space where two terraced houses had stood until fire-gutted, and clambered down to the canal.

'They've lit a fire, sir.' Windsor pointed down the footpath.

'As long as that's all they do.'

They went single file. In the distance they could see a bridge. It was a place for miasmas, rotting vegetation, the sickly smell of groundsel, the stench of the canal.

The turning pool gleamed. Two hundred years before, commercial longboats had swung here to begin their return journeys. Now, the overgrown towpath by the bridge's arch housed the pollen factory, Noddo's dank country.

'How do, lads and lasses,' Hassall said to everybody.

'Who's yon sider, Hass?' an immense man asked.

Seven of them sat in near filth round a fire in an old diesel drum. A cat waited indolently for the first night rodent to make its pointless dash. A wall had fallen in since last time, Hassall saw.

'Don't be like that, Robar. My sider is Sergeant Windsor. It's bleedin' perishing here.'

Someone cackled. 'Try here when it's raining.'

Two women, five men. Two loles, one Pak, a halfie, and three probable island folk. Both women could have been fifty, but a still aged people faster than clocks.

'Anybody hear news of Jase?' Hassall asked straight out.

More cackles. 'Who?'

'Now, now,' Hassall chided. 'I've a message. His girlfriend's been poorly. The hospital wants him.'

'What fer?' a woman asked. She looked like a bundle of grey-black washing under a black shawl, straight off an old sepia photo.

'How the hell do I know? I said I'd pass it on. Tell Jase.'

'Right, Mr Hassall.'

'When'd he stop by last, Robar?' Into the silence Hassall said, 'Only, it's pretty urgent.'

'Coupler days gone, me.'

It was as much as they were going to get. Jase was still about. The cat, alerted by some sound, slid into the gathering dark.

'If you see him, then. Night, folks.'

Somebody made a muted remark and laughed. Hassall let Windsor walk ahead with his flashlight. He could fall in first.

'It's called a still because they used to distil spirit, what they called "flash". Now they're places for coch factoring. Bring in a weight of scag, divide it up.'

'I know.' From Windsor, it was virtual rebellion.

'Pollen's their word for scag, ganja, yellow jellies, Gwaddy gold, King White,' Hassall continued. 'Any powder that makes happiness while you're dreaming in slutch. You and me are anachronisms, see?'

'No,' Windsor said. The stubborn sod'd say no even if he meant yes.

'The Medicines Control Agency couldn't even curb herbal ecstasy. What'd they do? Analysed the bloody gunge – what, eight ounces to sample the entire kingdom? Decided there was too much methylamphetamine or ephedrine in the base clags, so slammed it on the 2130 Schedule as a Schedule drug.'

'A *legal* move, Mr Hassall.'

'Which made it even more illegal. Sell openly in the streets, you're not just naughty, you're *very* naughty.'

'We've got to beat them, sir.'

Hassall increasingly marvelled at optimism. Was it any wonder? 'You think any druggo couldn't afford the nineteen thousand quid needed for a *legal* herbal retailer's licence? They'd pay it off in a fortnight. So why don't they? Answer: they'd then be subject to law, whereas now they're beyond it.'

'That's despair, Mr Hassall.'

They reached where they had come through, a space of fallen houses.

Windsor waited, shone the torch for Hassall. 'Can you manage?'

'I'm not in my frigging dotage, for God's sake.'

Their motors were intact, bumper to bumper, like conspirators having a gossip.

'Know what they calculated? That more people now take dope – pardon the antique term – than don't. Get it? We're outnumbered.'

They went towards the cars. A noise made Hassall long to hold the torch, but he deliberately kept mum.

'That means, sergeant,' he said loudly, 'we're increasingly outnumbered by junkheads. Minorities breed out. We're the minority. Being a junkie is the norm. We're extinct, sergeant.'

Hassall got into his car and fired the engine.

'And seeing places like this makes you believe it. Ta for your flashlight. That matron say anything more?'

'No, sir. Just contact urgently.'

They flashed their headlights to signal readiness. Hassall deliberately made Windsor do the three-point turn on all that broken glass. No sense in ruining his own tyres just for nothing.

Bonn and Rack walked down Market Street, Rack shouting joke insults at the stallholders. The street market closed late, and it was almost half-seven. Girls were already clustering up into twos and threes. For car jobs, mostly the top of Waterloo Street, they went single. Pairing was to keep an eye on each other, talk number plates if a punter went ape.

'This way, Bonn.'

Rack was proud, walking through the manor with the key all the girls eyed. Bonn looked embarrassed, when it was sheer frigging fame people would pay for.

'Good heavens, Rack.' Bonn stared at the facade.

The building looked like a cobbler's shop. It had ornate cast-iron railings, awnings gaudy in green, gold and pink, edged in red bunting. Cellar windows reached the pavement. Music blared from its open doorway. A commissionaire paraded in a red and gold uniform arrayed with phoney medals.

It was the tackiest place Bonn had ever seen. BOUNCING BLOCK flashed in neon letters. Banners hung from the third storey, announcing MECCA OF MUSCLE.

'Toby, this is Bonn.' Rack leapt the steps.

Toby doffed his ludicrous topper. Bonn hesitated. Did one shake hands with a commissionaire, especially when one had just deposed his employer?

'How do, Toby.'

'Message, sir. Please phone Miss Martina. Office to your left.'

Bonn entered. Rack danced down the hall shouting good cheer. The girls wore white, prepared for action in gym or sauna, smiley and eager.

Bonn heard Rack shout. 'This is my chief, name of Bonn. He's new here. I'll introduce you if you like. Ask me, he'll do a few lengths in your pool. Know how you tell a good swimmer?'

Et cetera, Bonn thought. The office was vacant. He ignored it, rang Martina from the corridor pay phone. She answered second ring.

'Hello. You wanted me.' No names with Martina.

'Yes. I've been thinking about it.'

Bonn felt really down. 'I take it there is a revision.'

'Yes. Leniency is in order.' Bonn thought, what now? 'I wondered how you'd feel.'

'My feelings are out of the question.'

'Not in this case,' she said with asperity. 'Be frank.' She paused, then continued, 'Try leniency. No time like the present.'

'Very well.'

'If you have any feelings, will you let me know?'

He ignored the barbed sarcasm. 'Certainly. Thank you.'

He replaced the handset, stood looking at the apparatus. Vandal proof, indestructible metal flex. It would outlast everybody.

The problem was, why Martina's change of heart? Word must have got about that Bonn had ditched Galahad, yet now everything was rescinded.

'No time like the present,' Martina's lovely mellifluous voice had told him. Wrong. There was no time *but* the present, no such thing as future time for some, past time for others. He ought to ask Posser what was going on, but the old man would be having his sleep, Dr Winnwick's insistence.

He told Rack to curtail the visit.

'But we can't!' Rack cried in anguish. He'd been looking forward to seeing Prand's face when he learned he was going to get Galahad's half of the gym for nothing. 'I've teed Prand up and everything.'

Bonn noted his stander's disappointment. 'We'll go to the Palais.'

'Bloody typical,' Rack groused, Toby doing his doff.

'That's just it, Rack,' Bonn said as they took to the pavement. 'It isn't.' He couldn't remember a final sanction revoked.

'Bloody mogga dancing,' Rack muttered. 'Everybody's sick of it. Know why it'll never catch on? Because of fumes. Know why?'

The street market was closing patchily. Rack took an apple from a stall, and sulked when Bonn made him pay. This, Rack thought with utter disgust, in a street market where Martina's writ ran. He paid the grinning hawker. Rack's job was to see Bonn right, but Bonn had some crazy fucking ideas.

He'd work out why, tell Bonn where his life was going wrong. They headed for the Palais Rocco, where that idiot Lancelot would sit in a knot, yogaing himself ready to dance.

Rack bit the apple. Too hard. He'd have fired it at a passing bus, except Bonn would have sent him to pick it up, un-fucking-believable.

# 20

**Scrip** – a legitimate drug prescription from a doctor

BONN DECIDED THE two women who welcomed him were simply curious. His old theologian tutor used to say, each day you meet your world's guise; care for it, as God instructs.

He would care. He advanced, smiling.

The lady extended her hand, a footballer's wary welcome to an opponent. Bonn thought, but I've done nothing.

'Bonn, is it?' the lady said. Bonn said hello. She seemed to have expected volubility, and coloured a little. 'I am Mrs Winstanley, secretary. This is Jane Livingstone, deputy chairperson.'

The other lady was younger, twinset and beads, brogues. Mrs Winstanley was a galaxy of accessories, brooches galore, bracelets, rings. Posser's dictum was, 'Never a group, always lone,' for a man climbs to paradise one step at a time. But Martina ruled, and knew best.

'I am pleased to be invited.'

They seemed stultified. Had they expected a guest to say it was rotten coming here? Mrs Winstanley led into the building, a low church hall recently restored.

The room was nothing more than a small chamber. Bonn instantly thought, trick? Fourteen women were distributed round a mahogany table. The scent – Bonn wondered, Yardley? Givinchy? – was as if they'd agreed on some aromatic plan.

Mrs Fennimore rose, out for combat.

'So glad you could come.' She swirled away before he could offer his hand. 'Ladies, this is the . . . gentleman. Bonn.' She trilled a laugh. 'Please sit down.' Mrs Fennimore walked to the far end.

The table was a long rectangle, the ladies seated formally at the sides. Mrs Fennimore sat at the head facing the one vacant chair, clearly to be his. He was to be interrogated, an exotic specimen they could dine out on.

He remained standing. Martina's terrible mistake, but Bonn's cross to carry.

'Take a seat.'

Mrs Fennimore was adamant. Sit down, he'd become a supplicant.

'No, Emily,' he said. There was a stifled gasp at his use of the chairlady's name. 'You know I like to stand.'

Mrs Fennimore spoke harshly.

'Very well, then. I call the meeting to order. We shall hear our speaker's explanation of his escort agency—'

Bonn started shaking his head almost immediately. 'No, Emily.'

'What do you mean?' Two red doll's dots appeared on Mrs Fennimore's cheeks. 'You distinctly agreed—'

'No, Emily.'

She almost shouted, 'It is a firm contract! My husband is a council lawyer! You must—'

Sadly, a score of marvellous escapes would occur to him the moment he got free. Hindsight, blindsight. He was overcome with sympathy. She must be feeling terrible, her impregnable position lost in seconds.

'Ladies, please forget this incident. I seem to have misunderstood. Please don't blame Mrs Fennimore.' He took in each face, said with sorrow, 'I deplore my clumsy assumption. Goodbye.'

Jane Livingstone caught him up outside, breathless.

'The least I could do is give you a lift, Bonn. The bus takes hours.'

No, twenty minutes, Bonn thought.

'You are so kind,' he said.

He reported frankly to Martina. She sat glowering.

'Catastrophe is rather an emotive word.'

'Hardly.' He felt on trial, in a day of trials. 'Mrs Fennimore is on some crusade. I simply escaped.'

'And the ladies, potential clients by the hundred?'

'She had promised her guild a witch hunt.'

'So much belief, so little evidence?'

He thought, Martina should have been a theologian, her mind.

'I was there, Martina. You were not. One client, though, will book me. She gave me a lift.'

'Very well.' Martina held the pause. Another person would have ahemed, shuffled papers. 'We'll subtend the coaches.'

'Er, coaches.' Bonn strove to remember.

'Holland. You know Holland? The smoke coaches you disliked the idea of?' Her sarcasm revealed her distress at the guild fiasco.

'Yes.' It seemed months since Martina had argued this.

'We'll guarantee eighty coaches the first year, three hundred the second.'

'I have no contribution there, I surmise.'

'Surmise as you wish. And who's Jase?'

'Jase is a male who lived with a girl who died of AIDS. Clare Three-Nine-Five asked me. She's to pass him the deceased's dying words.' He admitted, 'I haven't tried much, I'm afraid.'

'The police are hunting him over some killing,' Martina prompted, and when he made no reply, said, 'That's all.'

He stayed a little to watch old Osmund's patience. The snooker matches were individual and intense. Bonn hadn't heard the place so quiet since he'd first walked in out of the rain.

'Robar?'

They called them buildings, areas of rubble where houses became mounds of broken bricks, springs, tarred unburnable timber. It was as if the city's sleepers clung to terms, generations since, when every place where brick met earth showed where some edifice was about to spring, stone flowering for mankind to rule.

The big man didn't looked round. The others were still at their bonfire, light not reaching where he'd gone for a pee.

'Yih?' he said into the dark.

'I need some.'

Robar let his bladder drain, flourished off the drop, tried to squirt but failed. With a sigh he zipped his fly.

'You got wealth?'

'Nar. I can owe.'

'Noddo don't know owe, Jase.' Robar had more sense than peer.

'Aye. But I need now. We'm negotiate.'

Robar considered. Beggie was already at the aperture

where customers came for their bags. She even had a calculator that actually wrote it all down for Coffee when he came for the hand-in. Rounders, his oppo, was out there in Wharf Street, like a shadow, him, despite size.

The thing was, Jase was quiet, secretive, the way of some loles. And he was a sharp tube man. It was Robar's serious opinion that Coffee should stay the money man, the humble collector, with Bunce and Beaky Divine as support, Sanj the ultimate wheels. Robar's job was to factor, which meant cut, sort, sell. Now this, a voice out of the rat-infested dark, no sense playing cops and robbers.

Robar was sure he heard Jase's teeth chatter. An ecstasy fall, or maybe overdone Mersey White, cocaine cut with chalk, even baking soda, these kids stretch to infinity and back. Selling satches with bugger all inside except grandma's flour mix.

'They been down along,' he told the darkness, whistling to show the still he was hoping to spray his shoes.

'Who?'

Robar snorted in disgust. 'Who? *They* is who.'

See? Stupid. No wonder these young idiots didn't last. It got you down, the way they behaved. Like, Robar'd bet his dick Jase wouldn't last three days, top whack. He wondered where all the sense went. One time, Robar sixteen, the world woke and there it was, all sense gone and everybody bad news.

'What'd they want?' the dark asked quietly.

In the street somebody yelped and a scuffle started. Shouts rose, customers wanting quiet so they could get served. Robar listened, no, it would settle, a few residual thumps, then back queuing to collect doom, the way of the world.

'Your girlfriend, hospital want to see you. Next of kin, sumth'n.' Robar snickered. 'The man said call the plod.'

'You know him?'

'Hassall, he. Some sandy-haired lole his sider, wired, I reckon.'

'I need now. I'll pay before Coffee comes to bag up.'

Now here was a problem, Robar thought, because word would out that he'd given Jase credit, which Noddo would down Robar for. The scag didn't matter. The money, Christ, didn't matter. But, credit? That mattered.

And why wasn't Jase on the towpath talking like, hey, here's wealth so give me two, three satches?

Something wrong here. Jase was Noddo's yard's tuber. See? Sense out of the window. It was a sick world. He was supposed to argue with a tuber in canal blackness? Fuck that.

'Hang on. I'll drop you a satch, okay?'

'Two. And the doings.'

Jesus. He'd have him doing his teeth. 'Okay. You owe, right?'

'Don't forget the matches.'

Matches. He, Robar, who ran Haleys Wharf, tight ship, fetch matches? Yissuh, masser, I bring matches.

He strolled back, the others joshing him about having some bird on the towpath rubble. He laughed, nicked some satches, foil, matches, straws, broken glass, syringe, needles so scagged at the tip they could have hooked fish. Bit of dirt, what did it matter, Jase that bad? It was a sick world.

Mrs Mandel was altogether different from how Hassall had imagined. He took Windsor, after that smart performance with the Truro couple.

'Marie Cullokin, deceased, gave this Jase as her next of kin. Were they married?'

'That we don't know.' The SNO had a reproachful sigh. 'One can never tell these days, Mr Hassall.'

'One can't indeed,' he said. 'My wife deplores the way they carry on. This address. No such place exists now, Mrs Mandel.'

She consulted the notes. 'It wasn't a staff doctor who did the admission. Perhaps Dr Burtonall made a mistake.'

Even before she'd finished her admonitory sniff, Hassall cut in.

'Dr Burtonall admitted her?'

'A Cardiac locum. Comes,' she said, and added witheringly, 'and goes.'

'Does she now!'

'The fact is,' the SNO said confidingly, 'that this Jase person is making a formal complaint. Dr Burtonall hasn't seen fit to fully inform me of his precise grievance. It might be to do with Dr Burtonall's treatment. It makes me wonder about Dr Burtonall's role in all this.'

Windsor barged in. 'Is she concealing details?' he thundered.

Mrs Mandel brightened. 'That is certainly a—'

'Sorry,' Hassall said. He had more chance of getting a word in with his daughters than here. He'd been daft to bring Windsor, the tact of hailstone. 'I might speak with Dr Burtonall. Focus her mind, so to speak.'

'Certainly, Mr Hassall! Any help—'

'One thing, Mrs Mandel.' Hassall went for it. 'Was Dr Burtonall's handling of Marie Cullokin according to hospital procedure? I don't mean unethical.'

'Her behaviour was highly eccentric, Mr Hassall.'

She only needed a nudge. Hassall provided it. 'As a doctor, though?'

'Dr Burtonall was called to the ward and arrived after Marie died. She instructed Nurse McHenry's nurses to lay out the cadaver. They refused.'

'There was some sort of row?'

'Dr Burtonall herself did the laying out – carried out the "last offices" of cleaning the deceased.'

'Why? As a kindness?'

'I prefer to see her actions as deliberate trouble-making. Dr Burtonall's behaviour set hospital tongues wagging.'

'So you went on television.'

'Purposely, to obviate the brewing criticism!'

They left, Hassall with a grievance at Windsor, the sergeant annoyed at Hassall for having left the interview half undone. Hassall was fed up. He decided to issue Jase's artist-fit drawing. Much good it would do.

Clare was nervous about going to the Café Phryne. Would Bonn even agree to see her? She parked her Humber behind the Weavers Hall and walked down Market Street among the street barrows.

She passed the café, checking it was still there, *still* still there. The olive-green sign glowed as before, discreet and muted. Three anonymous phone messages were too many, though. Each had asked about Marie's doctor. It was scaring her. The hospital telephonists by some fluke hadn't given the male enquirer Clare's mobile-phone number, thank God. She'd seen the midday tabloids depicting some police artist-fit sketch of a haggard youth. 'Wanted in connection with . . .' said the black type.

For an instant she hesitated, glancing back at the taverns,

the burger places, dry goods shops, leather accessories all wrong for the fashion but with advertising claiming they weren't. It was homely, she realized with a shock. Café Phryne's exterior seemed in character. Somebody was clever.

Was the facade intended to conceal the café's true purpose? But, goodness, she was only dropping in for tea. Had any possible gossip-critic thought of *that*? Ergo, her visit was legitimate. She was here on a whim, for God's sake.

'Good day, madam. Please sit anywhere.'

The girl by the entrance barely looked up. Lovely smile, enormously long tresses, hinting she was there to be noticed only on request. Clare entered, pleased by the wall recesses with the displays of gardening implements. It could have been garish to the point of irritation, but instead was a subtle blend of pleasantries with even the occasional surprise.

Clare sat in a bay opposite a miniature bank of flowers. Colours pastel, illumination moderate. Several people were in, all women, she observed. Were they regular – what had been Bonn's revealed word – uppers, waiting for their goers? The thought brought colour to her face, but she ordered tea and scones calmly enough.

'Our last display was materials,' the young waiter said. 'Created quite an interest. Textiles, you see.'

Clare tried not to wonder about him. 'Professional decorators?'

'No. Carol does them. She's our clever one.'

Her first conversation in the Café Phryne. She'd looked the name up in an encyclopaedia. Phyrne was a courtesan who'd famously gone to the bad, scandalizing the Ancient World. It had made Clare smile.

'Trellises are a terrible risk.' The desk girl – clever

Carol? – paused by Clare's table. 'Sometimes I really want to go over the top, but find myself cutting back. Restraint is everything.'

'It's quite beautiful. Carol, is it?'

'Yes. Thank you.' The girl concealed a laugh. 'I once had an epidemic of fans – *fans*! I ordered a hundred, every style imaginable! Japanese, African, Regency. The boys could hardly move. Finally I reduced it to three.'

'I wish I had your talent.'

The waiter arrived, served. 'Please don't advertise on my time, Carol!' he said, camp.

'Sorry, sorry!' The girl moved through a Thai silk curtain. Clare glimpsed a corridor, floral stands hinting at lounges set apart.

Clare was left solitary. As Carol passed on her return journey minutes later, Clare caught her eye.

'Don't tell me!' Carol said, joking. 'That alcove's trugs and fawn grasses are driving you mad!'

Clare didn't even hesitate, was proud of herself coming out with it. 'Bonn told me I could leave a message here.'

'Of course.' Nobody was in earshot, some mastermind having also seen to acoustics. Clare wondered about the expense of creating such a place. 'Just tell me. Bonn will get it within the hour.'

Sixty minutes? It took Clare aback. 'It's not exactly urgent.'

'I can give you the agency number, if that will help?'

'I already have it, thank you,' Clare said, admiring her own boldness. 'It will have to wait.'

Carol went to her desk while Clare pondered. There were two places Bonn could be. One was here, so he'd once said. The other place was the Palais Rocco, where the mogga dancing went on.

On the way out, she paused to compliment Carol.

'I shall come again,' she said.

'Thank you,' Carol said. 'We do quite well, though so many places are in competition.' She added confidentially, 'The balcony café of the Palais Rocco has become quite smart lately!'

Minutes later, Clare walked into the dancehall entrance. Another tea, she'd be waterlogged, but it was all in the cause. She climbed the stairs, and her heart almost stopped. Bonn was at a balcony table overlooking the band, with a dark-haired youth of about his own age. No women, thank God. For an instant she hesitated, then her fear of that anonymous caller returned, and she advanced.

She sat at the next table.

# 21

**Firm** – a group of goers, usually three or four, directed by one key goer

'Eleven couples is too many. It's a bleedin' insult!'

Bonn looked over the balcony's ornate scrolling. The place numbed the eye, all red plush and gilt. He wondered if Rack ever got into a truly savage temper. Joviality, exuberance, certainly. But how many of Rack's responses were decided by Martina? Like some exploding nova, determinants were out there, observers simply registering events of times long gone. This disturbing feeling was becoming more frequent.

'There can't be too many, Rack,' Bonn reasoned. 'Dancers like a crowd.'

'Not when they're the flaming enemy, they don't.'

The tune was an ancient foxtrot. Rack sang tunelessly . . . *My pretty little poppy, you're pretty as the stars that shine abo-hove yooo* . . . which surprised Bonn, Rack knowing old melodies. Bonn had another goer to appoint. When he'd first been made key, Martina had forced him to accept Galahad and Lancelot. Posser had insisted Bonn be promoted, but Martina hadn't been able to go all the way.

'Rack,' he said, 'it's only a rehearsal.'

Rack posed on the balcony like some dictator about to harangue.

'That's the point, Bonn!' It sounded genuine anguish. 'Lancelot needs space! They're crowding him out!'

Lancelot was the showiest in his exotic clobber – bolero, cossack trousers, neck chains, glitter gloves.

'Lancelot's worried his bird's a dud.' Rack's mood suddenly went. 'Gets up my fucking hooter.'

'Language, please. Public.'

'Sorry.' Rack said, lips not moving, 'That bird's here. Don't look.'

'Thank you.' Bonn had already seen Clare. He was saddened by her visit. Which would it be: apology, or more recriminations?

The dancers changed. Lancelot switched from a tango to a military two-step.

'Eighteen leps,' Rack counted. 'English slow waltz twice, the goon.'

'He is allowed.'

'Judges fail you for that.' Rack snorted. 'I've got money on him.'

It was all rigged anyway, Bonn had heard. Rack squared the judges. Bonn inspected Lancelot's partner, a bonny pale girl with an intent face. The flair had gone and the girl knew it. Bonn felt sympathy; she didn't look capable of fighting her corner.

'I trust Lancelot has kept up with his goes,' he said quietly.

'Yeah. One homer, we had camera trouble. I had Akker lift tackle.'

'And that there has been no bother?'

'Lancelot? He's clean. His dancing partners'll drive him unglued, then watch out.'

So far Clare Three-Nine-Five had said nothing, simply

paid attention to the dancers. She went for a coffee, returning as the music ended.

'One thing, Rack,' Bonn went on as the spectators started analysing the dancers' 'leps' when they changed styles. 'I should like to see Prand.'

Rack weighed things up, when Rack was usually straight out, have him here in a sec. 'Now? He's at the Take Ten football club.' Rack showed disgust. 'Pays a subscription. Like, their bits of iron are brill, everybody else's iron is crap. Can you believe that?'

'Please arrange it.'

'Prand heard about the Bouncing Block, Bonn. Okay,' Rack added after the briefest hesitation. 'Lancelot's bird. She's duff.' He went, shaking his head. Rocco Randle the band leader called his combo as new dancers eased on to the floor. They seemed so aloof. It puzzled Bonn.

'Bonn?' Clare didn't know whether to speak directly, and was taken aback when he immediately smiled her way.

'They do dance well.' He pointed ostentatiously. 'I hope it's a tango.'

Clare wondered if she was to maintain the fiction that they were strangers. It was as if he'd quite forgotten her outburst. 'I'm just getting the hang of this dancing. I'd be hopeless.'

'I met you before. We spoke about mogga dancers.'

'That's right.' She was relieved, on a shakily acceptable footing. 'They switch styles every few bars. How skilled!' She coursed swiftly on now that she'd got going. 'Please. I need your help. It's become pressing to find Jase. I told you, his girl died.'

'Jase, no surname.'

'Marie Cullokin. There've been some anonymous calls,

a male wanting details of the doctor who treated Marie. Me.'

A rhumba struck up, the most difficult but Lancelot's favourite, the hand of Rack in there somewhere.

Bonn took notice as Lancelot moved instantly to the centre of the dance floor, claiming the high ground, guessing – knowing? – that the music would be the favourable Latin-American.

'You think it was Jase.'

'I'm apprehensive. The city feels, well, dangerous.'

'I shall expedite it.'

She felt frankly confused. In ordinary conversation he would offer to make contact, a number he might ring. She said her thanks.

'Not at all.'

Was that it, then? Not at all, wench, be on your way? She was about to say more, but the swarthy youth emerged on to the balcony, speaking volubly with a larger tougher-looking young man. In near anger she clutched her handbag and left without another word. Expedite, indeed!

She stalked down the stairs. Was she the only one who considered polite manners? His job must have ablated the social niceties in his character. It was her own stupid fault, consorting with ruffians, the dregs of the city. Serve her right.

The more she thought about Bonn the angrier she became. Once he'd found this Jase, she'd pass on the poor girl's last message, send Jase to the Infectious Disease clinic, then cut all ties with Bonn. Graceless and obscene. She'd been a fool. She would remake her life with Clifford, salvage her own brands from the burning, then leave Bonn in his weird world.

*

'Prand.' Rack indicated the man he'd brought. 'Body-builder.'

'Thank you, Rack. Please sit down, Prand.'

Rack glared down at the dancing. Two couples were arguing, one girl stalking off belligerently, the end of an era.

'Look at that!' Rack dragged a chair to the balcony rail, knelt to see better. 'Supposed to be fucking champions!'

Prand sat, wondering. He glistened, skin oiled, long hair waved.

'Prand, please tell me about your past,' Bonn said.

Rack yelled encouragement at the dancers. Tables filled up, friends arriving for the practice session.

'I've done nowt wrong, Bonn,' Prand said. 'I didn't leave the Bouncing Block till Rack said.'

'Good, Prand. I take it you are local.'

'Aye. I won second in the Carlisle–Wolverhampton Open. My trainer'd been ill, or I'd have got first place.' He waited. Bonn waited. Rack yelled. The nervous iron-pumper resumed, 'Er, that's my best so far. I'm in the jump-pumper next week. Is it a bet?'

Bonn pondered. What bet? He wanted Rack to translate, but Rack was screaming for Lancelot to change to a cha-cha, Christ's sake, anything but the valeta. Prand was scared that Bonn even knew of him.

'Look, Bonn. My dad does all my bets. If you say I've got to do it different, I will, but . . .'

'Your father wouldn't like it.' Bonn was lost. What *was* this?

'I'm not saying no, Bonn, honest,' Prand said. 'Just, it'll take time to talk Dad round. He wants me to get somewhere.'

'Thank you for that frank disclosure, Prand. I appreciate it.'

'Can I carry on?' Prand sounded astonished.

Bonn's thoughts floundered. With what? 'For the whilst.'

Prand was bemused. If he wasn't to fix a bet, then what?

Bonn heard a row break out. Dancers squabbled below, girls screeching, the males being pulled apart, two bouncers suddenly on to the floor. He prayed Lancelot was not involved.

'You live at home, Prand.'

'Yes. My mam's poorly. I have a sister. I was no good at school.'

'And your job isn't all that well paid.'

'I deliver for that supermarket.'

'Where,' Bonn chose words, 'you occasionally find a partner.'

Rack was almost apoplectic, reaching so far over the balcony that he was in danger of falling, hollering abuse. Spectators surged on to the dance floor to join the dispute. The music stopped, Rocco making an appeal through the squealing tannoy. 'Listen, everybody.' His saxophonist played a mocking intro to the national anthem.

Prand fidgeted, afraid at Bonn's mention of women.

'Honest, Bonn. I don't go out of my way. I just load up for customers.'

Bonn gave the body-builder a prolonged look.

Prand was now sweating. 'I don't, well, pick them up or anything. Honest. I was going with Mandy till last week. Ask anyone.'

'Mandy, on the end check-out.'

Which remark made Rack pause a millisec. He was now listening more than yelling.

'That's her.' Prand seemed pleased Bonn knew.

'Until last week. Rather sad, Prand.'

'Aye.' Prand shrugged. The gesture was an immense business, mounds of muscle rising beside his neck. His trunk melted into a squatter, broader form. 'She saw a bird give me her phone number. I don't charge, Bonn.'

'Ah, now,' Bonn said, 'there was that problem, Prand.'

Rocco was pleading for calm, the rehearsal frankly out of control.

'It was okay, Bonn,' Prand told him earnestly, leaning to explain, get out of this unscathed. 'The bird's husband got wind. I always say what if your bloke finds out.'

'But it wasn't okay, Prand.'

'She told me wrong. He belted her. She come to the supermarket. That's when Mandy got the hump.'

Bonn tut-tutted, watching Prand for clues. 'The woman, though.'

'My dad said swap until it blows over, see. I changed to driving.'

'Very good. I'm pleased, Prand.'

'Straight up?' Prand said, surprised. 'Ta, Bonn. I appreciate it, you not minding. I'd have left if the bird had come stronger.'

'You tried to invest money in the Bouncing Block, Prand.'

'Me and my dad.' He grimaced. Bonn suddenly realized the body-builder's head seemed disproportionately small. What age was Prand, a couple of years older than Bonn himself, say twenty-two? 'Dad couldn't raise the deposit. Never mind.' Prand tried a smile, feeling almost in the clear.

'You are in training today.'

'Aye.' Prand inspected his arms with admiration. 'I could do well, if I had the money.'

'I hear everybody does steroids.' Bonn tutted. 'Such a shame.'

'Not me, Bonn,' Prand said earnestly. 'They make your brain funny, Dad said. It's not right. Like having a crazy person inside your body. Look at my pal.'

Bonn hadn't heard. He said evenly, 'Your pal. Sad, that.'

'Aye. Me and Galahad did training circuits together, the RAF line-rounders, all that. I don't mean anything, Bonn,' Prand added, suddenly remembering that Galahad was one of Bonn's goers. 'Great bloke.'

'I know,' Bonn said with sorrow. 'Prand. I want you as a goer. Speak with Doob this evening. Please cancel your training.'

Prand gaped. 'Cancel . . . ?'

Down below the Palais was quieter, apart from occasional shrieks.

'I am appointing you a goer, Prand.'

'Me?' Prand looked about as if wanting people to explain this new world order. 'Me? A goer?'

'That is correct, Prand.'

'Who with?' the muscler asked, bewildered. 'You can't just start up on your own, Bonn. You've got to have . . .' Realization dawned.

'Congratulations, Prand. It will mean a deal of money, funds in the syndicate. You, Doob, Lancelot, will be the goers on my firm. Rack bosses the standers. He will explain.'

'Rack?' Prand looked at Rack, who'd gone quiet, just looking down as the music struck up.

'Meet tomorrow at the snooker hall. You know it.'

'Me?' Prand asked. Another muscler, even more huge, peered through the balcony's end curtains, and lumbered among the tables.

'Thank you for coming, Prand.' Bonn gave a smile that was almost all apology. 'Sorry about your training.'

Prand dithered over whether to shake hands or not, scrapped the notion. 'Ta, Bonn.'

'I hope you won't let me down, Prand.'

Bonn saw the newcomer and Prand meet, converse with heads lowered. Then Prand's mate grinned, wrung his hand, glanced towards Bonn as they left.

'What was all that about?' Rack asked, sliding into his chair.

'I've appointed Prand a goer.'

Bonn didn't add that that might mean four goers now, or only three, depending on Galahad's fate.

'And Martina?' Rack huddled his elbows on the table.

'I shall tell her.'

'You might have fucking well asked me first,' Rack said, aggrieved.

Bonn smiled his so-sorry. 'You already knew.'

Rack didn't know how to take that, but luckily for Bonn another fight broke out among the dancers, this time somebody shouting that it was time Lancelot got binned. Rack was off like a bolt, so Bonn had time to think.

Half an hour, he was due another client at the Hotel Vivante. Jase, though. A shooting out beyond Deansgate, the Liverpool Road. He'd get Askey to ferret the details. He wouldn't mention it to Rack, which was unusual.

# 22

**Coch** – any illicit drug

The problem, Jase worked out with hardly a conscious thought, wasn't a problem at all. There were simply three places, and that was that.

One was the end of Haleys Wharf, where dingy pub lights showed. The middle of Haleys Wharf was another place where he could do Bunce. The last was no place, for it was anywhere – taxi rank, Liverpool Road, Bunce's dosser while he slept.

Think about a problem made it pros and cons, a mess in your head. You got nowhere, just sicker.

Jase dialled and asked for Mr Hassall.

'He's not here at the moment,' a clipped voice said.

'It's about Marie Cullokin.'

Jase hated phone boxes. They stank of piss, and always some nerk told you to hang on while he did sod-all.

'Hello?' Amazing, an answer, some grandad, a lollies-for-grandbabs voice. 'About Miss Marie Cullokin?'

Jase felt really proud, hearing her talked of like that. Serious.

'Aye. She were with me.'

'Is it Mr Jase?'

'Aye, Jase.' He listened, wary, waiting for plod to jump out of nearby buildings. They traced everything these days.

'I'm afraid I have some rather sad news, Mr Jase. Please accept my condolences. Miss Cullokin passed away in hospital.'

'Some tart said so on telly.'

A pause, then, 'Miss Cullokin gave her doctor a message.'

'What message?'

'The doctor said it was confidential. You can ask her.'

'Who'd I ask for?'

Another pause. This grandad was past it, a think an inch.

'Dr Clare Burtonall.' Hassall carefully spelled it. 'You'll have to check when Dr Burtonall is on duty.'

'Right. Ta.' Jase marvelled, I've done it, got the cow!

'There's one other thing, Mr Jase. Would you—?'

Jase cradled the receiver. They must think he was a moron. Hang on while I send out the vans.

He had Robar's satch to see him through until he got Bunce. He'd never felt so frigging rough.

Hassall got Dr Burtonall third go.

'This is the sort of phone call I hate making, doctor,' he said straight out. 'I have to apologize.'

'For what, Mr Hassall?'

'That Jase called. Inadvertently, I gave him your name. About Marie Cullokin's message.'

Clare said, heart in her mouth, 'The SNO.' She couldn't resist adding, 'Broadcast some confidential information.'

'I'm afraid it's more complicated, doctor. We're trying to find this Jase, to help us with enquiries. Can you let me know urgently if Jase shows up?'

'You mean here? The shooting?'

'We don't know, it's early days. He could be the criminal, but then we say that about millions.' He gave an unconvincing chuckle.

Hassall gave her his mobile-phone number, glad he was alone in the office. Windsor would have reported him.

The public phone Jase had used turned out to be near the football ground, waste of time. It was one of over seventy drug drops in the city. It would all come down to luck, typical police work.

Jase could smell it a mile off. Noddo had been warned. Since he'd got the satch from Robar he'd used twice, and got lucky in the football changing rooms, a locker with money.

Waiting, he'd played his mouth organ and was alight, that inner wheel spinning his mind to glories other people couldn't know. His reflexes were electrons. Watch out, you lot, here comes Jase. He liked the words, said them over and over.

Even the Filth had shown Marie respect. *Miss* Marie Cullokin, he'd said, that Hassall, *Miss* Cullokin. And *Mister* Jase.

But she was gone. It was only fair that Noddo's yard should pay. Then Dr Clare Burtonall, before he skipped south.

Jase felt smart, in the dark by the canal. At the Harbour changing rooms, three pavilions by the A666 curve, he'd got proper clothes, ditched his stolen clobber. No satch, from them upstanding soccer jockers bent on kicking a ball between two sticks, occupation for fucking life, that. He felt normal, first time since the Janesons.

Okay, so the group now had flashlights, enough torches

to do a night search, fine by him. Like Blackpool Illuminations down the turning pool. These were new, since he squeezed satch from Robar. That'd be Noddo's orders, not give Haleys Wharf a bad name.

He wondered, in the crumbling terraced house, how the streets were talking of him, Jase on the loose. Druggos huddled round brazier fires would go endlessly on about it, dream what tubing somebody felt like.

Since Robar, Jase had tried to work out who, and guessed tonight would be Sanj. Bad times, Noddo kept his oppos close. Oppos like Beaky Divine, nonentity, and Coffee of the giant intellect who Jase thought thick as grapefruit. Sanj was different. He knew engines, could do one-eighty on a tin lid, second gear up to fourth in three seconds. Jase'd seen him do it.

Tonight's big question was, would Noddo send some third yardie with Bunce and Sanj, lying doggo in the back seat, surprise? For all his talk Noddo hadn't all that many shelts.

The queue had formed up a good three hours since. Jase dozed off. He'd not eaten lately, which came as such a surprise that he started working out when. Marie's norm was, no money no satch. No scrip no food. Pollen came first. And quality doses lengthened the time to come down. Christ, he felt so frigging tired, had this endless cough. Even doing sod-all he was sweating like a pig.

He found he'd stiffened, stood and did some exercises. The canal stank. Rats or something splashed, no fish for sure, poisoned water black as oil.

Further down, the lock gate was now so weed-choked that even water couldn't get past. There, illicit lovers shagged, calling out in rut before shuffling off in silence. He didn't mind them. What harm? He'd phoned the hospital, but that doctor had just left and wasn't on until morning.

It was time. He could have nicked a watch down at Harbour pavilions – Mummy's birthday present, so sad – but he'd forgone the pleasure. Watches were traceable. Marie had given him this one, nicked it from Preston's in Ormonde Street.

Jase slipped from the derelict house. The mistake would be to step on to the towpath. It was almost pitch, the only light now from the city skyglow and the glim of Robar's brazier by the turning pool. All it'd need was somebody's electric torch, half a second, for the canal to light up. Just his luck to be there the one time they clicked on. Eight minutes to walk the length of Wharf Street.

No, he'd clamber through the ruined cottages. He knew which planks would carry his weight, where the ceilings gave way.

He made the canal bridge and stayed immobile while a nearby couple groped themselves to exhaustion. They began arguing in whispers, she saying had he been careful and him lying blind yes, yes, some hopes.

They left, hissing argument, until they reached flagstones, solid pavement to pretend propriety. Jase heard her heels clip to silence.

The car came about, what sort of time, two in the morning? The city cathedral clock didn't chime any more. The wheels did that cobble-street flop. Bunce's wheels. Who else'd want a big old Merc like that bloody thing? Car people were mental.

'Ten minutes.' Jase realized with a shock that he'd spoken aloud. He felt his tubes, three remaining cartridges in his trouser pocket.

He tried to count seconds, but got lost. He started

thinking, hey, haven't I already done thirty-three? He gave up.

Bunce was a fast collector, hence his name, got the bunce quicker than anybody. Coffee didn't do collecting – he'd have unloaded computers, taken hours just to heft a bag. Bunce once done Jase a favour, got him a huge old Rudge motorbike. No good, but it looked the part. Jase thought himself real flash on it, posing for Marie to take pictures. Never had the snaps developed, shame.

The car started back. Somebody shouted. Jase saw the flash of a torch, Robar's mob showing how careful they were so Bunce would tell Noddo. All he wanted was Bunce to come over the canal bridge, not go straight on.

It came.

Jase hauled up the great cobble for his one shot, hit or forget tonight, and lobbed as the car took the bridge. It crashed satisfyingly, crazing the windscreen and making the motor career into the wall. The car crumpled with its engine whirring, lights like eyes of some great landed fish.

'What the fuck?' Bunce after all.

Nobody came running, good. This time of night, the plod always keeping well out, ta very much.

Jase yanked open the door, stuck his tubes into Bunce's face. He had the sense to check the driver. Sanj sure enough, or rather no longer Sanj. The cobble had stoved his head in. It stuck on his forehead like a great tumour. Jase whistled. Jesus, he couldn't have done that if he'd tried. The car and the driver, one cobble. Goodnight Sanj, the wheels a wrapper.

He said, 'Out, Bunce.'

'You can't do this, man,' Bunce said.

Jase jabbed the tubes into his eye. 'Let's count to three. One—'

'I'm coming, see? I'm out, man.'

Jase turned the engine off, though reaching past Sanj the state he was in made him retch a bit. He dowsed the lights and took the satchel Noddo always used.

'Walk down to the towpath.'

'Jase,' Bunce quavered, 'you're not going to do anything, right?'

'No. We're going to Robar's still, talk about an idea I've got. I'll give you a message for Noddo. Understand?'

'Right, right, man.'

'Stay steady, Bunce. I don't want to tube you.'

The tall man scrabbled down to the canal. Jase was going by the skyglow, ducking to see the faint sheen.

'Count steps as you go, okay? One, two, three.' All fucking counting.

'One, two,' Bunce went earnestly, trudging. 'Three, four.'

Following was easier with Bunce silhouetted against the brazier's firelight. At thirty, Jase clobbered Bunce sideways. He splashed, attempted a shriek before his mouth filled.

Jase crouched. Robar would have the sense not to come looking, knowing what sudden sounds meant.

He listened, saw ghostly pallor of flailed water come and go, heard the gulping and threshing of Bunce. The trouble was, the canal was filled with sediment. It was shallow. Old bikes, nicked cars, mattresses, somebody would find a footing and stop themselves drowning. The thought of that put Jase into a fury so bad he almost tubed the bastard's drowning head off. But he stayed sensible, thought how Marie would have thought, cool.

No counting now. Bunce managed one enormous howl, then bubbled to silence. Jase moved away, listening every yard for noises like a possible escape, Bunce climbing from the water covered in filth.

He found Sanj, still dead, wearing his extra stone head. He opened the satchel of money, held the handle. Take the money, drop the empty bag on to the London express for Euston Lost Property. Everything felt better. Tired, he went coughing hack-hack into the crumbling warehouses.

# 23

**Wadge** – an amount of money

MARTINA'S HOTEL-PAYMENT system Bonn hadn't quite worked out. It would be wrong to try. He told the new woman this when she asked. Meena lay against him, her leg over his waist. It was something in her manner.

'Why don't you ask, Bonn? It'd be really interesting.'

'Not to me, Meena, darling.'

Endearments were Meena's insistence. She couldn't do without them. Coffee, darling? The heating enough, lover? Let me lift your skirt, honey. She'd all but given Bonn a prescriptive list of terms.

She reached to hold him. 'You have so many rules, Bonn.'

'They're to protect the lady, sweetheart.'

'Always?' She looked at him. Her long hair was coiled. Even after they made love not a hair was out of place. Meena planned.

'Bonn.' She looked down at her hand on him, parting the bedclothes to see. 'What if a lady got pregnant by you?'

'That is virtually impossible, Meena darling.' Maintain the lady's myths at all costs, Posser's rule. 'Precautions for the lady's sake.'

'But what if a goer got careless?'

'That too, darling.' Blackmail, Bonn diagnosed. Poor Meena.

'Only,' she weighed her words, 'that's what's happened.'

She was lying. Sorrow rose in him. This go was a ploy, then, in some unknowable marital strategy. He felt such pity for Meena, the goers, for the grim sequelae.

'I'll have to tell my husband.'

The popular term 'human condition' was spurious, it always seemed to Bonn. As if there was an alternative to existence, and complaint obligatory. Here was a quite attractive woman of, say, thirty-eight, who implied that her very existence condoned any act. Life was the excuse, everything everyone else's fault.

'He'll go mad. Unless . . .'

Back in the seminary, theologians had the difficult task. Liturgy was never straightforward, and history was a nightmare. Apologetics he'd always found filled with unexpected uncertainties. But poor theologians. He'd once argued that theology ought to be simply a branch of rhetoric, got into trouble with his tutor over it. What was Meena saying now?

'I don't want to lose his love, you see, Bonn.'

Hadn't Cronin once written that was the most spurious reason for demanding an abortion? In fiction, of course.

'It'll take money to keep him quiet.'

Strange that blackmail didn't happen more often. Meena might see the Pleases Agency as a kind of giant supermarket, her stratagem simply a kind of moral shoplifting. He knew that shoplifters Meena's age rarely operated alone, unlike teenagers. Her husband an accomplice.

' . . . don't *want* to do this, Bonn.'

'Darling, please be frank.'

'The last thing I want is anybody to suffer, Bonn.'

Bonn had always found moral – his tutor said emotional

– difficulty in the opposed concepts of duties and obligation. They never quite balanced. Meena might think blackmail a way of making equitable an unjust system, that she had an inalienable moral right to loot. Tautology – good old rhetoric – returned, spectre at a troubled feast.

He was hardly listening.

'Yes, darling, I do see.'

Meena sighed, snuggling close. 'What can we do, Bonn?'

'Tell me what you want, darling.'

He dozed as she started to speak, her breath warm on his chest, her words defining consequences. His mind wandered. Aristotle laid down the axiom for the validity of the categorical syllogism, *Dictum de omni et nullo* . . . He made himself concentrate.

'. . . not much, Bonn, for what I'm going through . . .'

Bonn remembered the complexities of logical reason, how he had tortured his mind in the night hours learning to think. The great philosopher De Morgan once said that the mnemonic jingle, sung by students down the centuries, formed the most meaningful words ever created. He drifted, his brain singing silently, *Barbara*, *Celarent*, *Darii*, *Ferioque* . . .

He'd had to leave the seminary. Too perfect, too serene. In a word, heaven. Too good to be true, simply not in the evident world. Was she still speaking?

He said with sorrow, 'Meena, darling, phone in and explain. They have a system.'

'Will it be all right?'

'Like night follows day,' he said sadly, 'darling.'

Clare found the Pickard Private Clinical Laboratory in Droylsden, went through the athletes' names with the receptionist and handed the sealed freeze-containers over. She felt duped and angry, Clifford up to something and she didn't know what. The laboratory's senior Ph.D., Julia Pickard, was too busy to be introduced, which was fine by Clare.

'What account, doctor?' Clare gave the finance number Clifford had provided, and signed brusquely. She drove to the city.

Clare's day worked itself out. The cardiac surveillance was going well. Dr Porritt's suggestion to involve shops and supermarkets had paid dividends. All investigations were free, and GP liaison had been readily accepted. Women, more aware of health issues, talked openly about their men's reluctance. The ripple effect brought in diverse groups – factories, sports clubs, navvies. Road hauliers were the most difficult, working always against the clock. None the less, Clare accumulated a series of occupational clusters.

Her nurse was a part-time SRN trained at the city hospital. Nurse Partington had ambitions in district work, and saw this post as community experience. A bit grand, put like that. Clare encouraged her even though she knew she would soon lose Jill Partington to midwifery.

'Nine takers today, Dr Burtonall,' Jill announced as Clare arrived. 'Our mixed bag.' She liked handling the men, had developed a fine line in banter.

Clare pretended weariness. 'I'd rather they came in neater. Separate codings can be messy.'

Jill was a bony girl, her figure belied by astonishingly neat small hands. 'Like children. I'd rather have mixtures.'

Clare had accidentally overheard Jill phoning a motorcycle courier, and guessed the nurse had other than career reasons for liking case variation.

The small surveillance unit was enough, though outside

visits proved unexpectedly difficult. Jill was good with records. It was during a brief interval that morning that she brought Clare the record book with a disturbing problem.

'This very first case, doctor.' Jill showed the page. 'Same name as yours!'

'It's my husband.' Clare laughed. 'My guinea pig! I ran him through the tests – electrocardiograph, sphygmo, lipoproteins, erythrocyte sedimentation rate, leucocytes, everything I could think of. He actually asked if it would hurt! Infantile!'

'But there's no follow-up, doctor.'

Clare looked ostentatiously at the book, startled by Nurse Partington's remark. 'Ah. He couldn't make the appointment.'

'What date?' Jill moved to the terminal and sat at the screen.

Clare silently cursed her carelessness. 'Four weeks since?'

'Isn't it unusual for a doctor to examine her own husband?'

'There is that!' Clare kept it light. 'I was trying the system out.'

'I can't raise it, doctor.'

Clare thought, shut *up*, drop it. 'It must be there.'

'Did you book him yourself, Dr Burtonall?' Jill sounded worried. 'Only, how many more defaulters have slipped through?' She prided herself on aptitude, and now this.

'Yes, I think so.'

'Are you sure?' Jill clicked the program menu. 'I'd have picked it up.'

'I had no help, remember. Is that the next patient?' But no buzzer had gone in the waiting room. Clare felt Jill's sidelong glance.

'I joined three weeks into the survey. Remember my

first day? Those lads from the canal lumber yard mucking about?'

'Yes,' Clare said brightly. 'Our first real mob! I was so relieved—'

'It's not here.' Nurse Partington fixed on the screen. The buzzer went, the next patient. 'I'll do a numbers tally.'

'Better get him in,' Clare urged. 'The lab will only create.'

Jill shot her another look. They had plenty of time before clinical pathology's watershed for specimens. Clare tried to carry it off, but it didn't work.

The record was the false one she had prefabricated to give Clifford an alibi. She had backed it up with lab tests, ECGs, the lot. If Jill hadn't been so meticulous, Clare's slip would have gone unnoticed. As it was, Clifford's failure to attend follow-up examinations would stand out as a gross anomaly. She had committed the deceiver's cardinal blunder, failed to support the first lie with a second, the second by a third, and so for ever and ever.

Now she would somehow have to darn over the problem. And is any repair ever truly invisible? She felt worn out, thought damn Clifford and his money schemes. And damn the obsessional Nurse Partington.

The phone went. Clare answered. Nobody spoke.

'Hello? Dr Burtonall, cardiac surveillance. Hello?'

She replaced the receiver, frightened, thinking of Bonn as the next patient entered.

Bonn was explaining to Martina. 'Meena Three-Eight-Oh.'

'Is she really pregnant?'

'I wouldn't know.'

Exasperation made Martina seethe. He'd done

everything sexual to this Meena bitch that she demanded, and he still hadn't a clue? It was becoming hopeless. Every time she set eyes on Bonn she finished up drained and angered. She wondered how long this could go on.

'I think it's plain blackmail, Martina.'

'Leave it with me.'

'Please.' He hesitated. It struck him how little Martina used his name. 'I do hope sanctions will be minimal, Martina.'

'Don't worry,' she said, as if to a child. 'Meena's punishment won't fit the crime.'

He never did know what she meant. The next time he glanced through Miss Faith's code book Meena Three-Eight-Oh had been deleted.

# 24

**Mosh (adj.)** – secret, disguised (esp. of motorcars)

MOTORWAY SERVICE STATIONS were the pits, in Akker's opinion. They looked terrific in daytime – cars, families, glittering signs, the great pantechnicon HGVs – at night they were dire. He wanted to smoke, but never on a job, when you might find yourself being interviewed by some copper.

Akker sat in his motor watching Galahad and Danielle toking their heads into orbit across the parking lot. Heap big deception, them hiring a car. Like announcing it on frigging BBC Radio One, them thinking they'd got away.

Truth was, Akker was the one in the mosh wheels. His van was marked for an unknowable electrical company, logos hardly dry and registration from Belgium or somewhere vague. They were stoning themselves stupid, inhaling God-knows-what from God-knows-where. Were folk barmy, or what?

The service station was marked on every map, not like those masquerading clever-clevers that tricked you in, buy a cardboard burger or you couldn't even go for a piss. This was huge, arcades of games machines, jerk bandits, shops, a vast expanse for cars next to the mainroaders' wagons. Like, just the place. Secret as the Cup Final.

Their grey saloon wasn't much, considering the money they'd nicked. The city was full of talk even before Galahad got ruled on, Danielle taking satches, selling the drug on to punters, even giving them the doings, syringes, foil and all. Her real crime though was dosing her customers then nicking their wadges, being a right busy little cunt, spreading the habit when punters only wanted a shag.

It wasn't right. Anybody but a log would know that. The girls on Grellie's strings, especially from Riversgate, were well pissed with Danielle. They reported her to Grellie – and nobody hates telling on each other more than a working lass – complaining that she was going separate, so busy that other stringers were being approached as if they were doing it too. That had made them scared, meaning Rack. No knowing where *that* would end for an honest working lass.

The one person Akker couldn't fathom in this mayhem was Galahad. The burke's savings growing like moor grass, all the cunt a bloke could ever wish for. Money and honey heaven, and what does he do? Chucks it away, cavorts with some dopehead bint booked for the slice anyway. The ultimate gormlessness. Got everything, so you throw it away?

'Course, Galahad was thick as a doctor's door. Maybe she'd shot him some line about setting him big in films, movies like that big Continental bloke with the wrong teeth, fame, game and fortune? Or maybe she'd got the nerk hooked on the odd satch? But Grellie kept a medical book on her stringers that the girls called the Card – Akker had never seen it – when lasses had to go to the doctor, poorly or no. Danielle only had to turn up to be made better.

He'd had six reports from Rack, well primed, about pollen Danielle had bought since she'd been caught crossing. He snorted in disgust. They'd pulled in and parked, then fallen on the stuff, keeping their car windows closed to get there faster. Fucking ridiculous. If it had been him he'd have escaped first, then crashed up in safety. As it was, Birmingham smog enveloping the Midlands and them halting in puffer's paradise was asking for it. But who could argue with a druggo? Life expectancy was done. Time wasn't just running out, it was just a question of who did the topping.

The answer to that was always themselves. If Galahad hadn't crossed the line with Danielle. If Danielle hadn't crossed with Galahad. If she hadn't started pollen. If she hadn't started Galahad down the cracktrack. But there never were enough ifs. The most useless word in the language, if. Like asking a corpse what it wanted instead.

He clicked the radio on, some woman wanting everybody to exercise three times a day, silly moo. A background piano didn't quite make it. He pressed the digital, got some starched git reading the news. Galahad got out of his car, reeling, probably wanting the loo but forgetting what he'd got out for. See? Druggos thought they were clever, because they managed to keep some brown King Kong for themselves. Just look, Galahad singing, daft prat. A family arrived in a red estate car, children laughing thinking the big handsome man was singing booze out.

Galahad got back in, still singing, Danielle illuminated in the courtesy light, head back for one more laugh. Akker thought, aye, luv, make it last. Time.

They had parked by the concrete perimeter fence. Akker gave silent thanks. He'd already picked out a roadie's monster double-loader, the cabin an incredible height from the tarmac. His own van was near the garage exit. He didn't want to get checked by some RAC man out for glory.

The best was, who'd notice a bloke in overalls, night time, among parked cars? Akker had watched the enormous container wagon arrive. The two – driver and mate – stretched, went into the building rubbing their eyes. They'd pee, wash, shop a bit, then nosh. Akker's belly rumbled at the thought. Sausage, beans, toast, fried bread, bacon, eggs, but it was like smoking. Before a job, no.

The wagon's alarm was a simple rod-and-click, what he'd been brought up on. A laugh. The real joke, they had those Midland double switchers, that only took a second to set and were a pig to de-set. Rod, his mate, could de-set a Midland, but Rod'd done an apprenticeship – seven years, City and Guilds. The silly sods hadn't even bothered! Maybe the drivers theirselves didn't understand it.

He climbed into the cabin, slumped down as another hauler rumbled past. A serious risk. These roadies were a clan and looked out for each other. Last thing he wanted was for some other driver say to those two, hey, mate, I just saw somebody in your wagon. Also, longhaulers were a law to theirselves. No asking the police to come and arrest the bugger, none of that polite stuff. It'd be kick the bastard senseless, break a couple or three bones, and only then let's think whether to bother writing police statements half the bleeding night when they should be trundling into Carlisle.

Cautiously Akker raised his head. No lorries on the move, no drivers coming out talking football and women, docking their fags after a last drag. No saloons, with tired motorists ready to snap into wakefulness at the sight of a massive transporter rolling forward in eerie silence.

Galahad and Danielle were there still. He did the engine, his penknife stripping the wires like putty. He pocketed a small piece of insulation. No trace was best evidence.

The vehicle was ready. He fired the engine – Christ, double bass, shuddering – and drove forward, first gear. Galahad's car was a hundred yards off. Akker flicked the lights once, making doubly sure it really was the silly sods and not somebody innocent. Aye, there they were, flicking their lights playfully back, laughing.

He drove easily, not making too much of the powerful engine's revving. Steady did it, circumstances like this.

Their laughing faces turned dozily towards him and froze in the windscreen. He spun the wheel like a serving plate in his hands so the cabin slewed.

Almost lovingly the vehicle moved on to their motor. He drove over rather than at them. Their expressions changed for their final moment. Before, in bliss. The wagon rose as it crunched, seeming to gnaw at the car beneath. He gunned power, shoving the saloon and Galahad and Danielle. Them concrete barriers were good things, Akker decided, protecting the public from petrol station calamities, thousands of gallons of octane. Think of all those happy families in the service station.

Akker felt he'd gone a little too slow, perched up there with the engine muttering, but you couldn't rub out and start again. He opened the cabin door. Somebody far away screamed. He nipped behind Galahad's wheels – him well crushed, Danielle just a leg showing, blood everywhere, the sweet stench of whatever pollen.

He chose near a tree on the banking, was over the tall fence almost before folk started coming out. He drove the opposite way. Alibis weren't always wise. Distance was best. No, constable, I was miles away at the time, where was it, exactly?

The accident would go down as some yobbo trying to nick a wagon, losing control and crashing it into a young couple's car, poor dears. The haulage drivers would get ballocked for leaving their vehicle's alarms unset, only fair. They shouldn't be so fucking sloppy.

And Galahad and Danielle would be marked down as dopeheads too stoned to get out of the way when they saw a great vehicle bearing down. Shouldn't take those nasty drugs. Young people nowadays, tut frigging tut. Akker could write tomorrow's tabloids.

'This is hardly the right restaurant for business, is it?'

Clifford wore his charm smile, believing it his best selling point. The scientist Julia Pickard seemed interested, but then she would be, him the bringer of business.

They made a pretence of studying the menu.

'We chose your laboratory,' Clifford began, 'because—'

'Because I've only been going two months, because my pattern hasn't yet been established among taxmen, county pharmacists, government scientists, et cetera?'

'Well, yes.' Clifford saw she would not be disarmed, suspected she was already ahead of him. And she didn't think much of his subterfuge.

'My wife, Dr Clare Burtonall, handed in some samples, a coded fund for payment.'

'And?' Julia wrinkled her brow, said something about how were the peas done, not like French? The waiter sprinted for answers.

'The same code can be used for any other analyses,' Clifford said carefully.

'Fine. Once we have the payment code, we supply a block of chits. One chit per sample.'

Was it so easy? Was this how athletics officials sent in tests at the Olympics, then? Clifford smiled. She was attractive, this enviably cool scientist. Alert, in command, perhaps some father funding her?

'Can we start with wine?' she suggested. 'I'm in no hurry.'

He answered the waiter's interrogation, and went for it, laying it down on the table. 'What *kind* of specimens?'

'Any.' She watched the waiter's wine mysteries.

She'd given him a tour of the laboratory, wondering what was the matter with the man. Couldn't he see the lengths she was willing to go to for her new business? It was a cut-throat world. Was he secretly thick?

'Julia. Suppose we wanted some sample powders analysed?'

She hadn't yet addressed him by name. Names were selling points, and she was pricey. A given name was persuasion and acceptance. Also, the freedom thing could be overdone.

'Your doctor signs the request forms,' she said, having towed him serenely through the reef into the lagoon. 'Send one with each.'

'And you send reports to Dr Burtonall?' he said, as if to a dolt.

She could have hit him, but he represented a longterm contract. Which equalled profit. She would bugger about all evening to win.

'Of course,' she said, shaking her head prettily at the hovering waiter for one more minute, please. She was starving. Was the penny dropping? Julia Pickard sighed inwardly, give it to the moron in syllables.

'My staff check every sample container and its form.' She gave him a wide-eyed stare. Perhaps he wanted a bimbo?

'What if her signature isn't quite . . . ?'

At last. Name time. It was like pulling teeth.

She used her eyes in the candlelight. 'Good heavens!'

she cried mockingly. 'A doctor whose handwriting isn't copperplate? Whatever next!'

'I get it.' He gave her his dashing smile. What a nerve.

She raised her eyebrows. The waiter gunned over, ready.

Clifford relaxed. He'd won. The tests could be anything at all: specimens from an athlete; drugs whether cut or not. Clare had played her unwitting part. Clifford could now decide which and what were tested. All samples would be coded. And whoever sent Julia the samples could even decide the results. Just keep up her payments.

He set out to enjoy the attractive woman's company. He felt lucky.

# 25

## **Satch** – one dose of illicit drugs

QUESTIONS COME TO a woman. Clare saw the beautiful Dr Anita Carrillon approach down the ward, and felt her hackles rise. She had just completed her examination of the patient in Intensive Care.

It was as if Dr Carrillon had some cue mechanism, the bitch. Her smug moral certitude was enough to make everyone agnostic. Clare tried to control her temper. She began to write her notes, fuming.

'Thank you,' she told the student nurse specialing Janeson.

The girl went, starched apron crackling, as the beautiful Dr Carrillon wafted fragrantly down the ward linoleum, her hair more lustrous than hair could possibly be. The scene was set for a morality play, Clare thought with anger.

'Dr Burtonall!' Dr Carrillon whispered, tiptoeing up, clasping files to her admirable bosom. '*So* glad I caught you! Could we discuss this case, please? I'm particularly interested, you see.'

Like Clare wasn't? Like all other doctors lazed in idleness, while dedicated Dr Carrillon battled alone against disease and death?

'What is it?' Clare thought, This PVS case might be me.

Dr Carrillon smiled sweetly, gently inclined her gracious head. Clare grabbed her notes. Her work must come second. They left the greenish gloaming and entered the vacant glass-panelled side room. Clare switched on the consols, checking the nurse had returned to special Hebrew Janeson.

'Shall we sit, Clare?' Dr Carrillon sank elegantly to a chair. 'It's such a pleasure to get one's weight off one's feet!'

Global note: Dr A. Carrillon, exhausted by life-saving tasks, alone deserved rest. Obstinately Clare remained standing before the screen monitors. She'd been manipulated too often by this woman.

'Janeson, Clare,' Dr Carrillon began. 'Rather a problem, don't you think?'

Clare said pointedly, 'In what way?'

'In a *moral* way, Clare,' was said with reproach.

'All patients present moral issues.'

'*That's my point*, Clare! It is a dilemma for us all!'

'Your *it* is my *he*.'

Anita did her woebegone sigh. 'I'm truly sorry to ask your attention, but I want *some* assurance that you will consider a *proper* evaluation.'

'Meaning I work improperly?'

Dr Carrillon smiled wistfully. 'Clare. Please *do* try.'

'I'll try, Anita,' Clare ground out. She knew the other's reasoning.

'When I heard that Dr Burnden had asked *you* to perform an assessment, I felt immediate anxiety.'

The woman had a galling effect. There was no doubting her beauty. Good figure, hair titian, pale face bringing out contrasts. From an excellent medical school, Anita soared up the hospital's ranks. That she was the daughter of the medical director of the giant St James's Hospital hadn't exactly impeded her progress, though that was the sort of catty thought Anita always evoked. Was it simply that her beauty riled?

Or was it her ineffable compassion, so sweetly displayed? Dr Carrillon might be so slow in clinics that other doctors invariably had to finish her work, but always she thanked colleagues with saccharine allure. Clearly, no blame attached to one so devoted.

Worst of all was Clare's suspicion that Anita's morality was abuse. Therapeutic abortion – for medical reasons, to protect the mother – Dr Carrillon flatly condemned, her group battling unrelentingly for blanket anti-abortion legislation. Clare had even found her own name added to Anita's petition without Clare's knowledge. Anita had opposed the PVS revisions by a vigorous letter campaign.

Clare believed that Anita was unscrupulous, manipulation a coercion game to support some crusade.

'My anxiety, Clare,' Dr Carrillon said reproachfully, 'is that you will score this patient down.'

'I record the observations I find, Anita.'

'But don't you realize that the clinical signs, level of consciousness, eye movements, responses to stimuli, reflexes, will be coloured by your own attitude? *I'm* continually aware of it.'

'Meaning I'm not? Meaning,' Clare said, 'that I give a mere unthinking glance at a comatose patient then condemn him to death?'

'Certainly not!' The other was shocked. 'I *know* you'll take care this time! It's just that some other doctor might inveigle you into deciding what he wants.'

Clare fought for control as a thought struck her. 'Has Dr Burnden asked you to assess this PVS patient?'

'No.' Anita smiled sadly. 'A telling comment! He only invites doctors he can manipulate.'

Clare kept her eyes on the monitors. 'Anita. The young male was shot. After six months as a PVS patient, the chance of recovery is meagre. After a year, virtually nil. I shall advise Dr Burnden to take a twelve-month shut-off time as final.'

Dr Carrillon rose, pale and angry. 'Have you performed the *right* tests?'

Clare became aware that nurses were listening from the adjoining cubicle where they were specialing a post-diabetic comatose patient, but she was determined to oppose Anita's badgering.

'The ice-water caloric test, Clare? Nystagmus response? Visual tracking of movement? Looked for the 'menace' response? Drug exclusion? Search for reversible metabolic causes?'

'Read my notes – all done and repeated, thank you.'

'What about computed tomography? Magnetic resonance imaging? Electroencephalography? Evoked potentials?'

'What's your evidence that those improve clinical diagnostic appraisals, please?' Clare demanded, enraged. 'But yes, yes, yes.'

'Please side with morality, Clare!'

'Meaning prolong intolerable agony so we can continue playing God?'

Dr Carrillon smiled, angelic. 'Morality should not be intolerable to any doctor worth her salt, Dr Burtonall!'

And the woman swept out. Clare tasted bile. The insufferable bitch always had the last word.

'Sorry, Dr Burtonall,' Hassall said. 'Butting in, am I?'

'Not at all.' Clare felt compassion at his discomfiture. 'Come in.'

He obeyed. She sat to keep an eye on the screens.

'I called to say sorry, disclosing your name to Jase.' He shrugged. 'It's probably not made much difference, after your Mrs Mandel went on telly.'

'You heard of the anonymous calls?' She felt suddenly down. 'Why *are* you here?'

'Making sure he's still with us.' Hassall nodded at the screens. 'What did you think of Haleys Wharf?'

She shivered. 'Miserable place.'

'The quicker your husband redevelops it, eh?' He smiled. 'Do you have any contacts in Victoria Square, doctor?'

'Not really.' She kept her voice even, unsure what he was asking. 'I have no contracts with the hotels for GP services, if that's what you mean.'

'No calls to Waterloo Street, those places?'

'No. Some doctors do locums for voluntary organizations, but you'd have to ask.'

'What're his chances, doctor? The Janeson lad.'

She sighed. It was always difficult, confidentiality versus the law. 'See for yourself, Mr Hassall. He's out, no responses to speak of.' She became wintry and self-condemning. 'You must have heard our differences. Dr Carrillon thinks he's to be preserved for ever.'

'You favour withdrawing life support?'

She gazed at him. 'After a year of PVS, yes, Mr Hassall. To me, a year of PVS is equivalent to a patient's announcing his demise.'

He nodded. 'Like old folk, isn't it? My old mum was helpless at the finish. It was a blessing when it came. She'd have said so. Thanks for your time, doctor. Oh, forgot. How's Mr Burtonall?'

'Fine, thank you.'

He left Clare wondering. His asking after Clifford again was more than a ritual politeness.

Leaving the hospital late that night, she saw a thin youngish figure among the cars. Just standing there, facing the hospital. It wasn't Bonn. She looked about, wanting to see Mr Hassall, anybody, but she was alone. Quickly she entered her Humber. She locked the door, first time ever, from the inside. When she drove away, he was nowhere to be seen.

Jase watched her go, went inside to ask at Reception. He learnt that Dr Burtonall had just this minute gone. Jase smiled, told the receptionist never mind. He was gone before they could offer to let Out-Patients make another booking for him.

# 26

**Stripe** – stolen goods

Martina had left Bonn a message in the kitchen. He read it while making his Lancashire porridge. The note was folded, one margin serrated. That more than anything revealed Martina's anger. It had been ripped from the spring-bound notebook she used for the housekeeper.

*Please call, S.P., ten-fifteen.* Unsigned.

A command performance, then, at the Shot Pot. He made tea, one small dose of sugar for the first cup of the day. Was it deliberate ostracism? He mustn't start reading motive into things. Motive was the road to dementia, which came soon enough. Posser last night had started talking over something with Mrs Ainsworth, who'd hired him for her lifespan then died, *requiescat in pace*.

Today, he would grasp the nettles as they sprang.

Fat George gave him a newspaper unasked, nettles shooting early.

Bonn read, walking along the pavement. Rack usually happened by at this point, but today was missing. Neither had Grellie yet surfaced. Even the traffic seemed indolent. Two stringers trolled the gardens with little hope.

CAR CRUSHED IN MOTORWAY TRAGEDY wasn't much of an epitaph for the blond giant. The paper gave Galahad's real name, which only now Bonn remembered. Danielle wasn't Danielle. She had a plainer born name. The two had been on drugs, which police had found in the damaged vehicle. Witnesses remembered the big young man singing, possibly drunk, beside the car. Two drivers were being questioned by police. A police spokesman pointed stern morals.

Bonn consulted another two columns. An accident near Haleys Wharf in the dark hours was still being investigated, individuals helping police with enquiries. A motorcar had crashed against a canal bridge, the driver dying immediately. Coincidentally, a man's body had been seen in the canal by a dawn jogger.

'Excuse me. So sorry.'

Having to apologize to pedestrians made Bonn smile wrily. Rack usually bounced along, shoving folk aside so Bonn could progress unharassed. None of this in the cloisters when reading his breviary office of the day. There, priests and brothers had all gone in one direction, except for Father Brockhurst.

The Butty Bar was open, a few people in for breakfast.

'Bonn? Can I join you? I'm prepared to wait.'

Bonn looked up at the youth's public-school face. 'Please do, Bertram. I have five minutes only, I'm afraid.'

'Quite follow, Bonn.'

Bertram sat, a veritable Peter Pan. Smooth of face, tanned, suited, he looked everything he wasn't. He seemed rich, and wasn't. Looking efficient, he couldn't drive or earn a crust. Rack said it was a wonder Bertram came out dressed of a morning, he was that useless.

'Please say if I may help,' Bonn said.

Today brimmed problems, and here came Bertram. Mabs

the counter girl was desperately trying to catch Bonn's eye, offer him a coffee. But Mabs's coffee was execrable. Bonn would be too kind to leave it, so he would drink it and then get a headache because her coffee always gave him one. If he left it, she'd be mortified. If he ignored her, she would then know he didn't like her coffee, which would be cruel.

Another thing. The accident had 'taken place'. Why did accidents 'take place', as if they came along in due season? He gave up.

'About the accident, Bonn.'

Bertram was smart, give him that. English gentleman from some old B film – inept at banking, hopeless in the navy, failed trying for the police, slung out of university. Bertram was hollow.

'Extremely sad, Bertram. May they rest in peace.'

'Yes, indeed.' Bertram claimed to have been at Harrow, Eton, somewhere, but hadn't. Even his accent was sham, but sham what, when Bertram was totally phoney? Bertram conned punters at the city racetrack.

'I suppose you did not see it.'

'Me? Gosh, no. Bonn. Nowhere near.'

Bonn wasn't sure if they were talking about Galahad and Danielle, crushed to death under the transporter, or Sanj and Bunce at Haleys Wharf.

'Coffee, incidentally?' A measure of Bertram's hopelessness, trying to con free coffee.

'No, thank you.'

'Oh. Well, is there a vacancy? Galahad's gone, right? I'm an educated man, Bonn, fit the bill, know what I mean?'

'Not really, Bertram.' Bonn hadn't the heart to glance at the clock.

'Can I put in for goer, on your firm?' Bertram made it an offer, giving Bonn the benefit of first refusal. 'I'd prove my worth.' He gave a dashing laugh, depressing Bonn still more.

'I'm afraid an appointment has already been made, Bertram.'

'Already?' Bertram looked at Bonn in alarm.

'Thank you for offering. You know,' he put in quickly to prevent the other pressing his question, 'I keep no waiting list.'

He eyed Bonn doubtfully. 'How did you know it'd happen?'

'I appointed the new goer some time back, Bertram,' Bonn said sadly, sad because similar suspicions occurred to him also. 'Poor Galahad.'

'Then you still need a replacement, Bonn? I've always been popular . . .'

Bonn thought wearily, where is Rack? He should be here saying which clients and which hotels by now.

'No, thank you, Bertram.'

'Oh.' Bertram lost impetus. Fascinated, Bonn watched the man's aura fade. Strange that synthetic brashness kept deception alive. Pop one balloon, and the whole man actually vanished. 'Well.' Bertram glanced longingly at the counter, where Mabs stirred eagerly, but Bonn shook his head. Bertram left, waving to baffled people who did not know him, phoneyness returning. Down the street he'd be strutting like the Man Who Broke The Bank At—

'What's all this, then?' Rack plonked himself down. 'Beans and bacon, Mabs, and not streaky. Yesterday it was horrible. And an egg in a cup, not soft.' He spread his elbows on the table, staring at Bonn. 'Know what gets me? They don't ever hot the pan, women. Know why?'

'Good morning, Rack.' For all Rack's lateness Bonn was relieved.

'They think of gas bills, the electric. Chefs don't, see? Know why?'

'I'm to see Martina.' Bonn guessed she was the delay.

'Quarter past ten, row about Prand. And Servina's playing hell.'

'I'm afraid I quite forgot. That cruise.'

'Unquite it, then, mate.' Rack guffawed. 'Because Martina's remembered it and so's Servina.' Rack shouted for Mabs. 'Where's that grub? It's sodding afternoon!' He lowered his voice. 'That Jase did the canal thing. And you've two uppers today, two-fifteen and seven o'clock.'

'I see,' Bonn said, who didn't. 'Jase? God rest them.'

'Shame about Galahad and Danielle. Stoned, the plod.'

'I think I should go, Rack. Martina.'

'Grellie's at the bus station talking in a new stringer.'

'Thank you, Rack. Oh, I told Bertram no.' Bonn paused. 'And please get that Trish.'

'Trish,' Rack said, thinking through faces. 'That older bird who wanted into Grellie's line, no idea? You can't mean her?'

'That is she,' Bonn said.

'Right. First in the Vivante, Room 362. She's a broadcaster.'

'Thank you, Rack.'

Bonn left, mercifully without a headache from Mabs's coffee, but suffering another of life's devising.

Grellie was sitting outside the bus-station café, trees and bushes bending in a freshening breeze. The girl with her almost drooping with fatigue, eyes hollow and features void of make-up. Bonny, marked for Grellie's blue string.

'Morning, Bonn,' Grellie said. 'This is Maureen from the pickings. Maureen, you don't talk to Bonn unless he talks first, see?'

'Yes, Grellie.' The girl's wavering large blue eyes took Bonn in.

'All right if I finish, Bonn?' Grellie asked, and went on, 'No gob jobs straight, Maureen, understand? You gob sidewards on – I don't want you going down with pneumonia. Charge punters on the nail. If the mark says, oh, my pal over there'll pay, you scream blue murder. And clear car jobs first.'

'Who with, Grellie?'

'Your string leader's Eve. Do as she tells. And no foreign money. We've had hell of a time with old Finnmarks. They mean sod-all.'

'When do I ask for the money?'

'Always up front, love. Collect first, then do it.'

'What if they don't like the room?'

Grellie avoided Bonn's eye. 'He won't even *see* the room. He's on fire, see? Fifteen minutes is plenty.'

'What if he wants something different?'

'That's up to you, love. No trolling in the shopping mall. Did Lorraine tell you? They've CCTV systems there for shoplifters, one operator in a control room, one on the thief. And shops have link radio, three buttons, tuned in.'

'Lorraine said I'll have a set beat.'

'Go to see Eve now. She'll be in Waterloo Street.'

'Good luck, Maureen.' Bonn watched her go. She wobbled on the paving, heels impossibly high. 'A nice lass.'

Grellie sighed. 'I feel like her mother. I ought to shop with her, kit her out. What's this Trish business?'

'I want to ask her some questions.'

Grellie stared, incredulous. 'You? *Ask?* What has Trish got that I haven't, except twice my age?'

'She might solve a problem.' He added, 'Posser.'

She touched his hand. 'Remember, Bonn. You want, choose me.'

'I am worried it will be thought crossing of the worst kind, Grellie.'

'I've already told you it'll be safe, Bonn.'

'Yet everybody knew about Trish, no sooner had I spoken her name.'

'Rack has this numbers system. He teaches the girls, numbers mean things, changes them every morning. Notice he's never drunk, never forgets a thing? Loony mind, that's all. Nothing spooky.'

'I should like to, Grellie.'

Her face lit up. 'Try me, darling, and see.'

She watched him go. Sooner or later Posser would pass, then Martina would be alone. An enterprising girl might make a stab at taking over. With Bonn on her side there'd be no contest. Rack was less of an enigma than he seemed. Bonn was the key, more ways than one.

Sergeant Windsor was ecstatic, scurrying between seniors like a dog wanting sticks thrown. Hassall stood at the bridge looking where the jogger had found Bunce. Hassall hadn't had final ID.

'Where's the SOCO?'

Windsor managed to stand still long enough to reply. 'Mr Ventris? Under the bridge with the druggos.'

Hassall clambered to the towpath. 'Not druggos, Sergeant Windsor, until conviction. Possible witnesses.'

There'd be some coffee-time carping at the nick after that little exchange, Hassall thought.

'Roy,' he greeted the Scene Of Crime Officer. Roy Ventris spent his morose time crown green bowling. Crime was an unwelcome interruption, to be quickly got rid of. He had surprising girth. Dr Burtonall ought to get him on her scales, guinea an ounce.

'This cobble business.' Ventris had laid out scores of cobblestones under the arch. 'Take a hefty kid to lob one, eh?'

'Kids are all hefty, Roy.'

'It's their game, isn't it? Wait, chuck, car crashes, theirs for the looting.'

'We used to think putting a penny on the line in the Salford railway sidings was daring, I was a kid. Bunce?'

'The floater. Druggo, wasn't he?'

'The point is, Roy, could it have been this Jase?'

'A tube man would have popped them.'

'The pathologist will test for drugs?'

'It's Dr Wallace. Takes his time, though.' Ventris beckoned a uniformed constable. 'Get the dabs man.' He shrugged at Hassall's expression. 'There might be the odd print.'

'If kids did Sanj, and a druggo falling in, then Jase will go unhindered.'

'And do what?'

'To pop others – like Noddo, maybe.'

Roy Ventris said as the fingerprints man came slithering, dragging his box, 'I reckon you've got a criminal mind.'

# 27

**Straightener** – punishment of one who disobeys

Being frightened was not new. A year ago, driving her old maroon Humber into Bowton, a waste-disposal vehicle had slewed across the A666. To this day she couldn't work out how the massive yellow truck, in the spraying wet, had avoided slamming into her. But she remembered the fright.

On Farne Island, too, returning one night across the Causeway, the tide had suddenly risen about her car wheels. The relief, bumping up out of the dark waters on to stone!

Now? Since Mr Hassall's blunder she looked at people in a new way. Folk at bus stops, disembarking passengers on Station Brough. Even patients, for doctors were vulnerable, more than most. Any public library, the General Medical Register, doctors were clearly listed.

She was at the police station, feeling put out. She'd failed to book Bonn beforehand, and smarted at Hassall's cackhandedness telling Jase her name. Nurse Partington was having a high old time flirting when Clare got there.

A small lecture room had been allocated. Jill had brought screens from hospital, three officers helping with apparatus. Clare had a nasty moment when two women police officers came asking when females would receive the same checks, and had to explain she was studying male morbidity, not providing health services.

'But we're as entitled,' one WPC said hotly.

'To health services, yes,' Clare said a third time. 'But the research is in male cardiac problems alone.'

They would not let up, and only left when Hassall put his head round the door.

'Can I be first?'

'We're almost ready.' Clare made an attempt at cordiality. 'I ought to put you last, telling that Jase about me.' She found power points, plugged in the ECG. 'I've been scared ever since.'

Hassall pulled a face. 'Sorry. You were already in the firing line, Mrs Mandel on telly. Do I have to take off my coat?'

'More than that.' Jill came. 'Please fill in the card. Strip to the waist.'

'The lads are doing these cards.' Hassall found a pen. 'You'll get Mickey Mouse, 1, Hyde Park Gate. Watch out for film stars. We're juvenile.'

Nurse Partington smiled. 'It's carnival out there.'

Hassall said, writing. 'More jokes about nurses' uniforms than that. Will this hurt?'

Clare gave an obvious sigh.

'You're all the same. Look.' She pointed to the instrumentation. 'Body fat measurements. Simplest indices, shape, weight, height. A few elementary tests – blood pressure, a small pinprick, an ECG. For heaven's *sake*. Exercise tolerance, then lie down.'

'Did your husband object, doctor?' Hassall asked mildly.

'My husband?' Clare maintained innocent exasperation.

Hassall shelled his clothes. 'He was your first patient, wasn't he, that time?'

She was aware Jill was looking across. 'I'd forgotten. Yes, he kept asking, will this hurt, what's that for. Women are much more sensible.' She tried to bring Jill in. 'It was women got this research going. Right, Jill?'

'Yes, doctor,' Jill said evenly, but Clare knew she'd not managed to skate over the ice. She glanced at Hassall, but he said no more.

Twenty-five policemen were processed in a little over four hours. Nurse Partington stayed to chat. Clare drove into the city, and stopped to call the Pleases Agency from a public phone, to book Bonn but he was not available.

'Can I book for tomorrow?'

Mercifully, 'Yes, that will be in order. The Hotel Vivante, nine o'clock.'

'Room 571. Thank you, Clare Three-Nine-Five. We aim to offer—'

'Thank you.' Clare rang off. She wanted Bonn. She felt vulnerable. Her earlier anger at Bonn had faded, become depression, longing. He might have news of Jase. Maybe Hassall and Nurse Partington were already poring over the records back there, setting Hassall wondering.

'Prand,' Martina said the instant Bonn entered her non-office. 'You made him a goer. Why?'

Bonn delayed his reply a pulse or two. Normally, Martina was up and down, like the rest, but lately she'd been vixenish.

'I need a fourth goer, not to say a third.'

'What exactly does that mean?'

Her beauty was enhanced by pallor. How far could that equation, anger and a pale countenance, go?

'To my surprise I find I have appointed Galahad's substitute.'

She waited, tense, but he out-lasted her. 'What are you implying?'

'Nothing, Martina. I make the observation.'

'Do you mean I ordered Galahad's death?' She coursed on before he could speak. 'I wouldn't do such a thing.' She took the risk, her voice choked with anger. 'There's no future in the agency for someone who loses trust. You see why?'

'Yes.'

'Trust has to be reciprocal. One-way trust is a lost cause.'

'I know.'

'Very well.' She scanned her blank paper for vital messages. 'Servina Four-One-Nine. She has had phone fights with Miss Rose, and me, about her precious cruise.'

'I remember her saying the Mediterranean.'

'You didn't explain that the agency bars cruises with clients? Why not?'

'All goes are unique, Martina. No two alike.' He tried to slow her rage, work cool sense in. 'To pause and explain the agency's policies would create havoc.'

She spat, '*What* havoc?'

Bonn couldn't help wondering about beauty. Some women seemed perversely determined to reduce their loveliness. Did they know what they were doing, and, conscious of a mistake, do it all the more?

'Screaming fits, abuse.' He pondered. 'Rage. A client sets her mind on delighting her goer, can become maniacal if denied.'

'Enough to bring in the stander?'

'More than enough. Rack had a fireman by.'

'Really?' That took her aback. She hadn't known.

'Rack will tell you.'

He wished he hadn't said that, for she coloured as if caught out. She lowered her head to stare at her hands.

'I think the agency can explain its limits best, Martina.'

'All right. I'll have Miss Rose put Servina through to me.' She seemed tired, avoided his eyes. 'This Jase. It's Noddo's yard, isn't it, that Haleys Wharf thing?'

'I hear so.'

'Your instinct was right about the Dutch smoke coaches. I'm revoking the arrangement. We stay out.'

'Very well.'

She'd wanted to infuriate, force him to be white with anger, leer, gloat at having proved her wrong. Instead, she got a very well.

'Another thing.' It was harder to go on. 'Trish.'

'I told Rack to find her.'

She couldn't resist saying, 'That old woman who wanted in?'

'I have many uppers older. In fact—'

Martina said, 'No sociology. I want to know why.'

'You asked me to solve the problem of your father. I have a solution.' Her stare returned. 'I must see Trish alone first.'

She thought a moment. 'The client you have later. Broadcaster?'

'Yes.'

'It's her first time with us. Maybe she's been an upper somewhere else.' Martina judged him. 'I want to be absolutely sure. I don't want late-night TV documentaries on the agency, be careful what you say.'

'I shall.'

'Another lady booked you for tomorrow. I agreed. Mrs

Fennimore, the guild chairwoman you found hard to manage.'

He ignored the pointed remark. It was a strange development, and he said so. 'I thought she was an enemy.'

'Evidently we were wrong. Take care – a woman can bear malice.'

She let him go then. A solution, to Posser's problems? That Trish hadn't looked at all remarkable, and as a street prostitute she'd be simply wrong. Bonn was normally so reticent, perhaps she ought to listen when he came out with something, anything, so direct.

He'd been calm about the tigress Mrs Fennimore. And he'd somehow got round her accusation about Servina Four-One-Nine. He must heed her warning about the woman broadcaster. It was too soon to have Akker straighten some over-ambitious media mare, seeing she'd used him so recently for Galahad and Danielle. Her word ought to be good enough for Bonn. His innocence made him gullible, yet his instinct was sometimes unerring – those damned smoke coaches. Unless he knew something that her people and Rack's shelts hadn't yet sussed?

A blinding headache came on. She decided to go home and lie down. She didn't know what was the matter with her these days.

Money had only ever come to Jase in trickles. He opened the leather case and gasped, never seen so much. The notes he divided, low denominations, high, different pockets. He caught the Bowton train, got kitted out in their market, cheapest in the north, and felt himself again. He returned by bus, took a bed-and-breakfast, grot he was used to.

The big question was where now. He had Marie to settle

for. Noddo might think that losing wadge plus two shelts made it quits. Wrong. Jase cooked foil and inhaled greedily in his pit. Marie's death was down to Noddo. If Noddo didn't set prices so high Marie wouldn't have had to use filthy needles, syringes. No wonder she got ill, going to druggos who cut with fucking toothpowder to flour. Crappy pollen killed Marie.

The reasoning was clear. Noddo owed. And that doctor owed.

Jase bought from an Aincoats teenager. Marie was the expert, somehow knew good from bad. Grass was easier, one peck you knew what you were in for. The old biddy that ran the B&B, give her a few notes to buy Gwaddy Gold or Jammy Red she'd come back with a tin of fucking salmon. Like she lived on frigging Mars. Marie'd said that. They laughed about it.

That Dr Burtonall. He'd watched at the hospital. It was her, all right, the one he'd handed Marie to. AIDS killed people, Jase knew. No doubt, the lady doctor owed. No problem doing her. Save the best wine till last?

Noddo's lot must have known, them thinking tee fucking hee, the car won't be there, wharra laugh, Jase's face. Nobody gave him so much as a nudge, and them his oppos. The slightest hint, Jase wouldn't feel like this. But from none?

With this much money he'd be right for ever in the south. First, the work.

He went to hunt Coffee and Beaky Divine.

The TV broadcaster was a professional people meeter. Bonn imagined her wafting about in her dressing-gown in her flat, but never at a loose end. She was directional, like now.

He wasn't taken aback so much as saddened. Women, he'd excitedly come to realize, were a myriad changing facets, chameleon-like, not in a biologic sense but emotional. Rita Seven-Two-Five, though, seemed to lack a dimension – perhaps honed off in all those encounters? She was slim, her physique burnished by activity.

He watched her pad to the bathroom, return to bed, practised, sure. She seemed to look at the carpet a lot. Bonn doubted Rita would be able to picture his face after leaving.

'Who picks the rooms?' She clasped him. 'How much longer've we got?'

'The agency. Ten minutes.'

'I've a pig of an afternoon coming.' She smiled. He could feel her mouth change form against his chest. 'I'm in for a corporate row. Blood will flow.'

'You sound delighted.'

'Of course!' she purred. 'Every woman wants to be a murderess.' She looked up at him, dark blue-grey eyes, a German kissing mouth in Pritchett's words. 'You in your trade, you don't even know that?'

'Does your meeting have to end thus, Rita?'

'Thus!' she mocked, laughing. 'Of course – if everything goes right!' She enjoyed his sobriety. 'There'd be no point otherwise! I can't understand you, in your trade.'

Trade. She kept on about it. 'It isn't a trade, Rita.'

Surprise jolted her out of her shell. She drew away to stare. 'Then what is it? Look, Bonn. Don't take this personally. You're not exactly unique.' She shifted so they lay side by side.

'I'm sure that is so.'

'And okay, fine, you're good value.' She let her smile out for a few seconds, dog on a leash. 'But what you do is, let's face it, not an all-time first. Man and woman *happens*.'

'I acknowledge that, Rita.'

Now she was curious, how he'd not lose the argument with no escape. 'Give service for a fee, it's a trade by definition. Capeesh?'

'Not to me.'

Rita Seven-Two-Five, broadcaster, was often in the papers on account of some documentary she'd been the mutter on, meaning TV presenter who'd read the idiot scroll. The fifty-minuter concerned transgressions of some noble lady in a stable. A fifth-form script had punned heavily, drawing on schoolday verbs. The programme was a popular success, got Grellie's girls talking and Rack theorizing on decadence. She'd hired Fret Dougal, lanky Accrington goer. Bonn was Rita's second incursion into the agency. She was cool, fame was the only game.

'Now you *are* fibbing, darling. I can prove it. Is Bonn your real name?'

'I thought I'd made it up. It means "worthless" in French argot.' He wanted the conversation over.

'Whatever contract you're on, I can buy you out.' Mischievously she teased the moment. 'I really do mean, take you away from all of this. You'd come.'

'No.' Cynicism foundered on the reefs of penitence and presumption. He felt such sympathy for her.

She laughed. 'Pay and conditions, Bonn dear, are chains. I can free you.'

'Please don't be sad.'

She said with asperity, 'Sad? In case you haven't noticed, I'm the one here who defines terms. You can't – you want more money.'

'That is so for some.'

'Now you're simply irritating, dear.' She said it singsong,

punishment coming. He'd heard parents and wives speak so in their power. 'Everybody's for sale. Right?'

He shook his head. 'I'm afraid it's time, Rita.' He should be out on the hour, so Rack could breathe again.

'Not so fast. My exact meaning, dar*ling*, is that you're *hired*, and I *pay*. Support for my argument in there somewhere, mmmh?'

'No, Rita, there is not.'

Bonn smiled an apology and went to run a bath. A few minutes, Rack would come in like Arapaho, delay being a goer's signal of things gone awry. She followed him, sharp anger rising.

'Then you tell me, mister,' she shouted, her expression dark, 'how come I make one call and you run up with your fucking dick out? It's money, lov-err!'

He paused, standing there naked, the bath running, steam enveloping. 'I almost wish that were true. Morality would be so much less of an issue. I'm sorry. You omit something really vital.'

'Lerve, dear?' she said, trembling with rage. 'You do it for romance? Above all that filthy lucre, are we?'

He thought, am I superior to commerce? The way of arrogance; worse, pride.

'I would have to think, Rita.' He turned the taps off and embraced her. 'Please don't be mad,' he said quietly into her hair. 'You and I have different modes. I do this because I do. Freedom would not appeal.'

She wrestled out, shouting, 'Total freedom, with money to choose?'

He said, 'It would be hell, Rita.'

She stared at him in the steam. 'Jesus H. Christ. I almost believe you!'

'I wish I could say the same.'

'You're ignorant or innocent.' She was frankly intrigued, fury forgotten.

'To be either is a monstrous arrogance,' he told her like that settled it. 'Get in the bath. I'll do your back.'

'I don't believe this,' she said, baffled. He lifted her in.

'If we are late out, somebody'll be for it.'

'Who?' she asked. 'You or me?'

'That'd be telling. Is this hot enough?' She kept her gaze on him. 'Sit still. I'll bath you. Get a move on, or we'll be sorry.'

# 28

**Plant** – one who will perjure for money

So cheap it was laughable, the phone business costing only a couple of hundred, Jase paying it out of Noddo's wadge in a schoolbag.

He paid two voices to do the arranging, fixed in an unbelievable twenty minutes. Strangers linked Noddo with Bunce's walktalker Jase found in the bag. The phone checks Noddo made, suspicious sod, would prove that the call came from Birmingham, no anxieties and thank you caller.

Coffee and Beaky Divine, pollen shovellers for Noddo's yard, would be in the old mill elevenish to gather the Morocco pollen. Seventh floor, using the old pull-rope counterweight lift for heavy cotton bales. Jase would be in position.

He felt so frigging tired, could sleep for a week, his cough enough to wake the dead. He kept barking for nowt, sweating cobs. It must be the scag. That sometimes happened, but he'd promised the druggo a kneecapping if it turned out duff. No honesty even on the manor. His luck had gone with Marie. What was he doing still here? He could be on the London express.

Waiting in a mill for Coffee and Beaky Divine, that's what.

He'd reported three-and-a-half bales of Gwaddy Green, in Noddo's code, meaning one hundred and seventy-five kilos of untouched, a bale being fifty pounds weight, ignorant cunts pretending they knew metric.

He slept on the top floor. He saw the massive counterweight, clever buggers them Victorians, no electricity needed. And then there was one, he thought, hacking drowsily, kipping on empty sacks. He had three sets of tools. Leave them unguarded, they'd vanish like snow off a duck. That's how it should be, or they might become evidence.

'Trish. I'm Bonn. You saw me at the Barn Owl.'

The woman stood like before a jury. Rack rolled his eyes and left. He'd sulk, not even knowing what Bonn was doing.

'Please be seated.'

She sank into the chair, clutching her handbag like a staff of office. She'd done her hair differently, perhaps protective colouring.

He smiled her to ease. 'I have quite forgotten my manners. I should have offered you tea, coffee.'

'Coffee, please.' She looked about warily.

The Butty Bar was its grottiest. He'd deliberately chosen there, knowing it would make her doubt her wisdom in coming. He wanted uncertainty, not the vehemence of a convert. She was attractive, despite Martina's animosity and Grellie's flat-out rejection. Longish hair on to her collar, fawn coat from a multiple stores, decent shoes, she might have been going to the pictures. He thought nice, but that word was on its last legs from precisionists. I like her, he amended, found that better.

The coffee came instantly, separate sugar, milk, cream. She was quick to notice that the other tables were sleazy.

Bonn hadn't lifted a finger or asked to be served. She told the waitress thanks, wondering.

'You came to be picked, Trish,' he suggested.

'Yes.' She coloured. 'I felt so ashamed. I'd just assumed.' She wanted to spoon sugar, pour milk, for him but he shook his head. 'I just assumed that I would do,' she said, face flaming.

'You must have heard about the syndicate circuitously.'

'Yes.' She was defiant. 'My friend went to Liverpool to be one. She hasn't written yet. She'll be all right, won't she?'

'There is no way to tell, Trish.'

'I cried all night. I'm stupid. They only want young girls.'

'You could be a working lass if you choose, Trish.'

'But I was told I couldn't.'

'I am considering making a special position for a lady such as you, but I need to consider first.'

Her hand crept to her throat. 'What would I have to do?'

'Tell me what you imagine the life of a working girl to be.'

'Well, it's . . .' she reddened, plunged on in a whisper. 'I mean, going with men who pay you. It's that, isn't it? I've seen them at the station.'

'Women have a certain fascination with that sort of life, I find.'

Her guilt returned. 'I know it's wrong. I want out of myself.'

A group of football supporters entered, crowding the counter and cheeking the serving girls, clapping in synchrony, chanting.

'Those, Trish, might want girls tonight. It isn't all sweetness and light, romance, carriage-and-pair moonlight rides.

It might be raining. You might have to give your services to, say, three in less than an hour, drunks among them. One might demand unorthodox intercourse, what the genteel call perversion, as others watch. One might be ill.'

He ran on, drawing the gloomiest picture. She watched his mouth.

'One might want to ignore sexual precautions. Some might create fights, sordid arguments, injuries. It is not pretty. On the other hand . . .'

She stayed in there, with him. 'Yes?'

'A syndicate lass is protected from the worst.'

'Is that what I'd have been?'

'What you still can be, if you will consider a new arrangement I wish to propose to the bosses.'

'I thought you were the boss!' Trish exclaimed, eyes wide. 'Everyone—'

'Trish.' He let her mind settle. 'If I were to make you a special, you must honour it.'

She breathed. 'Can you, Bonn?'

He decided to trust his judgement. 'It will be part time. You'll have to move house.'

She said, 'I'm not in a relationship or anything. I've thought about it.'

'Be on standby for three days, please. You will have to meet some people.'

'Thank you, Bonn.'

He let her go, waited a while, then left. Outside, moving away with Rack, Bonn said nothing until Rack exploded, 'I don't believe what you're doing, straight up I don't.'

'Martina will never rest until Posser is helped.'

'You're a key, Bonn!' Rack was beside himself, bludgeoning his way along the pavement. 'And you're going to use that old mare to—'

Bonn halted. 'Rack. I keep asking you to moderate your language. There are children, respectable people all around.'

They walked on. Rack said, 'I've guessed, you silly bleeder! A frigging brothel! Are you off your trolley?'

'Please be silent on the issue, Rack. My next go.'

'That broadcaster wants you for a Norway TV documentary, nine days. Martina's thinking of banning her. And that City Ladies' Guild bird with the big bristols now wants a homer. Martina sez you can take or leave.'

'Thank you, Rack. I shall go to the Conquistador for supper.'

Bonn didn't feel like it. Fridays meant fish, Christianity dying hard.

Clifford would be late home. He had okayed it with Clare, who told Mrs Kinsale.

Julia Pickard had her own schedules.

'My husband's a stick-in-the-mud academic,' she revealed to Clifford at the Royal and Grandee. It was getting on for nine. They had supper in the bedroom. She insisted on choosing the wine, after that restaurant. 'Criminology. Can you imagine?'

That gave them a laugh. He thought her vivacious. She reserved her opinion about him, despite his financial talents.

'Who earns the bread?' he asked, straight being her style. She'd asked bluntly about Clare, intimate details women normally euphemized.

'I do. He writes articles. They live longest.'

He could never tell when she was being mischievous. Even when she said she'd booked a room, he'd not been sure. Over coffee in the hotel's imposing lounge, she said be in Room 558 in five minutes. Then matter-of-fact sex, she looking past him as he worked into her and he'd glimpsed, what, boredom? For a fleeting second he'd thought of her analysing a chemical reaction. And who lived longest, exactly?

'Academics outlast the lot of us.' She smiled, shoving his hand away. A reflex offering, reflexively declined. 'Longevity is a doubtful benefit, I imagine.'

This woman's imagination was dangerous, Clifford warned himself. Yet what could be simpler than this? In business, in bed. But that absent look, sex an incidental in the service of. No friendliness.

'This contract will be good value, Clifford.'

'When the sport centres get going.'

'I want you to widen your specimen catchment. Forget the public health labs – government's always a pain. My lab could serve as many yardies as want drug analyses, make a killing.'

His throat dried. 'Many? Don't risk it, Julia. They use guns.'

She teased, 'Why so scared?'

'Suppose you test one bale as eighty percent pure, another bale thirty. And suppose one bale's from one yard, and the second's from a rival. They'd slang that you'd been nobbled to report wrong results.'

'You see, Clifford? You *can* do it!' She tutted. 'Jeremy's home at ten We'll do this again.'

And that was it, her dressing, frowning at her stockings for a run and ignoring him before the mirror. It was as if he had never been with her. He wondered how exactly he'd earned her praise.

*

The deserted mill held its silence, making up for years of endless noise, engines on the go, looms clashing. Jase liked mills. You could hear rats a mile off, floors vast as parks, iron pillars propping ceilings.

Earlier in the afternoon, Jase had gone to the scrap-metal yard beyond Market Street. He'd never seen such a mass of dross, old looms, gantries, fly-wheels galore, ball-jointed governors, cogs by the hundred.

The old man explained.

'You want to cut a cable that carries weight? Do distance, lad!'

Addin was an old mill engineer, lived for ancient craftsmanship, wasting his time everybody into computers, but Jase liked the daft owd git. Addin looked like a mobile walnut, cased in a rough leather apron and shod in pit clogs.

'Cut it first.' Addin gave Jase a great thing with double bolts and stubby blades.

'Here?'

'No, son.' Addin had learned patience for ignorance. 'Link the cable where you're going to cut first, see?'

'Link what with?'

'This.' A metal bar with clamps. 'Fasten it where you want to cut *before* you cut anything. Then fasten this rope to the *top*, move away a good twenty feet.'

'Then what?'

Addin sighed. In the mills from the age of nine, he couldn't understand how folk didn't know what it had taken him a lifetime to learn and now couldn't forget.

'Then when you pull on the rope, the cable will part.'

Jase still couldn't see. 'Why the rope?'

Addin had lived next door to Jase's auntie down Haleys Wharf when the city had been alive.

'Because, lad, a cable carrying weight will snap like a

whiplash, snake anywhere it wants. I've seen one cut a man's head off.' And before Jase could draw breath to ask, added, 'That's why it's a *long* rope, lad.'

Jase was humbled by all that knowledge. 'I'll bring the doings back when I've finished.'

'Don't,' Addin said, clumping in his great pit clogs back to his wooden shed. 'I'll list it as owffed.'

That hurt Jase. He'd known the old man ever since he could remember.

'Owffed, Addin? I'd never steal from you.'

'Aye, son,' Addin said over his shoulder. 'But others would.' He'd eyed Jase, hawked and spat. 'You awreet, son? You look poorly.'

'I'm fine, Addin, ta.' Two hundred, Jase gave him.

In the mill, he settled to work. He was ashamed, the exertion causing him to throw up twice. He ended up shivering, wondering what was the matter. Addin would have laughed. Old men like that were good, not carping, mildly amused at incompetence.

He got the clamp on the cable by the caged winding-pulley. The size of the hanging counterweight unnerved him, the cable so thick it seemed impossible to bend. In its day it had lifted mill workers and bales to the roof.

The clamps he fastened as Addin had showed him, then set to cutting through the cable. It took him two scary hours, the metal complaining. Done for, he had a sleep, woke in panic at seven, slept in relief for another hour, then had fish and chips from Edgworth Street gone cold in the newspaper. He spewed most of it up, probably all that exertion. His eyes felt puffy, sores all round his lips.

But they were coming, his false phone messages making

sure. He rigged the rope. Frightened by Addin's description of the lashing cable, he lay down as far as the rope would reach. He kept his loaded tubes beside him. You could never tell.

Coffee and Beaky Divine would be on time. He dozed, woke in alarm, dozed.

'Brothel?' Martina stared at Bonn. 'Are you out of your mind?'

Posser had been put to bed, arguing for another whisky. Martina had diluted his late-nighter, and Posser knew it. Bonn said why not ask Dr Winnwick, see if whisky mattered. Martina brusquely told him to mind his own business.

'It will solve the problem, Martina.'

'The problem, in case it slipped your notice, is my father.'

'Hence my suggestion. Buy two next doors, freehold.'

'Clients coming in and out?' she cut back.

'By arrangement, at a rate we determine.'

'With my father in the doorway as a male madam?'

'No. Here, a spare wheel, book-keeping, whatever.'

'And who will run this?'

'Trish can supervise a couple of shift nurses. And run the girls' rota.'

Women's beauty was enhanced by anger, ravished by worry, nullified by concern. By the fire, Martina's facial contours called for Gainsborough's painterly justice. Bonn thought her the prettiest woman alive. Waiting to speak the minute Posser had gone to bed, he felt her beauty to be a tangible thing.

She said with slow sarcasm, 'How will Saint Trish's natural talents enable her to run the girls?'

'Not street lasses, Martina,' he said patiently. 'Posser's carers. As reward, make her a part-time stringer in the working house.'

'We have no part-timers. They're always trouble. Look at those Middleton bitches. They riled every watch committee in the kingdom.'

A cluster of part-timers, taken on by an Ancoats syndicate, had pupped off no fewer than nine franchises between Middleton and Pendleton. There were still repercussions. Grellie had forewarned Martina. It had been a near and dangerous thing.

'This will be next door, Martina, and concern only one lass, with a legal job.'

'And will you be responsible?' Martina's voice went harsh.

'Yes,' Bonn said, calm. She was challenging him to mention Grellie. 'I don't know how to manage a working house, but I would try. Knock through on two floors.'

'Losing your room,' she said, sarcasm again.

Bonn smiled. 'Architects could devise a way.'

'My father, next door to a brothel?'

He said patiently, 'It's the very best plan.'

Martina watched the flames shine on the fire grate. 'I'll have your Trish in, give her the once-over with Connie.'

Connie, not Grellie? Still, Martina was boss, in a woman's world.

'I believe Posser will be really quite pleased,' he said. He took the chair opposite, the fire warm on his cheek.

'It's your responsibility,' she said, cold, and limped off to bed.

# 29

**Franchie** – to franchise illegally

'Dr Burtonall's called one of us back,' Windsor told Hassall. 'That desker Ramton, beer gut.'

Hassall was relieved. 'I knew I was fit.' Hassall couldn't wait to bell his missus. She'd been on at him, diet here, exercise there. She'd be suspicious, though, want the letter to check the doctor's very words. 'Come on. There's been a sighting.'

'The other shooter we wanted to see, Walsall, turned up on holiday in Rome.'

'Since when?' Hassall asked.

'Since before. His wife's doing a religious thing, him toping himself stupid in the trattoria. Leaving Jase.'

'Makes me wonder why the law bothers.'

Windsor looked his question.

'Herbal ecstasy's legally on sale. Contains that pseudo-ephedrine, ephedrine proper, and damn near every herb from Asia, South and Central America, and Africa. You can get it in biscuits, fags, printed labels and all. Makes me wonder. Doesn't it you?'

'Jase is in the city, Mr Hassall.' Windsor ignored meanders.

'Who saw him?'

'Two of his old mates. The scrap dealer isn't sure, though.'

'If it's Addin, he's a lying old sod. You go, there's a good chap.' Hassall shouted after Windsor, off like a hare, 'And check if the hospital's seen him.'

That left Hassall clean off in free time, to stir things.

Jase heard the lift go, just had time to unloop the rope. You needed to pull it the instant you wanted the cable to part, send them plunging when the lift was slowing. *Don't pull otherwise*. He struggled to control his cough, dried his sweating hands. Christ, he'd pissed himself while dozing, first time since a little lad. He felt really rough, but he'd a job on.

The lift-shaft interior was dark. He peered down, somebody shining a flashlight in the cage. The huge counterweight sank past his face. He spat on it for luck.

They were talking! He heard Coffee's quietish voice, Beaky Divine's insistence. And Noddo himself, three birds with one stone. Jase checked his tubes, in case luck wasn't along.

'I want it done quick,' Noddo was saying. 'Engine running, ma man.'

'Right, Noddo. You got it.'

Jase's lip curled. Like American gangster films, y'goddit, man, crapster talk. Shootouts, sheriffs closing. You'd think they'd frigging grow up. He seriously began to wonder if they were worth it, the effort he'd put in.

'Hush now. We here.'

The lift cage slowed. The clamp was almost opposite Jase's face, linking the metal cable across his cut.

He tip-trotted away over the bare boards. The pulley was almost still. Now? Yes, pull now.

The clamp lever flipped off like it was an elastic band, the cable parting with a great *twang*. Shouts rose. The cable vanished, the pulley like a missile slamming the suspension beam so hard it drove in. Something huge and solid crashed up through the flooring less than four paces away sending showers of splinters, Jase trying to scramble away. He could only think of that enormous counterweight coming after him.

Something whined, screamed, went shriller, but it was only machinery, until a single thump stopped all the malarkey, thank Christ. Dust set him choking, splinters firing around and cutting his face, from where for fuck's sake when it was done with?

A length of floorboards twisted inexplicably rising up like some giant was pushing it, slewed and fell with a crash. He bum-shuffled away, kicking his legs like an infant, dragging his tubes. The fucking rope had burned his hand. It stung like hell, bleeding, just what he needed. Old Addin ought to have told him things would happen that fast. The rope should have been a mile long.

Could he hear moaning? Were there other people in the mill? What the fuck, here this hour?

He made his way out, allowing himself loud relieving coughs now. The stairs were stone, quiet if you kept clear of the glass shards.

'Going down,' he said, a joke. There was no lift now.

The stairs seemed endless. By the bottom he was so exhausted, he could have slept. He'd used a hankie to stifle his coughs while waiting, but no use trying now. They'd have maybe a tube or two, but so? If they were still alive after falling that far, he'd seriously miscalculated. He was too tired to change things.

He came on them. Well, it didn't take a genius. Pull the plug when they were up high, it was all fall down. They showed in his flashlight, blood everywhere, them sprawled like dolls. They'd have been ashamed if they'd known how stupid they seemed, dead like that. Funny both ways, haha *and* odd.

Noddo looked daftest, one eye crushed under a corner of metal, the other staring. Beaky Divine was worst. He was kneeling, the cage roof folding him like paper, head back almost touching his arse. Coffee's chest was opened so all sorts of gruesome things showed, red, purply, really naff. Jase thought it disgusting, made you ashamed you were made of the same stuff.

Finding the clamp, lever, cutters, and chucking them over Addin's wall was out. He took his tubes and walked out of the mill.

Their motor was there. Jase was tempted. Why walk all that way back into the centre when he was so weary, this terrible chest he couldn't shake? Except it was Noddo's game to have somebody close by in case.

No. Safer, not easier, to climb the mill wall and walk. Let Robar and the others scrap over who was boss. It had been a success.

Only Dr Burtonall left now, and he could go south, have a rest. He deserved it bad.

'I have made a suggestion, Posser,' Bonn said.

'Oh, you have, have you?'

Breakfast had ended, things cleared away and Mrs

Houchin clattering pots in the kitchen. Martina gave a glance, and Bonn closed the door.

Posser smiled bravely. 'You're up to something, our Martina.'

She quietly told him about Bonn's proposal. He listened, looking from one to the other, weighing it.

The window was open, unusual because traffic noise could rebound from the terraces opposite. But today was Sunday, the city quiet. Bonn had already been to church. The curtains blew gently, air refreshing the room. Bonn thought it as pleasant as life could ever be.

'Me on the scrap?' Posser's joke.

'No. You will do the tally, Dad, like Bonn says, if you want.'

Bonn started when Martina looked to him for support. 'It won't be the sinecure it seems, Posser. The difference is, it is on your doorstep.'

'Can the houses be knocked through? City ordinances.'

'They can be got round, Posser.'

'Aye, that's true as death. When?'

'I'm seeing this Trish – somebody Bonn happened on – with Connie today. She's a bit older, a starter, no idea yet. Bonn's keen.'

Bonn did not rise to her taunt. If only Martina didn't flail about.

'Friend of yours, Bonn?' Posser asked, eyes twinkling.

'No, Posser.' That was enough.

'How come, then?'

Bonn explained how he'd been forced in on the pickings, and called Trish back.

'I'm advised,' Martina put in icily, 'that this Trish is preferable to our own girls.'

'Carol'd do it brilliantly, from the Café Phryne,' Posser said directly to Bonn.

'You need a family woman to supervise you, Posser. All Grellie's lasses would love the promotion. But could they take care of you while learning the working house?' Martina made to interject, but Bonn asked if he could speak on. 'The need stems from you, Posser, not the girls or the goers. Forgive my bluntness.'

'That's telling me,' Posser said, trying not to laugh but setting himself off all the same.

Martina glared, but he saw the time had come for frankness. Posser was no fool.

'Your wisdom is valuable, Posser,' he said candidly. 'A nursing home would be a waste of resource, that being you. Therefore you ought to stay, fulfil an agency duty here.'

'Is he telling the truth, love?' Posser asked Martina.

'Yes, Dad.'

'How soon does all this happen?'

'We saw nursing homes,' Bonn told him bluntly. 'I propose that the agency buys both next doors, urgently. Start Trish off in one while adapting the other. Take on nurses but let Trish be in on it. Martina has veto.'

'And the working house?'

Bonn looked his apology at father and daughter.

'I'm sorry,' he said, 'but how on earth can I know?'

They let him go then, Martina accompanying him to the door, and instructing out of Posser's hearing. 'I don't want this getting out.'

He was surprised she even doubted. 'Of course not.'

'And you take no part in running the working house.' She saw how taken aback he was. 'And your Trish lives elsewhere.'

'Whatever, Martina.'

'I shall send for Grellie after Connie's been over. Rack is already on his way.'

'I believe there is no reason to worry, Martina.'

'I'm not worried.' She didn't quite slam the door, but came close.

Posser was waiting for her, having to prop himself up to give his chest enough play. 'Well?' he got out. 'Is this what you want, luv?'

'Is it what you want, Dad?'

'It'll do. It's the best, for me at any rate.'

'Do you mean me?' she asked, stung.

'What is it? You're worried Bonn's getting drawn by some other bird?'

She went to the door to see that Mrs Houchin really had gone upstairs to do the beds.

'Today, Bonn has one go. It's with that Clare Three-Nine-Five woman. She's become a regular upper, only him. She's the doctor who's married to that investor services man Burtonall, in George Street. He once wanted to broker a takeover of the agency. Remember?'

He got her to bring him his glyceryl trinitrates, shoved a white tablet under his tongue. 'It got quelled.'

'Bonn did well, yes. But I don't want this Clare on the scene.' She wondered how much to admit. 'I listen in on her bookings.'

'Then get rid.'

She looked at him, startled. 'What, Dad?'

'Not that,' he said impatiently. 'I mean neutralize her.'

'Neutralize? Get her shifted from the city? But—'

He made a cross gesture, shut up for what breath he had.

'I've sussed her too. She did locums in GP surgeries and

hospital units, does some heart survey, men in work. Short term.'

Martina marvelled that he'd been so percipient. 'I think she lives in the Wirral,' she added weakly, her only news.

'No children yet. Doctoring's just what she does.'

'Dedicated,' Martina observed caustically.

'So take her on.'

'*What?*'

'We've never had a doctor, just sent the goers for medical checks. Grellie runs the Card, medicals for the street girls.'

Martina was astonished. 'Can we do that? Just go out and hire a doctor?'

'Martina,' he said carefully, 'we're setting up a brothel. How many girls, twenty-five? Surely you can write a letter of appointment?'

'But that will mean . . .' Martina's cheeks reddened. 'Meeting Dr Burtonall.'

'Correct,' her father said drily. 'And it certainly won't be me. Any chance of a coffee?'

'No. You had two cups at breakfast. I saw you.'

'I'll be bloody glad when this Trish takes over,' Posser wheezed as she pushed his cushions into some sort of order. 'I'll stand a better bloody chance.'

'Mind your language.'

'You're beginning to sound like Bonn. I've been meaning to warn you.'

'That will do from you.' She called Mrs Houchin. 'It's time for your rest.'

# 30

**Ploddite** – a policeman

THE WORD HIT the papers. Bonn heard from Rack, who had Askey the messenger digging before the story came out.

'Seems Jase did the snip in the old Ramsden Mill, Bonn,' Askey reported. 'Noddo and two yardies. That Fluella's in hospital, attempted suicide, but she does that.' Askey waxed indignant, his sister laid up and Fluella, fit as a flea, making herself poorly for nothing.

'Robar's taking over, Bonn. Some say it was him got it done.'

'God rest them. I thought Jase was a gunman.'

'Aye. He did the Janesons. His girl was that lass who died, the telly?'

'Askey. Please listen out, for where Jase is.'

'Right, Bonn. Oh, my sister sends love.'

Bonn wondered, watching the diminutive figure scoot back among the couriers loafing outside the Triple Racer, where that left Dr Burtonall. More vulnerable.

The obvious, as Martina thought it, was that Dr Burtonall would no longer be able to use the agency, once she became the goers' doctor. She'd been so slow to see it. The implications came to her while having coffee with the architects, Snape, Breenon, Fazackerley. She'd drawn the uncontrollable Vincent Fazackerley, and his old dad.

'I've had more brawls with draughtsmen than anyone,' he lectured her proudly. 'My father says that, who founded us.'

'Your logo says Founded 1708,' the girl behind Martina said.

'Oh, we bought Snape out in 1826,' young Vincent said.

He was boisterously suited in pinstripes, had violent hair. Martina felt definitely attracted. Posser was too unwell to attend, but she was going to buy number eleven and number fifteen.

'Miss Martina knows that, Vin,' the old Fazackerley said. 'The freehold—'

'Dad,' Vincent said, rushing to serve more coffee ahead of his secretaries, who rolled their eyes in exasperation. 'I'm dealing with it, okay? Miss Martina wants it done today – right?'

'Miss Martina wants speed.'

The girl sitting behind Martina rustled no papers, sharpened no pencils. Lavinia served as Martina's pretend secretary. She knew little but could transcribe and had a phenomenal memory. Grellie farmed out two lady clients weekly to Lavinia, whose value as an AC-DC working girl kept her tied to Grellie, which was Martina's instruction. Lavinia was sensible. Her peculiar proclivity, Martina said bluntly, was her own business, as long as she fronted well.

'Fine, fine! Purchase guaranteed in an hour, surveys done in two!'

Lavinia was unmoved by boyish exuberance. 'Then

where is the contract?' She spoke over Vincent's voluble response. 'It could have been finalized while Miss Martina was journeying here.'

Journeying, Martina thought, Lavinia earning her crust. The architects' office was only three hundred yards away.

'Look, we've got absolutely no doubt—'

'Please.' Archibald, Vincent's father, interrupted. 'This is binding. We guarantee that numbers eleven and fifteen will be purchased and surveyed in two hours.'

Lavinia asked, 'Which is the better?'

Vincent couldn't resist blundering in. 'For what purpose?'

'For Miss Martina's purposes,' Lavinia said, cold. 'Which?'

'Number eleven,' the elder architect said firmly. 'I know the building.'

'Fine. Have it ready for use seven days from now.'

'Very well. Will Miss Martina specify structural alterations?'

'They are ready.' Lavinia enjoyed displeasure.

'Hold on there!' Vincent waved his hands as if slowing a runaway. 'There's things to consider—'

Archibald Fazackerley advanced smiling to take Martina's hand.

'Thank you for choosing us. We shall be expeditious.'

Martina said her goodbyes while the younger architect spluttered. In the motor, she sat as Lavinia fussed.

'Thank you, Martina. Did you *see* that *ape*?'

'You did well. Now get on with it. Bye.'

Lavinia flushed at Martina's rebuke and quickly closed the car door.

'George Street,' Martina commanded her driver, curt. She was on edge, having this Clare Three-Nine-Five thing.

She looked out of the dark-tinted windows as the saloon car drove two miles out of the city before heading back. It returned south of Greygate where the Phoenix Theatre stood in Bridgewater Street. It was virtually a back alley. A disused half an acre of pressed cinders, had a forlorn old guardian smoking in a wooden Charlie hut. Martina's saloon reversed and let her out. No pedestrians.

Martina judged she was not seen. A few hobbled paces to the narrow ginnel. Across the car park was the blank wall of the Phoenix Theatre. She limped down the thoroughfare, unlocked the door, switched on the light, and sat at her desk.

Posser had seen it all coming, this Clare problem. Did men talk over their loves? Instinctively she knew that men didn't. Possibly teenage bragging of improbable seductions, but men as men? No.

Therefore Bonn had said nothing to Posser about being attracted to this Clare beyond the call of, what, duty. She felt instinct warn her that Bonn gave this Dr Burtonall far more consideration than, say, that broadcaster Rita Seven-Two-Five. Nothing new. Women often did feel for a goer, convincing themselves they were in a 'relationship' – hateful word. There'd been a homer – Pixie Four-Five-Something, was she? – who'd tried posting envelopes of money to him, until Martina had put a stop to it, used Akker to straighten the woman.

No, women liked Bonn, came back for more. She could cope with that, the agency's proper business when all was said and done. This Dr Burtonall, though, had to be stopped.

In the circumstances, Posser's advice was wise. Use Clare Three-Nine-Five's own doctoral chains to bind her, and do it soon. You could wait too long. Her dad had told her, 'Passion is dangerous stuff. It risks the love that creates it,' so perceptive. She should have asked him how to cope with Bonn a long time ago. Maybe she thought she had, and hadn't?

Old Osmund entered after a knock. 'Hello, luv.'

'I want a company secretary and a lawyer, not our own, today.'

'Right.' He hesitated. 'Martina. Is this waistcoat too bright? Only, Toothie and Beppo've been ribbing me.'

'No, Osmund. It is perfectly acceptable.'

'Thanks, chuck.' He left in relief.

His waistcoats had not varied in years, black silk, back-strap and black buckle. Today's waistcoat had faint grey piping, hardly noticeable. The old man was being joshed, but in the way of those with unchanging lives was unable to shake the suspicion of some lurking truth in there.

Like, she compared bitterly, a lame girl who on a whim stupidly fancied the garrulous Vincent Fazackerley, who fancied himself more than he ever would anyone else. She had almost let him shut out thoughts of Bonn. Bonn, with his absurd apologetic smile that never quite got there, whose books – she'd visited his bare cell-like room when he was out – were a strange self-effacing admix of thrillers and ancient religious themes.

Osmund returned with two names and phone numbers. Martina told him she wanted a secretary, not Lavinia, in thirty minutes, mobile phones. By the time Osmund had carried out those intructions, Martina noticed, he had changed back into his older waistcoat, no decorative grey at all.

The boxing booth only came alive at dusk when the fair-ground lights, raucous clamour and the crowds made it.

Jase had worked a fair once, lasted a fortnight because of a shag-nasty. There, Jase first experienced pollen, learnt to get max from least.

Now he knew the answers to most things. Like, where do you hide a bloke? In a crowd. Where do you hide if you'd no place to go? Answer: in a fairground.

Life was opposites. Poor Marie had done more than just light his pipe. She'd even gone on the game for him, got him winnings. Not many birds'd keep the faith, scratch satch for her bloke. He had to do this for her, before he lit out south.

So far he'd done brilliantly. Now, he just had to be careful, his tubes an embarrassment. No yardies left, so why did he need them? For the woman doctor, that's what. He'd agreed to meet Barley after the interval bouts. Maximum crowd, minimum plod.

The ring inside was raised. People stood about on ordinary cinder, ramjam packed between gaudy canvas walls. Garish bulbs lit the ring. A hooded man leant casually on the ropes, staring from holes in his black hood. He wore a tight one-piecer.

No sign of Barley. The referee was yelling promises to anybody willing to take on Black O'Vengeance for a mint.

'Pay nowt and win a hundred!' he kept booming through a whistling mike. 'One swing, you've earnt yoursels a fortune!'

A man, egged on by his pals, got shoved forward, women oohing and aahing. All right for them, Jase thought, they wouldn't get kicked silly like him, first round, no messing.

'Give this challenger a big hand, ladies and gen'lmen!'

'Challenger?' Somebody nudged Jase. 'I've shot 'em. Not a chance.'

'I reckon he'll do the business,' Jase told Barley.

People around were taking bets, sizing the champion.

Barley was stout, thirties, what they called a straw man, who provided false alibis. But affluent days were gone. A straw man had to be sound of memory, and drink had taken Barley. Now he did the bins for hotel rubbish, losing luggage on airport nights.

'Wait till they start, lad,' he told Jase in scorn.

'Him? Against that hooded bloke?' Jase laughed, not too much.

'He won't last a round. I'd bet a quid.'

'Evens?' Jase taunted. 'That what you're asking, evens?'

'Give us three to one, and you're on for a hundred.'

They settled for that, Jase laughing inwardly at the ease of it. The so-called champion kneed the challenger in the groin and beat him senseless. There was a near riot, the crowd angry their man had been unfairly defeated, the referee screaming invented rules as Jase and Barley pushed outside. In the glittering night they stopped behind the rollercoaster, where Jase paid Barley.

'All in twenties, Barley. Where?'

'The lass died like they said. District General Hospital. AIDS, it was. The doctor was Dr Clare Burtonall. She's an upper.'

Jase stared in the gloaming. 'An upper? She buys shags?'

'Word is. Drives an old maroon Humber Supersnipe, know the sort? They say youngish, smart. Bonny herself.'

'What the fuck's she playing at?'

'Don't ask me.' Barley felt narked. 'Look, I've done a good job.'

'Where's she tek him?' This was the only question left.

Barley sniggered, chance of a joke, but this young bloke was a right loon, tube man for yardies, so Barley wasn't going to crosstalk. Also, this druggo was on his last legs, sick as a parrot. Too many youngsters lost it, on the sharp end. It was beyond him. Cunt and booze was good enough ruin.

'The Hotel Vivante mostly, but the problem is when.'

'How do they book?'

'Goers? Don't know. They're a close lot of buggers.'

'Don't they go in groups?'

'Aye, firms of three or four, under a key. The phone number's in the book, the Pleases Agency, Inc. It's Posser's, so go very careful.'

Barley was uncomfortable. He didn't want this feverish tuber flying off the handle. He looked frantic enough to tube you for nowt. And unless Barley mistook the lad's posture, he was already tooled, dee-bee down his trouser leg. They thought themselves in-fucking-visible.

'Do you deserve my money, Barley?' Jase asked, ice. A score of chanting hoolies swung on the ride's canvas so it ripped and bawling gangers came running.

Barley went for it, gave Jase everything.

'A bloke in the Vivante kitchens gets me jobs. I pay him in greyhound tips from Burnden.'

'Who?' The city lived on these compact arrangements.

'Ask for Vol, kitchen side door.'

'Okay, Barley.' Jase prevented the bigger man leaving. 'Not a word.'

'Aye, Jase. Ta. I appreciate it. Have you time for a drink, celebrate?'

That saved him, because Jase changed his mind. He didn't trust Barley. Too much worry in the man, anxiety to be gone. To phone somebody? But now Jase saw Barley the wino was only keen to be off and get sloshed.

'No, ta, Barley. Have it on me.'

Barley left, the wadge in his pocket. Repercussions if

word got out, so Vol would have to look out for himself. Barley didn't like things heavy, but what could you do when a tube crazo makes rules? It was money or suffering. Was that a choice?

He got a taxi, rolled into the city in style. He'd have a drink in the Volunteer, then if he had time he might give Vol a ring. Or not? He felt really great, new lasses in Waterloo Street. He felt owed, long deprived of pleasure for lack of gelt. There'd be time for phoning later, when he'd had a few, knew what to say.

# 31

**Grass** – an informer to police (from 'Whispering Grass', a song made popular by the Ink Spots)

THE TEMP SECRETARY did unexpectedly well. Margaret was an older woman, majored in taciturn, impeccable. Martina was pleased.

Dr Burtonall was contacted through the local medical society, and the nature of the contract briefly outlined. The meeting convened that evening in the Weavers Hall.

The Hall epitomized the city in Victorian times. With luxurious banqueting rooms, its club was a cut above others. Its hotel was restricted to thirty guests. Panelled withdrawing rooms for members overlooked its shopping mall, posher than the busier Deansgate. Balconies rimmed by ornate ironwork ran around the central well above the tea lounge. Glazebrook, a tubby fair-haired man, was on retainer from Posser, which was all Glazie would ever get.

'Dr Burtonall will be here presently, Miss Martina,' Margaret announced. 'To meet the company gentlemen.'

'I shan't want them until the contract is settled, Margaret.'

Two of the three company men were elderly. Paradoxically, the younger was the principal. Martina knew that Posser had employed the oldest man years before. By the time Dr Burtonall was ushered in, Margaret had them placed at the mahogany table, Martina at the head. Stagey, but right.

With difficulty Martina avoided inspecting Clare Three-Nine-Five. She represented herself as deputizing for her father, unfortunately indisposed.

'You know, Dr Burtonall, that we need a sessional doctor to perform medical examinations for a registered charity. Our funds are adequate. Please ask questions.'

Clare was startled, glanced at the three gentlemen.

'That brusque? Might I ask what is the patient pool?'

'Socially disadvantaged in the city centre, Dr Burtonall. Male to female ratio one to eight. You would be given a new surgery.'

Clare considered. 'Would that be . . . ?'

'You would be your own principal. Forty patients a month. You would guide us.'

'What is the charity exactly?'

Martina said gravely, eyes on her blank paper, 'You must be aware of the controversy surrounding charities. The Lord Chancellor's problems with the Charities Act, governmental wrangling. Our funding is anonymous. These gentlemen are eminent legal authorities.'

'How have you managed until now?'

'Piecemeal, doctor.' Martina allowed her gaze to touch Clare, judging that enough had been said to establish credentials. She was desperate to have the woman pose on some catwalk for detailed scrutiny. 'The socially disadvantaged are down to the Directorate of Health and Social Services. But we take a wide moral stance. We believe it is time for the more fortunately placed to improve the lot of these unfortunate young.'

'They are drug addicts, then?'

'Some,' Martina said smoothly. 'You will have full medical control. Your cardiac surveillance—'

Clare eyed the blonde girl. 'This is rather out of the blue. I'll be frank, Miss Martina, I came from curiosity. You know about me, while I know little about your charity.'

'Our sources are your current and past employers, the General Medical Register, the research papers cited in the Index Medicus. We also enquired about your husband, a prominent developer.'

'You have been very thorough.'

'We don't want a doctor who might leave after a week. Establishing a GP surgery in a busy city will be costly. Your participation would contribute to the city's recovery. Remuneration would of course reflect responsibility. You would not be disappointed.'

'It's very tempting,' Clare said, trying to put the offer in context.

'Start whenever you can. "Start" meaning establishing your office and surgery, buying the instrumentation you need. We want it functioning within a calendar month.'

'Would there be an escape clause?'

'Escape.' Martina savoured the word a moment. 'You can give a week's notice in the first month. Our charity will have no such option.'

'I could withdraw, but your charity could not?'

'You have two hours to decide, doctor.'

'Two *hours*?' Clare stared. 'I need to see—'

'Dr Porritt? A fulltime doctor for your cardiac survey programme would be subsidized by the charity, effective Sunday.'

'Fulltime?' Clare said. She was on sessional part-time. 'By leaving the hospital's heart survey, I will be doing them a favour? A part-time doctor replaced by fulltime?'

'Yes.'

'Were I to take it on, I would need laboratory support. Microbiology, serology, immunochemistry, haematology are notoriously costly.'

Martina said calmly, 'We can run to the expense.'

'I know a private laboratory that might undertake the work,' Clare said. 'Pickard of Droylsden.'

'Then the problem is already less, doctor.'

'Why me?' Clare asked. 'There are many other doctors.'

'Once our charity has firm recommendations, we go ahead immediately.'

'Are other doctors involved?'

'No. You will be autonomous.'

Clare asked about the nature of the work. Martina described some itinerants, drug addicts, plus various undetermined categories. The medical work would be paid for on a fee-for-service basis on a generous retainer. Dr Burtonall could publish medical papers unhindered.

At the conclusion of the interview, Clare retired to speak with the contract lawyers. Martina sat a moment, then told Margaret to make tea. The moment she was alone, she rang Posser on the mobile.

'Dad?' she said quietly. 'It's go. I'm certain of it. Set up a charity.'

Posser's wheezy chuckle gravelled into her ear. 'I'll call it something better than Pleases Agency.'

'Have her computers hacked into.'

'Any problems?'

'One thing.' Martina thought over Clare's words. 'She mentioned some laboratory. I want it gone over. Pickard, in Droylsden.'

'I'll see to it. Did old Patterson show? He's sound as a bell.'

'Yes. He nodded off at one point. Must they always be old?'

Posser was croaking laughing as she put the phone away and waited impatiently for Dr Burtonall to return. She watched the doctor walk smilingly in through the double doors, finally registering, so this is Clare Three-Nine-Five, is it? Attractive, level stare, decent figure, poisonously good legs, the bitch who hired Bonn far too often. Martina composed herself.

'I hope,' she said innocently, 'your decision is in our favour, doctor?'

Not without concern, Clare was to see Bonn at nine. The charity idea definitely appealed. Clifford's city project had taken off, and government funds had stockpiled. The newspapers were full of it, and twice Clifford had been in the *City Journal* and *Guardian* colour supplements, fame and wealth together. No problems there. But, Bonn. And Jase.

She went to have a moment's quiet in the entrance hall of the Textile Museum. In the very heart of the city, she would provide a GP surgery. Marvellous that there were charitable people, silently funding such projects. Anyone disadvantaged, homeless, lost. It warmed Clare just to think of the good she could do.

Advise the indigent, checking the health of the children *before* their vulnerabilities became illness. She might even help the blatant prostitutes in Waterloo Street, anyone.

Miss Martina had been right to say that Dr Porritt would not be at all put out, his part-time doctor being replaced by a fulltimer. Clare felt a twinge of regret. She had set up the whole project. Now somebody else would take over the second phase. Still, wasn't that medicine all over? Do your best, then move on to the next need?

And she was definitely needed here, in the city she had made her own.

That Miss Martina, though. Was there something odd? That super-efficient Margaret had been almost insultingly taciturn, yet desperately eager to please the wary young blonde. The gentlemen had been grovellingly deferential. Who *was* she? Was her charity some inherited fortune, she the darling daughter of a doting father of imponderable wealth? Or was she one of these enviable adamantine women who took financial worlds by storm? Her accent, faintly there, was local. Local but unknown, this Miss Martina.

Could Miss Martina be fronting for some organization concealed by its constitution? There were such clubs, Clare knew, women and men. Clifford belonged to some – mention the good you do, you got drummed out of the Brownies, all charity to be secret.

Perhaps it was Miss Martina's look? There was something penetrating in the girl's gaze, at once opaque yet laser-like. Still, she would need to inspect the doctor her charity was taking on. The gentlemen were *bona fide*.

Clare liked the whole thing. Dr Porritt knew, when she finally called him. She pulled his leg, playfully accusing him of wanting to get rid of her now she'd done all the donkey work.

She had three hours to kill before Bonn. For a second she panicked, thinking she had mislaid the Hotel Vivante room number, but found it in her notebook. She would have hated phoning that agency voice to make sure. Her heart lifted. Bonn lived here, *was* her city. Forget her stupid tantrum, as Bonn seemed to have done, and take what was on offer. They would be partners, of a kind.

She remembered the girl's stare – accusatory, or merely hard to understand? Maybe she would get to know her, something to look forward to. They might become friends, even.

What a momentous day! She might tell Bonn, though he evaded confidences, asked her not to make revelations. Surely this was exceptional?

Today felt her day, something wonderful on the horizon.

Vol spent the whole supper hour finding out details. Easy, once you knew where to look. Short bookings were in a special log by the registration desk, and Vol could bribe for that, no problem. The difficulty was, a woman might use any name. The Pleases Agency, Inc. was a reserved code.

He broke through by paying the money Jase gave him, the fucking *lot*, to the comi chef, who was on his uppers from horses same as everybody else in hotel kitchens. The comi was thick with the manager, who did him favours. The Pleases Agency had booked four rooms over the next twenty-four hours. When Vol saw Rack joking his progress through the staff sitting rooms, Vol guessed the fifth-floor reservation was for Bonn. Bonn was famous, who never said boo to a goose, was polite like it was a sickness, girls talking of him in whispers.

Vol told Jase his news in the side alley, pretending to be out for a smoke. Vol'd had to pay a tenner for the comi chef's mobile phone to raise Jase at the Volunteer. Jase paid Vol just enough, which narked Vol. Jase looked fucking dying.

Back in the kitchen Vol seethed. All risk, no profit was

insulting, real diss. And got ballocked by the sous-chef for loitering, Vol's day on the stock pot. Grievance grew, but what could he do? Barley was a juggo who'd kick Vol silly, step out of line, and Jase was a tube hooligan. People like himself lived pig in the middle. Do as you're told, get sod all.

It made him morose enough to bubble Barley, serve the stingy bastard right. But he'd do it round about, stay clean. He'd see Rack heard of Jase's interest.

# 32

**Dooze** – a yobbo, tearaway, troublesome rapscallion

The new halfie called May caught Bonn outside the Volunteer, not her patch and sure to get reported for it but she didn't care.

'Bonn? I walk along?'

'Good evening, May. Please do. I trust you are well.'

Bonn worried. May was the tall one who was going to get herself pasted by the diminutive Connie, now front runner for Grellie's deputy. He hadn't heard the details. The Waterloo Street lasses seemed to see him as an intercessor.

She said outright, 'Fuck it, Bonn. Sorry, sorry. I mean I dunno what, when youse talk like tha', straight I done. Say, How yer doin', May, I know where I is.'

'I'm a poor conversationalist. I apologize.'

'See?' she said, riled. 'I *steel* dunno!'

They waited for the lights at Bolgate Street. To the left, Bonn could see the Triple Racer couriers talking in the light from the newsagent's. Ahead, a cluster of exotic males moved, posturing, towards the Rum Romeo. They grouped close as they passed the Butty Bar. There was often trouble. Why? Bonn could never fathom.

'But I forgeeve you, hone.'

May collapsed with laughter. The last shoppers were

leaving, Deansgate proprietors locking up and heading, also grouped, to the bank night-safes on Manchester Road. Bonn reddened at May's joshing. She sobered, looking about for girls who'd report her walking with Bonn. Cecile had warned her, Grellie was all eyes for Bonn.

'Listen, Bonn. I'm friend with the Forester Dep stores man.'

'Oh.' He didn't know what that was.

'The chain of hotels, y'know? Vivante?'

So many questions were inexact, Bonn observed. Was that the reason he only ever asked questions of himself, where he was safe from the answers?

'I suppose you're allowed.' See? He couldn't even ask that outright.

'I heared something. Asking after you, and the agency? They call him Vol. Skivvy, fetch 'n' slop, he. Sells news.'

'It would be good were you able to discover more, May.'

'Vol sussed the agency code. My friend heard Vol giving it to some thin bloke in the back entry.'

'Thank you, May. You've done well. You could have told Rack.'

'I want a favour. Rack give no favours. And what'd Grellie say when Rack does ax her favours except piss off? You'd do it, the girls all say.'

'Thank you.' Bonn was uneasy, what was coming.

'My friend, he's halfie but Bermuda, y'know? From Wigan, footballer but never got there. Well, he wants on your list, y'know, be goer?' She looked abashed as three lads in a passing car leaned out, whistling. 'Sorry 'bout that, Bonn. Mountbatten, you call him County.'

'May, I can't promise, because I keep no lists. However, I shall see him.'

'Ta, Bonn. I appreciate it.' She waited for him to ask

more. 'That Vol told the lad a room number, fifth floor, nine o'clock.'

'Lad, May,' Bonn said, thinking. 'Before, you said bloke.'

'Say, twenny two-three. He couldn't see.'

'Thank you. County Mountbatten in the next two days, please.'

'He'll be there, Bonn. Now, 'less you want to hold ma hand . . . ?'

She left, mischievously swinging her body when she saw him looking after.

He went slower along the pavement towards the Hotel Vivante. Room 571. Clare Three-Nine-Five would be there at nine.

The old Humber had had its day. Not the motor's fault. Only one scrape, from the Farnworth General car park.

'It's going so well, poor thing,' she told Paul Porritt as he walked her down. 'Everything comes to an end.'

'Like your appointment.'

'You gain a fulltimer, Paul. The NHS will send you a turkey at Christmas.'

'Without you we'd never have got it off the ground.'

'Not true, Paul.' She faced him, collar up against the chill breeze. 'You'd have spread yourself thinner. I just helped out.'

'You've opportunities now, eh? Draw the prostitutes in.'

She mocked herself. 'Dedication! Money *and* morality!'

'You'll do more good than the rest of us put together, Clare.'

'Now you're being gross.' She bussed him and said her thanks.

'Can we drop in, see how rich doctors live?'

'Any time. Gin and tonic by my swimming pool.'

'Just don't pinch our nurses.' He opened the car door for her.

'Guilty as charged, Paul. I'll give you a ring once I've got going.'

She gunned the engine. She saw him in the driving mirror. He waved, and walked up the ramp into Casualty.

She turned right into the traffic, not much this time of an evening, the juggernauts gone to rest. Odd thing for Paul to say, or was it? Prostitutes. If some came, she would hope they'd spread the word.

Plenty of time, the journey a mere unhindered twenty minutes. Bonn would already be on his way.

Her body filled in expectation, her past annoyance with him evaporating. Did Bonn feel the same subdued excitement? Was it different for a man, for Bonn, hired to love women on command? Or did he reserve his true feelings for a selected client, perhaps herself, and towards the rest only acted? Yet Bonn *was* as he seemed. That poem, what was it, *be* being the ending of *seem*? Bonn was beyond 'seem'.

Could it come to the end of pretence for them both?

She tutted as a car cut in sharply, and slowed to keep her distance. For the whilst, she would remain as she had the night she'd first hired him for sex. The payment had been difficult. God, how she'd worried over that.

Emotionally, she must stay aloof. The only other way was love, which might prove fatal. Bonn had indicated as much. Her marriage was troubled, she herself not exactly obeying her vows. And with Bonn's job – keep it as that – love was out. Dalliance, the old word, would have to suffice.

The lights of Victoria Square were already gleaming in the rain as she reached the city, cars swishing round, a bus loading up by the Granadee Studios, the last tourist package of the day for the wonders of TV soaps.

She was on time.

Suite 571 was too large, Bonn thought, but it was too late to change. He readied tea, coffee, juices.

The bed was freshly aired. The flower vase he moved into the sitting room because he disliked that particular Royal Doulton design, let it lurk by the curtains in case Clare took pity on the freesias. He opened the quarter-light because heating was always a problem, women preferring it warmer, but that was only gender. Hotels cunningly knew this, but so far had eschewed those great downward blasts of hot air.

Ready? Clare last time had mentioned the female contraceptive, wanted to discuss how people responded. Was sex noise a complaint? she'd asked him, or lubrication? The *British Medical Journal* had gone on about those lately. As ever, he'd tried hard to remain at a distance and had changed the subject, which amused her.

He would have sat on the couch but had the idea – from where, for heaven's sake? – that an impression left on cushions would somehow seem slovenly. Instinct? Did a woman, seeing a dent in a sofa, think, God above, I've entered a zoo?

Unknowable. He shelved the problem. Odd how these theorems came to mind. He had little contact with the other keys, so no way of discovering the evolution of the goer trade. That 'trade' word again, that had caused, who was she, Rita the broadcaster, such unease. Did it imply the craftsmanship of an artisan? Curiously, he believed that other goers would be silent on this, and that the real source of opinion would be Grellie's stringers. It wasn't the girls' loquacity, more likely that they'd face up to their thoughts. A nice problem in semantics. Once he had been shocked to see Rack send no fewer than three honchos to separate a street scrap between Grellie's lasses – one girl, jealous of another's promotion, had openly called her a whore. It had been truly terrible, two sackings resulting. Martina had fined the whole blue string. Grellie too had suffered, been docked day money, mutterings going on for days afterwards.

Soon, he would speak with Grellie; answers might lie in her deep core. He would particularly like to ask why euphemisms, why on earth *did* folk, women particularly, want to prettify any mention of sexual congress, intercourse, the maulings, frigging, the rest? It was an ancient taboo. Ancient World philosophers had condemned their young who, intellectuals all, had defiantly copulated in the streets in the name of freedom. Hadn't there been, in Georgian Society days, furniture specially made for undetectable groping?

Grellie was a different problem. He felt drawn to her. Attractive, innately beautiful, in control of the stringers. Grellie had real power, could punish girls who transgressed, by calling on Rack. The girls stayed in line or else. They could appeal to Martina, of course, but Martina was a stickler for discipline and several times had imposed a worse sanction.

The no-crossing rule kept goers and stringers apart. Galahad and Danielle had crossed and look what happened, accident or no accident. Bonn knew the risk Grellie was taking hoping that he would accept her. *Could* it be secret?

He liked, even wanted, Grellie, in a different way than he wanted Martina. Both drew him. Martina carried the whole responsibility, Posser fading as he was.

The door. A knock, two gentle taps. This was the moment. He swallowed and went to the door. As he opened it somebody pushed in, shoving him back.

The intruder was not tall, but looked exhausted and sick. He had a crust of sores round his lips. One eye ran with sticky yellow glutinous tears. He stood skewed, like a bad actor trying to seem lame, and coughed with a dry hacking sound.

Bonn smiled, extended a hand, and grasped the other's right.

'Hello. You must be Jase.'

'What?' Jase looked about. He looked feverish.

'Ta for what you did, Jase. You did a great job.'

'Job? Who the fuck? Where's the woman?'

'Been expecting you,' Bonn said with what nonchalance he could. 'I've got your money.'

Jase twitched his left arm. Here it came, Bonn thought. He went cold. His grin felt plastered, the silly welcome ritual Rack had made him memorize.

'Have a drink, Jase. You look worn out. The money's over there. There's Newcastle Brown, or lager.'

'What the fuck *is* this? You're Bonn, right?'

'That's me, Jase.' Bonn went to the fridge, Jase moving swiftly aside to watch. 'Magee Pale is rotten stuff. Newcastle, I suppose. Cheers.'

He removed a tin of beer and pulled the ring seal. It hissed, frothed. Jase took it doubtfully, stepping away instantly.

'Where's that doctor bitch?'

'Oh, her. Due any sec. Have a sit.'

Bonn pulled the seal ring on a Magee's and sat in the armchair. Jase took the room's centre, edgy, glancing. All the interior doors were ajar. Jase checked that nobody lurked behind the couch and sat.

'You tell me what the fuck this is, Bonn.'

'You did Noddo, Jase.' Bonn toasted him. 'You did everybody a favour there, pal.'

He wondered if his slang sounded convincing. It didn't to himself.

'Favour? Who for?'

'Noddo had rivals.' Bonn remembered that his speech had to be peppered with questions, and added, 'Am I right?' Of course it all sounded wrong. Should he revert? But he had explicit instructions. 'I'm the bloke who passes money. Do the job, you get the gelt. It's on that stand.'

'Where?'

'That flower thing.' Bonn indicated the corner. 'It's pretty generous, considering.'

'Considering what?'

'The effort you put in. They said tell Jase it was clever stuff, and would you consider doing something else. I told them, look, I am no telephone.'

'You talk funny.' Jase didn't move to the money, guessing something was wrong. 'Are you really Bonn?'

'Yes, I am Bonn.' Let the slang and the act go. 'You are not well, Jase. Please see a doctor. Your lady Marie was very ill, God rest her.'

'Shut your fucking face, you!' Jase bawled, shaking. 'I've had enough crap!'

'Do please say if there is anything I can do.'

'I'm not ill!' Jase yelled. 'I'm fine! Marie was poorly from the sick scag they sellt her, bastards.'

Bonn really wanted to know. 'I'll bet she was generous to a fault. She must have been a lovely girl.'

'She was terrif, her.' Jase's eyes filled. Yellow pus poured down his cheek. 'If she'd had money like what I've got now, they'd have doctored her right.'

'I doubt that, Jase,' Bonn said, when Rack had specifically said not to contradict. 'You know what she died of.' He rose for another can of beer, seeing Jase stiffen. Bonn would have a headache all night now. Half a pint was enough to cause it, wine in moderation hardly ever, but drink Magee's was what he'd been told to do. 'They've a car for you. The registration number's on the money packet, the keys inside. Hang on.'

'What?' Jase followed him, took the different can Bonn offered.

'I've forgotten something.' Bonn stood, frowning, bad acting. 'Money, motor, keys, registration number. Oh, aye. There's a map. The plod have been asking, somebody called Hassall. You've to go north. They've pull-outs along the motorways.'

He affected relief, went to sit down. 'That's it. The doctor should be here soon. Count the money, please. I don't want to be here when she comes.'

'Wait.' Jase glanced round. 'Something's not right. Why's she late now?'

'Time,' Bonn said sadly. 'A doctor's time isn't her own. She has been delayed five times out of eleven occasions.'

'You talk funny. Why?'

'I was in a seminary before.'

Jase eyed him. 'A priest?'

Bonn felt himself redden. 'I had taken vows, but not them all. I was a brother. I left. Things changed in me more than in the priesthood.' He shrugged. 'Religion is no mere administration, as folk presently assume.'

'What you being a goer for then? And passing gelt.'

Jase's eyes looked hollow, sunken. He leaned back. 'Because you've chucked it in, you want to do the opposite.'

'Is it?' Bonn asked outright, astounded. He sounded dismayed.

'If you think anything else you're a prat.'

'I don't really believe that I would consciously—'

'Listen,' Jase said. It was a real effort to keep his eyes open. Bonn wondered if it was his imagination, or was Jase's speech slurred? He tried to think how Jase had sounded when he'd pushed in. 'I knew this mate. He's doing time, year maybe with remmo.'

'Also a religious—?'

'Nar. Listen. He supported City, see? Even as a kid. Scraps every Saturday, year in year out. Then he switched to United. Now, he can't even talk of another team. See?'

Bonn didn't. 'I suppose he had a reason.'

'That's just it. He's forgot what it were.' Jase's eyes shut. He wore a smile of remembrance. 'What's it called when you do that?'

'Conversion.'

'Conversion.' Jase's hand relaxed. The beer spilled, frothing.

'Is that what I've done, Jase, converted and forgotten?'

'Aye, Bonn,' Jase said drowsily. 'You've gone over to the enemy. You don't know it yet, but you have. It's people. You're nowt special just because you're you, and you're more worried because of it. We're *all* special, to usselves. You go over completely or not at all.'

Bonn's eyes were moist. He dabbed them. 'Excuse me, please.' Jase slumped. He tried to speak. Bonn sat watching through blurred vision.

Jase began to snore, utterly relaxed, legs splayed.

It was several minutes more before Rack came silently

from the bathroom. He went across and drew Jase's shotgun out. He patted Jase's pockets, took out money, cartridges, a canvas roll. Bonn said nothing, watching Rack.

Rack went to the flower stand in the corner, bundled the packet and Jase's materials into a plastic bag he got from the alcove cupboard, and beckoned.

'Please don't forget Jase,' Bonn said.

'He'll get took.' Rack walked to the door.

Jase's breathing worried Bonn. He asked, 'Should he be snoring quite like that?'

'Him? He's fine. Hospital in forty minutes. Course,' Rack said, grinning, 'I'll see his tubes get discovered by the nurses. They'll tell the plod, and Bob's your uncle.'

'Clare Three-Nine-Five—'

'Trouble with you, Bonn,' Rack said, a joke coming, 'is you ask too many fucking questions. She was warned off when she arrived, on Martina's orders. She's been given a booking for tomorrow. Don't worry. Miss Faith done it. Clare Three-Nine-Five knowed her voice.'

'I would have done it myself, Rack.'

'You know Martina's rule. Goers isn't risked.' Rack held the door. 'Out. Never say I don't never do nuffin', okay?'

# 33

**Working house** – a brothel

ASKEY THE MESSENGER arrived breathless at the Volunteer.

'Christ's sake, Askey, you're puffed out. Get your breath.'

It was twenty to eight. Askey wouldn't have come this far, but a Butty Boy lass told him Rack was in the pub arguing bets.

'It's that Jase,' he gasped, sweating.

'Oh, aye?' Rack was telling Medals, the Volunteer's potman, stellar reasons why boat races went wrong. 'What's he done now?'

'He's snuffed it, in some cellar. Had his tubes with him, but did it with the old pollen.'

'Who sez?'

'Everybody. There's a crowd in Inkerman Street, and the plod.'

'I expect things'll go quiet for a bit, eh?'

'Er, aye.' Askey was put out. Rack seemed unperturbed. 'Rack?'

'Go and tell Osmund. Then catch Grellie in Quaker Street. Stand there until she shows. It'll be at half ten. Don't miss her. Today'll be a right pig.'

'Right!'

'And take your time,' Rack called after the fleeing messenger. He told Medals, 'That one'll give hisself a stroke. Know why folk get strokes? It's yawning, scientific fact.'

'Thirteen to eight they'll say it's murder.'

'Never in a million years. Jase was a druggo.'

'The plod don't know any different. Everything's murder to them. Dead in a landlady's yard? No chance.'

'You're on, Medals. Tenners?'

They spat and slapped hands. Rack told him he'd already lost because he had inside knowledge; he laughed and laughed.

Hassall went on television news.

'The individual appears to be the person wanted in connection with recent incidents,' he intoned. 'A further statement will be made tomorrow.'

'Jase did the mill killings then?' a journalist shouted.

'That is not known,' Hassall said.

'The canal slayings?'

'Results are awaited from Forensics.'

Hassall had learnt it off by heart, Windsor drilling him from a script he'd produced, the lads in the police canteen laughing at Hassall stumbling over answers. The reporters worried questions like dogs a bone.

'They are connected, surely?' a gorgeous lass from the City Press demanded.

'We are not yet able to say that.'

'Who caused Jase's death?'

'We are awaiting the outcome of investigations.'

'Further . . . investigations,' the girl wrote, making a painstaking joke out of it. 'Mr Hassall, are police hiding behind "drug-related accidental death"?'

He controlled himself, wishing he'd got Windsor, glib pillock, to do this.

'When we have any firm facts, we will make an announcement,' he said woodenly, then managed to fight clear of the lot of them. His missus had their measure, good enough for writing obituaries of their mates, nothing else. She kept telling him not to read newspapers.

The lawyers sat with the chairman and secretary of the city hospital's trustees. Dr Wallace, for Pathology, signed the agreement for Clinical Pathology to provide a standard fee-for-service for the charity. The sole consigning doctor would be Dr Clare Burtonall.

Martina's seniormost lawyer was Marcus Atherington. She did not attend.

Two hours later, Atherington called at the house in Bradshawgate, saying how pleased he was. Posser asked the only question that mattered.

'This means what?'

'Dr Burtonall will send her lab investigations to the hospital's clin. path. laboratories.'

Posser insisted, 'Can we *restrict* which lab she uses?'

'Yes. Your charity has a binding contract to use the hospital labs.' The lawyer did face-play with his spectacles. 'As you instructed.'

'The Pickard Lab in Droylsden,' Martina said. 'Can she use a payment code there?'

'No. This supersedes all Dr Burtonall's previous arrangements.'

They thought in silence. Posser looked at Martina.

'You did well, Marcus.'

Atherington ahemed, glanced at Posser. 'Concerning fees.'

Posser nodded, settlement time. 'Martina? Would you like to phone word through? Miss Janet can do the donkey work.'

'Yes, Dad.'

The elderly lawyer leant forward, checking that Martina had gone.

'There's a new girl, Posser. May, is it?'

'Aye. Good lass, her.'

'She looks a bit' – the lawyer licked his lips – 'rough.'

'Just a bit. But reliable.' Posser peered round in his chair at the closed door, and quickly gestured to the bureau. 'There's a bottle of Dow's, Marcus. Make sharp.'

The old lawyer moved with speed, poured them both a measure.

'Can I have her, Posser? A couple of nights?'

'God Almighty, Marcus. Be reasonable. They're not a gang of navvies.'

'No,' the lawyer said, trembling. 'One night, then? Only, I put a lot of quality thought into this contract, Posser.'

'All right. I'll swing it. Who else?' The lawyer's usual charge was two.

Marcus Atherington quietly began debating the girls in Waterloo Street.

Posser listened gravely. He was delighted. Martina now had a completely new beginning. She deserved it.

The post-mortem examination was being conducted in the Class 100 enclosure. Dr Wallace called through the glass panel when he saw Clare in the observer gallery.

'If it isn't Dr Burtonall!' he exclaimed. 'The arch traitor!'

'The what?' Clare's heart almost stopped. Then she saw Bruno's grin.

'You've sold us out! Leaving the Health Service for schemer's gold.'

'Stop it and get back to Fife. What've you found?'

'Come to gloat at the menagerie?' Wallace said. He loved his pipe, but had ruled against smoking in Pathology on safety grounds.

Bruno the PM technician pointed gleefully. Clare stepped back to look. Above her somebody had scrawled MENAGERIE. She smiled to appease.

The new facility was almost completely glassed in. The pathologist and Bruno moved in their cumbersome garments under the downward draught. Class 100 microbial containment rooms were ventilated solely by filtered air that entered by parallel downward displacement through HEPA ceiling sieves. The High Efficiency Particulate Air flow streamed invisibly down. The Class 100 area gave virtually complete containment, and had been adapted in Morbid Anatomy as a safe autopsy suite.

Dr Wallace was almost done. The cadaver that had been Jase lay displayed. Bruno waved at the automatic weighing devices. Clare pretended to applaud when the technician posed, clowning with barmy pride at his controls for automatic specimen handling.

'I'd ask you in for coffee, young Burtonall, but . . .'

The remark made Clare laugh. The prolonged ritual of admission, through airwash vestibules and repeated wet-wash spray disinfection procedures, required for a single person to get in or out had had the pathologist and his technician devising silly and meaningless extra gambits.

'Know what?' Dr Wallace called, resting his hands on Jase's opened thorax. The speakers above Clare resonated tinnily. 'This lad has more Schedule drugs in him than the High Street chemist's.'

Clare leant towards the microphone set into the window, caught the foolishness in her movement and reddened. Bruno grinned, and scored a large 1 in the air. Spectators were clearly audible inside.

'How do you know?' she asked.

'Clumsiest self-administration of drugs I've ever seen.' Wallace called Bruno. They partly raised the corpse on the slab so Clare could see.

Neither of them was yet used to the suspended angle-mirrors in the ceiling, controlled by foot-tapper switches. Dr Wallace blamed Bruno for designing them arse-about-face, making them operate in the reverse direction to that intended. Bruno retorted that you had to be an MD to devise instruments that cackhanded.

'What am I looking at?' Clare called.

'This extravasation, doctor.' The pathologist lowered the body with a grunt and said to Bruno, 'Sorry for that delay, Bruno. She went to an inferior medical school. She learned her morbid anatomy from Vesalius.'

The corpse was blotched by a large smudge of haemorrhage into the body tissues below the ribcage.

'What's that from, Dr Wallace?'

'It's got a punctum, where the needle went in. I've sampled the tissues.' He glanced at Bruno. 'If we've understood the new automatic sampler. Bruno tells me that I pressed the right buttons, but he's daft as a brush.'

'Like the killer!' Bruno said, laughing.

'He means Jase was right-handed. The killer assumed he was left-handed, because he had a poacher's canvas gun slot cobbled inside the left leg.'

'The police wouldn't let us keep it,' Bruno mourned. 'A

dee-bee is three hundred quid down Pleasance Street. And they say this country's fair!'

Wallace snorted. 'Don't blab our secrets. She's the opposition now.'

'Right, left, so?' Clare said.

'See, Bruno? She's ignorant. If he was right-handed, doctor, would he have injected himself on his *right* front side under his diaphragm?'

Bruno said, 'Can't be done.' He mimed a graphic negative.

'Why,' Bruno worked up to a joke, 'change the habit of a lifetime?'

They laughed, sharing the pun. Clare smiled weakly. She found their comedy act a little gruesome.

'Get it?' Bruno was delighted. 'Change the *habit*? Habit like in—'

'Thank you, Bruno,' Dr Wallace said heavily.

'What's the significance?' Clare badly needed to know.

Wallace said, 'A person might have assumed that he was left-handed, and lethally needled him on the wrong side.'

'*Was* he injected?'

'I think so. The tissues, the site. We'll be able to say with what later on, if the biochemists start work.'

'Biochemists? We wait for biochemists?' Bruno groaned theatrically. 'Make it next year. This week is Ascot Week. Flat racing.'

'They're not that bad, Bruno. They got one result out last month.'

'Stop it,' Clare scolded. 'Jase was killed?'

'Seems to me, Clare.' Wallace sliced into lung tissue to inspect its parenchyma. 'God knows what our microbiologists will grow from this lot. Bronchopneumonic consolidation. See?'

Clare saw the patchy apprearance of the lung tissue.

'Couldn't he have done it himself?'

'The injection? By dint of much contortion.' The pathologist sighed. 'That's what the police will say. So will the useless Crown Prosecution Service, hopeless sods. It's so tempting for authorities. Unless there's hard forensic evidence, they'll say he was a drug user who had money – did Bruno tell you the police wouldn't let us keep that either? – and died of self-administered bliss.'

'Which raises the question,' Bruno prompted his boss.

'He was the Jase I was looking for,' Clare faltered. She felt demoralized by their crosstalk act. 'He was the partner of Marie Cullokin.'

'Was he?' The pathologist looked at a glowing screen on the wall. 'That name's familiar. Hang on. PM'd her yesterday, acquired immunodeficiency syndrome, her. Every feeble organism that fancied its chances of claiming pathogen status jumped on her bandwagon, God rest her.' His eyes twinkled. 'You had a scrap with the SNO about her.'

'Permanent partners now!' Bruno said. 'Jase and her.'

'Diagnosis?' Clare thought Bruno's guffaw was in singularly bad taste. 'I'll not quote you.'

'Well, he's riddled with infection. At a pinch, I'd say an acute-on-chronic drug incident, in an AIDS patient. *Possibly* self-administered.'

Bruno laughed. 'Hundred to one against!'

Clare thanked them and left. The quips were disturbing, but if jokes were their way of coping what harm was done? She had seen the pathologist broken-hearted over an autopsy on a child. People compensated by different tricks. Clifford had his tricks. She had hers.

# 34

**Viller** – an innocent bystander, person of no account

She went to sit in the hospital park. It was cold, the wind blustery. It seemed important to be where she had first spoken with Bonn, this very bench.

The question was, after effecting her reunion with Bonn – she had him this evening after that hitch – what was on her mind? That she and Bonn could now be more than casual lovers? Very well, she crossly chided herself, users, clients, whatever term applied, but lovers in truth.

As a couple, though? She and Clifford had no children. Living with Clifford for ever, now that they each recognized their separation, was remote. But *living* with Bonn?

What would he do? Teach something, somewhere? If so, what? Work in some bank, then? Was he qualified? And would he want a routine job, day in day out? What exactly was she proposing? That she buy him from his Pleases Agency and keep him, as Victorian gentlemen bought pretty girls and kept them in Whitechapel or St Giles's? And, she asked herself with contempt for her slipshod logic, would *that* arrangement last long?

Shelve it for the whilst, she decided. For now, she would meet Bonn full of joyous expectation, and express no doubts. He deserved that as, she told herself in a glow of pleasure, she deserved him. She was sure now; bide her time, and win in the end.

He heard Rack in the Bouncing Block. Workmen were everywhere, far too noisy. Bonn took refuge in the coffee bar.

Rack must have thought himself alone or, Bonn wondered, not. His voice was clearly audible over the thumping music.

'It was worth it, boss,' Rack said at the phone. He insisted that there'd been no other choice, but twice hesitated, when Rack never hesitated.

Bonn accepted a coffee, and paid against the girl's protests. A smile was hard to come by today. The receiver clumped down and Rack came in, grinning.

'Know what, Bonn?' he said. 'Prand's got a certificate in fucking French. Would you believe it?'

'Good heavens,' Bonn said politely.

'And he's started an accounts course. Well weird!'

'Amazing.'

'I'll make him teach me French,' Rack said. 'I mean it. Scientists proved we'll soon want three languages. Know why?'

Bonn silently appraised his stander.

'It's our brains. They keep going. Know what's best for brains?'

'Languages.'

Rack shrugged. Bonn was usually easier than this. 'Italian's best, because it's not Chinese.' He almost faltered before Bonn's silent look. 'Chinese is bad for counting.'

'Poor Jase,' Bonn said. Reports were in all the papers.

'Poor bugger. You heard he snuffed it?'

'I trust it was accidental, Rack.'

Rack recovered in an instant. 'AIDS, him.'

'I thought that disease was downhill but gradual.'

'Nar, Bonn. I've seen them die quick as a flash.'

Bonn listened while Rack invented spectacular medical details to prove his argument. He wondered about his stander. Rack only called Martina boss. He wondered too about Martina. What exactly was 'worth it, boss'?

'After I left, you took Jase to hospital,' Bonn said.

'Quiet lodgings. Changed my mind about the hospital. They've security cameras. Made sure he was okay.' Rack was back explaining options. 'I couldn't have let him loose, the state he was in.'

'The beer was doped, I suppose, Rack.'

'You did good. Hey!' Rack was suddenly indignant at the way Bonn's mind was going. 'I was there, Hawkeyes. I wasn't fucking dozing. I'd have stopped anything going wrong, Bonn.'

'I know,' Bonn said resignedly. 'It still seems a mess.'

'I'd got four more plans, Bonn.' Rack thumped his chest gorilla fashion, making the counter girls laugh, his thing. 'Me great!'

'That place he was discovered, Rack.' It still niggled.

'Inkerman Street? Old dear's crappy boarding house.'

'I was wondering if she is on our books.'

'Not that I know. Why?'

'I heard you on the phone a moment ago.'

'Eh? Oh, just checking about Prand. You got a good instinct for folk.' Rack hitched closer, the ultimate confidence. 'Know what? I was against Prand when you picked him for a goer. No, honest. Martina was, an' all.'

'I surmised so, Rack. But Jase—'

'I'm not saying Prand's not a nice bloke, got the makings,

not saying that. But I did wonder. Prand's straight. Good eye for people, Bonn.'

'Thank you.' After all, Bonn reasoned, it was Rack's function to suss.

'Finish your coffee,' Rack told him. 'You've Clare Three-Nine-Five in twenty minutes.'

'So I have,' Bonn said, thinking, full circle, but only for some. For others, circles were broken for ever.

'What d'you reckon?'

Windsor worried the remark was some trick. Hassall didn't usually want opinion. They were in the old mill, yellow warning tapes everywhere, Hassall grumbling about sloppy sods in the uniformed branch. The SOCO was a new intent bloke Hassall had never seen before, too many changes in the Division lately.

'The Proceeds of Crime Act? The £20,000 shut-off was a pig. But go for the lot, seize any assets we know were obtained by crime. Now the POCA is law, we don't have to prove the buildings, money, whatever, stem from a specific bludge, right?'

'Right. Do we dig bank accounts?'

'Confiscate all cash. That'll end Haleys Wharf.'

Hassall kicked a cola tin thinking brilliant goal, Wembley Cup Final, last second of extra time. It skittered across the glass-strewn floor. A rat scurried for cover.

'Not for good. They'll simply shift.'

'Without money?'

That was the difference in age-related beliefs, Hassall thought. Police of Windsor's youth were cavalry, charge any windmill, knock buggers down and break your lance you got a heroism medal. Twenty years and scores of crime epidemics later, you know it's all balloon squeezing. Crush here, it swells there; compress the top, the bottom bulges. Am I, he wondered with a twinge of guilt, past it?

'We just watch our ship sail, occasionally nudge the steersman.'

Windsor got the sarcasm. His lips thinned. 'That's ignoring law!'

'Is it?' Hassall kicked another can, missed the blanket. No goal.

# 35

**Manor** – a crime district

SHE ENTERED WITH her brightest smile. New clothes, Bonn guessed, secretly wishing there was some way a man could tell how radical a woman's new hairstyle was to her. Revolutionary, or a slight transition?

His admiration was transparent. She was delighted and said so. The meeting felt like a reunion with a loved one, familiar, warming, nothing to do with any hiring business or past row. For an instant, as she led him – as *she* led *him* – to the window banquette, her thought recurred that there was now something immutable between herself and Bonn. She was to blame for her plight, having prematurely linked her life to Clifford in marriage. But everything had changed now, surely for the better.

'Don't say anything, Bonn.' She pressed her fingers on his lips. 'That Miss Faith lady positively *glowed* on the phone. She explained everything, the postponement on account of increased police activity. Poor Jase.'

Miss Faith glowed? Did she now, Bonn thought. Opinion was frankly barred, Martina's rule. He wondered about giving Miss Faith a quiet warning.

'Amen, Clare.' Poor dead Jase.

'Bonn. I have something to tell you.'

'Not about your private life, I trust.'

She mimed astonishment, amused. 'And why not?'

'It is' – he searched words – 'not requisite.'

'I beg to differ.' She almost hugged herself, sure he too would be delighted. 'It's about my future.'

'I wish you wouldn't, Clare.'

'Hear me out, darling.' She put her arm through his. They sat, evening sun streaming through the louvred blinds. 'You know what I do?'

'Of course. A doctor.'

'I'm to have a surgery and office in the city centre!'

He tried to register surprise. 'No more hospital or GP work, then.'

'Not NHS. It's private. I'm looking for locations.'

He looked blankly at her. 'I can't imagine it.'

'To serve vagrants, lost children, the homeless, disadvantaged! Isn't that marvellous?'

'If you say.'

'Can't you see? We'll be able to meet virtually any time!' She teased, 'If your profits soar, can I have a piece of the action?'

'The agency determines those,' he replied gravely.

She clouted him with a cushion. She hadn't felt so animated for a long time. 'Don't be dour, Bonn. There's nothing wrong, is there? Street girls, worried teenagers, anybody! All for charity!'

'Street girls,' he said.

'They have a right to medical screening, Bonn.'

'The stringers might actually be sent, Clare.' It was as near as he could go.

'Sent? Stringers?'

He said carefully, 'If you were a male doctor and hired

a girl, you couldn't be her doctor. I've heard that is medical law.'

'No, of course. That would mean . . .' She sobered.

'That you would be struck off practice, being your lover's doctor.'

'That's true,' she said, not knowing where the argument was heading. 'But it's not quite the same, you and me, is it?'

'It would be, Clare, if you accepted me as a patient.'

Mechanically she tidied the cushion and looked into space.

'Is that what you think might happen?' She swung to face him. 'Could it?'

'For sure, Clare, yes it could.'

They stared at each other. Clare stood over him, looking down.

'I'm caught, you mean?' She suddenly remembered the implacable gaze of the blonde girl Martina who'd never moved yet who'd been the power in that room, dominating the lawyers and contract men. And suddenly saw it all too clearly. 'Getting me under contract puts you beyond my reach?'

'It occurs to me, Clare.'

'Did you know of this earlier?'

'So many things came together. I worry that I helped to kill somebody.'

'Jase?' She sank beside him, let her hands fall into his. 'I was at his autopsy.' She remembered the feeble jokes between pathologist and technician. 'You wouldn't do such a thing, darling. You've no need to convince me.'

'Convincing myself is the problem.'

'Bonn. Why grieve over something that might not have been?' She almost cried it aloud in exasperation.

'Unknowing is no help, Clare. The Greeks believed you were simply fated, and so things came to pass.'

Savagely she took his head between her hands and kissed him full on the mouth, drawing away only when breathless.

'Sod the Ancient Greeks, Bonn. Sod the agency. I'm going to have you. Just as we are, if that's all we can be. Go to a doctor somewhere else.'

'That might not be allowed.'

'I shall make it a condition of acceptance.'

'They've already bound you legally.'

So he'd suspected it from the beginning, seen the inevitable chessboard moves? Clare said calmly, 'Then I shall abrogate my medical oath. I'll continue hiring you despite them.'

'You'll be vulnerable to blackmail.'

'Who is she?' Clare asked, harsh. 'Small, good figure, blonde, ruled the roost. Miss Martina.'

'That name will do,' Bonn said.

'Is there anything between you?'

'Please know that I would never broach a lady's confidence.'

'Do you mean not yet?'

'I mean no.' He stood. 'I feel I ought to apologize. I've got you into difficulties, and I'm not even sure what those difficulties are. I'm really pathetic.'

She smiled, her lips tight, ferociously determined. 'You warned me, Bonn. No special feelings allowed, no chance of a permanent union.'

'I remember.'

'Well, I was the pathetic one. I used to think that a woman who settled for less was hopeless. Now, I see there are times when that's all that can be. Fine. I'll settle for less, Bonn, if less includes you.'

'I don't deserve it, Clare.' He wouldn't have blamed her if she'd simply walked out. 'I'm the sordid part of the city. With me you'll only get gutter reasons, criminal logic, street chances. I can't change.'

She gazed at him in appalled awe. 'Why on earth can't you, Bonn? It would solve all our problems. I'd leave Clifford. We could be permanent any way you wished.'

'For me there is no way to the outside. Thank God. I survive.'

'The agency wouldn't let you go?'

'I must assume so, Clare.' He thought, and if they would I'd never leave.

'Then we – I – stay. Arrangement as usual, darling.' She smiled. After all, it was as much as she'd hoped when arriving this evening. 'Say it, please.'

'Arrangement as usual, darling.'

'Not bad.' She tugged him towards the inner room. 'You can develop the endearments when we're resting.'

'Whatever the lady wishes,' he said.

'Again, darling, please. This time with fervour.' She kicked off her shoes and turned to him with a bright new ferocity. 'We'll get away with it, darling, you'll see.'

'As the lady says.' He tried to match her conviction, slowly undoing her skirt with his murderer's hands.

She said thickly, 'Curtains, darling. Do hurry.'

**Above** Ang Thong National Marine Park (p224)

### Choltanutkun Tun-atiruj

*linkedin.com/in/choltanutkun*

Choltanutkun is a native Thai former music student who found a love for writing when she took up a job after graduation as a Nightlife Writer for a Bangkok's online *BK Magazine* in 2016. She always fights for equality in society and that reflects onto her work, which it always has a political angle tied to it even if it's a lifestyle piece. She is currently living in Bangkok's nightlife neighbourhood, Thong Lo, fighting for the (unfair) Alcohol Control Act in Thailand to be revised, and still writes every day.

### Barbara Woolsey

*@barbara.woolsey*

Barbara is Canadian-born, of Filipina, Irish and Scottish heritage, and has been living and working on and off in Thailand since 2010. She's currently living on Ko Samui, obtaining a Masters of Global Studies and in her free time, DJing and learning Thai and Tagalog.

# Contents

TUPUNGATO/SHUTTERSTOCK ©

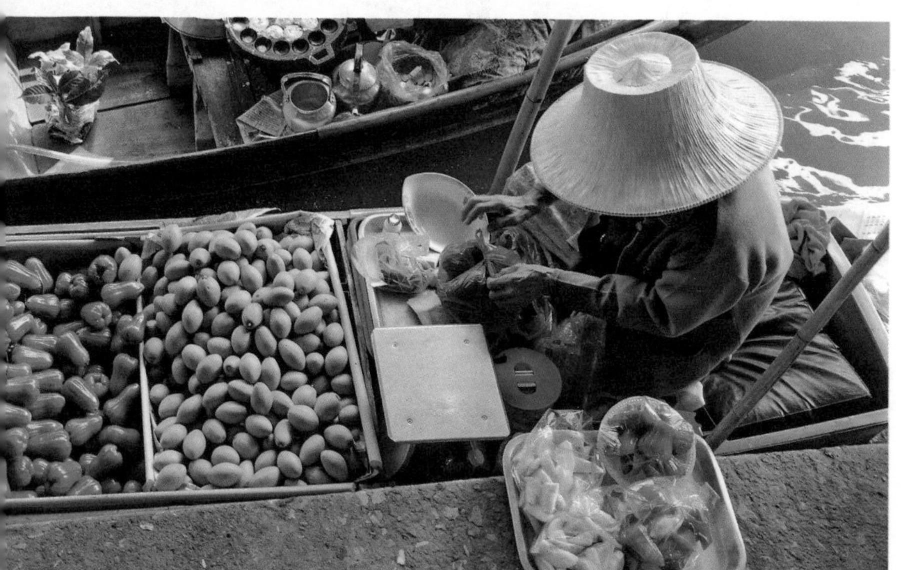

**Above** Damnoen Saduak floating market (p73)

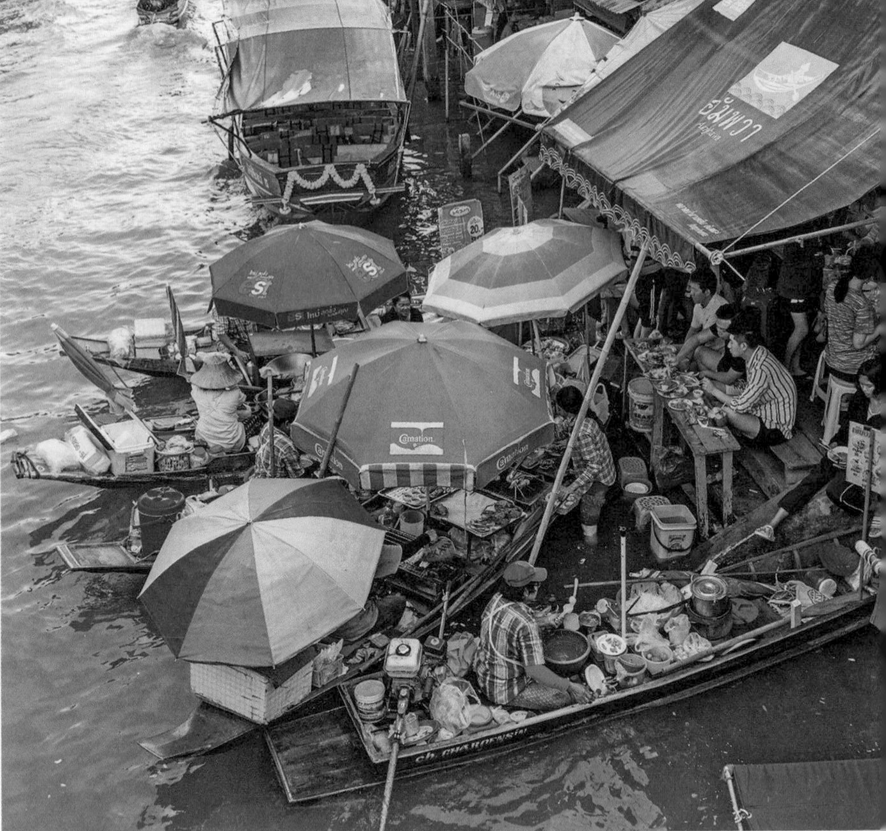


# COMMUNITY **SPIRIT**

Thailand's villages are where tradition thrives. Societies are based on togetherness, respect and ritual. From mountain hill tribe settlements to rural and fishing villages, spending time in smaller places is a way of more deeply understanding Thai people and their values. Homestays, traditional markets and courses in foraging and plant medicine bring context to the culture.

FOKKE BAARSSEN/SHUTTERSTOCK ©



**Left** Amphawa floating market (p73). **Right** Cottage, Nan Province (p108). **Below** Bun Bang Fai Rocket Festival (p133)

## → HOMESTAYS

In northern Thailand, homestays offer unique proximity and access to remote mountain villages – although probably not the electricity nor toilets that you're used to.

▶ See p112 for more about homestays in Chiang Mai

## MINORITY HISTORY

Learning the history of minority communities, including the Chinese and Muslim Malay cultures, is the key to unlocking Thailand's oft-misunderstood south.

▶ See p234 to learn about the cultures of Thailand

RIGHT: THARAMUST/SHUTTERSTOCK © LEFT: GLEN PHOTO/SHUTTERSTOCK ©

## ↑ FESTIVALS

Research the dates of local festivals like the incredibly unique **Bun Bang Fai Rocket Festival** (p133). They provide unforgettable snapshots into Thai cultures and lifestyles.

▶ Learn more about festivals on p132 and p146

## Best Unique Experiences

- **Shop at a floating market outside Bangkok, including the lesser-knowns like Bang Phli and Tha Kha.** (p72)
- **Camp out in Mae Wang and learn ancient practices from Karen hill tribes.** (p107)
- **Delight in fresh seafood at stilt restaurants around the eastern Gulf's fishing villages.** (p163)
- **Try a unique local take on Isan cuisine in Baan Phue village in Udon Thani.** (p131)
- **Explore customs from fabric dyeing to elephant training by village-hopping northeastern Thailand.** (p116)

Thailand has more than 100 national parks.

The first was Khao Yai National Park, opened in 1962.

Over 20 more national parks are in the works.

The country plans to dedicate 55% of land to protected forest by 2037.

# INTO THE JUNGLE

Thailand's rugged tropical rainforests are gateways to pure seclusion and hidden spectacles: misty mountains, deserted beaches and bays, river cascades and waterfalls. Diverse flora and fauna abounds. National parks across the country offer chances to trek, sleep rough under the stars and learn the true meaning of a digital detox.

**Left** Elephants, Kui Buri National Park (p182). **Right** Khao Chang Phueak (p88). **Below** Camping, Khao Yai (p77)

### → NATIONAL PARKS

Thailand's national parks are wild and strong-willed. You may be required to have a licensed guide or ranger accompany you for safety.

ARTMAN7007/SHUTTERSTOCK ©

### CAMPING OUT

Rent a tent to pitch on the beach or stay in a jungle-canopied bungalow via the Thai park authority's website ▶(dnp.go.th).

RIGHT: PONPUN WICHAINSAN/SHUTTERSTOCK ©
LEFT: TANES NGAMSOM/SHUTTERSTOCK ©

### ↑ SEASONAL HIKES

Consider jungle trekking closer to rainy season when foliage and waterfalls are at their lushest. High humidity can make dry-season hikes more demanding.

## Best Wild Experiences

▶ **Watch wild elephant herds roaming and bathing in Kui Buri National Park.** (p182)

▶ **Trek the dense jungle interiors and rocky coasts of Mu Ko Chang National Park.** (p143)

▶ **Tackle the challenging 'knife's edge' Khao Chang Phueak on Myanmar's border.** (p88)

▶ **Take your pick of untamed northern peaks including Thailand's highest, Doi Inthanon.** (p101)

▶ **Discover Thailand's first national park, Khao Yai, and its wine growing.** (p77)

★Thailand has 3219km of coastline.

# COASTAL PARADISE

Thailand's shores, formed by soft sands, rocky outcrops and primeval forest, offer a landscape for every kind of island lover. Snorkelling and diving, feasting on seafood, or becoming a golden god on the beach – take your pick of fun in utopian surrounds. Marine parks are perfect for barefooted boat adventures and island-hopping.

Left Ang Thong National Marine Park (p224). **Right** Kitesurfing. **Below** Jet-skiing, Pattaya (p158)

## → CITY BEACHES

You'll find the best beaches near to Bangkok at Hua Hin and Ko Samet – and can even take a taxi from downtown to get there.

## DRIVE YOURSELF

Ride services around islands like Ko Samui and Ko Chang are scarce. Drive yourself to skip between coasts and experience incomparable freedom.

## ↑ WATER SPORTS

Pattaya is famous for its jet-skiing, while Hua Hin is an amazing spot for kitesurfing.

▶ Check out water activities on p157 and p176

### Best Coastal Experiences

▶ **Take a traditional long-tail boat to hang with the pigs on Ko Madsum.** (p225)

▶ **Discover coral reefs in the Ang Thong National Marine Park.** (p224)

▶ **Dip into clear waters framed by limestone karsts along the Andaman Coast.** (p188)

▶ **Escape the crowds on the delightfully quiet beaches of Ko Mak and Ko Kut.** (p154)

▶ **Join an evening boat ride with a squid fisher from Hua Hin Pier.** (p177)

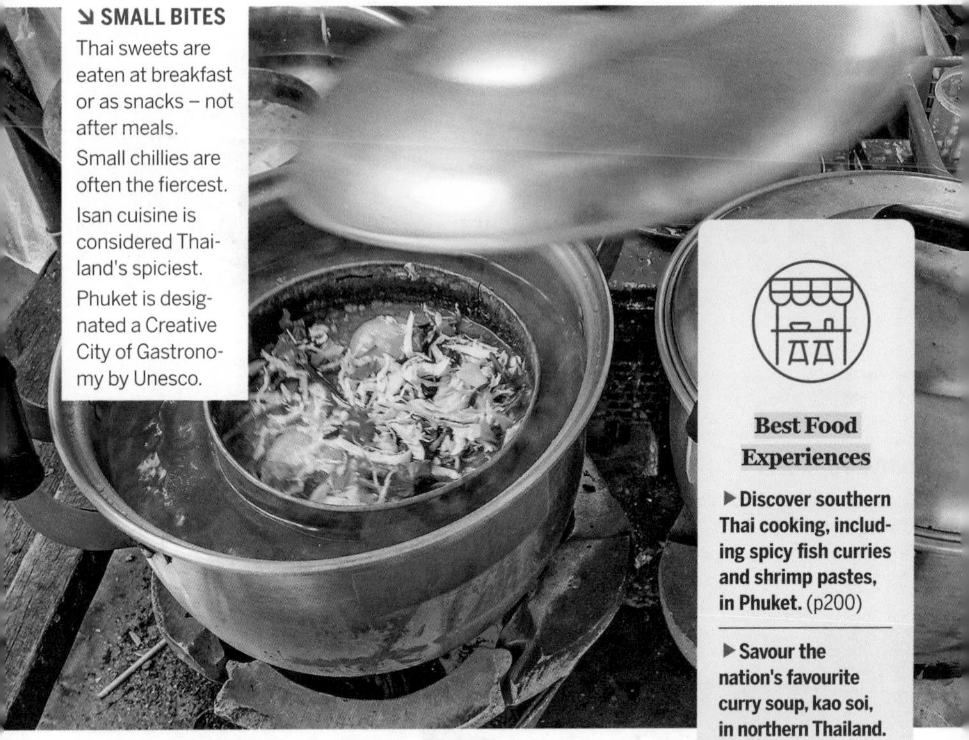

**↘ SMALL BITES**

Thai sweets are eaten at breakfast or as snacks – not after meals.

Small chillies are often the fiercest.

Isan cuisine is considered Thailand's spiciest.

Phuket is designated a Creative City of Gastronomy by Unesco.

**Best Food Experiences**

▶ **Discover southern Thai cooking, including spicy fish curries and shrimp pastes, in Phuket.** (p200)

▶ **Savour the nation's favourite curry soup, kao soi, in northern Thailand.** (p95)

▶ **Slurp spicy seafood noodles on the banks of Chanthaburi.** (p150)

▶ **Try sôm đam (spicy green papaya salad) in its ancestral homeland of Isan.** (pp121 & 131)

▶ **Burn your mouth on a piece of Lampang's spicy grilled pork or fish sausage, sâi òo-a.** (p104)



# BRINGING **THE HEAT**

Thailand's food has an incendiary reputation for being spicy, but it is actually one of the most harmonious – and complex – cuisines of the world. Street food stands, market stalls and shophouse restaurants showcase the flavours of various regions and ethnic groups. Get ready to sweat it out over chilli-spiked soups, curries and salads.

# LIFE OF **THE PARTY**

Thais know the meaning of a good time. Fun *(sà·nùk)* is more than an adjective, it's a cultural ethos. Celebrating makes life worth living – think parties, good tunes and turning up on the dance floor. Island life is about live beats and sunset buckets, while Bangkok's underground bars are the definition of midnight magic.

### → PARTY BOATS

In Bangkok, boat parties cruise the Chao Phraya, serving up fancy drinks, good DJs and sparkly sightseeing by night.

LEFT: VISUN KHANKASEM/SHUTTERSTOCK ©, BOTTOM: MATT HUNT/SOPA IMAGES/LIGHTROCKET VIA GETTY IMAGES ©

### Best Nights Out

▶ **Party with the locals at Ko Pha-Ngan's hidden Eden Bar.** (p238)

▶ **Visit a hidden Chinatown gin bar in Bangkok.** (p56)

**Raise a vodka bucket at sunrise at Ko Chang's Ting Tong Bar.** (p145)

▶ **Track down a secret rave on the shores of Ko Mak.** (p145)

▶ **Catch international DJs on Patong Beach at KUDO Beach Club.** (p211)

### ← KO PHA-NGAN

Ko Pha-Ngan, Thailand's raver's paradise, is much more than Full Moon. The best parties happen far off Haad Rin on secluded beaches and cliff sides.

▶ See p223 for more information

**Far left** *Kôw soy noi* **Above left** Full moon party (p225). **Left** River cruise party

# COFFEE CULTURE

In every sip of Thailand's here-only Arabica strain, there's a story of hardship – and also a true taste of Thai pride and success. The unique coffee culture can be discovered at charming cafes, of which there's no shortage across the kingdom – especially up north where beans are grown.

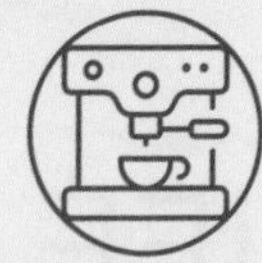

### Best Brews

▶ **Drink a cup from Phuket's original coffee roaster, Hock Hoe Lee.** (p193)

▶ **Discover Mars. cnx, a small coffee bar posing as an alien diner.** (p114)

▶ **Enjoy sleepy artisan sips in Lampang's MAHAMITr Microroaster Cafe.** (p114)

LEFT: I AM JIFFY/SHUTTERSTOCK ©, BOTTOM: NONGNINGSTUDIO/SHUTTERSTOCK ©

### ← ARABICA SOLUTION

In the 1970s, Thailand's Arabica was developed to provide northern communities with a crop-growing alternative to opium poppies.

▶ For more coffee culture, see p96.

### →LATTE ART CLASSES

Demonstrating Thailand's obsession with latte art (a Thai barista even won the world championships in 2017), Bangkok's **Le Cordon Bleu** offers classes in foamy design.

**Above** Fresh Arabica coffee beans. **Left** Coffee with latte art

# HEALTHY **ESCAPES**

From massage to meditation and aromatherapy, Thailand's ancient wellness traditions offer opportunities for recalibration and growth. Spas and wellness sanctuaries range from simplistic to bespoke and over-the-top. In island paradise, you'll find a yoga retreat around every bending road. Moo-ay thai (Thai boxing) is also a beloved fitness activity.

LEFT: JM TRAVEL PHOTOGRAPHY/SHUTTERSTOCK ©; BOTTOM: SATIT_SRIHIN/SHUTTERSTOCK ©

### →FOOT MASSAGES

When you're short on time and energy, there's nothing more refreshing than a half-hour of foot reflexology. Tipping is a must.

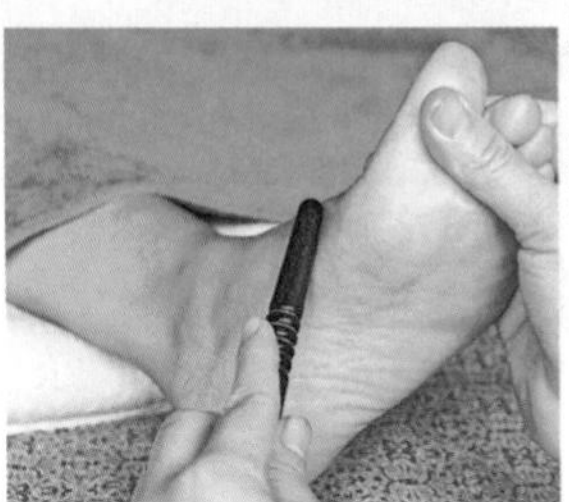

## Best Wellness Activities

- ▶ **Learn to meditate from monks at the Samui International Meditation Center.** (p219)
- ▶ **Get your first Thai massage at a Bangkok spa.** (p60)
- ▶ **Stay at one of Samui's luxury wellness resorts.** (p218)
- ▶ **Work up a sweat at moo-ay thai gym, Yodyut.** (p239)
- ▶ **Shop natural health products at Foods & Roots on Ko Pha-Ngan.** (p237)

### ★ VISUALLY IMPAIRED MASSAGE THERAPISTS

Find a spa employing visually impaired massage therapists. Such therapists are trained at special schools in Thailand and are highly talented.

**Above** Traditional Thai four hand massage **Left** Foot massage

# MERGING CULTURES

Thailand is highly multicultural. Over centuries, migrant communities of Chinese, Indian and other ethnic minorities have infused their traditions into Thai societies from north to south. While 85% of the population is Buddhist, Islam, Christianity and other religions are also represented. From landmarks to unique dishes, discover Thailand's stories of tolerance and diversity.

### Silom Soi 2 & 4

**Rainbow fun**

On the edge of the Patpong red-light district, Bangkok's main LGBTIQ+ area is bubbly and welcoming. You can catch drag shows, dance to bongos and electronic beats, and even do karaoke until the wee hours.

*15 minutes from downtown Sukhumvit*

▶ p57

### Nguan Choon Tong

**Ancient remedies**

Of the many Chinese herbal medicine shops in Phuket Old Town, this is the oldest. Fruit, bark and roots are weighed onto antique scales. Afterwards, sip a *kopitiam* at the family's small restaurant next door.

*25 minutes from Patong Beach*

▶ p209

Mae Sai
Chiang Rai
Mae Hong Son
Chiang Dao
Phayao
Chiang Mai
Doi Inthanon
Lampang
Ping
Salween
Sukhothai
Tak
Mawlamyine
Mae Sot
Kamphaeng Phet
MYANMAR (BURMA)
Mae Klong
Chao Phraya
Sangkhlaburi
Suphanburi
Kanchanaburi
Nakhon Pathom
Bay of Bengal
Ratchaburi
Phetchaburi
Hua Hin
Myeik Archipelago
Prachuap Khiri Khan
Port Blair
Andaman Islands
INDIA
Andaman Sea
Chumphon
Ko Tao
Ranong
Ko Pha-Ngan
Nicobar Islands
Ko Samui
Surat Thani
Ko Phra Thong
Nakhon Si Thammarat
Phang-Nga
Krabi
Ko Yao
Phuket Town
Phatthalung
Ko Phi Phi
Ko Lanta
Trang
Satun
Ko Tarutao
Pulau Langkawi
Strait of Malacca

0 200 km
0 100 miles

Baan Rak Thai
Tea village
Nestled in a permanent mountain fog, this tranquil Chinese village up north is significant for its authentic Yunnan culture, cuisine and nearby tea plantations. Stop by for a cuppa with the locals in a teahouse.
5 hours northwest of Chiang Mai
▸ p101
Cathedral of the Immaculate Conception
Christian worship
Chanthaburi, along the eastern gulf, is home to one of Thailand's largest Catholic churches. The cathedral is a historic devotion place for the local Vietnamese Christian minority which first fled from persecution here in the 19th century.
3 hours southeast of Bangkok
▸ p148
Chao Mae Lim Ko Niao
Chinese shrine
This beautiful shrine paying homage to a local heroine has a fascinating connection to the nearby Krue Sae Mosque. Every year, worshippers gather here at a post–Chinese New Year fair.
1½ hours east of Hat Yai
▸ p233
Krue Sae Mosque
Siamese-Islamic architecture
This 500-year-old mosque is one of Thailand's oldest and most prominent. Bullet holes on the walls represent a tragic 2004 showdown here taking place as part of southern Thailand's ongoing insurgency conflict.
1 ½ hours east of Hat Yai
▸ p234
Chiang Saen
Mekong
Nan
LAOS
Yom
Phrae
Vientiane
Nong Khai
Uttaradit
Loei
Udon Thani
Sakhon Nakhon
Nakhon Phanom
Phitsanulok
Phetchaburi
Khon Kaen
Chi
Mukdahan
South China Sea (East Sea)
Danang
Chaiyaphum
Roi Et
Amnat Charoen
Mekong
Nakhon Sawan
Mun
Nakhon Ratchasima (Khorat)
Si Saket
Ubon Ratchathani
Pakse
Surin
Lopburi
Saraburi
Ayuthaya
VIETNAM
Prachinburi
Bangkok
Aranyaprathet
Chonburi
Battambang
CAMBODIA
Pattaya
Tonlé Sap
Chanthaburi
Rayong
Trat
Ko Chang
Ko Kut
Koh Kong
Phnom Penh
Koh Rong
Mekong
Ho Chi Minh City
Phu Quoc Island
Gulf of Thailand
South China Sea (East Sea)
Con Dao Islands
Songkhla
Hat Yai
Pattani
Yala
Narathiwat
Alor Setar
Kota Bharu
MALAYSIA

Demand for accommodation peaks during the cool season. Book tours and overnight adventures in advance at lonelyplanet.com/activities/thailand/activities.

**↙ Lopburi Monkey Banquet**

Villagers court good luck by cooking for the 3000-plus monkeys in town on the last Sunday of November.

Lopburi

▸ p83

### Surin Elephant Festival

Considered the symbol for good luck, elephants from all over converge on this northeastern town to show off their skills.

Surin

### Loy Krathong/Yi Peng

On the evening of the 12th lunar month, Thais 'float' the sins of the past year away on makeshift water rafts or sky lanterns.

**NOVEMBER**

Average daytime max: 32°C (Bangkok)
Days of rainfall: 5 (Bangkok)

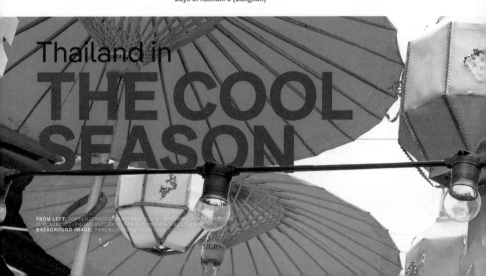

**DECEMBER**

Thailand in

# THE COOL SEASON

FROM LEFT: TOPTEN22PHOTO/SHUTTERSTOCK ©, APCHANEL/SHUTTERSTOCK ©, BLACKCATZ/SHUTTERSTOCK ©, VARIOUS IMAGES/SHUTTERSTOCK ©;
BACKGROUND IMAGE: PHAGALLEY/SHUTTERSTOCK

**↘ King's Birthday/Father's Day**

Thais celebrate Father's Day on 5 December, the birthday of Rama IX, which is usually a public holiday.

**↘ Chinese New Year**

At the start of the lunar new year, businesses owned by Chinese-Thais are shuttered and Chinatown (Yaowarat) erupts with celebrations.

Bangkok

**Wonderfruit**

Aimed at exploring art, music and food, this festival is expected to return in 2022 on the fringes of Pattaya.

▶ wonderfruit.co

▶ p145

**JANUARY**

**Average daytime max: 32°C (Bangkok)**
**Days of rainfall: 0 (Bangkok**

**Average daytime max: 32°C (Bangkok)**
**Days of rainfall: 1 (Bangkok)**

**Packing Notes**

Although it's the 'cool' season, you'll only need a jacket if you're in the north/northeast.

It's scorching outside, but a silver lining: the variety of tropical fruit in the markets is at its most bountiful.

### → Songkran

Also known as the 'water festival', Thai New Year on 13 April usually lasts three days. You will get splashed.

▶ p146

### ↓ Waterfalls

Beat the heat with a trip to some of the most beautiful waterfalls in Thailand at Kaeng Krachan.

▶ thainationalparks.com

▶ p187

**FEBRUARY**

Average daytime max: 34°C (Bangkok)
Days of rainfall: 2 (Bangkok)

**MARCH**

**APRIL**

# Thailand in THE HOT SEASON

**↓ Forest Monastery**

Since it's so hot outside, why not head to a cooling forest sanctuary for some enlightenment?

▶ p142

**→ Samui Wellness**

For something a little high-end, head to one of Ko Samui's famed wellness retreats.

▶ kamalaya.com

▶ p219

**↘ Phi Ta Khon (Ghost Festival)**

At this colourful festival, usually held in June, people dance in the streets wearing 'scary' masks and ringing bells to wake the spirits.

Loei

▶ p133

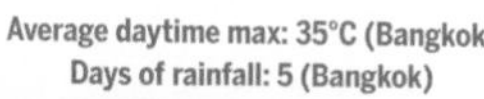

**MAY**

Average daytime max: 35°C (Bangkok)
Days of rainfall: 5 (Bangkok)

**JUNE**

Average daytime max: 35°C (Bangkok)
Days of rainfall: 14 (Bangkok)



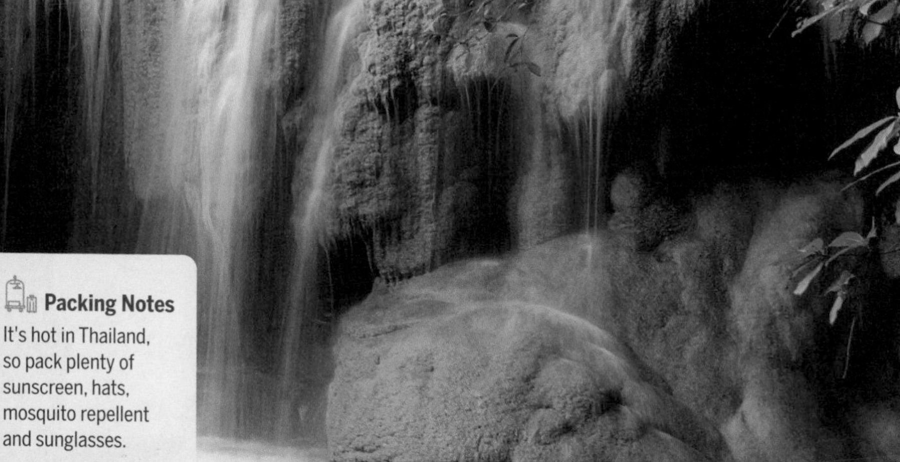

**Packing Notes**

It's hot in Thailand, so pack plenty of sunscreen, hats, mosquito repellent and sunglasses.

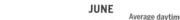

### ↘ Bun Bang Fai (Rocket Festival)

Adopted from the Laotians, this three-day northeastern festival features music and parades, culminating in a competition involving home-made rockets.

Yasathon

▶ p133

### ↙ Mekong Naga Fireballs

Every year people meet at the Laotian border to watch 'fire-balls' – a natural phenomenon – appear along the Mekong River.

Mekong River

### Candle Festival

Parade floats decorated with carved candle sculptures flood the streets of Ubon Ratchathani every July to mark the start of Buddhist Lent.

Ubon Ratchathani

▶ p133

Phuket and Samui experience the least rain in the country at this time, so now – when rates are down – is a good time to visit.

**JULY**

**Average daytime max: 33°C (Bangkok)**
**Days of rainfall: 14 (Bangkok)**

**AUGUST**

## Thailand in THE RAINY SEASON

**FROM LEFT:** YUPA WATCHANAKIT/SHUTTERSTOCK ©, BIRDBYB STOCKPHOTO/SHUTTERSTOCK ©, HOMAS FOO/SHUTTERSTOCK ©, MC 243/SHUTTERSTOCK ©, APCHANEL/SHUTTERSTOCK © **BACKGROUND IMAGE:** SANGKHOM HUNGKHUNTHOD/SHUTTERSTOCK ©

### ↓ Phuket Vegetarian Festival

Every 9th lunar month, festival participants celebrate the virtues of vegetarianism by displaying 'extreme' skills such as body piercing.

Phuket

### → Whale Watching

Whales can be spotted in the upper gulf between May and November, but October is considered the high season.

▶ bangkokwhale.com

### ↘ Running of the Water Buffalo

This nearly 200-year-old farmers' festival in Chonburi centres on the racing of water buffalo, an important animal in Thai agriculture.

Chonburi

**SEPTEMBER**

**Average daytime max: 33°C (Bangkok)**
**Days of rainfall: 18 (Bangkok)**

**OCTOBER**

**Average daytime max: 33°C (Bangkok)**
**Days of rainfall: 15 (Bangkok)**

### Packing Notes

A raincoat or umbrella is essential. Quick-drying clothes and non-slip shoes are important.

# UPPER GULF Trip Builder

**TAKE YOUR PICK OF MUST-SEES AND HIDDEN GEMS**

Sun, sand and slow life start just a couple hours' drive south from the capital, driving along the Gulf of Thailand's coasts. Hidden beaches and outdoor adventures abound.

## Trip Notes

**Hub towns** Hua Hin, Chumphon

**How long** Allow 2 weeks

**Getting Around** Hire a car for the highest convenience. Otherwise, taking minivans and trains between towns is also possible and quite economic, although much slower and potentially crowded.

**Tips** Destinations along the Gulf get very busy during weekends and public holidays such as Songkran. Book ahead to beat the Bangkok exodus.

0 50 km
0 25 miles
Pranburi
Escape on a motorbike into mangrove forests and hidden beaches.
30 mins from Hua Hin
Kui Buri National Park
Encounter wild elephants, and a plethora of other wildlife, in one of Thailand's most beloved national parks.
1½ hours from Hua Hin

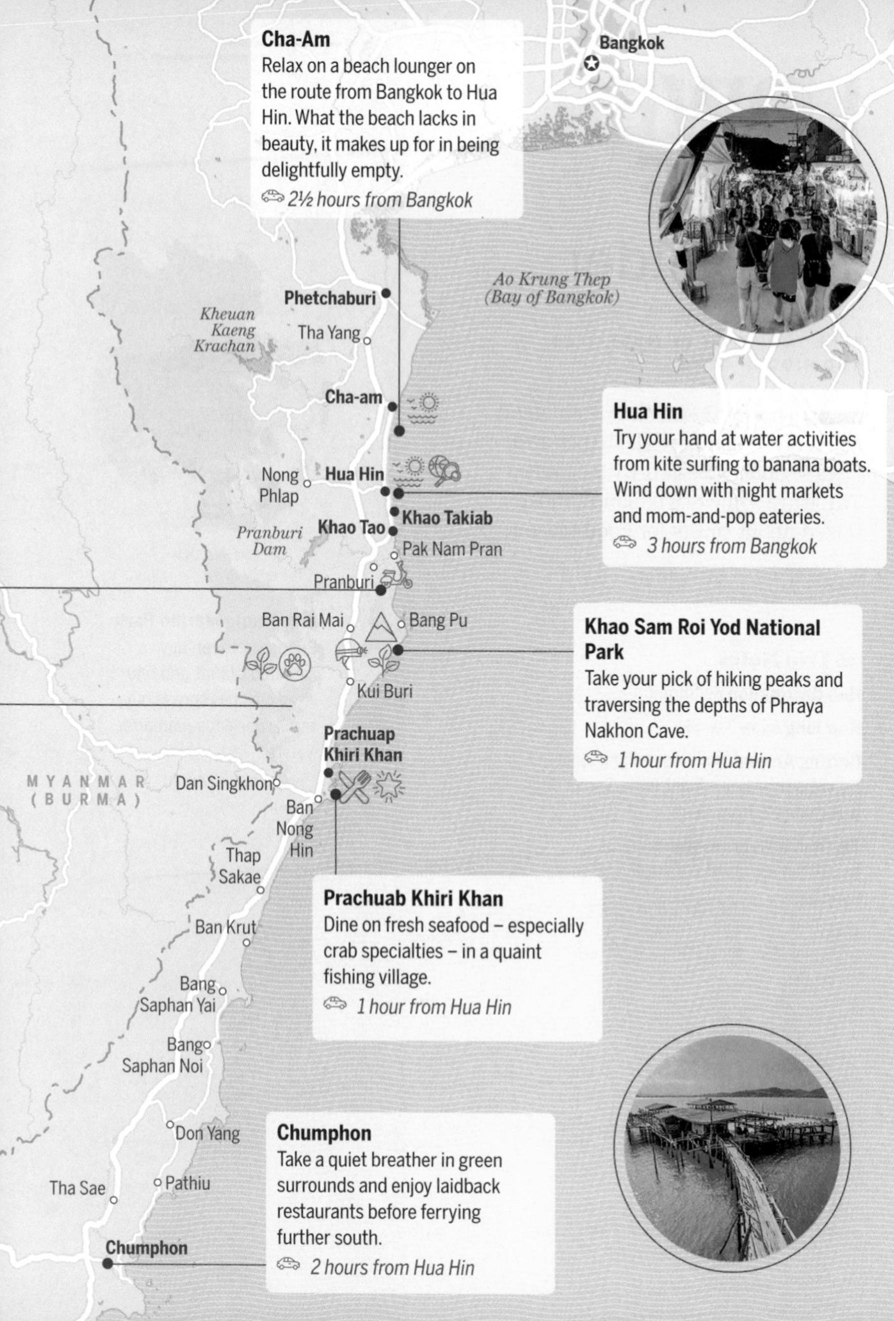
Cha-Am
Relax on a beach lounger on the route from Bangkok to Hua Hin. What the beach lacks in beauty, it makes up for in being delightfully empty.
2½ hours from Bangkok
Bangkok
Ao Krung Thep (Bay of Bangkok)
Phetchaburi
Kheuan Kaeng Krachan
Tha Yang
Cha-am
Hua Hin
Try your hand at water activities from kite surfing to banana boats. Wind down with night markets and mom-and-pop eateries.
3 hours from Bangkok
Nong Phlap
Hua Hin
Khao Takiab
Khao Tao
Pranburi Dam
Pak Nam Pran
Pranburi
Ban Rai Mai
Bang Pu
Khao Sam Roi Yod National Park
Take your pick of hiking peaks and traversing the depths of Phraya Nakhon Cave.
1 hour from Hua Hin
Kui Buri
Prachuap Khiri Khan
MYANMAR (BURMA)
Dan Singkhon
Ban Nong Hin
Thap Sakae
Prachuab Khiri Khan
Dine on fresh seafood – especially crab specialties – in a quaint fishing village.
1 hour from Hua Hin
Ban Krut
Bang Saphan Yai
Bang Saphan Noi
Don Yang
Tha Sae
Pathiu
Chumphon
Chumphon
Take a quiet breather in green surrounds and enjoy laidback restaurants before ferrying further south.
2 hours from Hua Hin

# LOWER GULF
## Trip Builder

**TAKE YOUR PICK OF MUST-SEES AND HIDDEN GEMS**

The southern slice of Thailand has it all – islands of all shapes and sizes seriously blessed with beauty. These are some of Thailand's most talked-about coasts for good reason.

### Trip Notes

**Hub destination** Ko Samui

**How long** Allow 3 weeks

**Getting Around** The most comfortable arrival is boarding a flight to Ko Samui and hiring wheels from there.

**Tip** Grab taxis are available on Ko Samui but are quite expensive and very unreliable.

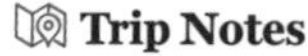

CLOCKWISE FROM LEFT: EXOXIDEZ/SHUTTERSTOCK ©, JOHN BACK/ SHUTTERSTOCK ©, ANNA EWA BIENIEK/SHUTTERSTOCK ©

0 — 20 km
0 — 10 miles

**Ang Thong Marine Park**
Bounce between tiny deserted islands and bite-sized beaches spread out across perfect aquamarine waters.
*1½ hour from Ko Samui*

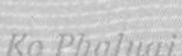


Don Sak

**Ko Tao**

Explore Ko Tao's bohemian spirit on diving trips, cliff jumping expeditions and sunset beach walks.

*1½ hours from Ko Samui*

Gulf of Thailand

Chong Tao

**Ko Pha-Ngan**

Rave on secluded sands until the sun comes up. Recharging is easy with plant-based food and coffee fixes.

*1½ hours from Ko Samui*

ng Thong Marine National Park

Chong Pha-Ngan

**Ko Samui**

Escape on a wellness journey with yoga, meditation, a digital detox or moo·ay thai. Seek out other island paradises.

*1 hour from Bangkok*

**Ko Madsum**

Take a day trip on a long-tail boat to befriend the island's hog inhabitants.

*30 minutes from Ko Samui*

# NORTHERN PROVINCES
## Trip Builder



**TAKE YOUR PICK OF MUST-SEES AND HIDDEN GEMS**

Beyond mountain tips and hairpin turns, expecting the unexpected is key up North. You never know what kinds of treasures you'll find. The roads can be challenging, but those who've visited swear that it's worth it.

### Trip Notes

**Hub towns** Chiang Mai, Chiang Rai

**How long** Allow 10 days

**Getting Around** A scooter will do just fine – although the bigger the bike, the more you can roam off the beaten track.

**Tips** Carry cash as most establishments in this part of Thailand do not accept cards. ATMs become scarcer the further you meander into remote areas.

0
100 km
0
50 miles
MYANMAR (BURMA)
Pai
Drive the Mae Hong Son Loop, rambling across wild jungle thickets and pretty rice paddies, to find reprieve in a backpacker's paradise.
3½ hours from Chiang Mai
Ban Rak Thai
Salween
Mae Hong Son
Khun Yuam
Mae Sariang
Mae Hong Son
Discover the culture and cuisine of local Yunnanese communities between magnificent mountain panoramas and deserted trails.
5½ hours from Chiang Mai
MYANMAR (BURMA)


CLOCKWISE FROM LEFT: LEMARET PIERRICK/SHUTTERSTOCK ©, OPPORTUNITY_2015/SHUTTERSTOCK ©, MAMINAMI/SHUTTERSTOCK ©

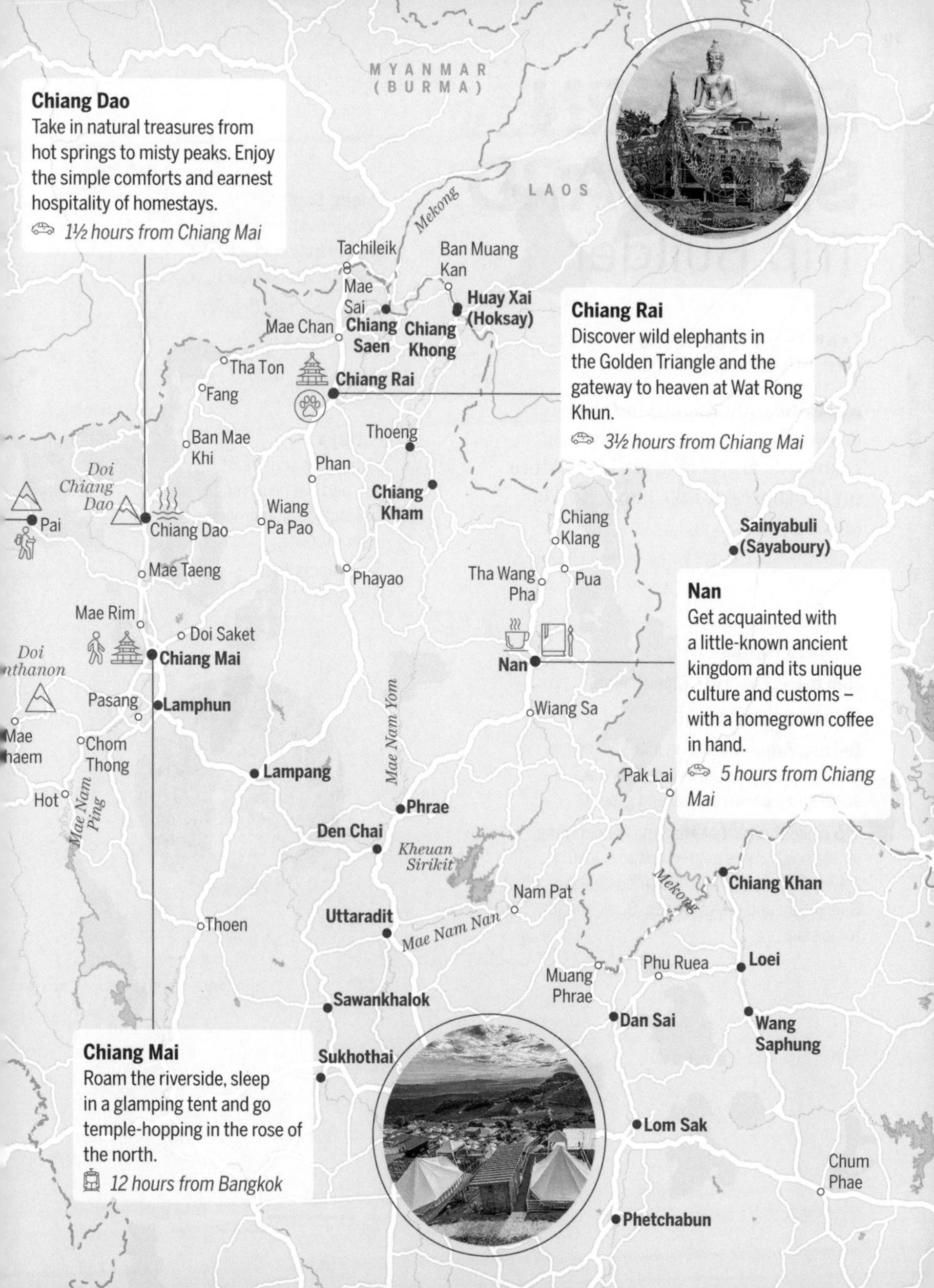
MYANMAR (BURMA)
LAOS
Chiang Dao
Take in natural treasures from hot springs to misty peaks. Enjoy the simple comforts and earnest hospitality of homestays.
1½ hours from Chiang Mai
Chiang Rai
Discover wild elephants in the Golden Triangle and the gateway to heaven at Wat Rong Khun.
3½ hours from Chiang Mai
Nan
Get acquainted with a little-known ancient kingdom and its unique culture and customs – with a homegrown coffee in hand.
5 hours from Chiang Mai
Chiang Mai
Roam the riverside, sleep in a glamping tent and go temple-hopping in the rose of the north.
12 hours from Bangkok
Mekong
Tachileik
Ban Muang Kan
Mae Sai
Huay Xai (Hoksay)
Mae Chan
Chiang Saen
Chiang Khong
Tha Ton
Fang
Chiang Rai
Thoeng
Ban Mae Khi
Phan
Doi Chiang Dao
Chiang Kham
Pai
Chiang Dao
Wiang Pa Pao
Chiang Klang
Sainyabuli (Sayaboury)
Mae Taeng
Phayao
Tha Wang Pha
Pua
Mae Rim
Doi Saket
Chiang Mai
Nan
Lamphun
Pasang
Wiang Sa
Chom Thong
Lampang
Mae Nam Yom
Pak Lai
Hot
Mae Nam Ping
Phrae
Den Chai
Kheuan Sirikit
Chiang Khan
Nam Pat
Thoen
Uttaradit
Mae Nam Nan
Phu Ruea
Loei
Muang Phrae
Sawankhalok
Dan Sai
Wang Saphung
Sukhothai
Lom Sak
Chum Phae
Phetchabun

# EASTERN SEABOARD
## Trip Builder

**TAKE YOUR PICK OF MUST-SEES AND HIDDEN GEMS**

Beating the beachcomber crowds can be as easy as heading eastwards and seeing what's in store on the shores of Ko Chang, Ko Mak and the like.

### Trip Notes

**Hub towns** Ko Chang, Chanthaburi

**How long** Allow 3 weeks

**Getting Around** Jump on a bus, minivan or flight to Trat or Rayong and rent a scooter once you're on island ground.

**Tip** While this part of Thailand is becoming increasingly more geared towards luxury travellers, you can still find good deals in Baeng San and on Ko Chang. Book ahead to be safe.

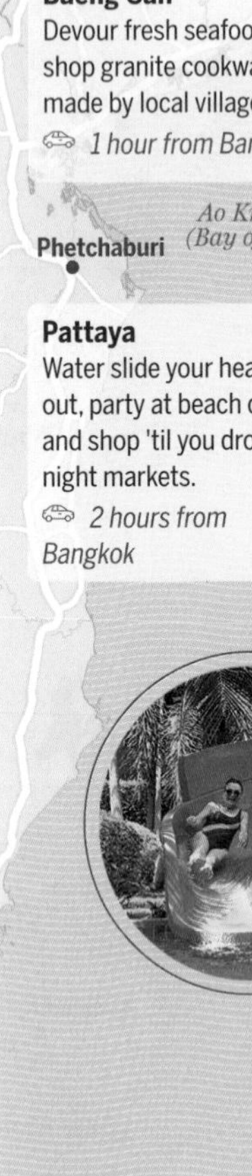

**Chanthaburi**
Discover the charms of a multicultural city and its historic waterfront quarter – from jewels and noodle soups to graffiti art.
*3 hours from Bangkok*

**Si Racha**
Reap the bragging rights of visiting the ancestral home of Sriracha chilli sauce. Do a little karaoke with the Japanese locals.
*1½ hours from Bangkok*

**Ko Samet**
Relax and indulge in resort life. Boat to little secluded islands all around the marine national park.
*2 hours from Rayong*

**Ko Mak**
Kayak all your cares away. Discover hidden beaches and dive into incredible turquoise depths.
*1 hour from Trat*

**Ko Chang**
Hike between pristine jungle and coastline. Discover coral reefs, aquatic life and shipwrecks off the coast.
*30 minutes from Trat*

**Ko Kut**
Mix it up between snorkelling and kayaking in crystalline waters. Laze around on white-sand beaches.
*1½ hour from Trat*

# 7 Things to Know About THAILAND

**INSIDER TIPS TO HIT THE GROUND RUNNING**

## 1 Food everywhere, literally

Thais are super innovative and entrepreneurial when it comes to turning anything into a food stall. Motorbikes turned into a food cart or a stall on the side of the road where you can sit and dine in are common sights throughout Thailand. And don't assume that because it's sold on the street, the food is substandard. Choose something from a freshly cooked, busy stall and enjoy!

▶ See more about street food on p46

## 2 Anything can be breakfast

Thai breakfast options go beyond cereal, eggs and bacon, and toast. You are more than welcome to eat your green curry or pad thai for breakfast without judgement.

## 3 Bum guns

This bathroom invention will change your life. Forget wiping your behind with toilet paper; in Thailand, people use water for cleansing. Don't be scared to try it!

## 4 Don't wait to be approached

Getting ripped off is probably on a lot of people's minds when travelling to Thailand. To avoid paying pumped-up prices, do your research and find your own operators. When someone approaches you to offer a service, it's good to ask a lot of questions.

## 5 Alcohol sale restrictions

Ironically, for a country that many tourists dream to party in, you cannot buy alcohol around the clock in Thailand – only from 11am to 2pm and 5pm to midnight. There are also no alcohol sales on Buddhist holidays. These rules impact the income of local businesses, which is why you will always find some places who sneakily let the regulations slide...

## 6 Bowing to tradition

Despite the nation's sometimes modern facade, Thais still bow to tradition, praying and worshipping the supernatural. You will find all sorts of shrines all over Thailand that the locals pray and give offerings to, whether it's a spirit house at a residence (believed to be the home of angels that protect your abode from bad things) or a sculpture. Some trees can also be considered sacred – look out for those wrapped in colourful fabric. No one really knows why, but red soda is a common offering throughout Thailand. It's okay if you don't believe in any of these superstitions, but it doesn't hurt to be humble and respectful when you see locals praying at the stump of a tree.

▶ See more about the supernatural on p84

## 7 Hands off!

It's not common for Thais to greet each other by hugging or kissing on cheeks. In fact, it could make locals uncomfortable. However, if an old lady who you've never met before starts playing with your toddler, touching their cheek and calling them *na rak* (cute), that's totally normal...

▶ See more about etiquette on p253

# Read, Listen, Watch & Follow

## READ

**Thailand's Best Street Food** (Chawadee Nualkhair; 2015) The ultimate guide to everything street food around Thailand.

**The Blind Earthworm in the Labyrinth** (Veeraporn Nitiprapha; 2013) The first female writer to win SEA Write Award twice.

**Very Thai** (Philip Cornwel Smith; 2005) A complete guide looking into modern contemporary Thai culture.

**Bangkok Eight** (John Burdett; 2003) A Bangkok-based thriller about a devout Buddhist policeman, Sonchai Jitpleecheep.

## LISTEN

**Rasmee** Up-and-coming Thai indie artist; perfect combination of jazz and *molam* (Thai northeastern folk) music, often sung in the orginal dialogue.

**The Bangkok Podcast** Cultural commentary about what's happening in Thailand from an expat's perspective.

**Carabao** Legendary Thai blues/rock music known as the icon for *phleng phuea chiwit* (songs for life).

**The Suntharsphon Band** Traditional Thai popular music from the early '30s, with a delicate and gentle sound.

KAN SANGTONG/SHUTTERSTOCK ©

**Rap Against Dictatorship**

Thai rap group famous among the democracy protest movement, with lyrics criticising the unfairness and inequality of Thailand.

## WATCH

**Street Food Asia (2019)** Explore the best street food culture in Bangkok.

**Mae Nak movies** (pictured bottom right) Watch a movie, then visit the shrine at Wat Mahabut in Bangkok.

**The Serpent (2021)** The story about 1970s conman and murderer Charles Sobhraj; partly filmed in Bangkok.

**The Promise (2017)** Thai horror/drama movie based on Sathorn 'Ghost Tower' and Asia's financial crisis.

**Midnight Asia (2022)** Explore what goes on in Bangkok at night via food, drink, music and more.

ANANSING/SHUTTERSTOCK ©

PANIDA WIJITPANYA/GETTY IMAGES ©

## FOLLOW

**@ohhappybear**
Instagram page on Thai food and culture.

**@BKKFatty**
Twitter community about food in Bangkok.

**@Thai Enquirer**
A fresh take on local news.

**Mark Wiens**
Food video tours on YouTube.

**@BK Magazine**
English-language magazine on the hip and happening in Bangkok.

**Sate your Thailand dreaming with a virtual vacation at lonelyplanet.com/thailand#planning**

BANGKOK
VIBRANT | CHAOTIC | LIMITLESS
Experience Bangkok online
Panasonic
MITSUBISHI ELECTRIC
TISCO
TAXI
TOYOTA

Jump on a boat and eat your way through the floating market along **Khlong Lat Mayom** (p42)

*20 minutes from the city centre*

Wake up early to catch the action at the **Flower Market (Pak Klong Talad)** and grab breakfast nearby, followed by a walk around the Old Town (p43)

*3 minutes from MRT Sanam Chai underground train station*

Check out the Portuguese touches to Thai architecture in the **Kudi Chin** area (p44)

*8-minute ride on a tuk-tuk*

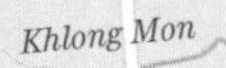

TALING CHAN

Th Boromaratchachonanee

Khlong Bangkok Noi

Chao Phraya River

BANG LAMPH

DUSI

BANGPHA

Ratchapruk Rd

KHLONG BANGKOK NOI

PHRA NAKHON

Khlong Mon

KHLONG BANG LUANG

KHLONG BANGKOK YAI

Th Prachathipok

KHLON SAN

Khlong Bangkok Yai

Th Phetkasem

THONBURI

Th Charoen Nak

Chao Phraya Riv

Th Taksin

THANO TOK

Th Suksawat

# BANGKOK
## Trip Builder

Bangkok is the city that never sleeps, which means there's something going on 24/7. Whether it's getting out of bed at dawn to catch the city waking up or staying out so late at night you see local breakfast stalls preparing for their day, plan to experience Bangkok at any hour of the day.

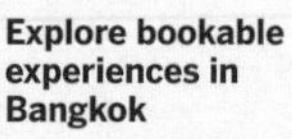

**Explore bookable experiences in Bangkok**

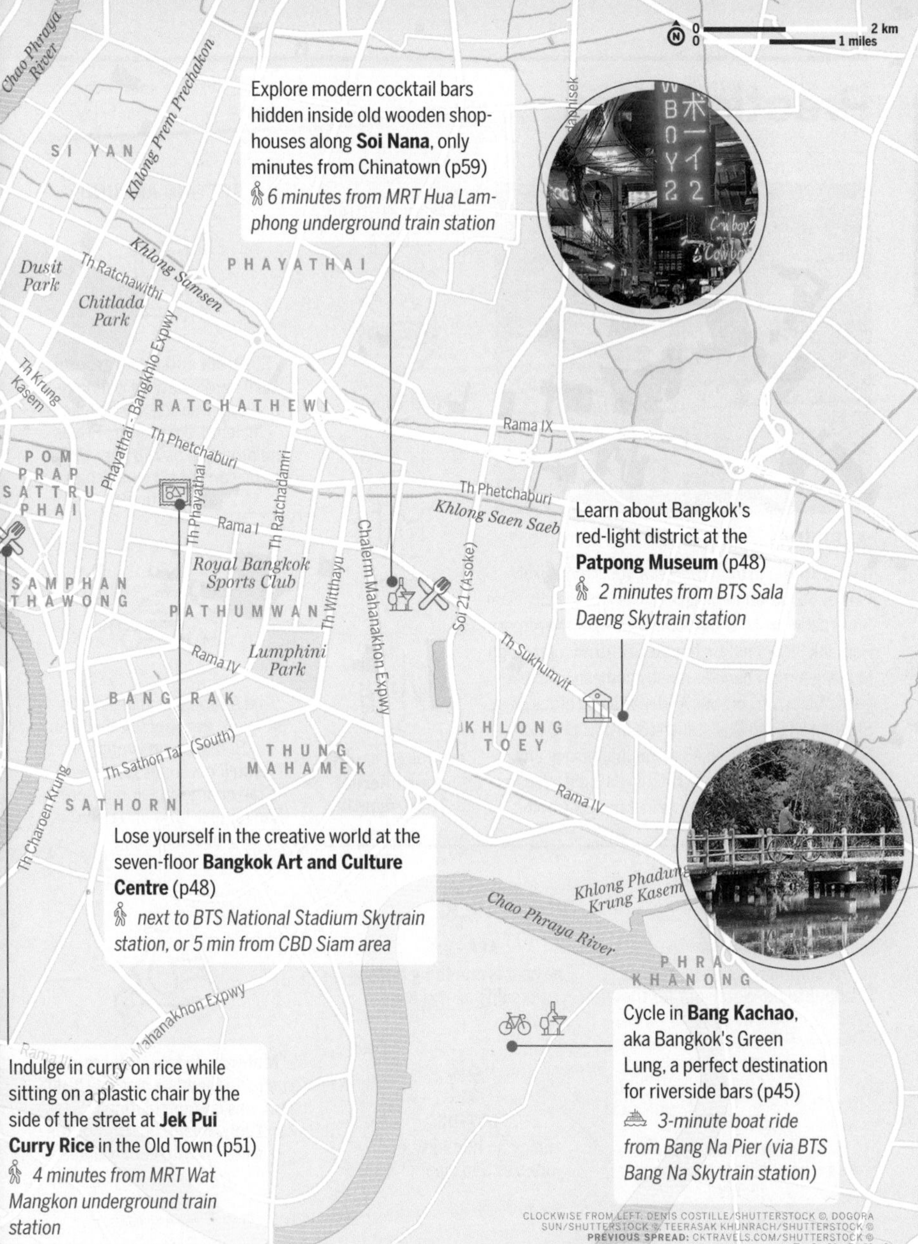


Explore modern cocktail bars hidden inside old wooden shophouses along **Soi Nana**, only minutes from Chinatown (p59)
*6 minutes from MRT Hua Lamphong underground train station*

Learn about Bangkok's red-light district at the **Patpong Museum** (p48)
*2 minutes from BTS Sala Daeng Skytrain station*

Cycle in **Bang Kachao**, aka Bangkok's Green Lung, a perfect destination for riverside bars (p45)
*3-minute boat ride from Bang Na Pier (via BTS Bang Na Skytrain station)*

Lose yourself in the creative world at the seven-floor **Bangkok Art and Culture Centre** (p48)
*next to BTS National Stadium Skytrain station, or 5 min from CBD Siam area*

Indulge in curry on rice while sitting on a plastic chair by the side of the street at **Jek Pui Curry Rice** in the Old Town (p51)
*4 minutes from MRT Wat Mangkon underground train station*

# Practicalities

NITINUT380/SHUTTERSTOCK ©

## ARRIVING

If you're flying in from overseas, you'll most likely land at Suvarnabhumi Airport. Get into the city from Suvarnabhumi by taxi (around 200B) or the Airport Rail Link Skytrain (less than 100B, 45 minutes). Don Mueang Airport handles mostly domestic and budget services. Airport bus A1 departs and drops off at Skytrain BTS Mo Chit station (30B); A2 at Victory Monument (30B); and A3 at Ratchaprasong and Lumphini (50B). If you're catching a flight, plan for extra time for your commute in Bangkok's traffic.

## HOW MUCH FOR A

**Pàd gàprow 50B**

**Local beer 4B**

**Unlimited smartphone internet 200B/month**

## WHEN TO GO

**JAN–MAR**
Pre-summer, not as humid but about to be. Watch out for the air quality.

**APR–JUN**
The heat is one thing but the humidity is next level.

**JUL–SEP**
Rain, storms, monsoon. But also fewer visitors and cheaper flights.

**OCT–DEC**
Enjoy no humidity, cool breezes and clear skies.

## GETTING AROUND

**Skytrain and underground** You'll hardly have to wait longer than four minutes on Bangkok's efficient train system. Prices are as cheap as 17B per station. Trains can get extremely packed at busy times.

**Taxi** As soon as you arrive in Bangkok, get yourself the Grab and Bolt apps on your phone – you'll never get lost again. Grab charges a fair bit more than regular taxis and Bolt only accepts cash.

**Motorcycle taxi** If you're in a rush and there's a massive traffic jam, this is your solution. It's fast and convenient, but it's not the safest way to get around.

## EATING & DRINKING

You'll always be able to find food in Bangkok – 24 hours of every day. Apart from the city's ubiquitous food stalls and famed eateries, you can also order food on apps like Grab, Robinhood or foodpanda.

Make it your mission to try as many of Bangkok's noodle dishes as possible. Likewise the enticing array of fruit; try them all – even the durian. And if you've got a sweet tooth, hunt down Thai chocolate brands like Kad Kokoa or Shabar.

There are plenty of local brewers to support; try Outlaw, Devanom, Sandport (pictured bottom right) or Stone Head.

For a Thai coffee experience, most cafes in Bangkok use beans sourced from the mountains up north.

**Best Thai chocolate**
Kad Kokoa

**Must-try beef noodles**
Wattana Panich Beef Broth (p64)

## CONNECT & FIND YOUR WAY

**Wi-fi** Internet quality in Bangkok is good, but free public wi-fi is rare. It's cheap to buy a local Thai SIM card with unlimited internet.

**Navigation** You could ask a local, but not everyone speaks English fluently. You can't go wrong with Google Maps or transport apps like Grab or Bolt.

## TRAIN PASSES

Unlike other big cities, there's no such thing as one ticket for all transport. You have to buy a pass for each different train system. Walking around town is totally doable.

## WHERE TO STAY

Whether you're looking to throw yourself into the chaos or want something slower, you'll be able to experience it all in Bangkok.

| Neighbourhood | Pros/Cons |
|---|---|
| Old Town | Close to the river; blend yourself into the local community. Can be touristy. |
| Sathorn | CBD area that's close enough to both the Old Town and Sukhumvit area. |
| Lower Sukhumvit (Ploen Chit-Nana-Asoke) | Very busy, but if you like the vibrancy, it could be fun. |
| Mid Sukhumvit (Phrom Phong-Thong Lo-Ekkamai) | A busyish area, but more residential. |
| Upper Sukhumvit (Phra Khanong and beyond) | Further out from the city centre, but with BTS Skytrain stations, commuting is not a problem. |

## MONEY

Your bank cards will work in Thailand, however, to be completely sure, contact your bank before departing home. Always, always carry cash, especially small notes for taxis or street food.

# 01 Thai Food CANALSIDE

FLOATING MARKETS | FRESH | FOOD

Floating markets are the best way to eat everything and experience all Thai cuisine at once, so arrive hungry. To get the best out of this adventure, aim to snack on small bites so you can leave room for the next delicious thing you see.

### How to

**Getting there** Taxis will get you here.

**When to go** Any time, but expect high water levels in the rainy season.

**Travel light** Fresh markets are usually in confined spaces and crowded, so avoid bringing a big backpack. You could be eating standing up or hopping on canal boats too, so travel light.

**Cash up** Make sure you bring enough cash, especially small notes. ATMs can be hard to find.

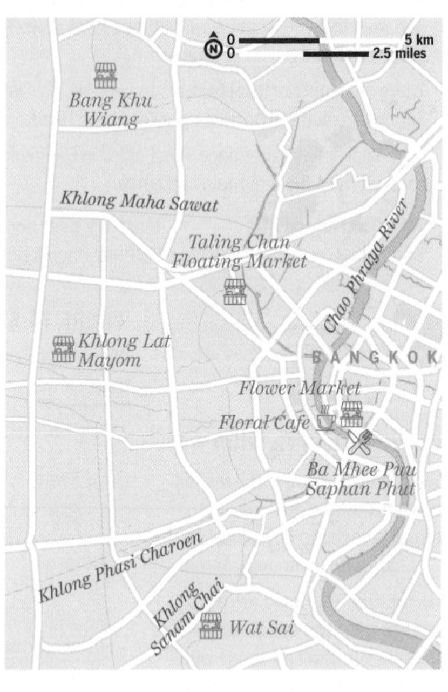


## Step Back in Time

**Khlong Lat Mayom** (as seen on Netflix's *Street Food Asia*) is the perfect place to spend a day! Surrounded by nature and just 20 to 40 minutes drive (depending on traffic) outside Bangkok, it has a preserved culture and way of life that will transport you back to a time when living next toa river or canal was the equivalent of living next to a main street today. Find a riverboat to rent for the day and float through the neighbourhood, exploring small temples nearby, like **Wat Theppol** or **Wat Chang Lek**.

When visiting a floating market, not only do you get to eat traditional Thai dishes, you'll also experience how the Thai business district would have looked and functioned about 200 years ago. You'll be surprised how much cooking can be done on the water – even making a bowl of noodles can be done right from the canal boat.

Today, the majority of floating markets have moved onto land and are big tourist attractions for both internationals and locals. Everyone here, except the vendors, are tourists, even the Thais. While there is still definitely some language barrier, it's OK to ask questions about the food in English, as the vendors are familiar with daily foreign visitors. Must-sees include **Taling Chan**, **Bang Khu Wiang** and **Wat Sai**.

## Bangkok Flower Market

**Bangkok Flower Market (Pak Klong Talad)** is the biggest wholesale and retail fresh flower market in the city. It's open 24 hours but the best time to visit is pre-dawn when street vendors from all over Bangkok stop by to grab their fresh supplies for the day. The market is located in the Old Town, minutes from **Wat Pho** and other historical landmarks, like **Saphan Phut (Memorial Bridge)**.

After your visit, grab a coffee nearby at **Floral Cafe** at Napasorn, then move on to crabmeat noodles for lunch at **Ba Mhee Puu Saphan Phut** (at Memorial Bridge) that will only set you back 50B.

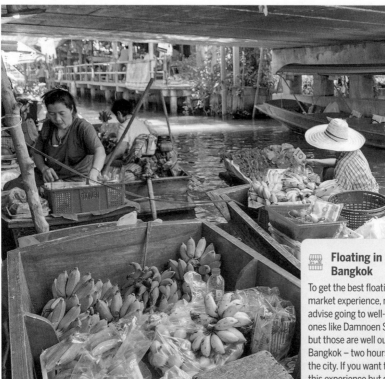

### Floating in Bangkok

To get the best floating market experience, many advise going to well-known ones like Damnoen Saduak, but those are well out of Bangkok – two hours from the city. If you want to have this experience but still make it back in time for dinner reservations, try **Khlong Lat Mayom**, which is more navigable and less crowded.

■ **By Chawadee Nualkhair,** *author of Thailand's Best Street Food, Instagram @BangkokGlutton*

**Above** Khlong Lat Mayom floating market

# 02 Heart of Bangkok: CHAO PHRAYA

**HISTORIC | SLOW LIFE | MIXED CULTURE**

The Chao Phraya is the main river that flows through Bangkok and into the Gulf of Thailand. While the riverside in Bangkok is a tourist-magnet, with popular landmarks like Wat Arun and Asiatique, the riverside's history goes far beyond that. For Thailand's capital, the river used to be the heart of everything and was the main source of life before urban establishments.

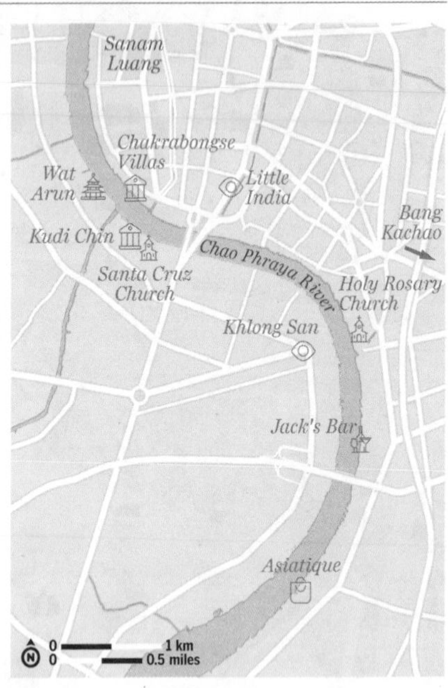


### How to

**Getting there** Skytrain or underground train.

**When to go** Late afternoon for late lunch or early dinner, with sunset at a riverside bar, a cocktail in Soi Nana and post-drinking food in Chinatown.

**Flooding** Any time after heavy rain, but especially from late June to the end of October, the Chao Phraya River can flood. Usually the water will disappear in a few hours but add extra time to your commute if you're using the road.

## Cultural Remnants

You can expect to see a hint of other cultures this side of Bangkok, like Chinese (red lanterns), Japanese (the minimal wooden buildings often found housing onsen spas or cafes), Indian (the colourful Phahurat Rd) and Portuguese (Kudi Chin). Foreigners have been living and working in the city since the early era, leaving architectural crumbs as they go.

Unlike the high-rises in the centre, this part of town has more historic buildings and thanks to Thailand's Urban Plan Law (disallowing tall buildings here), much of the architectural beauty dates back many centuries.

## Historic Architecture

**Kudi Chin**, on the bank of the Chao Phraya, dates back to King Taksin's formation of Thonburi as the capital in 1767. Here, you'll find some Portuguese influence – visit the **Holy Rosary Church** or **Santa Cruz Church**.

Other highlights include **Chakrabongse Villa** (1908), which welcomes guests to visit and stay, or you can walk through **Khlong San**, **Little India** and **Talad Noi**. This is the perfect spot to blend into local communities, sampling foods from roadside stalls. As the sun sets, find a table at a riverside bar, such as **Jack's Bar** or **Samsara Cafe & Meal**, or head to the rooftop

DAVID BOKUCHAVA/SHUTTERSTOCK ©



bar at **sala rattanakosin** for a sundown cocktail.

## Bangkok's Green Lung

Take a boat from Bang Na Pier across the Chao Phraya River into **Bang Kachao**, a preserved neighbourhood surrounded by forests, and with no high buildings in sight. Spend a day cycling around this green island and stop for a drink at a riverside bar to catch the sunset. Bring mosquito repellent!

## Private Canal Boat Tours

If you're unsure where to start or what to see, bangkokriverboat.com offers the chance to explore with no schedule. It's an open-ended canal experience that lets you choose where to stop. It can even take you to Ayuthaya for the night. The old wooden boat comes with a cooler so you can bring beverages and food if you wish. Starting at B2000 per hour, the boat can take up to 10 people.

### Relax by the River

Bangkok is a chaotic city but the riverside offers a mini escape from the hustle and bustle. Gazing at the water and catching one of the best sunsets the city has to offer can help you unwind after a fast-paced day.

■ **By Nopparat Thongsuk**, *owner of Samsara Cafe & Meal, a drinking spot located inside a charming, wooden riverside house*

**Above** Cycling, Bang Kachao

# Street Food Vendors: The Unsung Heroes

**MORE THAN JUST FOOD SERVED STREET-SIDE**

The City that Never Sleeps... Bangkok is vibrant, full of life and there's always something going on. That also goes for the food. It doesn't matter what time you're hungry, there will always be street vendors cooking something, ready for you to stuff your face with.

DAY2505/SHUTTERSTOCK ©

**Left** Woman cooking Thai noodle soup in a floating market.
**Middle** Vendor, the Khao San area
**Right** Khao San Road street food

'*Kin khao rue yung*?' Or 'Have you eaten (rice) yet?' is a common saying in Thailand as a way of greeting each other. It's kind of like the British 'You OK? Would you like some tea?', the Aussie 'How you goin'?', or the French '*ça va*?'.

Asking someone if they have eaten yet in Thai culture is a way of saying you care for them, without actually having to say that you care for them out loud. Thai country-folk music singer Tai Orathai sings exactly about this. In her lyrics, she sings about how the man that she loves had to leave their hometown to work in the big city of Bangkok, and she would ask him this question on the phone over and over, to show that she cares and misses him.

Food is a very big part of Thai culture – you'll never go hungry in this country. And eating out won't necessarily break the bank either. Bangkok's food scene has so much to offer that you will be able to find memorable eats in all price categories, from very cheap street food to very expensive fine-dining paired with wines. Here, there will always be food: food carts, food vendors, food on motorbikes-transformed-into-vendors...There's pretty much food at every corner. It doesn't matter what you're craving or what time you're craving it, there's a good chance that you'll be able to find it in Bangkok.

That's because street food vendors are not only just trying to feed you, they are also trying to feed themselves and make a living out of selling food. Street vendors have

1000 WORDS/SHUTTERSTOCK ©

THITIKORN/SHUTTERSTOCK ©



to continue to sell and make money even when the streets are flooded after heavy rain, when the pollution outside is unhealthy to breathe in and even during Covid-19. Street vendors hold a responsibility to feed this city through any hardship, and they do so with no support from the government or social security.

> It doesn't matter what you're craving or what time you're craving it, there's a good chance that you'll be able to find it in Bangkok.

This is fortunate for locals – and tourists – because everybody has to eat. Food from street food vendors is usually hot, freshly cooked, very affordable and ready to be eaten. In a city that moves fast, where people are always busy and where most affordable accommodation for locals doesn't usually come with a cooking space, street food vendors enable people to live without having to prepare any meals themselves.

So while your stomach is being taken care of by street food vendors, keep in mind you are also helping them survive by supporting their business too.

## Supporting Each Other

The street food scene has developed over this landscape that the people are trying to feed themselves. Some locals don't always have a kitchen, when you walk out of your hotel you don't really get to see that perspective of how Thai people live. For some people, space, time and finance can be very limited, and they have to rely on the street food vendors to feed them. And the food is delicious, the people are nice, but the reality is there's more to the story – the people are trying to eat and the vendors are trying to make ends meet as well.

■ **By Dwight Turner**, *runs cooking classes and street food tours in Bangkok, Instagram/ Twitter @bkkfatty, Instagram @ courageouskitchen*

# 03 Bangkok off the BEATEN TRACK

QUIRKY | ARTSY | SPIRITUAL

If you're bored of the tourist trail, regular food tours, drinking at bars and temple visits, these experiences are for you. These activities will let you glimpse another side of Bangkok – one that's unexpected, less known to the world and uniquely Thai. Most people wouldn't even know what to Google to find encounters like these!

SOPA IMAGES LIMITED/ALAMY LIVE NEWS ©

## All That's Quirky

While the surrounding area keeps developing, travel back in time to '70s Thailand by heading to the **Nightingale Olympic** shopping mall. Note that no photos are allowed inside.

Learn about the history of Bangkok's red-light district at **Patpong Museum**, which brings the Cold War, the Vietnam War and the Secret War in Laos into the context of Bangkok's 'soi of sex'.

PERCULIAR BOY/SHUTTERSTOCK ©

## Artsy Pursuits

Art has always pushed boundaries and here is no different; talented locals create controversial works to challenge the political climate. Alex Face (BTS National Stadium Skytrain station and

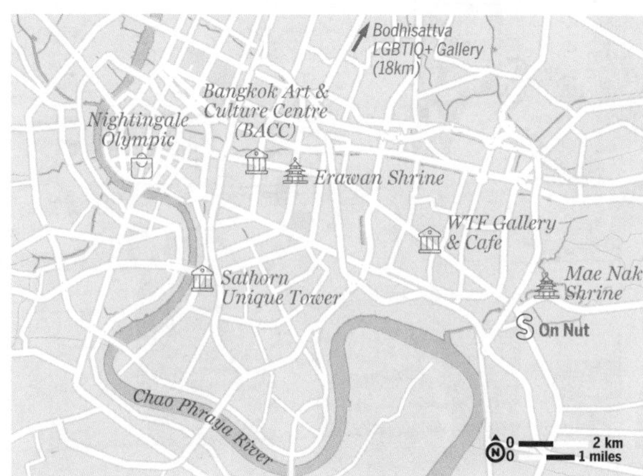


Bangkok CityCity Gallery) and Muebon (Charoenkrung Soi 28) are two of the big graffiti artists. Baphoboy is an up-and-coming Thai political artist to keep an eye on. His works exists mostly on Instagram and exhibitions at various galleries.

For gallery visits, check out the **Bangkok Art and Culture Centre (BACC)**, **WTF Gallery and Cafe** (evenings are the best as it's also a bar!) and cute **Kathmandu** photo gallery in Silom, where you can also buy affordable prints.

## Feeling the Spirits

The ghost story of Mae Nak (Nang Nak) is a tale every Thai remembers (p86). Her shrine is located at **Wat Mahabut**, a 10-minute walk from the Skytrain On Nut station. Visit the night before lottery day (1st and 16th each month) to see the temple in full action and to ask for the winning lottery numbers.

Visit **Erawan Shrine** in Chidlom, to see Thai traditional dancers around the four-face shrine. These dancers are hired as thanks by those whose prayers to the shrine have been answered.

Another spectral sight is the 47-storey **Sathorn Unique Tower**, or 'Ghost Tower', a victim of the 1997 Tom Yum Kung financial crisis. You can spot it when travelling from Sathorn to Chinatown. It now hosts street graffiti, and homeless people also take shelter here.

## Photo Tours to Go-Karts

A great way to explore Bangkok on foot is a photography walk with **@sweetfilmbar**. The walk usually takes you to an area that makes you question if you're actually still in Bangkok! There's no need for an analogue camera; your phone or digital camera is welcome, too.

Speed through the city centre, skipping traffic jams on an **E-Gokart by Monowheel** tucked away in the middle of the Siam Centre area.

## How to

**Getting there** It doesn't matter which part of Bangkok you are in, you'll always find a taxi, motorbike taxi or tuk-tuk to get you to your destination.

**When to go** All year round; some places are great for rainy days.

**Get lost** Most of these places are off the beaten path, but thanks to apps like Grab or Bolt, you can never really be truly lost.

**Left** Patpong Museum.
**Below** Erawan Shrine

### Art Reflecting Life

While the state constantly tries to erase and reconstruct the nation's narrative, one can see the reflection of what's truly Thailand in its art scene – a constant contradiction and flux. You will see a portrait of the king in gold, facing queer artists painting [democracy movement] protest posters. That's what makes us the most exciting place for art lovers in Southeast Asia.

■ **By Oat Montien**, *artist, writer and owner of Bodhisattva LGBTIQ+ Gallery, Instagram @oatmontienstudio, @bodhisattava.gallery*

# 04 Have You EATEN YET?

**ACCESSIBLE | NON-STOP | VARIETY**

The question 'Have you eaten yet?' is one of the many ways Thais greet each other. It's a way of showing that they care, as if when your stomach is full, everything else in the world is fine. You will never go hungry in Bangkok. It doesn't matter what time you're hungry or what you're craving...this city *will* feed you.

FEELGOODLUCK/SHUTTERSTOCK ©

## How to

**Getting there** Bangkok is easily accessible. You can walk or use motorbike taxis, regular taxis or the Skytrain or underground systems, depending on where you are going.

**When to go** Whenever you're hungry.

**Spoilt for choice** On top of international cuisine, you'll find native food from all around Thailand in Bangkok.

**Street food** Don't be scared to try street vendors – you might be surprised at what you can find. It goes without saying that everything is affordable.

OSAZE CUOMO/SHUTTERSTOCK ©

### Protein Cravings?

Thai-French beef is so underrated and deserves more recognition. It's originally from the north-eastern part of Thailand, which is dense with farms. Anywhere around Bangkok you will see meat on a stick – and it's a must try whether it's pork, beef, or beyond!

Thais love to get together and eat, and *mŏo krata* (literally, pork pan) is a fun experience to have. A group of people sit around a charcoal stove, grill meat and eat together. Of course, you can do this as a one-person experience, but it's not quite the same.

One food innovation you can't miss is *mŏo grob* (crispy pork): try it in a *phat kaphrao* (basil stir-fry) dish. For meat curry, **Jek Pui Curry Rice** in the Old Town is both tasty and a great Thai street food experience where you get to sit and eat on a plastic chair with no tables.

PUMPUI/SHUTTERSTOCK ©

### Gub Glam

Thais have a specific name for 'drinking food': gub glam. These dishes are commonly fresh and hot and go together nicely with icy cold beer (you'll find it's common to drink beer with ice in Thailand). The favourites among drinkers are various kinds of yum (spicy salad) dishes. For your first gub glam experience, visit Samlor in Charoenkrung for elevated gub glam dishes and natural wines or Thai craft beer.

**Above left** Jek Pui Curry Rice. **Above** *Sôm đam* (spicy green papaya salad). **Left** *Mŏo Krata*.

You can't leave Thailand without trying *sôm·đam* (spicy green papaya salad)– originally from the north east, *som tum* is ordered pretty much everywhere in Thailand. It's best with grilled chicken, grilled pork neck or *nham tok* (a spicy meat dish). **Baan Somtum** is a good first experience as it serves northeastern cuisine to a milder Bangkokian taste. Check out **100 Mahaseth** for more elevated northeastern dishes.

### Simply Seafood

Seafood is very popular in Thailand. A **Jay Fai** Michelin-starred crab omelette is the ultimate must-try for anyone in Bangkok. Or head over to **Jeh Oh Chula** for its signature tom yum mama noodle special that comes with an ocean of seafood and is served only after 10pm.

### Oodles of Noodles

Just like Italians with their huge variety of pasta, Thailand also has different types of noodles: *sen yai* (big noodles), *sen lek* (small noodles), *sen mhee* (tiny noodles), *ba mhee leung* (yellow noodles), *giam ee* (short noo-

### The Future of Food

Bangkok is a very multicultural destination, whether it's different cultures from all over Thailand or the world, and that unavoidably translates to its food scene. In recent years, local farmers have been stepping up their agricultural skills massively, trying to grow everything organically with many restaurants happy to source their goods from them.

**By Napol Jantraget**, *chef and co-owner at Samlor Restaurant in Charoenkrung, Instagram @samlor.bkk*

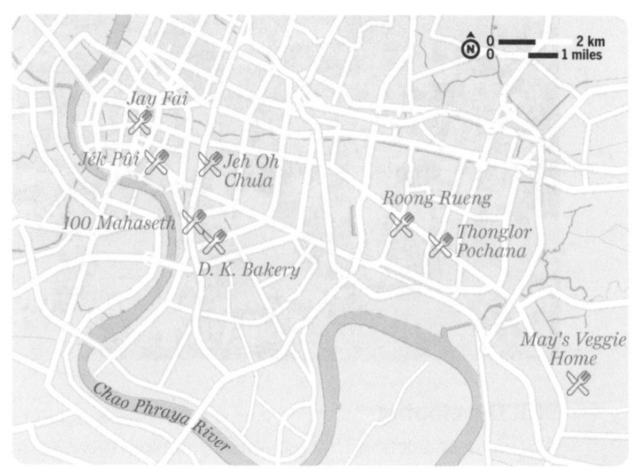

## Vegetarian Offerings

It used to be tricky to get a completely vegetarian meal in Bangkok, but it has been getting easier in recent years, with the menu being more creative, too. May's Veggie Home, Vistro and Arawy are the top three must-visits.

**Left** Jay Fai.
**Below** Paithong coconut ice cream

dles), *guay jub* (curled-up noodles – these come with their own kind of soup and style) and *mama* (instant noodles).

The way to order noodles in Thailand is simple: just pick what type of noodles you want, whether you want them with or without broth (dry noodles are good!), and then wait to be served!

Visit **Thonglor Pochana** for beef noodles or **Roong Rueng** or **Zaew Noodle** on Sukhumvit Soi 49 (not to be confused with the one on Sukhumvit Soi 57) for tom yum pork noodles.

### Sweet Treats

A large part of what makes Bangkok so vibrant is its street food vendors – and desserts can be found among them. If the food gods are smiling and you come across an ice-cream cart called **Paithong**, try the coconut ice cream. Or grab any coconut ice cream from any cart, chances are they will be just as tasty and refreshing in the Bangkok heat.

For bakery lovers, head over to **D.K. Bakery** in Silom, a local Thai bread shop that has been open for 70 years. The pandan custard buns are to die for.

Don't forget to eat your fruit, too. There's more to local fruit than just mango sticky rice and they are all equally tasty. Thai tea is also a must-try.

# Bangkok Is & Is Not Thailand

**CONSCIOUS TRAVEL FOR A BETTER WORLD**

There are approximately 70 million people in Thailand, with almost 11 million of those in Bangkok and the rest spread out over the other 76 provinces. Bangkok doesn't represent what the nation is really like, but you'll be able to find every little part of Thailand in Bangkok due to decentralisation – or lack thereof.

**Left** Protest against Prime Minister Prayuth Chan-o-cha. **Midde** Democracy Monument (p66). **Right** Protest with three-finger salute

## Still Developing

When you speak to a Thai person in Bangkok, there's a high chance that they are not a native Bangkokian. And if you visit Bangkok during the nation's important holidays, like Songkran (water fights festival in April) or New Year's, you'll find the streets are empty, as everyone has left to go back to visit their hometown.

According to the Country Classification list by the Department of Economic and Social Affairs of the United Nations Secretariat (UN/DESA), Thailand is listed under 'Developing Economies', meaning the country is still being developed, albeit inequitably across the nation. As the capital, Bangkok has more developments than the rest of the country, which in many ways is still way behind. This means a lot of Thai people from all over the country come to Bangkok for its job opportunities, bringing little pieces of their native provinces with them, whether it be cuisine or dialect.

While you'll be able to find Thai food from every part of the country in Bangkok and the Thai accent of the local language might sound a little different to you at some point, what Bangkok has to offer is not what the whole of Thailand really looks like. So when planning your trip here, make sure you get out of Bangkok and explore the real Thailand in other provinces, too.

## Military Coups & Recovery

Behind beautiful beaches, delicious food and glorious summer sun, the people of Thailand are still fighting for real democracy. The country's latest coup – number 13

SAIKO3P/SHUTTERSTOCK ©

ADIRACH TOUMLAMOON/SHUTTERSTOCK ©



in Thai history – began in 2014 and ended in 2019 with an election. Many still debate today whether it was a fair election. Beginning in late 2020 and continuing through 2021, a political awakening movement saw Thailand's younger generations fighting for their rights and democracy.

While Thailand's economic potential is clear, the disruption caused by coups and political unrest have hampered the country's growth. Emerging from each military coup the constitution gets rewritten, everything gets reset, and the people of Thailand start from square one – again.

> Behind beautiful beaches, delicious food and glorious summer sun, the people of Thailand are still fighting for real democracy.

You don't really need to understand the whole political climate fully, but just be mindful that sometimes, while you're holidaying in Bangkok, you might run into a protest or roadblocks. It could be annoying, but it's also part of the process of Thais fighting for their rights.

Sometimes, you might also come across things that don't make any sense in Thailand, like an almost unwalkable pavement, or messy cables and wires hanging alongside the street. You may wonder why the locals don't change these 'simple' things. It is important to know that the locals know better and want these things to change, but because of political reasons, changes just don't come easy in this country.

### The Pros & Cons

While Bangkok has a lot to offer as a city, it's good to be mindful while you're visiting that it does not represent Thailand as a whole. Thailand is and continues to be among the Top 10 most unequal countries in the world for wealth distribution, meaning the rich are getting richer and the poor are getting poorer.

■ **By Emilie Palamy Pradichit,** *founder and executive director of Manushya Foundation, a feminist and human rights organisation based in Bangkok. Instagram @manushyafoundation*

# 05 Meander the MIDNIGHT CITY

**EARLY | DIVERSE | HIDDEN TALENTS**

A night out in Bangkok usually starts quite early compared to Western countries. That's because, by law, alcohol can only be sold until midnight. You can buy alcohol from 11am to 2pm and 5pm to midnight, but you will still be able to find somewhere open past midnight. Bar-hopping is totally doable here, but with Bangkok's famous traffic jams, it's best to stick to the same neighbourhood. Each neighbourhood has its own character and style, so pick an area and explore.

## How to

**Getting there** Evening after-work traffic can be hectic, so stick to the train systems or motor-bike taxi – or walk.

**When to go** Some riverside or rooftop bars offer beautiful sunsets with the city views; otherwise, aim to get started around 9pm.

**Alcohol regulations** You'll find creative local business owners who have to stay low-key because of the Alcohol Control Act.

**Left** 72 Courtyard, Thong Lo
**Below** Miss Srimala performing at the Stranger Bar

### Art Pride Night

It couldn't get more gay-friendly than Silom Soi 2 & 4. This area was where all the partying pioneers started. Back in the days, it used to be the cool spot for locals to meet up and hang out. Try and catch a drag show at the **Stranger Bar** while you're here.

It's good to keep in mind that Bangkok may seem like a super LGBTIQ+-friendly city and on the fun-and-game part – yes, it is. However, Thailand has absolutely no laws or regulations to support this community at all.

## Sukhumvit

Sukhumvit is one of the longest roads in Thailand, and in Bangkok it's one of the main roads that cuts through the city centre. You can easily separate each neighbourhood based on the Skytrain BTS stations; the character of each neighbourhood can be very similar, except for Nana. Before Covid-19, Nana was the go-to place for tourists seeking fun and wild nights out. Post Covid-19, it has quieted down, but if you're looking for a super fun place to dance, head over to **Havana Social**, a Cuban bar-club. It does get crazy packed, though – you've been warned.

For something less wild and dancey, move towards the bigger soi numbers. Next to Nana is Asoke, one of Bangkok's business districts, followed by Phrom Phong – here, you will find that the majority of food and drink venues are Japanese.

Next is Thong Lo, one of Bangkok's main nightlife districts. It's packed with fancy bars and elevated restaurants that serve a slightly younger, cooler crowd who will most likely arrive in a supercar. Visit **Beam** in 72 Courtyard for the coolest night-club in town, where you won't be hearing any chart Top 100 tunes. For cocktails, it's always fun to try to find the entrance for speakeasy bar, **#FindTheLockerRoom**. Finish your Thong Lo night out at **Saeng Chai** for some hot *khao tom* (rice soup) and Thai-Chinese stir-fried dishes to wake up to no hangover the next day.

## Sathorn/Silom

If you go out in this area on a weekday, chances are you'll run into a lot of locals in work clothes as this is another one of Bangkok's business districts. **Vesper** is perfect for a sit-down and drink. You'll be able to see street food stalls out your window while enjoying your cocktails inside.

## Charoen Krung/Old Town

Packed with so much Thai and Chinese culture, fewer high-rise buildings and more old, wooden shophouses, this area is well-kept and treasured. It's where you can see what all of Bangkokwas before its more modern development. Behind the old shophouses

### Experience the Real Bangkok

A night out in Old Town provides you the opportunity to dive deep into Thailand's cultural roots. On top of a modern cocktail bar hidden behind an old shophouse, you'll also get to see the other side of Thailand that doesn't exist to serve tourists, like homeless people, the older generation making a living and more. Unlike Thonglor or other Sukhumvit drinking spots, in Old Town, we don't care about dress code or 'being posh', so you can show up as the real you and enjoy the real Thailand.

■ **By Niks Anuman-Rajadhon**, *founder of Teens of Thailand Bar, Asia Today Bar and Tax Bar; partner of Issan Rum – craft Thai rum; Instagram @ niks_anuman*

### Thai Craft Beers

You will find that Thai craft beers are just as expensive as imported ones – because Thai craft beers are actually imported. Thai alcohol regulations don't support local craft breweries, so Thai brewers have to make their craft beers in neighbouring countries then import back into Thailand (facing the same taxes as any foreign booze).

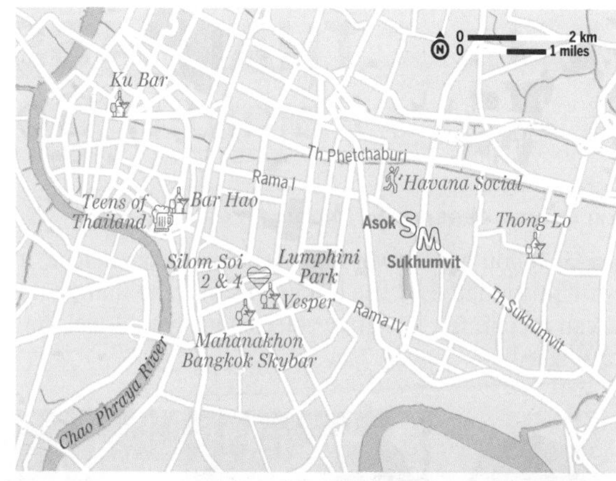






along the small road of Soi Nana (not to be confused with Sukhumvit Soi 11 Nana), you will find a gin bar, **Teens of Thailand**, and honey-based cocktail bar **Asia Today**. **Bar Hao** is the perfect spot to snack on modern Chinese bites while drinking.

If you fancy a bit of an adventure, the journey to find the super-hidden speakeasy **Ku Bar** is amazing; it's worth the trek out.

Drinking in this area is amazing for many reasons but proximity to Yaowarat Rd (also known as Chinatown) and its amazing food is reason enough to head here. Backpacker-centric Khao San Rd is also just around the corner. Bangkok's party organising pioneer-slash-art and fashion installer, Dudesweet, just opened a bar here called **Mischa Cheap**.

## Bangkok's Rooftop

Everyone loves a good rooftop bar, and what's good about the rooftop bars in Bangkok is they are very affordable. Check out **Mahanakhon Bangkok Skybar** for some spectacularly high city views (76th floor). For a close-up river and Wat Arun view, head to the humble **Deck** by Arun Residence.

**Left** Kratom tea shots, Teens of Thailand. **Above** Observation deck, Mahanakhon Bangkok Skybar

# 06 THAI MASSAGE: Painfully Good

**RELAXING | BENEFICIAL | ADDICTIVE**

If you have never had a Thai massage before, it's very common to feel a little intimidated by the unknowns and the many tales of how painful it is. Yes, it can be painful, but after you're done, you'll feel that your body isn't as stiff afterwards.

ANEK.SOOWANNAPHOOM/SHUTTERSTOCK ©

## How to

**When to go** Any time! But especially good when your body is sore or tired.

**Pain vs pleasure** Thai massage focuses on deep tissues and the 'lines' (sen) on your body, but at the end of the day, you should enjoy it, too. If you find yourself in a situation where the massage therapist is being too intense, tell them. Try to work out a pressure that feels OK for you and is still beneficial for your body.

CHATCHAI SOMWAT/SHUTTERSTOCK ©

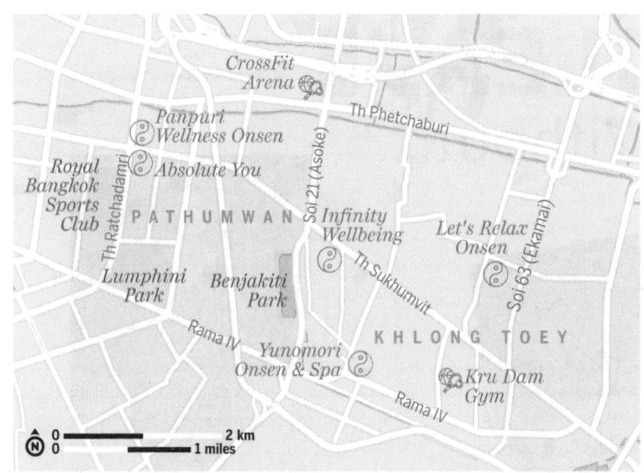


**Left** Thai massage.
**Bottom left** Moo·ay thai

Believed to date back thousands of years, Thai massage is listed as part of the Thai medical system due to its emotional and physical benefits. It uses no oils, and you wear loose and comfortable clothes – usually provided by massage places. Unlike massages with oil, a Thai massage therapist combines hard pressure with stretching which is helpful for your ligaments; you'll remain fully clothed.

Bangkok is the best place to try any massages in general as not only is it very cheap, it's also very common and accessible.

## Getting Your First Massage

**Infinity Wellbeing** This place is so warm and welcoming, if you're still scared of getting a massage in Thailand, you'll feel comfortable here.

**Panpuri Wellness onsen and cannabis dining experience** You could easily spend an entire day at this place, deep in the smell of the products. Come to remove stress from body and mind.

**Let's Relax Onsen** A very common onsen chain throughout Bangkok; the quality is equally good in all the branches.

**Yunomori Onsen & Spa** Experience the comfort and minimalism of being in Japan all in the chaos of Bangkok! You'll forget you're in the city while you're here.

## Exercising with Locals

**Moo·ay thai** Kru Dam Gym, Elite Fight Club, BigBox Muay Thai.

**CrossFit** CrossFit Arena, Training Ground.

**HIIT** F45 Training.

**Yoga and Pilates** Absolute You, Divine Yoga, Pilates Station.

### Work up a Sweat

Bangkok is a city full of life and distraction. Walking on the street of Sukhumvit feels like walking in a concrete jungle, and sometimes you feel out of place. One great spot to find your tribe is to visit a box/gym. Expats, travellers and locals with the same goal are gathered in their local gyms. More than just working out, people hang out together afterward and refill their calories to make sure they have enough to burn the next day.

■ **By Lu, Yen-Ju**, *fitness coach, Instagram @ yen_ju04*

# DON'T LEAVE
## Bangkok Without...

**01 Thai silk**
However you like it, whether in a tote bag, scarf or dress. The texture is so unique and perfect for cooler weather. Remember, dry clean only!

**02 Anything by a Thai designer**
Whether it's clothes or home decorations, Siam Discovery and Emporium has a whole section dedicated to Thai designers.

**03 Artwork**
Support a local artist and have something totally different hanging on your wall that will always remind you of your time in Thailand.

**04 Curry pastes**
The pastes found in Thai supermarkets are the second best thing to having real curry made for you at a Thai restaurant (and better than the stuff you get back home).

**05 Thai coffee beans**
Visit coffee shops like Kaizen, Single Lane and Roots, or order online from Left Hand Roaster and you can still have Thai coffee

when you're back home.

### 06 Thai chocolate

Thai chocolate culture is still considered pretty niche and small, but brands like Kad Kokoa, Shabar or Pridi offer high-quality, well-crafted chocolate made from locally grown beans.
was exclusively made for the royals but is now available for everyone.

### 07 Sampheng bag

The multicolour Balenciaga's Barbes East-West shopper bags have been around in Thailand for decades, often used by street vendors when buying supplies at Sampheng Market. They are known locally as Sampheng bags.

### 08 Benjarong

Considered an art form in their own right, Thai ceramics painting is believed to have been around since the 13th century. Benjarong

# Listings

**BEST OF THE REST**

### Soul Food

Baan Nual $$

Before the pandemic, this place would be fully booked for six months in advance. It offers simple, comforting ancient Thai recipes in a stylish decorated old wooden house. Advance reservations only.

Sorn $$$

Some fine dining can feel like a science project rather than a dinner, however, this two-Michelin-starred restaurant secialising in southern cuisine has the perfect combination of luxury and comfort. Book ahead.

Wana Yook $$$

This place offers an elevated version of the famous and well-loved street food dish, *khao kaeng* (curry served on top of hot rice).

Sri Trat $$$

If you're searching for delicious eastern Thai food for a slightly fancier occasion, this place is perfect. The Thai-inspired cocktails go down well with the dishes.

Wattana Panich Beef Broth $$

Famous for its beef noodles cooked in a giant pot that has never been emptied, so your noodle soup is actually mixed with soup from years ago. It gives rich and thick flavour unlike any other. Try the goat noodles as well.

Nong Rim Klong $$

Basically what Jay Fai (p52) is, but cheaper. It's easy to find located right in the city centre in Ekkamai neighbourhood (next to a not very attractive looking canal that somehow is one of its unique selling points).

W District $

A night market popular with locals. Offers many options for food, in case you can't agree on the same restaurant, and cheap beers.

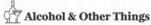

### Alcohol & Other Things

Laoteng $$

What looks like your typical dim sum place or an entrance to a bar might also not be. Have fun finding this speakeasy located on a busy street in Chinatown.

Tep Bar $$

A modern Thai cocktail bar serving drinks mixed with Thai fruits, herbs and spices, and home-infused *ya dong* (Thai herbal whisky). Musicians perform traditional Thai music.

Rabbit Hole $$

A simple-looking, gigantic wooden door on busy Thonglor Rd marks this three-storey bar that has been serving Bangkokians craft cocktails for years.

Bar Yard $$

Comfort in the posh Langsuan neighbourhood can be found at this rooftop garden-bar serving tropical drinks and homey barbecue dishes.

*Khao kaeng*

ABar Rooftop $$

Perfect for gin lovers who want to enjoy 360-degree city views. If you're hungry, head down a floor for Japanese fusion food at Akira Back.

SEEN Restaurant & Bar $$$

Located on the 26th floor overlooking the Chao Phraya River, with a swimming pool to maximise the water views. Favoured by locals who want something a little fancy.

Changwon Express $$

Thai craft beer and Korean fried chicken – what could be a better combination? This small corner bar is so casual everyone ends up becoming friends by the end of the night.

Philtration $$

Learn about 19th-century Thai herbal medicine through cocktails inspired by the herbs, spices and teas found in Moh Mee. The bar can be found hidden inside the basement of a century-old house.

12 x 12 $$

This one-of-a-kind dive bar where none of the decorations match offers cheap local beer; dance to world music played strictly on vinyls only.

Yoshibar $$

Sake can seem like an intimidating liquor to get started on, but this small, super casual bar will make your sake-learning experience easy to understand and fun. The dishes are also good to pair with.

Jack's Bar $

One of the legendary riverside bars well loved by locals, expats and everyone in Bangkok. If you drop your phone, there's a chance it will fall into the river.

ARTAPARTMENT/SHUTTERSTOCK ©

Emporium Shopping Mall

## One-Stop Shops

Emporium

Located next to BTS Phrom Phong Skytrain station, Emporium offers many Thai designers' work ranging from clothes to home decorations. Its sister centre EmQuartier is just across the road.

Siam Discovery

Much smaller and easier to walk around than neighbouring Siam Paragon or CentralWorld; you'll find many Thai designer brands here.

MBK

A tourist-centric centre selling everything from fake goods to food and services from plastic surgery to dentistry. You could also walk to Platinum Mall from here for cheap fashions.

Chatuchak Market (JJ Market)

Offers cheap local goods. Keep in mind that it's located outdoors in the blasting sun and if it rains, there's hardly any shelter to hide under.

Phahurat

Known for being the textile market and the 'Little India' of Bangkok. You'll also find gems, jewellery and amazing food.

Terminal 21

Has all the brand stores you'd typically find inside a shopping centre, plus local vendors.

River City Bangkok

If you're looking to buy art or antique goods, this is a place to go. While here, you could also hop on a river boat and check out the touristy IconSiam, too.

Srinagarindra Train Night Market

A little bit out of the city with no public transport, this market offers local food vendors and cheap goods, as well as antiques.

## Caffeine & Sugar Rush

Chu $$

Missing your favourite Western-style breakfast while you're travelling? Visit this cafe situated in a house with a nice green yard; loved by many Bangkokians.

Ceresia $$

This simple-looking coffee shop is very serious about coffee, with a big selection from around the world. On the same road, there's an amazing Japanese bakery, Custard Nakamura, that forms a queue out front before it even opens.

Holey Artisan Bakery $$

If you need a break from Thai cuisine, this bakery offers homemade pastry (sweet and savoury) that will remind you of your favourite pastry shop back home.

Bartels $$

This two-floor cafe hosts many WFH office people on weekdays. It serves good coffee, amazing sourdough and is dog-friendly. What else can a stressed office person ask for?

H Dining $$

While you might come here for caffeine, the food is also worth ordering. Serves a slightly modern/fusion take on Asian-inspired cafe food; has outdoor seating and is dog-friendly.

Flower in Hand by P. Cafe $$

This flower-themed cafe is located in the hipster-centric Ari neighbourhood. You could easily spend a day cafe-hopping here with local Instagrammers.

## Green Lungs & Touristy Stuff

Benjakiti Park

Located just minutes walk from Terminal 21 shopping mall, this park recently got revamped and is now greener than ever. There's also a secret skywalk path that takes you straight to Lumpini Park.

Benjasiri Park

Trees are not a common sight in the city centre but this pocket-sized park located in the middle of two shopping malls offers a quick city break. It also has two playgrounds for little ones.

Lumpini Park

This park is one of the important landmarks in Bangkok that offers trees as well as cats and monitor lizards.

Democracy Monument

A monument filled with the history of how people have been fighting for their rights. It

Benjakiti Park

has been one of the main spots to hold a protest in Bangkok in recent years.

### Wat Phra Kaew

This could be a good starting point for you to explore surrounding landmarks like Grand Palace, Ananta Samakhom Throne Hall and more. Remember to dress respectfully or you'll be denied entry.

## Art & History

### Museum of Contemporary Art (MOCA)

MOCA bangkok is one of the biggest contemporary art museums in Asia, featuring work by many Thai artists. It is owned by one of the richest Thai business executives.

### Art Gallery at Ban Chao Phraya

This riverside gallery used to be the palace of Prince Sathittamrongsawas and years later, the Italian architect Mario Tamagno lived there for a while. It's now showcasing works by renowned and emerging artists.

### National Museum of Royal Barges

Located on the banks of Bangkok Noi canal, this is where the royal barges from the Royal Barge Ceremony – a ceremony used by a monarch for processions and transport on water – are kept.

### Suan Pakkad Palace

The first ever museum in Thailand opened in 1952 and was originally a private residence of Royal Highnesses Prince and Princess Chumbhot of Nagara Svarga who decided to turn it into a museum.

## Offbeat Activities

### Dasa

Book lovers should definitely visit this three-storey secondhand bookshop. Dig away and you might find your next favourite book here.

National Museum of Royal Barges

### Fox Hole Art Shelter Cafe

While this place could be listed as a cafe serving coffee beans from Chiang Rai, it offers much more, including Thai craft beers and a cinema club upstairs.

### Doc Club & Pub

If you have run out of things to do in Bangkok or just want to catch a movie, Documentary Club is where you can drink, socialise, and catch a film that you probably haven't heard of anywhere before.

### Dream World

The majority of Thais grew up visiting this theme park as a kid, and it remains a trip down memory lane. This is one of the very few theme parks in Thailand.

**Scan to find more things to do in Bangkok online**

# CENTRAL THAILAND

ADVENTURE | HISTORY | FOOD

Experience Central Thailand online

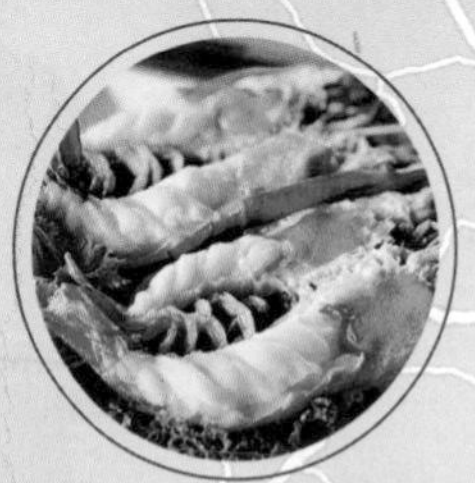

Feast on river prawns waterside at **Ruan Thai Goong Pao** in Ayutthaya (p81)
*50 minutes from Bangkok*

Go monkey spotting in Lopburi at **Pa Prang Sam Yod** (p83)
*2 hours from Bangkok*

Hike the infamous **Death Railway** on the River Kwai (pp83 & 85)
*1 hour from central Kanchanaburi*

Bike your way through **Ayuthaya Historical Park** (p82)
*19 minutes from central Ayutthaya*

Challenge your senses at **Damnoen Saduak** floating market (p73)
*90 minutes from Bangkok*

Commune with nature in **Sakaerat Biosphere Reserve** (p77)
*1½ hours from Khao Yai*

Hankha
Tha Ngam
Singburi
Sam Chuk
Si Prachan
Ang Thong
Suphanburi
Lopburi
Phra Phutthabet
Kaeng Khoi
Saraburi
Nakhon Ratchasima (Khorat)
Pak Thong Chai
Bo Phloi
U-Thong
Sena
Ayuthaya
Ban Na
Thung Khok
Bang Pa In
Nakhon Nayok
Sai Yok
Lat Ya
Kamphaeng Saen
Pathum Thani
Prachinburi
Kabin Buri
Kanchanaburi
Mae Nam Mae Klong
Ban Pong
Nakhon Pathom
Nonthaburi
Mae Nam Chao Phraya
Minburi
Phanom Sarakham
Sa Kaeo
Bangkok
Sam Phran
Chachoengsao
Samut Prakan
Ratchaburi
Samut Sakhon
Bang Pakong
Phanat Nikhom
Samut Songkhram
Ao Krung Thep (Bay of Bangkok)
Chonburi

# CENTRAL THAILAND
## Trip Builder

Central Thailand contains some of the most quintessentially Thai settings to be found anywhere. Considered the rice basket of the country, this region teems with both traditional and less-than-traditional experiences, from outdoorsy hikes to good old retail therapy.

**Explore bookable experiences in Central Thailand**

CLOCKWISE FROM LEFT: BULAN PHOTO LOVER/SHUTTERSTOCK ©, SEJI GOTO/SHUTTERSTOCK ©, JOEY56/SHUTTERSTOCK © PREVIOUS SPREAD: WAJ/SHUTTERSTOCK ©

# Practicalities

## ARRIVING

Just as all roads in Italy are said to lead to Rome, all points in central Thailand are accessible from Bangkok's two airports, the closest point of entry from abroad.

### CONNECT

Like in Bangkok, wi-fi is available in all public spots, or you can rent pocket wi-fi (muaythai-wifi.com).

### MONEY

Many shophouse restaurants outside of Bangkok will only take cash, so bring bills in different denominations.

## WHERE TO STAY

| Place | Pros/Cons |
|---|---|
| Ayuthaya | Easily accessible via boat or car from Bangkok; close to historical landmarks. |
| Sukhothai | The gateway to the north, a sleepier version of Ayutthaya with excellent food. |
| Kanchanaburi | Full of things to do and see; accessible via plane, train or automobile. |
| Lopburi | Charming and often overlooked; bursting with natural beauty. |

## GETTING AROUND

**Car** The easiest way to explore the region; a driver can be hired from Bangkok (bangkokbeyond.com).

**Boat** Tours to Ayutthaya depart from Bangkok regularly (ayutthaya-boat.com).

**Train** Departures from Bang Sue station reach all major regional cities (thailandtrains.com).

TOP: SIRAWIT KHO/SHUTTERSTOCK © BOTTOM: GAN CHAONAN/SHUTTERSTOCK ©

## EATING & DRINKING

Obviously popular in its namesake city, Sukhothai noodles(pictured top left) feature minced pork, crushed peanuts, blanched long beans and the region's reknowned palm sugar and limes.

Invented by a boat vendor at a market, Ayutthaya boat noodles (pictured bottom left) feature either pork or beef and are thickened with the animal's blood.

Thais travel from far and wide for river prawns.

**Best Sukhothai noodles** Ta Pui Noodle (p88)

**Must-try Ayutthaya boat noodles** Pa Lek Boat Noodle (p88)

**NOV–FEB**
Pleasantly balmy weather, but also the most travellers and highest hotel rates.

**MAR–MAY**
The height of the heatwave, it's also the best time for fruit.

**JUN–OCT**
Monsoon season, punctuated with brief, strong downpours. Beware of flooding.

# FLOAT YOUR BOAT at a Market

**CULTURE | SHOPPING | FOOD**

From the outskirts of Bangkok to a two-hour drive south of the capital, floating markets may be the most evocative diversions of central Thailand, showcasing what was once part of a traditional way of life. Today, many may consider floating markets tourist traps, but locals still frequent a handful of markets for everything from dishes to fruit.

VISUAL STORYTELLER/SHUTTERSTOCK ©

### How to

**Getting here** If you're in Bangkok, rent a car (thairentacar.com) or take a floating market tour (foodtoursbangkok.com).

**When to go** Usually mornings are best, the earlier the better.

**Beware** When going to the markets in Samut Songkhram Province, expect up to a two-hour drive from Bangkok.

**Quick visit** Bang Nam Pueng – though technically in Samut Prakan – is the closest market to get to from downtown Bangkok.

MONGKOL UDOMKAEW/SHUTTERSTOCK ©

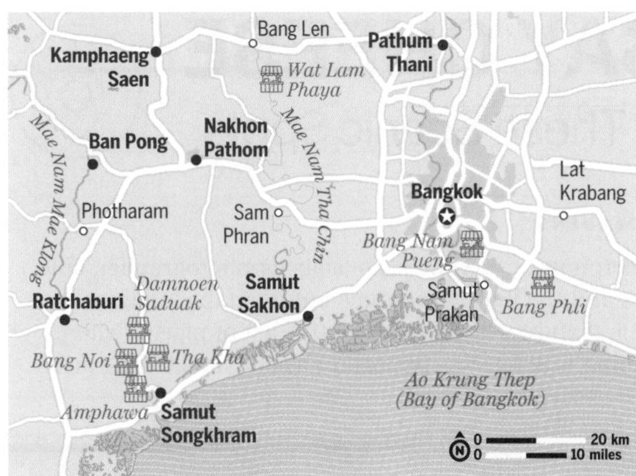


## The Big Two

The subject of many a Thailand poster, **Damnoen Saduak** epitomises the chaotic bustle of a typical market, as floating vendors vie for customers' attention on boats piled high with fruit. While conventional wisdom says the action is best viewed in the early morning, there is activity all day.

Unlike the daytime shenanigans of Damnoen Saduak, **Amphawa** (open Friday to Sunday) truly comes alive when the sun comes down, bars open up, and the boat tours for spotting fireflies begin. Guesthouses along the canal allow revellers to continue their fun into the night.

## Loved by Locals

Although the Big Two are exciting, they can also be overwhelmingly crowded. Those in search of something more sedate can go to centuries-old **Bang Phli**, a series of rickety floating shophouses known for its snacks, particularly sweets; it opens at midday.

Meanwhile, early birds may prefer tranquil **Tha Kha** (weekends only), best seen before the heat sets in. Expect a lot of vendors of *maprao nam hom* (coconuts with fragrant water).

Like Tha Kha, **Bang Noi** serves as a weekend community centre, where locals congregate at the noodle shop to warble karaoke at lunchtime. Besides singing, there are woven baskets, traditional Thai clothing and coffee. Make sure to visit the nearby Wat Bung Kung, an ancient temple set inside a banyan tree.

If you have time for only one smaller market, head to the rice paddies west of Bangkok for weekend-only **Wat Lam Phaya**, which abounds in papaya salads, fried noodles and Thai sweets.

**Left** Damnoen Saduak floating market. **Bottom left** Coconuts, Tha Kha floating market

### My Favourite Central Thai Floating Market

I enjoy Tha Kha the most. It has friendly people, all the local people do homemade cooking, and they sell what they grow in their gardens, not like the big businesses at some of the other floating markets. They still use rowboats and when there is a full moon and new moon, many local people come together in their boats to sell and trade their produce in the early morning, like in the olden times. Also at night, the fireflies come out. It is beautiful because they fill up the trees, and it looks like Christmas trees with all the lights.

■ **By Chin Chongtong**, *founder of Chili Paste Tour, Instagram @chilipastetour*

# 08 SAY CHEESE in These Scenic Spots

**PHOTOGRAPHY | NATURE | GARDENS**

In the age of the smartphone, everyone is an aspiring photographer, able to manipulate filters, angles and the light to produce unforgettable images. Orchestrate your next profile picture with the help of this list of places, where the photo you end up snapping is at least as important as how much fun you're actually having.

TAVARIUS/SHUTTERSTOCK ©

### How to

**Getting around** From Bangkok, it's easiest to rent a car with (black-lane.com) or without (sawasdeerentacar.com) a driver.

**When to go** Photos are best without sudden monsoons, so avoid rainy season (June to October).

**Close to Bangkok** Find lily pads big enough to serve as your personal stage at **Victoria Water Lily Garden**.

**Bad at photography?** No sweat, just hire your own photographer (shootmy travel.com).

TOEFOTO/SHUTTERSTOCK ©

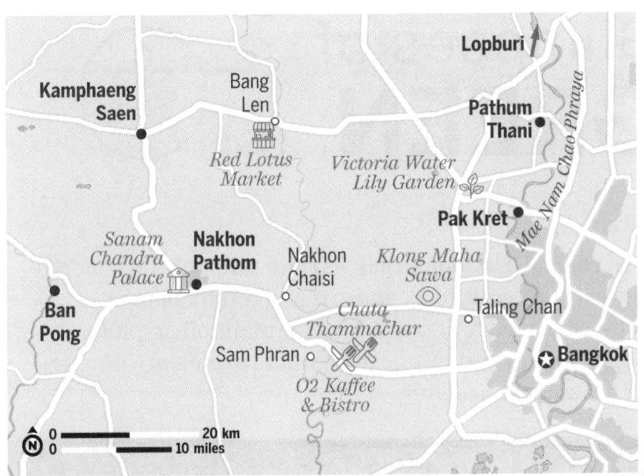


**Left** Sunflower fields, Lopburi. **Bottom left** Sanam Chandra Palace. **Below** Red lotus flower

## But Wait, There's More

Not enough? **O2 Kaffee & Bistro** has outdoor tables set atop a series of small canals, where you can attempt to row a boat and snap a photo simultaneously. Be careful!

## Photogenic Scenery

A cruise down **Khlong Maha Sawat**, listed as a national heritage ite by the Thai government, in Nakhon Pathom affords a charming view of orchid and fruit gardens, enormous lily pads and old-fashioned houses on stilts, all from the comfort of a sun-kissed boat on tranquil waters.

Water lilies also take centre stage at **Red Lotus Market**, where visitors can change into traditional Thai clothing before posing in wooden boats surrounded by the aforementioned blooms. You can even take photographs by drone for that perfect shot.

Less Monet and more Van Gogh, the famous sunflower fields of the eastern Thai town **Lopburi** burst into full bloom during the cool season, providing a colourful backdrop to your Instagram feed.

But if fairy-tale castles are more your jam, you can put on your Cinderella gown for **Sanam Chandra Palace**, a former royal residence built by Rama VI over 80km west of Bangkok. The charming European-style exterior, reminiscent of a Swiss ski chalet, is accented with Thai touches like traditionally carved railings.

## Photo-Friendly Cafes

You can also do as the Thais do and combine your two favourite activities: photography and eating. **Chata Thammachart cafe**, comprising conical bamboo buildings set in verdant rice paddies, offers its own speciality coffee, while **Say Hay Cafe Cuisine** features real, cuddly animals in a waterside restaurant-farm.

# 09 Glimpses of GREEN

NATURE | HIKING | RAFTING

When people think of central Thailand, they usually think of the concrete jungle that is Bangkok. However, green forests and rivers liberally blanket the north of the capital, providing plenty of sport for mountain bikers, hikers and kayakers. If you are not that sporty, don't despair: there are plenty of tour guides happy to drive you through the scenery.

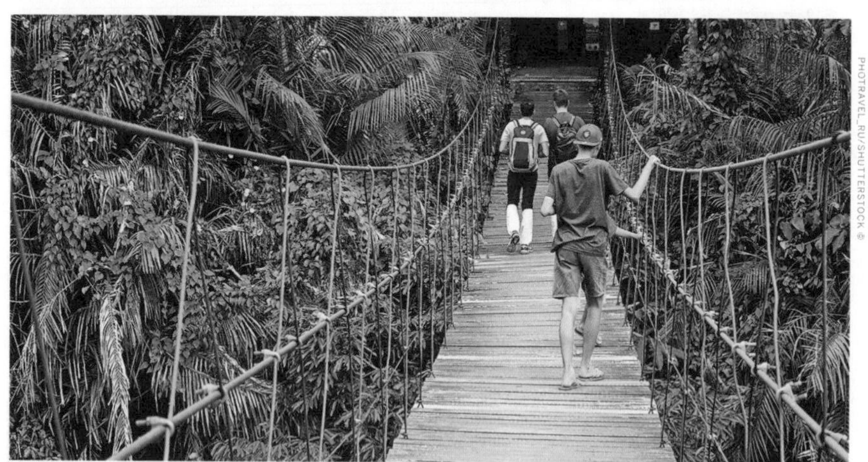

PHOTRAVEL_RU/SHUTTERSTOCK ©

## How to

**Getting around** If coming from Bangkok, rent a car (rentalcars.com) to drive to the park or book a tour which can arrange transport for you (thainationalparks.com).

**When to go** The cool season from November to February is the best time to go. Remember to bring a jumper and wear sturdy footwear.

**From Bangkok** You can cross the river and rent a bicycle to explore Bang Krachao, the 'lungs of Bangkok'.

NACH-NOTH/SHUTTERSTOCK ©

**Left** Khao Yai National Park. **Bottom left** Erawan Falls. **Below** Butterly, Sakaerat Biosphere Reserve



## Flora & Fauna

Out of all the national parks in Thailand, **Khao Yai** – two hours' drive north of the capital – is arguably the most well-known, where well-heeled Bangkokians spend the weekends sipping wine in local vineyards. Like Las Vegas, it's a place geared towards people from elsewhere. Luckily, this Unesco World Heritage Site also boasts seven major trails and a host of English-speaking guides.

Those interested in a more educational experience should visit the famous red-leafed forests *(pa dang)* of **Sakaerat Biosphere Reserve** east of Khao Yai, one of five Unesco reserves in Thailand.

## River Wild

Guaranteed to work off any jet lag, white-water rafting tours can be found on both the jade-tinted **River Kwai** in Kanchanaburi (where floating raft hotels also drift) and the limestone cliff-lined **Mae Klong** in Tak.

The water-averse can visit the 500m-long **Lawa Cave** near Kwai Noi River, with stalactites and bats aplenty.

## Chasing Waterfalls

Explore **Erawan Falls** with its seven tiers, turquoise water and little fish that nibble at your toes. Or try Umphang Wildlife Sanctuary's towering **Thi Lo Su** waterfall, Asia's sixth-largest, open to visitors October to May (before the rainy season). Closer to Bangkok, the **Sa Lad Dai** waterfall in Saraburi rewards visitors willing to hike for an hour with a sparsely populated water playground.

### Best Trails in Khao Yai

My favourite trail is Nong Pak Chi (trail No 3) because it is mostly level and easy to walk. The most challenging trail is to the Heo Suwat waterfall (trail No 6).

■ **By Duangjai Somroob**, *park ranger at Khao Yai National Park (thainationalparks.com)*

JOEY56/SHUTTERSTOCK ©

# 10 From the Palace TO THE STREET

FOOD | RESTAURANTS | HAWKERS

Of course, no Thailand experience can be considered complete without an in-depth exploration of its cuisine. Thailand is rightly famous for its street food, but excellent central Thai cuisine can be found in all types of dining experiences, from streetside to the old-fashioned shophouse to the Michelin-starred royal Thai specialist.

RAKRATCHADA/GETTY IMAGES ©

## How to

**Getting around** Renting a car is the easiest way to zip around, especially to some off-the-beaten-track places.

**When to go** River prawns are considered to be best in the cool season, but are readily available all year round.

**Oh no** Thais see an upset tummy as a fact of life. If your stomach hurts from overindulging in chillies, activated charcoal tablets from the convenience store can help.



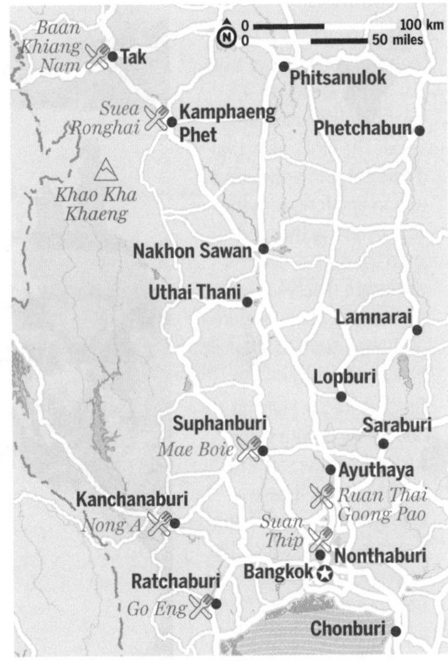


### Platonic Ideal

Of all the eateries spanning Thailand, none embody the platonic ideal of Thai cuisine as thoroughly as the ones in the central region. Coconut-milk-infused curries, tart and spicy salads bristling with lemongrass and *magrood* lime leaves, sugary egg-yolk sweets: it's all here. One purveyor of such a meal is **Baan Khiang Nam** in Tak, revered among locals despite its stiff decor. Another favourite in Tak is **Krua Samosorn**, famed nationwide for its *tod mun pla* (fried fish cakes garlanded with a fresh cucumber-and-chilli relish). In Kamphaeng Phet, a town flying under the typical travel radar, **Suea Ronghai** (Crying Tiger) traffics in the fiery cuisine of the northeast, boasting grilled meats tasty enough to make

FOTOERRO/GETTY IMAGES ©

**Above left** *Tod mun pla.*
**Left** Thai street food vendor, Kamphaeng Phet

a jungle cat weep in envy. And just on the outskirts of Bangkok in suburban Nonthaburi, the sprawling riverside restaurant **Suan Thip** boasts a Michelin star and hard-to-find *gaeng khi lek* (a thick curry of Siamese senna), beloved by chefs all over the country.

## Main Attraction

But of all the delicacies beckoning the Thai food gourmand, none perhaps beckons as brightly as the true star of the show in central Thailand, the gigantic river prawn. Typically spanning the length of a forearm, these prawns are usually simply grilled over an open fire and served sliced in half, accompanied by a spicy dipping sauce (*nam jim* seafood) of lime juice, fish sauce, chillies and coriander leaves. The tail is juicy and sweet, for sure, but the prize for most Thais is the head, where the ochre-coloured *mun goong* (fat) resides. This admittedly acquired taste

### Thai Table Manners

Liking spicy food is very well and good, but to truly eat as the locals do, it's best to follow a few key rules. The first one is that Thais eat primarily with a spoon and fork, with the fork ushering the food onto the spoon. Chopsticks are reserved for dishes that are considered 'Chinese', such as soup noodles or chicken rice.

Since dishes are served 'family style', with diners taking from the same plate, each plate must have a *chon glang* (central spoon), which is used to scoop the food onto your plate. Never eat from this spoon.

■ **By Chef McDang,** *Thai food expert and host of McDang's Travelogue, Instagram @ chefmcdang*

## A Few Tasty Things in Central Thailand

Kanchanaburi's **Nong A** offers *khao mok talay* (an unusual seafood biryani), while **Tabasco Restaurant** nearby has a herb-encrusted salad of fresh prawns.

In Ratchaburi, **Go Eng**'s razor clams reign supreme. The speciality of the house in Samut Songkhram's **Gong Meng Jan** is stir-fried noodles.

VELAART/SHUTTERSTOCK ©

is mixed in with white rice until it resembles a risotto on the plate.

Eateries specialising in this delicacy can be found all along wherever the Chao Phraya River wends its way, but some of the most famous are located in the former Siamese capital of Ayutthaya. Famous would surely describe the riverside shack known as **Ruan Thai Goong Pao**, but be sure to arrive early or the speciality of the house will be gone before you get there. If this is indeed the case, try **Baan U Thong**, also along the Chao Phraya.

### Prawn Paradise

Another city famous for its river prawns is Suphanburi, where **Mae Boie** can probably claim the mantle for most well-known restaurant in town. But stiff competition comes in the form of **Kui Mong**, which also fries the prawns in salt, and the tiny **Wang Goong Yai Chai Suwan** next to the town's clock tower, with only four tables. If you truly want to venture off the beaten path, **Jay Dum** in Patum Thani will fit the bill nicely.

LEFT: PEEMAI WONG/SHUTTERSTOCK ©; RIGHT: QUYNH ANH NGUYEN/GETTY IMAGES ©

**Left** Chinese noodle soup.
**Top right** Grilled fresh river prawns.
**Above right** *Yum talay*, mixed seafood salad

# 11 Historical INSIGHTS

HIKING | CULTURE | RUINS

Bona fide history buffs will find a treasure trove of sites to explore in central Thailand. Bike your way through the region's archaeological parks, learn about the tragic legacy of the River Kwai, play hide and seek with the monkeys of Lopburi, or travel back in time to ancient Siam.

## Learn about Thai History

Khu Bua displays textiles by its northern Tai-Yuan community, who wrap its Dvaravati-era stupa in red cloth. Potharam has a Mon minority museum and hosts Nang Yai shadow puppetry at Wat Khanon. In Ratchaburi town you can see Dragon Jars being made in Chinese settlers' potteries like Tao Hong Tai, whose artist owner founded the contemporary gallery d'Kunst.

**By Philip Cornwel-Smith**, *author of Very Thai and Very Bangkok, Instagram @verybangkok*

## Trip Notes

**Getting around** The most convenient way to zip around is via rented car or a car and driver from a central point like Bangkok (drivecarrental.com).

**When to go** The cool season is most popular, but the rainy season affords sunshine in between (usually) brief downpours.

**What it costs** Renting a bike for a ride around Sukhothai or Ayuthaya Historical Parks should cost no more than 50B per person.

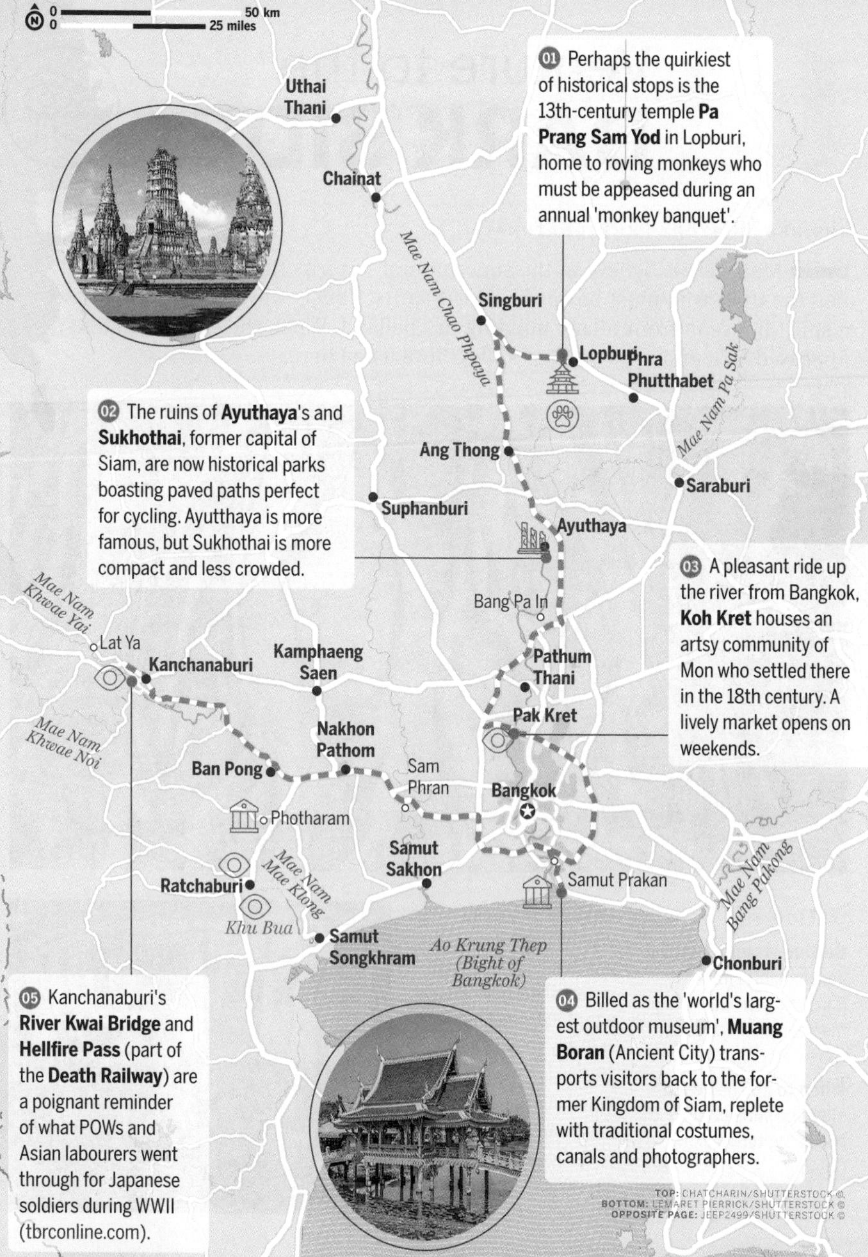

0 50 km
0 25 miles
01 Perhaps the quirkiest of historical stops is the 13th-century temple **Pa Prang Sam Yod** in Lopburi, home to roving monkeys who must be appeased during an annual 'monkey banquet'.
02 The ruins of **Ayuthaya**'s and **Sukhothai**, former capital of Siam, are now historical parks boasting paved paths perfect for cycling. Ayutthaya is more famous, but Sukhothai is more compact and less crowded.
03 A pleasant ride up the river from Bangkok, **Koh Kret** houses an artsy community of Mon who settled there in the 18th century. A lively market opens on weekends.
04 Billed as the 'world's largest outdoor museum', **Muang Boran** (Ancient City) transports visitors back to the former Kingdom of Siam, replete with traditional costumes, canals and photographers.
05 Kanchanaburi's **River Kwai Bridge** and **Hellfire Pass** (part of the **Death Railway**) are a poignant reminder of what POWs and Asian labourers went through for Japanese soldiers during WWII (tbrconline.com).
Uthai Thani
Chainat
Mae Nam Chao Phpaya
Singburi
Lopburi
Phra Phutthabet
Mae Nam Pa Sak
Ang Thong
Saraburi
Suphanburi
Ayuthaya
Bang Pa In
Mae Nam Khwae Yai
Lat Ya
Kanchanaburi
Kamphaeng Saen
Pathum Thani
Pak Kret
Mae Nam Khwae Noi
Nakhon Pathom
Ban Pong
Sam Phran
Bangkok
Photharam
Samut Sakhon
Mae Nam Mae Klong
Ratchaburi
Samut Prakan
Mae Nam Bang Pakong
Khu Bua
Samut Songkhram
Ao Krung Thep (Bight of Bangkok)
Chonburi


TOP: CHATCHARIN/SHUTTERSTOCK ©, BOTTOM: LEMARET PIERRICK/SHUTTERSTOCK © OPPOSITE PAGE: JEEP2499/SHUTTERSTOCK ©

# 12 Venture to the DARK SIDE

**SHRINES | HISTORY | SUPERNATURAL**

Many Thais believe in the supernatural - spirits that reside in the land and the trees who must be appeased with gifts. This is why you will usually see a spirit house in front of any building in Thailand. When the spirits can't be appeased, you end up with places like those listed here.

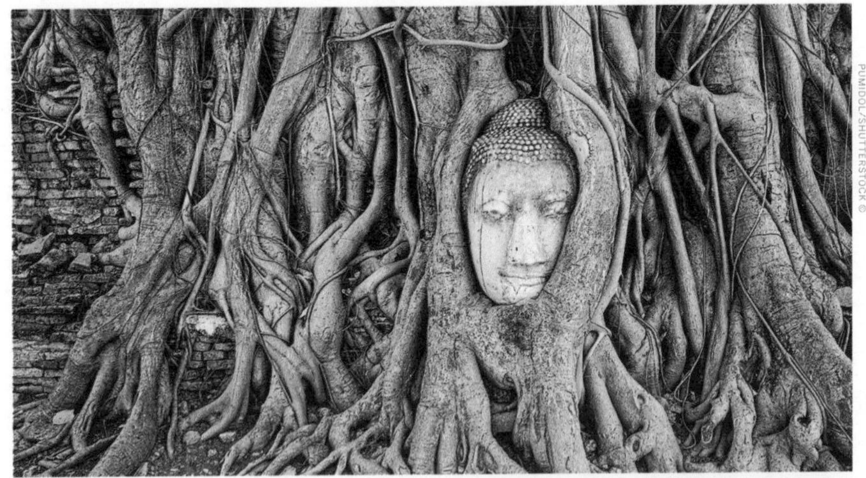

PUMIDOL/SHUTTERSTOCK ©

## How to

**Getting around** If visiting Kanchanaburi from Bangkok, consider taking the train (thailandtrains.com).

**When to go** The region might be subject to floods September to October.

**Unlike in the West** Visiting a *mor doo* (fortune teller) is a mainstream thing. You can find one at the street market or in any community in Thailand.

**When visiting a temple** Remember to keep your shoulders and legs covered.

JUAN HUNG-YEN/SHUTTERSTOCK ©

WARAPHORN APHAI/SHUTTERSTOCK ©

**Far left** Buddha head in a banyan tree, Ayuthaya. **Below far left** Erawan Buddha, Bangkok **Near left** Monks walking along the Death Railway. **Below** Rubbing powder on a sacred hopea odorata tree

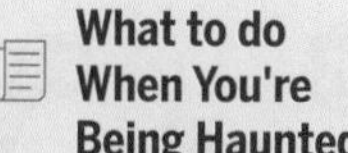

### What to do When You're Being Haunted

Feeling a tug on your leg or a weight on your chest when you drop off to sleep? Tell the spirit that you're grateful and they should leave you alone.



## Getting Spiritual

Thais typically go to the temple to petition the spirits to grant their wishes, but shrines such as Bangkok's Erawan Shrine are also known for their ability to fulfill hopes and dreams. A different kind of shrine – the one devoted to one's ancestors – is set up at the homes and businesses owned by Thai-Chinese proprietors.

And then there are the spirit houses: mini-structures that exist specifically to placate spirits living in the land and trees. Typically set next to a building, they provide alternative shelter for spirits displaced by inconvenient construction.

## Dark Side

But what happens when these spirits can't be placated? That's when you go to see a fortune teller, able to hear or see what the spirit desires. These fortune tellers are valued by many businesses, included on the payroll and used to cleanse new properties of bad juju.

Not surprisingly, the most restless spirits haunt the places where they died violent deaths. That of course includes Sukhothai, Ayutthaya and Kanchanaburi's Death Railway, considered one of the most haunted spots in the kingdom. But the decrepit bunker known as Brothel 35 – aka the Prostitute Graveyard in Kanchanaburi – is also believed to contain the spirits of enslaved women left to die after falling sick. It has since been abandoned, although lookie-loos continue to walk the trash-strewn corridors.

ANIRUT THAILAND/SHUTTERSTOCK ©

# THE GHOSTS of Thailand

**01 Khwai Tanu**
This spirit appears as a buffalo and acts at the behest of its voodoo master, for good or bad outcomes.

**02 Krasue**
A floating woman's head with entrails attached, these females are being punished for their evil pasts.

**03 Krahang**
The male version of the Krasue, presumably the husband, these spirits are paired even after death.

**04 Kuman Thong**
The spirits of young boys wearing traditional dress trapped in the service of a voodoo master for eternity.

**05 Mae Nak**
Dying in childbirth while her husband was at war, Mae Nak pretends to still be alive when he returns. She now protects mothers and children and helps lottery seekers.

**06 Phi Tai Hong**
The spirits of other women who died in childbirth. Because of their unexpected deaths, they are angry and aggressive.

**07 Nang Tani**
A beautiful young woman in a green tradi-

tional dress, she haunts banana tree clusters on the full moon.

**08 Nang Takian**

This beautiful young woman also wears traditional dress, but in brown or red tones. She haunts takian *(hopea odorata)* trees.

**09 Phi Am**

Fond of sitting on people's chests as they sleep, this pale, angry woman is believed to cause 'sleep paralysis'.

**10 Phi Dip Jeen**

Adopted from the Thai-Chinese community, this vampire wears traditional Chinese clothing and a Chinese rune on its face.

**11 Phi Kong Koi**

A one-legged phantom that travels by hopping, it sucks blood from people's toes as they sleep in the forest.

**12 Phi Pop**

This spirit usually possesses a living female host and eats the intestines of others as they sleep.

**13 Pret**

Tall humanoid forms, these spirits have tiny needle mouths because of gluttony and greed in their former lives.

# Listings

## BEST OF THE REST

### Inspired Temples

Wat Ban Tham

While cave temples are nothing new in Thailand, this one in Kanchanaburi is especially picturesque, with its entrance resembling a dragon's mouth and mountaintop views of the surrounding river.

Wat Tha Khanun

Across the river from Kanchanaburi proper, this temple features a hilltop golden stupa, accessible via suspension bridge lending up-close and personal views of the water.

Wat Sam Phran

This temple is famous for the enormous dragon wrapped around its 17-storey cylindrical structure painted a vibrant shade of candy pink, a 1½ hour drive from Bangkok.

### Noodle Fixes

Ta Pui Noodle $

If you are in Sukhothai, you can't leave without trying a bowl of Sukhothai noodle. This charming open-air eatery on the outskirts of town offers a stellar version.

Yai Krieng $

Another Sukhothai fixture, this open-air stop sells its own unique version of Sukhothai noodles without the broth called *guaythiew bae*, as well as fermented rice crepes on a stick.

Pa Lek Boat Noodle $

Ayutthaya is famous for its boat noodles, first made by floating vendors on the river and thickened with pork or beef blood. This shop is by far the most famous.

Kai Tong $

Chinese-style *guaythiew lard na* (fried rice noodles with pork or beef) are the speciality at 'Gold Chicken', drawing foodie crowds from nearby Bangkok, especially on weekends.

### Remote Camping

Huai Mae Khamin Waterfall

Not only is this stunning seven-tier waterfall considered one of the most beautiful in Thailand, it also offers camping opportunities nearby with tent and sleeping set rentals available.

Khao Luang

Like its similarly named sibling down south, this beautiful mountain trail in Sukhothai's Ramkhamhaeng National Park allows camping on the mountaintop. The hike is considered difficult for newbies.

Thong Pha Phum National Park (Khao Chang Phueak)

Experienced hikers will enjoy exploring this mountain on Myanmar's border, nicknamed 'the knife's edge' for its dramatic views. Hiring a guide is considered essential; hikes are cancelled in bad weather.

### Night & Floating Markets

JJ Night Market Kanchanaburi

Thais love their night markets, and this one in Kanchanaburi is no different. Street food, cute souvenirs, cheap clothing, and, of course, coffee loom large at this nightly market.

Wat Tha Khanun

Ayuthaya Weekend Night Market

Also known as Krungsri Walking Street, this market offers everything you'd expect of a Thai night market, plus martial arts shows. As the name suggests, it's open on weekends.

Ayuthaya Floating Market

This is not a real floating market – one in which floating vendors actually conduct business – but it still sells souvenirs and snacks to visitors in a charming setting.

## Historical Sites

Thailand-Burma Railway Centre

No visit to the River Kwai is complete without a stop at this interactive museum, dedicated to educating guests about the Thai-Burma Railway, otherwise known as the Death Railway.

JEATH War Museum

The first museum in Kanchanaburi devoted to telling the story behind the infamous Death Railway, JEATH focuses on the POWs' experiences and operates out of a former WWII detention hut.

Si Satchanalai Historical Park

Less famous than its neighbour Sukhothai Historical Park, this attraction is also less crowded and offers a breezy bike ride through the ruins of the second-largest city after Sukhothai.

Bang Pa-In Palace

Also known as the Summer Palace, this former royal residence in Ayutthaya dates as far back as the 17th century before its restoration by Rama IV 200 years later.

## Just for Kids

Alpaca Hill

Restless kiddos would be hard-pressed to find something more fun than this sprawling petting zoo and working farm in Ratchaburi. Come for alpacas, stay for mini-kangaroos.

Boon Lott's Elephant Sanctuary

This rescue sanctuary for elephants in Sukhothai allows overnight guests to follow the pachyderms about on their day-to-day activities. Meals and transport from Sukhothai airport included.

Million Toy Museum

Toy aficionados of all ages will enjoy this private museum in Ayutthaya founded by a local professor and featuring both Thai and Western toys from as far back as 1880.

## Nature Walks

Sap Lek Reservoir

If you just want a nice easy walk with beautiful scenery, this reservoir on the outskirts of Lopburi affords calm and serene strolls on weekdays.

Giant Rain Tree

Located in Kanchanaburi Province and more than a century old, this massive tree measures 20m tall with a 52m-wide canopy. An elevated walk protects the tree's roots.

## Veggie Friendly Eats

Kaffa Bistro $$

This pizza specialist in Ayutthaya is not just vegetarian-friendly, but also provides gluten-free menu items. Small and cozy, it's helmed by a gregarious, *Star Wars*–loving owner.

Aurra Ammie Vegetarian Restaurant $

This vegetarian spot in Pak Chong sits next to the river and puts forth a menu peppered with both Thai and Western standards. Mosquito repellent is recommended.

**Scan to find more things to do in Central Thailand online**

# CHIANG MAI & NORTHERN THAILAND

COFFEE | ELEPHANTS | MOUNTAINS

Experience Chiang Mai & Northern Thailand online

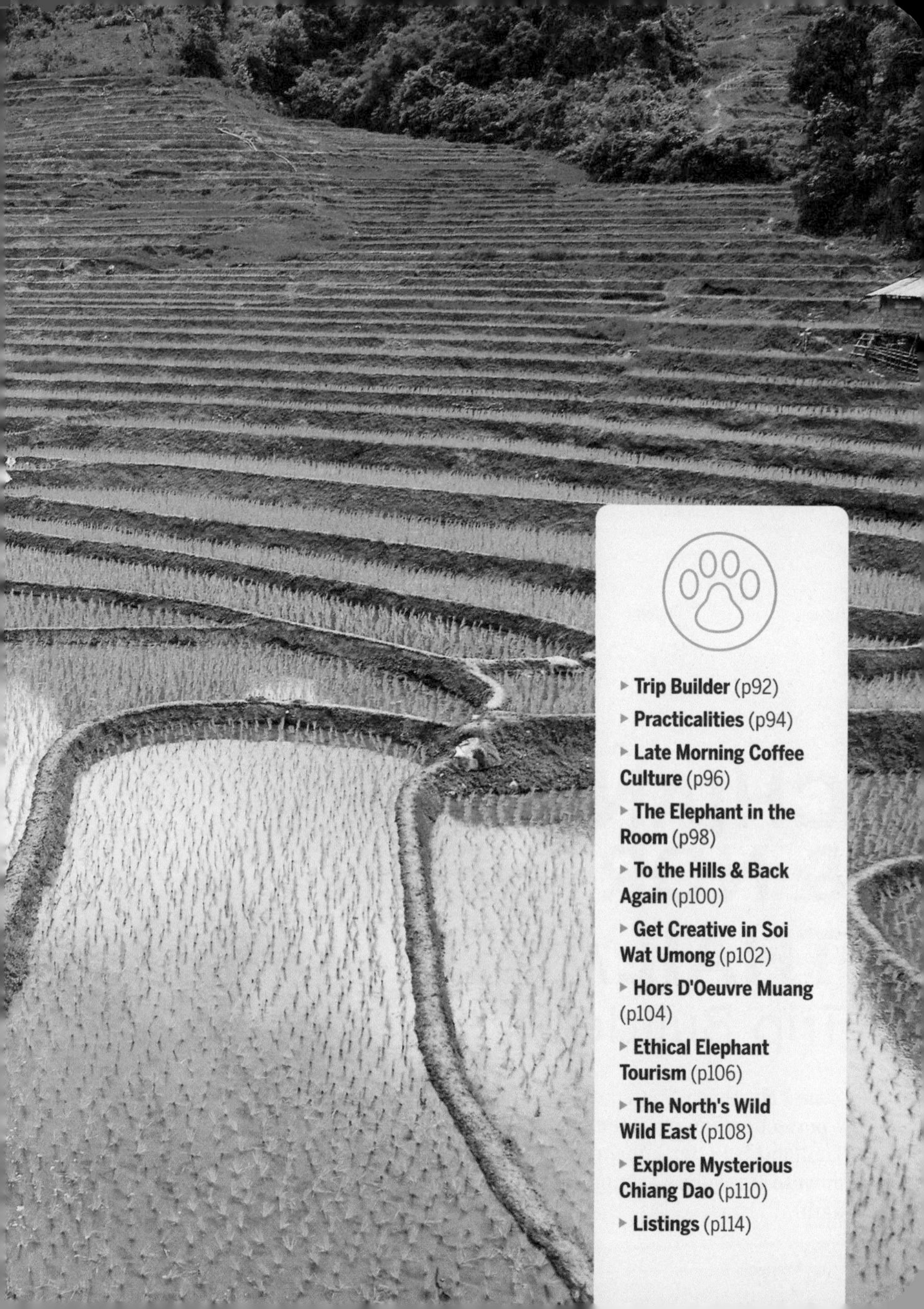

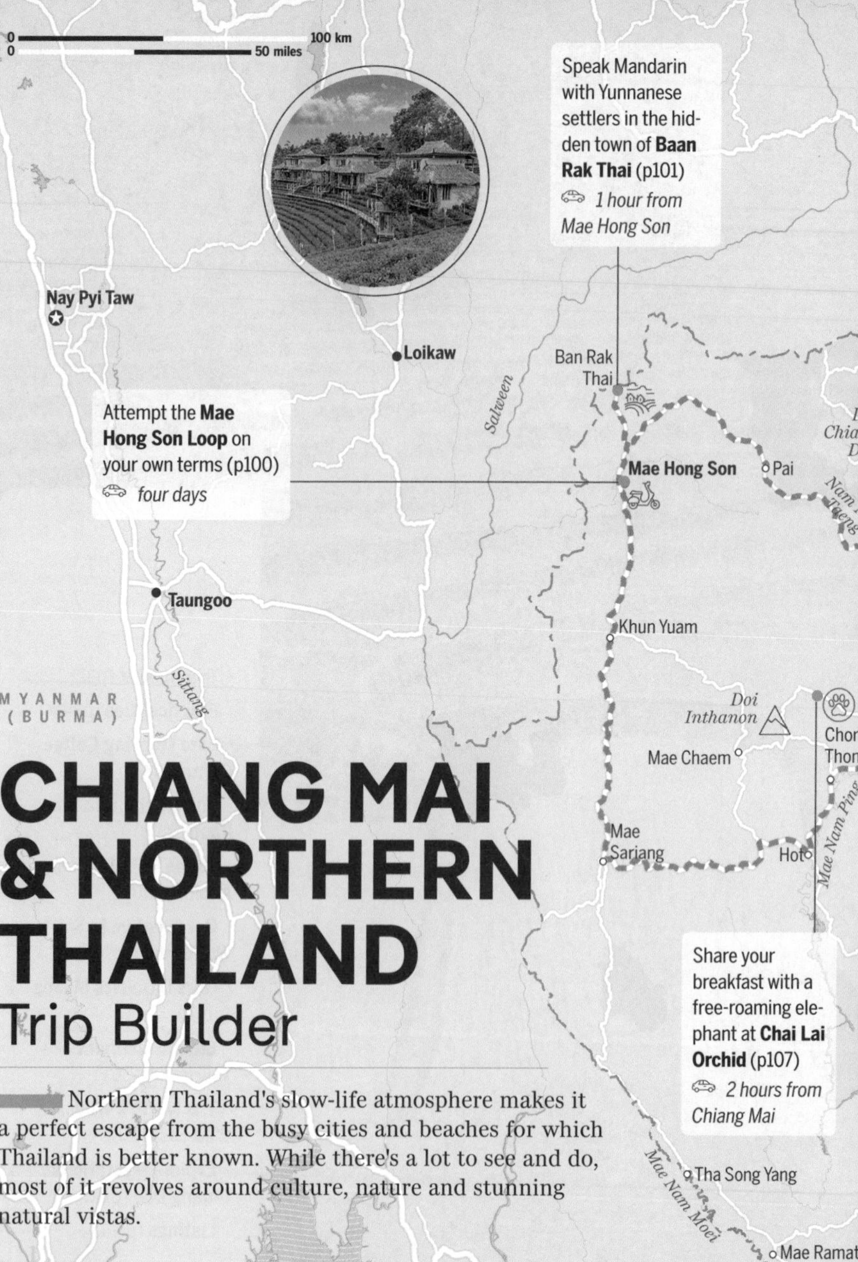


# CHIANG MAI & NORTHERN THAILAND

## Trip Builder

Northern Thailand's slow-life atmosphere makes it a perfect escape from the busy cities and beaches for which Thailand is better known. While there's a lot to see and do, most of it revolves around culture, nature and stunning natural vistas.

Soak in the hot springs of **Chiang Dao** (p110)
1 hour from Chiang Mai
Sit sidecar on a Royal Enfield ride along the edges of the **Golden Triangle** (p107)
5 hours from Chiang Mai
Go without electricity and live fire to fist in the mountain town of **Mae Mae** (p112)
2 hours from Chiang Mai
Discover the wild land of bandits and boatmen in **Nan Province** (p108)
4 hours from Chiang Mai
Get lost down hidden Chiang Mai sois and underground temples on **Soi Wat Umong** (p102)
15 minutes from Chiang Mai Old City
Sip on locally grown coffee, roasted by the socially conscious **Akha Ama** (p96)
10 minutes from Chiang Mai Old City
Explore bookable experiences in Chiang Mai & Northern Thailand
Tachileik
Mekong
Ban Muang Kan
Mae Sai
Huay Xai (Hoksay)
Chiang Saen
Chiang Khong
Mae Chan
Mae Nam Ing
Tha Ton
Fang
Chiang Rai
LAOS
Ban Mae Khi
Thoeng
Phan
Chiang Kham
Wiang Pa Pao
Chiang Dao
Mae Mae
Chiang Klang
Mae Taeng
Phayao
Pua
Tha Wang Pha
Mae Rim
Doi Saket
Chiang Mai
Nan
Lamphun
Pasang
Wiang Sa
Phrae
Den Chai
Kheuan Sirikit
Nam Pat
Uttaradit
Mae Nam Nan
Thoen
Si Satchanalai
Sawankhalok
Dan Sai
Wang Saphung
Nakhon Thai
Sukhothai
Tak

# Practicalities

AMNAT PHUTHAMRONG/SHUTTERSTOCK ©

## ARRIVING

Buses and trains give the most flexibility for visiting northern Thailand, as you can jump on and off at any stop along the way. Chiang Mai also operates as a hub for the region, with hundreds of connecting routes to neighbouring cities and provinces. The sleeper train from Bangkok may be slow but it is a fun experience in and of itself. Flights destined for Chiang Mai International Airport are frequent and inexpensive.

## HOW MUCH FOR A

**Local coffee** 50–100B

**Cocktail** 150–300B

**Kôa soy** 50–100B

## WHEN TO GO

**NOV–MAR**

Cool and balmy, this is the north's most popular season despite smog from agricultural burning. Late November is the best time to visit, before the smog but after the rain.

**APR–JUN**

Hot and dry, but still cooler than Bangkok. Expect an influx of people during Songkran.

**JUL–OCT**

The rainy season revives parched jungles and fills waterfalls.

## GETTING AROUND

**Walking** Despite the heat and humidity, the best way to navigate the main cities of northern Thailand – which are considerably smaller than the capital – is by foot.

**Red trucks** Chiang Mai is home to the ubiquitous red trucks *(rót daang)* that drive set-price but unplanned routes around the city depending on passenger requests. You can also negotiate prices for return trips or a full-day adventure.

**Taxi and Grab** Most major northern Thai cities have taxi services and cars with the ride-hailing app, Grab. In Chiang Mai, traditional taxi cabs can be booked for advanced trips and travel greater distances. Grab only operates within city limits, so be sure to arrange return transport if going far away.

## EATING & DRINKING

A northern speciality best described as a curried noodle soup, *khao soi* is most commonly made with beef or chicken, egg noodles and served with a topping of shallots, pickled greens, lime and crispy fried noodles in one generous bowl.

Another northern classic, *sâi òo·a* (heavily spiced pork or fish sausage) is a must-try (pictured bottom right). Lampang claims to have the best, but each province contends with their own recipe.

A locally brewed form of rice whisky fermented with bark and herbs, *ya dong* is undergoing a revival in Thailand, with bars serving this traditionally medicinal alcoholic beverage in cocktail form.

**Must-try local coffee**
Akha Ama (pictured top right; p97)

**Best northern dining atmosphere**
Chiang Dao Nest (p112)

## OUT ON TWO WHEELS

Although Thailand's roads can be dangerous at times, driving two wheels around the inner cities of northern Thailand is a safe way to explore on your own terms. Renting bicycles and motorbikes is incredibly easy and inexpensive; just beware of police checkpoints that will fine you if you don't have the proper documentation.

## BREATHE SAFE

If you're visiting between December and March, it's advisable to wear an N95 mask when air quality gets bad to protect against the smog caused by agricultural burning. During this season, particulate matter can blanket the city, ruining the views and your health.

## WHERE TO STAY

Each northern capital is its province's namesake, and each one boasts its own culture, dialect and cuisine. Locals say that you've not seen the north until you've seen more than one capital.

| Town/Village | Pros/Cons |
|---|---|
| Chiang Mai | The hub for your northern adventure. The old city is best for tradition, the riverside is best for romance. |
| Chiang Rai | Home to the Golden Triangle, Black House and White Temple. |
| Mae Hong Son | A charming mountaintop town infused with hill tribe culture. |
| Nan | A former hidden kingdom with its own unique cultures and customs. Popular with hip domestic travellers. |
| Tak | Connects with the central plains; the busiest Thai–Myanmar border town in Thailand. |
| Lampang | A hot and quiet backwater with incredible mountaintop stupas and quaint horse-drawn taxis. |

## MONEY

Carry cash; in the north most restaurants, bars and shops still don't accept cards. ATMs are plentiful, and you can always change big notes at 7-Eleven.

# 13 Late Morning COFFEE CULTURE

COFFEE | CULTURE | ART

Chiang Mai's love affair with coffee may be new, but the history of Thai-grown coffee is rich: in each cup, a story of drug addiction, poverty, deforestation, royal intervention and international cooperation. Today, there's a coffee shop on every street corner, from aunties roasting freshly harvested coffee beans in their homes to latte art champions serving cups topped with their award-winning patterns.

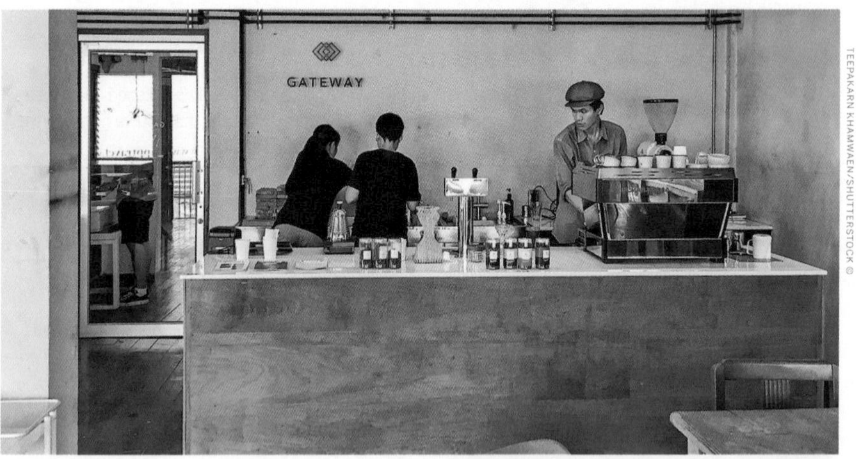


TEEPAKARN KHAMWAEN/SHUTTERSTOCK ©

### How to

**Slow risers** People in the north live on a slower schedule than other coffee drinking cultures. Most coffee shops open at 10am or later.

**Presentation tops taste** Taking photos (and selfies) in coffee shops is a key part of the experience; bring a camera and give in to the trend.

**Working coffee** With so many digital nomads in the city, almost all cafes have high-speed internet and everything you need for a full day's work.

AYDAN STUART/LONELY PLANET ©

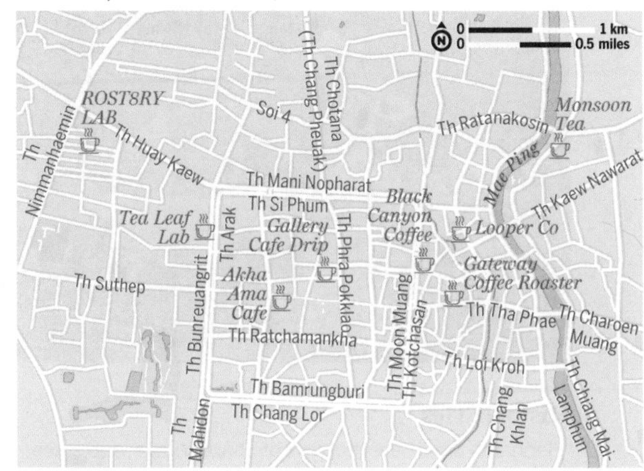


**Left** Gateway Coffee Roaster. **Bottom left** Coffee, ROST8RY LAB

## Locally Sourced

The scent of freshly brewed coffee is ubiquitous with the Chiang Mai experience. It all started with King Bhumibol Adulyadej's Royal Projects that developed a unique Arabica strain to provide local communities with an alternative to opium poppies. As a result, a coffee culture unlike anywhere else emerged – born out of a genuine passion for this much-loved bean.

For a taste of locally grown coffee, there's no place better, or more famous, than **Akha Ama**. More than just a cafe, it also runs a social enterprise that empowers hill tribe villages to grow coffee in more sustainable ways. **Gateway Coffee Roaster**, just steps from Tha Phae Gate, also brews Thai single-origin cups made from beans grown in Doi Chiang and Huay Chomphon.

## International Sensations

When it comes to international blends, **ROST8RY LAB** is legendary. Taking first place in the 2018 and 2019 World Barista Championships and the 2017 World Latte Art Championship, they definitely know their coffee.

The international **Black Canyon Coffee** is likely Chiang Mai's biggest success story, with branches across Southeast Asia.

## Creative Cultures

With creativity (and caffeine) in their blood, many local cafe owners strive to take coffee to new heights. **Looper Co** has the city's most minimalist, Instagrammable interior, and **CottonTree Roasters** serves some of the most creative cold brew concoctions in town.

If tea is more your thing, then **Tea Leaf Lab** and **Monsoon Tea** both brew up a storm.

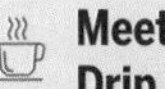

### Meet Thailand's Drip King

Drip coffee may not be the fastest way to enjoy a cup, but the stories and legends told by Thailand's Drip King are well worth the wait.

**Gallery Cafe Drip** is home to the city's first 'Barista-table' experience, a sit-down journey for those curious about the origins of Thai coffee and its unique flavour profiles. With no way to book in advance, this experience is a slow and holistic walk-in journey, led by the Drip King's passion for helping people understand the coffee they are drinking – from the mountain soil it was grown in to the curated blends he designs for your palate.

# The Elephant in the Room

**TALKING GOOD AND BAD ABOUT ELEPHANT TOURISM**

Interacting with captive elephants is a controversial topic, sparking great interest and activism the world over. However, much of this outrage comes from a place of misinformation or misunderstanding. Captive elephants have always been a key character in Thailand's development, and without a chance to earn their keep through interaction, education and tourism, their future is uncertain and perilous.

**Left** Mahouts bathing their elephants. **Middle** Sculpture, Wat Phra Singh. **Right** Elephan, Chai Lai Orchid

MATYAS REHAK/SHUTTERSTOCK ©

## Historic Ties

'Elephants are a beautiful part of Thai heritage, and since Covid things have been pretty terrible for them,' said Alexandra Pham, founder of Daughters Rising, an organisation that empowers at-risk Karen women in northern Thailand, and Chai Lai Orchid, an eco-resort that rescues elephants and lets guests interact with them.

Elephants have lived and worked with humans for the better part of four millennia, and have played a crucial role in Asia's development. After forests were left decimated by logging in the mid-20th century, there was not enough space to release elephants back into the wild. Even if there was, releasing captive elephants is a complex process, not to mention illegal.

As income dried up, elephants could no longer pay for their own survival. Around 250kg of food every day and a full-time mahout, who himself needs to eat and raise a family, does not come cheap. Luckily, tourism filled this void, seeing just three elephant camps in the '70s turn into over 160 sanctuaries (of various welfare standards) today.

## A Complicated Issue

There is an ongoing debate about the ethics of modern-day elephant keeping.

'A lot of tourists believe that every elephant is abused and believe that any interaction with elephants must be bad,' said John Roberts, Anantara's Director of Elephants, who also oversees sustainability and conservation projects for Minor hotels. 'But in reality, it's all about how it's done.'

Some sanctuaries are guilty of inhumane treatment, but there are also sanctuaries that do everything in their power

CYRILLE REDOR/SHUTTERSTOCK ©

JAMES DE LA CHOCHE ©



to give elephants the best care possible. Either way, if tourists boycott both types, all elephants become homeless.

'Because of Covid, we have seen first hand what a lack of tourism can do to the elephant,' explained Pham, who recently saved a 60-year-old matriarch after a lack of tourists forced her owner to abandon it. 'The elephants in camps nearby are all suffering from gastrointestinal issues as all they're doing is standing all day; at least rides keep them active and healthy.'

Some sanctuaries are guilty of inhumane treatment, but there are also sanctuaries that do everything in their power to give elephants the best care possible.

## A Valued Solution

Although there's no perfect way to keep an elephant in captivity, there are things tourists can do to ensure they visit the right places.

'There are so many highly skilled camp managers, mahouts and staff that work around the clock to provide excellent levels of enrichment and support for elephants,' said Dr Ingrid Suter of Asian Captive Elephant Standards (ACES), a leading elephant camp accreditation organisation. 'I believe these venues should be showcased and supported.'

Roberts adds that sanctuaries who are in the process of applying to any accreditor who bases their standard in scientific or veterinary experience are worthy of respect, as they're already trying hard to do the right thing.

To find out more and learn how elephant tourism can help the animals thrive, explore the resources of ACES (elephantstandards.com), Asian Captive Elephant Working Group (ACEWG), and Global Spirit (globalspirit.biz) who all work to dispel myths and better the quality of elephant tourism across Asia.

### Evidence Speaks

Various research measuring stress hormones in Asian elephants found that elephants who did not give rides but were left to roam in large fields were more stressed than those giving rides to tourists every day. 'Probably due to inappropriate bonding, lack of exercise and obesity,' John Roberts, Anantara's Director of Elephants, suggests. 'That's not to say that free roaming is worse than riding or vice versa! It is just that both can be done badly and both can be done well. What's great is that photos of bad conditions or negative reviews on social media are keeping places in check. And although it's not necessarily the right motive to change, the result is a positive one for elephants as a whole.'

# 14 To the Hills & BACK AGAIN

BIKING | VILLAGE LIFE | ADVENTURE

Motorised or pedal-powered, a tour of the northern provinces can be a thrilling experience on two wheels. But of all the routes, taking two wheels around the Mae Hong Son Loop is a rite of passage for any adventurer. And for good reason.

SCOTT BIALES DITCHTHEMAP/SHUTTERSTOCK ©

### Trip Notes

**When to go** Riding a bike in monsoon rain can be dangerous. The cool season is best, the hot season a very close second.

**What bike is best** A rental scooter will more than suffice, but the bigger your bike, the more freedom you have to explore.

**Practise your Mandarin** Yunnanese communities that settled in the mountains of Mae Hong Son after fleeing the Communist revolution still speak a form of Mandarin today.

### A 600km Round Trip

Starting and ending in Chiang Mai, the Mae Hong Son Loop takes four or five days to complete, depending on how adventurous you feel. With literally no restrictions except time, an extra day in Pai or a half-day detour to a remote Chinese village can make this shared experience truly yours.

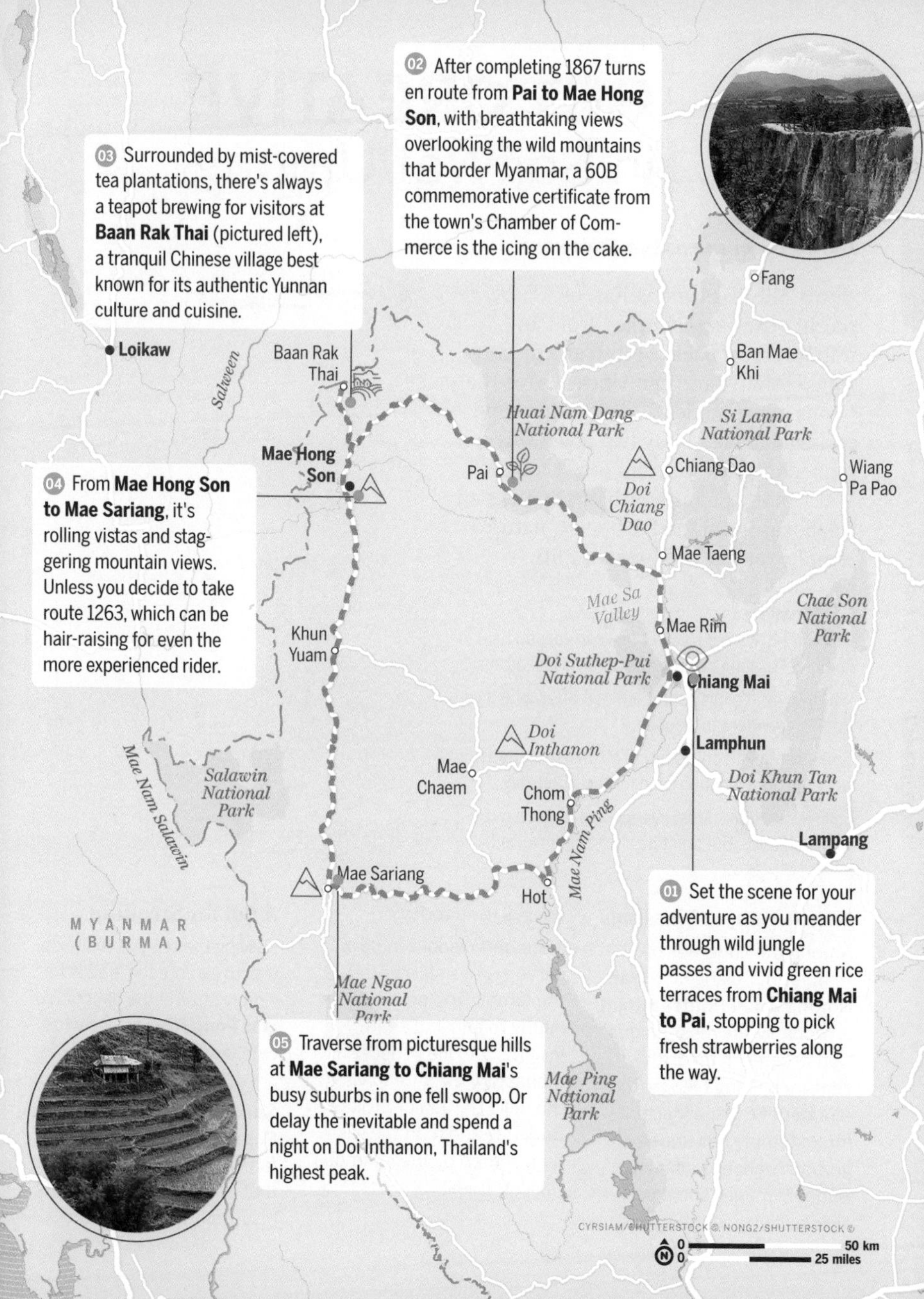

01 Set the scene for your adventure as you meander through wild jungle passes and vivid green rice terraces from **Chiang Mai to Pai**, stopping to pick fresh strawberries along the way.
02 After completing 1867 turns en route from **Pai to Mae Hong Son**, with breathtaking views overlooking the wild mountains that border Myanmar, a 60B commemorative certificate from the town's Chamber of Commerce is the icing on the cake.
03 Surrounded by mist-covered tea plantations, there's always a teapot brewing for visitors at **Baan Rak Thai** (pictured left), a tranquil Chinese village best known for its authentic Yunnan culture and cuisine.
04 From **Mae Hong Son to Mae Sariang**, it's rolling vistas and staggering mountain views. Unless you decide to take route 1263, which can be hair-raising for even the more experienced rider.
05 Traverse from picturesque hills at **Mae Sariang to Chiang Mai**'s busy suburbs in one fell swoop. Or delay the inevitable and spend a night on Doi Inthanon, Thailand's highest peak.
Fang
Loikaw
Salween
Baan Rak Thai
Ban Mae Khi
Huai Nam Dang National Park
Si Lanna National Park
Mae Hong Son
Pai
Chiang Dao
Doi Chiang Dao
Wiang Pa Pao
Mae Taeng
Mae Sa Valley
Chae Son National Park
Mae Rim
Khun Yuam
Doi Suthep-Pui National Park
Chiang Mai
Doi Inthanon
Lamphun
Mae Nam Salawin
Salawin National Park
Mae Chaem
Chom Thong
Doi Khun Tan National Park
Mae Nam Ping
Lampang
Mae Sariang
Hot
MYANMAR (BURMA)
Mae Ngao National Park
Mae Ping National Park
0 50 km
0 25 miles

# 15 GET CREATIVE in Soi Wat Umong

**ART | COMMUNITY | SHOPPING**

Soi Wat Umong has, in recent years, transformed from an unimpressive back soi into an epicentre for creativity (and gentrification) at the hands of art students, cafe owners and residents alike. A day trip down this soi, named after the ancient forest temple Wat Umong Suan Phutthatham, ticks all the boxes: local food, bars, art, nature, temples, culture and community.

### How to

**Getting here** A red truck or taxi can get you here in no time. Flagging down a ride home is just as easy.

**When to go** It's best to set out mid-afternoon if you want everywhere to be open.

**Carry cash** With only a few ATMs that are often not working, bring enough cash for the whole day.

**Follow the locals** Most events here target a more local audience. But don't be shy to get involved.



## Forest Temple Blessings

Among the hundreds of temples in Chiang Mai, **Wat Umong Suan Phutthatham** is probably the most unique. Constructed in the 13th century by King Mengri, the founder of Chiang Mai, this forest temple has underground tunnels containing Buddha images and dark alcoves for meditation that are still used today.

Buddhist monks in dark saffron robes still reside at the temple and are often happy to talk and share insights into life in a forest monastery. Be sure to visit the Relic Garden of Broken Buddhas and read the wisdom shared by the infamous 'Talking Trees'.

## A Soi for Strolling

Leaving the temple, the best way to explore the area is to simply stroll in the direction of **Wat Pong Noi** and see what catches your fancy.

Tucked behind **Paper Spoon** coffee shop, is **Book: Republic**, Chiang Mai's famed activist bookshop that regularly organises discussions on Thai and

JEWN_YEEP/SHUTTERSTOCK ©



## Eat Your Way Around

Thai food is made for grazing, so it's not unusual for people to eat as they go. Ask any local, and they'll recommend **Laap Lung Noi** for the best grilled meats, northern-style *lâhp* (spicy, herbal mince-meat salad)and *sôm·đam* (spicy green papaya salad) in the city. and **Sri Payong Seafood** for, well, seafood. For tastes more similar to home, **Dinky's BBQ** offers the best smoked Southern American cuisine in the city. **L'amour Cafe**, with its hard-to-miss bright yellow building, is a good halfway house for a caffeine boost and Instagram-friendly slice of cake. If you make it to Wat Pong Noi, there's a generous offering of street food outside its gates.

international literature, film and culture.

Further down, **Lansieow Freeative Art Space** is a fun community of bars and restaurants, with regular family-friendly concerts, pop-up markets and charity events.

### Community Squared

Temples aside, **Baan Kang Wat** is probably the most well-known destination along the soi. Set up as a sustainability-focused community market square, it gives back to society with shops, galleries, restaurants and art schools that share a similar ethos.

Join a workshop or watch a movie in the mini amphitheatre. If art is your thing, right behind is the **Wattana Art Gallery** that has some fantastic local Thai and contemporary art on display.

**Above** Inside Wat Umong tunnels

# HORS D'OEUVRE

## Muang

**01 Lâhp mŏo krua**
A northern meat salad flavoured with cumin, turmeric, pigs blood and ginger for a deeper taste profile than its northeastern cousin.

**02 Yam nòr mái**
A spicy salad made from young bamboo shoots, lemongrass, kaffir lime leaves and ginger; brought together with a nice dollop of crab paste.

**03 Kôw soy**
Egg noodles in a rich coconut curry broth, garnished with deep-fried crispy egg noodles, pickled mustard greens, shallots, lime and chilli oil.

**04 Sâi òo·a**
Every region has its own take on this spicy pork sausage, infused with lemongrass, kaffir lime leaves, galangal and red chilli paste.

**05 Nám prík nùm**
Northern Thailand is renowned for its chilli dips. Made from young green chillies, this dip is best enjoyed with crispy pork crackling and fresh vegetables.

**06 Nám prík ong**
This chilli dip is like a Thai ragu; made by simmering pork, tomatoes, shrimp paste and fermented soy beans for hours.

**07 Gaang hoh**
'*Hoh*' in the northern Thai dialect means to put

together, so this stir-fried curry is usually made by mixing leftover curries with glass noodles and fresh herbs.

**08 Gaang kà·nŭn**
A northern spin on tom yum soup that is hot, sour and layered. Unripe jackfruit, cherry tomatoes and pork bones are the stars of the show.

**09 Aab ong orr**
Pork brain mixed with local herbs and spices, wrapped in a banana leaf and grilled to perfection. Sounds awful, tastes great.

**10 Kà·nŏm jeen nám ngée·o**
Fresh rice noodles served with a spicy tomato broth flavoured by the unusual ngiao flower *(Bombax ceiba)* that naturally grows in the north.

**11 Gaang hung le**
Popular at holiday feasts, this Thai-Burmese curry has a distinct masala-style aroma brought to life with tamarind, pickled garlic and ginger.

**12 Gaang gae gòp**
A very local curry (read: spicy) made using chilli paste, betel leaf, vegetables and frog meat with a soup-like consistency.

# 16 ETHICAL Elephant Tourism

**ELEPHANTS | TREKKING | CONSERVATION**

If there's one animal that comes to mind when you mention Thailand, it's the elephant. With over 160 sanctuaries around the country, there are many experiences to be had. And although it's true that not all elephant sanctuaries are equal, it takes just a little bit of research to ensure a pleasant experience for you and the elephants you meet. Here are two we guarantee do elephant tourism right.

JAMES DE LA CHOCHE ©

### How to

**Understand the ethics** See p98 for an insight into what ethical elephant tourism really means.

**Do your research** Before going anywhere with elephants, do proper research into what sanctuaries are good and bad.

**Get a second opinion** For peace of mind, it can be good to find a second opinion to corroborate the claims made by elephant sanctuaries.

STEVE CUKROV/SHUTTERSTOCK ©

## Immerse Yourself in Conservation

**Anantara Golden Triangle Elephant Camp & Resort** is probably the most spectacular elephant experience in Thailand, if you can afford its high price point.

Perched on the border with Myanmar and Laos, this is all about deep immersion in a one-off experience. Elephants freely roam the property, continually cared for by their mahouts. Big on conservation, the team has spent years finding the best ways to keep elephants active and socialised in sustainable and educational ways.

Learn about the mahout way of life, watch elephants roam their natural habitat from your balcony, ride sidecar in a Royal Enfield along elephant pathways, or sleep amid these majestic animals in luxury from the comfort of a jungle bubble room.

## Hands-On Social Development

**Chai Lai Orchid** is a more accessible alternative to enjoying the company of elephants, with a social development twist. Over the last eight years, Chai Lai Orchid has cared for, fed and rescued dozens of Asian elephants from abusive practices.

As a non-profit eco-lodge, all proceeds go to elephant care and social projects through Daughter's Rising that empower and provide education to marginalised Karen refugees to overcome intergenerational poverty and uplift their communities.

As a guest, you not only live among elephants and their mahouts, but are encouraged to get hands-on with elephant care, including feeding, bathing and forest tree exfoliation – three things elephants love the most. Most importantly, you can learn how to better support elephants and maintain their home, the forest. The highlight of any stay is the elephant wake-up call and balcony banana breakfast.

**Left** Elephant, Chai Lai Orchid
**Bottom left** Anatara Golden Triangle Elephant Camp & Resort

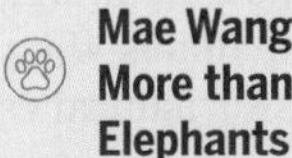

### Mae Wang: More than Elephants

Chai Lai Orchid is located in Mae Wang, the homeland of the Pga k'nyau indigenous people and a treasure trove of jungle experiences that go far beyond elephants. Surrounded by dramatic jungle landscapes and breathtaking green rice fields, visitors to this area can trek to waterfalls and hidden jungle temples, sleep rough in the forest with Karen hill tribe guides who share native knowledge about foraging, plant medicine and weaving, or lazily float down the river on a bamboo raft, local beer in hand.

■ **By Alexandra Pham,** *founder of Chai Lai Orchid (chailaiorchid.com) and Daughters Rising, Facebook Chai Lai Orchid, Instagram @Chailaiorchid*

# 17 The North's Wild WILD EAST

HISTORY | HERITAGE | MOUNTAINS

Often thought of as a rural backwater, Nan was once deemed a wild and inaccessible bandit-ridden land that sheltered violent Communists in its unmapped mountains. Today thankfully, with fewer bandits (ie none) and more boutique hotels, the province is slowly gaining popularity among city-dwellers looking for natural escapes and unadulterated northern Thai culture.

THANAKORN HONGPHAN/SHUTTERSTOCK ©

### How to

**Getting here** You can reach Nan via car or bus but expect a tiring drive. There are no trains, but direct flights from Bangkok are quick and inexpensive.

**Wrap up warm** There's something special about Nan in the winter months. The sky is clear and temperatures are nippy. Misty mornings are guaranteed but don't forget a scarf.

**Rent a car** With little infrastructure, it can be easy to get stuck unless you rent a car from the airport.

BOUYBIN/SHUTTERSTOCK ©

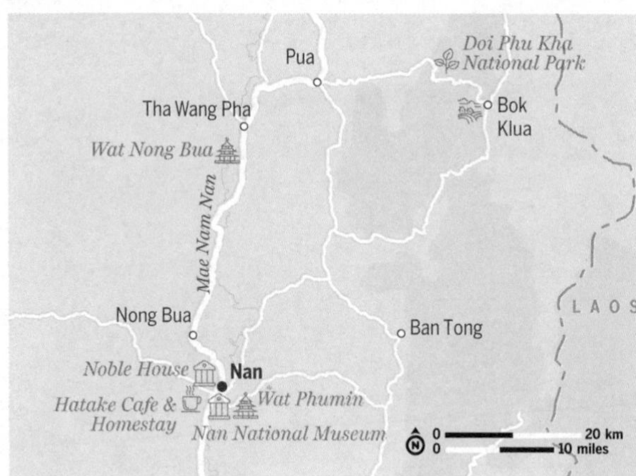


## Artistic Old Town

As the last province officially incorporated into Siam in 1932 after centuries as an autonomous state, Nan struggled with the reputation of being a barbarian backwater for decades. Left unconnected to the rest of the country until the 1980s, Nan's ethnic heritage is distinctly different from its northern peers.

Nan's claim to fame is **Wat Phumin**, a 16th-century temple with Thai Lü murals painted by the legendary Thit Buaphan. The 'Whisper of Love' is the most well-known, printed on countless souvenirs sold at the **Weekend Night Market** just outside.

**Nan National Museum** provides a unique glimpse into its intriguing history, and the **Noble House** offers a snapshot of 1900s Lanna Royal living, complete with wearable outfits for that perfect selfie.

Like Chiang Mai, Nan's hills grow a bounty of coffee. **Hatake Cafe & Homestay** serves local coffee with a view, and **Rong Krua Cafe Lab & Roastery** has the freshest roasts you'll find.

## Well-Kept Wildlands

Further north, the outpost town of **Pua** is home to an ancient Mon temple, **Wat Nong Bua**, and is gateway to Nan's well-kept national parks, the most significant being the picture-perfect **Doi Phu Kha National Park** with its iridescent rice paddies and towering mountain views.

If you're driving, let the winding mountaintop roads lead you towards the small village of **Bok Klua**, an ancient settlement where locals extract and refine salt harvested from a single well, following a process that's over 800 years old.

**Left** Doi Phu Kha National Park. **Bottom left** The 'Whisper of Love', Wat Phumin

### Boating Mad

From around mid-July, the Nan River begins to fill with teams of rowers practising for boat racing competitions that have become a tradition of **Tan Kway Salak**, a northern merit-making festival for ancestors.

Festivities usually occur between October and November, where the river fills with brightly coloured dragon boats and cheering crowds armed with amplifiers, eager to watch the boat races.

Each village has a team of rowers, with winners earning bragging rights for the following year. At this time, Nan is transformed from a quaint mountain village to a town of raucous cheer and rivers of colour.

# 18 Explore Mysterious CHIANG DAO

**ADVENTURE | HOMESTAYS | MARKETS**

While only a stone's throw from Chiang Mai, Chiang Dao is different in almost every sense. A hidden jungle delight in the shadow of a mighty mountain that maintains a cool, damp rainforest feel year-round, it's popular among domestic wildlife enthusiasts and trekkers. Here, the howls of gibbons and the scream of cicadas are a familiar sound, escapable only in the depths of a legendary cave used as shelter and a place of worship from at least the 17th century.

RBK365/SHUTTERSTOCK ©

## How to

**When to go** Persistent cool temperatures mean there's never a wrong time to visit Chiang Dao.

**Moving around** As soon as you enter Chiang Dao, taxis and buses more or less disappear. Rely on hotel transportation or rent a motorbike for added freedom to explore.

**Bring a jacket** Chiang Dao tends to get more chilly than nearby Chiang Mai, and the cool temperatures of winter mean you almost always need a jacket.

AMNAT30/SHUTTERSTOCK ©



## The Must-Sees

With a name that translates to 'City of the Stars', it's not surprising that Chiang Dao is most famous for its towering limestone peaks and unobstructed starry night skies – as long as fog or pollution don't spoil the view.

Climbing the majestic **Doi Luang Chiang Dao** to take in the surrounding mountains that undulate into the hazy blue distance is the obvious highlight. Its gravity-defying slopes often blanketed in morning fog tower 2175m over the quaint northern city and require a guide to reach the summit (it can be reached in about four hours). Staying overnight on the peak and watching the sunrise is almost undescribable.

Going in the opposite direction, is a vast and eerily spiritual cave complex that is part temple, part natural wonder. There are two portions to visit: the main cave, which takes

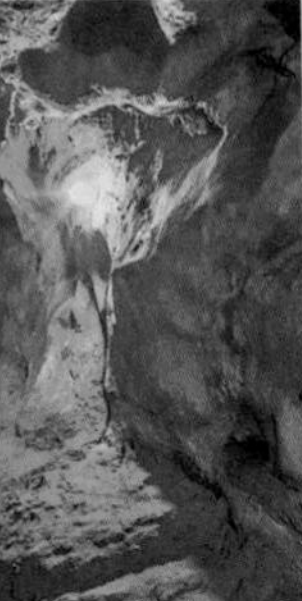
BLUR LIFE 1975/SHUTTERSTOCK ©

### Tuesday is Market Day

Every Tuesday morning, Chiang Dao's main market springs to life as locals and hill tribe villagers come together to trade garments, trinkets, spices and food foraged from the jungle. Walking between the disorganised stalls, you'll see everything from freshly harvested beehives and piles of wriggling ant eggs to hand-woven sun hats and bamboo rice steamers.

**Above left** Tents, Doi Luang Chiang Dao.
**Below left** Cave complex, Chiang Dao.
**Above** Market, Chiang Dao

about 30 minutes to an hour to explore unguided, and the deeper, pitch-black section, which only local guides and resident bats know how to navigate.

But the rarest of hidden gems is **Chiang Dao Hot Springs**. Found right at the foot of the mountain, there are free public pools and private pools that can be rented for around 50B an hour. As a shallow stream skips between you and a jungle village, while away the day in piping hot water tubs, snacking on grilled chicken and sticky rice while watching village life go by, cold beer in hand.

## The Homestays

Drive up into the hills of **Mae Mae**, and you'll discover countless homestays that grant remote access to distant mountain villages rarely seen by tourists.

**Tree House Hideaway** offers the best in unspoiled canopy views and proactively encourages guests to explore nature, interact

### A Refuge in Paradise

**Chiang Dao Nest** put Chiang Dao onto the tourist map when it opened its doors two decades ago. Charming bamboo cottages pepper well-tended tropical gardens of towering yang trees that are dwarfed by the mountain that looms over the resort at its foot. Natural beauty aside, owner and chef Wicha Cavaliero serves up some of northern Thailand's best Northern and European gourmet cuisine in the least pretentious of settings. Guest or not, this is a place for leaving maddening crowds far behind to indulge in the spectacular scenery, the friendly service and the fine fine food

**By Pim Kemasingki**, *founder and editor of* Chiang Mai Citylife *(chiangmaicitylife.com)*

with local culture and experience the outdoors. **Cher Cheeva**, on the other hand, provides a more intimate stay that focuses on community table dining and shared experiences between guests.

**Yu Tuan at Suan Koh** is for the more hardcore homestayer, with no electricity, outdoor toilets and little more than lighting fires, playing in the stream and swatting mosquitoes to pass the time. A private barbecue, complete with jungle whisky and views of the distant Doi Luang Chiang Dao, transports you to paradise.

## The Extremes

No trip to the jungles of northern Thailand is complete without taking a day to go head-to-head with the forces of nature.

**Kayak** along the river, **zipline** through the canopies, **trek** across razor-sharp peaks or battle **rapids** in a dinghy. Whatever catches your fancy, be sure to do your due diligence before committing to any operator. Some operators have a murky history, and not all experiences are fully safety checked or licensed. Stick to verified operators with good reviews and be willing to pay more for your own safety.

**Left** Chiang Dao Nest. **Below** View of Doi Luang Chiang Dao

# Listings

**BEST OF THE REST**

### Family Glamping

Camp Mai Mee Chue, Chiang Mai

Overlooking a valley in Pong Yaeng, this camp takes glamping to the next level with standalone tents and even a tent built atop a VW Beetle; complete with fancy drip coffee for the hipsters among us.

Camp Ta-Torn-Yorn, Chiang Mai

Named after the northern phrase for 'slow life', this glamping spot celebrates locally sourced cuisine and charmingly slow hospitality. Rural life with all the amenities.

Pang Ung, Mae Hong Son

Very close to the Myanmar border, this hidden village has several campgrounds and homestays that are worth the extra miles. Lakes, swans, forests and bonfires.

National Parks, Northern Thailand

Almost all national parks in northern Thailand have camping facilities. The campsites can be a little cramped, but you can rent everything you need and they're well maintained.

### More Coffee Please

Mars.cnx, Chiang Mai $$

With only 20 seats per night, this exclusive coffee bar made to look like an alien diner carved into a martian cave is an experience unlike any other in Thailand.

Zombie Cafe, Chiang Mai $

Don't be fooled by the name; this cafe is not zombie-themed but set in verdant green woodland, complete with treehouse and riverside seating where you can get your feet wet.

MAHAMITr Microroaster Cafe, Lampang $

Small, hip and artisan coffee serving the locals of Lampang, a sleepy town a few hours from Chiang Mai. Great for a detour on your way to somewhere special.

Baan Na Kang Tong, Nan $

A coffee shop and B&B, this misty mountain getaway is a popular destination with its own rice paddy and a curated selection of northern coffee blends.

Big's Little Cafe, Pai, Mae Hong Son $

Serving only one type of coffee – hot black – this simple-as-can-be hangout is where tourists rub shoulders and share secrets of must-see backpacking trails.

Cat' n' a Cup, Chiang Rai $$

Just off the Chiang Rai night bazaar, cat lovers can refuel on caffeine and cuddles at this petting-friendly cat cafe full of fuzzy furballs, local coffee and cute cakes.

### Chiang Mai Food Tour

House by Ginger, Chiang Mai $$$

A casual mix between a restaurant and bistro that fuses Western favourites with traditional northern fares that are all home-cooked. Quirky kitchenware and kitsch decor sets the scene.

Wat Chaloemphrakiet, Lampang

Huay Tung Tao, Chiang Mai $

North of the city is a reservoir that sits at the foothills of mountains, surrounded by floating bamboo huts that serve up some top-notch Thai food. Beer and swimming are (almost) compulsory.

RodYiam Beef Noodles, Chiang Mai $

A legend in Chiang Mai, this never-ending boiling pot of stewed beef served with a 'build-it-yourself' noodle soup menu that's to die for.

Laab Bunker, Chiang Mai $

Once an early morning, post-party mecca but now open afternoons; sample popular northern dishes served on tiny plates at extremely low prices.

Sudsanan Bar & Restaurant, Chiang Mai $$

Another legend of Chiang Mai, this time as a meeting place for artists, liberal politicians and laid-back hippies. Spicy northern food served with a generous helping of live music.

Tong Tem Toh, Chiang Mai $$

Long queues can only mean good things, so don't expect to find a seat for a quick bite at this traditional northern Thai restaurant. But when you do get seated, you'll not regret it.

## Special Mentions

Wat Rong Khun, Chiang Rai

Better known as the White Temple, it's not a temple at all but a private art exhibition that represents the gateway to heaven, designed and constructed by Chalermchai Kositpipat.

Wat Chaloemprakiet, Lampang

Ivory-white pagodas perched on a series of peaks in the mountains of northern Lampang. Be sure to bring a camera and some good walking shoes.

Baan Dam Museum, Chiang Rai

Otherwise known as the Black House, this is a local museum attraction made using a mix of traditional and contemporary architecture designed by Thawan Duchanee.

SIRICHAI PUANGSUWAN/SHUTTERSTOCK ©

Bua Thong Sticky Waterfalls

Baan Doi Pui, Chiang Mai

Although catering to tourism a little too much, this mountain top Hmong village is a great place to learn about the history and cultures of the many northern Thai ethnic groups.

Bua Thong Sticky Waterfalls, Chiang Mai

Ever wanted to climb up a waterfall? Well, now you can. The unique limestone riverbed is 'sticky' even as the water runs over it. Best to avoid weekends when it gets busy.

Kwan Phayao, Phayao

A giant lake in the heart of undiscovered Phayao. Boat rides to see the sunset are a must before a walk around the night market on its banks.

Mae Salong, Chiang Rai

Another ethnically Chinese village that makes little sense until you understand why they're here today. Walking down the street, you'd think you were in Yunnan Province, China.

**Scan to find more things to do in Chiang Mai & Northern Thailand online**

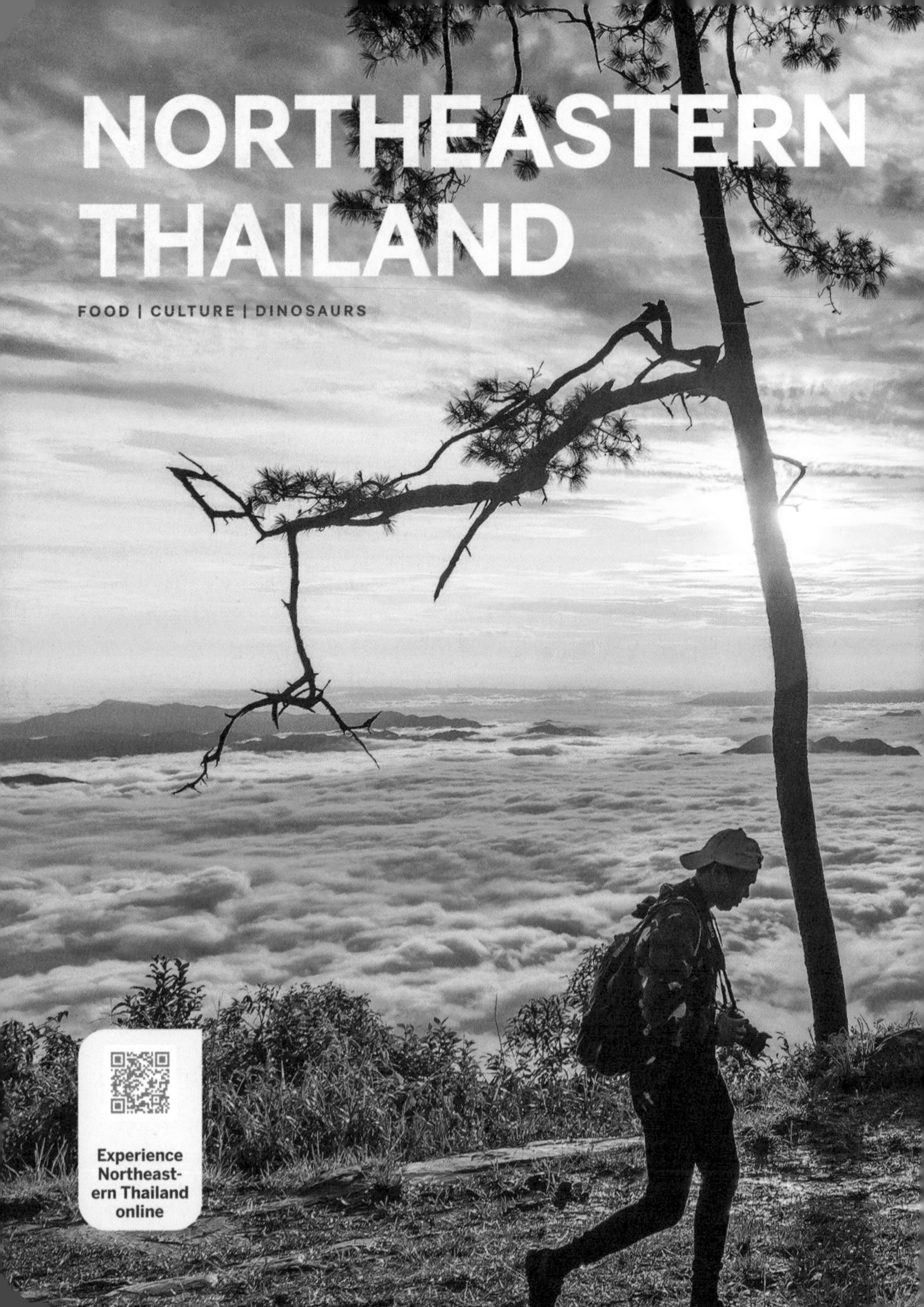
NORTHEASTERN
THAILAND
FOOD | CULTURE | DINOSAURS
Experience Northeastern Thailand online

Ang Nam Ngum
Mae Nam Ping
Lampang
Mae Nam Yom
Phrae
Mekong
Chiang Khan
Vientiane
Nam Som
Baan Phue
Uttaradit
Muang Phrae
Phu Ruea
Loei
Wang Saphung
Nong Bua Lamphu
Phu Kradueng
Si Buan Ruang
Tak
Kheuan Ubon Ratana
Chum Phae
Mae Nam Yom
Nakhon Sawan
Phimai
Nakhon Ratchasima (Khorat)
Pak Thong Chai
Kabin Buri
Sa Kaew
Aranya Prathet

Taste the most unusual Isan cuisine in **Baan Phue** (p131)
*1 hr from Udon Thani*

Rekindle your love of hiking at **Phu Kradueng** (p127)
*2 hrs from Khon Kaen*

Walk with dinosaurs at **Phu Wiang National Park** (p122)
*1.5 hrs from Khon Kaen*

Dance to Thai reggae at the **E-san Music Festival** (p133)
*Location changes every year, but usually near city of Khon Kaen*

# NORTHEASTERN THAILAND
## Trip Builder

Vast and under travelled, northeastern Thailand – more commonly known as Isan – is a sprawling wild land of verdant rice fields, sparse jungle and fun-loving communities. The incredible food and natural rhythm accompanying almost every interaction makes it the perfect region for off-the-beaten-track adventures.

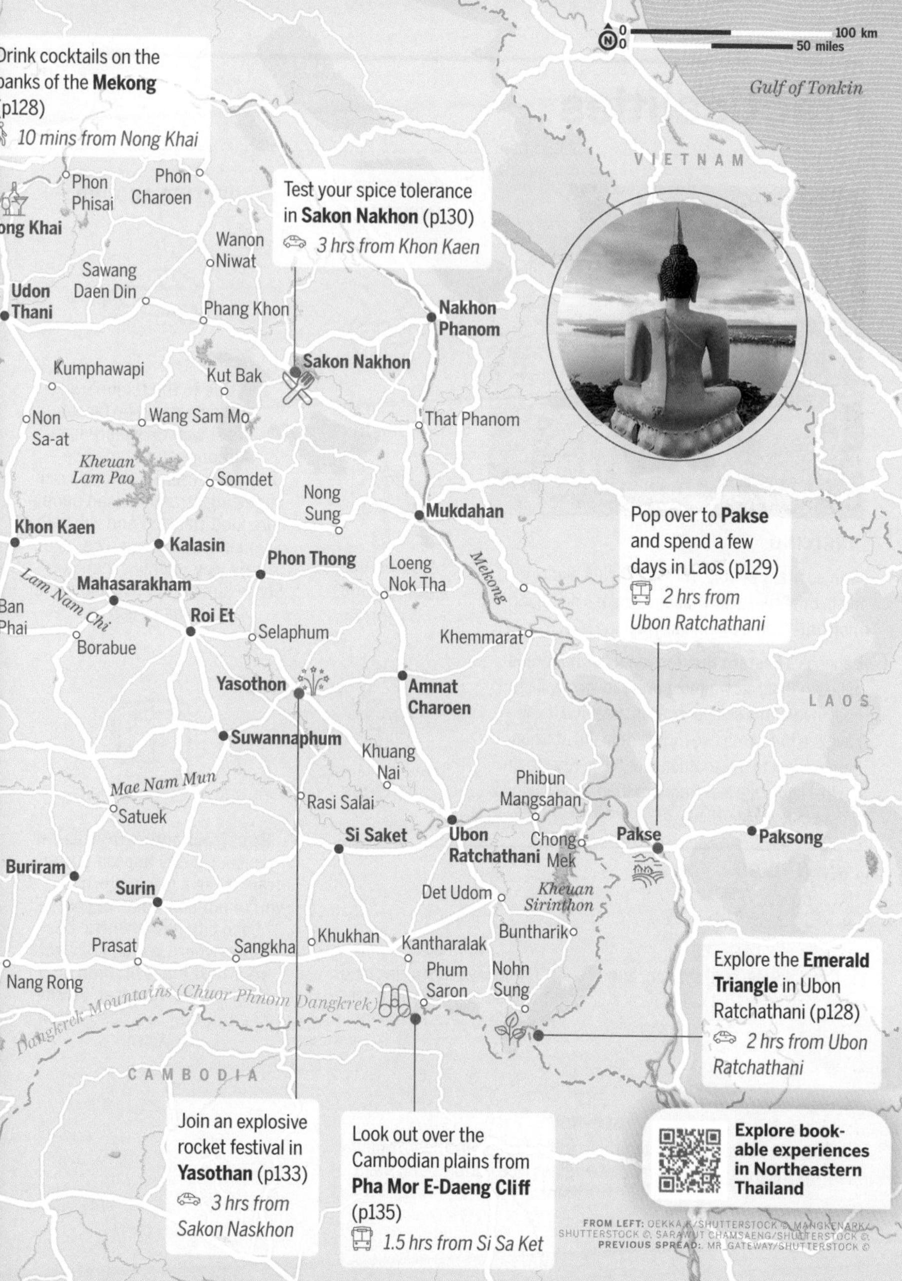


FROM LEFT: DEKKAR/SHUTTERSTOCK ©, MANGKENARK/SHUTTERSTOCK ©, SARAWUT CHAMSAENG/SHUTTERSTOCK ©, PREVIOUS SPREAD: MR_GATEWAY/SHUTTERSTOCK ©

# Practicalities

ATOMLINEARAN/SHUTTERSTOCK ©

### ARRIVING

With so many people from Isan living and working in other parts of Thailand, there's no region more interconnected than Thailand's 'rice bowl'.

Bangkok's **Eastern Bus Terminal** has hundreds of buses that reach almost every town or village imaginable. The sleeper train is great fun if you have the time, with two routes that end at Ubon Ratchathani to the southeast or Nong Khai to the north. Flights are less frequent than other regions but equally as affordable.

### HOW MUCH FOR A

**Sôm đam Lao**
**40–60B**

**Umbrella (for the sun)**
**100B**

**Souvenir sarong**
**200–300B**

### WHEN TO GO

**DEC–FEB**
Officially the cold season, but rarely that chilly.

**APR–JUL**
40°C middays turn green lands into desert in no time, often resulting in severe droughts.

**SEP–NOV**
The rainy season hydrates the parched red soil of Isan, quickly reviving a lush landscape of endless rice paddies and giant banana plants.

### GETTING AROUND

**Car** Due to the region's size, driving a car is by far the easiest way to explore Isan. Although buses may be frequent, there's always a risk of getting stranded. Isan people are kind-hearted and will help you in a pinch, but a car is a safe way to stay in control. Some hire companies offer one-way hires.

**Bus, Train and sŏrng·tăa·ou** For quick city hops, a bus or train make a great alternative if you're not able to drive yourself. Each city has a central bus station where you can navigate your next move or jump on a *sŏrng·tăa·ou* (the Isan version of a tuk-tuk) to a destination in town.

## EATING & DRINKING

**Sôm đam** (pictured top right) is a spicy salad made from unripe papaya (and often laced with preserved crab and fermented fish). It's of Lao-Isan origin but is enjoyed nationwide. What sets it apart here is the sheer volume of chillies added – spicy even by Thai standards.

**Gài yâhng kôw nĕe·o** (grilled chicken and sticky rice; pictured bottom right) is one of Isan's most popular dishes. While *năam neu·ang* is an Isan take on a Vietnamese dish of pork sausage, herbs, garlic and peanut-chilli sauce wrapped in rice paper and a fresh salad leaf. Adding unripe banana and green mango gives it a classic Thai sourness.

**Must-try authentic Isan food**
Samuay & Sons (p131)

**Best Vietnamese food**
VT Naem Nuang (p131)

## CONNECT

Coverage on wi-fi and mobile data is surprisingly good in Isan, but internet connections are spotty in remote areas. Stay connected with a data-loaded SIM card found at any 7-Eleven. Communicating where you need to go can be challenging as most people in Isan speak little to no English. Download a translation app.

## FOREIGN DIALECTS

Many people in Isan originate from neighbouring Laos or Cambodia, creating many different dialects across the region. For example, people in Surin and Buriram speak a Thai-Cambodian dialect, while those on the border to Laos speak more like a Laotian than a Thai.

## WHERE TO STAY

Isan is an expansive part of the country, roughly half the size of Germany. It's impossible to see everything in one go; instead find a city hub and explore from there.

| Town/Village | Pros/Cons |
|---|---|
| Khon Kaen | The capital of Isan, famous for silk and dinosaur remains. A great hub for regional exploration. |
| Ubon Ratchathani | A sleepy city with little in town but lots to see and do on the outskirts and some amazing Vietnamese cuisine. |
| Nong Khai | A bustling border town a stone's throw from Vientiane, Laos, and some beautiful Mekong surroundings. |
| Udon Thani | A hotspot for travellers and home to some of the better bars and restaurants in the region. |
| Loei | Technically part of Isan but more northern Thai in many ways given its proximity to the mountains. |

## MONEY

Cash is king in Isan. It's extremely rare for a shop or restaurant to take cards (big chains being the notable exception), so always have enough cash to cover expenses.

# 19 Explore the Capital KHON KAEN

**SHOPPING | DINOSAURS | FOOD**

Khon Kaen is the de facto capital of Isan, prophesied to become the new capital of Thailand after Bangkok sinks into the sea. There's a notably energetic feel to the city compared to the other major cities in the region, likely due to the combination of Lao, Thai and Vietnamese cultures, food and music, and an emerging middle class that's spearheading fast urban development.

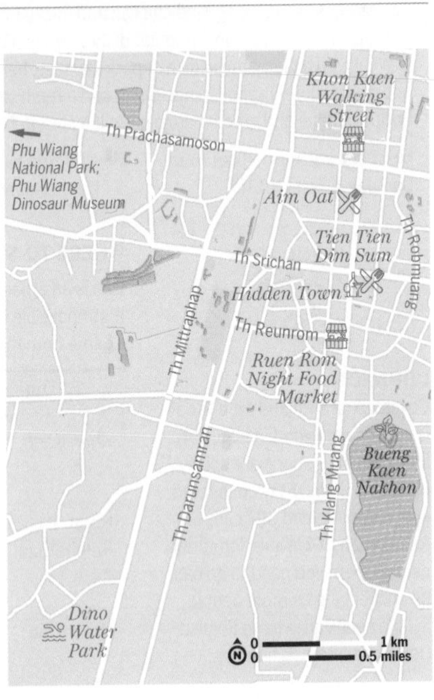


### How to

**Getting around** Khon Kaen now has Grab, the most convenient way to get around. There's also a light rail transit under development (the first outside Bangkok), scheduled to open in 2022.

**Smart city** Khon Kaen's Smart City Development Plan has significantly upgraded city infrastructure, including transport, waste management, green energy and sustainable agriculture.

**Silky souvenirs** Khon Kaen is famous for its high-quality Thai silk. A yearly silk festival is held to promote the industry.

## Prehistoric Pathways

Dinosaurs were the first inhabitants of Khon Kaen, with five of the 10 native dinosaur species to Thailand unearthed here. **Phu Wiang National Park** is the main centre for paleontology in Thailand, and its **Phu Wiang Dinosaur Museum** houses a large collection of specimens, replicas and a research library. As far as museums go in Thailand, this one is exceptionally well maintained and translated.

Maintaining the theme, **Dino Water Park** is an excellent place for kids and adults to cool off in the midday sun.

## Cosmopolitan Cultures

Jumping back to the 21st century, get a taste for the combined cultures of Isan by eating your way through the day. Try a Vietnamese breakfast of *kai kata* (fried eggs served in a pan), *kuay jap* (a thick Thai-style pho) and mini banh mi at **Aim Oat**, then gorge on as many 10 baht Chinese dumplingf as you can for lunch at **Tien Tien Dim Sum** before sitting down for a classic evening

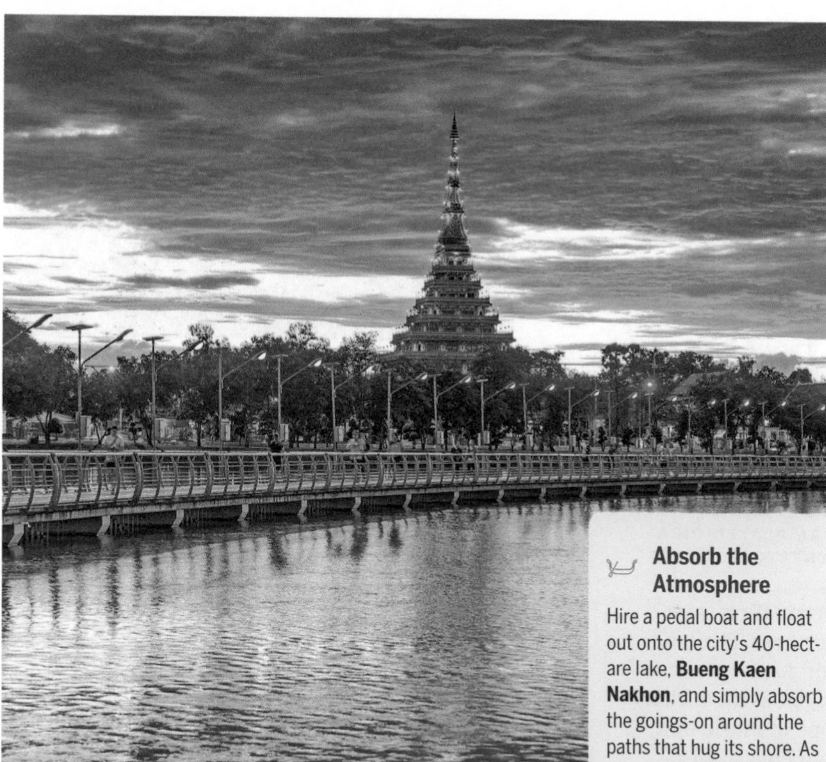



### Absorb the Atmosphere

Hire a pedal boat and float out onto the city's 40-hectare lake, **Bueng Kaen Nakhon**, and simply absorb the goings-on around the paths that hug its shore. As the sun begins to set, return to shore and do a few laps of the lake on foot or by rental bike before refuelling at the Rim Bung Market that seems to materialise out of thin air, complete with singing policemen, sweet Thai tea and grilled meaty morsels on sticks.

meal of *sôm·đam*, *gài yâhng* and sticky rice at **Teng Mo Zeb Werr**, a trans-owned restaurant famous for its extravagant service and authentic flavours.

If you can manage to walk off your full stomach, the **Khon Kaen Walking Street** and **Ruen Rom Night Food Market** (more food!) are both exceptional places to see how the city comes alive after the sun goes down. Finish off the night with a cocktail at **Hidden Town** and imbibe on the melancholy sounds of live jazz and local *mŏr lam* mixed seamlessly together by the talented resident band.

**Above** Bueng Kaen Nakhon with Wat Phra Mahathat in the backgrounf

# Mŏr Lam: Rhythm of Northeast Thailand

**THE SPIRIT OF ISAN PLAYED ON A PENTATONIC SCALE**

Originating from northern Thailand and Laos, *mŏr lam* began as an ancient type of music that told epic stories through a musical style best described as folk-tale rap. Today, its updated melodic rhythm has all but engulfed the old traditions and is now regarded as one of the most infectious cultural symbols of the northeast.

**Left** A *pin*. **Middle** Traditional Thai instruments. **Right** *Mŏr lam* dance show

SOMBAT MULMANEE/SHUTTERSTOCK ©

## Quintessentially Isan

At its best, *mŏr lam* is fast-paced, energetic and full of humour. Cowbell beats and surging organ swells accompany singers, musicians and troupes of dancers dressed in traditional Thai costume, sequined disco garb, or a stylised combination of both.

Although it didn't start out this way, *mŏr lam's* most ancient techniques can still be heard, creating a musical genre that is exceptionally varied and quintessentially Isan.

## Original Folk Tales

The term *mŏr lam* comes from the two Thai words. '*Mŏr*', the word for doctor, and '*lam*' meaning tune or rhythm.

In the early days, these 'doctors of rhythm' would sing stories about ghosts and perform spiritual rituals to the sound of a single *khaen* (bamboo mouth organ). But by the early 1900s, topics moved away from religion and focused on the tension between rural Isan and the Bangkok-based government. In the late '50s, American GIs introduced Western instruments, and the techno beats of the '80s further funk-ified the sound.

Yet despite the genre's evolutionist nature, the core instruments of *mŏr lam* survived its rolling modernisation. 'Instead of being replaced by a guitar, the *pin*, a Thai three-stringed instrument, became the hero sound of Thailand,' explained Rasmee Wayrana, a *mŏr lam* singer and songwriter from Ubon Ratchathani. 'Today you can hear it used across all Thai music, from pop-rock to reggae.'

## And Modern Twists

Today *mŏr lam* holds a tight grip on Thai pop culture. '*Mŏr lam* is still the bedrock of Isan society, but has more recently become the music of rich hipsters in Bangkok too,' shared

KILLABEE KHAIRUL FADHLI/SHUTTERSTOCK ©

ARTHIT PREMPRAYOT/SHUTTERSTOCK ©



Hatthayathiti Chouynukit, a *mŏr lam* vinyl trader from Chumphon. 'As few were printed in the day, original vinyls that once collected dust are now selling for tens of thousands of baht while businesses are fighting over licensing rights to print new ones.'

Taxi drivers in Bangkok, most of whom are from Isan, will likely pass the time by listening to *mŏr lam reung*, a simple rhythm built around long and enthralling folk tales, whereas malls and restaurants may play more *mŏr lam ploen,* an early Isan-style pop.

> In the late '50s, American GIs introduced Western instruments, and the techno beats of the '80s further funk-ified the sound.

At temple fairs, identified by hundreds of coloured strip lights directing you to the entrance like a runway, you may encounter a stage performance of *mŏr lam klon*, a comedic or religious poetry face-off between two singers. And in the bars and clubs of Isan cities, it will be high-tempo *mŏr lam sing* that dominates the airwaves.

'In the West, samples from *mŏr lam* and full *mŏr lam* tracks are showing up everywhere,' added Hatthayathiti. '*Mŏr lam* has a habit of adapting to the era, and its flexibility means it is now being enjoyed by many more people the world over.'

Back in Thailand, some venues have even made *mŏr lam* their calling card like **Tawandeng**, which puts on a lavish cabaret-style live music performance every night, perfectly choreographed to the most iconic *mŏr lam*, country folk and Thai pop of the day, with a wardrobe the puts the Brazilian carnival to shame.

And in the world of music, otherwise forgotten tracks and artists are brought back to life by organisations such as **Hear & Found** who have found a passion in connecting people to local Thai music, and producers such as Maft Sai, founder of **ZudRangMa Records**.

## Add To Your Playlist

Search for these artists and get hooked before you arrive.

**Thongmee Malai** A flamboyant singer and legend of *mŏr lam ploen*.

**Daoban Don** A novice monk who left the *sangha* to become a *mŏr lam* star.

**Ratree Sriwilai** Highly regarded as the Queen of *mŏr lam sing*.

**Jintara Poonlarp** Most famous for mixing old-school *mŏr lam* with modern pop.

**Paradise Bangkok Molam International Band** World-touring *mŏr lam* band famous for bass-filled classics.

**Khruangbin** Probably the first all-foreigner *mŏr lam* band outside of Thailand.

**Rasmee Wayrana** Jazzy, soulful *mŏr lam* with flourishes of Khmer, Lao and English verse.

# 20 TREK LOEI'S Heart-Shaped Plateau

HIKING | CAMPING | VIEWS

Although Thailand's trekking scene can leave a lot to be desired, Phu Kradueng is one of the few exceptions. A 9km hike up the side of Loei's stand-alone heart-shaped mountain is no doubt a sweaty experience, but the incredible panoramic views, winding forest trails and cool alpine climes are worth every arduous step.

SONGDECH KOTHMONGKOL/SHUTTERSTOCK ©

## How to

**When to go** The mountain is closed from June to September for forest recovery.

**Stay close by** An early morning start is highly recommended. Camp at the trailhead or find a cheap hotel nearby the night before to get going quicker.

**Dual pricing** Entrance fees for national parks in Thailand are almost always higher for tourists than locals, and haggling doesn't work with park officials.

PLATOO FOTOGRAPHY/SHUTTERSTOCK ©

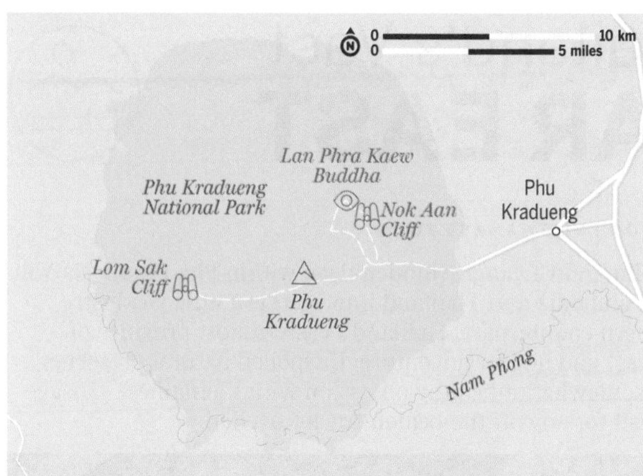


Without a peak, **Phu Kradueng** is more about what happens at the top than the hike it takes to get there. However, one experience obviously requires the other.

From trailhead to summit, the hike is split into two sections: a 5km, 1000m elevation scramble up the side of the mountain, followed by a 4km flat hike to the campsite.

Luckily, 30B per kilo will get you a porter who will do the heavy lifting, and the five rest stops along the way have everything you'll need to keep going, from water and coffee to grilled eggs and ice-cold refreshing towels.

At the top, 20km of plateau-top trails can be walked or cycled (find bike rental at the campsite) without much effort, taking you across alpine savannahs, deep into maple forests, and alarmingly close to sheer cliff edges. Each route is clearly marked, so there's no need for a guide.

**Lom Sak Cliff** is where most people aim to reach; if not to take a photo on the overhanging rock, it's to watch the sunset before a thrilling night hike back to camp. Treat yourself to a hot Thai BBQ from any stall to top off the perfect Phu Kradueng experience.

Next morning, wake before sunrise, dress warm, and follow the dimly lit trail east towards **Nok Aan Cliff** and watch the sunrise over a sea of clouds below. Before the sun warms your face, detour back via **Lan Phra Kaew Buddha** and get lost in the dense, eerie fog that blankets a pine forest trail that leads back to camp.

**Left** Phu Kradueng National Park. **Bottom left** Porters, Phu Kradueng

## We Keep Going Back

Phu Kradeung can be very colourful during the cold season, where the ground gets frosty and maple leaves turn red – something rarely seen in Thailand. We first did this hike with our families when we were kids. It was the first time we experienced the true serenity of nature, and cold temperatures in Thailand. Phu Kradueng holds a sentimental value for us and any Thai who loves hiking, which is why we keep going back again and again.

■ **By Pakawat Thongcharoen and Prichaya Suthivet**, *travel creatives, hiking enthusiasts, founders of PakaPrich (pakaprich.com), YouTube PakaPrich*

# 21 Thailand's Vast FAR EAST

**BORDER TOWNS | MEDITATION | VIETNAMESE FOOD**

Although the actual Emerald Triangle (hidden deep within Phu Chong Na Yoi National Park where Laos, Cambodia and Thailand intersect) is a little lacklustre when compared to its northern counterpart, Thailand's easternmost province of Ubon Ratchathani is wild, vast and hot for adventure. Unspoiled natural preserves, melting-pot cultures and a somewhat unhealthy obsession with Vietnamese sausage makes this region a must-visit for any off-the-beaten-track traveller.

TONOGRAPHER/SHUTTERSTOCK ©

## How to

**Getting here** Ubon, as it is locally known, can be easily accessed by bus, train or flight from Bangkok. There's even a bus from Chiang Mai if you can stand a 21-hour journey.

**When to visit** Ubon is hot all year round, but the rainy season floods in September and November can be treacherous.

**Bring sunscreen** Isan is notoriously hot, and most of Ubon lacks any real tree coverage. Sunscreen is a must, even on overcast days.

I VIEWFINDER/SHUTTERSTOCK ©

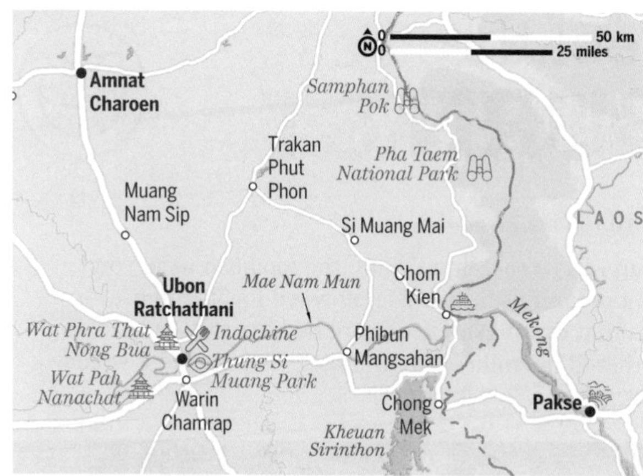


**Left** Hamuman sculptures, Wat Phra That Nong Bua. **Bottom left** Cave painting, Pha Taem National Park

## Start in the City

Any provincial adventure should start in its namesake capital. At its heart, **Thung Si Muang Park** is where most of the city's social activities take place, including dance classes, auntie aerobics and scrumptious food festivals.

Within a small radius of the park, you can find **Wat Phra That Nong Bua** (a replica of India's Sri Mahabodhi Temple), a prominent Catholic nunnery and **Wat Pah Nanachat** (Thailand's original English-language forest temple).

If food is your religion, **Indochine** and **Kuay Jub 99** are perfect examples of how locals have added a spicy kick to otherwise delicate Vietnamese flavours. Be sure to stock up on *moo yor*, a Vietnamese sausage wrapped tightly in banana leaves that locals claim is the best in Thailand.

## Venture into the Wild

Early risers can leave the city to catch sunrise from the edge of Thailand atop cliffs overlooking Laos at **Pha Taem National Park**. It's here where hundreds of prehistoric cave paintings can also be seen. Those who prefer sunsets can head to the desert-like **Had Hong Sand Dunes**, where only ice-cold local beers can keep you cool.

Aspiring astronauts can take a trip to the alien landscape of **Samphan Pok**, the biggest rock reef on the Mekong known for its thousands of oddly shaped craters. Further away is **Chom Kien** where a long-tail boat ride can get you within reach of Ubon's most watery phenomenon, where the muddy-brown Mekong and dark blue Mun rivers meet but do not mix.

### Pop to Pakse

Visas permitting, swing past **Sirindhorn Lake** and cross the border into the southern Laos city of **Pakse**, famous for its relaxing Mekong atmosphere and ubiquitous riverside restaurants and bars. Stay the night and take in the breathtaking scenery as the sun casts long morning shadows across the Bolaven Plateau before being transported back in time to Wat Phou, a 5th-century Unesco World Heritage Site said to rival Cambodia's Angkor Wat.

# 22 Feel the BURN

**FOOD | RESTAURANTS | CULTURE**

Although the Isan sun can be scorchingly hot, the food can burn you more. Salty, sour and rich in umami, Isan food is renowned for its intense flavours and fresh spiciness that can make your entire body sweat. And although Isan food isn't always smothered in chillies, the average Western palate would be hard pushed to believe it.

AIMPOL BURANET/SHUTTERSTOCK ©

## How to

**Expect the spice** Be prepared to deal with chillies. Even if you ask for something not spicy, there's bound to be a chilli somewhere.

**Eat with your teeth** It may look odd, but when locals take a bite of something spicy, they keep their lips far away from the spoon. You'll soon find out why.

**Looks can be deceiving** Small chillies are often the fieriest, and a red colour doesn't always mean hot.

SUPERMEE/SHUTTERSTOCK ©

**Left** *Sôm đam*. **Bottom left** Isan style dipping sauce

## Salt, Spice & Everything Nice

When the first dedicated Isan cuisine restaurants opened in Bangkok, popularity for extra spicy dishes quickly grew into one of the best (albeit unplanned) marketing campaigns for the region. This stereotype became so widespread that even the locals started to believe they had always eaten things this spicy.

From fruit dipped in little bags of sugar, salt and chilli flakes to pungent salt-fermented fish sauce known as *plaa ra* slathered over a papaya salad, the taste of salt and the tingle of spice are now considered signature elements of Isan food.

## Eat Your Fill

For authentic Isan tastes that are not doctored to Bangkokian and foreign palates, **Phai Lom Restaurant** in Sakon Nakhon can kick-start any culinary (read: spicy) adventure in the northeast. Alternatively, try the *sôm đam* at Udon Thani's **Jay Gai** that are literally swimming in chillies – perfect for throwing yourself into the deep end. More refined **Samuay & Sons** offers a menu dedicated to local ingredients and craft cooking techniques.

If you pass through the big four, these are your spicy go-to: **Gai Yang Rabeab Khao Suan Kwang** in Khon Kaen, **Aed Kai Yang Mahatthai** in Korat, **Laab Nuad** in Udon Thani and **Jae Kaek Jaew Hon** in Ubon Ratchathani.

## Guaranteed Spice-Free

With a big Vietnamese influence, some Indochinese staples have survived the 'great spicening'. As restaurants go, **VT Naem Nuang** is the national favourite. The flagship in Udon Thani is the biggest by far.

### A Taste of its Own

For a different taste of Isan cuisine that even most Thais have never experienced, I recommend visiting the village of **Baan Phue**, Udon Thani. This small community developed a cuisine unlike anything you'll find in Isan, complete with different cooking techniques, ingredients and flavours.

Imagine *lâhp* with a curry powder base or an ant egg soup made with wild herbs you've never seen. While this cuisine is becoming hard to find, **Yoy Pa Roj** is one of the few places that still serve this incredible ethnic cuisine. Unfortunately, this disappearing cuisine is not yet protected, but I think it should be.

■ **By Weerawat Triyasenawat, aka Chef Num,** *co-owner of Samuay & Sons, Udon Thani, Facebook Samuay & Sons, Instagram @samuayandsons*

# 23 The Land of FESTIVALS

MUSIC | RELIGION | ENTERTAINMENT

The people of Isan are intrinsically tethered to festivals, and Isan culture is born from a love of music and rhythmic storytelling. From traditional *mŏr lam* to high-tempo *luk thung* (p124), there's an undeniable rhythm to everything that goes on here. However, it's not just elegant religious festivals and village concerts. It's the biggest reggae festival in Thailand, the land of travelling folk musicians and homemade rockets that reach the edges of space.

ARNON POLIN/SHUTTERSTOCK ©

## How to

**Check the dates** Festival dates change every year as they follow the lunar calendar or align with a long weekend.

**It comes from the soul** Whatever the occasion, don't be surprised to see people dancing. Weddings. Funerals. In a market with earphones on. Dancing is an innate practice in Isan.

**Camping gets hot** No matter how cool it gets at night, the hot morning sun is enough to turn any tent into a sauna.

FORD CONTRIBUTOR/SHUTTERSTOCK ©

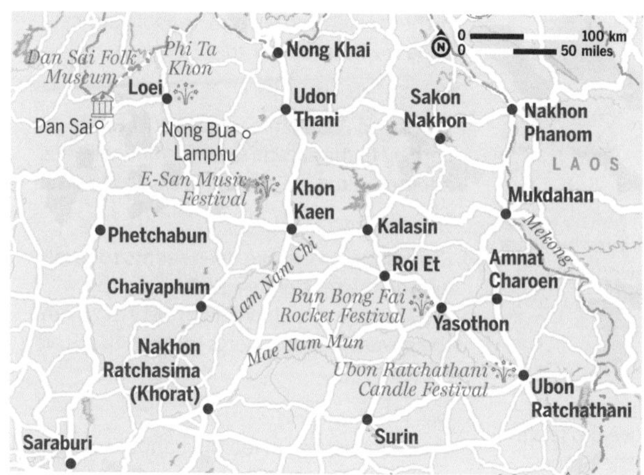


## Feel the Groove

Isan remains one of the most authentic parts of Thailand, and its undying love for *luk thung* has defined music scenes in Thailand for decades. Most events, and even most markets, will have some form of stage complete with live singers, backing dancers and a cabaret-like atmosphere that's seriously infectious.

Some of Thailand's biggest Western-style music festivals take place here during the cooler months, including the **E-san Music Festival** and **Barbarian Land**, where crowds of hippies and glad-ragged city dwellers join together to the sound of Thai reggae, rock and indie music.

## Dance with the Spirits

The other kind of festival in Isan revolves around religion, superstition or both. The wildest of these has to be Yasothon's **Bun Bang Fai Rocket Festival**, where the sound of *luk thung* and exploding rockets compete for attention for five days of total mayhem. Up to 10m in length, homemade rockets are packed with gunpowder and shot into the sky to ensure a good monsoon and bountiful rice harvest.

Keeping with superstition, Loei's **Phi Ta Khon** is one of the most colourful festivals, held in June. To worship ghosts and bring good harvests, people dress in bright costumes, wield phallus-tipped swords, and perform complex rain dances. The costumes are then displayed year-round at **Dan Sai Folk Museum**.

For something a little more elegant, the **Ubon Ratchathani Candle Festival** held in July sees two-storey candles paraded around the city to gawping crowds, each one intricately designed by local temples, villages or institutions.

**Left** Phi Ta Khon festival.
**Bottom left** Candle festival

### Songkran in Isan

Songkran swings around every 13 April and usually lasts three days. It is well-known for being Thailand's most important festival, hailing in the Thai New Year with a country-wide water fight. In Isan, bigger cities like Khon Kaen and Udon Thani will have more going on, but there's no village or town that won't have some type of celebration.

For foreigners in Isan, you'll tend to stand out more than other places, and with so much festivity, people will be eager to bless (ie splash) you. Strangers inviting you to drink, dance and feast can either be ridiculously fun or frustratingly repetitive, depending on how long you've been at it.

# Listings

BEST OF THE REST

### Natural Hotspots

Red Lotus Sea, Udon Thani

A seasonal winter boat trip out into the watery expanse of Nong Han Kumphawapi Lake blanketed in pink-red lillies that stretch as far as the eye can see.

Phu Laen Kha National Park, Chaiyaphum

Home to some striking and unusual rock formations that stand high above the ground, this park has been nicknamed the Stonehenge of Thailand.

Khao Yai National Park, Nakhon Ratchasima

Shared between the central plains and the gateway to Isan, this is Thailand's first national park and also one of the biggest.

Wat Phu Tok, Bueng Kan

The main attraction of Isan's newest province, this protruding mountain rock formation has rickety wooden stairs and bridges that connect visitors to dangerously placed shrines, statues and ordination halls.

Erawan Cave, Nong Bua Lamphu

Not to be confused with Erawan Falls in central Thailand, this gargantuan cave is said to be one of the most beautiful in northeast Thailand, guarded by a towering Buddha at its entrance.

Dong Ling Don Chao Pu Park, Amnat Charoen

Also known as the Phana Monkey Forest, this nature park maintained by the Phana Monkey Project promotes the safety and wellbeing of Thai monkey species and forest research.

### Speciality Villages

Chiang Khan, Loei

A quaint village on the banks of the Mekong with picture-perfect riversides, a buzzing night market, and a warm, friendly atmosphere wherever you go.

Sala Keoku, Nong Khai

A whimsical sculpture village park built according to the eccentric visions and religious interpretations of its founder, Bunleua Sulilat.

Ban Ta Klang, Surin

Everything this village does seems to revolve around the resident elephants and their respective mahout families, many of whom the government supports through the Surin Project.

Ban Don Koi, Sakon Nakhon

Those interested in learning about traditional indigo dyeing can get hands-on with the region's best indigo fabric dyers and can even have a custom dyed shirt or outfit made to order.

### Markets After Dark

Saveone Night Market, Nakhon Ratchasima

As busy and as populated as Bangkok's Chatuchak, this is the biggest night market in the biggest city in the Isan region.

Ton Taan Market, Khon Kaen

The smaller of the three main night markets in the city, there's a more rough and ready feel to proceedings, with a strong focus on food, ingredients, trinkets and cheap clothing.

Thung Sri Muang Walking Street, Ubon Ratchathani

Another Thung Sri Muang favourite, open only on the weekends and bustling with activity, music and snacks of all kinds and creations.

Indochina Market, Mukdahan

For a province whose most frequent tourist is the border-runner, this market capitalises on the transient nature of the Thailand–Laos border by selling cheap knockoffs from neighbouring countries.

Chaiyaphum Night Bazaar, Chaiyaphum

With a distinct country town feel, the night bazaar is clearly the highlight of the city's evenings. All the stalls you'd expect from a Thai market, but cheaper and more authentic.

## Significantly Cultural

Sirindhorn Museum, Kalasin

Housing one of Southeast Asia's largest collections of dinosaur bones and fossils, it was built around a perfectly preserved fossilised dinosaur skeleton that has been left in situ since 1994.

Phanom Rung Historical Park, Buriram

Detailed statues, beautiful architecture and sweeping terraces. This well-preserved, partly reconstructed 10th-century temple complex was built by the mighty Khmer Empire.

Million Bottle Temple, Sisaket

Recyclers rejoice! This temple is made entirely from recycled glass bottles. Even the Buddha statues are made from bottles, which begs the question: who drank all the beer?

Phra Maha Chedi Chai Mongkol, Roi Et

Like something out of a fairytale, this walled temple complex shimmers gold and white, with immaculately tended flower beds, fantastical water features and opulent temple interiors.

Buriram United Football Stadium, Buriram

Thais are mad about football, the English Premier League to be precise. But when it comes to local teams, Buriram is a national favourite, and the cheering crowds are like nothing you've seen before.

Pha Mor E-Daeng Cliff, Si Saket

The incredible views overlooking the much-disputed Preah Vihear temple ruins on the Thailand–Cambodia border (both sides claim ownership) are worth the very slim risk of getting caught in any crossfire is worth the incredible views.

AKARAT PHASURA/SHUTTERSTOCK ©

Ton Taan market

## Drink East, Northeast

U Bar, Ubon Ratchathani, Nakhon Ratchasima & Khon Kaen $$

A hip hangout for university students who still prefer the sound of Thai rock and hip-hop. As a growing Isan club franchise, you know where you stand with U Bar, which is usually around a table with a bottle of whisky.

Soi Rim Kong, Nong Khai $

A 3km strip along the banks of the Mekong with dozens of restaurants, bars, karaoke bars and live music clubs. Views of Laos and a lively Saturday market make this spot a must.

GranMonte Vineyard & Winery, Nakhon Ratchasima $$$

Located in the Asoke Valley of Khao Yai, this winery has 16 hectares of wine and table grapes, complete with guided tours, tastings and elegant sleepovers.

Taawandeng, Almost Every City $$

This is the authentic Thai party experience. Live music, extravagant cabaret dancers, whisky bottles, Thai food and cheering strangers guaranteed.

**Scan to find more things to do in Northeastern Thailand online**

# KO CHANG & THE EASTERN SEABOARD

NATURE | LAID-BACK | BEACHES

Experience Ko Chang & the Eastern Seaboard online

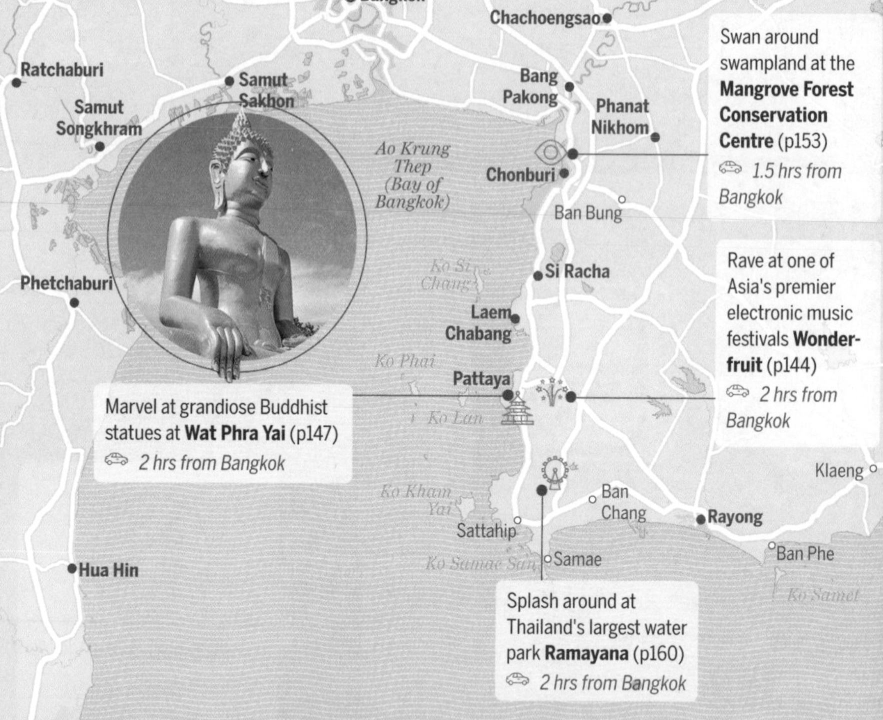




# KO CHANG & THE EASTERN SEABOARD

## Trip Builder

Thailand's eastern coastal region is for those who like things simpler and sleepier. Escaping into infinite jungle, wi-fi dead zones and beach bungalow life. While it's slowly but surely getting more developed, here, seclusion is the high spot.

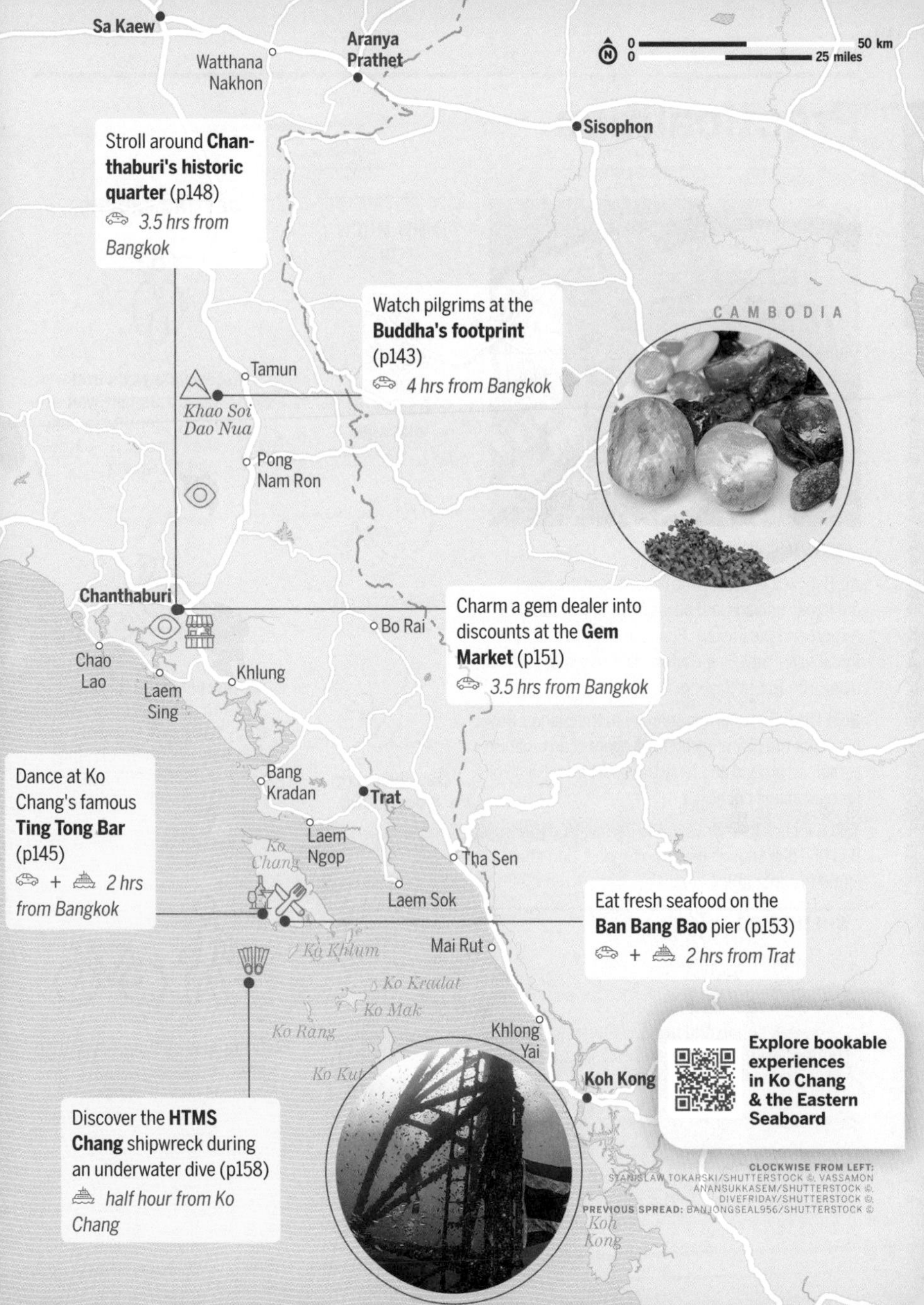

Sa Kaew
Watthana Nakhon
Aranya Prathet
0 50 km
0 25 miles
Sisophon
Stroll around **Chanthaburi's historic quarter** (p148)
3.5 hrs from Bangkok
Watch pilgrims at the **Buddha's footprint** (p143)
4 hrs from Bangkok
CAMBODIA
Tamun
Khao Soi Dao Nua
Pong Nam Ron
Chanthaburi
Charm a gem dealer into discounts at the **Gem Market** (p151)
3.5 hrs from Bangkok
Bo Rai
Chao Lao
Laem Sing
Khlung
Dance at Ko Chang's famous **Ting Tong Bar** (p145)
+ 2 hrs from Bangkok
Bang Kradan
Trat
Laem Ngop
Ko Chang
Tha Sen
Laem Sok
Eat fresh seafood on the **Ban Bang Bao** pier (p153)
+ 2 hrs from Trat
Ko Khlum
Mai Rut
Ko Kradat
Ko Mak
Ko Rang
Khlong Yai
Ko Kut
Koh Kong
Explore bookable experiences in Ko Chang & the Eastern Seaboard
Discover the **HTMS Chang** shipwreck during an underwater dive (p158)
half hour from Ko Chang
Koh Kong

# Practicalities

NARIN NONTHAMAND/SHUTTERSTOCK ©

### ARRIVING

**Air** Bangkok is usually the main departure point out here. Minivans and buses from Suvarnabhumi Airport and the Eastern Bus Terminal are most affordable for travelling eastwards. Some might prefer flying into Trat or Rayong.

**Boat** From there, ferries connect to the islands. Buy tickets at the pier or local travel agents can organise combined ground and ferry transport from Bangkok for reasonable prices.

**Taxi** Bangkok taxis drive out to Pattaya and Rayong's Ban Phe pier, though usually off-meter. Don't be afraid to negotiate!

### HOW MUCH FOR A

**Traditional massage 300B**

**Fresh coconut 45B**

**Day diving trip From 3000B**

### WHEN TO GO

**DEC–MAR**
Peak action and high temperatures. Pattaya and Ko Samet get busy.

**MAY–OCT**
Monsoon season. The islands wind down, except for Ko Samet with its drier microclimate.

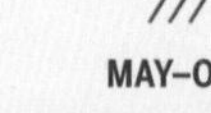

**NOV & APR**
Best times to go. Better rates except for Songkran when you'll need to book ahead.

### GETTING AROUND

**Motorcycle taxis and sŏrng·tăa·ou** Usually wait at piers and are plentiful in busy places like Pattaya, Ko Samet and Ko Chang.

**Motorcycle** Hire for about 200B to 300B per day; will always be most convenient, especially on smaller islands. Watch out for winding gravel roads.

**Walking and cycling** Around Ko Samet and Chanthaburi is an especially lovely experience.

## EATING & DRINKING

The regional fare here is more about lighter meals and lots of fresh seafood. Foodies are obsessed with Chanthaburi for its plentiful noodle shops and famous fruits sold at stalls and featured in sweets, salads and curries during the 10-day Fruit Festival in harvest season (May and June). Island resort restaurants will scratch the itch for eating Thai, but independent restaurants offer authentic tastes and surroundings. Pattaya, Ko Chang and Ko Samet have party scenes ranging from classy to really rowdy.

**Best noodle shop**
Tom Yum Sen (p149)

**Must-try beach dining**
Glass House (p154)

## CONNECT & FIND YOUR WAY

**Wi-fi** While most lodgings and restaurants have decent wi-fi, buying a Thai SIM is recommended. Tourist SIMs from 7-Eleven are fine for 30 days. Network providers offer better packages for longer stays (including unlimited data) directly at their shops.

**Navigation** Internet connectivity and navigation apps aren't always reliable. When motorbiking, carry a paper map (most lodgings provide them).

## WHERE TO STAY

The eastern shores offer some of Thailand's most underrated sceneries – and a charmingly snoozy, tropical vibe compared to more popular stops like Phuket and Ko Samui.

| Place | Pros/Cons |
|---|---|
| Ko Chang | Best infrastructure with busy nightlife and most dive sites; generally midrange resorts. |
| Ko Kut | Best beaches and tropical landscapes but limited activities (snorkelling and kayaking). |
| Ko Mak | Beautiful for beaches and snorkelling; quiet and undeveloped. |
| Ko Samet | Nice resorts with good restaurants, mostly family and couple visitors. |
| Pattaya | Closest beaches to Bangkok; notorious nightlife and some tourist traps. |

## RAINY SEASON VISITS

Don't count one out. Rates drop, big showers aren't always guaranteed and waterfalls are more spectacular. Ko Chang and Ko Kut mostly stay open.

## MONEY

The eastern seaboard is becoming ever more oriented to luxury travel and flashpackers. Those seeking beachy backpacker life and fun on a budget can still look around Bang Saen and Ko Chang.

# 24 Lose Yourself in a NATIONAL PARK

**NATIONAL PARKS | WILDLIFE | WATERFALLS**

This part of Thailand comprises around five national parks and two marine national parks ranging considerably in size and landscape. Nestled into deep swathes of jungle, there is unlimited natural splendour to become acquainted with – wildlife sanctuaries, walking trails, Buddhist architecture, waterfalls and hidden coastlines. Stunning coves and bays, in particular, provide epic Instagram moments and attract fewer visitors than similar scenery down south.

KWANCHAI/SHUTTERSTOCK ©

## How to

**Getting here** *Sŏrng·tăa·ou* and van rides are sometimes available from towns.

**When to go** January to April. Some park sights close during rainy season.

**Hire a guide** To enter a Thai national park, you must have a licensed guide or ranger present.

**Where to stay** Book accommodation via the park authority's reservation system (dnp.go.th).

SUPAKIT KAEWYOO/SHUTTERSTOCK ©

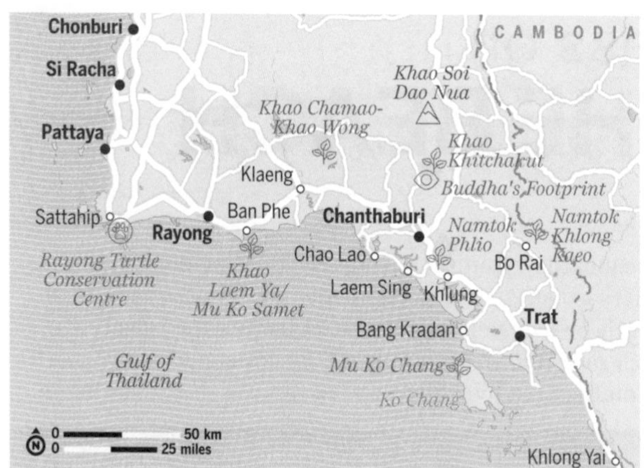


Thailand has more than 100 national parks, and over two dozen more have been opened or announced lately as part of Thailand's plan to dedicate 55% of the entire country to protected forest by 2037.

Near Chanthaburi, **Khao Khitchakut** is one of Thailand's most compact national parks and a great spot for sinking into waterfall plunge-pools and scaling mountain peaks. Diverse flora and fauna live here; wild elephant herds are sometimes spotted and the park borders an important wildlife sanctuary for birds and insect conservation. Further north, mountainous and cooler **Khao Chamao-Khao Wong National Park** also borders the sanctuary and is home to some wild banteng cattle and elephants.

On the opposite side of Chanthaburi, **Namtok Phlio** and the further afield **Namtok Khlong Kaeo** are also known among birders and waterfall-hunters, while the former has the added pull of several Buddhist worship sites.

Ko Chang and 46 other islands are encompassed within the **Mu Ko Chang National Park** which is known for great hiking, birds, assorted aquatic wildlife and its protected coral reefs. Meanwhile, the island of Ko Samet and the nine other small islands along the Rayong coastline comprise **Khao Laem Ya/ Mu Ko Samet National Park**.

**Left** Khao Chamao-Khao Wong National Park. **Bottom left** Crimson sunbird on a Chinese hat plant, Khao Khitchakut

## Best Nearby Sights

See rescued turtles at the **Rayong Turtle Conservation Centre** on Ko Man Nai, which provides a safe breeding place for endangered sea turtles.

Feel the spiritual energy at the **Buddha's footprint** mountaintop landmark in Khao Khitchakut National Park, a popular pilgrimage site for Thai Buddhists. Sunset here is a magical experience.

**Go chasing waterfalls** at Namtok Phlio National Park. A short nature trail leads around a string of pretty waterfalls including the park's star attraction, its namesake **Phlio Waterfall**.

Meanwhile, Khao Kitchakut's largest waterfall is **Krathing**, a sprawling 13-level cascade.

# 25 Bass on THE BEACH

**PARTIES | MUSIC | DANCING**

While the eastern seaboard's reputation is mostly associated with calm and tranquillity, it also offers isolation (aka deep jungle that absorbs acoustics) for partying hard. Whether it be live melodies at bucket bars or the velvety dance floors of secret beach raves (often with famed DJs), great gigs and festivals happen out here on the dreamy white.

FRED MARIE/ART IN ALL OF US/CORBIS VIA GETTY IMAGES ©

### How to

**Getting here** Never drink and drive. Check events' Facebook pages for organised transport (or get a group together with other party goers and organise your own).

**When to go** European DJs tend to flock to Thailand from November to March.

**What to bring** Party essentials that people usually forget (but are often thankful for) include a small flashlight, a folding fan, tissues, chewing gum and sunglasses.

FRED MARIE/SHUTTERSTOCK ©

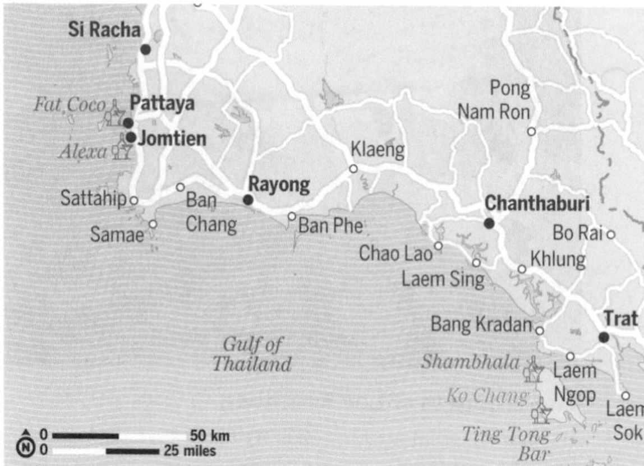


## Surviving Wonderfruit

Wonderfruit exploded onto Asia's festival circuit in 2014 and is now dubbed the region's Burning Man. Over 20,000 electronic music lovers from around Thailand, Singapore, the Philippines and beyond converge on the empty fields of Siam Country Club near Pattaya for three December days bursting with glitter, cloudy soil and unforgettable memories.

Tickets usually go on sale in February. Before you buy one, understand that Wonderfruit is a splurge. Most partygoers stay in nearby hotels or in the festival's glamping tent area, as the lack of shade from the hot Thai sun makes regular tenting tough. That means you'll need taxis to and from, plus there will probably be some gourmet food on the grounds you'll want to indulge in (Michelin-starred chefs from Bangkok cook at trucks and stalls).

## Experience of a Lifetime

But anyone will tell you it's the experience of a lifetime. The world's best DJs play across multiple stages, art installations instigate magical realism, and revellers take festival fashion to a whole 'nother level.

The festival is focused on sustainability and has a single-use plastics ban. So in addition to the party essentials above, bring your own cup (or buy a metal one on-site). Also, pack a light jacket for the evenings when it can get cool and windy.

Be sure to check out Wonderfruit's activity programme too. There are yoga meditations, môo·ay thai classes and talks on topics like gender, design and cannabis politics (plus plenty of family-friendly activities).

**Left and below** Wonderfruit festival.

### Other DJ Festivals & Clubs

Dance into daybreak at Ko Chang's infamous **Ting Tong Bar**. It pulls international house and electro DJs and technically never closes (although party primetime is midnight to sunrise).

Check out some of the more exclusive DJ festivals, like **Kolour Beachside** in Pattaya and **Fly To The Moon** (an annual New Year's festival on Ko Mak). Tickets are limited so it's an intimate experience.

Visit a beach club at cool, sophisticated Pattaya venues like **Alexa** or **Fat Coco** which eschew the sleaze of Walking Street.

Sip a cocktail poolside at Ko Chang's trendiest joint, **Shambhala**. It has perfect views and DJ beats for sundown boogies.

■ **By Dan Buri,** *DJ and music producer, Instagram @danburi, Soundcloud soundcloud.com/dan-buri*

# Festivals on the Beach

**SEA AND SAND SPICE UP TRADITIONAL FESTIVALS**

The eastern seaboard is a wonderful place to experience a Thai festival. Both the annual Songkran (New Year) and Loy Krathong (lantern and water vessel) festivals have a special meaning for small coastal communities. You'll be able to rub shoulders with Thai folks and see how they celebrate sacred holidays.

**Left** Songkran festival, Chiang Mai. **Right** Songkran festivities, Pattaya. **Far right** Monk, Wat Khlong Phrao

REDHATZ69/SHUTTERSTOCK ©

## The Wonders of Loy Krathong

The gulf is a great spot to celebrate another water festival called Loy Krathong. Locals make (or buy) intricately woven baskets and decorate them with offerings like lit candles, incense sticks and flowers. Then, they head to the nearest body of water to make wishes and send the *krathongs* afloat. Releasing sky lanterns is also popular (although it's a tradition that has its ancestral roots up north).

Floating a *krathong* is a beautiful ritual, and the more on the water there are, the more romantic it gets. It's an activity beloved by families and couples. Don't be surprised if you even see a marriage proposal (Loy Krathong is akin to Valentine's Day for young Thai lovebirds).

## Songkran Festivities

Every year in April, Thais celebrate Songkran (Thai New Year) with a three-day public holiday packed with water fights and blessing rituals. Water is symbolic of washing away sins and bringing good luck into the new year.

Pattaya and Bang Saen are both known for ruckus Songkran parties with huge stages, fireworks and live bands. The beaches get packed with partygoers toting boom boxes and revellers carrying Super Soakers. The streets evolve into a very Thai-style tailgate party – people sit in the back of pickups and throw water at each other.

The white talc slopped onto people's faces is inspired by monk blessings using chalk – if someone of the opposite sex playfully swipes some on your cheeks, it usually means they're crushing on you.

As a popular destination for Thai revellers, Bang Saen mixes the soggy chaos with downtempo Buddhist prayer ceremonies in local temples. Monks chant and receive alms of fresh rice, while worshippers wash Buddha statues and

GURKAN ERGUN/SHUTTERSTOCK ©

U_PHOTO/SHUTTERSTOCK ©



decorate them in gold leaf. An impressive sandcastle building competition where stupas and pagodas are the speciality is full of impressive feats.

## Songkran Survival Tips

**Buy a special plastic holder** to keep your cash, phone and other essentials dry (trust us, everything will be wet). They are sold at most convenience stores and some street stands.

**Book ahead!** The east is a popular destination for Bangkokians escaping the city heat (and the mayhem) for their holiday. Expect higher room rates.

> The beaches get packed with partygoers toting boom boxes and revellers carrying Super Soakers.

The streets and traffic tend to get chaotic, so **leave the wheels**. You're always fair game for getting splashed – driving a motorbike or not!

## Celebrating Sustainability

If you choose to take part in either Songkran or Loy Krathong, consider the environmental implications. Both festivals are known for generating litter, but you can avoid this.

Spend Songkran by the seaside and **source your water** from the shore directly (as opposed to in Bangkok where plastic water bottles pile up on the streets).

**Avoid sky lanterns** as they can catch fire, harming wildlife and their ecosystems.

Float a *krathong* made with banana leaves and not styrofoam. On Ko Chang's Ao Salak Phet beach, a new tradition has emerged of floating sustainable **coconut shell krathongs** which lay abundantly around the island anyway.

### More Waterside Ceremonies

On Ko Chang, **Wat Khlong Phrao** near Klong Prao Beach, is the island's main temple for festival celebrations.

**Wat Phra Sing** is a popular temple for Ko Mak locals on Songkran. The festival kicks off every year with a parade procession starting from here. A sacred image of Buddha is carried around town and bathed by locals in water.

Take in Songkran prayers at the hilltop **Wat Phra Yai** in Pattaya, where staircase dragons and gold Buddha figures (including the principal 18m Big Buddha) culminate in an otherworldly sundown experience.

# 26 A Cultural MELTING POT

HISTORY | ARCHITECTURE | ART

In Chanthaburi's historic Waterfront Community, restored landmarks and cute riverside shops and restaurants showcase the town's unique blend of Thai, Chinese, French and Vietnamese influences. On a short self-guided walk, get acquainted with the neighbourhood's charm and aesthetic.

SUMETH ANU/SHUTTERSTOCK ©

### Trip Notes

**Getting around** The historic quarter is easily discovered on foot. Rent a bicycle to explore nearby waterfalls in national parks and beach villages.

**When to go** Combine the Waterside Community's quaint ambience with local delicacies during Chanthaburi's 10-day **Fruit Festival** (late May to early June).

**Where to stay** Beautifully restored inns like **Baan Luang Rajamaitri** or **Tamajun Hotel** offer rooms with hardwood floors and riverside views.

### Must-See Cultural Sights

Note the Sino-Portuguese and gingerbread architecture (such as the fancy trims).

The **Baan Luang Rajamaitri** hotel has a free ground-floor museum with photos and archives.

Over the footbridge, the **Cathedral of the Immaculate Conception** (pictured) has a Virgin Mary statue blinged out in over 200,000 sapphires (pictured).

**05** For dessert, try a traditional Thai ice cream. **Rocket Ice Cream** makes homemade popsicles in traditional flavours like Thai tea and lime. Who screams for durian ice cream?

Th Tha Luang

**04** The restaurant at the **Tamajun Hotel** serves Thai food on a riverside wooden terrace packed with nostalgic photos and decorations. Sometimes, there is live music at night.

*Baan Luang Rajamaitri*

**03** Or if you prefer to down a burger, **Wacko Cafe** is not your average burger joint. The retro terrace with outdoor bar stools overlooks the river. Tacos are also on the menu.

Th Sukhaphiban

**02** The area specialises in good drip espresso and homemade cakes. Look for one of the modern cafes with trendy decor and air-con, like **Sweet at Moon** or **C.A.P**.

*Mae Nam Chanthaburi*

Th Benchamarachutit

Th Khwang

Th Sukhaphiban

*Cathedral of the Immaculate Conception*

Footbridge

**01** Slurp noodles by the water at **Tom Yum Sen**, an antique shophouse restaurant; *tom yum* fish soup is the speciality. Past the bridge, two more restaurants specialise in noodle soups with seafood (**Je Eed**) and pork (**Che Noy**).

N
0 200 m
0 0.1 miles

# 27 All-Out MARKETS

VILLAGES | SHOPPING | FOOD

Markets are an important, time-honoured component of everyday life here. Once a trading and transport hub to Cambodia and elsewhere in Thailand, the east coast still knows good shopping. Compared to Bangkok's mega-markets, the atmosphere is more inclined to chill perusing by the seaside – think friendly sellers, intimate atmospheres and better bang for your baht.

SARAYUTH3390/SHUTTERSTOCK ©

## How to

**Getting around** Most markets are in village centres except for (usually waterside) fish markets.

**When to go** Some markets only open at night or on weekends. Check with locals.

**How to haggle** Always negotiate at non-food stalls. Ask the price, counter with half, and meet somewhere in the middle.

**Going to Cambodia** Daily minivans and *sŏrng·tăa·ou* depart from Chanthaburi to the Ban Pakard border crossing.

KHWANJAI WANNASOOK/SHUTTERSTOCK ©

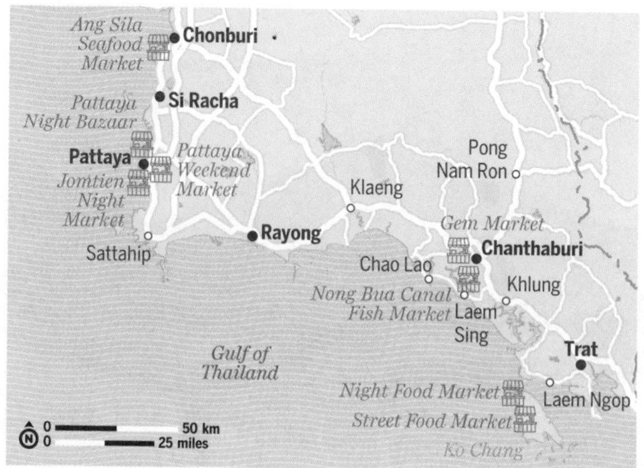


**Left** Pattaya Night Bazaar.
**Bottom left** Gem Market

Bordering Cambodia to the west, this stretch of Thailand's gulf spent its early days as a trading and transport hotspot – and that has contributed to a vibrant market culture continuing to define the region today.

For decades, Chanthaburi has been the historical heart of Thailand and Cambodia's gem mine and trade. In the town's surrounding hills, sapphire and rubies were once buffed and shipped to royal palaces and beyond. These days, Chanthaburi is no longer such a principal commercial hotspot, but its weekend **Gem Market**, run by Thai-Chinese traders over generations, is still a famous landmark (although now the bling is predominantly sourced from overseas).

Most fishing villages along the coast will also have their own market of varying sizes, either focused on fresh seafood, shopping, street food or all of the above. However, if you're seeking shopping paradise on the seaboard, look no further than Pattaya or Ko Chang. Pattaya, one of Thailand's most expat-heavy cities, has several night markets to choose from, including the **Pattaya Night Bazaar** and **Weekend Market** (the two busiest) as well as smaller, neighbourhood set-ups like **Tree Town**, **Rompho** and **Jomtien Night Market**.

In Ko Chang, you'll find markets like the **Night Food Market** and **Street Food Market** lined up along the western coast.

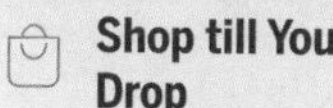

### Shop till You Drop

Waterfront markets like Chanthaburi's **Nong Bua Canal Fish Market** and the **Ang Sila Seafood Market** display colourful smorgasbords of the daily catches. Cooking stalls will grill your crustaceans fresh.

Ko Chang, Trat and Pattaya all have wonderful midsized night markets combining street food and snacks, plus clothing and trinket stalls and often live entertainment.

# 28 Coastal CHARMS

**BEACHES | FISHING VILLAGES | SEAFOOD**

Eastern Thailand has a slice of seaside life for everyone. There are endless beaches to explore, ranging from empty to bustling, and they tend to be expansive (perfect for long sunset walks or afternoons becoming a bronzed god). Soft sands are spliced between fishing villages – dining on a seafood meal in a stilted house is also moment you won't want to miss.

TANAPAT LEK.JIW/SHUTTERSTOCK ©

## How to

**Getting around** Transport infrastructure to beaches and fishing villages can be scarce – hire your own scooter for ultimate freedom.

**When to go** November to March.

**How to order** Fresh seafood is usually priced by the kilo – and differs according to what has been caught. Avoid bill surprises and ask your server if the cost is not on the menu.

TANATE PHUEAKKWANNAK/SHUTTERSTOCK ©

## Fishing Villages

North of Bang Saen, **Ang Sila** is known for producing granite cookware (like Thai mortar and pestles) and fresh-caught delicacies like prawns, mud crabs and mussels.

Ko Chang's time-warp fishing villages include the well-visited **Ban Bang Bao**, where you can pick and choose from a long dock of seafood restaurants, and the sleepy **Ban Salak Phet**, where there's not much to do aside from befriending pier dogs and embarking on a nearby jungle trek.

**Ao Yai** on Ko Kut is the island's hotspot for gorging on seafood. Restaurants on stilts pull in great local catches – if you're feeling fancy, there are flathead lobster and scallops.

IAMNOONMAI/SHUTTERSTOCK ©

## White-Sand Beaches

The region's most famous beach is the aptly named **White Sand Beach (Hat Sai Khao)** on

### Unique Experiences

The **Mangrove Forest Conservation Centre** in the fishing village of Ang Sila is a great half-day excursion for families and nature lovers. Pick your own jungle adventure with fun activities such as discovering an oyster farm, mud-skiing (a truly unique local activity!), planting mangrove saplings and feeding macaques in a mangrove swamp.

**Above left** Ban Bang Bao. **Below left** Granite mortars and pestles, Ang Sila. **Above** Mangrove Forest Conservation Centre

Ko Chang; beware, it's very busy and developed. The northern strip has a backpacker vibe.

Much lazier is **Ao Kao Beach** on Ko Mak, with just a couple of good resorts, or the undeveloped (yet tough-to-reach) **Ao Pra**.

Seeking sheer quantity? The western coast of **Ko Kut** is lined with long stretches of ivory sand. Note that these days, more beaches are starting to charge admission for non-resort guests. Top picks include **Hat Khlong Chao**, **Ao Noi**, **Ao Prao** and **Ao Tapao**.

## Beach Feasts

Look no further for Pattaya's best beachfront dining than **Glass House** on Jomtien Beach, where excellent Thai dishes complement a romantic candlelit vibe.

Much rowdier is Ko Chang expat institution, **Oodie's Place**, a fa·ràng (Westerner) favourite for Thai and international food and live blues performances.

Many Ko Samet resorts offer beach barbecues and fire shows. It's a very local affair

### Ideal Islands

Once a royal beach retreat, **Ko Si Chang** is worth a day trip for its fishing-village atmosphere and seafood joints. Between watery expanses with creaky squid rigs and fishing boats are a couple of interesting sights: **Phra Chudadhut Palace**, an ancient Victorian-style palace designed in teak and gold, and the striking Thai-Chinese temple **Chao Pho Khao Yai Shrine**.

The island is easily reachable by ferry from the fishing village **Si Racha** on the mainland. Spicy Sriracha sauce is said to have originated here, but these days the town is more known for sushi spots and karaoke bars catering to local Japanese industrial workers.

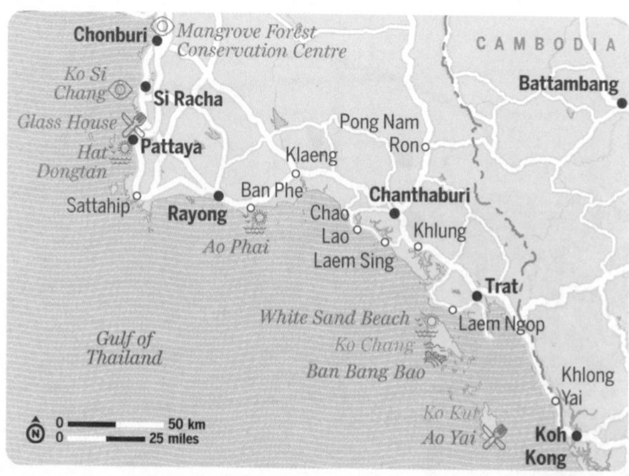


**Left** Ko Kut island. **Below** Glass House on Jomtien Beach, Pattaya

(albeit a little touristy). A better vibe can be found at the romantic restaurant **Kitt & Food** where the waves lap by your feet tableside.

## Rainbow-Friendly Beaches

The eastern region is typically known as a welcoming and tolerant place for LGBTIQ+ travellers. There are a couple of beaches to know about.

**Hat Dongtan** on Pattaya, part of Jomtien Beach towards the northern side, is a popular strand among gay visitors.

**Ao Phai**, a small but sweet white-sand beach on Ko Samet, is home to the well-known gay resort **Silver Sand**. It's got a bumping open-air bar and restaurant.

## Hidden Beach Gems

Ko Chang's **Khlong Kloi** is a tiny beach offering the best of both worlds – a lively daytime vibe but none of that in-your-face tourism feel. Think guesthouses and a simple treetop restaurant.

On Ko Samet, beaches away from the masses include **Ao Thian** for downing beer and listening to low-key guitar sessions and the lonely, delightfully underdeveloped **Ao Wai**.

Most of Ko Mak feels quite hidden, but those looking for completely deserted beaches might consider starting on the northwestern bay of Ao Suan Yai and renting a motorbike to discover eastern and northeastern shores like **Ao Nid** and **Ao Tan**.

# 29 Crystal Blue PERSUASIONS

SNORKELLING | KAYAKING | ISLANDS

You won't regret exploring the curvy coves and bays of the eastern gulf and its islands – crystalline waters, diverse aquamarine life and coral reefs, plus the ready availability of instructors make water activities one of the best things to do here. The snorkelling and scuba diving is especially famous, with sites ranging from expert to beginner-friendly.

DUDAREV MIKHAIL/SHUTTERSTOCK ©

## How to

**Getting around** Tour providers will generally include hotel pickup and drop off in most activities.

**Best time to go** October to December when seas are at their calmest. Many dive shops stay open during the rainy season (May to October) but visibility and water conditions will likely be poor.

**Cost** One-day diving trips typically start at 3000B. Budget about 15,000B per person for PADI or other certification courses.

BIRDPITS/SHUTTERSTOCK ©



## Diving & Snorkelling

Ko Chang offers the largest and best assortment of dive sites in the **Mu Ko Chang National Marine Park**, though underwater adventurers will be enthused with the coral reefs around Ko Mak and Ko Kut too.

**Hin Luk Bat** and **Hin Rap** are two beloved seamounts offering a good variety of fish and turtle sightings.

At **Hin Gadeng** and **Hin Kuak Maa** (Three Ringer Reef), spectacular coral reefs and rock formations steal the show.

For beginners, the shallow waters around **Ko Yak**, **Ko Tong Lang** and **Ko Luan** have an excellent array of fish and coral.

**Ko Wai**, off the coast of Ko Chang, is a popular little island for snorkelling. Consider

MAEMANEE/SHUTTERSTOCK ©

### Give Back to the Environment

Ko Chang's chapter of Trash Hero, an international volunteer-led organisation performing beach clean-ups, is very active on the island. Visit the Facebook page (facebook.com/trashhero-kochang) to find out about lending a hand and tackling the abundant garbage that washes up on shore here.

**Above left** *HTMS Chang* (p158). **Below left** Giant Barrel sponge, Mu Ko Chang. **Above** Mu Ko Chang National Parine Park

staying overnight to beat the day-tripper crowds to the coral.

Near Pattaya, **Ko Samae San** is a beautiful island that is part of a royal Thai conservation project. The snorkelling here won't disappoint.

Off Ko Mak, **Ko Phe** and **Ko Rayang** offer plentiful coral reefs and stunning rocky stretches.

## High Adrenaline

**Pattaya** and **Ko Chang** are the main points for water-sports thrills in the eastern gulf. The favourite activities include parasailing, Sea-dooing and jet-skiing.

Jet-skiing is a local speciality in Pattaya. The city annually hosts the Jet Ski World Cup.

## Bayside Adventure

Ko Samet's activities are based around coves and rocky headlands. Think stand-up paddle boarding, windsurfing, squid-fishing and other angling trips as well as diving and snorkelling.

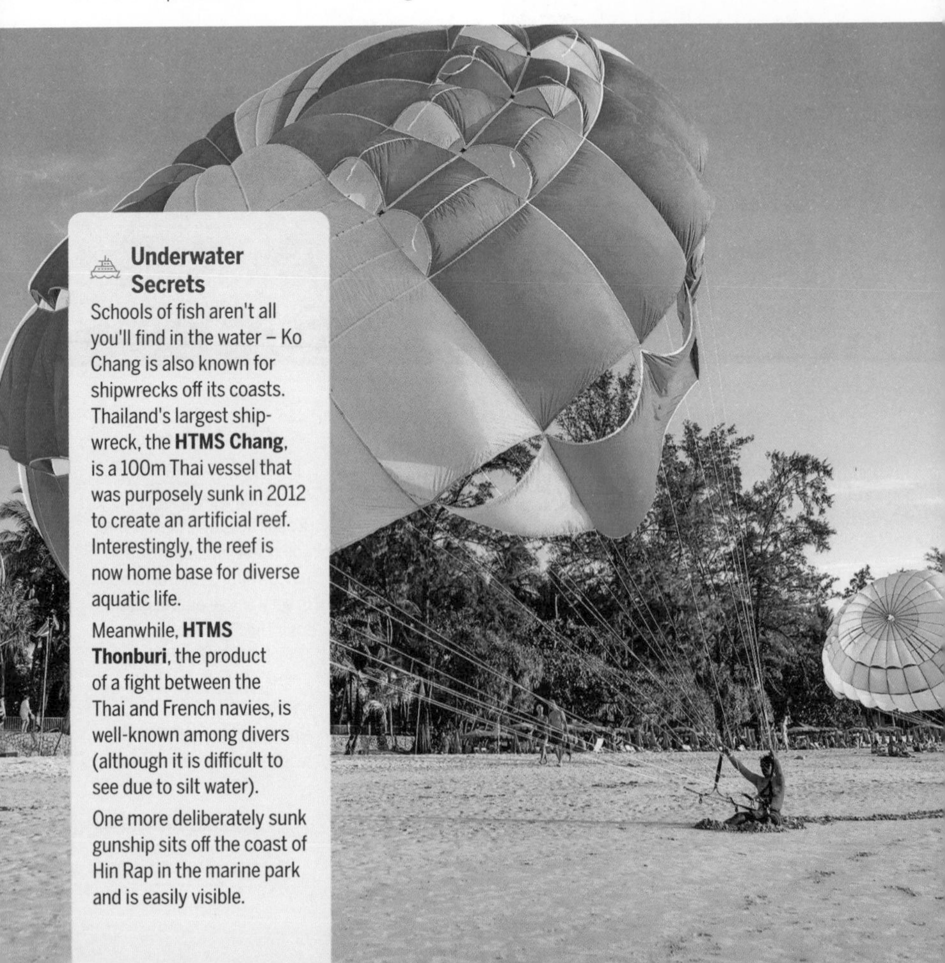

### Underwater Secrets

Schools of fish aren't all you'll find in the water – Ko Chang is also known for shipwrecks off its coasts. Thailand's largest shipwreck, the **HTMS Chang**, is a 100m Thai vessel that was purposely sunk in 2012 to create an artificial reef. Interestingly, the reef is now home base for diverse aquatic life.

Meanwhile, **HTMS Thonburi**, the product of a fight between the Thai and French navies, is well-known among divers (although it is difficult to see due to silt water).

One more deliberately sunk gunship sits off the coast of Hin Rap in the marine park and is easily visible.

**Left** Parasailing, Pattaya.
**Below** Kayaking, Ko Lan

The small rocky islands near Ko Samet, like **Ko Ku Dee** and **Ko Thalu** (also comprised in the Khao Laem Ya/Mu Ko Samet National Park), make great destinations for private boating and fishing tours.

From Pattaya, catch a ferry to the tiny island of **Ko Lan** for an afternoon of banana boating.

## Kayaking

The tranquil waters around **Ko Mak**, **Ko Kut** and **Ko Chang** are excellent spots for kayaking. Some hotels provide kayaks for free.

Ko Chang tour operators **KayakChang** and **SEA Kayaking** offer serious rigs and days-long kayak expeditions. Look for tour operators on Ko Chang and Ko Mak also offering kayaks with glass bottoms.

The **Salak Kok Kayak Station** is a one-of-a-kind kayaking experience focused on sustainability. Kayaks are available for rent on self-guided tours through the mangrove swamps of **Ao Salak Kok**. As you cruise, spot villagers hammering away at traditional houses or tilling the forestland. They are participating in an eco-project to protect nature and revitalise the traditional lifestyle here.

Renting a kayak from **Hat Tham Phang** on Ko Si Chang and paddling to Ko Khang Khao (a 45-minute kayak) is also a delightful journey.

# 30 Amusement Park MADNESS

SWIMMING | OUTDOORS | FAMILY

Just a two-hour drive from Bangkok, Pattaya is Thailand's destination of outdoor water parks and theme-park thrills. Water slides of all shapes and speeds, crazy rides and games – parks are a good action-packed alternative to sea activities when tides are poor. Mostly they cater to families, although your inner child may appreciate adults-only pools and swim-up bars.

### How to

**Getting here** Hire a taxi from Bangkok for an official flat rate (1500B from downtown, 1110B from Suvarnabhumi Airport plus toll charges).

**When to go** Pattaya's weather is mild yet sunny from November to February.

**What to bring** Umbrella and jacket in case of bad weather and a towel (or rent your own).

**Cost** Day admission covers rides only. Bring ID for student and senior discounts.

## Water Parks

Pattaya's amusement parks share one common philosophy: the bigger, the better.

Water parks boast dozens of superlative slides, wave pools and flow riding, making for wildly fun days (and sound sleeping at night). **Ramayana** is Thailand's biggest water park (and one of Asia's largest) with 18 hectares promising fun for everyone, including shaded play areas and adults-only sections. Unlike Thai tap water, it claims the water here is drinkable thanks to a high-tech filtration system.

Meanwhile, **Columbia Pictures Aquaverse** is the production company's first water park in the world, with slides and rides themed by its movie and characters. **Pattaya Park** and **Dream World** offer a funky fusion of water park and amusement park including roller coasters (the former also has the advantage of a private stretch of Jomtien Beach).

FOTOGRIN/SHUTTERSTOCK ©



## Raise Your Adrenaline

Jump off Pattaya's highest tower, take a zip-line fall or cable-car ride from the 55th floor at **Pattaya Park**. Or if that's too much, stand on the observation deck or dine at the revolving restaurant.

A colossal tangle of twists and turns, Pattaya Park's **Slalom** is one of the weirdest and wackiest roller coasters out there. A must for enthusiasts – just try not to throw up!

Get launched into swimming pools (if you dare). **Ramayana**'s biggest thrills include the AquaLoop and Freefall, where riders get thrown out of launch capsules into the depths.

## Cultural Theme Parks

For those looking to stay dry, cultural theme parks like **Legend Siam** and **Mini Siam** showcase ancient Siam history, while the **Nong Nooch Tropical Garden** is a science theme park focused around a centre for seed genes and a botanical garden full of tropical plants.

Prepare for a park visit to be mostly outdoors and an all-day affair. Many also offer live shows and demonstrations. While food is generally not included in the ticket price, the offerings tend to be well-priced and pretty good – think Thai cuisine buffet-style or a traditional food court with many stalls.

**Above** Zip-lining, Pattaya Park

# Listings

BEST OF THE REST

### Thai Cooking Classes

Blue Lagoon

Pound out your own curry paste at this friendly little eco-resort on Ko Chang. Once your work is over in the open-air kitchen, savour the final products in a little wooden stilt house on the lagoon.

Ka-Ti Culinary Cooking School

A Ko Chang cooking school with quite the reputation thanks to its excellent adjoining restaurant. You can learn the same family recipes served to diners.

Napalai Thai Cooking School

Come to Ko Chang to learn recipes for soups, salads and curries – leave with new techniques for cooking from scratch and fun memories of the instructor Bunny's smile.

### Volunteering

Koh Chang Animal Project

Abused, injured or abandoned animals receive comfort and care at this non-profit centre. Help doing odd jobs, and the skills of travelling vets and vet nurses, is always welcome.

Animal Voice Koh Chang

At this non-profit island sanctuary started by a local veterinarian and animal activist, volunteers can help out with daily feedings and walking stray dogs.

Cambodian Kids Care Center

Take part in an internship or educational project at this Ko Chang centre providing day care to Cambodian migrant kids.

### Live Music Bars

Filou $$

A fancy Ko Chang restaurant and cocktail bar on Kaibae's main street, it's known for its live bands which kick off nightly around 9pm.

Stone Free $

Your friendly Lonely Beach (Ko Chang) institution for hippie jam sessions and none of that DJ stuff. Think old-school rock, the blues and probably a sad guitar solo or two.

Long Tail Bar $

Nothing epitomises Thai island life more than this Lonely Beach bar on Ko Chang where you can enjoy reggae beats, vodka buckets and perhaps even a joint now that it's being decriminalised.

### Cosy Cafes

Sketch Book Art Café $$

This Pattaya cafe has good coffee and smoothies, and a comfy leafy ambience. Paint materials are up for sale in case the owner's artworks inspire you.

Shee Va Café $$

This delightfully retro artisan coffee joint in Pattaya has a focus on music, with lots of vinyl records to sift through and a piano. The espresso art and sweets are nice too.

Ploy Talay at night

Backstreet House $$

A Pattaya stop for serious coffee drinkers – beans are sourced from around the globe and roasted in-house. The outdoor terrace is a shady, relaxing spot that feels very European.

## Thai Eats

Cabbages and Condoms $$$

The Pattaya spin-off of the famous Bangkok institution is very similar with condom-art statues, true-to-form Thai food and lovely wooden terrace seating.

Leng Kee $$

At this popular Thai-Chinese Pattaya street kitchen, sauce-drenched duck and seafood dishes are sure to illicit a drool. Open 24 hours, it's perfect for a late-night snack.

Mum Aroi $$

This fishing-village restaurant is often touted as Pattaya's best seafood joint. Stare into the distance at swaying boats and sink into the speciality *bplah mèuk nêung ma · now* (squid steamed in lime).

## People Watching on Ko Samet

Ploy Talay $$

The busiest restaurant on Hat Sai Kaew. Join a crowd of mostly Thai diners perched on pillows at low tables on the sand, watching the fire show over cold beers.

Audi Bar $$

The upstairs bar provides the perfect vantage point for eyeing passers-by below. As the beach dancers start to head home, grab a nightcap and play pool.

Naga Bar $$

A beachfront bar to see backpackers get silly at happy hour. As the night progresses, don't be surprised if you also end up on the dance floor covered in body paint.

## Underwater Shenanigans

Koh Mak Divers

This well-known Ko Mak dive company organises trips to a variety of sites off Ko Mak and the Ko Chang National Marine Park. It also offers PADI certifications.

BB Divers

A centrally located dive shop behind the Ko Mak Resort (where most of the boats get in). Good options for beginners' dives and snorkelling.

Dive Seacret

Baan Ko Mak's dive shop offers a daily well-priced snorkelling trip to four nearby mini-islands (Ko Yak, Ko Kra, Ko Hin Bai, Ko Rung) with lunch and equipment included.

## Ko Kut Feasts

Fisherman Hut $$

Steak, seafood and burgers – with a side of awesome live music. Fisherman Hut is a great spot for refuelling after long days of diving and lounging.

Noochy Seafood $$

Get ready for a seafood extravaganza. Fresh catches come in from around Ko Kut and are served up in generous portions.

Chonthicha Seafood $$

Juicy seafood platters plus a cosy fishing-village atmosphere. Chonthicha is the kind of place you may never want to leave.

Chaiyo Restaurant $$

Cute bungalow restaurant run by a sweet Thai couple. You can't go wrong with anything on the menu, but the curry prawns are a top pick.

**Scan to find more things to do in Ko Chang & the Eastern Seaboard online**

# HUA HIN & THE UPPER GULF

BEACHES | NATURE | SEAFOOD

Experience Hua Hin & the Upper Gulf online

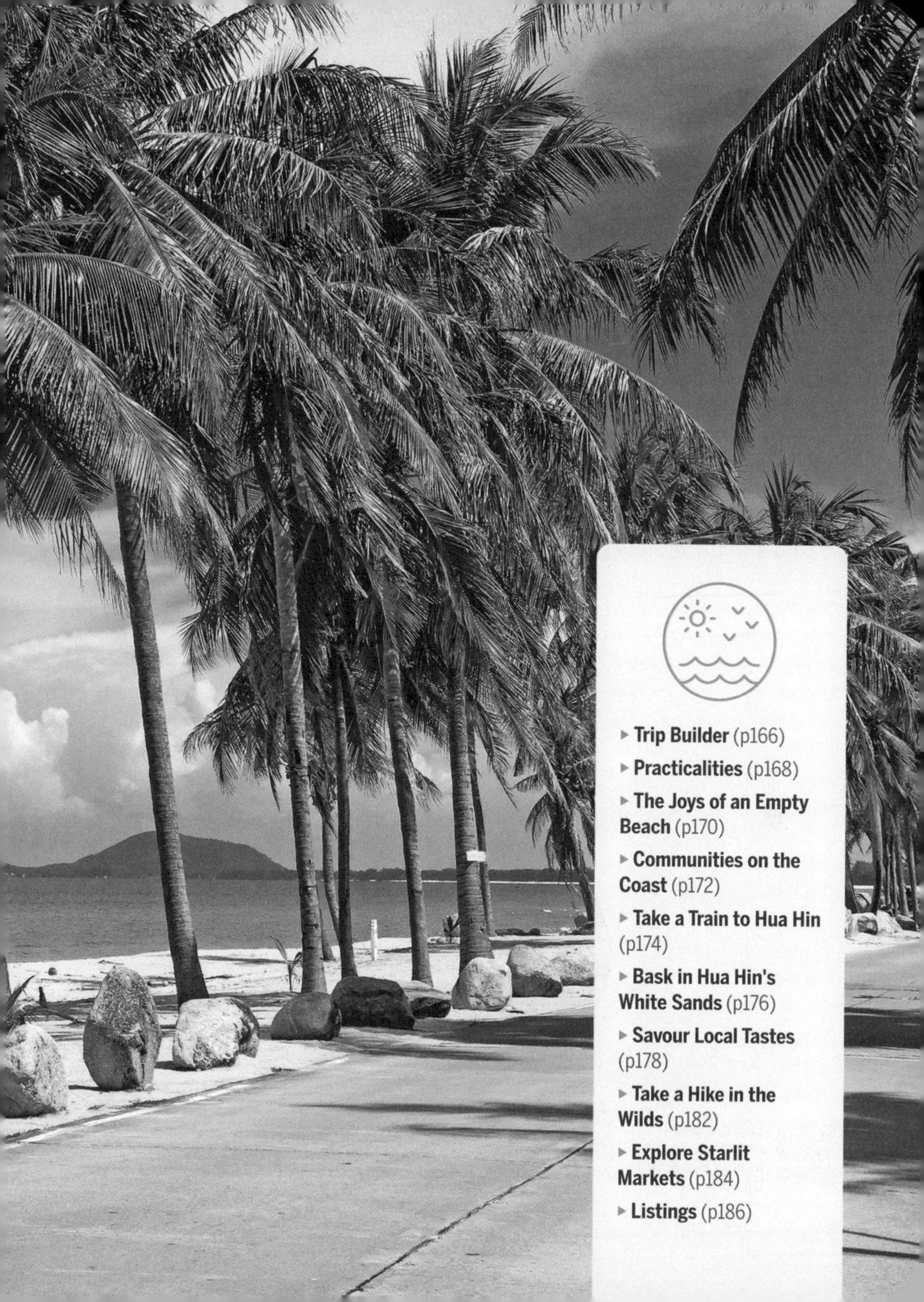

# HUA HIN & THE UPPER GULF
## Trip Builder



Ask most people what they want out of a trip to Thailand, and the answer usually involves sun, sand and the juice of a freshly opened coconut. Happily for them, all of those things are well within reach here, a mere two-hour car ride from the crowded capital. The cracked crab is fresh, the beer is ice cold and the oysters grow to the size of your hand.

Watch the elephants play in **Kui Buri National Park** (p182)
*1 hour from central Hua Hin*

Dip in the hot springs of **Raksa Warin** (p183)
*2 hours from Chumphon*

**Explore bookable experiences in Hua Hin & the Upper Gulf**

Myeik
*Myeik Archipelago*
Kawthoung
**Ranong**
*Ko Chang*
Ratcha Krut
*Ko Phayam*
Kapo

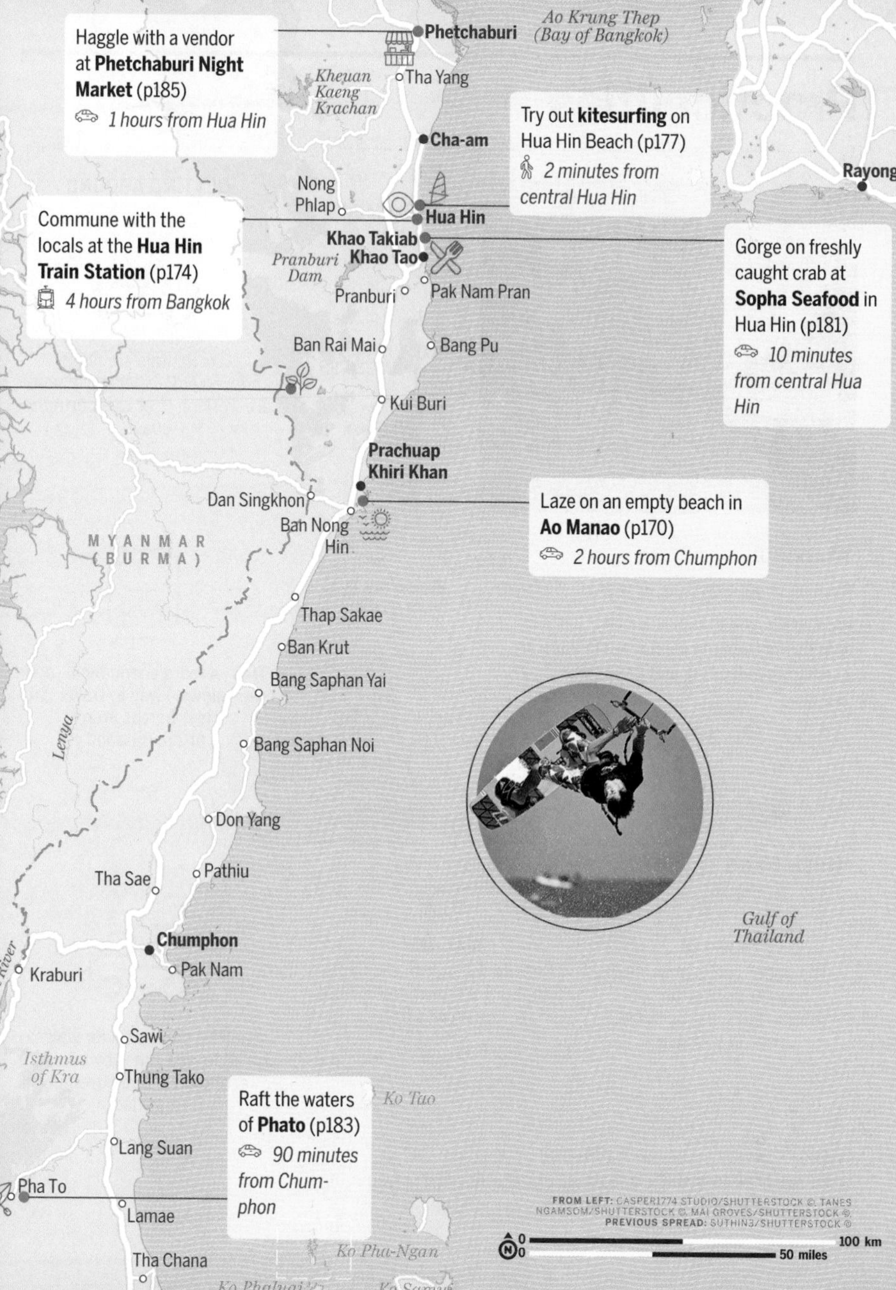


FROM LEFT: CASPER1774 STUDIO/SHUTTERSTOCK ©, TANES NGAMSOM/SHUTTERSTOCK ©, MAI GROVES/SHUTTERSTOCK ©. PREVIOUS SPREAD: SUTHIN3/SHUTTERSTOCK ©

# Practicalities

ANTONY MCAULAY/SHUTTERSTOCK ©

## ARRIVING

**Train** All major towns are accessible via train.

**Air** Hua Hin and Pranburi are two- to three-hour drives from the capital, while there are also flights to Ranong and Chumphon.

## HOW MUCH FOR A

**Beer 90–150B**

**Mango sticky rice 120B**

**100ml of sunscreen 290B**

## GETTING AROUND

**Car** Rentals are most convenient, especially if you are working your way down the coast.

**Train** A more economical (and much slower) way to travel; 3rd-class berths aren't air-conditioned.

**Van** The most popular way to travel to Hua Hin is by minivan; economical but extremely crowded.

## WHEN TO GO

**NOV–FEB**

The upper gulf is at its most popular during the cool season, but must be booked well in advance.

**MAR–MAY**

Despite the sweltering heat, Songkran celebrations in April are always fun.

**JUN–OCT**

There will be frequent – and usually brief – downpours, so bring a raincoat.

## EATING & DRINKING

Here, seafood is king. But Phetchaburi is also famous for its *kôw gaang* (curry rice; pictured top right), so try to stop by for a bite on your way south.

In Hua Hin, traditional sweets of sticky rice and coconut are prized, as is *kôw nĕe·o má·môo·ang* (mango sticky rice; pictured bottom right), arguably Thailand's most famous dessert.

**Best curry**
Kôw gaang
Jay Muay (p186)

**Must-try dessert**
Kanom Waan
Pa Prang (p187)

### REFRESHMENTS

When it comes to the upper gulf, fruit and herb juices rule the roost in the many markets that dot the region. Try *nam grajieb* (roselle juice) as a thirst quencher.

## WHERE TO STAY

The upper gulf is chock-full of interesting places to bed down, but these towns boast the most options.

| Town/Village | Pros/Cons |
|---|---|
| Hua Hin | An obvious hub, it is close to many attractions but can be crowded during holidays. |
| Pranburi | Much quieter than its northern sibling Hua Hin, it is still in a convenient location |
| Ko Mak | Green and isolated, it's beautiful but there's not much nightlife beyond the hotel or resort. |

### CONNECT

Most public spots will have wi-fi, especially cafes, but service in parts of Chumphon might be spotty.

### MONEY

If hiring a driver, it is customary to tip them 100B to 500B per day, depending on how many hours they have been working.

# 31 The Joys of an EMPTY BEACH

**BEACHES | DRIVING | SUN**

It's hard to believe, but Thailand is home to so many beaches that quite a few of them are pretty much deserted during hot weekdays. Take advantage of the Thai fear of the sun by exploring these glimmering – and empty – slices of coast and live out your *Cast Away* fantasies, one beach at a time.

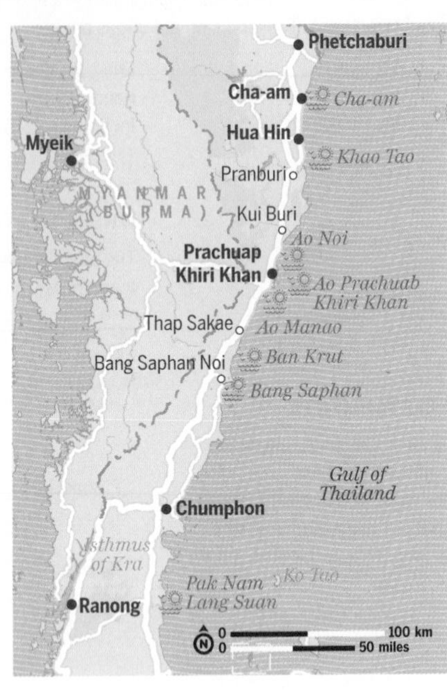


### How to

**Getting around** You can rent a car to flit from beach to beach (rentcarhuahinchaam.com) or book a taxi (huahintaxitravel.com).

**When to go** Early weekday mornings are best to avoid UV rays, but afternoons are also fairly quiet.

**Avoid crowds** Skip visiting in the cool season if you want empty beaches.

**Sun protection** Bring protection in the form of a hat and sunscreen.



## Fly & Flop

Just south of Hua Hin's main drag, the overlooked beach of **Khao Tao** feels like discovering a hidden treasure, especially at night when the area is almost completely deserted. Like Hua Hin's main beach, the sand is fine and white, and refreshingly silky in the cool night air.

Also overlooked in favour of its more glamorous sister, **Cha-Am** beach may not be as pretty as its southern sibling, but it is definitely less cluttered. The best time to come is on weekdays (except Wednesdays), when visitors are few and sling chairs are readily available.

Further south, **Ao Manao** (Lime Bay) is considered part of the Royal Thai Air Force's land and is thus largely free of the activity found on other beaches. Meanwhile, **Ban Krut** beach – also in Prachuap Khiri Khan – comprises a 20km-long stretch of golden sand that lures few interlopers, especially on weekdays. If you dare to walk the entire stretch, you will eventually

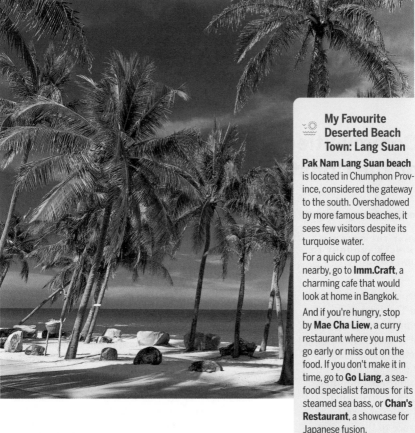

SUTHIN3/SHUTTERSTOCK ©



### My Favourite Deserted Beach Town: Lang Suan

**Pak Nam Lang Suan beach** is located in Chumphon Province, considered the gateway to the south. Overshadowed by more famous beaches, it sees few visitors despite its turquoise water.

For a quick cup of coffee nearby, go to **Imm.Craft**, a charming cafe that would look at home in Bangkok.

And if you're hungry, stop by **Mae Cha Liew**, a curry restaurant where you must go early or miss out on the food. If you don't make it in time, go to **Go Liang**, a seafood specialist famous for its steamed sea bass, or **Chan's Restaurant**, a showcase for Japanese fusion.

■ **By Panisha Chan**, *from Bangkok, vegan chef of kurrykween.com, Instagram @panisha*

reach **Bang Saphan**, another underrated curve of sand rimmed with coconut trees and aquamarine water.

Finally, another notable beach in Prachuab is **Ao Noi** (Little Bay), the little sister to **Ao Prachuab Khiri Khan**. Picturesque and quiet, the bay plays host to numerous fishing boats as well as the elaborately carved teak **Wat Ao Noi** and **Tham Phra Non** (Reclining Buddha Cave).

**Above** Ban Krut Beach

# Communities on the Coast

**WHAT THE COASTAL CHINESE BROUGHT TO THAI FOOD**

People typically think of Thailand as a homogenous blanket of 'Thainess', but the country is actually a tapestry of different ethnic communities, each contributing their own secret sauce to the concept of being Thai. The upper gulf illustrates this tapestry perfectly, and its cuisine has benefited greatly as a result.

**Left** Chinatown, Bangkok
**Middle** Dim-sum dumplings.
**Right** Food vendor, Chinatown, Bangkok

GIFTOGRAPHY/SHUTTERSTOCK ©

What we think of as the upper gulf is really an amalgam — a *yum*, or spicy salad, if you will — of communities that moved to the kingdom at various points in time, often fleeing upheaval at home in search of a better life. Happily for Thai food, many of those communities that migrated to the region hailed from China.

## Coming to Thailand

Few communities have made as much of an impact on Thai cuisine as the Chinese, who started coming en masse to Thailand in the mid-1800s. They moved everywhere in Thailand, but set up particularly vibrant communities in Bangkok and along the seafood-rich lands rimming the coast south of the capital.

Once there, the Chinese filled in gaps otherwise not served by the native Thais, who mostly worked in agricultural and civil service jobs. The niches that the Chinese carved out for themselves included toiling in tin mines and on rubber plantations along the gulf, and inventing the concept of the restaurant and street food in Bangkok, where their homes were too small to have kitchens in which to cook.

Unlike the Thais, who used earthenware pots, the Chinese used woks and brought the idea of frying and deep-frying to Thailand. The Chinese cooked duck meat instead of simply harvesting their eggs; introduced noodles; brewed stock for their soups instead of simply infusing water with herbs. They fried eggs in savoury dishes instead of saving them for desserts, seasoned with vinegar instead of lime juice, and showed Thais how to use chopsticks and the Chinese cleaver.

PJARUWAN/SHUTTERSTOCK ©

PERCULIAR BOY/SHUTTERSTOCK ©

Perhaps most importantly for the upper gulf, they steamed their fresh crabs and prawns, as well as whole fish in their native soy sauce and ginger. They put curry powder and eggs in their cracked crab stir-fries and flash-fried their rice with crab, shrimp, salted fish, or whatever other seafood was available at the market. It was a Thai-Chinese housewife on the coast who first came up with a concoction of pickled garlic, chillies and vinegar that would later become known as Sriracha sauce. These culinary contributions spawned an entire new category of Thai cuisine that could be referred to as 'Thai-Chinese seafood' – as found in famous restaurants such as Bangkok's Somboon Seafood – but which is really thought of among Thais as just 'seafood'.

> The Chinese . . . set up particularly vibrant communities in Bangkok and along the seafood-rich lands rimming the coast south of the capital.

### Roadside Treats

Get on the southbound highway from Bangkok, and you'll see it: roadside vendors, some beckoning for you to browse their wares, some with noses buried in their mobile phone screens. If you deign to make a few stops, you'll see that the offerings on the way change as you travel, giving great insights into the communities behind them. Sea salt harvested through the centuries-old process of evaporating sea water; salted eggs and steamed Chinese dumplings; and roti stuffed with candy floss are just a few of the surprises awaiting you on the side of the road.

## An Icon is Born

All the same, a darker period of ultranationalism in the 20th century led to a raft of laws targeted against the Chinese, with Chinese-language signs banned and Chinese vendors barred from selling near schools. It was during this period when a contest was held in the capital to come up with a recipe to make Chinese noodles more Thai. In typical Thai fashion, a government minister's wife won with her creation of noodles stir-fried with tamarind paste, lime juice and palm sugar. The result would eventually become known as pad thai, Thailand's most famous dish – an invention sparked by the Chinese community.

# 32 Take the Train to HUA HIN

**TRANSPORT | ADVENTURE | HISTORY**

If you have the time and inclination, the four-hour trip from Bangkok through the upper gulf gleans some of the best people watching to be had anywhere in the country. The sense of community, the stops, and, of course, the food, illuminate a part of life that is difficult to find in the Covid-era sterility of the modern airport.

FIAT NATTARAT/SHUTTERSTOCK ©

### How to

**Getting there** The train now departs from Bang Sue station, accessible via MRT (subway).

**When to go** Hua Hin is more popular during the cool season, but the beach is far more deserted in the rainy season. Just make sure to avoid big public holidays, when it will be packed.

**What it will cost** From 44B to 1000B, depending on class.

**For any additional info** Go to thailandtrains.com.

## What It's Like

Trains have been serving the kingdom since the late 19th century. While some travellers can claim to have traversed the length of Thailand by rail, the train journey from Bangkok to Hua Hin is by comparison a relatively painless affair. Once departing from Hua Lamphong station, the southbound train now leaves from Bang Sue station in the north of the city. Taking roughly four hours, the journey will haul you through the western reaches of Bangkok before veering south towards Malaysia. If the ride is overnight, your first or second-class

**Above** Hua Lamphong train station. **Above right** Hua Hin train station. **Right** Coffee and *patongko*

CASPER1774 STUDIO/SHUTTERSTOCK ©

SOMSIT/SHUTTERSTOCK ©

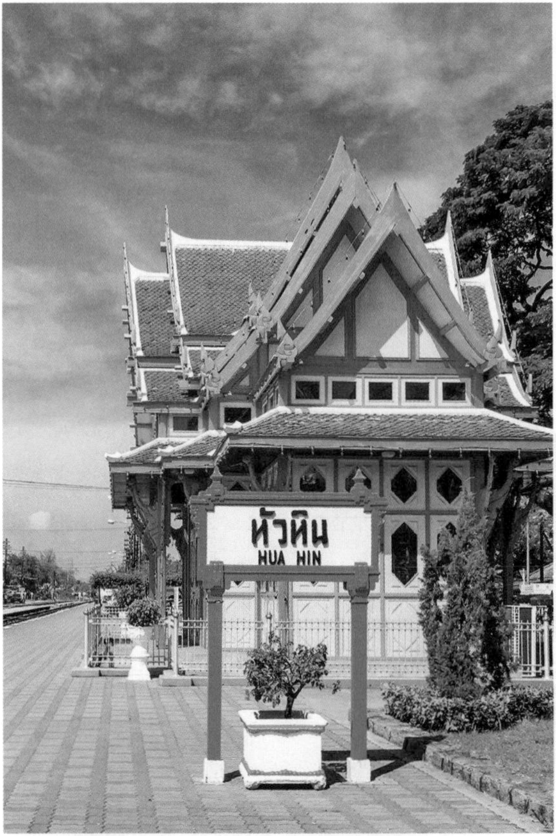

### Train Tips

To be extra safe, it is best to buy your tickets in person a few days in advance, as the websites aren't always up to date.

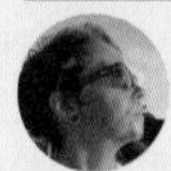

■ **By Minh Lowe,** *yoga instructor from Bangkok, yogatiquebangkok.com, Instagram @minh.lowe*

seat will be turned into a bed by the train attendant in the afternoon.

Pre-Covid, the train ride was a more boisterous affair, where trains would slow down at various stations for long enough for snack vendors to jump on the train. Today, such visits are no longer allowed, but simple menus are still provided for overnight travellers, with the Thai version of the continental breakfast — a *patongko* (deep-fried cruller) with coffee — available when you wake. Of course, as it is Thailand, most locals will be travelling with shopping bags filled with food, and they are usually happy to share. Unlike a plane trip, the train affords actual contact with Thai people, ever-changing scenery outside your window, and the romance of a slow journey.

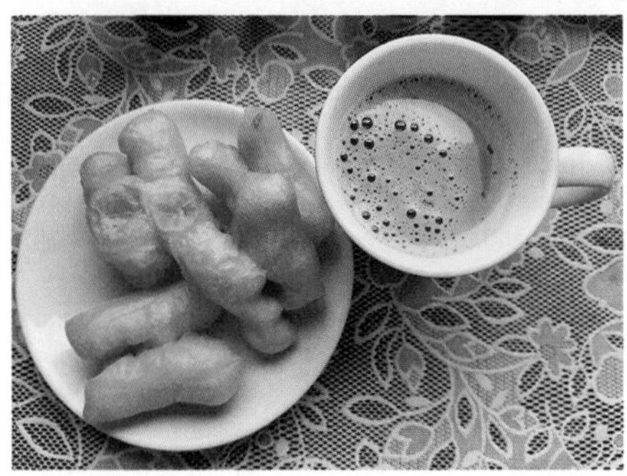

# 33 Bask in Hua Hin's WHITE SANDS

**BEACHES | SPORTS | WATER**

Of all the beaches in the upper gulf, the soft white sands of Hua Hin are the most popular among Thais. Despite the millions of people who visit every year, this beach remains, for the most part, pristine from the usual ravages that mar its Thai counterparts. Perhaps this is why so many activities can be found on Hua Hin's shores.

HINNAMSAISUY/SHUTTERSTOCK ©

**Recommended by Panarat Bunnag,** *actress and long-time resident of Hua Hin*

## Trip Notes

**Getting there** The most picturesque way to go is by train, but bus service (busonlineticket.co.th) and minivans (12go.asia/en/operator/nor-neane-transport) are also available. Or you can go by private car (privatetaxithailand.com).

**When to go** Hua Hin is most crowded during Thai holidays; watch out for outrageous hotel rates and traffic jams during New Year's and Songkran.

**Dangers** Beware jellyfish during rainy season.

### My Favourite Beach Activity

My favourite thing to do is to take a walk on the beach at sunrise, when there are few people around. You can find monks walking barefoot on the beach and Thais with offerings of food for them as they pass by, waiting to get their morning blessings.

### 01 Kite surfers
On windy days, the gulf is peppered with **kitesurfers** (and their instructors) as they navigate the choppy waves with varying degrees of skill.

### 02 Banana boats
The terrified shrieks you hear are thanks to the **banana boat**, as riders cling on for dear life on rough waters.

### 03 Horses
Considered a symbol of Hua Hin, **horses** (and owners) roam the beach in search of riders, charging 500B for half an hour.

### 04 Roti Vendors
Because you are in Thailand, you cannot go for long without a snack. Luckily **roti vendors** are easy to find, offering sweet flatbread doused in sugar.

# 34 Savour Local TASTES

**FOOD | NATURE | BEACHES**

Thais do not go to the beach armed with a pina colada, suntan lotion or trashy novel, expecting to snooze on the sand. Thais go to the beach for one reason only: to eat. And when you go to the beach to eat, steamed crabs are almost always involved, garnished with a Thai-style dipping sauce of green chillies and lime.

## How to

**Getting around** From Bangkok, a car is convenient, but if you are more than four travellers, why not travel in comfort in a van (bangkokvantravel.com)?

**When to go** Any time of year works, especially if you can brave the heat.

**Allergic to seafood?** No worries, stir-fried chicken and pork options are de rigueur on most Thai menus.

**Hua Hin food tours** Available at feastthailand.com.



## Road Trippin'

Yes, this is all about the upper gulf of Thailand, but first, you have to get there. And for many Thais, taking the car ride down to the Gulf of Thailand, the first point of call is always the first appealing seafood restaurant you can find on the coast. Typically shacks built next to the water to offer a picturesque view of the waves, these restaurants take all that is fresh from the ocean that day and transform it into the joy that, for most on this journey, embodies the real point of a trip to the Thai beach.

## Closer to Home

Unlike most of its brethren, **Maew** in Samut Songkhram, near Mae Klong, offers no lovely view. It doesn't even offer a chef that

**Above left** Beach shack, Bang Pu. **Left** Steamed crab with spicy dipping sauce

is eager to seat you. One must call ahead of time or risk a closed door – or worse, being turned away because there are simply too many people. But if you are one of the lucky ones with a seat, you will be rewarded with a gorgeously clear lemongrass soup rife with thick chunks of pomfret, or a perfect platter of crab fried rice.

But no seat, no worries, nearby await **Chaophraya Kitchen** and **Krua Wasana**, further along the highway and a stone's throw from each other (if the stone is thrown by a talented athlete). The former is the more famous of the two, with a beautiful view of the sunlit water, but the latter is set in a mangrove forest and features a coconut-milk-rich stew of fresh crab.

## In Town

But perhaps you'd like to wait until you are in a big town with more choices? If that is the

### Under the Sea

Thailand enjoys the best seafood from both the Gulf of Thailand and the Andaman Sea. There's also the diversity of seafood preparation – from Chinese influenced dishes (such as a pomfret hot pot, or steamed in soy sauce) to an astounding array of Thai seafood preparations like shrimp *pad phet* (spicy stir-fried shrimp), or fiery mud crab with green peppercorns. There are plenty of strongly spiced seafood dishes and there are seafood dishes that are simply prepared to let the freshness shine – both equally pleasing. Lastly, nowhere else on earth does seafood dipping sauce as well as Thailand!

**By Mark Wiens,** *food expert from Bangkok, eatingthaifood.com, Instagram @migrationology*

### Sumptuous Seafood

In Phetchaburi, **Raan Puang Petch** serves a catfish *pad cha* (a mountain of tender catfish stir-fried with a paste of green chillies and lime leaves).

Meanwhile, Prachuab Khiri Khan's homey **Pa Aung Pa Aing** specialises in fresh seasonal seafood like mantis prawns and slipper lobsters.

THITAP'A/SHUTTERSTOCK ©

NUCHUN/SHUTTERSTOCK ©

case, Hua Hin is obviously your town. Here, more than a handful of spots can claim their own groupies, but among the most voraciously followed is **Sopha Seafood**, home of *gaang sôm* (a particular type of sour curry) that includes holy basil and *prik nok*, a local chilli that is even spicier than the typical bird's eye. Closer to downtown lies **Nong May**, purveyor of spicy stir-fried scallops, and **Fah Mui** in the heart of town, with a view over the water.

## Decent Drive

If you like prolonging the anticipation for your meal, the town of Prachuab Khiri Khan hosts a fresh crab eatery called **Rub Lom**, with a view of Ao Prachuab Khiri Khan. And in front of the famous **Khao Sam Roi Yod** sits **Yok Sod**, which will reward you with an excellent Thai meal after your hike to **Phraya Nakhon Cave**.

MANANYA SOIRAYA/SHUTTERSTOCK ©

**Left** *Gaang sôm*. **Top right** Hua Hin seafood stall. **Above** Catfish *pad cha*

# 35 TAKE A HIKE in the Wilds

ADVENTURE | HIKING | NATIONAL PARKS

The upper gulf is more than just the sum of its beaches. A plethora of activities can be found among its waterfalls, mangrove forests, mountains, and even its marshes, provided you are willing, able and armed with the knowledge of where to go. From the mountains of Phetchaburi to the hot springs near Chumphon, these places have you covered.

Khao Wang
Phetchaburi
Cha-am
Myeik
Hua Hin
Pranburi
Mangrove Forest Walk
Tham Phraya Nakhon
Kui Buri
Kui Buri
MYANMAR (BURMA)
Prachuap Khiri Khan
Thap Sakae
Bang Saphan Yai
Gulf of Thailand
Chumphon
Isthmus of Kra
Ko Tao
Ranong
Raksa Warin
Phato
0 100 km
0 50 miles

## How to

**Getting around** If using Hua Hin as your base, you can rent a car with or without driver (huahin-cars.com). Or go for a company with multiple branches (nationalcar.com).

**When to go** These attractions are open all year round, but the cool season is when it's most crowded.

**Be prepared** Some of these attractions involve water so bring a towel for the car ride back.

## Out of Bangkok

Glimpsed from the road as a mass of white spires on a mountaintop, **Khao Wang** sits in Phetchaburi Province, where a trolley takes you up to a charming royal residence built by Rama IV.

## Near Hua Hin

Further south, myriad attractions are clustered around the hub town of Hua Hin. Roughly an hour south of town lies **Kui Buri National Park**, a mecca for animal lovers, where your chances of seeing an elephant in the wild are almost guaranteed.

Closer to town lies Pranburi's **Mangrove Forest Walk**, offering a (free!) stroll through quiet wetlands only 25km south of Hua Hin. Boat tours are available during high tide.

But if you desire a more arduous hike, head to **Phraya Nakhon Cave** in **Khao Sam Roi Yod National Park**, named for its 300 peaks. The limestone cave is famous for its stunning Royal Pavilion, bathed in sunlight from a

NATE SAMUI/SHUTTERSTOCK ©

hole in the roof resembling an oculus.

## Down South

In Chumphon, considered the gateway to the south, a maze of rivers marble the region, providing ample fodder for rafting enthusiasts. If you are one, head to **Phato**, where a number of tours operate. Or if you'd rather just sit and soak, try **Raksa Warin hot springs** further down the peninsula in Ranong, where people take turns dipping in open-air thermal waters believed to cure minor ills.

### How to Squat Toilet in the Wild

The squat-style toilet found in most public restrooms may be difficult to negotiate. Here are some tips:

- The roll of toilet paper next to the sink is there for use in the stall, as most stalls do not have their own toilet paper.
- You will find a receptacle full of water next to the squat toilet, with a plastic bowl floating on the water's surface. This is for 'flushing' when you are done.
- If you are wearing long pants, roll them up. If you are wearing socks, good luck.

**Above** Elephants, Kui Buri National Park

# 36 Explore Starlit MARKETS

SHOPPING | FOOD | NIGHTLIFE

Shopaholics can find their spiritual brethren in the Thais, who have made shopping a priority at any time of the day. Morning markets open at the crack of dawn for breakfast and stay open well past noon. But it's the night markets that are the most well-known, and there are many to choose from.

### How to

**Getting around** Renting a car is the easiest way to zip around the outdoor markets in the region.

**When to go** Since hot season is sweltering and rainy season is...rainy, cool season seems to be the way to go.

**Bargaining tip** The standard rule of thumb for where to start when you haggle with a vendor is to propose half of what you wish to pay.

In Hua Hin, **Cicada Market** – possibly the most popular night market outside of Bangkok – draws artists from all over the region to hawk their handmade wares. Expect paintings, home decor, live music and, of course, food.

Not one to slack, neighbouring Cha Am hosts a **Wednesday Night Market** that has become something of a tradition among the locals. There are the usual snacks and artsy tchotchkes, but unlike elsewhere, this market also boasts a Farang Husband Minding Centre

**Above right** Painter, Cicada market.
**Right** Crepe shop, Prachuab Khiri Khan Night Market

BANJONGSEAL956/SHUTTERSTOCK ©

BUBBERS BB/SHUTTERSTOCK ©

### Artsy Cicada

My favourite is Cicada, although a lot of vendors have disappeared. The market has unique artsy merchandise, fun entertainment and lots of good basic food selections to choose from.

■ **By Nong Tumsutipong,** *designer from Bangkok, Instagram* @seenyc

where wives can deposit their complaining spouses to shop at their own leisure.

Meanwhile, Prachuab Khiri Khan is the proud home of several night markets, including **Sam Ao Walking Street** on the waterfront, basically the centre of the town's social life on Saturdays and Sundays. But if you are in town on a weekday, check out the regular **Prachuab Khiri Khan Night Market**, open every evening from after 5pm, on the way to the train station.

Less frequented than its neighbours in Hua Hin or Cha Am, **Phetchaburi Night Market** offers just as much variety but at cheaper prices. Further south, visitors to the kingdom between February and April can enjoy the colourful offerings on display in Ranong's **Walking Street Night Market**, held on Saturday nights, and another nexus of activity for the town on weekends.

# Listings

**BEST OF THE REST**

### Not So Seafood-Obsessed

Tanya's Homemade Eatery $$$

Set right on the water's edge, Tanya's has drawn raves from foodies nationwide for its take on central Thai classics like crabmeat *lon* (a coconut-milk-based chilli dip).

Krua Kannikar $

A long-time fixture on the Hua Hin dining scene, this unassuming eatery near the train station is all about the chicken: try the green chicken curry and stuffed chicken wings.

Nai Pew duck noodles $

This duck noodle vendor is the go-to for Hua Hin locals who want a quick lunch. You have your choice of stewed thigh or breast meat.

Rabiang Rimnam $$

Foodies in search of a central Thai meal in a traditional setting should head to this riverside teak house in Phetchaburi, serving local favourites like toddy palm curry.

Pae Yuan $$

If you have time for only one meal in Phetchaburi, make it at this tucked-away restaurant specialising in *aharn pa* (jungle cuisine). One caveat: spice levels are high!

Kôw gaang Jay Muay $

This humble street-side spot offers *kôw gaang* (curry over rice), for which Phetchaburi is especially known. You can choose up to three curries to sample on one plate.

### Prayers & Reflection

Khao Luang

North of Phetchaburi, this cave temple comprises a series of caverns in which golden Buddha statues reside among the stalactites. It was a favourite spot of Rama IV for meditation.

Wat Khao Takiap

Another hilltop temple with great Hua Hin views, this one sits at the edge of Hua Hin beach. Beware of aggressive monkeys; they are always in search of food.

Wat Huay Mongkol

Visible from the highway, this temple is known for its enormous statue of Luang Phor Thuad, a famous monk, as well as a fallen teak tree believed to grant wishes.

Wat Kaew Prasert

Built in Chumphon, this temple harbours an incredible view of the sea and a nine-headed naga statue; don't miss the statues illustrating the various torments of hell.

### Kid-Friendly Activities

Black Mountain Waterpark

While the beach is right there, this water park provides enough bells and whistles to divert kids for days: slides, a lazy river and a sprawling wave pool.

Wildlife Friends Foundation of Thailand

This rescue centre in Phetchaburi focuses on neglected and confiscated animals. Outside of Kui Buri, this is your best chance to see elephants roam. Overnight stays are available.

Malai Farm at Cha Am

If you are travelling with especially young animal lovers, this farm provides opportunities

AFRIRAMPOE/SHUTTERSTOCK ©

Khao Luang cave temple

to get up close and personal with all manner of cuddly creatures hoping to get a treat.

## Sweet Tooth Cravings

Kanom Waan Pa Prang $

The most famous Thai desserts vendor in Hua Hin, this stall usually sells out by noon. Especially recommended is the hard-to-find *khao fang* (jade-coloured millet in coconut milk).

Mae Lamiad $

This spot serves a dessert particularly prized in Phetchaburi, *kà·nŏm môr gaang* (custard made with palm sugar and coconut milk with fried shallots on top).

Pa Jua $

Lovers of mango sticky rice need look no further than this long-time Hua Hin vendor, who also offers sticky rice topped with durian. Try to go before noon.

## Explore

Kaeng Krachan National Park

Only an hour's drive from Hua Hin, this national park is the largest in Thailand. It also boasts more varieties of animals than any other park, including leopards and tapirs.

Khao Nang Panthurat National Park

This park close to Cha Am highlights a series of caves which hosts five different species of bats, as well as a type of lizard unique to the park.

Hua Hin Hills Vineyard

Try different kind of exploration at this vineyard, where guests can sample local wines, paint a wine label or even cycle the 3km bicycle trail.

## Western Eats

Ogen $$

Somehow, a great Israeli restaurant managed to find its way to Hua Hin, offering tasty vegetarian options like falafel, a rice-stuffed whole chicken and a wide range of mezze.

MERCEDESS/SHUTTERSTOCK ©

Leopard, Kaeng Krachan National Park

Brasserie de Paris $$$

This charming Hua Hin eatery sits right on the beach and provides typical French bistro favourites like chateaubriand, bouillabaisse and escargots. Save room for desserts, which change daily.

Andreas $$$

One of the most popular restaurants in Hua Hin, this spot next to Cicada Market is packed most days and nights. Wood-fired pizzas, lobster pasta and risottos are especially recommended.

Mirabelle $$

This Hua Hin delicatessen/bakery may be difficult to find but is worth the journey for its fluffy croissants, creamy cheeses and buckwheat crepes. Takeaway is also available.

1d+ Day Artist cafe $$

Expect all the things you'd find at a typical cafe – coffee, smoothies, sweets, pasta – but right on the beach in Pranburi.

Volcano Restaurant & Bar $$

One of the few quality pizzerias in Chumphon, this charming restaurant also hosts a great seaside view and cooks Thai food for the pizza- and pasta-averse.

**Scan to find more things to do in Hua Hin & the Upper Gulf online**

# PHUKET & THE ANDAMAN COAST

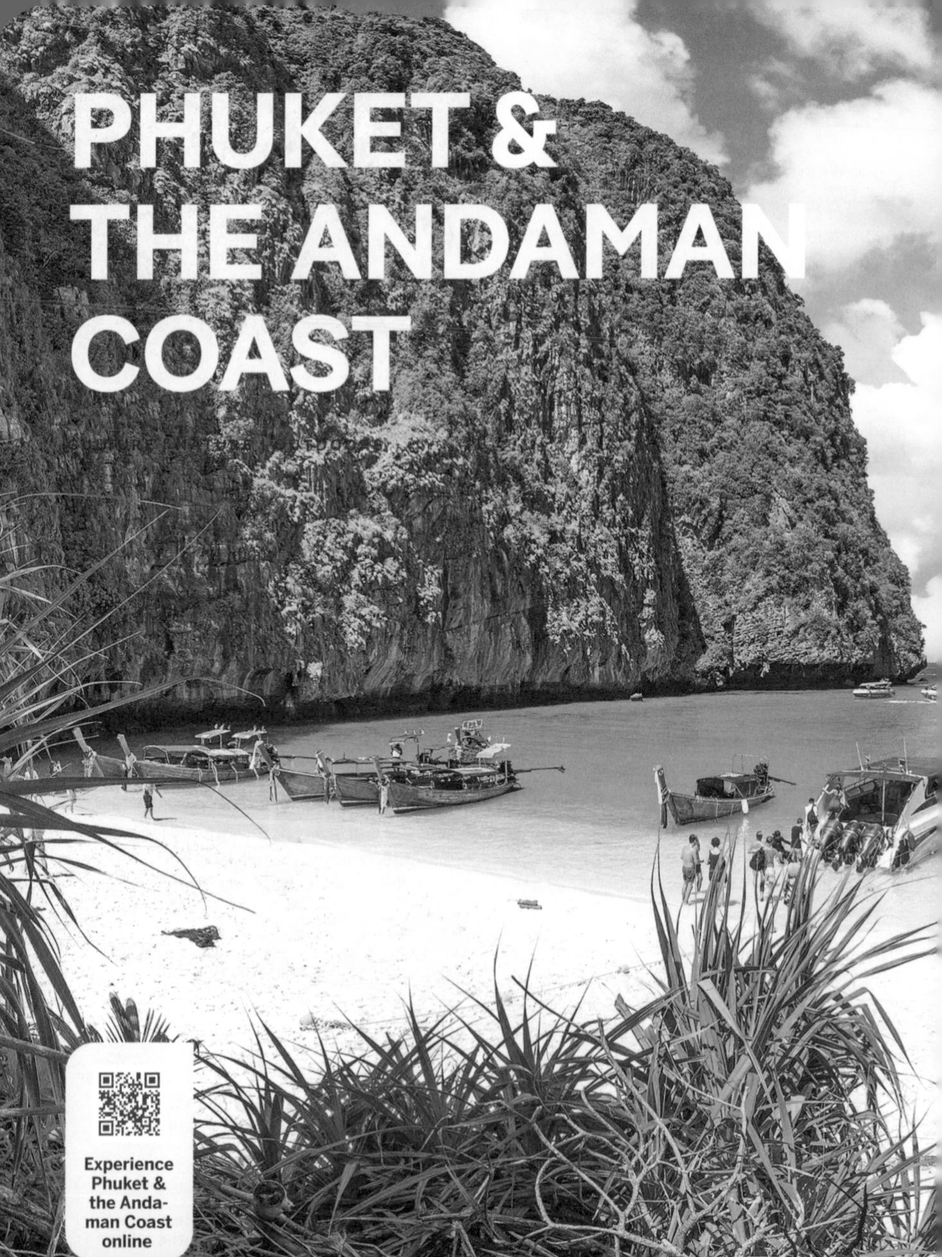
Experience Phuket & the Anda-man Coast online

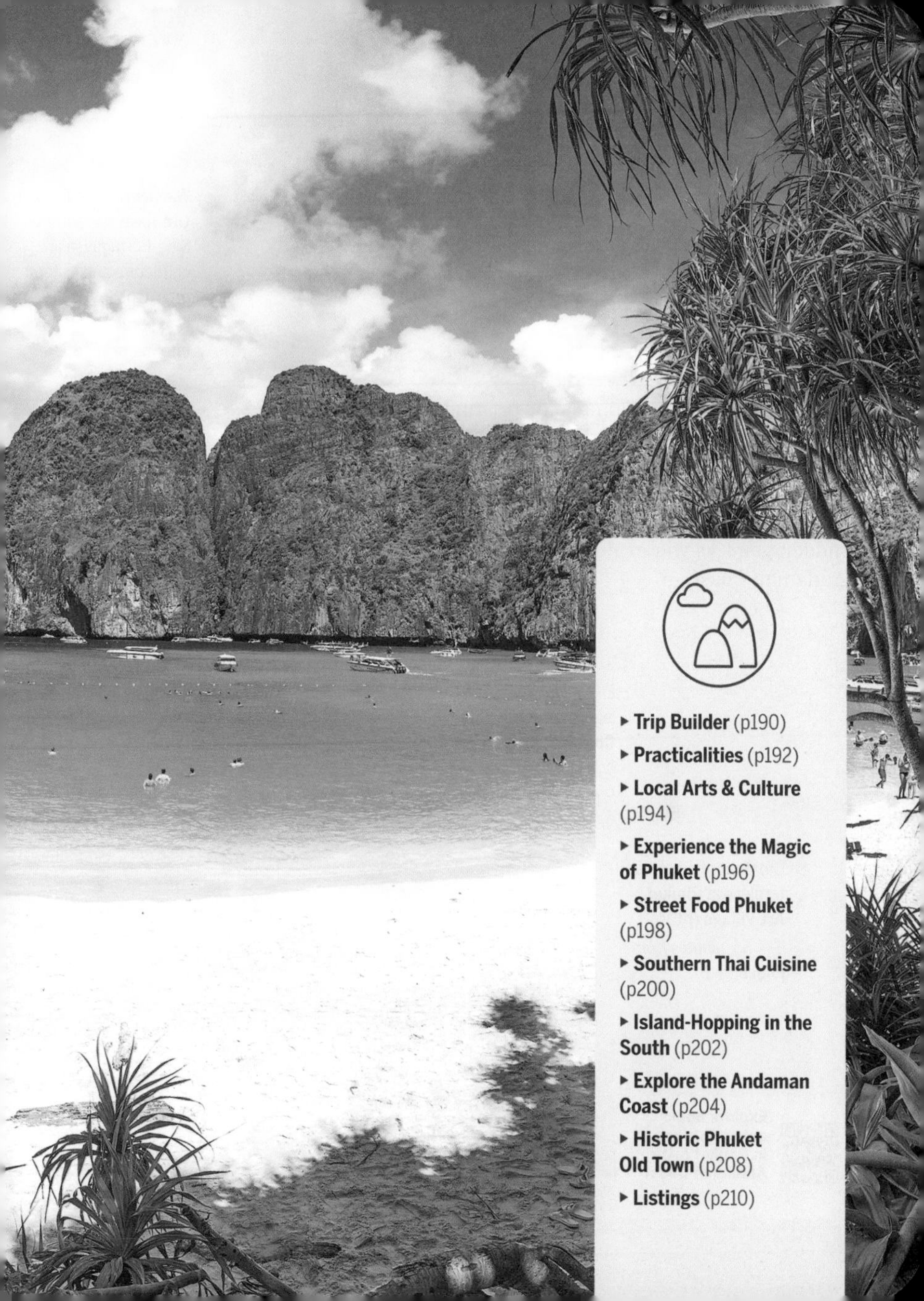

# PHUKET & THE ANDAMAN COAST

## Trip Builder

Although most famous for pristine beaches and jaw-dropping landscapes, Phuket and the Andaman Coast offer unique art and culture, along with culinary and outdoor adventures. Get off the beaten path and discover local charm, exceptional food and hidden gems as you explore Phuket and traverse the Andaman Coast.

Wander historic **Phuket Old Town** and admire Sino-Portuguese architecture and historic mansions (p208)
*1 hour from Phuket International Airport*

Enjoy a Burmese tea leaf salad at **Mingalar Coffee Shop** (p198)
*5 minutes from Phuket Old Town*

Create an original masterpiece at **Phuket Art Village** (p194)
*35 minutes from Phuket Town*

Go birdwatching at **Coral Island** (p202)
*15-minute speedboat ride from Rawai Beach*

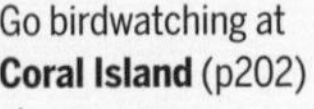

Bang Niang
Thap Lamu
Natai
Ban Khok Kloi
Ban Tha Chat Chai
*Andaman Sea*
Thalang
Patong
Phuket Town
Rawai
*Ko Lon*
*Ko Raya Yai*
*Ko Raya Noi*

**Explore bookable experiences in Phuket & the Andaman Coast**

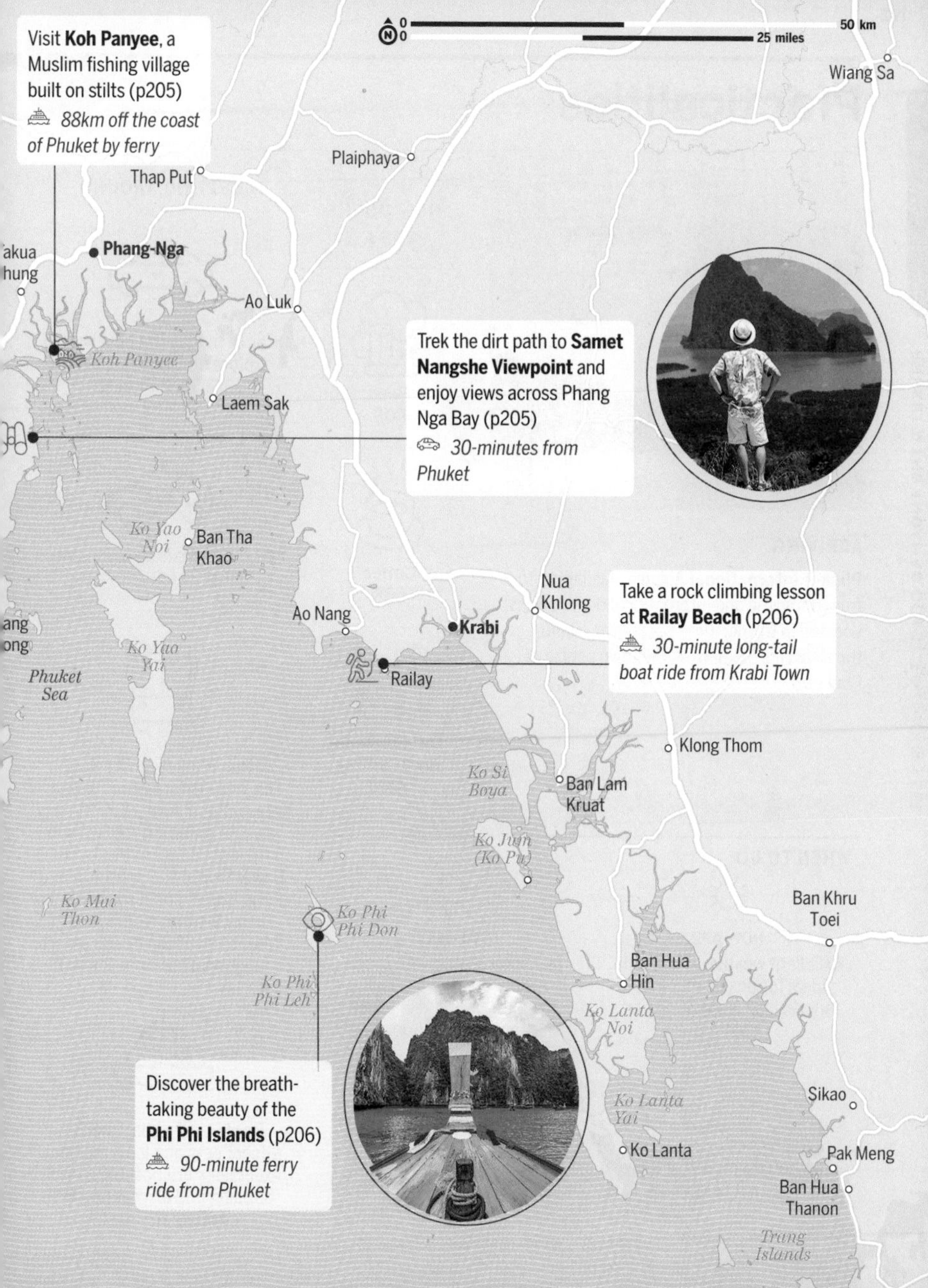

Visit **Koh Panyee**, a Muslim fishing village built on stilts (p205)
88km off the coast of Phuket by ferry
Trek the dirt path to **Samet Nangshe Viewpoint** and enjoy views across Phang Nga Bay (p205)
30-minutes from Phuket
Take a rock climbing lesson at **Railay Beach** (p206)
30-minute long-tail boat ride from Krabi Town
Discover the breath-taking beauty of the **Phi Phi Islands** (p206)
90-minute ferry ride from Phuket
0
50 km
0
25 miles
Wiang Sa
Plaiphaya
Thap Put
Phang-Nga
Ao Luk
Koh Panyee
Laem Sak
Ko Yao Noi
Ban Tha Khao
Nua Khlong
Ao Nang
Krabi
Railay
Ko Yao Yai
Phuket Sea
Klong Thom
Ko Si Boya
Ban Lam Kruat
Ko Jum (Ko Pu)
Ban Khru Toei
Ko Mui Thon
Ko Phi Phi Don
Ban Hua Hin
Ko Phi Phi Leh
Ko Lanta Noi
Ko Lanta Yai
Sikao
Ko Lanta
Pak Meng
Ban Hua Thanon
Trang Islands

# Practicalities

IAMDOCTOREGG/SHUTTERSTOCK ©

### ARRIVING

**Phuket International Airport** Has flights to/from domestic and international destinations. Located in the northern part of the island, the airport is 32km from the town centre of Phuket.

### HOW MUCH FOR A

**Beer 80B**

**Coffee 60B**

**Taxi (airport–town centre) 700B**

### WHEN TO GO

**NOV–APR**
Excellent weather conditions ideal for beach activities, snorkelling, swimming and boating.

**OCT–MAY**
Monsoon season with rough water conditions, cooler temperatures and cheaper accommodation.

**APR**
The hottest month of the year in Thailand, but also the month that celebrates Songkran, the Thai New Year.

### GETTING AROUND

**Car** Driving is the best way to explore off-the-beaten-path places in Phuket.

**Taxi** Public taxis are available in Phuket 24 hours per day.

**Bus** Phuket Smart Bus carries visitors from Phuket International Airport all the day along a standard route down the west coast of Phuket to Rawai Pier at the southern end of the island. Local *sŏrng·tăa·ou* carry visitors from Phuket Town to all of the beach resort neighbourhoods in Phuket.

**Boat** Private boat charter, speedboats and long-tail boat excursions are best for island-hopping and discovering the Andaman Coast.

## EATING & DRINKING

**Kôw gaang** refers to a hole-in-the-wall local restaurant with food that has already been made and is served in metal trays or pots. Pick what you like by pointing at the trays; dishes can be served with or without rice. These restaurants are a fun dining experience and a good introduction to local Thai food. Dishes generally start at an affordable 50B.

Phuket has a thriving coffee culture, with old-style *kopitiams*, local coffee roasters and Instagrammable cafes on every corner. Try **Hock Hoe Lee**, Phuket's original coffee roaster since 1958 with in-store shopping on Ranong Rd in Phuket Town, and a cafe on Viset Rd in Rawai.

**Must-try Phuketian specialities** Cham-Cha Local Food Court (p199)

## INFORMATION

A tourist information centre can be found on Thalang Rd in Phuket Old Town.

## WHERE TO STAY

Each major beach destination of Phuket has its own character. Choose the one that best matches your needs and preferences, and you are guaranteed to have a wonderful time.

| Town/Village | Pros/Cons |
|---|---|
| Bang Tao | Close to the airport, with lots of restaurants and hotel choices, but accommodation can be expensive here. Nice option for those wanting all-inclusive accommodation. |
| Kata/Karon | Beach towns within walking distance to restaurants, hotels and activities, but far from the town centre. Best for beach bums and nature lovers. |
| Phuket Old Town | In the heart of the city, with lots of restaurants and historic sites, and easy access to public transportation. Good jumping point for exploring the rest of Phuket. |
| Rawai | Charming fishing village with plenty of restaurants and tourist activities, but accommodation choices are limited. Rawai is sleepy at night. |

## MONEY

Money changers are readily available in Phuket, and major international credit cards and debit cards are widely accepted around the island.

# 37 Local Arts & CULTURE

ART | CULTURE | GALLERIES



Discover the diversity of Phuket's local art scene while visiting a variety of eclectic galleries, participate in online art workshops, or create a unique masterpiece in a pottery class. Let your inner artist shine and the creative juices flow with endless options for art and culture classes in Phuket.



### How to

**Getting around** Local buses, known as *sŏrng·tăa·ou,* run from 6am to 6pm daily. Buses leave Phuket Town every 30 minutes and visit all major destinations on the island.

**Recommendation** Stroll Phuket Old Town and discover the street art on Phang Nga, Thalang, Krabi and Dibuk Rds.

**Highlight** Visit **I Mon Art Gallery** on Phang Nga Rd in Phuket Old Town to observe a Thai master printmaker at work.

Although Phuket is wildly popular for its energetic nightlife, incredible beaches and delicious street food, the booming art scene on the island should not be ignored. With creative flair and a unique aesthetic, the local art scene in Phuket continues to grow rapidly. Whether you're a refined art connoisseur, looking for an imaginative, quirky painting or hoping to take a class, the Phuket art scene delivers.

If you're looking to get up close and personal to or create a masterpiece with local Thai artists, make your way to southern Phuket.

The Rawai neighbourhood is home to the eclectic **Phuket Art Village**, a contemporary arts and cultural community centre which features several art galleries and studios, each with their own style and artist. The artists here are passionate and friendly, hap-py to engage in conversation

and offer art workshops and private classes in a variety of mediums. Most of the art displayed within the Phuket Art Village is for sale, but even if you don't make a purchase, you're welcome to stay and hang out for the day.

There's a treehouse-style coffee shop at the entrance to the village which serves up basic coffee drinks and tea, and provides an ideal vantage point for watching the artists create their works throughout the day.

Aspiring ceramists can try their hand at **Art Studio Green Grey**, or visit **Rawai Ceramic Cafe** to learn clay modelling and ceramic hand-painting while enjoying coffee beverages and home-made cakes.

## Living Art Gallery

Located in the cosmopolitan neighbourhood of Cherngtalay, the Living Art Gallery, a lifestyle gallery at Blue Tree Phuket, is a creative hub which supports up-and-coming local Thai artists. The unique gallery is open daily to the public and exhibits one-of-a-kind paintings, ceramics, home decor and fashion from young Thai artists. The gallery also offers online art workshops and facilitates an online marketplace for artists to display and sell their work. The Living Art Gallery curates the annual **Thailand Art Festival** which is a vibrant showcase of art, culinary experiences, live music, discussion panels and masterclasses.

■ **By Sornchat Aom Krainara,** *owner of the Living Art Gallery and curator of the Thailand Art Festival, Instagram @thelivingartthailand*

**Above** The Living Art Festival, Phuket

PIYAWAT NANDEENOPPARIT/SHUTTERSTOCK ©

# Experience the Magic of Phuket

GET TO KNOW THE OTHER SIDE OF PHUKET

For decades, Phuket has been thrust into the spotlight for all of the wrong reasons. Often referred to as a tourist trap full of visitors looking to party hard, the island has been branded with an unfavourable reputation. While there is some seediness that still lingers, there is more to the Pearl of the Andaman than meets the eye.

**Left** Chinese temple, Phuket. **Middle** Fruit market, Phuket Old Town. **Right** Sunrise, Phuket

## Phuket's Spirit

Phuket has had its fair share of drama on the international scale. The island has made headlines for pristine, yet overcrowded beaches, bold nightlife, jet-ski scams, and over-the-top luxury lifestyle offerings. For years, Phuket has had the reputation of being a hedonistic playground in the form of the legendary Bangla Rd. It's the island's nightlife hotspot where everything is in your face, cheap and honestly, just a bit sleazy. In recent years, the island has started to change for the better. There is still magic to experience in Phuket, it just depends on how hard you are willing to look for it.

To know Phuket, the real Phuket, is to love it. Phuket is not Patong – it's not aggressive or abrasive. In fact, the real Phuket oozes historical charm, is home to friendly locals and showcases hidden gems and off-the-beaten-path locations. The true spirit of Phuket can be found in the small alleyways of Phuket Old Town, the massive pineapple plantations in the northern part of the island, and the discreet fishing villages scattered up and down the east coast where locals greet you with a wave and a trademark Thai smile.

## Natural Beauty

Move away from the tourist destination and head off the path to experience the magic of Phuket. It's in these hidden places nestled all over the island that it is possible to discover an island of yesteryear. There are still picturesque areas of Phuket that aren't developed and nature is abundant. It is at these places where you'll get to know another side of Phuket.

CHRISPICTURES/SHUTTERSTOCK ©

NADYA CHETAH/SHUTTERSTOCK ©



This other side of Phuket is one of natural beauty, one that is home to villages hundreds of years old, and it's a place where tradition, culture and religion blend in harmony. One of the most interesting aspects of Phuket is its diversity. Wander down any one street in Phuket Town, and it's possible to see a Chinese shrine, a mosque and a church all within steps of one another. Known as a melting pot since the tin mining days, Phuket's diversity is celebrated all over the island.

> Phuket oozes historical charm, is home to friendly locals and showcases hidden gems and off-the-beaten-path locations.

## Local Charm

To experience the real magic of Phuket, take the time to mingle with the local people. Give a friendly nod and say hello, because despite any language barriers, the people will acknowledge you and do their best to communicate in any way they can. Wander the streets, shop at the fresh markets, visit a hilltop shrine, explore one of the island's remote, secret beaches. Follow the dirt paths and don't be afraid to get lost because it's on these lesser-known paths where you will discover a softer, gentler side to Phuket.

Once you have met the real Phuket, there is nothing left to do but love it. The Pearl of the Andaman Sea is naturally stunning, possesses so much culture, boasts a unique history and is loaded with local charm.

### Spirit of Phuket

Behind the chaos of Bangla Rd and Patong Beach, the true spirit of Phuket can be found in the island's rich history, its strong cultural heritage, and the eclectic mix of locals and expats that call Phuket home. While it's true that Phuket doesn't suit everyone's tastes, there's no better place in southern Thailand for a magical beach getaway seasoned with cultural and historical experiences.

# 38 Street Food PHUKET

RESTAURANTS | MARKETS | FOOD

There's more to Phuket than just beaches. In recent years, the island has become a culinary hotspot for those looking to indulge in creative cuisine. Whether you're looking to sample street food, try your luck with spicy southern Thai specialities, grab a roti on the go or slurp up a bowl of Hokkien-inspired noodles, Phuket offers up a medley of interesting cuisine.

DENIS COSTILLE/SHUTTERSTOCK ©

### How to

**Getting around** Phuket Old Town is best explored on foot. Start at the fresh market on Ranong Rd and head to Phang Nga, Thalang, Krabi and Dibuk roads to find the best street food.

**Recommendation** Visit **Lock Thien**, a food court at 173 Yaowarat Rd, to sample some real Phuket specialities, including *po pia sot* (fresh spring rolls).

**Highlight** Located on Soi Talat Sot south of the fresh market on Ranong Rd, **Mingalar Coffee Shop** is a Burmese teahouse serving sweet coffee and tea and delicious bites.

MOSAYMAY/SHUTTERSTOCK ©

## Foodie Tours

Dubbed a Creative City of Gastronomy by Unesco in 2015, Phuket boastss cuisine shaped by Thai, Chinese, Malay and Burmese influences as well as secret family recipes passed down and adapted over the years. Throw in a splash of coconut milk and a spoonful of spicy curry paste from the south, and the end result is myriad flavours sure to please any palate.

One of the best ways to discover Phuket's diverse cuisine offerings is by embarking on a food tour. A food tour offers the opportunity to take a bite out of all of the best cuisine in Phuket as well as discover local restaurants and hole-in-the-wall eateries not usually known to tourists. Here the cuisine is authentic and as rich in flavour as any five-star restaurant.

A Chef's Tour provides an insider's look into Phuket's eclectic culinary scene. Led by a local foodie, the adventurous tour takes you to the streets of Phuket Old Town and the city's largest fresh market. Discover an array of local ingredients, breathe in the pungent aroma of freshly made curry paste and sample a few fresh spices. Then head out to tantalise your taste buds on tasty curries and wood-fired naan at a hidden Burmese teahouse, munch on freshly grilled meat satays dripping in peanut sauce, tuck your chopsticks into heaping bowls of Chinese noodles and devour an array of colourful, sticky Thai sweets.

## Eating Local

As you eat your way around Phuket, make sure to try the truly local dishes of *mee hokkien* (big yellow noodles served in a brown gravy with red pork, squid and vegetables), *kà·nŏm jeen* (a rice noodle served with the curry of your choice and topped with an array of condiments including pickled veggies, morning glory and thinly sliced banana leaves) and *por pia* (fresh spring rolls stuffed with red pork, shrimp, crispy pork, lettuce, turnip and slathered in a sweet brown sauce). Don't miss *o taw* (small stir-fried oysters with flour, crispy pork and taro), the famous *gaeng massaman* (a savoury beef curry cooked with peanuts, potatoes and chopped onions in a rich coconut cream sauce), and finish off with *a-pong* (a traditional Phuket snack of fried crepe made from rice flour, coconut milk, water and sugar). *A-pong* is crispy on the outside, soft on the inside and a scrumptious sweet snack for any time of the day.

**Left** Lock Tien food court.
**Bottom left** *A-pong*, Thai crepe

### The Original Phuket Foodie

Discover culinary gems and recommendations from one of the original Phuket foodies!

**Go Benz** Don't miss the restaurant's signature dried rice porridge with pork. It's worth waiting in the long queue!

**Hong Khao Tom Pla** Famous for its fish porridge; the owner-cook is loud and stern with his staff but the result is outstanding Thai-Chinese food.

**Go Song Khon Boran** Choose your dish from pictures on the wall and watch the married duo cook; try the stir-fried minced pork with salted fish.

**Cham-Cha Local Food Court** The best fresh spring rolls in town; make sure to slurp up a bowl of the noodle soup with pork ribs. Cool off with *o-aew* (ice with flavoured syrup).

**Roti Taew Nam** The roti is cooked on a massive charcoal flat pan. Don't forget to ask for a heaping bowl of the tender beef curry to dip it in!

■ **By Warin Mueanklew,** *known as Toon Kouran, Phuket local expert and tour guide, Instagram @toonkouran*

# Southern
# THAI CUISINE

**01 Kôw mòk gài**
Yellow rice and chicken flavoured with dried spices and turmeric cooked in the same pot. Served with coriander, cucumbers, a sweet sauce and fried shallots.

**02 Môo hong**
Pork belly braised in a sweet paste of black peppercorns, garlic and coriander root, and then stewed with star anise, oyster sauce and dark soy sauce. Popular in southern Thailand.

**03 Khua Kling**
A super spicy dry curry made from chilli, lemongrass, turmeric, garlic, salt, galangal and shrimp paste. The meat is roasted with curry paste and kaffir lime leaves.

**04 Gaang sôm pla**
A sour fish curry made of salt, shallots, turmeric, shrimp paste, dried chillies and boiled into a soup with bamboo shoots and fish. It's a spicy acquired taste!

**05 Kôw yam**
An aromatic rice salad featuring the colours of the rainbow, *kôw yam* consists of herbs, vegetables, dried shrimp, and roasted coconut mixed with lemongrass, chillies, kaffir lime leaves, turmeric and covered with *nam badu* sauce.

### 06 Gaang sataw

Green stink beans stir-fried with beef, pork, chicken or seafood, shrimp paste and curry paste. The result is a super spicy delicious concoction of authentic southern Thai flavours.

### 07 Moo tod kratiem

Deep-fried pork with garlic and black pepper served with coriander and a sweet chilli dipping sauce. Generally served as a side dish.

### 08 Gaang tai pla

Thick fish curry made from galangal, chillies, kaffir leaves, turmeric, fermented shrimp paste, bamboo shoots, eggplant and grilled fish. It is a spicy, salty curry.

### 09 Nám prík gûng sèe·ap

A spicy sauce made of dried shrimp, fermented shrimp paste, chillies, garlic, lime juice, fish sauce and sugar pounded in a mortar. Generally served as a dipping sauce for fresh vegetables.

### 10 Kà·nŏm jeen

Vermicelli rice noodles served with a curry of choice, usually fish curry or crab curry, and eaten together with a variety of fresh and pickled vegetables. A wonderfully spicy breakfast dish.

# 39 ISLAND-HOPPING in the South

**ISLANDS | NATURE | OUTDOORS**

Southern Thailand boasts a large number of islands off its coast. While Phuket is the largest, there are other lesser-known islands off the southwest well worth exploring. Whether you are looking for an idyllic beach to laze on, a stunning snorkelling destination, or an adventure on the Andaman Sea by boat, a day trip to these islands provides the perfect escape.



## How to

**Getting there** Bon, Coral and Racha islands are easily accessible via speedboat or long-tail boat. Speedboat charters leave from Chalong Pier, and long-tail boats from Rawai Beach. Prices for long-tail boats start at 1500B for the day, while speed-boat prices vary. Visit any of the street agencies on Chalong Pier for speedboat pricing.

**Highlight** Don't miss spotting the local hornbill population in the late afternoon on Coral Island.

There is plenty of outdoor fun to add to your Phuket experience. Exploring the islands off the southwest coast is the best way to escape from the crowds, reconnect with nature, have a great snorkelling experience, and enjoy the lesser-known beaches Phuket is so famous for.

**Bon Island** is a two-minute long-tail boat ride from Rawai Beach, Phuket's most southern point. The jungle-clad island has two picturesque beaches for spending a lazy day or frolicking in the water. Make sure to eat at **Bon Restaurant**, an idyllic spot of wooden *salas* with thatched roofs that serves up fresh seafood and Thai favourites such as pineapple fried rice with prawn.

**Coral Island** is famous for its different shades of turquoise water and shallow snorkelling sites. The island is postcard perfect with swaying palm trees and lush vegetation. There are two main beaches on Coral Island – Long Beach and Banana Beach. Long Beach offers beach bungalows to rent and is popular for water-sports

H-AB PHOTOGRAPHY/SHUTTERSTOCK ©



### Magical Koh Kaew

Explore magical Koh Kaew, home to Buddhist monks living a simple life and protecting an imprint of Buddha's foot and a Golden Buddha statue. Trek through the jungle interior to discover a chedi and various religious shrines. Located 4km from Rawai Beach, **Koh Kaew,** often referred to as **Buddha Island**, has a small, white-sand beach and a beautiful Buddha statue adorned by naga (mythical snakes) that wind around the statue's platform at the northern tip of the island. Koh Kaew is an interesting island to stop off at on an island-hopping tour.

activities. Banana Beach caters to tourists with beach chairs, restaurants, a beach club and activities throughout the day. To enjoy all that Banana Beach has to offer, book a tour from any street agency or enquire at your hotel.

Best reached by speedboat, **Racha Island** is located 12km off the southwest coast of Phuket. Popular for scuba diving due to its clear water and visibility, Racha Island is home to three luxury resorts and two outstanding beaches. Definitely visit the rocky east-facing cove of Ter Bay for a cocktail, and enjoy the white sand and crystal clear water of Patok Beach.

**Above** Patok beach, Racha Island

# 40 Explore the ANDAMAN COAST

BEACHES | NATURE | OUTDOORS

The Andaman Coast is postcard perfect with swaying palm trees, white-sand beaches, turquoise water, lush jungle and towering limestone karsts. The spectacular scenery provides the backdrop to outdoor adventures, leisure activities and a relaxed tropical holiday in a beautiful destination. To make the most of the Andaman Coast, visit these must-see recommendations.

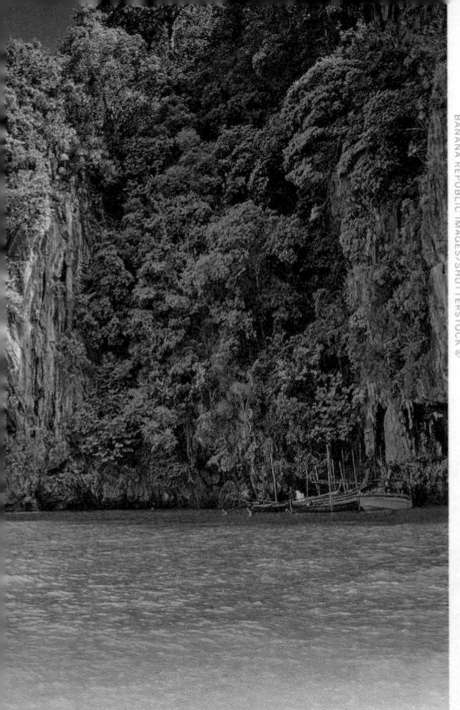

BANANA REPUBLIC IMAGES/SHUTTERSTOCK ©

## How to

**Getting there** The Andaman Coast is easily accessible by plane, boat, bus and minivan. During the wet season, from May to November, boat travel is less frequent due to dangerous waves. Day trips to Phang Nga Bay and the Phi Phi Islands can be booked at all street tour agencies.

**Getting around** The Andaman Coast is easy to explore on foot, but the Krabi International Airport and the main bus terminal are far from the town centre. Taxis, motorcycle taxis and local *sŏrng·tăa·ou* run from the main bus terminal to the town centre and are easily flagged down.

LUCY.BROWN/SHUTTERSTOCK ©



## Phang Nga Bay

Picturesque Phang Nga Bay with its emerald green water and limestone karst formations is wonderful for boating and sea kayaking. The two most famous spots located within the bay are James Bond Island and Koh Panyee.

Made famous by the 1974 James Bond movie, *The Man with the Golden Gun*, **James Bond Island** (Koh Tapu in Thai), is a rocky pinnacle located next to Koh Ping Ghan. The latter has a small beach and several small caves to explore.

**Koh Panyee** is a remarkable island. The Muslim fishing village is built out over the water on stilts and circles massive limestone karsts. There are several souvenir shops and restaurants here as well as a mosque, health centre and floating football pitch. Most of the islanders work in the tourism industry or are fishers.

### Jungle Views

Nestled into a hilltop covered with rainforest, **Samet Nangshe Viewpoint** offers impressive 180-degree panoramic views over Phang Nga Bay, including small gumdrop islands and towering limestone karsts. The viewpoint can be reached by a steep 20-minute hike up a dirt path.

## Krabi

The true gem of the Andaman Coast, Krabi has breathtaking scenery framed by ragged limestone karsts, white-sand beaches, dense jungle, waterfalls, caves, exotic wildlife and over 100

**Left** James Bond Island (Koh Tapu).
**Above** Long-tail boats, Koh Panyee

islands to explore. Laid-back, less developed and without the crowds of the Phi Phi Islands or Phuket, Krabi is a relaxing holiday destination with a variety of leisure activities for the whole family.

The bustling city centre of **Ao Nang** has a variety of hotels and restaurants to choose from, and is a short walk to **Noppharat Thara Beach**. The more remote **Railay** (also spelt Rai Leh) and **Tonsai Beaches** can be reached via long-tail boat and are famous for their serene atmospheres, jungle settings and expansive rock climbing routes which cater to beginners and families. One of the most reputable rock climbing centres on Railay Beach is **Tex Rock Climbing**, which offers half-day courses all the way up to three-day courses.

Head to isolated **Tubkaek Beach** to enjoy powdery white sand, shallow waters and stunning views of islands dotted across the Andaman Sea. From Tubkaek Beach, it's easy to access the **Dragon Crest Mountain** trail. Also

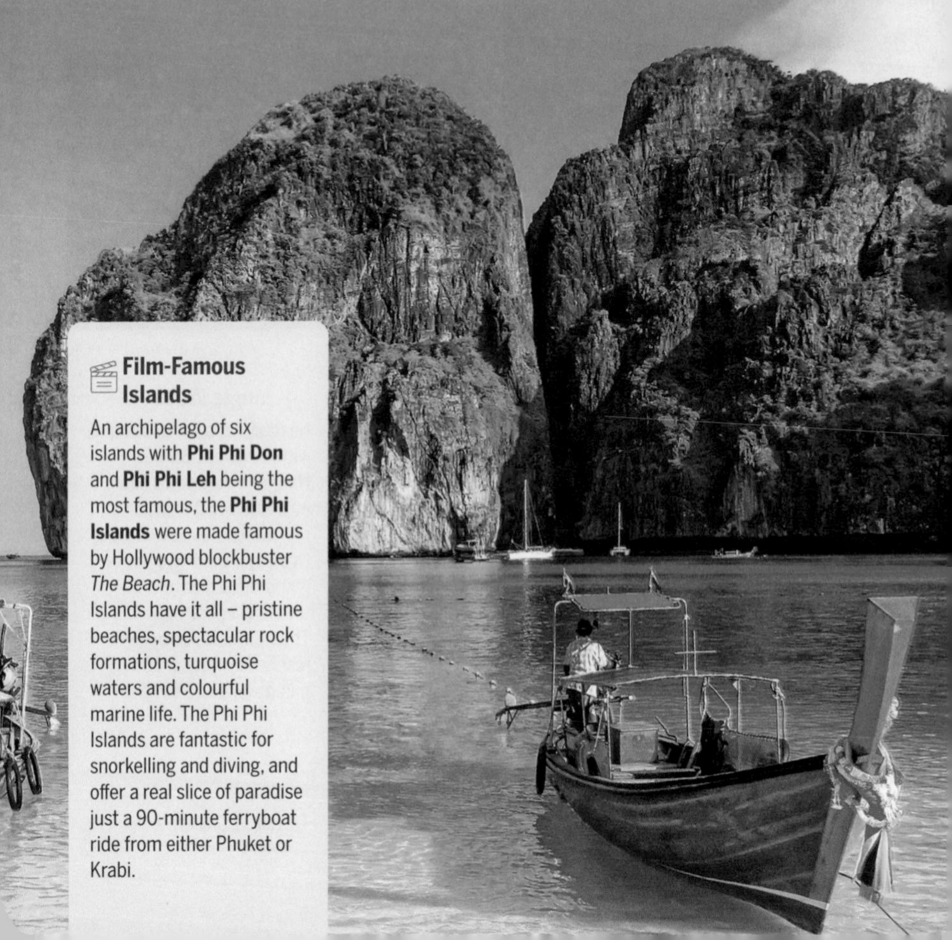

### Film-Famous Islands

An archipelago of six islands with **Phi Phi Don** and **Phi Phi Leh** being the most famous, the **Phi Phi Islands** were made famous by Hollywood blockbuster *The Beach*. The Phi Phi Islands have it all – pristine beaches, spectacular rock formations, turquoise waters and colourful marine life. The Phi Phi Islands are fantastic for snorkelling and diving, and offer a real slice of paradise just a 90-minute ferryboat ride from either Phuket or Krabi.

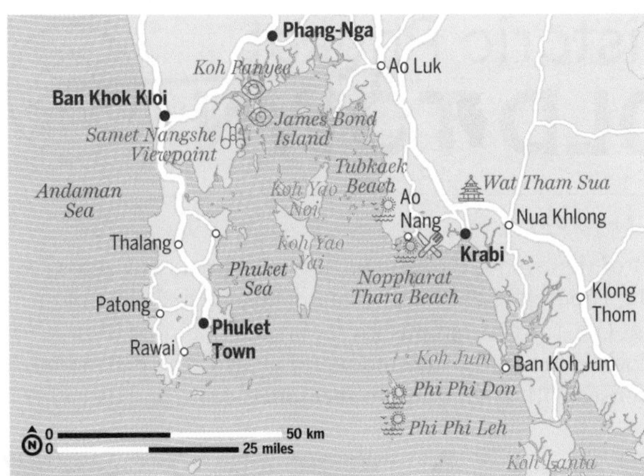


**Left** Maya Bay, Phi Phi Leh



known as Khao Ngon Nak or Hang Nak, the hiking trail winds through a lush forest and offers a sensational vantage point over Krabi. Advanced hikers will enjoy the 8km hike, while beginners can still get in on the action by taking the 4km route from the starting point to the top viewing point. You can hike the Dragon Crest Mountain trail without a guide, but there are several tour operators at the main beach road in Ao Nang that offer packages.

Visit laid-back **Krabi Town** to catch a glimpse of daily life. A busy market centre with a river filled with fishing boats, Krabi has its own local charm. The **night market** on Friday, Saturday and Sunday is worth visiting for great street food and small souvenirs, and **Wat Tham Sua** (Tiger Cave Temple) offers panoramic views over the city and the Andaman Sea.

There are lots of islands to explore off the coast of Krabi like Koh Poda, Chicken Island, Tup Island and Phranang Cave Beach. However, most travellers head further south to Koh Lanta and Koh Jum.

With its long coastline and dozens of beaches, **Koh Lanta** is a favourite. The island caters to all budgets, and is popular for its long-tail boat tours, scuba diving, snorkeling and a wide variety of outdoor hippie shacks that function as reggae bars. Make a point to visit **Lanta Old Town**, also known as Sri Raya, which once served as a commercial port for Arabic and Chinese trading vessels sailing between Phuket, Penang and Singapore. Modern-day Lanta Old Town is a sleepy village that oozes rustic charm.

**Koh Jum** is a small island with nine beaches to explore. The beaches in the southern part of the island can be easily reached by scooter. The northern beaches are more off the beaten path and provide a sense of adventure in reaching them as there are many gravel roads to cross. Life moves at a slower pace on Koh Jum, and the island is usually void of crowds, so it's the perfect spot to visit if you are hoping for a quieter holiday. The island also has some great snorkelling spots. Head to **Ban Koh Jum**, the biggest village on the island, to buy souvenirs or visit a travel agency to sort out the next stop on your itinerary.

# 41 Historic Phuket OLD TOWN

ARCHITECTURE | CULTURE | HISTORY

The historical heart of the island, Phuket Old Town is spread out across Thalang, Phang Nga, Krabi, Dibuk and Yaowarat roads. The true melting pot of the island's culture, Phuket Old Town is famous for its brightly painted Sino-Portuguese shophouses, lively atmosphere and old-world charm. The district is an amazing feast for the senses with something to see, touch, taste or experience on every corner.

DENIS COSTILLE/SHUTTERSTOCK ©

### How to

**Getting around** Phuket Old Town is best explored on foot. Phang Nga, Krabi, Thalang, Yaowarat and Dibuk roads make up the heart of the old town, and are all within close proximity of each other.

**Recommendation** Visit **Bookhemian**, an arty cafe located at 61 Thalang Rd, for a refreshing beverage or a bite to eat while exploring Phuket Old Town.

**Highlight** Don't miss the **Sunday Walking Street Market**, known as Lard Yai, that takes place every Sunday from 4pm on Thalang Rd.

TAYAWEE SUPAN/SHUTTERSTOCK ©

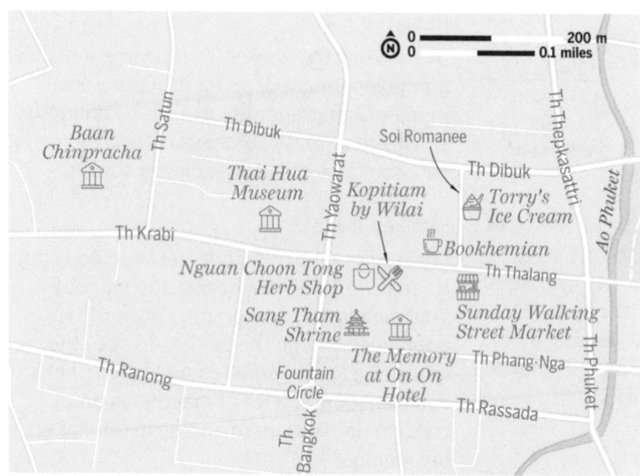




**Left** Soi Rommanee.
**Bottom left** Sang Tham Shrine

The best way to truly discover historic Phuket Old Town is on foot. Start on Phang Nga Rd, first visiting **Sang Tham Shrine**, known as the Shrine of Serene Light. Built in 1889 by a local Hokkien Chinese family, the shrine's walls are covered with murals showcasing old stories. Further down the road, stop and admire the Sino-Portuguese architecture of **The Memory at On On Hotel**.

On Thalang Rd, you will notice shops selling everything from batik fabric to bamboo brooms. Make a point to stop in at **Nguan Choon Tong Herb Shop**, the oldest Chinese herb shop in Phuket. Stock up on herbal remedies, or browse the compact wooden boxes that contain fruit, bark and roots which are all used for cleansing the body.

Don't miss the charming alley known as **Soi Romanee**. Originally a red-light district for Chinese labourers during the tin mining days, present-day Soi Romanee is lined with colourful Sino-Portuguese shophouses, and one of the best local coffee roasters in Phuket, **DouBrew Coffee**.

To explore more of Phuket Old Town's unique culture and history, drop into the **Thai Hua Museum** on Krabi Rd. Built in 1917, it's a Sino-Portuguese colonial mansion that was once the first Chinese-language school in Phuket. You'll learn a lot about the tin mining trade and the prominent figures from Chinese families who helped shape Phuket into the melting pot it is today.

## European-Chinese Intersections

Visit **Baan Chinpracha**, a gorgeous Sino-Colonial mansion on Krabi Rd that is still inhabited by the Tandavanitj family. Baan Chinpracha provides an outstanding glimpse into how wealthy families in Phuket used to live years ago. Most of the house is open to the public and filled with family heirlooms, original furniture that was imported from both China and Europe, and vintage Italian floor tiles. The open-air inner courtyard is breathtaking, and throughout the mansion you'll find old family photographs, clay cooking pots, vintage kerosene lamps and remnants of life from the past.

# Listings

BEST OF THE REST

## Local Favourite Eats

Kin-Kub-Ei $$

Kin-Kub-Ei translates in English to 'Eating with Auntie,' and dining here is a truly unique local experience. You'll come face to face with Auntie Tubtim, often only wearing a batik sarong, as she cooks up exceptional southern Thai specialities from age-old family recipes.

Tu Kab Khao $$

The elegant Tu Kab Khao restaurant is housed in a restored Sino-Portuguese building and serves up the best of Phuketian cuisine as well as southern Thai favourites. The extensive menu features almost 100 items to choose from. While the restaurant looks expensive from the outside, it is very affordable and makes for an excellent Phuket dining experience.

Krua Thara $$

A popular local favourite on Krabi's Nopparat Thara Beach, Krua Thara serves authentic Thai cuisine, fresh seafood cooked to perfection in a blend of spices, and simple dishes such as fried rice and stir-fried morning glory. The long-established restaurant is highly recommended by locals and delights tourists alike.

## Sunset Views

Promthep Cape

The iconic Promthep Cape is one of Phuket's most important landmarks and photographed locations. Located in the south of the island, the cape offers sweeping views of the Andaman Sea; ideal for watching the sunset.

Rang Hill

Overlooking the Phuket Town skyline, Rang Hill is popular among locals for its natural environment, smattering of local Thai restaurants, small temple and the occasional wild monkeys. Panoramic views are sweeping at sunset.

Monkey Trail

Located in Krabi Province between Ao Nang Beach and Pai Plong Beach, the Monkey Trail meanders through the jungle with openings through the bushes to spot the limestone karst known as Ao Nang Tower. You'll encounter a lot of macaques on this trail; do not feed them and be careful of your belongings!

## Market Highlights

Phuket Indy Market

Phuket Indy Market caters to a younger crowd, and is popular for its diverse food, live music and artist booths with handcrafted souvenirs. Held every Wednesday to Friday 4pm to 10.30pm.

Naka Market

Also known as the Phuket Weekend Market, Naka Market is a one-stop shop for souvenirs, quirky handmade items, clothing, household goods and delicious street

DENIS COSTILLE/SHUTTERSTOCK ©

Monkey Trail

Krabi Night Market

food. The large night bazaar is located near Phuket Town; open daily 4pm to 10pm.

Krabi Night Market

A walking street market located in the heart of Krabi Town; takes place every Friday, Saturday and Sunday. Visitors can find a wide range of products including arts and crafts from local artists, clothing and, of course, street food snacks.

##  Phuket Nightlife

Zimplex

A cool bar in Phuket Town, Zimplex serves molecular cocktails and is designed to look like a science laboratory. The Thai owner, known to everyone as Tom Funk, combines creative cocktails and shots with a stellar music soundtrack.

KUDO Beach Club

The only beach club located on Patong Beach with a swim-up bar, lounge area and on-site Italian restaurant. Expect great live tunes spun by international DJs, epic themed-parties, delicious food and excellent cocktails.

Tew Lay Bar

Located on Krabi's Railay East Beach, Tew Lay Bar has a vintage vibe. Made entirely of bamboo and thatch, the charming little bar is a great place to enjoy a cocktail, listen to reggae music and appreciate the views that look out into the mangrove forest.

**Scan to find more things to do in Phuket & the Andaman Coast online**

# KO SAMUI & THE LOWER GULF

BEACHES | NATURE | TRANQUILLITY

Experience Ko Samui & the Lower Gulf online

Cruise through extraordinary **Ang Thong National Marine Park** that consists of 42 islands (p224)

*1 hour from Lomprayah pier*

Ko Phaluai

# KO SAMUI & THE LOWER GULF

## Trip Builder

Sapphire blue waters, powder -soft sands and lush green jungles form the rich tapestry of Ko Samui and the lower gulf. The second-largest island in Thailand, sitting alongside siblings, hippie Ko Tao and vibing Ko Pha-Ngan, draws in travellers and revellers for its laid-back vibes, crystal clear waters and bohemian nightlife.

Take the family kayaking around the sun-dappled **Ko Taen** (p225)

\+ *20 miutesn from Lamai Beach*

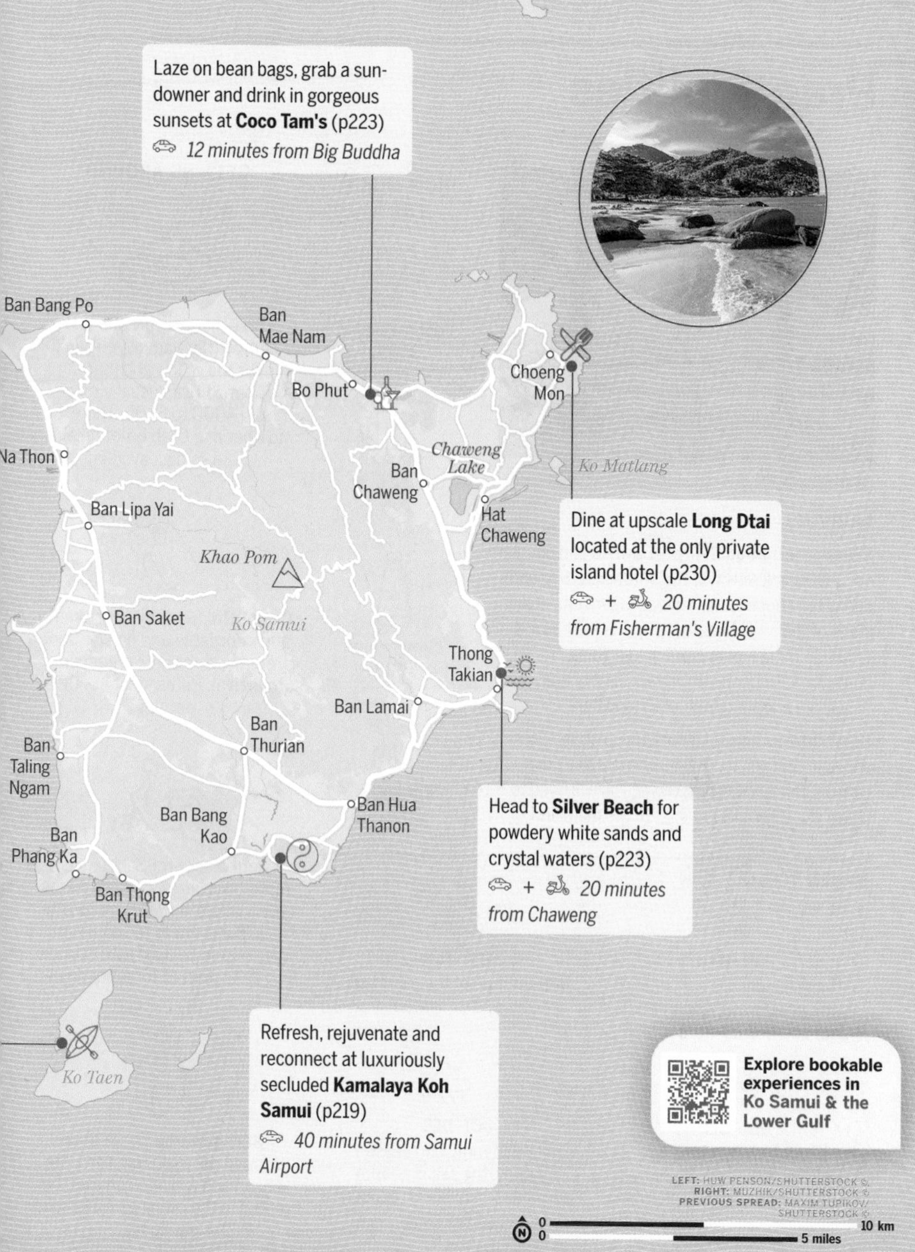


LEFT: HUW PENSON/SHUTTERSTOCK ©, RIGHT: MUZHIK/SHUTTERSTOCK ©, PREVIOUS SPREAD: MAXIM TUPIKOV/ SHUTTERSTOCK ©

# Practicalities

SUPAKIT_N/SHUTTERSTOCK ©

## ARRIVING

**Samui International Airport** Owned and operated by Bangkok Airways. The outdoor setting with dedicated shops under straw-fringed huts makes it one of the most beautiful airports in Thailand. Although most flights coming and going are domestic with Bangkok Airways, flights from Singapore and Hong Kong can land here.

**Surat International Airport** The cheaper alternative for getting to Ko Samui; more low-cost carriers can land here, however, you will need to take a car, then a ferry to get to the mainland.

## HOW MUCH FOR A

**Foot massage**
**350B**

**Singha beer**
**30B**

**Sunscreen**
**500B**

**Zip-lining**
**2000B**

## WHEN TO GO

**JAN–MAR**
High season; dry and sunny with great water conditions. Best and busiest time to visit.

**APR–JUN**
Hottest time of the year; falls around Songkran.

**JUL–SEP**
Weather is pleasant, but unpredictable with slight rain showers starting in September.

**OCT–DEC**
Height of monsoon season. It's rainy, the sea is choppy and water visibility is reduced significantly.

## GETTING AROUND

**Taxi** There is only one taxi company in Samui; you can't miss the yellow and maroon colours. Prices usually range from 400B to 800B. There is no Uber and Grab is not reliable here so best avoided.

**Car rental** Renting a car is easy and affordable and can be done from the airport or online prior to arrival. Rates start at 700B per day.

**Rent a scooter** Scooters or motorbikes are accessible almost everywhere, however, motorbike accidents are all too common; they should be used with caution. Prices start at 160B per day.

**Sŏrng·tăa·ou** These drive around the main ring road, are cheap and fun and can even be rented in the evenings for private transport.

## EATING & DRINKING

Southern Thai cuisine is chock-full of seafood and loads of heat. Try *gaeng som* (a sour soup made with tamarind, turmeric and fish; pictured above right) that can be found in most Thai restaurants. Muslim-style curry with roti is a must in the south, found in old shophouses or street carts. Roti with banana and condensed milk is the sweet version sold along the fisherman's Village walking street (pictured below right).

**Best goong sataw**
Krua Nai Nang (p231)

**Must-try ice cream**
Rossini's Ice Cream (p237)

## SUNSCREEN

Sunscreen in Thailand can cost a bomb, as much as US$20 per bottle. Stock up when packing and bring more than enough for your stay.

## MONEY

ATMS can easily be found on the main roads, in front of 7-Elevens or at shopping centres. Carrying cash is always a good idea for last-minute taxi rides or street food.

## CONNECT & FIND YOUR WAY

**Wi-fi** Readily available at most restaurants, cafes and even massage spots.

**Maps** Grab them at the airport on your way out from baggage claim.

## WHERE TO STAY

The almost circular shape of Samui can be explored in just over an hour, but the island is speckled with unique locations to stay that fit just about any budget.

| Town/Village | Pros/Cons |
|---|---|
| Bophut | Trendy area where you can stroll through the lively Fisherman's Village lined with restaurants, bars and shops of all kinds along the beach. |
| Lipa Noi | Remote beach located about 40 minutes from the centre filled with private villas and just a few restaurants. |
| Bangrak | Centrally located, near the big Buddha; not far from Chawaeng beach. Has affordable accommodation, international supermarkets, great bakeries and is near the pier. |
| Lamai | Loved by local expats; boasts a good mix of restaurants, clean beaches and affordable accommodations. There is a large French community here as well. |
| Choeng Mon | Not far from the airport; the area is dotted with luxury hotels and private villas, perfect for couples who want to laze all day. |
| Mae Nam | Quieter, more local and great for families; offers calm waves and activities like zip-lining, kitesurfing and Mae Nam walking street. |

# 42 Find Yourself in SAMUI

**MEDITATION | YOGA | DETOX**

It's not all sunsets and parties in Samui, the island is well known for its vast array of wellness resorts and yoga retreats that cater to any type of traveller. From open meditation workshops and mindful yoga classes to hardcore silent stays with monks, there is a little bit of everything for those seeking to reconnect with their inner selves.

PAULA BRONSTEIN/GETTY IMAGES ©

## How to

**Getting around** The best way get around Samui is by local taxi or a van service through your hotel. There is no Uber and Grab is scarce.

**When to go** Ko Samui is great for visiting all year. But if quiet is what you're seeking, April to August have fewer crowds and more tranquillity.

**Prices** The cost of meditative stays vary. Some are free of charge in exchange for daily chores or can be as much as US$270 per night for super luxe accommodations.

**Tip** Most resorts offer day passes for those who would like to experience luxurious amenities, lunch and relaxation.

ISLAMIC FOOTAGE/SHUTTERSTOCK ©

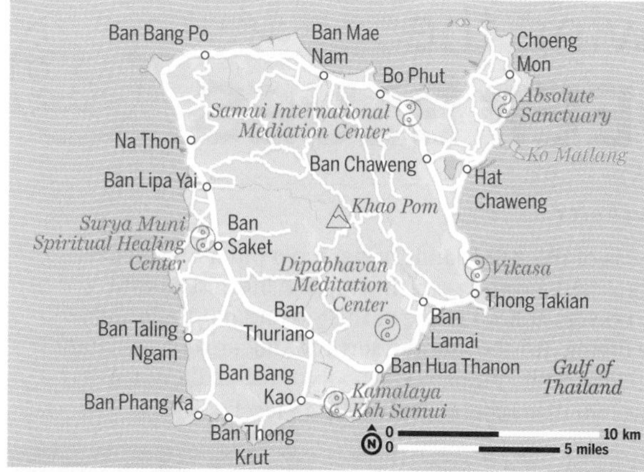


## Silent Samui

On top of a mountainous jungle lies **Dipabhavan Meditation Center**, a unique retreat that focuses on the practises of Dhamma, also known as the teachings of Buddha. The stay includes teachings conducted by the resident abbot or monks, highlighting techniques for mindfulness, concentration and vipassana meditation. Guests are encouraged to use the power of silence. The three-day course is free of charge, all set in an atmosphere meant to help find the 'place of light' as the name suggests.

## Spiritual Samui

If your spiritual journey desires deluxe accommodations, **Kamalaya Koh Samui** is for you. The wellness sanctuary and holistic spa, located on the southern coastline, is surrounded by lush greenery, discreet villas and peaceful pathways that offer a sweet escape from the hustle and bustle outside. Wellness services are the heart of the resort, which offers tailor-made programmes for everything from detoxification and weight management to managing stress and embracing change. The food is no afterthought, with good-for-you dishes available all day long.

## Serene Samui

Yoga enthusiasts can head to **Vikasa**, a stunning retreat that prides itself on the study of yoga amidst serene surroundings perfect for those seeking personal transformation. The holistic approach the hotel takes is eminent through its teachings all the way to its organic way of cooking. Yoga training courses are also taught here for those who would like to teach back in their home countries. This retreat offers day passes that give full access to its infinity pool, cafe, gardens and beach.

**Left** Kamalaya Koh Samui.
**Bottom left** Absolute Sanctuary

### Spiritual Healing

**Absolute Sanctuary**
Reboot in luxury at this award-winning, Moroccan-inspired wellness resort in a secluded area of Choeng Mon. Everything from detox programmes to fitness regimens, including a restaurant dedicated to nutritious meals.

**Surya Muni Spiritual Healing Center** This Lipa Noi centre is run by a loving septuagenarian who teaches and practises spiritual healing with the goal of connecting one with themselves. Daily sessions are available for those with little time.

**Samui International Mediation Center**
Spend three harmonious days learning the art of meditation by the resident monk who will guide you through the spiritual foundations of Buddhism. Meals and accommodations are included.

# 43 Diving the DEEP BLUES

DISCOVER | DIVING | BIODIVERSITY

The azure tempered seas of the gulf islands bring underwater aficionados from all over the world for its pristine waters, striking marine life and vibrant coral reefs. What some expert divers believe is one of the top and most affordable destinations in the world for diving, Ko Tao and the surrounding area has a handful of dreamy spots laced with giant granite pinnacles, schools of fish and even WWII shipwrecks while boasting over 70 dive schools geared for all levels.

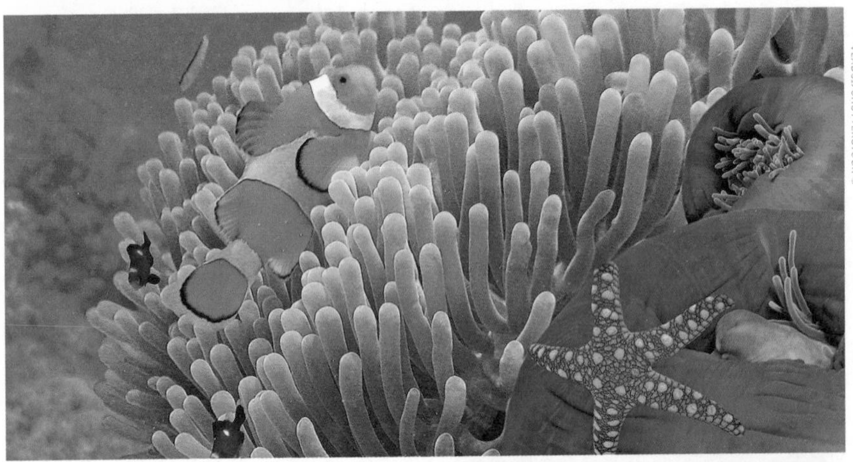

VLAD61/SHUTTERSTOCK ©

### How to

**Getting there** Take the Lomprayah high-speed catamaran (lomprayah.com) from Ko Samui or a private speedboat when booking with a dive school.

**When to go** Ko Tao's calm waters are great all year, however, the best time to visit is from May to September (April to May are clearest).

**How much** Basic dives from US$100, up to US$400 for PADI certification and US$900 for one-month instructor courses.

**Sundowners** Head to **Whitening** for a drink while catching the last rays of sun.

ISRA.HONG/SHUTTERSTOCK ©

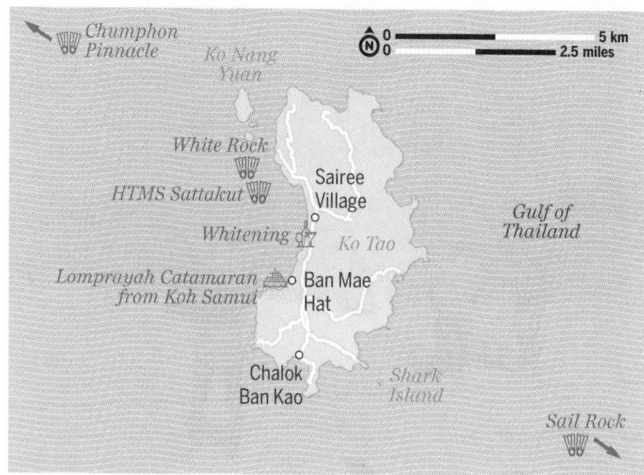


## Diving Around Ko Tao

One of the most commonly visited sites in the area, **White Rock** is just a few minutes from the Ko Tao pier. It is perfect for all levels and is loaded with marine life, including the occasional sea turtle. Night dives can also be done here, especially to see the pickhandle barracudas.

Although technically not in Ko Tao, **Sail Rock** is one of the most popular dive sites on the gulf and should not be missed. Just under a two-hour boat journey from the island, you'll know you've reached the site when you see a granite pinnacle ascending the surface. Underneath, you'll encounter a vertical cave known as the Chimney which exits about 18m deep, bringing spectacular aquatic life with schools of batfish, queenfish, snappers and smaller creatures.

To the west of Sairee beach on Ko Tao, the **HTMS Sattakut** shipwreck lies 18m below the surface. The artificial dive site is popular for advanced open divers looking to further their speciality courses. The wreck is known to have a variety of reef fish like yellowtail barracudas, Malabar groupers and, if you're really lucky, the occasional whale shark.

**Left** Anemone and clownfish, Ko Tao.
**Bottom left** *HTMS Sattakut*

### Best Dive Spots

**Sail Rock** A great dive spot for spotting giant trevally and groupers.

**Chumphon Pinnacle** Around 45 minutes from Ko Tao, this is one of my favourite dives spots where you might be lucky enough to spot whale sharks.

Overall **Ko Tao** has the main advantage of being close to most scuba diving locations, making it the ideal place for first-timers looking to be certified but who don't want to spend all day out at sea.

■ **By Darren Gaspari**, *PADI course director, owner and CEO of Aussie Divers (aussiediversphuket.com)*

# 44 Island-Hopping SEASCAPES

**BEACHES | DAY TRIPS | SUNSETS**

The Samui Archipelago in the lower gulf might be known for the indie side of Ko Tao and the infamous party island of Ko Pha-Ngan, but there is more than meets the eye. With over 60 islands, on top of the countless pristine beaches on the Samui mainland, here are some of the best to get your fill of soft white sands and idyllic palm-tree-fringed shorelines no matter where you turn.

PE3K/SHUTTERSTOCK ©

## How to

**Getting here** The best way to get to Ko Tao and Ko Pha-Ngan is with the Lomprayah high-speed boat (600B one way, 1½ hours) from Bangrak Pier.

**When to go** January to March is the best season for snorkelling, diving, hiking and tanning. July to September has fewer crowds and better deals.

**Tips** Boat rides can be choppy and unpredictable, so keep a stash of motion sickness pills handy.

**Visit** Hin Ta and Hin Yai (grandpa and grandma rocks) in Ko Samui have a striking resemblance to male and female genitalia and are popular with locals.

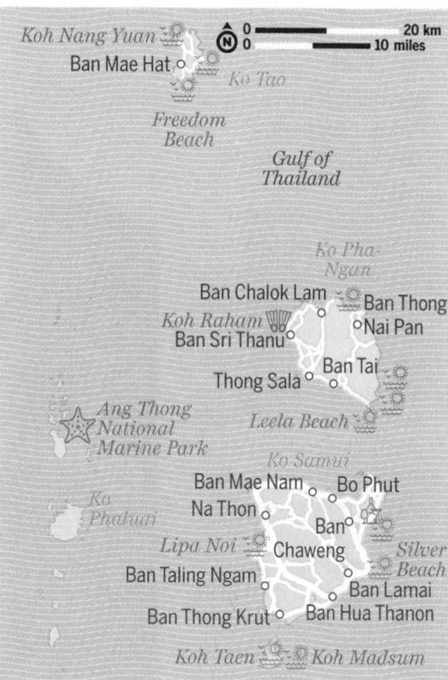


## Ko Samui

Sunbathe at stunning spots like dreamy **Silver Beach**, a stone's throw from the sometimes congested **Chawaeng**, with its crystal clear waters dotted with boulders of all sizes where small fish swim at your feet. A little further down is family-friendly **Choeng Mon** beach, a fan favourite for its powdery sands, calm waters and restaurants lining the 1km stretch. Sunset seekers should head to quiet **Lipa Noi** beach for its breathtaking views and shallow shorelines or to buzzing **Bo Phut** beach for rays and sundowners at **Coco Tam's** beach bar.

## Ko Pha-Ngan

The island might have a rep for all-night parties but there is a peaceful side that is dotted

**Above left** Lipa Noi beach.
**Left** Coco Tam's, Bo Phut

with hidden beaches and green escapes. Skip the infamous **Haad Rin** and head next door to **Leela Beach**, for its photo-friendly beach swings and crystal clear water. About 3km further north is **Haad Yuan**, harder to reach but completely worthy of its rocky surroundings, hikes and stunning viewpoints. **Bottle Beach**, situated in the most northern point of the island, is a must for hikers who like a challenge, with a sweet reward of crashing waves on a secluded beach. Snorkellers should head to **Ko Raham** where you can find hundreds of small fish swimming around large boulders at the foot of the self-named beach bar.

## Ko Tao

The small, free-spirited island of Ko Tao is surrounded by idyllic scenery, starting with its main beach, **Sairee**, a buzzing area that

### Ang Thong National Marine Park

Ang Thong National Marine Park is made up of 42 diverse islands along the Gulf of Thailand and no visit to the south is complete without stopping here. Accessible only by tour operator, its an ethereal preserve where you'll get lost in the sapphire blue sea studded with jutting rock formations and massive limestone cliffs with hidden caves underneath. Ang Thong was the original inspiration for *The Beach* by Alex Garland and appeared in his novel, not in the film. Stop at **Ko Mae Ko**, home to the breathtaking emerald saltwater lake that is completely surrounded by limestone cliffs and can only be reached by a 20-minute hike. The only place that offers bungalows is the nomadic village of **Ko Wua Ta Lap**, considered the main hub of the marine park.

### Full Moon Party

Said to have originated back in 1985 by a group of travellers, the Full Moon Party still grooves on in its original location at Haad Rin beach in Ko Pha-Ngan. Crowds pour in once a month when the moon is at its fullest for live music sets, beach views and meeting new friends.

PTTRAVELPHOTO/SHUTTERSTOCK ©

never feels dated. Perfect for sunsets and strolling. **Chalok Baan Kao Bay** is the third-largest beach with views of the main islands nearby and calm waters perfect for small children; it never feels crowded. **Freedom Beach** might be popular for its coral reef not far off, but the beach is beloved for its turquoise waters and shady shorelines. Not on the island but just a 10-minute boat ride is **Ko Nang Yuan**, consisting of three small islands that are connected by a dreamy sandbank and stunning corals that are known to have the occasional sighting of manta rays and sea turtles. Although busy, **Tanote Beach** just hits the mark with its cliff jumping, people watching and exquisite sunrises.

## Island Day Trip

Book a traditional long-tail boat and escape for the day to **Ko Madsum**, which inhabits an adorable family of pigs that happily hang around the island. After a morning swim, head to neighbouring **Ko Taen** for a busy day of snorkelling, swimming or kayaking in calming waters.

LEFT: DON MAMMOSER/SHUTTERSTOCK ©, RIGHT: SUTTIRAT WIRIYANON/SHUTTERSTOCK ©

**Left** Ang Thong National Marine Park.
**Top right** Ko Tao Island.
**Above** Sleeping pig, Ko Samui

# Outdoor **WONDERS**

**01 Hin Lad (Wat namtok)**
The second-largest waterfall on the island offers a tranquil setting with a 4km to 5km hiking trail along a river.

**02 Na Muang 1**
Part of a duo near Nathon Bay, Na Muang 1 offers a stunning setting of cascading waters into natural pools.

**03 Na Muang 2**
This fan favourite is surreal, with semi-hidden rock formations that perfectly overlook the sparkling sea.

**04 Khun Si**
Hike challenging trails hidden among durian plantations near Bophut; take a dip in pools around the naturally tiered rocks.

**05 Secret Falls (Tang Rua)**
Dense jungle trails lead you to exceptional vistas from Ko Samui's third-largest waterfall.

**06 Khao Yai**
Though incomparable to the rest, this waterfall is the most accessible

with a backdrop of tropical jungle and a Secret Buddha Garden.

### 07 Lady slipper orchid

If you are spending time in Ang Thong National Marine Park, look for this unique flower that is only found here.

### 08 Grand imperial butterfly

This stunning species (*Neocheritra amrita*) flits around Ko Pha-Ngan with its yellow and brown wings.

### 09 Dipterocarpus alatus

This towering Ko Tao forest tree is home to the rare white-bellied sea eagle that is a protected animal of Thailand.

### 10 Domsila viewpoint

Stop at the Phaeng waterfall before you reach the panoramic ocean views that await you at the top of Domsila on Ko Pha-Ngan.

# 45 A Great Day IN SAMUI

WELLNESS | ADVENTURE | LIBATIONS

With a beautiful sense of community sweeping across the island, my great day in Samui explores a range of wellness and indulgence, revealing a selection of heartfelt homemade foods and exciting activities.

DEV_MARYNA/SHUTTERSTOCK ©

**Recommended by Shannon Pert**, *co-founder of Hot Mess and resident advocate, Instagram @hotmess_samui*

### Trip Notes

**How much** A drop-in yoga class at **Vikasa** is 690B.

**Give back** Volunteer at **Pariah Dog Foundation** where playing with the dogs helps with socialisation, increasing their chances of adoption.

**Photo op** Brush up your photography skills at **Dusit Dheva Cultural Center** (pictured above) which showcases an other-worldly sculpture garden full of Khmer deities and replicated ruins.

**Drinks** One of the last remaining authentic reggae bars, **Beryl** is located quite literally off a beaten path in Baan Makham.

### Best Spots

**Silver Beach** is an excellent place for a dip on a tropical day after yoga at Vikasa. Bring your own towel or try Crystal Bay Yacht Club for more facilities.

**Wann Gram** in Bang Por is a tiny bistro with huge flavours combining modern Thai and Western classics. The creative menu features and Insta-worthy foie gras flambé.

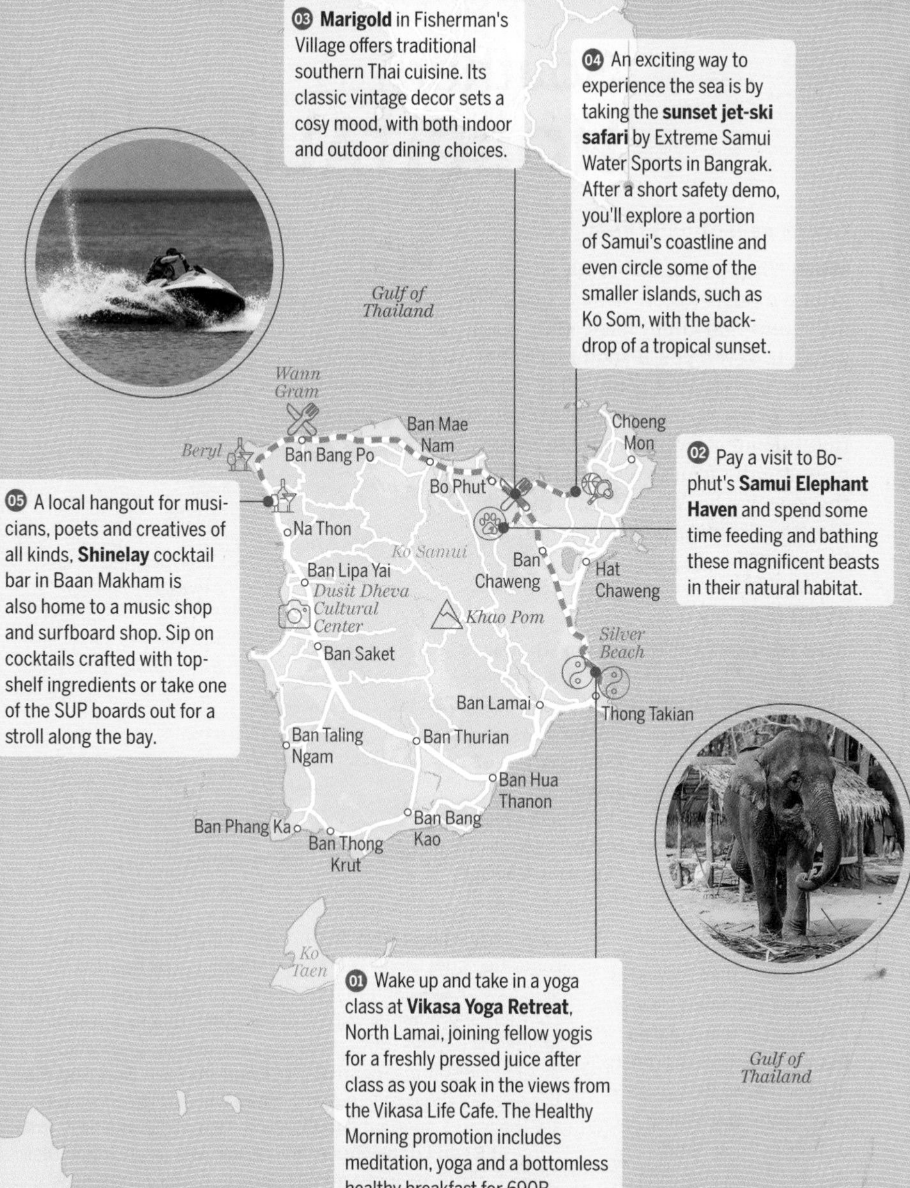

03 **Marigold** in Fisherman's Village offers traditional southern Thai cuisine. Its classic vintage decor sets a cosy mood, with both indoor and outdoor dining choices.
04 An exciting way to experience the sea is by taking the **sunset jet-ski safari** by Extreme Samui Water Sports in Bangrak. After a short safety demo, you'll explore a portion of Samui's coastline and even circle some of the smaller islands, such as Ko Som, with the back-drop of a tropical sunset.
Gulf of Thailand
Wann Gram
Beryl
Ban Mae Nam
Ban Bang Po
Choeng Mon
Bo Phut
02 Pay a visit to Bo-phut's **Samui Elephant Haven** and spend some time feeding and bathing these magnificent beasts in their natural habitat.
05 A local hangout for musi-cians, poets and creatives of all kinds, **Shinelay** cocktail bar in Baan Makham is also home to a music shop and surfboard shop. Sip on cocktails crafted with top-shelf ingredients or take one of the SUP boards out for a stroll along the bay.
Na Thon
Ko Samui
Ban Lipa Yai
Ban Chaweng
Hat Chaweng
Dusit Dheva Cultural Center
Khao Pom
Silver Beach
Ban Saket
Ban Lamai
Thong Takian
Ban Taling Ngam
Ban Thurian
Ban Hua Thanon
Ban Phang Ka
Ban Bang Kao
Ban Thong Krut
Ko Taen
01 Wake up and take in a yoga class at **Vikasa Yoga Retreat**, North Lamai, joining fellow yogis for a freshly pressed juice after class as you soak in the views from the Vikasa Life Cafe. The Healthy Morning promotion includes meditation, yoga and a bottomless healthy breakfast for 690B.
Gulf of Thailand
N
0 10 km
0 5 miles

# 46 Southern HOSPITALITY

**FIERY | SEAFOOD | ETHNIC**

The food of the south is synonymous with one thing: heat. The fiery kind that could make your head spin. However, you'll soon learn that southern Thai food is not all it initially seems. With myriad outside influences that include flavours from Malaysia mixed with Chinese techniques plus the glorious bounty of local seafood, you'll leave spicy notions behind and let the discovery begin.



## How to

**Spice control** If the spice gets too much, head to your nearest 7-Eleven and grab a bottle of Flying Rabbit, Thailand's answer to Pepto-Bismol.

**Balancing flavours** Thais share food with the table, typically ordering a dip, salad, soup, curry and stir-fry, all paired with fragrant jasmine rice.

**Cutlery** The only utensils you'll find in Thai restaurants are a spoon and fork. Chopsticks are typically only used with noodles or in a Chinese restaurant.

## Culinary Journey

Surat Thani, the gateway to the lower gulf has a slew of local restaurants like **Keo Pla**, famous for its silky fish balls and wontons served in clear broth. **Yok Kheng** specialises in Surat Thani pork noodles called *long tong* as well as various Thai sweets.

On Samui, **Long Dtai**, from renowned chef David Thompson, takes inspiration from southern ingredients and recipes, like Kolae mussels, in an upscale sharing menu at the swanky Cape Fahn hotel. Try the warm, coconut shoot curry at **Baan Luang Suan**, tucked in the midst of a coconut plantation. The menu highlights local seafood.

Food mecca Nakhon Si Thammarat is known for *khanom jeen* (sticky fermented rice noodles). Start at **Khanom Jeen Sen Sod Mae Aed** where it is served with intense curries like *nám yah*, paired with fresh vegetables and herbs to counter the heat. **Kopi** is perfect for

Singaporean/Malay-style *ba kuh teh* (pork rib broth infused with aromatics that can be paired with a rich black coffee). **Krua Nai Nang** is known for southern favourites like *goong sataw* (plump prawns sautéed with green peppercorn and stink beans) or the turmeric-laced deep-fried Thai whiting (Silago) that are topped with fried garlic.

Hat Yai, further south, has shopping and it has fried chicken. Head to **Meenah** street cart for delectable deep-fried chicken served over aromatic biryani rice that is topped with crispy shallots.

## Essential Ingredients in Southern Thai Cooking

**Coconut milk** Coconut milk is extracted and added to unique curries like *nám yah kati* (yellow-tinted curry served with fermented noodles).

**Fresh turmeric (*kha-min*)** This orange-hued fragrant, peppery root is like gold in Thai cooking. It's used in curry pastes, sour soups like *gaeng som* and in Muslim-style biryani rice.

**Shrimp paste (*kapi*)** Made using crushed tiny shrimp or krill mixed with salt before being fermented for a few weeks, the paste is used in curries, stir fries and in dips like the famous *nám prík kapi*.

**Chillies and pepper** Fresh and dry chilli, in particular *prík karieng*, and black pepper lend local cuisine different types of heat.

**Above** Kopi coffee shop

# 47 Songkhla: Old City, NEW VIBES

**ARCHITECTURE | LAKES | ART**

If you're looking for a unique change of scenery, head south to the charming province of Songkhla City, where you can marvel at historic Sino-Portuguese–style houses sitting between the largest lake in the country and the gulf. Venture down small alleyways peppered with shophouses. Immerse yourself in the rich Chinese culture that has been embedded in this historical fishing town since the 19th century.

BEN BRYANT/SHUTTERSTOCK ©

## How to

**Getting here** Fly to Hat Yai airport then grab a taxi (45 minutes) to reach town.

**When to go** Visit December to March for good weather.

**Hot tip** Have an aperitif at the super chill **Songkhla Lagoon Bar** before catching a long-tail boat to Songkhla lake as the sun sets.

**Language** With few foreign visitors, it can be tough to communicate with southern people; phone translators help a bunch.

KANOK SULAIMAN/GETTY IMAGES ©

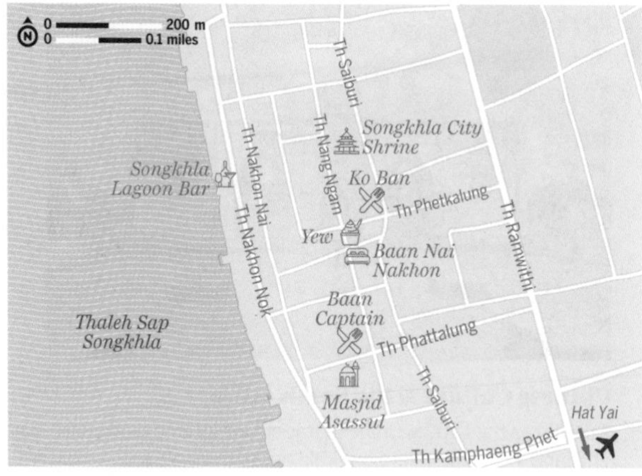


**Left** Songkhla City Shrine.
**Bottom left** Masjid Asassul mosque

## Explore the Historic Town

In 2016, the local provincial governor decided to bring new life to the area by adding murals designed by art students from local universities around the old quarter. Peruse the area around Nang Ngam Rd where you'll discover **Nang Talung** shadow puppets dressed in suits à la Beatles. Pop by the iconic **Songkhla City Shrine**, built in 1879, then visit the **Masjid Asassul** Islamic mosque on Phatthalung Rd that was built in 1850.

The food in Songkhla comes at you fast and furious, with southern delights to be found on every corner. Start your morning with milk tea at the nearly 100-year-old **Hup Seng** shophouse before venturing into the halal street for some chicken curry with vegetables and dips at **Baan Captain**. Cool down at **Yew** ice cream shop; the star is the creamy ice cream topped with egg yolk and sprinkled with Milo chocolate. Dinner should be at **Tae Hiang Aew** for Thai Chinese-style dishes like *rad na* (a concoction of tofu, veggies and crab tossed in a gravy) or tender squid sautéed with tons of garlic.

Stay at **Baan Nai Nakhon**, located in the heart of the old town and owned and operated by a former Thai airways attendant. The six-room boutique hotel is full of antiques and has colourful mosaics, a blooming garden and excellent service to match.

### Keeping it Local

Savour Songkla-style noodles at 100-year-old legendary **Ko Ban** or **Ko Yao**, which are sibling restaurants known for Teochew Chinese-style noodles served with a clear broth on the side.

The sunset in Nakorn Nok alley has my favourite view of the lake, located next to the Singha Beer Store with beautiful bougainvillea along the way. Go between 5.30pm and 6.30pm for the best light.

The Songkhla food scene is something you should not miss. Sip milk tea with the locals at **Hup Seng** teahouse, then discover Chinese-influenced food like a meaty pork stew or giant steamed buns at **Kiat Fung** on Nang Ngam Rd.

■ **Bby Aey Pakorn Rujiravilai,** *local Songkhla ambassador and owner of A.E.Y space Art Gallery (140 Nang Ngam Rd), Instagram @aey.pakorn, @aeyspace*

# Southern Cultures

**CULTURES COLLIDE IN THE SOUTH OF THAILAND**

Southern Thailand is rich with influences from neighbouring places. The further south you travel, the more this becomes apparent – and the more the region's unique culture starts to stand out.

**Left** Krue Sae Mosque.
**Right** Chao Mae Lim Ko Niao shrine

LOVESEEN/SHUTTERSTOCK ©

## Chinese Culture & the South

As early as the 1200s, Chinese traders emigrated to modern-day Thailand. Port cities like Songkhla housed immigrants who were escaping instability, searching for work or looking simply to wed. Made up of what are now the provinces Yala, Narathiwat and Pattani, as well as parts of Malaysia, the booming trade hub attracted traders from around the world: Persians, Indians, Arabs, Malay, Siamese, British, Japanese, Portuguese and Dutch.

Hokkien immigrants were known to be good sailors, and most relocated to the lower gulf and Andaman regions, where they hold jobs as rice merchants even to this day. These constitute the largest dialect group among the Chinese in Songkhla, Satun and Phuket. And while Songkhla is located in the mainly Muslim and Malay-influenced 'Deep South', its architecture, food and dialects are mostly Chinese, as are the local people.

Today, you'll find various Chinese ethnic groups across the south: Hainanese in Samui, Hokkien in Surat Thani and Hat Yai and Cantonese in Betong and Yala.

Chinese immigrants were key in the development of the entire Thai state, not just the south. Under the reign of King Taksin, who claimed Teochew ancestry himself, the Chinese community prospered in businesses across the land, controlling most of the shipping and export industries that involved sugar, fish, rice and rubber, and marrying into Thai families. From Bangkok's bustling Chinatown to the shophouses that dot the southern provinces, to the cooking techniques, ingredients and flavors they've added to Thailand's culinary traditions, their influence remains today.

## Islam Influences

While Chinese immigrants have played a huge role in the make-up of the south, Islam's influence is just as prominent. The

Muslim Malay community is the second-largest minority group after the Chinese. Although Islam is located all across the country, the spiritual centre for the Muslim community lies in the south, especially along the border with Malyasia.

WIBLACKANGEL/SHUTTERSTOCK ©

The provinces of Pattani, Yala and Narathiwat is where you will find the biggest concentration of Malay-Thai Muslims. Since the 16th century, if not earlier, this group has long held a sizable place in the fabric of Thai identity. The once-powerful Sultanate of Patani is where Islam was introduced to the predominately Buddhist country. It was also, then as now, a battleground between the ruling Buddhist powers and locals seeking autonomy due to their distinct cultural identity and religious beliefs.

In the early 20th century, the relationship between Patani and Siam soured following the Bangkok Treaty of 1909, which ceded several southern provinces to the British in return for their recognition of Siamese rule over the three flashpoint provinces of Pattani, Yala and Narathiwat. That effectively ended Patani's sovereignty, even if it had truly ended centuries earlier.

Today, you can find [Malay culture] in cuisine like heavily spiced, coconut-laced curries served with roti, in beautiful mosques and in attire such as the hijab.

### Battle for Autonomy

Tensions remain across the south. Separatists have cited the loss of their cultural identity at the hands of the ruling Buddhist powers in their decades-long battle for autonomy, a battle that has often turned violent. Since the early 2000s, thousands have died and many more have been injured in the ongoing battle for autonomy. Beyond the stigma of being labelled dangerous, the Deep South is not considered a tourist destination either, and its cities are less developed than most across the country.

Its rich Malay culture, however, never faded. Today, you can find it in cuisine like heavily spiced, coconut-laced curries served with roti, in beautiful mosques and in attire such as the hijab. And perhaps nothing says more about the diversity and identity of southern Thailand than one site in Pattani. Here, two distinctive houses of worship stand side by side: the 500-year-old Krue Sae mosque (Masjid Kerisik), made entirely of stone in a European style, and a national heritage site, and the Chao Mae Lim Ko Niao graveyard, an important Chinese burial ground and shrine to a legendary heroine-turned-goddess praised by the local community.

### Worship Houses

The 500-year-old **Krue Sae Mosque** is one of the oldest and most prominent mosques in Thailand. It's said it was built during the reign of King Naresuan the Great (1578–93). The structure is completely made of red bricks with round pillars and Gothic-like archways and was listed as a national heritage site in 1935.

Connected to the story of the mosque, is the Chinese **Chao Mae Lim Ko Niao** shrine dedicated to the Goddess, Lim Ko Niao. Legend has it that Lim travelled from China to Pattani in search of her brother. When he was found, she learned he married the daughter of the sultan, converted to Islam and started to build Krue Sae with no plans to return home. Riddled with sadness, she hung herself from a cashew tree, that is now where the shrine stands.

# Listings

**BEST OF THE REST**

### Thai & International Eats

2 Fishes $$$

Ko Samui chef Leo highlights local seafood in both classic and modern Italian takes such as crispy halibut with herbs, garlic and green chilli sauce, and linguini vongole.

Federicos $$

This unassuming Ko Samui restaurant doles out Italian favourites; expect quality ingredients in pasta dishes and addictive pizzas loaded with porcini, parma ham and mozzarella.

Suppatra $$

Enjoy an array of Thai dishes at this homey *sala*–inspired restaurant located in Bangrak, Ko Samui. The service is warm and the dishes are homemade.

Haad Bang Po $

The head chef, who has over 20 years of experience in hotel kitchens serves up southern Thai classic fare on a beachfront setting that is adored by Ko Samui locals and tourists.

P.Oys Place, $

Savour homemade Thai dishes at this family-run restaurant situated on Ko Tao between Mae Haad and Chalok Baan Kao. Also offers off-menu specials that can hail from northern Thailand all the way down the coast.

### Coffee & Daytime Bites

Fisherman's House x Sasatorn Coffee $$

This trendy Ko Samui cafe and hotel is in the heart of the Fisherman's Village but feels secluded thanks to the numerous potted plants and tropical vibes that fill the warm space.

Sirtaki Taverna $$

This beloved Ko Pha-Ngan taverna deals in the flavours of the Greek islands: tender grilled octopus, juicy lamb, chicken and pork souvlaki, hearty moussaka and more.

Bubba's $

For Bangkok coffee culture with a distinct Ko Pha-Ngan vibe, join the digital nomads at Bubba's (two locations: in Haad Yao and Baan Tai) for eggs Benedict and fair-trade coffee.

K.O.B by the Sea $$

Known for homemade sourdough, breakfast favourites and great coffee, there are three locations but K.O.B by the Sea, in the heart of Bangrak (Ko Samui), is where you can sit on the terrace feasting with stunning sea views.

Karma Sutra $$

This buzzing all day restaurant on Ko Samui sits at the foot entrance to the Fisherman's Village making it a perfect place to start or end your day. Low-key, Mediterranean vibes backed up by Indonesian furnishings are the perfect backdrop for an easy lunch or early happy hour.

Sairee Cottage Restaurant $

This restaurant sits right on the beach on Ko Tao and offers a spacious setting with wooden touches. The menu is Thai mixed with an array of Western dishes.

Avocado on toast

Foods & Roots $$

This airy eatery overlooking Chaloklum beach (Ko Pha-Ngan) sells a bunch of natural products – from hemp-based goods to natural cleaning supplies – and loads of vegan dishes.

## Snack Food

Nang Sabai $

This bohemian Bangrak (Ko Samui) spot caters to all kinds of dietary restrictions. Choose from vegan and non-vegan bites, including everything from nachos to vegan burgers.

Le Fabrique $

The bright yellow building that houses this loved Ko Samui French bakery might be understated inside but the food speaks otherwise. Indulge in the massive French-inspired menu.

Rossini's Ice Cream $$

Cool down at this iconic artisanal ice cream shop in Lamai (Ko Samui) that's been around since 1992. Savour flavours like caramel fleur de sel, forest berries, guava and creamy peanut butter.

Nui Bakery $$

This urban Ko Tao bakery offers a refreshing vibe. The warm setting mixes well with the good-for-you food like lacto-sourdough, vegan sandwiches, kombucha and coffee from the Royal King Project.

## Sunsets, Cannabis & Sundowners

Chi $$$

Sexy beach bar and restaurant in Bangrak (Ko Samui) serving creative modern fare paired with a lengthy cocktail list as well as a cannabis menu. Come here for the open bar and live DJ set.

Tham Khao Wang Thong (p239)

Dragonfly $$

Rooftop restaurant and cocktail lounge; offers a great Lebanese spread for lunch and dinner. Sundowners are a must to catch the last rays of the sun off Ko Samui while lounging on the rooftop terrace.

Magic Alambic Rum Distillery $

This French-owned Samui distillery is perfect for a late afternoon visit; you can swim in the pool, dine in the outdoor covered patio and try locally made rum.

Beryl Bar, Laem Yai $$

Authentic reggae bar located quite literally off a beaten path in Ban Macam (Ko Samui). Complete with its own tree house, private cove and a humble but generous cafe, this hidden jewel is the perfect place to slow down, mellow out and sip the afternoon away.

Jungle Club $$

Take in panoramic Ko Samui views at this restaurant and bar that sits high on the mountain amidst a coconut plantation. Choose from both Western or Thai dishes then grab a camera to capture the glorious sea vista.

## Late Nights & DJs

Eden Beach

Party from dusk 'til dawn at the isolated Eden Beach (Ko Pha-Ngan); only accessible by 4X4, a super tough hike or by boat. The restaurant is open daily but parties only happen on Saturdays.

Sand and Tan

The DJ sessions and chic decor of this bar/restaurant shows how Ko Pha-Ngan culture is evolving past its party roots.

Maya Beach Club

This loungey Ko Tao beach club brings music lovers together for electronic or drum and bass tunes by international and local DJs. Weekend BBQs and cool drinks are served with ocean views and daybeds under the shade of palm trees.

## Shop till You Drop

Saona

This Ko Samui clothing boutique offers colourful beachwear including flowy dresses, swimsuits and accessories that are all Thai made.

Central Festival

Ko Samui shopping haven with pharmacies, Thai knick-knacks and a gourmet supermarket, all in an open-air complex. Also has a large outdoor terrace complete with restaurants and a children's play area.

Bangrak Fish Market

Fresh market located just past the Seatran Pier in Bangrak (Ko Samui); filled with the freshest seafood the gulf has to offer (also has fruit and veg and a few eat-in restaurants).

## Unique Experiences

Koh Sanuk Tours

Charter a luxurious catamaran for the day; fitted with two trampolines, a BBQ, sleeping rooms down below and a gracious crew that will take you snorkelling around the gulf islands.

Island Organics Thai Cooking School

A unique farm-to-table Thai cookery experience that takes you through the owners' organic micro-farm where you can wander the grounds learning about the aquaponics system before picking fresh herbs and vegetables for your class with Chef Lat.

Luxsa Spa

Splurge on massage package from this award-winning Ko Samui spa located in the opulent Hansar resort. Indulge in traditional Thai massage, facials or body wraps.

## Getting Active

Ban's Diving School

Around since 1993, this Ko Tao diving school is known around the world. This PADI 5 Star Career & Instructor Development Centre specialises in scuba diving, freediving and snorkelling.

Scuba diving, Ko Tao

John Suwan Viewpoint

Put on your sneakers and start your morning with an adventurous hike up to this spectacular Ko Tao viewpoint with stellar panoramic views of the gulf. You must pay to enter, but it's worth every penny.

Yodyut MuayThai

Limber up on Ko Samui and take a muay thai class for a hands-on Thai experience. Choose between a private or group class.

Srithanu

A village on Ko Pha-Ngan known for its spiritual community. Take yoga, tantra and sound-healing workshops or visit one of the detox centres for a reboot.

## Contributing to Conservation

Plastao

Team up with the Plastao crew turning rubbish from Ko Tao beaches into colourful and reusable coasters, cups and plant pots. Workshops gather beachgoers to clean up the beach, collect plastic materials and bring them back to be recycled.

Coral Tribe

Devoted to marine conservation, on Ko Tao, Coral Tribe focuses on training divers and non-divers to get involved in coral restoration internships and community action.

## Back to Nature

Pink Dolphin Tour with Ocean Samui Tours

Hop on a boat for a day trip to spot rare pink dolphins, a unique subspecies of the Indo-Pacific humpback dolphin; Nakhon Si Thammarat.

Tham Khao Wang Thong

This limestone cave Nakhon Si Thammarat is worth the visit for its stalagmites and stalactites; you might need to climb, crawl or slither through openings.

EM7/SHUTTERSTOCK ©

Singora Tram

Khao Sok National Park

Reconnect with nature by heading inland to Surat Thani to this richly dense rainforest that sits between Phuket and Ko Samui. Lose yourself in a place filled with majestic waterfalls, limestone mountains and picturesque lakes, and renowned for a richness of flora and fauna.

## Souvenirs & Tours

Sin Adulayaphan

This very unique Songkhla shop has been around since 1923, selling edible souvenirs including airy shrimp crackers, soy sauce, shrimp paste and chilli paste.

Singora Tram

The Singora Tram Tour is a great way to see Songkhla, museums and Tang Kuan hill, which is a bit further away. The tour is free of charge and usually in Thai.

May and Co

This adorable Ko Tao general store sells unique environmentally friendly artisan products like candles or jewellery. You can grab a drink from the small bar.

**Scan to find more things to do in Ko Samui & the Lower Gulf online**

# Practicalities



**Right** Camping in Thailand (p246)

## EASY STEPS FROM THE AIRPORT TO THE CITY CENTRE

***Bangkok's Suvarnabhumi Airport, Southeast Asia's largest airport, is the main entry point for visitors to Thailand. It is located around 30km east of Bangkok. The arrivals hall has a selection of restaurants and coffee stops, including a 24-hour food court with decent, well-priced Thai dishes on level 1.***

### AT THE AIRPORT

**SIM CARDS**
SIM cards from providers such as AIS, True and dtac can be purchased in the arrival hall. Stalls tend to form long queues; if you're knackered, hit a shopping mall in the city (7-Eleven and mini-markets also sell 30-day tourist SIMs).

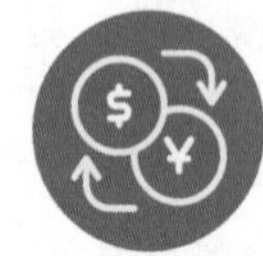

**CASH**
Cash counters at Suvarnabhumi's Airport Exchange Zone (5.30am to 8.30pm on the basement level) offer slightly better rates than the bank booths after baggage claim (though those are fine for ATM withdrawals). ATMs have cash limits of around 20,000B.

I VIEWFINDER/SHUTTERSTOCK ©

**ATMS** Bank counters after the baggage claim area such as Kasikorn and Bangkok Bank have ATMs taking foreign cards.

**WI-FI** Suvarnabhumi Airport offers free wi-fi for two hours (after that you'll have to reconnect) on the network 'AOT Free WiFi'.

**CHARGING STATIONS** Free charging stations are offered throughout the airport connecting to two-pronged plugs.

### IMMIGRATION TIPS

When arriving, be prepared to queue upwards of 30 minutes at immigration. If you have a tight window to catch a bus or train, consider purchasing a VIP fast-track online.

Leaving Thailand, overstaying your visa a few days is okay. You pay the penalty (500B per day) at immigration. Reaching the 20,000B maximum, however, is serious.

## GETTING TO THE CITY CENTRE

**METRO** The basement-level Suvarnabhumi Airport Rail Link operates daily from 6am to midnight (around every 10 minutes) and interchanges with the BTS Skytrain line at the Phaya Thai station (45B, one hour to 90 minutes). Also used by locals, it gets packed during weekends and morning/evening rush hour.

**GRAB TAXI APP** Grab is not necessarily cheaper than the taxi stand. Coordinating pickup might take effort. Pickup is on arrivals level 2.

**CAR RENTAL** Also available on level 2. All the well-known rental companies (Budget, Sixt, Avis, Hertz etc) have counters.

**TAXI** The level 1 taxi stand (arrivals hall) is a faster yet pricier option (around 350B plus tolls, 30 minutes to an hour). The driver will usually ask, 'Tollway?' Taking expressways slightly ups the price but shortens the drive considerably, so it's usually a good idea.

**BUS** Services connect travellers to Khao San Rd and there is also a free shuttle to Don Mueang Airport. Buses and minivans make Suvarnabhumi Airport a useful gateway to the coast, with service to Hua Hin, Pattaya and Rayong.

## OTHER POINTS OF ENTRY

**Don Mueang Airport** Bangkok's smaller, ageing sister airport to Suvarnabhumi, is serviced by domestic flights and budget providers such as AirAsia, Nok Air and Thai Smile. It is a far ride from the city centre due to high traffic, and a pain to leave with public transport.

**Phuket Airport** Thailand's third-largest international airport after Suvarnabhumi and Don Mueang, Phuket acts as a gateway to the country, particularly the southern islands.

**Samui Airport** A private airport serviced only by Bangkok Airways. It offers flights into Thailand from Singapore, Phnom Penh and Hong Kong.

**Bus and minivan services** Enter Thailand overland from neighbouring countries such as Cambodia, Laos, Myanmar and Malaysia. 'Visa runs' – one-day trips over a border and back promising fresh 30-day tourist visas – are also available.

**Train** Rail travel into Thailand is also possible from neighbouring countries. Splurge on the Belmond Eastern & Oriental Express luxury train from Kuala Lumpur and Singapore to Bangkok in a restored antique carriage.

**Cruise** Popular for entering Thailand from other Southeast Asian countries.

## TRANSPORT TIPS TO HELP YOU GET AROUND

***Bangkok aside, there's no freedom in Thailand quite like having your own wheels. While the capital has metro transport,* motorsai *(motorcycle taxis) and taxis aplenty, such options are scarce elsewhere – and become even more so the deeper you escape into island and rural life. Scooters are Thailand's most popular mode of transport and should be ridden with much caution.***

**CROSSING BORDERS**

Entering neighbouring countries with a rented vehicle is generally not allowed. It's easier to take a bus, train or plane, and then rent a new set of wheels at your destination.

**ENTERING CAMBODIA OR LAOS**

You will need to supply a passport photo as well as US$30 to US$42 for the tourist visa (crisp bills are better). Additional documents like health certificates aren't needed; ignore offers from non-border guards for them.

Car rental per day
800B
FREE
Motorbike rental per day
300B
Short-distance *motorsai* ride
15B


**TRAVEL AGENTS** In Thailand, brick-and-mortar travel agencies are still alive and well, and in many cases, a convenient means of booking transport. The booking process can be confusing for non-Thai speakers, especially in the case of tickets combining ferry with bus or train. Commission varies, so compare prices if you can. You should only have to pay (most likely cash) once the tickets are in hand.

**TRAIN** The favourite means of getting around for most visitors. It's inexpensive and a chance for scenery and people watching. Ticket prices range from 1st to 3rd class. Overnight trains offer beds and meal service over long distances like Bangkok to Chiang Mai.

**MINIVANS** A unique way to travel between Thai villages. Each town has a meeting point (often, an unassuming booth) where a vested staffer collects cash and coordinates pickups. The driver will remember where to drop you – and the other guests hopping on and off.

### DRIVING ESSENTIALS

Drive on the left; the steering wheel is on the right.

You technically need an international driving permit (IDP) although it's rarely enforced.

The speed limit is 50km/h on urban roads, 80km/h to 100km/h on highways.

You may be fined for driving without an IDP or helmet.

Watch for parking signs reading 'No Parking on Even/Odd Days'.

## BOATS

Convenient for hopping from bigger to smaller islands (like Ko Samui to Ko Pha-Ngan, for example), or in some cases, a faster means of travel from one side of an island to another. *Reu·a hăhng yow* (traditional long-tail boats) are common on canals and rivers. Wooden boats are standard for small islands, while bigger ones also have speedboats.

## CYCLING

An excellent idea for travelling in less-trafficky parts of Thailand, such as Pai and Hua Hin. It's especially popular around the Ayuthaya and Sukothai Historical Parks where the roads are flat and you can cruise between all the ancient ruins.

## TAXIS

Run on meters in Bangkok; less so on the islands. Grab app taxis and *motorsai* are only plentiful and affordable in the capital – elsewhere in Thailand, not always when you need them.

## KNOW YOUR CARBON FOOTPRINT

A domestic flight from Bangkok to Chiang Mai would emit about 210kg of carbon dioxide per passenger. A bus would emit 77kg for the same distance per passenger. A train would emit about 42kg. There are a number of carbon calculators online. We use Resurgence at resurgence.org/carbon-calculator.

## ROAD DISTANCE CHART (KM)

| | Bangkok | Chiang Mai | Hua Hin | Ko Samui | Phuket | Ayuthaya | Pattaya | Khon Kaen | Ko Chang | Krabi | Chanthaburi |
|---|---|---|---|---|---|---|---|---|---|---|---|
| Chiang Mai | 685 | | | | | | | | | | |
| Hua Hin | 183 | 869 | | | | | | | | | |
| Ko Samui | 769 | 1545 | 572 | | | | | | | | |
| Phuket | 862 | 1536 | 667 | 343 | | | | | | | |
| Ayuthaya | 79 | 607 | 262 | 834 | 929 | | | | | | |
| Pattaya | 149 | 919 | 343 | 903 | 970 | 205 | | | | | |
| Khon Kaen | 440 | 604 | 633 | 1206 | 1300 | 397 | 569 | | | | |
| Ko Chang | 346 | 1119 | 529 | 1089 | 1170 | 405 | 268 | 611 | | | |
| Krabi | 782 | 1569 | 585 | 258 | 163 | 859 | 908 | 1230 | 1108 | | |
| Chanthaburi | 249 | 1021 | 432 | 992 | 1072 | 307 | 171 | 527 | 96 | 1010 | |
| Chiang Rai | 775 | 191 | 1039 | 1545 | 1706 | 777 | 919 | 774 | 1119 | 1569 | 1021 |

## UNIQUE & LOCAL WAYS TO STAY

***Accommodation in Thailand spans from no-frills huts to luxury resorts, and both can offer picture-perfect seclusion and scenery. Expect good value from midrange lodgings, such as amenities like a swimming pool and room service, but not necessarily a view unless you request it. All-inclusive resorts are also not very common.***

HOW MUCH FOR A NIGHT IN...
Guesthouse 700B
Resort room 1000B
Beach villa 5000B

NAPAT INTAROON/SHUTTERSTOCK ©

### HOSTELS

The dark, dingy backpacker hostels and guesthouses of yore are becoming less standard across Thailand, being replaced by budget accommodation with modern flair. In beach destinations like Hua Hin and Phuket, there's a new emphasis on travellers who have cash but prefer simplicity. These modern hostels usually encompass a hip cafe with good wi-fi and a communal hangout area, and rooms that are small and minimalistic yet still stylish. Honestly, shared toilets aren't even such a thing anymore!

### HOMESTAYS

Homestays, or living with a Thai family, is a unique means of acclimatising to local life – and certainly more personal than hotel stays. Homestays are becoming popular across Thailand, although the concept is most established in remote northern villages where accommodation is scarce. Usually, stays are organised among villagers as a community effort.

SIRIPATWONGPIN/SHUTTERSTOCK ©

### LUXURY CAMPING

Some of Thailand's most extraordinary accommodation lies in luxury tenting camps, especially around the jungle-heavy Golden Triangle where Thailand, Laos and Myanmar meet. Eco-resorts offer luxury services and delightfully slow hospitality. Days are spent swanning around rice paddies and relaxing by bonfires, and in some cases, elephant trekking is included.

KEEPSMILING4U/SHUTTERSTOCK ©

## HERITAGE HOMES

Thailand's most architecturally special hotels are restored traditional houses or *reu·an thai* (Thai houses). Commonly, *reu·an thai* are teak or bamboo structures raised onto stilts with a curved gable roof, but styles can differ wildly (some Thais even oppose the term *reu·an thai* since Thailand comprised many ancient kingdoms and cultures). Therefore, design elements of heritage homes are very specific to each Thai region and its social, religious and cultural customs.

Traditionally, houses were built onto stilts to protect dwellers from storms, flooding and wild animals. The space underneath provided extra storage and a 'living room'. Meanwhile, the steep gabled roofs and large windows allowed for better airflow and sunlight and appeased the spirits with ample space.

Today, heritage houses are perfect setups for hotels. Many were built together to accommodate extended families after marriages. Revamping them is, however, expensive and not only done for tourism purposes. Maintaining these structures is also a means of honouring ancestral traditions and appeasing the spirits who live there.

Once close to the water for transport reasons, Thai heritage homes are still commonly found along canals and rivers. They are truly scenic places for cityscapes and sunset panoramas. Be forewarned though, creaky floorboards and a dust bunny or two will likely add to the charm!

## BOOKING

Travel search engines will pull up accommodation at hotels and resorts, while searching for more boutique accommodations is possible on specialised online platforms.

Booking in advance is highly recommended during public holidays such as Songkran. Sorting out accommodation on the ground will require your own set of wheels and some time, but can also help secure a nice discount or room upgrade.

**Lonely Planet** (lonelyplanet.com/hotels) Find independent reviews as well as recommendations on the best places to stay – and book them online.

**Airbnb** (airbnb.com) Particularly good for searching homestays and boutique stays, especially long-term. Lots of private lodgings like beach condos are posted by owners.

**Park reservation system** (dnp.go.th) Book stays in bungalows and on campgrounds in national parks.

**Couchsurfing** (couchsurfing.com) Stays organised, typically for free, in private homes (and often literally on a couch).

**Hostelworld** (hostelworld.com) Site focused on budget accommodation like hostel dorms.

**Agoda** (agoda.com) Good for finding the most reasonable rates on last-minute bookings.

NETFALLS REMY MUSSER/SHUTTERSTOCK ©

## BEACH STAYS

Wake up and jump in the ocean. Beach lodgings range from simple bungalows with mattresses and nets to fancy villas with pools. Prices range from a couple hundred to thousands of baht.

## SAFE TRAVEL

***According to the WHO, Thailand has the second-highest rate of traffic-related deaths in the world – most, unfortunately, occur on motorcycles. In addition to road safety, taking precautions against infectious diseases and insects is recommended.***

### WEAR A HELMET

It's common sense, but you would be surprised how many people don't. The best helmets are well-fitted, have visors and cover both sides of the head. A helmet should always be included in the price of a motorbike rental.

### BUY INSURANCE

Health insurance covering overseas medical expenses is a must. Most hospitals require an upfront guarantee of payment (from yourself or your insurer) for admission.Registered vehicles only include minimum liability insurance and any repairs (outside of tyre damage) will need to be paid out of pocket.

### DRIVE CAREFULLY AT NIGHT

The majority of road accidents happen after dark – especially when alcohol is a factor. Drive more cautiously late at night and, if possible, through well-lit areas. Bags are best placed under motorbike seats or strapped securely around the body in busy tourist areas, as bag-snatchings do occur.

### MOSQUITO-BORNE DISEASES

Illnesses like dengue fever and malaria are serious in Thailand. Using repellent, sleeping under a mosquito net and taking malaria medication in high-risk rural and remote areas is advised.

TECHA BORIBALBURIPUN/SHUTTERSTOCK ©

TOSHIO CHAN/SHUTTERSTOCK ©

### PHARMACIES

Found everywhere; pharmacies sell a variety of medicines and antibiotics over the counter (for a cheaper price than in most other countries). Stock up upon arrival, and especially before heading into remote areas.

### TRAVELLER'S DIARRHOEA

Also known as the 'Thai chilli sting ring' and a common health issue for travellers. Staying hydrated and antibiotics such as Norfloxacin and Ciprofloxacin can help.

### MOTORBIKE SCARS

Locals call them fa·ràng (foreigner) tattoos – scars from motorbike accidents. They're best avoided by driving a reasonable speed, indicating, avoiding wet and gravel roads, and learning how to use your brakes correctly.

## QUICK TIPS TO HELP YOU MANAGE YOUR MONEY

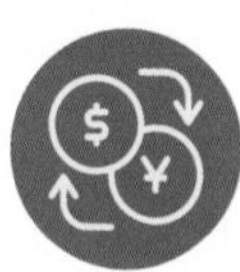

### CURRENCY

Paper currency is issued in 20B (green), 50B (blue), 100B (red), 500B (purple) and 1000B (beige) bills. Keep a variety for tips and paying street vendors.

Cash is king in Thailand. Many bars, restaurants and massage parlours will not accept plastic, although paying for transport and food over apps is becoming increasingly possible.

### VAT

A 7% value-added tax (VAT) is applied to goods and services. On shopping, it can be refunded later at the airport. Ask store staff about the documents and process.

### CREDIT & DEBIT CARDS

Visa and Mastercard are most accepted, American Express typically only at high-end places. Call your bank before travelling so overseas transactions aren't blocked.

### ASKING FOR THE BILL

Telling your server '*Check bin kâ/kâp*' is considered a polite way of asking for the bill. If they are across the restaurant, signing a checkmark in the air also works.

### CURRENCY

Baht

### HOW MUCH FOR A...

Thai massage 300B

Cocktail 200B

Bag of fresh fruit 10B

### WITHDRAWING CASH

Banks or private money changers offer better rates than hotels or ATMs. The US dollar is the most accepted currency, followed by pounds and euros. Commission varies, so shop around for the best rate.

### TIPPING

It's not expected in Thailand but appreciated by those in the low-wage service industry. Rule of thumb is leaving the loose change from your bill. On a massage, a 20B or 30B tip suffices. Note that nicer restaurants might already add a 10% service charge.

### HAGGLING

Haggling is a delicate art and not always appropriate. Prices are only flexible at stalls selling goods (such as clothing or souvenirs), and not at mom-and-pop shops or street food vendors.

The seller's suggested price is usually a starting point for negotiation. A common strategy is countering with half and meeting somewhere in the middle. Theatrics, like pretending to walking away, also make for good bargaining tactics! Asking for a discount is also fine when buying more than one item.

## RESPONSIBLE TRAVEL

***Tips to leave a lighter footprint, support local and have a positive impact on local communities.***

### ON THE ROAD

**Calculate your carbon** Try an online calculator like Resurgence (resurgence.org/carboncalculator).

**Do your research** Asking questions of hotels and tour operators will help improve ethical and sustainability practices in Thailand overall, and soothe your conscience.

**Learn to use a 'bum gun'** Practise using a bidet instead of toilet paper – just like the locals do.

**Leave only footprints** Take part in protecting ecosystems by not touching corals or marine life or feeding wild animals.

**Eat locally and mindfully** Although they may be tasty, popular imports like Wagyu and Aussie steaks have a considerable carbon footprint. Know the controversies behind dishes with shark and bird's saliva.

**Avoid flying when you can** Train, minivan, bus – Thailand's road transportation is plentiful and often quite comfortable.

**Above** Beach clean, Hua Hin.
**Far right** Reusable bags, Thailand



### GIVE BACK

**Support organisations conserving wildlife and biodiversity** Seek out groups working within protected areas and national parks.

**Research volunteering opportunities** Spend time with organisations that don't take work opportunities away from local folks and skillfully contribute to communities. Open Mind Projects (openmindprojects.org) places volunteers in healthcare and education roles.

**Take part in a beach clean-up** It really does protect marine life and is a great way to make local friends.

**Donate to strays** Poor *soi dogs* are often left forgotten. At urban and island initiatives, you can drop off food or take the pups on walks.

**Empower migrants** Cultural Canvas (culturalcanvas.com) advocates for marginalised populations and places volunteers in migrant learning centres.

## SUPPORT LOCAL

**Book direct** Small, independent lodgings will profit more if you don't book through third-party websites.

**Visit villages** Helps keep locals and their traditions thriving.

**Try a farm-to-table restaurant** The concept is flourishing in Thailand.

**Buy clothing from artisans** Cheap clothes and fake goods on the street are generally poor quality – and mighty susceptible to winding up in the trash.

SUTTHA BURAWONK/SHUTTERSTOCK ©

## DOS & DON'TS

**Know the law** Be aware of Thailand's lèse-majesté laws. Always stand still for the royal anthem.

**Respect Buddhist tradition** Act quietly and modestly in holy places. Exporting Buddha images can be illegal.

**Treat the body as a temple** Heads are sacred, so never touch a stranger's hair, nor put your feet up (they're considered unholy).

## LEAVE A SMALL FOOTPRINT

**Bring reusable bags and water bottles** Although Thailand has banned single-use plastics, they are still ubiquitous and difficult to recycle.

**Rough it** Camping in national parks, kayak expeditions and multiday hikes will reduce your emissions.

**Try natural bug repellents** Citronella products are available in convenience stores, smell nice and are more eco-friendly than DEET.

**Switch to natural sunscreen** Sunscreen is harmful to coral reefs. Non-nano zinc formulas are available in Thai pharmacies.

## CLIMATE CHANGE & TRAVEL

It's impossible to ignore the impact we have when travelling, and the importance of making changes where we can. Lonely Planet urges all travellers to engage with their travel carbon footprint. There are many carbon calculators online that allow travellers to estimate the carbon emissions generated by their journey; try resurgence.org/carbon-calculator. Many airlines and booking sites offer travellers the option of offsetting the impact of greenhouse gas emissions by contributing to climate-friendly initiatives around the world. We continue to offset the carbon footprint of all Lonely Planet staff travel, while recognising this is a mitigation more than a solution.

## RESOURCES

tourismthailand.org/Search-result/tagword/Ecotourism

thailandinsider.com/experience/responsible-tourism

trashhero.org

warthai.org

thairt.org

## ESSENTIAL NUTS & BOLTS

### 'FREE' TUK-TUKS

Be wary of tuk-tuk drivers who offer 'free' tours outside major landmarks. These tours usually end up in uncomfortable, high-pressure sales pitches.

### PUBLIC EMBARRASSMENT

There's nothing worse for a Thai person than losing face (feeling publicly embarrassed or disrespected).

### SHOES

Always take off your shoes at places like spas, temples and private residences. Easy-to-remove footwear and house slippers are nice to bring with you.

### FAST FACTS

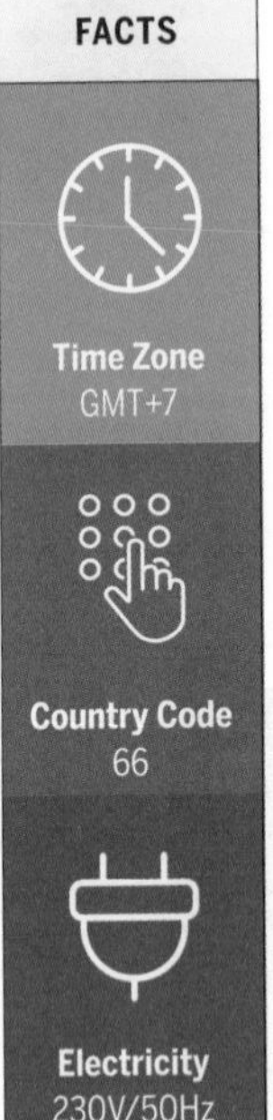

**Time Zone**
GMT+7

**Country Code**
66

**Electricity**
230V/50Hz

### GOOD TO KNOW

Passport holders from 19 countries are automatically eligible for a 30-day tourist visa on arrival.

Extending a visa is possible at immigration offices for a fee, but it may be cheaper to overstay your visa (500B per day).

The phone number for ambulances and other emergencies is 191.

The 24-hour tourist police service (1155) can help in cases of scams and theft.

Thailand is no stranger to ATM skimming. Check machines and use a credit card not directly linked to accounts.

## ACCESSIBLE TRAVEL

**Significant improvements** need to be made to accessible travel in Thailand overall.

**Urban landscapes** present challenges including uneven and crowded sidewalks, high kerbs and traffic congestion.

**Larger hotels** have more thoughtful designs and potentially extra staff for assistance.

**Top-end beach resorts** have wheelchair-friendly rooms (book in advance) and may offer buggy service on spread-out properties.

**Bangkok's public transport** (BTS Skytrain and MRT metro lines) is not wheelchair-friendly and best avoided. When taking taxis, planning for traffic jams is key.

**Download Lonely Planet's free Accessible Travel Guide** (lptravel.to/accessibletravel) for more info.

**ETHICAL TOURISM**
Before booking an elephant activity or hill tribe treks, research and consider all the socioeconomic implications.

**GREETING**
A very high *wâi* is only necessary for greeting monks and royalty. Don't *wâi* kids.

**NO PDA, PLEASE**
Egregious displays of affection between couples are considered to be quite rude.

**BIGGEST FANS**
Babies get a lot of attention in Thailand. Even the most tough taxi drivers and police officers tend to melt. Don't be taken aback if a Thai person asks to hold your baby or take a photo with them.

**FAMILY TRAVEL**

**Prams** Avoid using them on crowded streets and Bangkok's Skytrain. Slings and foldable strollers with umbrellas are helpful.

**Public transport** Bangkok stations lack elevators and have high stairwells, making travelling with prams and little ones difficult.

**Children's Day** The second Saturday of January, is when little ones get particularly special treatment.

**Children's amenities** High chairs and changing facilities tend to be scarce outside larger hotels and chain restaurants. Time to get creative!

**KID-FRIENDLY FOODS**
Hotels and resorts will have kids' menus with typical dishes like chicken fingers and spaghetti. Non-spicy street food dishes that children should like include *kài jee·o* (plain omelette), *kôw man gài* (white chicken breast and rice) and *kôw něe·o* (sweet sticky rice).

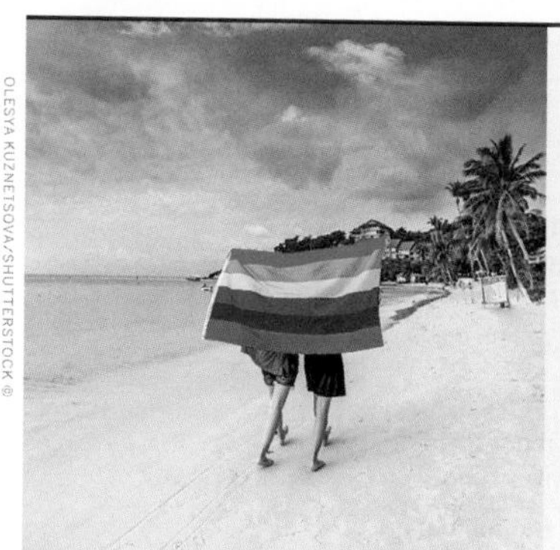

OLESYA KUZNETSOVA/SHUTTERSTOCK ©

**LGBTIQ+ TRAVELLERS**

**Tolerance** Thailand is very tolerant of LGBTIQ+ travellers. Bangkok, Pattaya and Phuket have the best gay circuits.

**Ladyboy** This derogatory, outdated term is best avoided.

**Gender identity** In Thailand, gender identity is complex. Lessons in Thai culture and history help to foster understanding.

**The Tourism Authority of Thailand** Has a website dedicated to LGBTQII+ travel (gothaibefree.com) with tips for hotels, restaurants and more.

**Utopia** Publishes LGBTIQ+ travel content and guidebooks to the kingdom. (utopia-asia.com)

## LANGUAGE

There are different ways of writing Thai in the Roman alphabet – we have chosen one method below. The hyphens indicate syllable breaks within words, and some syllables are further divided with a dot to help you pronounce them. Thai is a tonal language – the accent marks on vowels represent these low, mid, falling, high and rising tones.

Note that after every sentence, men add the polite particle *káp*, and women *ká*.

To enhance your trip with a phrasebook, visit **lonelyplanet.com**.

### BASICS

**Hello.**
สวัสดี — *sà-wàt-dee*

**How are you?**
สบายดีไหม — *sà-bai dee măi*

**I'm fine.**
สบายดีครับ/ค่า — *sà·bai dee kráp/kâ (m/f)*

**Excuse me.**
ขออภัย — *kŏr à-pai*

**Yes./No.**
ใช่/ไม่ — *châi/mâi*

**Thank you.**
ขอบคุณ — *kòrp kun*

**You're welcome.**
ยินดี — *yin dee*

**Do you speak English?**
คุณพูดภาษาอังกฤษได้ไหม — *kun pôot pah-săh ang-grìt dâi măi*

**I don't understand.**
ผม/ดิฉันไม่เข้าใจ — *pŏm/dì-chăn mâi kôw jai (m/f)*

### TIME & NUMBERS

**What time is it?**
กี่โมงแล้ว — *gèe mohng láa·ou*

| | | |
|---|---|---|
| **morning** | เช้า | *chów* |
| **afternoon** | บ่าย | *bài* |
| **evening** | เย็น | *yen* |
| **yesterday** | เมื่อวาน | *mêu·a wahn* |
| **today** | วันนี้ | *wan née* |
| **tomorrow** | พรุ่งนี้ | *prûng née* |

| | | | | | |
|---|---|---|---|---|---|
| **1** | หนึ่ง | *nèung* | **6** | หก | *hòk* |
| **2** | สอง | *sŏrng* | **7** | เจ็ด | *jèt* |
| **3** | สาม | *săhm* | **8** | แปด | *Ƀàat* |
| **4** | สี่ | *sèe* | **9** | เก้า | *gôw* |
| **5** | ห้า | *hâh* | **10** | สิบ | *sìp* |

### EMERGENCIES

**I'm ill.**
ผม/ดิฉันป่วย (m/f) — *pŏm/dì-chăn Ƀòo·ay*

**Help!**
ช่วยด้วย — *chôo·ay dôo·ay*

**Call a doctor!**
เรียกหมอหน่อย — *rêe·ak mŏr nòy*

**Call the police!**
เรียกตำรวจหน่อย — *rêe·ak đam·ròo·at nòy*

# Index

**'A new "white Christmas" for me – a Christmas feast on Ko Chang's White Sand Beach with a Thai children's choir.'**

BARBARA WOOLSEY

**'My favourite experience involves camping in national parks and getting lost on wild mountain trails before searching local villages for live music and whisky-infused atmospheres.'**

AYDAN STUART

**'Bangkok will ruin your diet. The anything-can-be-breakfast culture is so amazing. Who made the rule that toasts or cereal must be the only acceptable breakfast food?'**

CHOLTANUTKUN TUN-ATIRUJ

**TOP TO BOTTOM:** RALF LIEBHOLD/SHUTTERSTOCK ©, CGN089/SHUTTERSTOCK ©, NAPHASSAPHORN NA PANKAEW/SHUTTERSTOCK



**THIS BOOK**

**Design development**
Lauren Egan, Tina García, Fergal Condon

**Content development**
Anne Mason

**Cartography development**
Wayne Murphy, Katerina Pavkova

**Production development**
Mario D'Arco, Dan Moore, Sandie Kestell, Virginia Moreno, Juan Winata

**Series development leadership**
Liz Heynes, Darren O'Connell, Piers Pickard, Chris Zeiher

**Commissioning editor**
Daniel Bolger

**Product editor**
Alison Killilea

**Cartographer**
Anthony Phelan

**Book designer**
Clara Monitto

**Assisting editors**
Carly Hall

**Cover researcher**
Kat Marsh

**Thanks** Ronan Abayawickrema, Gwen Cotter, Clare Healy, Sandie Kestell, Amy Lynch, Darren O'Connell, Monique Perrin, Gabrielle Stefanos, John Taufa